NEW TOEIC
一本攻克新制多益
聽力＋閱讀
850⁺

**完全比照
最新考題趨勢精準命題**

不容錯過的多益應考攻略，透過短期密集訓練，培養高效解題思維，
一網打盡聽力閱讀 Part 1~Part 7 所有題型！

Eduwill語學研究所——著　關亭薇——譯

音檔使用說明

STEP 1

掃描書中 QRCode

STEP 2

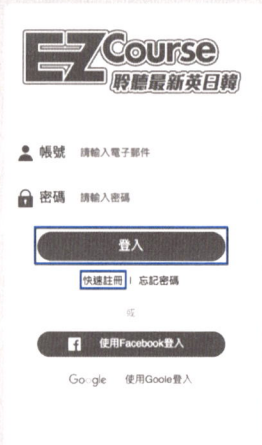

快速註冊或登入 EZCourse

STEP 3

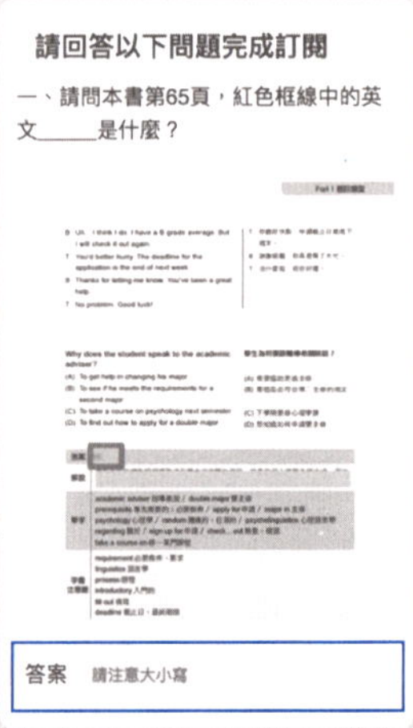

回答問題按送出

答案就在書中（需注意空格與大小寫）。

STEP 4

完成訂閱

該書右側會顯示「**已訂閱**」，表示已成功訂閱，即可點選播放本書音檔。

STEP 5
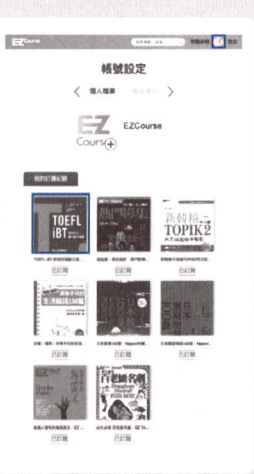

點選個人檔案

查看「**我的訂閱紀錄**」會顯示已訂閱本書，點選封面可到本書線上聆聽。

序言

考多益就選 EZ TALK！

700-850 分學習者的最佳學習書

本書編寫目的在於解決多益分數停滯在 700 至 850 之間的學習者。我們找來分數落在此區間的學生組成一個測試小組，針對他們在聽力和閱讀測驗各大題中遇到的困難和經常答錯的題目進行分析，並根據這些分析結果和各大題出題方向，設計相對應的學習步驟。因此，本書會對一些大題進行簡單說明，對於其他大題則會提供更詳盡的解說。例如：在聽力部分的 PART 3 和 PART 4 中，圖表題是一種固定出現的考題類型，但對分數停滯在 700-850 分之間的學習者來說，常常會為此陷入苦戰。因此我們分析了近三年的歷屆試題，編寫出各種實戰考題，幫助學習者做好萬全準備來應對該類型考題。在 PART 5 的文法題部分，我們僅精選出測試小組經常答錯的題目，重新編寫成難度較高的練習題。

高分祕訣在於紮實的基本功和充分練習常考題型

若想獲取高分，很容易想到要多做一些困難的題目。然而取得高分的祕訣在於練習經常出現的題型，累積紮實基礎。舉例來說，在聽力部分，若能自然聽出日常對話中的常見模式，就有餘力去注意穿插其中的艱深詞彙；而在閱讀部分，若能確實了解常考詞彙的意思和用法，同時具備掌握基本句型結構的能力，即使遇到陌生詞彙，也能透過上下文推敲其含義，不至於感到慌張。若在處理基本的出題模式、句型結構和詞彙時經常卡住，那將精力投入到出題頻率較低的困難詞彙或考題上也只是浪費時間。

多益測驗中出現的對話和文章，大多是基於一般人在工作中的常見情境。因此，測驗中有 85% 以上的內容為過往反覆出題的對話情境、文章、詞彙。只要能正確答對這些常考題型，考取 850 分以上絕非難事。本書分析大量歷屆試題，將常考題型整理出來，並透過改寫考題，編寫成各種練習題。重點在於培養學習者準確又快速作答任何相似考題的能力。

祝各位善用本書儘快考取理想多益分數，朝更遠大的目標邁進。

目次

LC

PART 1

照片描述		16
UNIT 01	人物照片	18
UNIT 02	事物照片與風景照	20
常考用法大全		22
PRACTICE 高難度		23
PART TEST 1		24
PART TEST 2		27

PART 3

簡短對話		50
UNIT 01	說話者的職業或對話地點	52
UNIT 02	對話目的或主旨	54
UNIT 03	建議或要求	56
UNIT 04	疑難問題或擔憂	58
UNIT 05	特定時間	60
UNIT 06	下一步的行動	62
PRACTICE UNIT 01~06		64
UNIT 07	掌握意圖＋PRACTICE 高難度	66
UNIT 08	三人對話＋PRACTICE 高難度	68
UNIT 09	圖表題＋PRACTICE 高難度	70
PART TEST		74

PART 2

應答問題		32
UNIT 01	Who/What/Which問句	34
UNIT 02	When/Where問句	36
UNIT 03	How/Why問句	38
UNIT 04	Yes/No問句	40
UNIT 05	表示建議或要求的問句、選擇疑問句	42
UNIT 06	直述句	44
PRACTICE 高難度		45
PART TEST		46

PART 4

簡短獨白		80
UNIT 01	會議摘錄	82
UNIT 02	電話留言	84
UNIT 03	廣播通知與公告	86
UNIT 04	電視、廣播節目與網路廣播	88
UNIT 05	廣告	90
UNIT 06	演說、介紹、參訪/觀光導覽	92
PRACTICE 高難度 （掌握意圖、圖表題）		94
PART TEST		96

4

RC

PART 5

句子填空		102
UNIT 01	名詞	104
UNIT 02	代名詞	108
UNIT 03	形容詞與限定詞	110
UNIT 04	副詞	112
UNIT 05	動詞、主動詞單複數一致性、語態、時態	114
UNIT 06	不定詞與動名詞	118
UNIT 07	分詞	120
UNIT 08	介系詞	122
UNIT 09	連接詞	126
UNIT 10	關係詞	130
UNIT 11	高分必備名詞詞彙	132
UNIT 12	高分必備形容詞詞彙	136
UNIT 13	高分必備副詞詞彙	140
UNIT 14	高分必備動詞詞彙	144
PRACTICE 高難度		148
PART TEST		151

PART 6

段落填空		156
UNIT 01	文法	158
UNIT 02	詞性	160
UNIT 03	詞彙	162
UNIT 04	連接副詞	166
UNIT 05	句子插入題	168
PART TEST		

PART 7

閱讀理解		174
UNIT 01	主旨或目的	176
UNIT 02	事實與否	178
UNIT 03	推論或暗示	180
UNIT 04	相關細節	182
UNIT 05	句子插入題	184
UNIT 06	找出同義詞	186
UNIT 07	雙篇閱讀	188
UNIT 08	多篇閱讀	192
PART TEST		196

實戰模擬試題		206

本書特色

LC

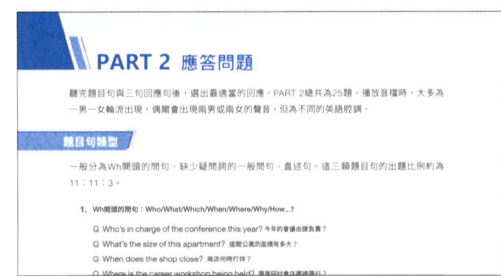

命題方向與解題策略
徹底分析各大題的特性、命題方向、考題類型、解題步驟、常見答題陷阱等，以這些內容為基礎，便能準確掌握學習方向。

UNIT
各單元準備了精選內容，包含 PART 1 常考用法大全、PART 2 高難度考題類型、PART 3 和 PART 4 的常考題型、代表題型範例等，幫助學習者鞏固基礎同時培養獲取高分必備的實力。

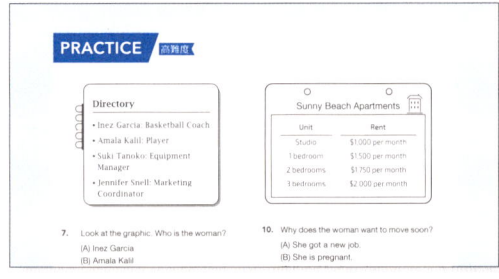

PRACTICE & PART TEST
簡單的考題類型為「PRACTICE」；難度較高的考題類型為「PRACTICE 高難度」，最後以「PART TEST」作結，檢視最終實力。

RC

命題方向與解題策略
徹底分析各大題的特性、命題方向、考題類型、解題步驟，有助學習者掌握正確的學習方向。

UNIT
PART 5 整理出重點文法和常考題型，並濃縮成一至兩頁的精華內容。學習完文法後，透過「PRACTICE」練習題立即測試實力，同時作答高分挑戰單元，做好應對高難度考題的準備。

PART 6 和 PART 7 按照考題類型劃分單元。PART 7 列出解題策略、題目類型、代表題型範例，只要掌握各單元重點，並完成練習題，便能有效減輕負擔，高效率學習。

學習計畫表

兩週速成學習計畫表

第1週

	DAY 1	DAY 2	DAY 3	DAY 4	DAY 5	DAY 6	DAY 7
	PART 1 UNIT 01~02 PRACTICE PART TEST 1 & 2	**PART 2** UNIT 01~06 PRACTICE PART TEST	**PART 3** UNIT 01~06 PRACTICE	**PART 3** UNIT 07~09 PART TEST	**PART 4** UNIT 01~04	**PART 4** UNIT 05~06 PRACTICE PART TEST	**PART 5** UNIT 01~05
	月　日	月　日	月　日	月　日	月　日	月　日	月　日

第2週

	DAY 8	DAY 9	DAY 10	DAY 11	DAY 12	DAY 13	DAY 14
	PART 5 UNIT 06~10	**PART 5** UNIT 11~14 PRACTICE PART TEST	**PART 6** UNIT 01~05 PART TEST	**PART 7** UNIT 01~05	**PART 7** UNIT 06~08 PART TEST	實戰 模擬試題	複習答錯 的題目
	月　日	月　日	月　日	月　日	月　日	月　日	月　日

四週速成學習計畫表

第1週

DAY 1	DAY 2	DAY 3	DAY 4	DAY 5
PART 1 UNIT 01~02 PRACTICE PART TEST 1 & 2	**PART 2** UNIT 01~06 PRACTICE PART TEST	**PART 3** UNIT 01~03	**PART 3** UNIT 04~06 PRACTICE	**PART 3** UNIT 07~09 PRACTICE PART TEST
月　　日	月　　日	月　　日	月　　日	月　　日

第2週

DAY 6	DAY 7	DAY 8	DAY 9	DAY 10
PART 4 UNIT 01~04	**PART 4** UNIT 05~06 PRACTICE PART TEST	實戰模擬試題 聽力測驗	**PART 5** UNIT 01~03	**PART 5** UNIT 04~06
月　　日	月　　日	月　　日	月　　日	月　　日

第3週

DAY 11	DAY 12	DAY 13	DAY 14	DAY 15
PART 5 UNIT 07~09	**PART 5** UNIT 10~12	**PART 5** UNIT 13~14 PRACTICE PART TEST	**PART 6** UNIT 01~03	**PART 6** UNIT 04~05 PART TEST
月　　日	月　　日	月　　日	月　　日	月　　日

第4週

DAY 16	DAY 17	DAY 18	DAY 19	DAY 20
PART 7 UNIT 01~03	**PART 7** UNIT 04~06	**PART 7** UNIT 07~08 PART TEST	實戰模擬試題 閱讀測驗	複習答錯 的題目
月　　日	月　　日	月　　日	月　　日	月　　日

多益測驗介紹

何謂多益測驗？

TOEIC為Test of English for International Communication（國際溝通英語測驗）的簡稱，測驗目的為測試英語非母語人士，是否具備在日常生活或商務上所需的實用英語能力。

測驗題型

題型	Part		題數		時間	分數
聽力 (LC)	Part 1	照片描述	6	100	45分	495分
	Part 2	應答問題	25			
	Part 3	簡短對話	39			
	Part 4	簡短獨白	30			
閱讀 (RC)	Part 5	句子填空	30	100	75分	495分
	Part 6	段落填空	16			
	Part 7	閱讀理解	單篇閱讀	29		
			雙篇閱讀	10		
			多篇閱讀	15		
總計	7 Parts		200題		120分	990分

命題範圍與主題

命題範圍涵蓋實際用於日常生活和工作中的主題，不會針對特定文化或職業出題。聽力測驗包含美國腔、英國腔、澳洲腔等各國發音。

一般商務	簽約、協商、業務、宣傳、行銷、商業企劃
金融財務	預算、投資、稅金、請款、會計
研發	研究、產品開發
製造	工廠管理、生產線、品管
人事	徵人、升遷、退休、員工培訓、新進員工
辦公室	會議、備忘錄、電話、傳真、電子郵件、辦公室設備與用具
活動	學會、宴會、聚餐、頒獎典禮、博覽會、產品發表會
房地產	建築、房地產買賣和租賃、企業用地、水電瓦斯設備
旅遊和休閒娛樂	交通工具、機場、車站、旅遊行程、飯店與租車預訂、延期或取消、電影、展覽、表演

報名方式

如何報名多益測驗？

- 採網路報名，請至台灣多益測驗主辦官網（https://www.toeic.com.tw）查詢報名時間。
- 報名測驗需提供近6個月內拍攝的照片，請提前準備好照片的jpg檔案。
- 多益追加報名約在考前3週開放，需另外支付追加報名費用。建議提前確認報名時間，並於規定時間內完成報名。

應試當天攜帶物品

身分證	有效的身分證件（中華民國國民身分證正本或有效期限內之「護照」正本）。
書寫用具	2B鉛筆、橡皮擦（不可使用原子筆或簽字筆）。

測驗流程

上午場次	下午場次	測驗流程
09:30-09:45	14:30～14:45	說明如何填寫答案卡
09:45-09:50	14:45～14:50	休息時間
09:50-10:05	14:50～15:05	確認身分證件
10:05-10:10	15:05～15:10	發放試題本與確認是否有破損
10:10-10:55	15:10～15:55	聽力測驗（Listening Test）
10:55-12:10	15:55～17:10	閱讀測驗（Reading Test）

成績查詢

測驗分數	考生可於成績開放查詢期間內至多益官方測驗服務專區查詢成績。
成績單寄送	成績單將於測驗結束後的第12個工作日以平信方式寄出。期限內可申請補發，免費補發僅限一次。

聽力測驗題型

PART 1 照片描述（6題）

題本

1.

音檔

Number 1. Look at the picture marked number 1 in your test book.

(A) He's staring at a vase.
(B) He's pouring a beverage.
(C) He's spreading out a tablecloth.
(D) He's sipping from a coffee cup.

PART 2 應答問題（25題）

題本

7. Mark your answer on your answer sheet.

音檔

Number 7.
When will the landlord inspect the property?

(A) No, it failed the inspection.
(B) I'll e-mail him about it.
(C) Do you like the apartment?

PART 3 簡短對話（39題） & PART 4 簡短獨白（30題）

題本（PART 3）

32. What is the conversation mainly about?
    (A) A boat ride
    (B) A history lecture
    (C) A nature hike
    (D) A bicycle tour

33. What does the woman ask the man to do?
    (A) Select a size
    (B) Show a receipt
    (C) Provide a phone number
    (D) Show an ID card

34. What does the woman suggest purchasing?
    (A) A map
    (B) A beverage
    (C) A gift card
    (D) A parking pass

音檔

Questions 32 through 34 refer to the following conversation.

M Hello. I'd like to sign up for the historic district bike tour. When does the next one depart?
W At eleven o'clock… um… about twenty minutes from now. And there are still a few spots left.
M Oh, that's great. I'd like one ticket, please.
W All right. And we provide all participants with a helmet and a safety vest. Please choose which size would be best for you.
M Sure. I'll take a medium.
W You might also want to buy something to drink to take with you. There's a convenience store right across the street.

Number 32. What is the conversation mainly about?

Number 33. What does the woman ask the man to do?

Number 34. What does the woman suggest purchasing?

閱讀測驗題型

PART 5 句子填空（30題）

101. If the parade goes ------- as planned, the planning committee members will be pleased.

(A) preciseness
(B) precisely
(C) precise
(D) precision

PART 6 段落填空（16題）

Questions 131-134 refer to the following article.

BALTIMORE (April 9)—The fitness club chain Power Gym ------- changes to its membership options. A spokesperson from the company's head office, Frank Jacobs, said they are adjusting their policies based on customer feedback.
131.

-------. The new policy will allow people to purchase one-day, one-week, or one-month passes, depending on their needs. This will support the company's commitment to making the gym convenient and -------. A parking garage will also be added to the gym's main site downtown. ------- will begin on that project sometime in June.
132.
133.
134.

PART 7 閱讀理解（54題）

Questions 153-154 refer to the following article.

Recall of Bratton Smartwatches

September 3—Smartwatch manufacturer Bratton has announced the recall of its Dola-9 line of smartwatches after being on the market for only 2 weeks. No serious injuries have been reported, but the product presents a risk of burns to the user, as the battery in the device may get too hot. Customers with a faulty device are eligible for a replacement or a full refund. Those who own a Dola-9 smartwatch are asked to contact the company at 1-800-555-7932. Once connected, you can input the serial number and automatically be informed of what steps to take next. Those with further inquiries can also leave a message for the customer service team.

153. What is indicated about the Dola-9 smartwatch?

(A) Its battery can overheat.
(B) It takes two weeks to be replaced.
(C) Its mileage is not recorded correctly.
(D) It has caused severe injuries.

154. What does the article recommend that Dola-9 owners do first?

(A) Visit a store
(B) Reset the device
(C) Call a helpline
(D) E-mail customer service

13

PART 1

照片描述

UNIT 01 人物照片

UNIT 02 事物照與風景照

常考用法大全

PRACTICE ［高難度］

PART TEST 1

PART TEST 2

PART 1 照片描述

該大題測驗內容為看試題本上的照片，聽完四個短句後，從中選出最符合照片的描述。聽力測驗共有100題，PART 1 佔6題。題本上不會印出選項 (A), (B), (C), (D)的內容。

照片類型

照片大致可分成有人物出現的照片和僅有事物或風景的照片兩大類。人物照片部分，單人獨照的出題頻率最高，一般會考2至3題。事物與風景照通常會考1題，少數情況會出2題。大部分照片為與工作或工作場合有關的情境，偶爾會出現日常生活照。

P1_命題方向與解題策略　解析p.2

單人獨照

🔊 音檔

1. (A) She's fixing a printer.
   (B) She's putting on a jacket.
   (C) She's examining some papers.
   (D) She's photocopying a document.

雙人照片

🔊 音檔

2. (A) They're removing their helmets.
   (B) They're folding some paper.
   (C) One of the men is marking a drawing.
   (D) One of the men is measuring a windowpane.

多人照片

🔊 音檔

3. (A) Customers are picking out some groceries.
   (B) Customers are waiting in a line.
   (C) A cashier is taking out some cash.
   (D) A cashier is opening a cash register.

事物與風景照

🔊 音檔

4. **(A) Some pictures are hanging on a wall.**
   (B) Some artwork is propped against a sofa.
   (C) A light fixture is mounted on a wall.
   (D) A potted plant is positioned on a table.

16

解題策略及步驟

STEP 1 | 聆聽音檔時請看著照片關鍵處
每一題會先說出指示「Look at the picture marked number（題號） in your test book.」，接著播放四個選項。此時請盯著該題對應的照片，把目光放在照片最關鍵的人物上。聆聽音檔時，請特別注意照片中最突出人物的動作、服裝以及手上拿的東西，可忽略照片背景和邊緣不明確的人事物。

Examples

1.

STEP 2 | 使用刪去法選出答案
PART 1播放選項 (A), (B), (C), (D) 的時間差不會超過1秒，若在聽完一個選項後，才思索是否為答案，便會來不及聽下個選項。因此請於聆聽各選項時，迅速判斷當中提到的事物是否出現在照片中、是否正確描述人物的服裝或動作、事物的狀態，並刪去錯誤選項。

2.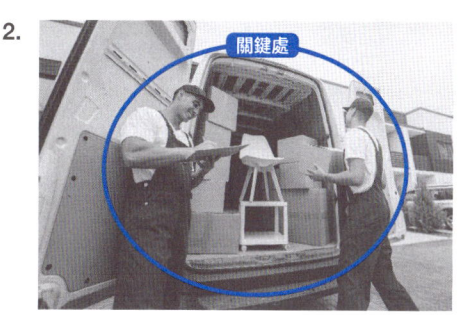

Look at the picture marked number 1 in your test book.

(A) She's putting items in a basket. (✗)
(B) She's holding a vegetable in each hand. (○)
(C) She's displaying some products. (✗)
(D) She's slicing some cabbages. (✗)

(A) 她正在把東西放進籃子裡。
(B) 她雙手都拿著蔬菜。
(C) 她正在展示一些產品。
(D) 她正在切高麗菜。

STEP 3 | 不要糾結於已播完音檔的題目
PART 1各題目的播放間隔時間約為5秒，需在5秒的時間內選好答案，並準備好看下一張照片。因此，請果斷放下已播完音檔的題目，否則可能會來不及確認下一題的照片，因而錯過後面的題目。

請熟記常考的事物名稱與人物動作用法

如欲在PART 1 取得高分，建議確實記下多益測驗中出現的各種事物名稱和人物動作用法，並正確辨別其發音差異，及小心避開誘答的陷阱選項。

UNIT 01　人物照片

💡 奪高分關鍵點

🎧 P1_U1

1. 陷阱選項會用照片中出現的東西搭配與人物動作無關的動詞，或提到照片中未出現的東西。

(A) He is pushing a wheelbarrow. ➔ 動詞 (✗)
(B) He is trimming some branches. ➔ 動詞 (✗)
(C) He is raking some leaves.
(D) He is clearing up some debris. ➔ 東西 (✗)

(A) 他正在推手推車。
(B) 他正在修剪樹枝。
(C) 他正在耙樹葉。
(D) 他正在清理碎片。

答案 (C)

2. 區分表示狀態的動詞與表示動作的動詞

(A) The man is organizing a toolbox.
(B) The man is lifting some furniture.
(C) The man is carrying a wooden plank.
(D) The man is putting on a helmet. ➔ 動作 (✗)

(A) 男子正在整理工具箱。
(B) 男子正在抬起傢俱。
(C) 男子正在搬運木板。
(D) 男子正在戴上安全帽。

答案 (C)

▶ is putting on指的是穿戴的「動作」；is wearing指的是穿戴的「狀態」，因此(D)應改寫成「The man is wearing a helmet.」才是正確的。工地人員戴的安全帽也可用hard hat表示。

動作 vs. 狀態

He **is putting on** a jacket.
(✗) is wearing
他正在穿夾克。

He **is wearing** a helmet.
(✗) is putting on
他正戴著安全帽。

She**'s wearing** glasses.
(✗) is putting on
她正戴著眼鏡。

She**'s riding** a bicycle.
(✗) is getting on
她正在騎腳踏車。

▶ 身上穿戴著衣服、鞋子、領帶、眼鏡、帽子、手套、圍巾時，要使用is wearing表示「穿戴著」。
▶ 使用「is taking off」和「is removing」表示正在脫下來的動作。

3. 選項可同時描寫人物與事物，通常其中兩個選項的主詞為事物，另外兩個選項的主詞為人物。

(A) **Some papers** have been stacked on the floor.
(B) **Some binders** have been lined up on a shelf.
(C) **A woman** is photocopying some documents.
(D) **A woman** is adjusting a computer monitor.

(A) 有些紙張被堆在地板上。
(B) 有些活頁夾被排在架上。
(C) 女子正在影印一些文件。
(D) 女子正在調整電腦螢幕。

答案 **(B)**

4. 事物當主詞時，可用「現在進行式的被動語態（is / are being p.p.）」描寫人物動作。

(A) A tree **is being planted**.
(B) A shovel is leaning against a fence.
(C) A woman is filling up a watering can.
(D) A man is emptying out a bucket.

(A)（有人）正在種樹。
(B) 鏟子靠在柵欄上。
(C) 女子正在為澆水壺裝水。
(D) 男子正在清空水桶。

答案 **(A)**

▶ (A) 把「They're planting a tree.」改寫成現在被動進行式。

Examples

 She **is painting** a wall.
她正在粉刷牆壁。

A wall **is being painted**.
牆壁正在被（某人）粉刷。

 He **is repairing** a roof.
他正在修理屋頂。

A roof **is being repaired**.
屋頂正在被（某人）修理。

CHECK-UP

🎧 P1_U1_Check-up 答案與解析 p.2

1.

(A)　(B)　(C)　(D)

2.

(A)　(B)　(C)　(D)

19

UNIT 02　事物照與風景照

💡 奪高分關鍵點　　🎧 P1_U2

1. 描寫事物和風景時，主要會使用「have / has been p.p.」或「are/is p.p.」的形態。陷阱選項經常針對照片中事物位置或狀態，進行錯誤的描寫。

(A) A lamp has been mounted on a wall.
(B) Some cushions have been set on an armchair.
(C) Some curtains have been laid out on the floor.
(D) A potted plant has been placed on a windowsill.

(A) 有盞燈被安裝在牆上。
(B) 扶手椅上放了一些靠枕。
(C) 地板上鋪著窗簾。
(D) 窗台上放著盆栽。

答案 (B)

2. 針對事物進行描寫時，可使用「be -ing」的形態。多益測驗中經常出現該用法，請務必熟記。

hang 懸掛、吊著	Clothing **is hanging** on racks. 衣服掛在衣架上。 Some pictures **are hanging** on a wall. 牆上掛著一些照片。
face 面對	Some chairs **are facing** each other. 有些椅子面對面擺放。 Some chairs **are facing** the sea. 有些椅子面向大海擺放。
lean 倚靠	A ladder **is leaning** against a fence. 梯子靠在柵欄上。 A bike **is leaning** against a building. 自行車靠著建築物。
line 沿著…排列	Some trees **are lining** a walkway. 有些樹木排在人行道上。 Some vehicles **are lining** both sides of a street. 有些車輛停在街道兩側。

Clothing **is hanging** on racks.
衣服掛在衣架上。

Some chairs **are facing** the sea.
有些椅子面向大海擺放。

A ladder **is leaning** against a fence.
梯子靠在柵欄上。

3. 針對事物進行描寫時，有時也會用「There is / are」或「介系詞片語」。

There are some vehicles lining the side of a street.
街道旁停著一些車輛。

Some shoes **are on display** on a shelf.
有些鞋子陳列在架上。

Some floor tiles **are in a pattern**.
有些地磚有圖案。

4. 若照片中未出現人物，選項卻以「事物＋is / are being p.p.」描寫時，通常為錯誤選項。

(A) A rear door of a van has been left open.
(B) Some boxes are being carried out of a building. → 進行式 (✗)
(C) Some crates are being unloaded from a truck. → 進行式 (✗)
(D) A vehicle is stopped at a traffic signal.

(A) 貨車的後門開著。
(B) 有些箱子正被搬出建築物。
(C) 有些貨箱正從卡車上被卸下。
(D) 車輛停在交通號誌處。

答案 **(A)**

▶ 下方所示的某些特定情境，即使照片中未出現人物，仍可使用現在進行式的被動語態描寫事物，請特別留意。

Merchandise **is being displayed** in a case.
商品陳列在展示盒裡。
→ 意思等同於Merchandise is on display。

The grass **is being watered**.
正在草坪上灑水。
→ 指的是靠機器灑水。

CHECK-UP

P1_U2_Check-up 答案與解析 p.2

1.

(A)　(B)　(C)　(D)

2.

(A)　(B)　(C)　(D)

常考用法大全

① 描寫動作

arranging some chairs　正在整理椅子
writing on a document　正在文件上書寫
taking some notes　正在做筆記
talking on a phone　正在打電話
packing some luggage　正在打包行李
watering some flowers　正在澆花
cutting the grass　正在除草
tying his shoes　正在繫他的鞋帶
facing a screen　正面對著螢幕
standing in line　正排成一列
photocopying a document　正在影印文件
operating some machinery　正在操作機器
looking through her handbag
正在翻看她的手提包
loading some bricks onto a cart
正在把磚塊裝上手推車

examining a flyer　正在檢視傳單
studying a drawing　正在研究設計圖
lifting some furniture　正抬起一些傢俱
carrying a shopping bag　正提著購物袋
exiting through a door　正穿過門出去
handing out some flyers　正在發送傳單
leaning against a railing　正靠著欄杆
sweeping a sidewalk　正清掃人行道
washing a window　正清洗窗戶
wiping down a countertop　正在擦拭檯面
removing his gloves　正脫下他的手套
clearing snow from a car　正清除汽車上的積雪
crouching to grab an item　正蹲下來拿東西
bending down to use a saw
正彎下腰來使用鋸子

② 描寫事物

常見動詞

Some pillows have been **placed** on a bed.　床上放了一些枕頭。

Sets of utensils have been **arranged** on napkins.　餐巾紙上擺放著成套的餐具。

Some bags have been **set** on the floor.　有些袋子被放在地上。
A tent has been **set up** near some cars.　汽車附近搭起了帳篷。
Food has been **set out** for an event.　為活動準備了食物。

A drawer has been **left** open.　抽屜開著。

Some boxes are **stacked** in a warehouse.　有些箱子堆放在倉庫裡。

常見介系詞片語

Some bricks are stacked **in a pile**.　有些磚塊堆成一堆。
Some vehicles have been parked **in a row**.　有些車輛停成一排。
The audience is seated **in a circle**.　觀眾圍坐成一圈。
A potted plant has been placed **on top of** a desk.　書桌上擺著盆栽。
Some chairs have been placed **by** a fountain.　噴水池旁擺放著一些椅子。
A toolbox has been set down **next to** some tires.　一輪胎旁放著工具箱。
Buildings are located **along** the shoreline.　建築物沿著海岸線分佈。
Two monitors are positioned **side by side**.　兩台顯示器並排放置。
A garden has been planted **outside of** a building.　建築物外面設有一座花園。

PRACTICE 高難度

🎧 P1_Practice 答案與解析 p.3

PART 1

1.

2.

3.

4.

5.

6.

23

PART TEST 1

1.

2.

3.

4.

5.

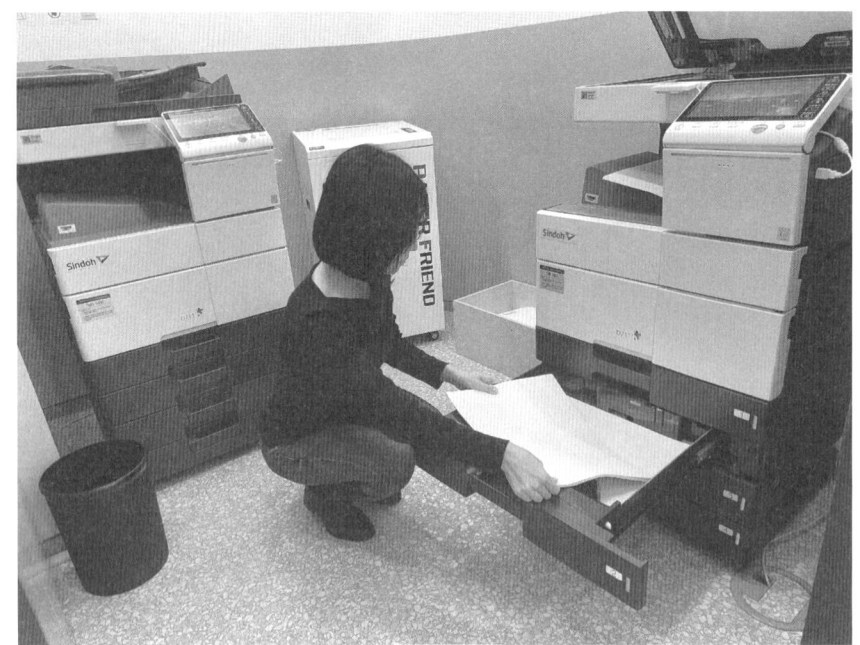

6.

PART TEST 2

P1_PT2 答案與解析 p.5

1.

2.

3.

4.

5.

6.

PART 2

應答問題

UNIT 01 Who/What/Which 問句

UNIT 02 When/Where 問句

UNIT 03 How/Why 問句

UNIT 04 Yes/No 問句

UNIT 05 表示建議或要求的問句、選擇疑問句

UNIT 06 直述句

PRACTICE ［高難度］

PART TEST

PART 2　應答問題

聽完題目句與三句回應句後，選出最適當的回應。PART 2總共為25題。播放音檔時，大多為一男一女輪流出現，偶爾會出現兩男或兩女的聲音，但為不同的英語腔調。

題目句類型

一般分為Wh開頭的問句、缺少疑問詞的一般問句、直述句。這三類題目句的出題比例約為 11：11：3。

1. **Wh開頭的問句：Who/What/Which/When/Where/Why/How...?**

    Q Who's in charge of the conference this year?　今年的會議由誰負責？
    Q What's the size of this apartment?　這間公寓的面積有多大？
    Q When does the shop close?　商店何時打烊？
    Q Where is the career workshop being held?　職業研討會在哪裡舉行？
    Q How was your vacation?　你的假期過得如何？
    Q Why did William move to Boston?　William為何會搬到波士頓？

    ▶ Wh開頭的問句有時會以「間接問句」的形式呈現，例如：Do you know when the library opens? 你知道圖書館何時會開嗎？

2. **一般問句＋直述句**

    [助動詞] Q Did you finish preparing for your presentation?　你的演講準備好了嗎？
    [助動詞] Q Will you be at the meeting this afternoon?　今天下午你會來開會嗎？
    [be動詞] Q Is there a café on this floor of the hotel?　飯店這層樓有咖啡廳嗎？

    ▶ 助動詞和be動詞開頭的問句有時會以「否定疑問句」或「附加問句」的形式呈現。
    　eg. Didn't you...?（否定疑問句）　You finished..., didn't you?（附加問句）

    [建議] Q Why don't we hold a fundraiser?　我們為何不舉辦募款活動？
    [選擇] Q Do you prefer to take the bus or the train?　你偏好搭公車還是火車？
    [直述句] Q I haven't received the updated employee list yet.　我還沒收到更新的員工名單。

解題策略及步驟

Example

Who's picking up the clients at the airport?

(A) In Terminal 2.
(B) Martin is. (O)
(C) She's my new client.

STEP 1｜聆聽題目句時，請專注於句子開頭處，尤其是疑問詞。有時只要聽清疑問詞，就能選出答案，因此請特別留意題目中出現的疑問詞為何。

STEP 2｜使用刪去法選出答案。(A)使用terminal，僅與題目句中的特定單字airport有關；(C)重複使用題目句中出現的單字client，兩個選項皆不是答案。

選項中常見的陷阱

1. 刻意使用發音相似的單字

    Q Who gave the presentation on the launch event? 誰在發布會上演講?

    A (×) I already had lunch. 我已經吃過午餐了。 → launch ≠ lunch

    A (○) The project manager, I believe. 我認為是專案經理。

2. 刻意使用意思相近或相關單字

    Q You transferred to this branch recently, didn't you? 你最近調到這間分公司了,不是嗎?

    A (×) No, we used a moving company. 不,我們用了搬家公司。 → move的意思與transfer相近

    A (○) Yes, just last week. 是的,就在上週。

3. 適合回答其他疑問句的答覆。

    Q When will the printer be repaired? 何時會修理好影印機?

    A (×) On my desk. 在我桌上。 → Where

    A (○) Probably this afternoon. 大概是今天下午。

4. 重複使用題目句中的單字。

    Q Do you think our customers will like our new logo? 你覺得我們的客戶會喜歡新商標嗎?

    A (×) I stayed late to help some customers. 我為了幫一些客戶留到很晚。 → 重複使用題目句中的customers

    A (○) Yes, it's very attractive. 是的,它非常有吸引力。

適用多種題目句的答覆方式

有些答覆方式適用於多種題目句,建議一次記下這些用法,有助於解題。

Question	Answer
Q Who's going to select a candidate for the position? 由誰選出該職位的候選人?	I'm not sure. 我不太清楚。
Q When are you going to interview the candidates? 你打算何時面試應徵者?	Brian will know. Brian會知道。
Q Did you select a candidate for the position? 你選出該職位的候選人了嗎?	You'll have to ask Sam. 你應該去問Sam。
Q Was it James or Chris who interviewed the candidates? 面試應徵者的是James還是Chris?	You'd better ask Sam. 你最好去問Sam。

UNIT 01　Who/What/Which 問句

Who

題目主要詢問某項工作的負責人是誰，答句經常直接回答人名或職稱。

1. **回答人名或職稱**

   Example 01　　　　　　　　　　　　　　　　　　🎧 P2_U1_Ex01

   Who's designing our new logo?
   (A) Terry is working on it.
   (B) Yes, the cover design is great.
   (C) In about two weeks.

   由誰設計我們的新商標？
   (A) Terry正在做。(○)
   (B) 是的，封面設計很棒。(×)
   (C) 大約兩週後。(×)

   常見回答
   A1　Paul takes care of that. Paul會處理。
   A2　Paul, as far as I know. 據我所知，是Paul。
   A3　Paul said he would. Paul說他會做。
   A4　Paul's in charge. 由Paul負責。
   A5　The chief designer. 首席設計師。

2. **回答公司名稱**

   Q　Who's going to sponsor this year's fundraiser? 誰將贊助今年的募款活動？
   A　A new hotel called Paradise View. 一間名為天堂視野的新飯店。

3. **常見的其他回答方式**

   Q　Who's leading the focus group meeting next week? 由誰主持下週的重點小組會議？
   A1　It's been delayed until July. 已延期至七月了。
   A2　It hasn't been decided yet. 還沒決定。
   A3　We're still deciding. 我們還在決定。
   A4　I'll have to check my notes. 我需要看我的筆記來確認。
   A5　That will be announced later today. 將於今天稍晚公布。
   A6　Didn't you get the e-mail this morning? 今天早上你沒收到郵件嗎？

4. **高難度** 雖然題目句為Who開頭問句，但有時答案為看似針對When開頭問句回答的內容，包含時間或日程的答覆，屬於難度偏高的回答方式。

   Example 02　　　　　　　　　　　　　　　　　　🎧 P2_U1_Ex02

   Who's going to submit the budget report today?
   (A) I thought it's due tomorrow.
   (B) Donna should be in the office.
   (C) The quarterly report.

   今天由誰來提交預算報告？
   (A) 我以為期限是明天。(○)
   (B) Donna應在辦公室裡。(×)
   (C) 季度報告。(×)

What/Which

What或Which開頭的問句，答案通常由疑問詞正後方連接的名詞決定，因此聆聽題目句時，請特別留意前半段的內容。

1. What kind / type of...?　What 名詞...?　What is / 助動詞...?

    Q What kind of food does your restaurant serve?　貴餐廳提供什麼類型的食物？
    A Italian, mostly.　主要為義式料理。

    Q What flight should I book for our business trip to Boston?　我應為前往波士頓出差預訂什麼樣的航班？
    A The earlier we arrive, the better.　我們越早抵達越好。

    Q What is the marketing department's phone number?　行銷部門的電話號碼多少？
    A All the information is available online.　所有資料均可在線上找到。

2. What do you think about...?　你對⋯有何看法？

    Q What do you think about our new company brochure?　你對我們公司新的宣傳手冊有何看法？
    A We'd better reduce the size of the title.　我們最好縮小標題大小。

3. 題目為Which開頭的問句時，答案通常會避開題目中出現過的名詞，改用one或ones來回答。但若選項中未出現one，仍可能為正確答案。

    Q Which bus stop is closest to your workplace?　哪個公車站離你工作的地方最近？
    A The one on Maple Street.　Maple街上的車站。

    Q Which training session are you going to attend tomorrow?　明天你打算參加哪一場培訓？
    A Well, **the ones** in the morning filled up quickly.　嗯，上午的場次很快就滿了。

    Q Which restaurant do you usually go to?　你通常會去哪間餐廳？
    A I always eat at the company cafeteria.　我都在公司的員工餐廳吃飯。

4. 高難度　題目句為Which開頭的問句時，並非只要出現one的選項，就一定是正確答案。

    ### Example 03

    Which company was hired to renovate the building?

    (A) That project has been postponed.
    (B) One of our most popular designs.
    (C) A 7-story building.

    哪家公司被聘請來翻修大樓？
    (A) 該工程已被延期了。(○)
    (B) 我們最受歡迎的設計之一。(✗)
    (C) 一棟7層樓高的建築。(✗)

CHECK-UP

1.	(A)	(B)	(C)	4.	(A)	(B)	(C)
2.	(A)	(B)	(C)	5.	(A)	(B)	(C)
3.	(A)	(B)	(C)	6.	(A)	(B)	(C)

UNIT 02　When/Where 問句

When

請仔細聆聽題目句為When還是Where開頭的問句。兩者聽起來有些微相似，容易聽錯，因此選項中常會同時出現回答地點和時間的答覆。

1. 同時出現與When和Where有關的選項

   Example 01　🎧 P2_U2_Ex01

   When will the prototype be ready for testing?
   (A) On the third floor.
   (B) By Thursday morning.
   (C) Just a few components.

   何時準備好測試樣機？
   (A) 在三樓。(✗) → 與Where有關的答覆
   (B) 星期四早上。(○)
   (C) 只有幾個零件。(✗)

2. 各時態的題目句與答句

過去式	Q　When did we last conduct a safety inspection? 我們上次何時進行安全檢查？ A1 About two months ago. 大約兩個月前。　　A2 Sometime last week. 上週某個時段。
現在式	Q　When does the museum open? 博物館何時開放？ A　Not until 10:00 in the morning. 早上十點之後。
未來式	Q　When are they going to replace the copy machine? 他們何時會更換影印機？ A　Before the end of the month. 本月底前。

3. 其他回答方式

   Q　When will our pasta be ready? 我們的義大利麵何時能準備好？
   A　I'll check with our chef. 我會向主廚確認一下。

   Q　When are the new employees starting? 新員工何時入職工作？
   A　There are two people left to interview. 還要再面試兩個人。

4. 【高難度】有時要等到句末才會出現與時間相關的內容，因此聆聽選項時，請務必聽到最後。

   Example 02　🎧 P2_U2_Ex02

   When will the new partnership be announced?
   (A) She's a partner in a law firm.
   (B) At the board meeting next week.
   (C) I'm happy to work with you.

   何時會宣布新的合作夥伴？
   (A) 她是律師事務所的合夥人。(✗)
   (B) 下週的董事會會議上。(○)
   (C) 我很高興能與你共事。(✗)

Where

答案一般為用到介系詞的選項，通常陷阱選項為適合回答When問句的答覆。

1. 回答地點或位置

    Q Where is the investment seminar being held this year? 今年的投資研討會在哪裡舉行？
    A The same hotel as last year. 跟去年一樣的飯店。

    Q Where can I find an extra stapler? 哪裡可以找到多的釘書機？
    A In the bottom desk drawer. 在活動櫃的最下層。

2. 採反問方式答覆

    Q Where is the presentation remote clicker? 簡報用遙控器在哪裡？
    A Didn't Helen use it at the meeting yesterday? 昨天開會時Helen不是有用到嗎？

3. 其他回答方式

    Q Where are the keys to the storeroom? 儲藏室鑰匙在哪裡？
    A Helen had them last. 最後使用的是Helen。

    Q Where did you buy this coffee machine? 你在哪裡買到這台咖啡機？
    A It was a gift. 這是收到的禮物。

    Q Where should I park when I go to the conference? 我去開會時該把車停哪裡？
    A It's better to take a taxi. 最好搭計程車去。

    Q Where should we examine these product samples? 我們該在哪裡檢查這些樣品？
    A No one is in the conference room. 會議室裡沒人（表示建議在會議室裡檢查）

4. **高難度** 切勿一聽到與地點或位置有關的介系詞（in, on, at, by）就馬上選該選項為答案。

    ### Example 03　　　　　　　　　　　　　　　　　　P2_U2_Ex03

    Where's the nearest pharmacy?
    (A) In the first drawer.
    (B) The closest one is on Hewes Street.
    (C) Dr. Martin is not available today.

    最近的藥局在哪裡？
    (A) 在第一個抽屜裡。（✗）
    (B) 最近的一間在Hewes街上。（○）
    (C) Martin醫生今天沒空。（✗）

CHECK-UP　　　　　　　　　　P2_U2_Check-up 答案與解析 p.8

1.	(A)	(B)	(C)	4.	(A)	(B)	(C)
2.	(A)	(B)	(C)	5.	(A)	(B)	(C)
3.	(A)	(B)	(C)	6.	(A)	(B)	(C)

UNIT 03　How/Why 問句

How

How開頭的問句，回答方式通常由正後方連接的單字決定，因此聆聽題目句時，請特別留意前半段的內容。

1. 詢問數量、頻率、期間等：How many/much/long/often/soon...?

    Q **How many** chairs need to be set up for the seminar?　研討會需擺設多少張椅子？
    A At least twenty.　至少二十張。

    Q **How much** does this toaster oven cost?　這個烤吐司機多少錢？
    A It's on sale for 450 dollars.　特價450美元。

    Q **How long** have you worked with John?　你和John一起共事多久了？
    A About four years.　大約四年。

    Q **How often** does the tennis club meet?　網球社團多久聚會一次？
    A Once every two weeks.　每兩週一次。

    Q **How soon** will the company brochure be ready?　公司宣傳手冊多久能準備好？
    A Not until next week.　要等到下週。

2. 詢問意見：How was...?/How did you like...?

    Q **How was** the trade show yesterday?　昨天的貿易博覽會如何？
    A It was very successful!　非常成功！

    Q **How did you like** the café?　你覺得這家咖啡廳如何？
    A It was great. Well worth the drive.　很棒。值得特地開車過去。

3. 詢問方法：How do I...?

    Q **How do I** sign up for the seminar?　我要如何報名參加研討會？
    A You need to fill out a form online.　你需在線上填寫表單。

4. 高難度 "How did ~ go?" 經常以「某事進行得順利嗎？、某事狀況如何？」之意出題。

    Q **How did** the product demonstration **go**?　產品演示進行得順利嗎？
    Q **How did** the sales presentation **go**?　銷售簡報進行得順利嗎？
    Q **How did** your interview **go** yesterday?　昨天的面試如何？

    ### Example 01　🎧 P2_U3_Ex01

    How did yesterday's meeting with the clients go?
    (A) Our biggest customer.
    (B) It went well. Thanks.
    (C) I go to Amsterdam every year.

    昨天與客戶的會議進行得順利嗎？
    (A) 我們最大的客戶。（✗）
    (B) 進展很順利。謝謝。（○）
    (C) 我每年會去阿姆斯特丹。（✗）

38

Why

題目為Why開頭的問句時，答句經常直接使用because/for或不定詞to V來回答。尤其當選項中出現Because，幾乎可以肯定為正確答案。

1. 回答原因或理由

    > **Example 02**　　　　　　　　　　　　　　　🎧 P2_U3_Ex02
    >
    > Why will the museum be closed tomorrow?　　為什麼博物館明天不開放？
    > (A) It's a week from tomorrow.　　(A) 從明天起一週後。（✗）
    > (B) It was an exhibit on ancient Egypt.　　(B) 是有關古埃及的展覽。（✗）
    > (C) Because it's a national holiday.　　(C) 因為是國定假日。（○）

    ▶ 有時答案會省略Because。

    A1　It's closed on Mondays.　每週一公休。
    A2　It's being renovated.　正在重新裝修。

2. 回答目的

    Q　Why did Mitchell leave early today?　為什麼Mitchell今天提早走？
    A1　To pick Mr. Torres up from the train station.　為了去火車站接Torres先生。
    A2　For a client meeting.　了與客戶開會。

3. 高難度　採反問方式答覆

    Q　Why do we have another meeting about the budget?　為什麼要再開一次關於預算的會議？
    A　Have you seen last quarter's sales figures?　你看過上個季度的銷售數據嗎？

    Q　Why haven't the tables been set up in the garden?　為什麼庭院裡還沒擺設桌子？
    A　Have you seen the weather forecast?　你看過天氣預報了嗎？

    Q　Why aren't the trainees in the conference room now?　為什麼學員現在不在會議室裡？
    A　Didn't you get an e-mail with the updated schedule?　你沒收到一封附上更新時程表的電子郵件嗎？

    Q　Why are they moving the bookshelves now?　為什麼他們現在要搬書架？
    A　Is the noise bothering you?　噪音對你造成困擾了嗎？

CHECK-UP　　　　　🎧 P2_U3_Check-up　答案與解析 p.9

1.	(A)	(B)	(C)	4.	(A)	(B)	(C)
2.	(A)	(B)	(C)	5.	(A)	(B)	(C)
3.	(A)	(B)	(C)	6.	(A)	(B)	(C)

UNIT 04　Yes/No 問句

一般問句（助動詞／be 動詞）

題目為助動詞或be動詞開頭的一般問句時，答句經常直接回答Yes或No，但有時也會出現省略Yes和No的答案。

1. Do/Have…?

    Q　Did you take the bus to get here?　你是搭公車過來的嗎？
    A1　Yes, it took longer than I thought.　對，花費時間比我想像中還久。
    A2　No, I drove.　不，我是開車。

    Q　Have you met Mr. Lee, the new HR director?　你見過新任人力資源總監Lee先生了嗎？
    A1　Yes, we just met at the meeting.　是，我們剛在會議上見過。
    A2　No, I just got back from vacation.　沒有，我剛度假完回來。
    A3　I've been in meetings all day.　我整天都在開會。

2. Will/Should…?

    Q　Will you be at the staff meeting this afternoon?　你會參加下午的員工會議嗎？
    A1　Yes, I'll be there.　是的，我會參加。
    A2　I have a dentist appointment.　我已預約看牙醫。

    Q　Should we reserve a conference room for the interview?　我們應該要為面試預約會議室嗎？
    A1　Yes, could you do that now?　是的，你現在方便預約嗎？
    A2　I heard it was canceled.　我聽說面試被取消了。

3. Be動詞開頭的問句

    Q　Is Jamie Lopez attending today's seminar?　Jamie Lopez會參加今天的研討會嗎？
    A　Alex has the guest list.　Alex有賓客名單。

    Q　Are these bookmarks for sale?　這些書籤有在販售嗎？
    A　Feel free to take one.　可隨意拿取一張。

4. 高難度　有些陷阱選項會於Yes或No後方連接答非所問的內容，或是相關單字混淆視聽，請特別留意。

    Example 01　　　🎧 P2_U4_Ex01

    Do you have Paul's e-mail address?
    (A) He moved to Miami last year.
    (B) Sure, I'll text it to you.
    (C) Yes, by mail will be better.

    你有Paul的電子郵件地址嗎？
    (A) 他去年搬到了邁阿密。（✕）
    (B) 當然，我用訊息傳給你。（○）
    (C) 是的，用郵寄比較好。（✕）

    ▶ (C)雖然回答Yes，但後方內容使用e-mail當中的mail，僅為相關單字並非答案。

否定疑問句／附加問句

無論是否定疑問句、還是附加問句，皆可用Yes / No來回答。

1. 請把否定疑問句和附加問句當成一般問句，只要答案為肯定，就回答Yes；否定則回答No。

    一般 Q Are you organizing our launch party? 你正在規劃我們的發布會嗎？
    否定 Q Aren't you organizing our launch party? 你不是正在規劃我們的發布會嗎？
    附加 Q You are organizing our launch party, aren't you? 你正在規劃我們的發布會，不是嗎？
    A1 Yes, with Harry in Human Resources. 是的，跟人力資源部的Harry一起。
    A2 No, Ms. Derby is handling it. 不，是由Derby女士負責處理。

2. 無論是肯定句或否定句，附加問句皆可替換成 "..., right?"。

    Q The last train to Boston hasn't departed yet, has it? 往波士頓的末班車尚未發車，是嗎？
    Q The last train to Boston has departed, hasn't it? 往波士頓的末班車已經開走了，不是嗎？
    ⇨ The last train to Boston has / hasn't departed (yet), right? 往波士頓的末班車已經／尚未發車，對吧？
    A1 Yes, it just left. 是的，它剛開走。
    A2 No, you've got 10 minutes. 不，你還有10分鐘。

3. **高難度** 聽到Don't/Didn't you...? 等以主詞you詢問的題目句時，千萬不要直接選擇以 "I" 開頭的選項作為答案。

    Example 02　　　🎧 P2_U4_Ex02

    Don't you need to order a flowerpot for the lobby?
    (A) Linda took care of it last week.
    (B) I water the plant once a week.
    (C) In numerical order, please.

    你不是要訂一個花盆放在大廳嗎？
    (A) Linda上週處理好了。（○）
    (B) 我每週給植物澆一次水。（×）
    (C) 請按數字順序排列。（×）

    ▶ 針對Don't you...? 開頭的問句，(B)刻意使用主詞 "I" 加上與flowerpot有關的單字plant，屬於陷阱選項。

4. **高難度** 題目為否定疑問句或附加問句時，答案可使用問句，或採反問方式答覆。

    Q Can't you reschedule the interview? 你不能重新安排面試時間嗎？
    A Can I get back to you later? 我可以稍晚再回覆你嗎？

    Q You're going to attend the training session tomorrow, right? 你明天要去參加培訓，對吧？
    A Do you think that's necessary? 你覺得有必要嗎？

CHECK-UP　🎧 P2_U4_Check-up 答案與解析 p.9

1.	(A)	(B)	(C)	**4.**	(A)	(B)	(C)
2.	(A)	(B)	(C)	**5.**	(A)	(B)	(C)
3.	(A)	(B)	(C)	**6.**	(A)	(B)	(C)

UNIT 05　表示建議或要求的問句、選擇疑問句

表示建議或要求的問句

題目為表示建議或要求的問句時，答句一般會使用Sure, Okay, Sorry等字詞開頭，直接回應同意或拒絕。有時也會省略這些字詞，直接回答具體內容。

1. 表示建議的問句：Why don't/How about/Would you like to/Can I...?

    Q Why don't we interview the two candidates at the same time?　我們何不同時面試兩名應徵者？
    A Okay, that sounds good.　好的，聽起來不錯。

    Q How about hiring more temporary workers?　招募更多臨時工如何？
    A There's not much money in the budget.　預算不夠充裕。

    Q Would you like to come on a hike with us this Sunday?　這週日你願意和我們一起去健行嗎？
    A There's a lot of rain in the forecast.　天氣預報顯示會下雨。

    Q Can I help you move your desk?　需要我幫你搬桌子嗎？
    A I think I can manage on my own.　我想我可以自己處理。

2. 表示要求的問句：Could/Can/Would you...?

    Q Could/Can you give me a ride to work tomorrow?　你明天能開車載我去上班嗎？
    A Sure, I'd be happy to.　當然，我很樂意。

    Q Would you please take notes at the meeting?　可以請你在會議上做記錄嗎？
    A Okay, I'll take care of that.　好，我會處理。

    Q Would you be willing to give a speech at the ceremony?　你願意在典禮上致詞嗎？
    　= Would you be interested in giving a speech at the ceremony?
    A I'm leaving on an urgent business trip tomorrow.　我明天臨時要去出差。

3. 高難度　鄭重拜託他人時會用「Would you mind...?」，直譯為「你介意…嗎？」，因此回答No或Not at all的話，即表示同意。

    > **Example 01**　　　　　　　　　　　　　　　　　　　🎧 P2_U5_Ex01
    >
    > Would you mind looking for more boxes?　　　　　　你介意幫忙尋找更多箱子嗎？
    > (A) I found it very useful.　　　　　　　　　　　　(A) 我發現它非常有用。(✗)
    > (B) Not at all.　　　　　　　　　　　　　　　　　　(B) 當然不會。(○)
    > (C) Yes, that's the cheapest one.　　　　　　　　　(C) 是，那是最便宜的。(✗)

4. 高難度　使用問句回答

    Q Would you mind forwarding those e-mails to Mr. Ruskin in Human Resources?
    　你介意將這些電子郵件轉寄給人力資源部的Ruskin先生嗎？
    A What's his e-mail address?　他的電子郵件地址是什麼？

選擇疑問句

選擇疑問句的句末通常以「A or B…?」呈現，因此答句最常直接從兩者中擇一回答。

1. 兩者擇一

Q Would you like a refund or an exchange? A A refund, please.	你想要退款還是換貨？ 請幫我退款。
Q Would you like to see the doctor on Monday or Thursday? A Thursday works better.	你想在星期一還是星期四去看醫生？ 星期四比較好。
Q Do you want your commercial to run at eight or nine P.M.? A I'd prefer nine.	你希望你的廣告在晚上八點還是九點播放？ 我偏好九點。

2. 兩者皆可／提出第三種選項

Q Would you prefer to fly in the morning or the afternoon? A Whichever is cheaper.	你喜歡早上還是下午的班機？ 看哪一班比較便宜。
Q Have you finished reviewing the report or do you need more time? A I'm finishing it now.	你已經審閱完報告了嗎？還是需要更多時間？ 我現在完成了。

3. 高難度 有時答案為兩者擇一，但不會使用題目句中出現的單字。

Example 02 P2_U5_Ex02

Have you moved or are you at the same address?

(A) The same time next week.
(B) I still live at Greenwood Street.
(C) They're a great moving company.

你已經搬家了，還是住在同個地址？

(A) 下週同一時間。（✗）
(B) 我還住在Greenwood街。（○）
(C) 他們是間很棒的搬家公司。（✗）

CHECK-UP

P2_U5_Check-up 答案與解析 p.10

1. (A) (B) (C)   4. (A) (B) (C)
2. (A) (B) (C)   5. (A) (B) (C)
3. (A) (B) (C)   6. (A) (B) (C)

UNIT 06 直述句

平均每回測驗出三題。直述句包含各式各樣的句子，沒有固定出題模式，因此屬於Part 2難度最高的題型。在一來一往的對話中，題目句為直述句時，答句可為直述句或問句。

1. 直述句 ─ 問句：以問句答覆直述句。

   Example 01 🎧 P2_U6_Ex01

   We need a project assistant by the end of this month.
   (A) Thanks for your assistance.
   (B) Have you considered Ella Morita?
   (C) It's next to the projector screen.

   本月底前我們需要一名專案助理。
   (A) 感謝你的協助。（✗）
   (B) 你有考慮過Ella Morita嗎？（O）
   (C) 它就在投影機螢幕旁邊。（✗）

   更多範例
   A I'm going to try to fix this copy machine. 我要嘗試修理這台影印機。
   B Are you sure it can be repaired? 你確定可以修好嗎？

   A This month's training schedule has been revised. 已修改好本月的培訓時間表。
   B Which dates have been changed? 更改了哪些日期？

2. 直述句 ─ 直述句：經常是提出特定問題、建議或要求。

   Example 02 🎧 P2_U6_Ex02

   I tried turning the projector on, but it didn't work.
   (A) Why is it being moved?
   (B) That place isn't far from here.
   (C) The sales department used it yesterday.

   我試圖打開投影機，但無法使用。
   (A) 為什麼要移動它？（✗）
   (B) 那個地方離這裡不遠。（✗）
   (C) 昨天銷售部門使用過。（O）

   更多範例
   A I'm having trouble finding a carpenter to repair the roof. 我找不到木工來修理屋頂。
   B Marty's had a lot of work done on his home. Marty為他家做了很多工程。

   A I can help set up the tables if you'd like. 如果你願意，我可以幫忙擺設桌子。
   B Thanks, but you don't have to do that. 謝謝，但你不需要這麼做。

CHECK-UP

🎧 P2_U6_Check-up 答案與解析 p.11

1.	(A)	(B)	(C)	4.	(A)	(B)	(C)
2.	(A)	(B)	(C)	5.	(A)	(B)	(C)
3.	(A)	(B)	(C)	6.	(A)	(B)	(C)

PRACTICE 高難度

P2_Practice 答案與解析 p.12

UNIT 01~03

1. (A) (B) (C)
2. (A) (B) (C)
3. (A) (B) (C)
4. (A) (B) (C)
5. (A) (B) (C)
6. (A) (B) (C)
7. (A) (B) (C)
8. (A) (B) (C)
9. (A) (B) (C)
10. (A) (B) (C)
11. (A) (B) (C)
12. (A) (B) (C)
13. (A) (B) (C)
14. (A) (B) (C)
15. (A) (B) (C)

UNIT 04~06

16. (A) (B) (C)
17. (A) (B) (C)
18. (A) (B) (C)
19. (A) (B) (C)
20. (A) (B) (C)
21. (A) (B) (C)
22. (A) (B) (C)
23. (A) (B) (C)
24. (A) (B) (C)
25. (A) (B) (C)
26. (A) (B) (C)
27. (A) (B) (C)
28. (A) (B) (C)
29. (A) (B) (C)
30. (A) (B) (C)

PART 2

PART TEST

1. Mark your answer on your answer sheet.
2. Mark your answer on your answer sheet.
3. Mark your answer on your answer sheet.
4. Mark your answer on your answer sheet.
5. Mark your answer on your answer sheet.
6. Mark your answer on your answer sheet.
7. Mark your answer on your answer sheet.
8. Mark your answer on your answer sheet.
9. Mark your answer on your answer sheet.
10. Mark your answer on your answer sheet.
11. Mark your answer on your answer sheet.
12. Mark your answer on your answer sheet.
13. Mark your answer on your answer sheet.

14. Mark your answer on your answer sheet.

15. Mark your answer on your answer sheet.

16. Mark your answer on your answer sheet.

17. Mark your answer on your answer sheet.

18. Mark your answer on your answer sheet.

19. Mark your answer on your answer sheet.

20. Mark your answer on your answer sheet.

21. Mark your answer on your answer sheet.

22. Mark your answer on your answer sheet.

23. Mark your answer on your answer sheet.

24. Mark your answer on your answer sheet.

25. Mark your answer on your answer sheet.

PART 3

簡短對話

UNIT 01 說話者的職業或對話地點

UNIT 02 對話目的或主旨

UNIT 03 建議或要求

UNIT 04 疑難問題或擔憂

UNIT 05 特定時間

UNIT 06 下一步的行動

PRACTICE ［UNIT 01~06］

UNIT 07 掌握意圖＋PRACTICE ［高難度］

UNIT 08 三人對話＋PRACTICE ［高難度］

UNIT 09 圖表題＋PRACTICE ［高難度］

PART TEST

PART 3 簡短對話

聽完雙人或三人對話後，針對相關的三道考題選出最適當答案。PART 3總共有13組對話，其中固定會出現2篇三人對話文。

對話類型

PART 3的對話主題涵蓋範圍廣泛，主要為在公司可能發生的情境對話，包含公司內部業務、人事、活動、辦公設備及設施等。多為一男一女的對話組合，偶爾會出現兩男或兩女的對話。

考題類型

基本常見題型為詢問對話的地點或主旨、說話者的身分、說話者的建議或要求事項、說話者下一步的行動、需要討論的議題等。高難度題型為掌握意圖的考題，指定說話者提及的特定話語，詢問話語意圖（2題）。還有每回測驗固定出現的圖表整合題（3題），如欲取得高分，務必要充分練習這些題型。

解題策略及步驟

STEP 1 | 迅速瀏覽題目，並標出題目關鍵字。
請於各對話播放前，快速瀏覽三道題目的內容，並標出題目關鍵字。接著請根據關鍵字，判斷需要專心聆聽對話中的哪些部分。下方範例中，根據對話脈絡，需要專心聆聽的部分依序為「對話地點＞男子想買的東西＞女子要求男子的事」。

1. **Where** is the conversation taking place? → 前半段對話中要確認對話地點！
2. What will the man most likely **purchase**? → 接著要仔細聽男子打算買什麼東西！
3. What does the woman **ask** the man to do? → 對話最後女子會要求男子做什麼事！

通常只要透過三道題中的第一題，便能確認整篇對話的情境與說話者彼此間的關係。

eg What type of business is the woman calling? 女子打電話給什麼類型的公司？
▶ 在聆聽對話前，透過「calling」便能得知對話情境為女子打電話給某間公司。預先判斷可能的情境，有助於稍後聆聽時更快速聽懂對話內容。

STEP 2 | 聆聽開頭說明，確認對話為雙人對話還是三人對話。
題本上不會寫出對話人數，因此請留意對話前方播放的說明。聽到說明中出現「three speakers」，得知說話者有三人時，便能冷靜聆聽接下來的三人對話。

Questions 47-49 refer to the following conversation **with three speakers**.

STEP 3 | 題目內容通常會依序出現在對話中。

一般來說，前半段對話中會出現第一題的答題線索；對話中間會出現第二題的答題線索；後半段對話中會出現最後一題的答題線索。因此，聆聽前半段對話時，請邊聽邊查看第一題的選項，並在對話播放過程中，依序查看第二題和第三題的選項。

Example

🎧 P3_U0_Ex 答案與解析 p.19

W　Thank you for visiting the Kaysville Aquarium. How may I help you?

M　I'd like admission tickets for two adults, please.

W　The regular ticket is 22 dollars. However, you can get a season ticket for just 75 dollars. That allows you to visit our site as many times as you want for one year.

M　Hmm... Since we live locally, we'll probably come back many times. I guess I'll take that.

W　Great! All I need is for you to fill out this application form.

1. Where is the conversation taking place?
   (A) At a movie theater
   (B) At an aquarium
   (C) At an art museum
   (D) At a stadium

2. What will the man most likely purchase?
   (A) A group ticket
   (B) A half-day ticket
   (C) A season ticket
   (D) A student ticket

3. What does the woman ask the man to do?
   (A) Complete a form
   (B) Call another branch
   (C) Show an ID card
   (D) Make a phone call

聆聽時切勿錯過告知答題線索的提示字句（cue）

對話中，經常會出現一些「提示字句（cue）」，提前預告後方即將出現答題線索。像是「Thank you for visiting...」後方出現公司或店家名稱，其便是詢問對話地點的答題線索。另外，對話最後女子提到：「All I need is...」，後方便出現第34題詢問要求的答題線索。除上述兩種提示，若能事先掌握多益測驗中經常出現在特定考題的提示字句，便能在不用完全聽懂對話的情況下，透過答題線索輕鬆選出答案。本書按照各考題類型整理出提示字句，方便讀者學習。

選項經常會採取換句話說的方式改寫

選項經常會把對話中的單字換成其他意思相近的單字，或直接換句話說，改寫選項內容。如上方範例，女子的對白為「fill out this application form」，第34題選項改寫成 (A) Complete a form。

fill out this application form ➡ complete a form

雖然意思並非完全劃上等號，但換成同類別的單字後，只要重點概念相符即可。例如：party 換成event、shirt換成clothes、name and phone number換成 contact information。

UNIT 01　說話者的職業或對話地點

🔍 常見考題類型

詢問說話者的職業或身分

- **What industry [field]** do the speakers work in? 說話者在哪個行業［領域］工作？
- **What kind of business** do the speakers work for? 說話者從事什麼行業？
- **What type of business** is the woman calling? 女子打電話給什麼類型的公司？
- **Where** does the woman most likely work? 女子最有可能在哪裡工作？
- **Who** most likely is the man? 男子最有可能是誰？
- **What service** does the man's company provide? 男子的公司提供什麼服務？

詢問地點：地點包含商家、餐廳、醫院、博物館、工廠、展覽會場、飛機、火車等。

- Where are the speakers? 說話者在哪裡？
- Where is the conversation most likely taking place? 對話最有可能發生何處？

📎 代表題型範例

1. 說話者的職業與身分

Example 01　　　　　　　　　　　　　　美國男子／英國女子　🎧 P3_U1_Ex01

M　Susan, have you finished **the cover design for the March issue** yet? W　I didn't get the portrait for the main image yet. Without it, I can't start working on fonts and colors. M　The shooting was supposed to be finished yesterday, but the model's flight was delayed. I'll call the photographer to try and hurry him up.	男　Susan，你完成三月號的封面設計了嗎？ 女　我還沒收到主視覺圖的人物照片。沒有它，我就無法開始處理字體和顏色。 男　原本應在昨天完成拍攝，但模特兒的航班延誤了。我會打電話給攝影師，催促他加快工作進度。
What industry do the speakers most likely work in? (A) Magazine publishing (B) Interior design (C) Advertising (D) Aviation	說話者最有可能在哪個行業工作？ (A) 雜誌出版 (B) 室內設計 (C) 廣告業 (D) 航空業 答案 **(A)**

▶ 題目可能會詢問說話者的身分、說話者公司提供的服務及商品等。
　　Who most likely is the woman?　→ A designer（女子最有可能是誰？→ 設計師）
　　What does the speakers' company sell?　→ Magazine（說話者的公司販售什麼？→ 雜誌）

2. 對話地點

> **Example 02**　　　　　　　　　　　　　　　　　美國男子／英國女子　🎧 P3_U1_Ex02
>
> M　Hi, Ruth. How's **the order of cakes** for the Riverside Hotel coming along? They have to be ready by noon.
> W　I'm a little behind. It's a little more complex than I thought it would be.
> M　Hmm... Then, why don't you ask Tom for help?
>
> 男　嗨，Ruth。Riverside飯店訂購的蛋糕製作進度如何？中午前要準備好。
> 女　我的進度有點落後。它比我預想中的還要複雜許多。
> 男　嗯⋯那你何不請Tom幫忙呢？
>
> **Where** most likely are the speakers? → At a bakery　│　說話者最有可能在哪裡？ → 在麵包店

▶ the order of cakes → 透過有人訂蛋糕，可以得知對話地點在麵包店。

切勿錯過的答題提示字句（cue）

在電話情境中，下方字句後方會告知自己的身分或所屬單位，因此請務必仔細聆聽。

- Hello, **thank you for calling** Quint Computers customer service. 感謝您致電⋯
- Hello, **you've reached** the IT department. 您已接通至⋯
- Hi, **this is** Killian Scott, hiring manager at WeSoftware. 我是⋯

> **Example 03**　　　　　　　　　　　　　　　　　美國女子／澳洲男子　🎧 P3_U1_Ex03
>
> W　**Thanks for calling** Appleyard Flowers. How may I help you?
> M　I just ordered flowers online to be delivered today.
> W　Oh, yes. Was that the rose bouquet for the retirement party?
>
> 女　感謝您致電蘋果園花店。請問有什麼需要幫忙的嗎？
> 男　我剛在網路上訂購了今天會送達的花。
> 女　喔，沒錯。是為退休派對準備的玫瑰花束嗎？
>
> **What type of business** is the man most likely calling?　│　男子最有可能打電話給什麼類型的公司？
> → A flower shop　│　→ 花店

▶ 題目詢問男子打電話給什麼公司，指的就是女子工作的公司，因此答題提示字句最可能出現在女子所說的話中。Thanks for calling後方便提到公司名稱，可輕鬆選出答案。

CHECK-UP　　🎧 P3_U1_Check-up 1
　　　　　　　　🎧 P3_U1_Check-up 2　答案與解析 p.19

1. What industry do the speakers work in?

   (A) Publishing
   (B) Transportation
   (C) Construction
   (D) Finance

2. Who most likely is the man?

   (A) An interior designer
   (B) A real estate agent
   (C) A safety inspector
   (D) An apartment manager

UNIT 02　對話目的或主旨

🔍 常見考題類型

詢問來電、來訪、旅行等目的
- What is the **purpose** of the telephone call?　來電目的為何？
- **Why** is the woman calling?　女子為何打電話來？
- What is the **purpose** of the **man's visit**?　男子來訪目的為何？
- What is the **purpose** of the **man's trip**?　男子的旅行目的為何？

詢問對話主旨：詢問需要討論的議題、產品、活動等
- What are the speakers mainly **discussing**?　說話者主要在討論什麼？
- What does the woman want to **discuss**?　女子想要討論什麼？
- **What type of product** are the speakers discussing?　說話者正在討論什麼類型的產品？
- **What problem** is being discussed?　正在討論什麼問題？
- **What kind of event** is taking place?　正在舉行什麼活動？

📎 代表題型範例

1. 來電目的

Example 01
美國男子／英國女子　🎧 P3_U2_Ex01

M　Thank you for calling the Westfield Museum. How may I help you?
W　Hi, **I'm calling to** find out if the museum has any guided tour programs specifically for students.
M　Yes, we're running *Great Paintings* programs every Friday and Saturday. I can e-mail you an information packet, if you'd like.
W　That would be wonderful.

男　感謝您致電Westfield博物館。請問有什麼需要幫忙的嗎？
女　你好，我打來詢問博物館是否有專為學生提供的導覽服務。
男　有，我們每週五和週六都會舉辦絕佳畫作的課程。如果您願意，我可以用電子郵件發送相關資訊給您。
女　那太好了。

Why is the woman calling?
(A) To ask about a guided tour
(B) To confirm a schedule
(C) To sign up for a seminar
(D) To book a consultation

女子為何打電話來？
(A) 詢問導覽服務
(B) 確認日程表
(C) 報名參加研討會
(D) 預約諮詢

答案 **(A)**

▶ 對話情境為通話時，來電目的通常會出現在I'm calling to..., I'm calling because...的後方。

eg) **I'm calling because** I haven't received my order yet. → Answer: To make a complaint
我打來是因為我還沒收到我訂的東西。→ 答案：提出客訴

54

2. 來訪目的

> **Example 02**　　　　　　　　　　　　　　　　　　　　英國女子／美國男子　🎧 P3_U2_Ex02
>
> W　Hi, I'm Elaine Clifford. **I'm here for** an interview for a position as a sales manager.
> M　Good morning. May I see your identification? I'll need it to make a visitor's badge for you. All visitors must wear a badge while they're in the building.
>
> 女　嗨，我是Elaine Clifford。我來面試業務經理一職。
> 男　早安。我可以查看你的身分證嗎？我需要用它為你做一張訪客證。所有訪客在大樓內都必須佩戴識別證。
>
> What is **the purpose** of the woman's visit?
> → To have an interview
>
> 女子的來訪目的為何？
> → 來面試

▶ 來訪目的經常出現在I'm here to（動詞）/ for（名詞）... 後方。
　eg) Hi, **I'm here to fix** some damaged floor tiles. → Answer： To repair tiles
　　你好，我來修理一些損壞的地磚。→ 答案：修補地磚

3. 主旨

> **Example 03**　　　　　　　　　　　　　　　　　　　　澳洲男子／美國女子　🎧 P3_U2_Ex03
>
> M　Hi. I'm going to **rent a kayak** for my family. Do you have it available now?
> W　Yes, and if you rent it for more than two hours, we'll give you a 20% discount.
> M　That sounds great.
> W　Please wait over there for 10 minutes while I'm getting a kayak ready for you. And if you'd like to get some snacks to take along, we have a refreshment stand inside.
>
> 男　你好，我要為我的家人租一艘小船。現在能租嗎？
> 女　可以，而且如果您租用超過兩小時，我們會提供您八折優惠。
> 男　聽起來不錯
> 女　請在那邊稍候十分鐘，我會為您準備好小船。若您想帶一些點心，我們店裡有小販部。
>
> What are the speakers mainly **discussing**?
> → Boat rental
>
> 說話者主要在討論什麼？
> → 租船

▶ kayak屬於船的一種，選項改寫成boat，因此答案為Boat rental。

CHECK-UP　　　　　　　　　　🎧 P3_U2_Check-up 1
　　　　　　　　　　　　　　　　🎧 P3_U2_Check-up 2　答案與解析 p.20

1. What is the purpose of the telephone call?
    (A) To place an order
    (B) To arrange an interview
    (C) To confirm a contract
    (D) To cancel an appointment

2. What problem is being discussed?
    (A) An electric outage
    (B) A road closure
    (C) Bad weather
    (D) A broken vehicle

55

UNIT 03　建議或要求

常見考題類型

建議或要求對方做某件事
- What does the man **ask** the woman to do?　男子要求女子做什麼事?
- What does the man **tell** the woman to do?　男子告訴女子要做什麼事?
- What does the man **want** the woman to do?　男子希望女子做什麼事?
- What does the man **say** the woman should do?　男子表示女子應該做什麼事?
- What does the man **suggest** the woman do?　男子建議女子做什麼事?
- What does the man **suggest** doing?　男子建議做什麼事?

向對方提議做某件事
- What does the man **offer** to do?　男子提議要做什麼事?

代表題型範例

Example 01
美國男子／英國女子　P3_U3_Ex01

M You wanted to speak with me, Carol?
W Yes. I wanted to run something by you since you're the manager here. It seems like we don't get a lot of customers in the morning, but a lot of people want to go furniture shopping after they get off work.
M What do you mean?
W I think it makes more sense for us to push back our starting time and stay open later. That way more people can shop here after work.
M Aah, I see. That's a good idea. **Can you set up an employee meeting today**? I need to discuss this with everyone else.

男　你有話要跟我說嗎，Carol?
女　對。你是這裡的經理，所以我有些事想跟你商量。我們店裡早上的客人不多，但很多人在下班後會來買傢俱。
男　你的意思是什麼?
女　我認為應延後開店，並延長營業時間。這樣會有更多人可在下班後來店裡購物。
男　啊，我明白了。這是個好主意。你今天可以安排員工會議嗎？我需要跟其他人討論這件事。

[單字] run A by B　向B徵求對於A的意見

What does the man **ask** the woman to do?
(A) Schedule a meeting
(B) Contact a customer
(C) Set up a display
(D) Give a presentation

男子要求女子做什麼事?
(A) 規劃會議
(B) 聯絡客戶
(C) 擺設展示品
(D) 進行報告

答案 **(A)**

▶ 該類型考題一般會出現在三道題中的最後一題。只要看到題目中出現「ask... to do?」，便可預測答題提示字句會出現在後半段對話中。本題詢問男子要求女子做的事，因此請仔細聆聽男子所說的話，答題提示句為「Can you....?」。

▶ 答案將對話中的set up a meeting改寫成organize a meeting。

切勿錯過的答題提示字句（cue）

向對方提出 建議或要求	**Can/Could you** send me his e-mail address? 你可以把他的電子郵件地址發給我嗎？ **Will you** provide me with your account number? 能提供你的帳號給我嗎？ **Would you** consider promoting him to Susan's old position? 你會考慮把他升到Susan原本的職位嗎？ **Would it be possible** for you to give us a demonstration? 你能為我們演示一下嗎？ **Why don't you** do some research on that? 你何不對此研究一下呢？
	I'd suggest that you check it again before submitting it. 我建議你在交出前再檢查一遍。 **I'd highly recommend** you contact them right away. 我強烈建議你立刻聯絡他們。 **I'd appreciate it if** you'd fill out this form. 如果你願意填寫這張表格，我會很感激。 **I'd really like you to** tell me about your new book. 我真希望你能談談你的新書。 **Please** inform HR of which days you'd like to use for your vacation. 請告知人資部你想在哪幾天休假。
	You'll have to fill out this form. 你必須填寫這張表格。 **You'll need to** fill out an online request form on our website. 你需在我們的網站上填寫線上申請表。 **I need you to** submit the request in advance. 我需要你提前繳交請求單。
	Why don't we draw a blueprint for the plan? 我們何不製作一下計劃藍圖呢？ **How about** reaching out to tour guides? 聯絡一下導遊如何？ **Let's** switch to my laptop. 我們切換到我的筆電吧。
向對方提議 做某件事	**Why don't I** run a test first? 我何不先進行測試呢？ **I can** refund the amount to your credit card. **Would you like me to** do that? 我可以把款項退至你的信用卡，你同意我這樣做嗎？ **How about I** find out what events are coming up in our area? 我來查詢一下我們地區即將舉辦哪些活動如何？

CHECK-UP

🎧 P3_U3_Check-up 1
🎧 P3_U3_Check-up 2　答案與解析 p.20

1. What does the woman ask the man to do?
   (A) Modify a contract
   (B) Finalize a payment
   (C) Extend the deadline
   (D) Obtain a supervisor's approval

2. What does the woman suggest doing?
   (A) Conducting market research
   (B) Hiring more staff
   (C) Offering a rewards program
   (D) Finding a consultant

UNIT 04　疑難問題或擔憂

🔍 常見考題類型

- **What problem** do the women mention?　女子提出什麼問題？
- According to the woman, what might cause a **problem**?　根據女子所述，什麼可能會引起問題？
- What does the man say he is **concerned** about?　男子表示他擔心什麼事？
- What is the woman **concerned** about?　女子擔憂什麼事？
- What is causing a **delay**?　什麼原因導致延遲？
- Why does the man **apologize**?　男子為何要道歉？
- **What complaint** did customers have about the product?　客戶對產品有什麼不滿？

📎 代表題型範例

Example 01
美國男子／英國女子　🎧 P3_U4_Ex01

M　Excuse me, wasn't the train to Crayford supposed to leave at 11:00?
W　Right, **but the Bexley Transportation authority has suspended all rail service due to emergency railroad repair.**
M　I see. Then, is every train canceled all day?
W　The repair is expected to end in about 2 hours, and after that operations should return to normal.
M　Okay, then I guess I'll grab a bite to eat nearby.
W　There are some good cafés near the Bexley Hotel across the street. And we'll be posting updates on our mobile app, so be sure to check it regularly.
M　Thanks.

男　不好意思，請問前往Crayford的火車不是應該在11點發車嗎？
女　沒錯，但是由於緊急鐵路維修，Bexley交通局已暫停所有鐵路服務。
男　我明白了。那全天所有列車都停駛嗎？
女　維修工作預計在2小時內結束，之後應會恢復正常運行。
男　好的，那我就在附近吃點東西。
女　對面的Bexley飯店附近有些不錯的咖啡廳。我們會在手機應用程式上發布更新公告，因此請務必隨時查看。
男　謝謝。

What problem does the woman mention?
(A) The weather is bad.
(B) Some tickets are sold out.
(C) The railroad is under repair.
(D) Her car is not working.

女子提出什麼問題？
(A) 天候不佳。
(B) 部分票券已售完。
(C) 鐵路正在維修中。
(D) 她的車子壞了。

答案 **(C)**

▶ 只要看到題目中出現「What problem...?」，便可在聆聽對話時，預測當中會提到的特定問題。

▶ 題目詢問「女子提出的問題為何？」，表示答題線索在女子所說的話中。

▶ but或unfortunately後方有很高機率會提出問題所在，因此請專心聆聽後方的內容。女子在but後方提出由於緊急鐵路維修（due to emergency railroad repair.），暫停所有鐵路服務，因此答案要選 (C)。

切勿錯過的答題提示字句（cue）

The customers liked the fact that the new headphone is wireless. **But** there were complaints about the battery life. → [Answer] The battery life was short.	客人喜歡這款新耳機的無線功能，但對於電池使用壽命有所不滿。 → [答案] 電池使用壽命短。
I called the supplier this morning but **unfortunately**, the bricks we wanted are sold out. → [Answer] Some materials are not available.	今天早上我打給供應商，但不幸的是，我們想要的磚塊已經賣完了。 → [答案] 無法提供部分材料。

常見出題情境

I didn't have the hotel breakfast, but there's a charge for it here. → [Answer] A bill is not correct.	我沒在飯店用早餐，但卻被收費。 → [答案] 帳單不正確。
I'm stuck in traffic on the Johnson Highway. It looks like I'm going to be about 30 minutes late. → [Answer] Traffic is heavy.	我塞在Johnson高速公路上，看來會遲到約30分鐘。 → [答案] 交通阻塞。
Well, I just finished setting up the tables outside, but Browns Seafood is running late on their deliveries. → [Answer] A delivery has been delayed.	嗯，我剛在外面擺設好桌子，但Browns海鮮店的送貨延遲了。 → [答案] 交貨延遲。
The cost to install the solar panels is almost double what we anticipated. We don't have enough money for that. → [Answer] A project is too expensive.	安裝太陽能板的成本幾乎是我們預期的兩倍。我們沒有足夠的錢。 → [答案] 項目的費用太高。
Oh, unfortunately, I'll be attending a conference then. Could I reschedule for next week? → [Answer] She has a prior commitment.	哦，不巧的是，那時我要參加一個會議。我可以把時間改到下週嗎？ → [答案] 她有約在先。

CHECK-UP

🎧 P3_U4_Check-up 1
🎧 P3_U4_Check-up 2　答案與解析 p.21

1. What problem does the man mention?
   (A) A deadline was missed.
   (B) A product is out of stock.
   (C) An order was not delivered.
   (D) Some staff members are unavailable.

2. What does the man say he is concerned about?
   (A) Location
   (B) Available dates
   (C) Cost
   (D) Size

UNIT 05　特定時間

🔍 常見考題類型

題目中會出現具體的日期或時間，對話中會直接提及同樣的日期或時間。

- What does the woman say she is going to do **tomorrow**?　女子說她明天要做什麼？
- What has Reed Birney been working on **recently**?　Reed Birney近期在做什麼？
- What will the speakers do **this afternoon**?　說話者今天下午會做什麼？
- What does the woman want to do on **Friday morning**?　女子星期五早上想做什麼？
- What will happen **at the end of November**?　11月底會發生什麼事？

📎 代表題型範例

Example 01
美國男子／英國女子　🎧 P3_U5_Ex01

M　Thanks for calling Alabama Moving Services. What can I do for you?
W　Hi, I'm moving out of the neighborhood early next month. I have a lot of things I want to take with me, including furniture and some fragile items. I want them all to be taken care of at the same time.
M　That won't be a problem. You can take a picture of all the items you want moved, send them to our e-mail, and we'll show up on the designated day with moving vans to help you.
W　Will you be able to wrap my fragile items for me?
M　Yes, but that comes at an additional fee. And you need to **send us pictures of those items by the end of the week**.
W　No problem.

男　感謝您致電阿拉巴馬搬家服務公司。請問有什麼需要幫忙的嗎？
女　你好，我下個月初要搬離社區。我有很多東西想帶走，包含傢俱和一些易碎物品。我希望所有東西能一次處理好。
男　那應該沒有問題。您可以拍照所有您要搬運的物品，發送到我們的電子郵件信箱，我們會在指定日期派出搬運卡車幫您。
女　你們能幫我包裝易碎物品嗎？
男　可以，但要額外付費，且您需在這週前把那些物品的照片發送給我們。
女　沒問題。

What will the woman be doing **this week**?
(A) Renovating her home
(B) Sending some pictures
(C) Moving to a new place
(D) Starting a new job

女子這週要做什麼？
(A) 裝修她家
(B) 發送一些照片
(C) 搬到新地方
(D) 開始新工作

答案 **(B)**

▶ 雖然題目詢問的是女子要做的事，但答題線索可能會出現在男子所說的話中，因此聆聽對話時，兩人說的話都要專心聆聽。

▶ 通常對話中會直接提及題目中的時間點，但有時會像上方對話一樣，改寫成其他說法by the end of the week。另外，對話中還提及其他時間資訊（early next month），切勿搞混。

60

Example 02

美國男子／英國女子 🎧 P3_U5_Ex02

M Good morning, Ms. Sheldon. Is it possible to put some more money into the magazine's guest article budget?

W As you know, the budget has been the same for a while now.

M Yes, but this quarter is our 10 year anniversary special. I wanted to have a special guest author write an article praising the magazine. But I'm concerned if we get someone famous, they're going to ask for more money.

W Oh, I forgot about the anniversary special.

M We could try to find someone cheaper, but **Paul Adelstein is one of the most famous critics** these days.

W You're right. I have a management meeting to attend now, so **I'll try to get in contact with him in the afternoon**. I'm glad I have his number I got at the conference this spring.

男 早安，Sheldon女士。是否可在雜誌的客座文章預算中投入更多資金？

女 如你所知，預算已經有段時間沒變化了。

男 是的，但本季是我們的十週年紀念特刊。我想請一位特邀作者撰寫一篇讚賞我們雜誌的文章。但我擔心如果請了名人，他們會要求更高的費用。

女 喔，我忘記是週年紀念特刊了。

男 雖然我們可以嘗試找報價便宜的人，但Paul Adelstein是近期最知名的評論家之一。

女 你說得對。我現在有個管理層會議要參加，下午我會試著與他聯絡。幸好我在今年春天的研討會上有取得他的電話號碼。

What will the woman do **in the afternoon**?

(A) Contact a critic
(B) Review a report
(C) Host a meeting
(D) Consult with a supervisor

女子下午要做什麼？

(A) 聯絡評論家
(B) 審閱報告
(C) 主持會議
(D) 與主管商量

答案 **(A)**

▶ 雖然題目詢問女子要做的事，但答題線索可能會出現在男子所說的話中。女子表示：「I'll try to get in contact with him in the afternoon」，當中的him指的就是前方男子所提到的評論家Paul Adelstein，因此答案為(A) Contact a critic。

▶ (C) Host a meeting為陷阱選項，女子僅於對話最後提到「have a management meeting to attend」。

CHECK-UP

🎧 P3_U5_Check-up 1
🎧 P3_U5_Check-up 2　答案與解析 p.22

1. According to the woman, what will happen in three weeks?

(A) An inventory count
(B) An annual clearance sale
(C) An anniversary party
(D) A grand opening

2. What does the man say he will do later today?

(A) Give a presentation
(B) Fill out an online survey
(C) Reserve a vehicle
(D) Visit a community center

61

UNIT 06　下一步的行動

🔍 常見考題類型

預測後續行動為 PART 3 出題比例最高的考題類型之一，通常會出現在三道題中的最後一題。

- What will the man do **next**?　男子接下來會做什麼？
- What will the man most likely do **next**?　男子接下來最有可能做什麼？
- What is the woman most likely planning to do **next**?　女子接下來最有可能計畫做什麼？
- What does the woman say she **will do**?　女子說她會做什麼事？

📎 代表題型範例

Example 01

英國女子／美國男子　🎧 P3_U6_Ex01

W　Hello, West Square Apartments leasing office. How can I help you?
M　Hi, I currently live in unit 305, but I'm wondering if there are any larger units available to rent in the building.
W　Yes, we have one apartment which has three rooms and two bathrooms. Perfect timing, as the lease on it ends at the end of the month.
M　Sounds great. And is that facing south? I'm growing a garden on a balcony.
W　Yes, it gets sunlight for most of the day. **I'll call the current tenant** to figure out a time for a viewing.

What will the woman **do next**?
(A) Visit a client
(B) E-mail a contract
(C) Make a phone call
(D) Go on a tour

女　你好，這裡是西廣場公寓出租辦公室。請問有什麼需要幫忙的嗎？
男　你好，我目前住在305號房，但我想知道大樓內是否有更大的公寓要出租。
女　有的，有間三房兩衛的公寓。現在時機正好，因為本月底租約就會到期。
男　聽起來很棒。是朝南的公寓嗎？我有在陽台上種植花圃。
女　是的，幾乎一整天都有陽光。我會打電話給現在的住戶，確定看房時間。

女子接下來會做什麼？
(A) 拜訪客戶
(B) 用電子郵件發送合約
(C) 撥打電話
(D) 前往參觀

答案 **(C)**

▶ 題目句句末為「... do next?」時，答題線索通常會在後半段對話中，因此請專心聆聽後半段對話。

▶ 題目詢問的是女子接下來會做的事，請專心聆聽女子所說的話。

▶ 女子提到：「I'll call the current tenant...」，因此答案為(C) Make a phone call。

▶ I'll..., Let me..., I'm going to..., I'm planning..., Let's..., I can..., I have to..., I'd better... 等皆為「預測下一步行動」題型的提示字句，答題線索會出現在這些字句後方。

62

Example 02

美國男子／英國女子 P3_U6_Ex02

M Hello, I'm Leo from the IT department. I was told you need assistance setting up a video conference. I can help you with anything you need.
W Thank you so much. This meeting is very important to our team. We're looking to get funding from the government for our new project, so we have to speak with state officials.
M No problem. I can help with that.
W I can control the microphone to mute people if they make too much background noise, right?
M Of course.
W I also want to be able to share my computer screen with the participants. Can I do that?
M Sure, you can do all of that quite easily. **Let me use the manual to show you how**.

男 你好，我是技術部門的Leo。我聽說你需要協助安排一場視訊會議，有任何需求，我都可以幫你。
女 非常感謝你。這場會議對我們團隊來說非常重要。我們希望新專案能獲得政府資助，所以我們要與州政府官員洽談。
男 沒問題，我可以幫忙。
女 若與會者的背景噪音過大，我可以控制麥克風讓他們靜音，對吧？
男 當然可以。
女 我還想分享電腦螢幕畫面給與會者。可以做到嗎？
男 當然，你可以輕鬆做到這一切。讓我使用說明書並演示給你看。

What will the man **do next**?

(A) Consult a manual
(B) Speak with his supervisor
(C) Install a projector
(D) Arrange a meeting

男子接下來會做什麼？

(A) 查閱說明書
(B) 與他的主管談話
(C) 安裝投影機
(D) 安排會議

答案 **(A)**

▶ 題目詢問的是男子接下來會做的事，請專心聆聽後半段對話中男子所說的話。

▶ 對話最後男子提到：「Let me use the manual...」，因此答案為(A) Consult a manual。consult除了表示「商量、請教」外，還有為取得資訊，「查閱」書籍或資料的意思。（eg. consult a map 參考、查看地圖）

CHECK-UP

 P3_U6_Check-up 1
 P3_U6_Check-up 2 答案與解析 p.22

1. What will the man most likely do next?

(A) Make a phone call
(B) Prepare for a meeting
(C) Go to lunch
(D) Send out an announcement

2. What will the woman most likely do next?

(A) Inspect some equipment
(B) Speak with her colleagues
(C) Pick up clients
(D) Reschedule a demonstration

PRACTICE   UNIT 01~06

1. Who most likely is the man?
   (A) A marketing consultant
   (B) A news reporter
   (C) A construction manager
   (D) A web developer

2. What problem does the man mention?
   (A) Some materials are missing.
   (B) The project is too expensive.
   (C) The weather is bad.
   (D) A crew member quit.

3. What will the man do next?
   (A) Send an e-mail
   (B) Make a phone call
   (C) Write a report
   (D) Visit a government office

4. Who most likely is the woman?
   (A) A physician
   (B) A film director
   (C) An architect
   (D) An interior designer

5. What does the man say happened this morning?
   (A) He received an e-mail message.
   (B) He discovered a problem.
   (C) He met with a contractor.
   (D) He was late to work.

6. What does the man offer to do?
   (A) Conduct an interview
   (B) Submit a report
   (C) Arrange a conversation
   (D) Share some data

7. What does the woman's company sell?
   (A) Hiking gear
   (B) Mobile applications
   (C) Health food
   (D) Children's clothing

8. What point does the man emphasize?
   (A) A website has changed.
   (B) A customer is unhappy.
   (C) A product is reliable.
   (D) A price has increased.

9. What is the woman pleased about?
   (A) An advertising campaign
   (B) A delivery service
   (C) A skilled employee
   (D) A new supplier

10. Where does the woman work?
    (A) At a retirement community
    (B) At a university
    (C) At a recruitment agency
    (D) At a hospital

11. What is the purpose of the man's visit?
    (A) He is meeting a relative.
    (B) He is inquiring about a job.
    (C) He is delivering a product.
    (D) He is making a payment.

12. What will the man probably do next?
    (A) Watch a short film
    (B) Tour the facilities
    (C) Fill out an application
    (D) Write an e-mail

PRACTICE

13. Who is the woman?

    (A) A clothing salesperson
    (B) A grocer
    (C) A travel agent
    (D) A tailor

14. What does the man say will happen next week?

    (A) He will take a vacation.
    (B) He will host a meeting.
    (C) He will sign a contract.
    (D) He will attend an event.

15. What will the man probably do next?

    (A) Make a payment
    (B) Complete a form
    (C) Collect a receipt
    (D) Write a review

16. According to the woman, what recently happened at her business?

    (A) An investor was found.
    (B) Employees asked for higher pay.
    (C) The customer base grew.
    (D) The location was changed.

17. What can the man's company do?

    (A) Provide the wait staff
    (B) Arrange the dining room
    (C) Prepare quality meals
    (D) Make food deliveries

18. What does the woman say she could do to announce the partnership?

    (A) Plan a special event
    (B) Create commercials
    (C) Start a social media campaign
    (D) Publish a newspaper advertisement

19. Where is the conversation most likely taking place?

    (A) At an office building
    (B) At a fitness center
    (C) At a ski resort
    (D) At a sporting goods store

20. What does the man give to the woman?

    (A) A phone number
    (B) A receipt
    (C) A form
    (D) A website link

21. What will the woman most likely do next?

    (A) Make a phone call
    (B) Go to a waiting area
    (C) Submit a job application
    (D) Talk to a staff member

22. What problem does the man mention?

    (A) He injured himself.
    (B) He got a flat tire.
    (C) His engine malfunctioned.
    (D) His gas tank was leaking.

23. What does the woman suggest doing?

    (A) Going to a specific repair shop
    (B) Checking warranty information
    (C) Purchasing new insurance
    (D) Asking for a refund

24. What does the man say he will look for?

    (A) An invoice
    (B) A manual
    (C) A business card
    (D) A police report

PART 3

65

UNIT 07　掌握意圖

🔍 常見考題類型

此類題型通常只會出現下方三種句型，PART 3總共39題，此類題型固定會出2題。

What does the man imply when he says, "that happens all the time"?
男子說：「難免會發生那種事」，意味著什麼？

What does the man mean when he says, "I ran out of handouts"?
男子說：「我的講義用完了」，是什麼意思？

Why does the woman say, "It won't take that long"?
女子為何會說：「不會花那麼長的時間」？

📎 代表題型範例

Example 01

美國男子／英國女子　🎧 P3_U7_Ex01　答案與解析 p.27

M　Heather, we haven't planned anything for the Sheffield Summer Music Festival taking place next weekend. But it would be a good publicity opportunity.
W　There will definitely be a lot of people there.
M　Exactly. I thought that we could give out free cans of our line of sodas. And we could get limited edition cans printed with the festival's logo.
W　**That could take up to two weeks.**
M　That's true. Maybe we could think of another way to stand out.

1. What event will take place next weekend?
   (A) A music festival
   (B) A charity fundraiser
   (C) An anniversary party
   (D) A company picnic

2. What does the speakers' company produce?
   (A) Athletic gear
   (B) Clothing
   (C) Beverages
   (D) Outdoor furniture

3. Why does the woman say, "**That could take up to two weeks**"?
   (A) To offer an apology for an error
   (B) To suggest extending a deadline
   (C) To complain about a service
   (D) To express concern about a plan

▶ 此類題型通常出現在三道題中的第二或第三題。上方對話的最後一題為掌握意圖題，因此請專心聆聽後半段對話。此類題型屬於高難度題型，沒有明確的答題提示字句，因此聆聽時請務必掌握前後文意。

▶ 女子所說的話為回應男子的話，因此需先確認男子所說的話。男子提議在限量版飲料上印音樂節標誌發放，而後女子回應這需要長達兩週的時間，表示她擔心該方法會花費過多時間，難以實現。

※ UNIT 07~09屬於高難度題型，因此將簡易練習題Check-up換成完整版練習題PRACTICE，幫助學習者模擬實際測驗的作答模式。

PRACTICE 高難度

1. What type of business does the woman work for?

   (A) A marketing firm
   (B) A travel agency
   (C) A publishing company
   (D) A law firm

2. What does the woman mean when she says, "we're looking to hire as soon as possible"?

   (A) She will retire soon.
   (B) The timeline will be modified.
   (C) Additional funding is required.
   (D) The man should make a quick decision.

3. According to the woman, what does the company offer?

   (A) Free meals
   (B) A travel stipend
   (C) A company credit card
   (D) An employee discount

4. What industry do the speakers most likely work in?

   (A) Furniture
   (B) Fitness
   (C) Cosmetics
   (D) Clothing

5. What is the woman annoyed by?

   (A) Some materials are low quality.
   (B) Some equipment is broken.
   (C) Some designs are unusable.
   (D) Some decisions haven't been made.

6. Why does the man say, "Summer is coming in a few months"?

   (A) To stress the need for urgency
   (B) To remind the woman of a deadline
   (C) To fix a scheduling error
   (D) To express eagerness for a vacation

7. What problem does the woman mention?

   (A) Sales are down.
   (B) A delivery is late.
   (C) Data is missing.
   (D) A product is flawed.

8. What does the woman imply when she says "The project has already been a long haul"?

   (A) Employees have been working hard.
   (B) The company has hired new people.
   (C) The project should be stopped.
   (D) The game is for advanced players.

9. What will the man do next?

   (A) Do some online research
   (B) Write a formal complaint
   (C) Send an e-mail
   (D) Have a meeting

10. What field do the speakers work in?

    (A) Manufacturing
    (B) Finance
    (C) Architecture
    (D) Agriculture

11. Why does the man say, "I've narrowed everything down to two designs"?

    (A) To assure the woman that the meeting won't take long
    (B) To ask the woman for permission
    (C) To show surprise about blueprints
    (D) To express disappointment about a plan

12. What does the woman say she will do after work?

    (A) Attend an anniversary dinner
    (B) Grab a meal to take home
    (C) Go to a doctor's appointment
    (D) Plan for a vacation

UNIT 08　三人對話

- 該大題共有13組對話，當中固定會出現2篇三人對話文。
- 三人對話前方的說明為「Questions 00~00 refer to the following conversation with three speakers.」
- 三人對話的題目中，不會出現掌握意圖題和圖表整合題。

代表題型範例

Example 01

美國男子／英國女子／美國女子　P3_U8_Ex01　答案與解析 p.29

Questions 1-3 refer to the following conversation with three speakers.

M　Thankfully, Ms. Washington, it looks like your arm is all healed. We'll get you started on physical therapy during your next visit.
W1　Oh, but I thought my physical therapy appointment was also today.
M　I'm so sorry about that. There must have been a mistake when setting up your appointment. We only have you scheduled for an x-ray.
W1　Ahh, I see.
M　Ms. Rislov, could you please schedule a physical therapy appointment for Ms. Washington?
W2　Sure. But I should update your contact information. We normally send out reminders for appointments, but it seems we don't have your cell phone number on file. Do you mind filling out this contact form?
W1　No problem.

1. Where most likely are the speakers?
   (A) At a community center
   (B) At a fitness club
   (C) At a legal firm
   (D) At a hospital

2. Why does the man apologize?
   (A) Some equipment is not working.
   (B) A coworker arrived late.
   (C) A scheduling error was made.
   (D) A bill is not correct.

3. What will Ms. Washington do next?
   (A) Make an appointment
   (B) Fill out a form
   (C) Stop at a pharmacy
   (D) Contact an insurance company

▶ 第二題的考題類型屬於詢問男子或女子道歉的理由，PART 3和PART 4中經常出現該類題型。對話中通常會在sorry或apologize後方提及答題線索。

▶ 在三人對話的題目中，有時會像第三題一樣直接提到人名。這是因為對話中有兩名女子，如果題目為：「What will the woman do next?」，便無法確定the woman指的是哪一名女子，因此題目才會直接提到人名Washington女士。綜合上述，在三人對話的情況下，如果題目中出現人名時，請在聆聽對話時特別注意該人名。

PRACTICE 高難度

P3_U8_Practice 答案與解析 p.30

1. Where do the women work?
   (A) At a chemical plant
   (B) At a construction company
   (C) At an interior design firm
   (D) At a conference center

2. What is the man's job?
   (A) Sales representative
   (B) Building manager
   (C) Software engineer
   (D) Restaurant chef

3. What does Jolene plan to do in the afternoon?
   (A) Visit a property
   (B) Give a demonstration
   (C) Return to her office
   (D) Watch a presentation

4. What will be constructed near a factory?
   (A) A parking lot
   (B) A gas station
   (C) A storage facility
   (D) A waste site

5. What is the residents' biggest concern?
   (A) Safety
   (B) Noise
   (C) Funds
   (D) Traffic

6. Why has a new meeting location been chosen?
   (A) It provides more space.
   (B) The original venue was booked.
   (C) It is easier to travel to.
   (D) The residents preferred the new location.

7. What industry do the men most likely work in?
   (A) Hospitality
   (B) Media
   (C) Electronics
   (D) Architecture

8. What is the purpose of the telephone call?
   (A) To inquire about a field trip
   (B) To place an order
   (C) To set up an interview
   (D) To return some merchandise

9. What will be sent to the woman?
   (A) A warranty
   (B) Directions to a location
   (C) A copy of a contract
   (D) Some safety instructions

10. What kind of product are the speakers discussing?
    (A) Furniture
    (B) Office supplies
    (C) Kitchenware
    (D) Home appliances

11. What problem does the woman mention?
    (A) An item is out of stock.
    (B) A sale price has not been posted.
    (C) An item is damaged.
    (D) A bill is not correct.

12. What does the manager offer the woman?
    (A) A warranty
    (B) Express shipping
    (C) A store membership
    (D) A full refund

UNIT 09　圖表題

- 在PART 3中，固定會出現三個圖表題組。每個題組包含一段對話和三道相關考題，其中一題為圖表整合題。圖表類型包含目錄、表格、地圖、平面圖、圓餅圖、優惠券等種類。
- 圖表題偏向解題較為麻煩的類型，除了要確認三道題目的關鍵字外，還要同時掌握圖表中的重要資訊。圖表題中的對話僅會出現雙人對話。

📎 代表題型範例

Example 01

英國女子／美國男子　🎧 P3_U9_Ex01　答案與解析 p.32

Questions 1-3 refer to the following conversation and menu.

W　Hey, Marcus. **Our new employees are coming in for orientation next week**, and we have to decide the menu for their welcome lunch. Which of these dishes looks the best to you?

M　Hmm. Last time we had new employee training, we got the steak and potatoes. It was a big hit.

W　I remember that. Our budget is a little smaller this year, so I think we'll have to get something different.

M　Well, then **how about the pasta?**

W　**I think that's a good idea.** Chicken and curry sounds good too, but their restaurants are a little far from here.

M　Right, and before you call the restaurant to book a table, **we still need to prepare the exact schedule for orientation**, so I think we'd better get started on that right away.

Menu Option	Price
Chicken and Curry	$7 per person
Pasta	$10 per person
Fried Chicken	$11 per person
Steak and Potatoes	$16 per person

1. What are the speakers preparing for?
   (A) A retirement dinner
   (B) A county fair
   (C) An orientation
   (D) A client visit

2. Look at the graphic. How much will the speakers most likely spend per person?
   (A) $7
   (B) $10
   (C) $11
   (D) $16

3. What will the speakers do next?
   (A) Speak to their superiors
   (B) Ask guests to take a survey
   (C) Make a reservation
   (D) Prepare a schedule

▶ 聆聽時，不要僅專注於解答第二題的圖表整合題，而忽略第一和第三題。為了正確回答其中一題，卻因此答錯另外兩道相對簡單的題目，反而得不償失。

▶ 看到題目出現「Look at the graphic.」時，請根據題目中的關鍵字，迅速掌握圖表中的答題關鍵資訊。本題詢問的是每人最有可能花多少錢，表示對話中會提到表格中的餐點名稱。

▶ 男子建議餐點選擇義大利麵，女子回答「That's a good idea.」。查看表格中義大利麵對應的價格，答案應選 (B) $10。

70

PRACTICE 高難度

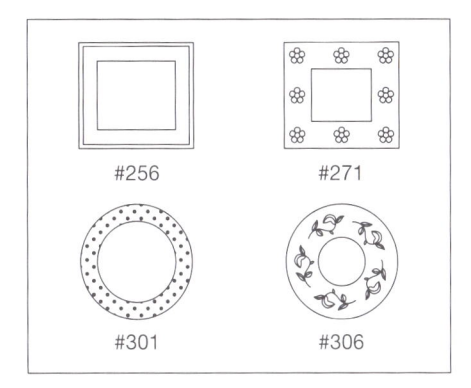

1. Look at the graphic. Which dish pattern is the man interested in?

   (A) Pattern #256
   (B) Pattern #271
   (C) Pattern #301
   (D) Pattern #306

2. What problem does the woman mention?

   (A) Some items are out of stock.
   (B) Catalogues are outdated.
   (C) Some items are limited edition.
   (D) Shipping fees will increase.

3. According to the man, what will happen in September?

   (A) A new employee will join his business.
   (B) A new product will launch.
   (C) A restaurant will have a re-opening.
   (D) A mall will open downtown.

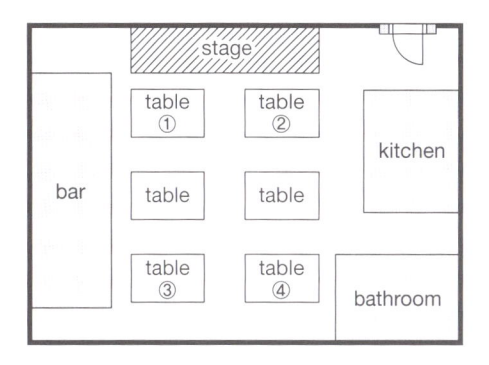

4. According to the man, what has caused the delay?

   (A) The roads are slippery.
   (B) Parking is unavailable.
   (C) Rush hour traffic is bad.
   (D) A location was changed.

5. Why is the man meeting with his business partner?

   (A) To discuss a potential merger
   (B) To talk about a job candidate
   (C) To analyze a product's sales
   (D) To prepare for a company launch

6. Look at the graphic. Where will the man sit?

   (A) Table 1
   (B) Table 2
   (C) Table 3
   (D) Table 4

請翻頁繼續作答

PRACTICE 高難度

Directory
- Inez Garcia: Basketball Coach
- Amala Kalil: Player
- Suki Tanoko: Equipment Manager
- Jennifer Snell: Marketing Coordinator

Sunny Beach Apartments

Unit	Rent
Studio	$1,000 per month
1 bedroom	$1,500 per month
2 bedrooms	$1,750 per month
3 bedrooms	$2,000 per month

7. Look at the graphic. Who is the woman?
   (A) Inez Garcia
   (B) Amala Kalil
   (C) Suki Tanoko
   (D) Jennifer Snell

8. What problem do the speakers discuss?
   (A) A game has been delayed.
   (B) The fans are angry.
   (C) The players are tired.
   (D) The team was sold.

9. What will the man most likely do next?
   (A) Post an advertisement
   (B) Purchase new uniforms
   (C) Upgrade flight tickets
   (D) Search for accommodations

10. Why does the woman want to move soon?
    (A) She got a new job.
    (B) She is pregnant.
    (C) Her building is unsafe.
    (D) Her rent is too high.

11. What does the man like about the bigger unit?
    (A) The interior design
    (B) The scenic view
    (C) The modern appliances
    (D) The large bathrooms

12. Look at the graphic. What is the price of the unit the woman wants to rent?
    (A) $1,000 per month
    (B) $1,500 per month
    (C) $1,750 per month
    (D) $2,000 per month

PRACTICE 高難度

Schedule

Emilio Lopez	9 am
Kate Marrone	11 am
Yeonsu Lee	2 pm
Leopold Fritz	4 pm

Flight	Departing From	Arriving At
156	Detroit	New York City
205	Atlanta	Miami
310	Honolulu	Los Angeles
644	San Francisco	Seattle

13. What kind of event is taking place?

    (A) A business seminar
    (B) A film festival
    (C) An award ceremony
    (D) A charity fundraiser

14. Look at the graphic. When will the man call a client?

    (A) 9 am
    (B) 11 am
    (C) 2 pm
    (D) 4 pm

15. What problem does the woman mention?

    (A) A lecturer might be late.
    (B) A conference room is closed.
    (C) The caterer missed a delivery.
    (D) The audience is too small.

16. Look at the graphic. Where is the woman departing from?

    (A) Detroit
    (B) Atlanta
    (C) Honolulu
    (D) San Francisco

17. How will the man help the woman?

    (A) By providing a refund
    (B) By checking an extra bag
    (C) By putting her in first class
    (D) By talking to airport security

18. What will the woman most likely give the man next?

    (A) Her flight ticket
    (B) Her credit card
    (C) Her voucher
    (D) Her e-mail address

PART TEST

1. What change is the company making?
   (A) It is offering flexible scheduling.
   (B) It is opening a new office location.
   (C) It is providing discounted meals.
   (D) It is reimbursing travel expenses.

2. What does the woman suggest doing?
   (A) Raising a concern to management
   (B) Submitting a preference quickly
   (C) Researching some products
   (D) Participating in a job interview

3. What will the man most likely do next?
   (A) Speak with a coworker
   (B) Call a customer
   (C) Ask for a refund
   (D) Conduct a training session

4. What kind of business do the speakers most likely have?
   (A) A convenience store
   (B) A landscaping company
   (C) A hardware store
   (D) A farm

5. What does the man suggest doing?
   (A) Purchasing more land
   (B) Offering a new product
   (C) Adding more plants
   (D) Building a new structure

6. What does the woman say she will do?
   (A) Check their inventory
   (B) Purchase materials
   (C) Hire a professional
   (D) Renew a contract

7. Why is the woman calling?
   (A) To discuss a property listing
   (B) To reserve a hotel room
   (C) To check on an application status
   (D) To submit a payment

8. According to the man, what affects the price?
   (A) The number of parking spaces
   (B) The usage of a shared room
   (C) The amount of customers
   (D) The presence of advertising

9. What does the man recommend bringing tomorrow evening?
   (A) A recommendation letter
   (B) A form of ID
   (C) A down payment
   (D) Proof of income

10. Why does the man need help?
    (A) An office has been moved.
    (B) A machine is malfunctioning.
    (C) A train route has changed.
    (D) An item is missing.

11. What does the man say he is frustrated about?
    (A) Spending too much money
    (B) Running late for an appointment
    (C) Receiving false information
    (D) Waiting in a long line

12. What will the man most likely do next?
    (A) Use an app
    (B) Take a taxi
    (C) Call a manager
    (D) Ride a bus

13. Where do the speakers most likely work?

(A) A concert hall
(B) A grocery store
(C) A restaurant
(D) A delivery service

14. What is the woman doing?

(A) Cleaning some equipment
(B) Talking to a supplier
(C) Preparing special orders
(D) Training new staff

15. What does Gerald suggest doing?

(A) Expanding their offerings
(B) Replenishing inventory
(C) Starting a marketing campaign
(D) Opening a second location

16. What are the speakers preparing for?

(A) A standardized test
(B) A game show
(C) A sporting event
(D) A public lecture

17. What problem does the woman mention?

(A) Some advertisements were wrong.
(B) A script is flawed.
(C) The participants are unprepared.
(D) A camera is broken.

18. Who is José Carrasco?

(A) An engineer
(B) A temporary worker
(C) A manager
(D) A screenwriter

19. What does the woman thank the man for?

(A) Submitting a proposal
(B) Closing a sale
(C) Recommending a vendor
(D) Leading a meeting

20. Why is the gathering being planned?

(A) The company had record sales.
(B) An employee is retiring.
(C) A manager is having a birthday.
(D) Some workers need a break.

21. What does the woman imply when she says, "I would be happy to prepare some homemade dishes"?

(A) A caterer is an unnecessary expense.
(B) The restaurant has bad reviews.
(C) The company will refuse to pay for catering.
(D) Everyone should bring their own dishes.

22. Where do the speakers work?

(A) At a bank
(B) At a sporting goods store
(C) At a health club
(D) At a credit card company

23. What does the man recommend doing?

(A) Changing business hours
(B) Lowering the prices
(C) Creating new advertisements
(D) Selling unused equipment

24. What does the man predict?

(A) The company will reduce wages.
(B) A new facility will keep its members.
(C) A location's rent will increase.
(D) Customers will post positive reviews.

25. What area do the speakers most likely work in?

(A) Marketing
(B) Information technology
(C) Research
(D) Human resources

26. What happened recently?

(A) New employees were hired.
(B) A department was moved.
(C) The company building was renovated.
(D) A computer was updated.

27. What does Mei Ling offer to do?

(A) Post a job listing
(B) Create some instructions
(C) Call some customers
(D) Host a meeting

28. Who is the man?

(A) A musician
(B) A photographer
(C) A film reviewer
(D) An actor

29. What does the man imply when he says, "taking it could help me gain some traction in the industry"?

(A) He does not have much experience.
(B) He is still earning a degree.
(C) He was given bad advice by his agent.
(D) He wants to switch careers.

30. What does the woman say she will do?

(A) Provide some contact information
(B) Attend an event
(C) Write a recommendation letter
(D) Read a contract

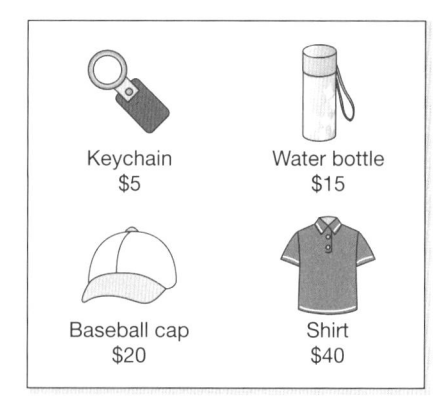

Keychain $5	Water bottle $15
Baseball cap $20	Shirt $40

31. Who will the woman give the gift to?

(A) Facility residents
(B) Upper management
(C) Family members
(D) Business partners

32. Look at the graphic. How much is the item that the man recommends?

(A) $5
(B) $15
(C) $20
(D) $40

33. What does the man say he will do?

(A) Contact a manager
(B) Do an inventory check
(C) Provide an extra item
(D) Offer a payment plan

Prices	
Plastic bag (4)	$3
Small basket (6)	$4
Large basket (9)	$6
Bucket (12)	$8

Underwater Diver

Level Name	Level Number
Coral Adventure	1
Swimming with Whales	2
Deep Ocean	3
Buried Treasure	4

34. What do the speakers sell?

    (A) Coffee beans
    (B) Fruit
    (C) Nuts
    (D) Dairy products

35. Look at the graphic. How much will the speakers charge for each sale?

    (A) $3
    (B) $4
    (C) $6
    (D) $8

36. What does the woman want help with?

    (A) Loading the truck
    (B) Setting up the booth
    (C) Transporting the product
    (D) Advertising the event

37. What are the speakers mainly discussing?

    (A) A research project
    (B) A product release
    (C) An advertising campaign
    (D) A supplier change

38. Look at the graphic. Which level is having issues?

    (A) Coral Adventure
    (B) Swimming with Whales
    (C) Deep Ocean
    (D) Buried Treasure

39. What does the woman offer to do?

    (A) Contact the sales team
    (B) Postpone an event
    (C) Request more funding
    (D) Create a job posting

PART 4

簡短獨白

UNIT 01 會議摘錄

UNIT 02 電話留言

UNIT 03 廣播通知與公告

UNIT 04 電視、廣播節目與網路廣播

UNIT 05 廣告

UNIT 06 演說、介紹、參訪／觀光導覽

PRACTICE ［高難度］（掌握意圖、圖表題）

PART TEST

PART 4 簡短獨白

PART 4是單人的獨白（talk），從第71題至第100題，共有10篇獨白。題型與PART 3相同，每篇獨白搭配三道相關考題，總共30題。

獨白類型

大致可分為下方五大類型，每回測驗一定會出現會議摘錄、電話留言、廣播通知，以及電視和廣播節目。

會議摘錄	從討論工作相關事項的會議擷取部分內容
電話留言	－ 來電者在答錄機留下的語音留言 － 公司或政府機關事先錄好的未接來電自動語音應答
廣播通知與公告	在機場、飛機上、商家、表演場地等公共場所播放的廣播通知或公司內部公告
電視和廣播節目	－ 播放當地新聞、天氣預報、交通資訊等的廣播節目與網路廣播節目 － 宣傳產品、服務、企業、活動等的廣告
演說、介紹、參訪、觀光導覽	－ 在會議、開幕式等各種活動上發表的演說 － 講座與人物介紹、觀光或參訪導覽、實地考察說明等

考題類型

與PART 3相比，並無太大差異。僅根據不同的獨白類型，特定題型出現的頻率更加頻繁。例如：獨白為電話留言時，詢問來電者打電話的理由；獨白為會議摘錄時，詢問會議上討論的議題；獨白為公共場合廣播通知時，詢問廣播通知所在地點；獨白為演講或廣播時，詢問其主旨為何；獨白為廣告時，詢問廣告對象。在PART 4中，掌握意圖題共3題、圖表題共2題。

與PART 3的不同之處

1. PART 4在播放新的獨白前，會事先告知獨白類型為何。

    • Questions 71 through 73 refer to the following **announcement**.

    請務必聽清楚the following後方出現的單字，有助於聽懂獨白情境。
    ▶ announcement（公告）、telephone message（電話留言）、recorded message（事先錄好的留言）、excerpt from a meeting（會議摘錄）、broadcast（廣播）、speech（演講）、advertisement（廣告）、tour information（旅遊資訊）等。

2. PART 3為雙人對話，因此題目中會寫the man、the woman或the speakers；而PART 4為單人獨白，因此會寫the speaker或the listener(s)。

    • Who is the speaker?
    • What are the listeners asked to do next?

解題策略及步驟

請於獨白播放前，提前掌握題目關鍵字，並隨著播放的獨白依序作答題目。在聆聽獨白時，請專心聆聽下方藍字標示的答題提示，不要錯過後方出現的答題線索。

Example 01

P4_U0_Ex01 解析 p.43

Questions 71-73 refer to the following field trip information.

I'm glad you all could join me on this tour of our rare books collection. **⁷¹ Here at the Jonestown Library**, we believe in the value of preserving literature from the past. That's why we have this unique collection of books that requires special care and handling. **⁷² Please make sure to avoid touching anything** here because all the materials are very sensitive. **⁷³ First, let's take a look at our medieval archives** on the basement floor. Follow me, please.

71. **Where** is the tour taking place?
答案 At a library

72. What does the speaker **remind** the listeners to do?
答案 Avoid touching anything

73. What will listeners **see first** on the tour?
答案 Some old archives

解題策略及步驟

獨白中會直接使用題目出現的特定關鍵字，此關鍵字常為答題提示字，後方會出現解題線索。

1. 題目中提及特定人名、時間、日期
   Q What did **Tom Clancy** start doing last December? → [獨白] Joining us today to walk you through the process is **Tom Clancy**, who started teaching coding at the public library in December.

2. 題目中出現動詞give, offer, send, receive, recommend, apologize
   Q Why does the speaker **apologize**? → [獨白] We **apologize** for the inconvenience the construction noise may cause.

3. 題目中出現impressed with, pleased/excited/concerned about, proud of
   Q What does the speaker say he is **pleased about**? → [獨白] I was really **pleased** by how much sales of the new wireless mouse have increased as well.

4. 題目詢問問題所在或擔心的事時，答題線索會出現在but, unfortunately等提示字詞後方。
   Q What **problem** does the speaker mention? → [獨白] I recently ordered a chair from your website. I chose a white one, **but** I received a black one.

5. 題目中出現remind時，答題線索會出現在remind, remember, please等提示字詞後方。
   Q What does the speaker **remind** the listener about? → [獨白] And **remember** there are only a few openings left for the training course, so be sure to sign up soon if you're interested.

81

UNIT 01　會議摘錄

獨白形式為摘錄會議上發言者的一段內容。主要討論工作相關內容，或告知公司內部新消息、政策變化等。每次測驗平均出現2篇。

代表題型範例

Example 01

美國男子　P4_U1_Ex01

Questions 1-3 refer to the following excerpt from a meeting.

I'd like to talk about a new initiative at our company. Reaching a larger audience has become **the number one priority** for us. The executives have decided we need to be more innovative when it comes to advertising our products. That's why we hired **Susan Hoover**, a digital marketing expert, to join our team. She is here to help us re-evaluate our current marketing strategy and make useful changes going forward. Right now, she is asking everyone to use their social media presence to gather data on our company. Instructions on how to do so will be sent out later today. I know we all have a lot of work already, but **this affects us all**.

1. What does the speaker say is **a top priority**?
   (A) Improving worker efficiency
   (B) Lowering manufacturing costs
   (C) Retaining quality employees
   (D) Advertising to more people

2. Who is **Susan Hoover**?
   (A) A marketing specialist
   (B) A course instructor
   (C) A renowned doctor
   (D) A human resources expert

3. Why does the speaker say, "**this affects us all**"?
   (A) To prevent future mistakes
   (B) To encourage participation
   (C) To apologize for a delay
   (D) To express opposition

我想談談我們公司的一項新計畫。吸引更多受眾已成為我們的首要任務。高階主管們決定，我們需在廣告產品上有所創新。因此，我們聘請數位行銷專家Susan Hoover加入我們團隊。她來此幫助我們重新評估當前的行銷策略，並在未來做出有效的改變。現在，她要求每人使用社群媒體來收集我們公司的數據。關於如何執行的說明將於今天稍晚發送給大家。我知道大家公務繁忙，但這會影響到我們所有人。

單字

initiative　新作法、主動
executive　幹部、高階主管
when it comes to　關於⋯
re-evaluate　重新評估
go forward　取得進展
instruction　指示說明

1. 說話者提到的首要任務為何？
   (A) 提高員工效率
   (B) 降低製造成本
   (C) 留住優秀員工
   (D) 向更多人廣告

2. Susan Hoover是誰？
   (A) 行銷專家
   (B) 課程講師
   (C) 知名醫生
   (D) 人力資源專家

3. 說話者為何會說：「這會影響到我們所有人」？
   (A) 防止未來犯錯
   (B) 為鼓勵大家參與
   (C) 為延誤道歉
   (D) 表達反對

答案　1. (D)　2. (A)　3. (B)

82

常見句型

告知消息	I'm happy to announce that... 我很高興宣布… I want to update you on... 我想向你更新… Before we end our meeting, I'd like to share... 在我們會議結束前,我想分享…
提出議題	To get started, I want to discuss... 首先,我想討論… The last thing I want to discuss at today's meeting is... 今天會議上我想討論的最後一件事是…
指出問題	But due to yesterday's equipment failure, we're behind on completing the orders. 但由於昨天的設備故障,我們未能完成訂單。 Unfortunately, we are more than two months past the scheduled completion date. 不幸的是,我們比預定的完成日晚了兩個多月。
話題轉換	Moving on, this quarter our sales are... 接著是,本季我們的銷售額為… Okay, next on the agenda... 好的,下一個議程為… Now onto the next item on the agenda for this board meeting. 現在來討論本次董事會議程上的下一個項目。

CHECK-UP

P4_U1_Check-up 答案與解析 p.43

1. Who most likely are the listeners?
   (A) Investors
   (B) Marketing specialists
   (C) Executives
   (D) Product designers

2. According to the speaker, what is the company going to change?
   (A) The type of car it makes
   (B) The location of its headquarters
   (C) The publisher for its catalog
   (D) The way it collects customer feedback

3. Why does the speaker say, "you'll probably change your mind if you look at this"?
   (A) To correct a mistake
   (B) To express doubt
   (C) To reject a suggestion
   (D) To offer reassurance

4. What industry do the speakers work in?
   (A) Advertising
   (B) Construction
   (C) Software
   (D) Shipping

5. What does the speaker thank the listeners for?
   (A) Filling out a survey
   (B) Meeting sales goals
   (C) Finalizing a contract
   (D) Creating a new device

6. Why does the speaker say, "we do have a limited hiring budget"?
   (A) To encourage the listeners to make more sales
   (B) To remind the listeners about losses
   (C) To tell the listeners that she will not hire more staff
   (D) To suggest that the listeners buy new software

UNIT 02　電話留言

主要為來電者留給對方的語音留言，有時會出現公司或政府機關事先錄好的未接來電自動語音應答。每次測驗平均出現2篇。

📎 代表題型範例

Example 01
美國女子　P4_U2_Ex01

Questions 1-3 refer to the following telephone message.

問候與自我介紹　Hello, I'm Dorothy Miller

來電重點　and I'm looking for someone to build a website for a new online clothing store I'll be opening in May. I saw the website you made for my friend, Maria Thompson, the other day. I was very impressed by how intuitive and sophisticated its design is, and Maria couldn't speak more highly of you. I'd like to meet you in person and discuss the project if you're available early next week. I'll have had a storyboard for the website ready to show you by then.

要求回電　Please call me at 525-9526 at your earliest convenience.

1. What type of business is the speaker planning to **start**?
   (A) A beauty salon
   (B) A bookstore
   (C) An online shop
   (D) A web magazine

2. What did **Maria Thompson** do for the speaker?
   (A) Repair an office
   (B) Design a dress
   (C) Develop a website
   (D) Recommend a business

3. What does the speaker want to **show the listener**?
   (A) An itinerary
   (B) A storyboard
   (C) A logo
   (D) A floor plan

問候與自我介紹　您好，我是Dorothy Miller。

來電重點　我正在找人為我將於五月新開幕的線上服飾店架設網站。前幾天我看到您為我朋友Maria Thompson所製作的網站。網站的設計既直觀又精緻，讓我留下深刻印象，Maria對您的評價也非常高。如果您下週初有空，我想親自與您見面，討論該項目。屆時我會準備好網站的故事板給您參考。

要求回電　有空的話，請您儘早回電，我的號碼為525-9526。

單字
look for　尋找⋯
intuitive　直觀的
sophisticated　精緻的、幹練的
can't speak more highly of　高度評價⋯
meet someone in person　親自與⋯見面

1. 說話者打算開設什麼類型的事業？
   (A) 美容院
   (B) 書店
   (C) 線上商店
   (D) 網路雜誌

2. Maria Thompson為說話者做了什麼事？
   (A) 修理辦公室
   (B) 設計裙子
   (C) 開發網站
   (D) 推薦公司

3. 說話者想向聽者展示什麼？
   (A) 行程安排
   (B) 故事板
   (C) 標誌
   (D) 樓層平面圖

答案　1. (C)　2. (D)　3. (B)

常見句型

問候	Hi, **this message is for** Brian. This is Selena from human resources. 您好，這是給Brian的留言，我是人力資源部的Selena。 **You've reached** the desk of Erika Watts. 已接通至Erika Watts的座位（自動語音應答）。
來電重點	**I'm returning your call regarding** the seminar I'll be giving at your company. 我回電給您，是為了討論關於將在貴公司舉辦研討會一事。 **I'm following up about** the hotel you asked me to book for next month's conference. 我打來更新進度，關於您要求為下個月會議預約飯店一事。 **I'm calling because** my computer suddenly went down. 我打電話來是因為我的電腦突然壞了。 Hi, it's Susan, your travel agent. **I'm calling about** the updated itinerary. 你好，我是旅行社的Susan，我打電話來更新行程。 Hey, it's Jeff. **I'm calling to see if** you're free on Thursday. 你好，我是Jeff。我打電話來確認你星期四是否有空。
結語	**Please call me back** at extension 618. 請撥打分機618回電給我。 **Call me** and let me know what you think. 打電話告訴我你的想法。 **Please call me** at your earliest convenience. 請盡快在你方便時回電給我。

CHECK-UP

P4_U2_Check-up 答案與解析 p.44

1. Why is the speaker calling?
   (A) To correct a mistake
   (B) To plan an upcoming trip
   (C) To ask for advice
   (D) To request a schedule change

2. What does the speaker say about a job candidate?
   (A) She has good references.
   (B) She speaks several languages.
   (C) She decided to work somewhere else.
   (D) She does not live in the area.

3. What did the speaker send in an e-mail?
   (A) A schedule
   (B) A cost estimate
   (C) A contract
   (D) A résumé

4. Why is the speaker currently unavailable?
   (A) He is attending an industry event.
   (B) He is taking time off.
   (C) His team is undergoing training.
   (D) His office equipment is malfunctioning.

5. What kind of business does the speaker most likely work for?
   (A) A computer software distributor
   (B) A magazine publisher
   (C) An electronics manufacturer
   (D) A recording studio

6. According to the speaker, what can be found on the website?
   (A) A job description
   (B) An event calendar
   (C) A photo gallery
   (D) An entry form

UNIT 03　廣播通知與公告

主要是在機場、火車站、登船碼頭、飛機上、商家、表演場地、圖書館等公共場所播放的廣播通知，以及公司內部向員工公告的內容。每次測驗平均出現1至2篇，有時甚至完全不會出現。

📎 代表題型範例

Example 01

美國女子　P4_U3_Ex01

Questions 1-3 refer to the following announcement.

Flyers, may I please have your attention? Starting next week, Terminal B will be out of operation, so no planes will be departing from there. All flights will either depart from Terminal A or Terminal C while **Terminal B is being renovated**. We expect renovations to take a few months, so we appreciate your patience until they are complete. Since Terminal A and Terminal C are on the far ends of the airport, **we recommend allocating extra travel time** to reach your gate before it closes.

1. **Where** is the announcement most likely being made?
   (A) At a ferry terminal
   (B) At a subway station
   (C) At a bus terminal
   (D) At an airport

2. **Why** is a change being made?
   (A) To renovate some facilities
   (B) To improve traffic flow
   (C) To save customers money
   (D) To increase energy efficiency

3. What does the speaker **recommend**?
   (A) Arriving earlier than usual
   (B) Postponing any travel plans
   (C) Reserving tickets online
   (D) Contacting customer service

各位旅客請注意。從下週開始，B航廈將停止營運，因此不會有任何班機從那裡起飛。在B航廈翻修期間，所有航班將改由A航廈或C航廈起飛。我們預計整修至完工需個月的時間，在此期間感謝大家的耐心等待。由於A航廈和C航廈位於機場兩端，我們建議您提前分配額外的交通時間，以便在登機口關閉前抵達。

單字
flyer　搭乘飛機的旅客
out of operation　停止營運
we appreciate your patience until...　直到…感謝您的耐心等候
allocate　分配（時間或金錢）

1. 該廣播通知最有可能在哪裡聽到？
   (A) 在渡輪碼頭
   (B) 在地鐵站
   (C) 在公車總站
   (D) 在機場

2. 為何要做出改變？
   (A) 翻修部分設施
   (B) 改善交通流量
   (C) 為客戶省錢
   (D) 提高能源效率

3. 說話者提出什麼建議？
   (A) 比平常早到
   (B) 延後旅遊計畫
   (C) 網路訂票
   (D) 聯絡客服

答案　**1.** (D)　**2.** (A)　**3.** (A)

常見句型

公共設施

Attention, passengers. Renovation work to upgrade our train station is underway.
各位乘客請注意，火車站正在進行升級改造工程。

Attention all passengers waiting for the 5 P.M. ferry to Jekyll Island. Due to a storm along the coast, the ferry has been canceled.
所有等待下午5點前往Jekyll島的乘客請注意。由於沿海發生風暴，本次渡輪已取消。

Attention travelers. The 7 P.M. Bluestar Airlines flight to Sydney has been canceled. We regret the inconvenience this may cause you.
各位旅客請注意，今晚7點飛往雪梨的藍星航空班次已取消。造成您的不便，我們深感抱歉。

Attention shoppers! Today is the first day of our summer sales event. All seafood is now on sale. Don't miss out.
各位顧客請注意！今天是我們夏季促銷活動首日。所有海鮮現正特價中，千萬不要錯過。

公司

Attention employees, a reminder that starting June 1st, the main entrance to the office building will be inaccessible while the road is repaved.
所有員工請注意，提醒自6月1日起，由於道路重新鋪設，辦公大樓正門將無法進出。

I have an announcement for the production line staff. As you've noticed, the main conveyor belt is temporarily out of order.
在此通知生產線員工，如同你們注意到的，主要輸送帶暫時發生故障。

CHECK-UP

1. What does the speaker say will happen this evening?
   (A) New books will be added.
   (B) The shelves will be rearranged.
   (C) The online catalog will be updated.
   (D) The reference desk will be moved.

2. According to the speaker, how can listeners get more information?
   (A) By speaking to a librarian
   (B) By checking the website
   (C) By picking up a handout
   (D) By calling the front desk

3. What is taking place tomorrow?
   (A) A group discussion
   (B) A book signing
   (C) An academic talk
   (D) A film showing

4. Where does the announcement most likely take place?
   (A) At a hair salon
   (B) At a grocery store
   (C) At a convention center
   (D) At a farmer's market

5. What is mentioned about Joe's Pickles?
   (A) He will hold a discount event.
   (B) He only accepts cash.
   (C) He is not present.
   (D) He went bankrupt.

6. What does the speaker encourage the listeners to do?
   (A) Arrive early
   (B) Greet people nicely
   (C) Work overtime
   (D) Ask for help

UNIT 04　電視、廣播節目與網路廣播

主要播放當地新聞、天氣預報、交通資訊等的廣播節目與網路廣播節目，每次測驗平均出現1至2篇。

代表題型範例

Example 01

美國男子　P4_U4_Ex01

Questions 1-3 refer to the following broadcast.

You're listening to *Business Today* on 167 F.M. Radio. For today's episode, we'll be **focusing on promoting your business through social media**. Getting enough engagement online is crucial to having a successful business. **It's important to separate yourself from your competition**. This involves creating a distinct social media presence that is associated with your company alone. For more advice on how to do this, we have **Stacy Lee**, **founder of Sell-it, a popular marketing consulting firm**. Welcome, Stacy.

1. What is the **focus** of the episode?
   (A) Promoting technological innovation
   (B) Offering training programs
   (C) Improving employee satisfaction
   (D) Using social media

2. What does the speaker say is **important**?
   (A) Creating a distinct presence
   (B) Attending networking events
   (C) Developing new products
   (D) Following industry standards

3. Who is **Stacy Lee**?
   (A) An office worker
   (B) A news reporter
   (C) A financial analyst
   (D) A marketing expert

您正在收聽的是F.M. 167廣播的《今日商業》節目。在今天的節目中，我們將聚焦於通過社群媒體來推廣您的業務。在網路上有足夠的參與度，對於一個企業的成功至關重要。重點在讓自己於競爭對手中脫穎而出。這包含建立一個與您公司相關的獨特社群媒體形象。如欲了解更多關於如何做到這一點的建議，我們請來人氣行銷顧問公司Sell-it的創辦人Stacy Lee。歡迎Stacy。

單字
focus on 聚焦於…
promote 宣傳
engagement 參與
crucial 至關重要的
distinct 獨特的、顯眼的
be associated with 與…有關

1. 本集的重點為何？
   (A) 推動技術創新
   (B) 提供培訓課程
   (C) 提升員工滿意度
   (D) 使用社群媒體

2. 說話者表示什麼很重要？
   (A) 創造獨特形象
   (B) 參加社交活動
   (C) 開發新產品
   (D) 遵循業界標準

3. 誰是Stacy Lee？
   (A) 辦公室員工
   (B) 新聞記者
   (C) 金融分析師
   (D) 行銷專家

答案　1. (D)　2. (A)　3. (D)

常見句型

活動	In local news, here's a reminder from the Bayland Community Center about their fundraising event this Saturday evening. 在當地新聞中，這是Bayland社區中心本週六舉辦的募款活動提醒。 You're listening to *Culture Hour* with Benjamin Feldom. First up in culture news is the Alvarado Art Museum's upcoming gala. 您現在收聽的是Benjamin Feldom的《文化時刻》。首則文化新聞是即將於Alvarado美術館舉辦的宴會。
交通	As of today, Hamilton Street between 3rd and 5th Avenues will be closed to traffic for emergency repair work. 即日起，第三大道與第五大道間的Hamilton街將禁止車輛通行，以便進行緊急維修工程。 It's 10 o'clock, time for the traffic update on Radio 105. A work crew is painting lines on Austin Street, so there have been reports of some delays in the area. 現在時間10點整，105電台為您播報最新交通消息。報導指出有工人正在Austin街上進行車道粉刷作業，導致該地區交通部分堵塞。
動工	The city broke ground on the new Houston Central Museum this morning. 今天上午，該市新的休士頓中央博物館開始動工。 The city's public transit agency has announced that construction has begun on the new Grantson train station. 該市公共交通機構宣布，新Grantson火車站已開始施工。

CHECK-UP

P4_U4_Check-up 答案與解析 p.45

1. What does Discover Works fund?
   (A) Park renovations
   (B) Music groups
   (C) Stage performances
   (D) Short films

2. According to the speaker, why should listeners arrive early?
   (A) To get a good seat
   (B) To save money
   (C) To meet the performers
   (D) To avoid heavy traffic

3. What is available on the town park website?
   (A) A discussion board
   (B) A series of videos
   (C) Membership information
   (D) A list of events

4. What is the podcast mainly about?
   (A) Chemistry
   (B) Video games
   (C) Travel
   (D) Astronomy

5. What did Kiran Buttar recently do?
   (A) She hosted a public fundraiser.
   (B) She started a business.
   (C) She created innovative technology.
   (D) She earned a scholarship.

6. According to the speaker, why should listeners subscribe to the annual plan?
   (A) To learn about private events
   (B) To download the transcript
   (C) To meet other members
   (D) To access the full episode

UNIT 05　廣告

主要宣傳產品、服務、企業、活動等的廣告，每次測驗平均出現1篇，有時甚至完全不會出現。

📎 代表題型範例

Example 01

美國男子　🎧 P4_U5_Ex01

Questions 1-3 refer to the following advertisement.

Looking for the perfect place to hold your next conference? Look no further than the Maple Square Convention Center. With our spacious auditoriums, extensive parking facilities, and easy access to public transportation, Maple Square Convention Center is the ideal location for both small and large gatherings. But there's another reason why you should hold your next convention here. **We're famous for our incredibly low prices.** If you are interested in booking with us, **please call our friendly staff at 555-0138 for pricing and available dates.**

1. What is being **advertised**?
   (A) A grocery store
   (B) A convention center
   (C) A restaurant
   (D) A travel destination

2. What is the business **famous** for?
   (A) Its amenities
   (B) Its modern design
   (C) Its prices
   (D) Its food

3. What does the speaker **suggest** listeners do?
   (A) Make a phone call
   (B) Visit a website
   (C) Schedule a tour
   (D) Place an order

您正在尋找舉辦下一場會議的完美場所嗎？楓樹廣場會議中心就是您的最佳選擇。我們擁有寬敞的禮堂，充裕的停車設施和便利的公共交通，楓樹廣場會議中心是舉辦小型和大型聚會的理想場所。但還有另一個理由，讓您更應在此舉辦下一場會議。我們以極為優惠的價格聞名。如果您有興趣與我們預約，請撥打555-0138聯絡我們親切的工作人員，詢問價格和可用日期。

單字

look no further　找不到更好的
spacious　寬敞的
auditorium　禮堂、會館
access to　允許進入⋯
gathering　聚會
incredibly　極為、難以置信地

1. 廣告內容為何？
   (A) 超市
   (B) 會議中心
   (C) 餐廳
   (D) 旅遊景點

2. 該企業以什麼聞名？
   (A) 便利設施
   (B) 現代感設計
   (C) 價格
   (D) 食物

3. 說話者建議聽者做什麼事？
   (A) 撥打電話
   (B) 造訪網站
   (C) 安排造訪行程
   (D) 下訂單

答案　1. (B)　2. (C)　3. (A)

常見句型

商品與服務	**Rest assured, we guarantee that** our work will be done by fully trained expert technicians. 我們保證工作將由訓練有素的專業技術人員完成,請放心。 Our hotel venue **features** several halls that can accommodate any event. 我們的飯店場地設有多個宴會廳,可容納任何活動。 **What sets us apart from our competitors**? You don't owe one penny until all pests on your premises have been eradicated. 我們與競爭對手的差別為何?除非消滅您家裡的所有害蟲,否則我們不會向您收取任何一分錢。 **In celebration of** our 5th anniversary, we're offering 10% off all your purchases in July. 為慶祝成立5週年,於七月購買的所有商品皆享九折優惠。
吸引客戶來訪	To get this deal, you must **schedule an appointment** either by phone or online. 如欲獲得此優惠,您必須撥打電話或線上預約。 For more information, **go online** and schedule a complimentary consultation with one of our representatives. 如欲了解更多資訊,請線上預約,與我們的客服人員進行免費諮詢。 For a list of all our locations, **visit our website** at www.alphachair.com. 欲了解我們所有分店地點,請至我們的網站www.alphachair.com。

CHECK-UP

1. What is being advertised?
   (A) An exterminator
   (B) A housecleaner
   (C) A pet care service
   (D) An interior designer

2. What is available for free?
   (A) A cleaning product
   (B) A home inspection
   (C) An hour of work
   (D) A membership card

3. How can listeners receive a discount?
   (A) By referring a friend
   (B) By creating a social media post
   (C) By using a promo code
   (D) By booking multiple appointments

4. How does each tour begin?
   (A) Refreshments are served.
   (B) A video is shown.
   (C) A lecture is given.
   (D) Safety gear is distributed.

5. What kind of gift do participants receive at the end of the tour?
   (A) A poster
   (B) A discount coupon
   (C) A bag of coffee
   (D) A postcard

6. What does the speaker warn the listeners about?
   (A) A health risk
   (B) An age restriction
   (C) Potential closures
   (D) Limited parking

UNIT 06　演說、介紹、參訪 / 觀光導覽

- 主要為在會議、開幕式等各種活動上的發言、主題講座、演講、講者介紹等。
- 也會出現觀光或參訪導覽、實地考察說明等。

📎 代表題型範例

Example 01
美國女子　🎧 P4_U6_Ex01

Questions 1-3 refer to the following introduction.

Thank you for coming to our ceremony today. We are pleased to host the ninth annual Art Awards **here at Grayson Academy**. I'm very excited to welcome our guest speaker, artist **Howard Penn. He recently wrote a book called How to *Paint Anything*, which has topped several bestseller lists**. During his talk tonight, he will explain how he became both a renowned painter and bestselling author. **After his speech**, we will announce the winners of this year's competition and then **offer some free drinks and snacks in the lobby**.

1. Where is the talk **taking place**?
   (A) At a museum
   (B) At an academy
   (C) At a club meeting
   (D) At a bookstore

2. According to the introduction, what did **Howard Penn** recently do?
   (A) He received an award.
   (B) He created a famous artwork.
   (C) He conducted some research.
   (D) He wrote a popular book.

3. What are the listeners invited to do **after the event**?
   (A) Buy some artwork
   (B) Enjoy some refreshments
   (C) Learn more about the venue
   (D) Take home a free gift

感謝大家今天前來參加我們的典禮。我們很高興在Grayson學院舉辦第九屆年度藝術獎頒獎典禮。非常熱烈歡迎我們的演講嘉賓，藝術家Howard Penn。他最近出版了一本名為《如何繪畫任何東西》的書籍，該書登上了多個暢銷排行榜。在今晚的演講中，他將解釋自己如何成為知名畫家兼暢銷書作家。演講結束後，我們將宣布今年比賽的獲獎者，接著在大廳會提供一些免費飲料和點心。

單字
be pleased to do　很高興能做到⋯
host　主辦
academy　學院、大學、研究院
top　在⋯之上、凌駕、超越
renowned　知名的
competition　比賽

1. 開場白在哪裡進行？
   (A) 在博物館
   (B) 在學院
   (C) 在社團聚會上
   (D) 在書店

2. 根據介紹，Howard Penn最近做了什麼事情？
   (A) 他獲頒獎項。
   (B) 他創作了知名藝術品。
   (C) 他進行了研究。
   (D) 他寫了人氣書籍。

3. 聽者於活動結束後受邀做什麼事？
   (A) 購買藝術品
   (B) 享用茶點
   (C) 了解更多場地詳情
   (D) 帶免費禮物回家

答案　**1.** (B)　**2.** (D)　**3.** (B)

92

常見句型

演說 講座	Thank you all for being here for this workshop for salespeople. 感謝大家前來參與本次為銷售人員舉辦的研討會。 I'd like to welcome you all to the grand opening of Newbury Park. 歡迎大家來參加Newbury公園的盛大開幕式。 Welcome to Harper Company's third annual conference on international business. 歡迎參加Harper公司的第三屆國際商務年會。 It's wonderful to see such a great turnout for this year's conference on hotel management. 很高興看到今年飯店管理會議有如此多的參與者。
參觀 導覽 旅遊	Thank you for joining this tour of our electric car manufacturing plant. Today, I'll be showing you how we produce our range of cars. 感謝您參加我們電動車製造廠的導覽行程。今天，我將向您展示我們如何生產各種汽車。 As we tour the Crescent Museum today, you'll see a wide range of artifacts from the Middle Ages. 今天我們參觀新月博物館時，您將會看到各式各樣的中世紀文物。 During today's bus tour, you will have a chance to see the city's legendary architecture. 在今日的巴士之旅，您將有機會看到這座城市的傳奇建築。

CHECK-UP

P4_U6_Check-up 答案與解析 p.47

[Tour information]

1. What is made at the farm?
    (A) Organic milk
    (B) Cotton
    (C) Beef jerky
    (D) Fresh fruit

2. What will listeners have the chance to do?
    (A) Take a walk with the animals
    (B) Taste the products
    (C) Provide food for the animals
    (D) Meet the owners

3. What will listeners receive?
    (A) A video link
    (B) Sauces for snacks
    (C) A leaflet
    (D) A brush

[Speech]

4. What location is the speaker discussing?
    (A) An art museum
    (B) An amusement park
    (C) A petting zoo
    (D) An athletic field

5. What special offer does the speaker mention?
    (A) A complimentary meal
    (B) A voucher for a friend
    (C) A discount for large groups
    (D) An annual membership plan

6. What will take place on Friday?
    (A) An art workshop
    (B) A guided tour
    (C) A live concert
    (D) A movie screening

PRACTICE 高難度（掌握意圖、圖表題）

P4_Practice 答案與解析 p.48

1. Where does the speaker most likely work?
   (A) At a car wash
   (B) At a moving company
   (C) At a car rental service
   (D) At an auto repair shop

2. What does the speaker imply when he says, "which will be a major job"?
   (A) A deposit must be paid.
   (B) The work will take him some time.
   (C) He needs to hire more people.
   (D) He is about to go on vacation.

3. What does the speaker say about this evening?
   (A) An employee will be present.
   (B) A part will arrive.
   (C) The business will be closed.
   (D) A payment system will be updated.

4. What is the purpose of the talk?
   (A) To tell the listeners about a lawsuit
   (B) To announce a new return policy
   (C) To prepare the listeners for complaints
   (D) To propose a team expansion

5. What does the speaker imply when he says, "We've radically changed our production process"?
   (A) The company once used dangerous chemicals.
   (B) Products are selling at a higher margin.
   (C) Productivity has increased dramatically.
   (D) A news report was wrong.

6. What are the listeners asked to do?
   (A) Read a handout
   (B) Take a short break
   (C) Write a report
   (D) Respond to some e-mails

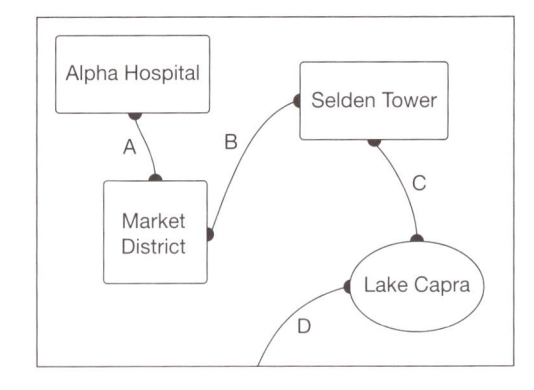

```
Alpha Hospital ──A── Market District
       │                    │
       B                    │
       │                    │
   Selden Tower ──C── Lake Capra
                           │
                           D
```

7. What project does the speaker mainly discuss?
   (A) A city hall
   (B) A walkway
   (C) A riverside park
   (D) A sports arena

8. Why was the project initiated?
   (A) A company offered to pay for it.
   (B) It was decided by the taxpayers.
   (C) The city mayor said it was necessary.
   (D) It was prompted by a research report.

9. Look at the graphic. According to the speaker, which segment of the project has been completed?
   (A) Segment A
   (B) Segment B
   (C) Segment C
   (D) Segment D

PRACTICE

Unit Features	Unit Type			
	A	B	C	D
Two bedrooms	✓			✓
Ocean view		✓		✓
Massage chair	✓		✓	

10. Look at the graphic. Which type of unit does the speaker mention?

    (A) Type A
    (B) Type B
    (C) Type C
    (D) Type D

11. What does the speaker emphasize about the hotel?

    (A) Its family-friendly atmosphere
    (B) Its low prices
    (C) Its high-quality food
    (D) Its cleanliness

12. What will happen tomorrow?

    (A) The speaker will take a day off.
    (B) The hotel will be closed.
    (C) The speaker will visit a client.
    (D) The hotel will be fully booked.

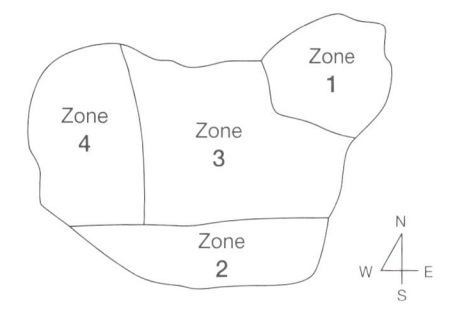

13. What does the speaker's company sell?

    (A) Stationery
    (B) Beauty products
    (C) Auto parts
    (D) Pharmaceuticals

14. Look at the graphic. Which region provided the least amount of sales last quarter?

    (A) Zone 1
    (B) Zone 2
    (C) Zone 3
    (D) Zone 4

15. According to the speaker, what will be launched at the end of the year?

    (A) A research project
    (B) Digital appliances
    (C) A new product line
    (D) Online advertisements

PART TEST

1. What position have the listeners been hired for?
   (A) Tour guide
   (B) Housekeeping staff
   (C) Receptionist
   (D) Supermarket clerk

2. What are the listeners asked to write down?
   (A) Their preferred working days
   (B) Their uniform size
   (C) A contact number
   (D) A password

3. What does the speaker say about a system?
   (A) It has recently been upgraded.
   (B) It is for managers only.
   (C) It takes a while to restart.
   (D) It does not get used very often.

4. What department does the speaker work in?
   (A) Purchasing
   (B) Marketing
   (C) Data management
   (D) Product development

5. What problem does the speaker mention?
   (A) He had to work overtime.
   (B) A conference room is locked.
   (C) Some lights are not working.
   (D) Some files were temporarily lost.

6. Where will the speaker most likely go at 2:00 P.M.?
   (A) To a department store
   (B) To a lecture hall
   (C) To a bank
   (D) To a train station

7. What does the speaker's company sell?
   (A) Paint
   (B) Pottery
   (C) Furniture
   (D) Jewelry

8. What does the speaker imply when she says, "those won't go on the website until April"?
   (A) She is experiencing some technical difficulties.
   (B) She thinks another task is more important.
   (C) She found an error in the schedule.
   (D) She wants to apologize for a delay.

9. What mistake does the speaker think the company made?
   (A) It set its prices too low.
   (B) It spent too much money on advertising.
   (C) It changed to an unreliable supplier.
   (D) It offered a fast delivery option.

10. Where does the announcement most likely take place?
    (A) On a ferry
    (B) On a train
    (C) On an airplane
    (D) On a bus

11. What are the listeners encouraged to do?
    (A) Refrain from eating
    (B) Fasten their seat belts
    (C) Move to another level
    (D) Stop using their phones

12. What will most likely happen next?
    (A) More information will be given.
    (B) The route will be changed.
    (C) More passengers will be picked up.
    (D) Luggage will be collected.

13. What is being advertised?
    (A) A concert hall
    (B) A tour company
    (C) A hotel
    (D) An airline

14. What benefit of the business does the speaker mention?
    (A) It offers full refunds for cancellations.
    (B) It can accommodate last-minute requests.
    (C) It uses environmentally friendly materials.
    (D) It provides customizable options.

15. What is being offered in March?
    (A) A meal voucher
    (B) A group discount
    (C) A free clothing item
    (D) An insurance policy

16. Who most likely is the speaker?
    (A) A fitness instructor
    (B) A park ranger
    (C) A bus driver
    (D) A research scientist

17. What does the speaker apologize for?
    (A) A fee increase
    (B) An unexpected closure
    (C) A delayed start
    (D) A printing error

18. What will some of the listeners most likely do next?
    (A) Fill a container
    (B) Watch a demonstration
    (C) Select some snacks
    (D) Put on name tags

19. Who is Terrance Hickman?
    (A) A potential investor
    (B) A new staff member
    (C) A university professor
    (D) A board member

20. Which department do the listeners most likely work in?
    (A) Graphic design
    (B) Technical support
    (C) Advertising
    (D) Legal

21. Why does the speaker say, "you all had the same opportunity"?
    (A) To give a warning about deadlines
    (B) To acknowledge the top employees
    (C) To encourage listeners to help
    (D) To explain a misunderstanding

22. Who is the speaker most likely calling?
    (A) A translator
    (B) An architect
    (C) An accountant
    (D) A financial advisor

23. What does the speaker mean when she says, "the board meeting is tomorrow"?
    (A) She cannot reserve the room she wanted.
    (B) She needs to reschedule an appointment with the listener.
    (C) She will have some information soon.
    (D) She would like the listener to give a presentation.

24. What does the speaker plan to do this afternoon?
    (A) Attend a conference
    (B) Train a colleague
    (C) Sign a contract
    (D) Visit a family member

Test Results	
Test	Distance
1	95 miles
2	121 miles
3	103 miles
4	99 miles

25. Where are the listeners?

    (A) At a staff orientation
    (B) At a job interview
    (C) At a press conference
    (D) At an awards banquet

26. According to the speaker, what happened in February?

    (A) An invention's patent was approved.
    (B) A safety report was publicized.
    (C) A department head was changed.
    (D) A company acquisition was finalized.

27. Look at the graphic. Which test run did the speaker participate in?

    (A) Test 1
    (B) Test 2
    (C) Test 3
    (D) Test 4

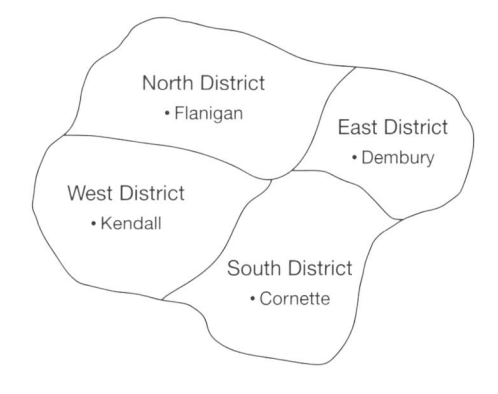

North District
• Flanigan

East District
• Dembury

West District
• Kendall

South District
• Cornette

28. Who did the speaker talk to in the morning?

    (A) Utility company employees
    (B) Department store managers
    (C) Emergency workers
    (D) Factory supervisors

29. Look at the graphic. Which district experienced storm damage?

    (A) The East District
    (B) The West District
    (C) The North District
    (D) The South District

30. What does the speaker ask Annabelle's team to do?

    (A) Review a document
    (B) Call some clients
    (C) Clear an area
    (D) Repair a vehicle

ENERGY

雨過天晴，方能迎來彩虹。
黑夜過去，方能迎來黎明。
歷經分娩之苦，方能迎來新生兒。
感動為苦難中結成的果實。

── 趙正敏《人生便是禮物》

PART 5

句子填空

UNIT 01 名詞

UNIT 02 代名詞

UNIT 03 形容詞與限定詞

UNIT 04 副詞

UNIT 05 動詞、主動詞單複數一致性、語態、時態

UNIT 06 不定詞與動名詞

UNIT 07 分詞

UNIT 08 介系詞

UNIT 09 連接詞

UNIT 10 關係詞

UNIT 11 高分必備名詞詞彙

UNIT 12 高分必備形容詞詞彙

UNIT 13 高分必備副詞詞彙

UNIT 14 高分必備動詞詞彙

PRACTICE ［高難度］

PART TEST

PART 5 句子填空

PART 5主要分成文法題和詞彙題，前者題型包含選出適當的詞性，以及選出正確的動詞形態（時態、語態、分詞、主動詞單複數一致性）；後者題型包含選出符合文意的詞彙，以及選出慣用語中的詞彙。文法題和詞彙題的出題比重差不多。在文法題部分，每次測驗出題比重最高的考題為選出適當的名詞、動詞、形容詞或副詞。掌握該類型考題，才能順利取得高分。在詞彙題部分，則為選擇符合文意的動詞、名詞、形容詞、副詞或介系詞，每次測驗考2至3題；選擇符合文意的連接詞或慣用片語，每次測驗考1至3題，出題頻率不固定。

作答PART 5時，為縮短作答時間，一般建議先查看選項，確認考題類型後，再根據所屬類型的解題策略作答。下方列出四種代表題型，請熟悉這些文法和詞彙題的基本作答方式。

[文法]

選出適當的詞性或詞類變化

Mr. Wood's ------- to the Paris branch was postponed until next year.
(A) transfer　　　　名詞、動詞
(B) to transfer　　　不定詞 to V
(C) transferred　　　過去分詞
(D) transferable　　 形容詞

中譯 Wood先生調職到巴黎分公司的時間延期至明年。

❶ 查看選項
四個選項的詞性皆不相同，但屬於同一字根transfer所衍生而成。

❷ 確認空格前後方
空格前方為限定詞Mr. Wood's，用來修飾名詞，表示空格應填入名詞。

❸ 選出答案
因此答案為名詞 (A) transfer。

選出適當的動詞形態

A retirement party will be held next week for Mr. Schmidt, who ------- for Melon Technologies for over 30 years.
(A) works　　　　　　單數主詞 現在式
(B) was worked　　　 單數主詞 過去簡單式
(C) have worked　　　複數主詞 現在完成式
(D) has been working　單數主詞 現在完成進行式

中譯 下週將為Schmidt先生舉辦退休派對，他已經在Melon科技公司工作超過30年。

❶ 查看選項
四個選項為不同的動詞形態，但皆由同一單字work所衍生而成。

❷ 確認文法並刪去錯誤選項
空格置於形容詞子句的動詞位置上，形容詞子句用來修飾前方的Mr. Schmidt，其先行詞與動詞需符合單複數一致性。先行詞Mr. Schmidt為單數名詞，表示答案要選單數動詞，因此可先刪去(C)。

❸ 選出答案
後方出現for over 30 years，適合搭配的時態為現在完成式，因此答案為(D)。

[詞彙]

選出適當的介系詞

------- coming to work early, Mr. Earl sometimes works on weekends to make sure he meets deadlines.

(A) As long as　　　連接詞：只要⋯
(B) After　　　　　連接詞、介系詞：在⋯之後
(C) In addition to　　介系詞：除了⋯之外（還）
(D) However　　　連接副詞：然而、無論如何

中譯 Earl先生除了提早上班外，有時還會在週末加班，以確保能趕上截止日。

❶ 查看選項
選項包含連接詞、介系詞、連接副詞，表示本題考的是選出適當的連接詞或介系詞。

❷ 確認空格前後方的「主詞＋動詞」
空格後方沒有主詞，直接連接coming，表示空格應填入介系詞。(A)為連接詞、(D)為副詞，因此可先刪去這兩個選項。

❸ 選出答案
根據文意，表達「除了提早上班外，還會在週末加班」最為適當，因此答案為 (C) In addition to。

選出適當的詞彙

During the interview, each candidate was asked to describe their previous work -------.

(A) experience　　經驗
(B) consumption　消費
(C) drop　　　　下降
(D) occasion　　　情況、場合

中譯 在面試過程中，每位應徵者都被要求講述他們過往的工作經驗。

❶ 查看選項
四個選項皆為不同意思的名詞，表示該題為測驗名詞詞彙的考題。

❷ 確認空格前後方字詞
把各選項套入空格中，確認是否適合搭配前後方字詞。
(A) work experience 工作經驗
(B) work consumption 工作消費
(C) work drop 業務下降
(D) work occasion 工作情況

❸ 選出答案
語意最通順的選項為 (A)，故為正解。若無法僅憑空格前後的字詞確認，可擴大確認範圍，例如：previous work experience（過往的工作經驗）、describe their previous work experience（描述他們過往的工作經驗）。

UNIT 01　名詞

1　冠詞／所有格＋名詞

空格前方為不定冠詞（a, an）、定冠詞（the）、所有格（her, Mr. Woods）等限定詞時，空格要填入名詞。

不定冠詞＋名詞　Because of unexpected competition, the store still had **an excess** / excessive of one hundred televisions left in stock.
由於意料之外的競爭，店內還剩下一百多台的電視庫存。

所有格＋名詞　Nicholas & Son and Johnston Co. have formed a mutually beneficial partnership to increase **their profits** / profitable.
Nicholas & Son公司和Johnston公司建立了互惠互利合作關係，以增加他們的利潤。

2　形容詞／分詞＋名詞

形容詞＋名詞　The restaurant on Mesa Street is having a **large celebration** / celebrate to mark its tenth anniversary.　Mesa街上的餐廳正在舉行盛大的慶祝活動，以紀念成立十週年。

分詞＋名詞　The **written agreement** / agreeable between HC Media and the band clearly outlined the terms for licensing the music.
HC媒體公司和樂團間的書面協議，清楚地概述音樂版權的條款。

3　當作主詞／受詞／補語

主詞　**Acceptance** / Accept to the law firm's internship program **depends** on university transcripts and recommendations.　能否錄取律師事務所的實習計劃，取決於大學成績單和推薦信。
→ 主詞為「Acceptance」、動詞為「depends」，介系詞片語「to the law firm's internship program」用來修飾主詞。

動詞的受詞　New employees should **obtain approval** / approved from their assigned mentors before leaving the office.　新進員工在離開辦公室前，應獲得指定導師的批准。

介系詞的受詞　Restaurant owners should make sure their kitchens are ready **for inspection** / inspect at all times.　餐廳老闆應做好萬全準備，讓廚房隨時可接受檢查。
→ 名詞可置於介系詞後方，當作介系詞的受詞。

主詞補語　The store's holiday season sales event **was** an unprecedented **success** / successful.
該商店的假期特賣活動取得了前所未有的成功。
→ 空格前方出現be動詞「was」，表示空格為主詞補語。加上空格受到不定冠詞「an」與形容詞「unprecedented」的修飾，因此空格應填入名詞。

高分挑戰　受詞補語

The department head **called Mr. Reuben** a great **leader** / leadership for finishing the project ahead of schedule.　部門主管稱Reuben先生是位優秀的領導者，因他提前完成該專案。
→ 空格置於動詞「call」後方的補語位置上，且受到冠詞「a」與形容詞「great」的修飾。雖然「leadership」也是名詞，但與Mr. Reuben屬於同格關係，不適合填入空格中。

4 複合名詞

複合名詞指的是「名詞＋名詞」。考題的空格會置於複合名詞中的第一個或第二個名詞位置，要求選出適當的名詞。

road repair 道路修繕	delivery receipt 交貨收據
repair service 維修服務	keynote speech 主題演講
product line 產品線	expiration date 有效期限、截止日
meeting agenda 會議議程	contract negotiation 合約談判
work site 工作現場	travel budget 差旅預算
hiring process 招募流程	quality standards 品質標準
baggage allowance 行李限額	e-mail reminder 電子郵件提醒

高分挑戰

The botanical garden is the most popular **tourist** / touristic **attraction** in Cincinnati.
植物園是辛辛那提最受歡迎的旅遊景點。

→ 「tourist attraction」為複合名詞，意思為「觀光地、旅遊景點」。空格置於名詞前方時，很容易讓人認定應填入形容詞或分詞來修飾名詞，請特別留意。

5 人物名詞 VS. 事物名詞／抽象名詞

選項同時出現人物名詞和事物名詞時，請根據文意選出答案。

Despite being **the largest producer** / production of textiles in the country, Grenadine's Fabrics has seen a steady decline in profits.
儘管Grenadine's織物場是國內最大的紡織品生產商，但其利潤持續下降。

→ 根據文意，空格指的是主要子句中的主詞「Grenadine's Fabrics」，因此空格適合填入「生產業者」，而非「生產」。

6 單數名詞 VS. 複數名詞

選項出現兩個名詞時，請先判斷為可數名詞、不可數名詞、前方是否有冠詞，以及其與動詞間的單複數一致性。

可數 VS. 不可數　If your copier is **in need of repair** / repairs, you're advised to select a certified technician.
如果你的影印機需要維修，建議你選擇經認證的技術人員。

→ 「repair」可以當可數名詞，亦可當不可數名詞使用，但搭配「in need of」使用時，僅能使用不可數名詞。

前方有無冠詞　The event organizer called the management office to ask **for permission** / permit to use the event hall. 活動主辦方打電話給管理辦公室，請求使用活動場地的許可。

→ 空格置於介系詞「for」的受詞位置上，應填入名詞。而空格前方沒有不定冠詞a / an，表示空格應填入不可數名詞或複數名詞。「permit（許可證）」為可數名詞，若前方沒有不定冠詞，得填入複數形態「permits」才行。因此答案為不可數名詞「permission」，意思為「許可」。

單複數的一致性　The museum cannot be opened to the public until structural **defects** / defect **are** repaired.
在建築結構缺陷修復前，博物館無法對外開放。

7 名詞 VS. 動名詞

Construction / Constructing **of** the Lowell Bridge has been postponed due to inclement weather.
由於天氣惡劣，已延後Lowell大橋的建設。

→ 雖然動名詞也具備名詞的功能，但後方受到介系詞「of」的修飾，因此空格只能填入名詞「construction」。「動名詞（constructing）」除了具備名詞的功能外，同時保有動詞的屬性，因此後方要連接受詞才行。

105

PRACTICE

答案與解析 p.55

1. According to the company newsletter, the vice president will hold a ------- on the firm's progress this Thursday.
   (A) discussing
   (B) discussed
   (C) discussion
   (D) will discuss

2. Speak with a supervisor if any safety ------- occur on the assembly line.
   (A) violated
   (B) violations
   (C) violate
   (D) violates

3. The lawyers carefully review negotiated ------- to check for any problems.
   (A) agree
   (B) agreements
   (C) agreed
   (D) agreeing

4. Irene Krakow intends to meet a ------- from her gym tomorrow morning.
   (A) train
   (B) trainer
   (C) trained
   (D) training

5. There is ------- among the bank tellers to accept the contract proposal put forth by management.
   (A) hesitate
   (B) hesitated
   (C) hesitation
   (D) hesitating

6. Mr. Cromwell was given a choice of ------- after he completed the Maxell Project successfully.
   (A) assigning
   (B) assigns
   (C) assigned
   (D) assignments

7. Dover Sporting Goods has a long-term ------- with several baseball teams in the local area.
   (A) affiliate
   (B) affiliated
   (C) affiliation
   (D) affiliating

8. ------- will be advised to avoid the roads in the mountains on account of the expected heavy snowfall.
   (A) Travel
   (B) Travelers
   (C) Traveled
   (D) Traveling

9. In ------- with the CEO's decision, all employees were given an extra day of paid leave.
   (A) accord
   (B) according
   (C) accordance
   (D) accords

10. During the holiday season, all hotel ------- made online will be completely nonrefundable.
    (A) booked
    (B) book
    (C) booking
    (D) bookings

PRACTICE

11. Mr. Hightower expressed ------- that his bridge design was selected by the mayor of the city.
    (A) satisfy
    (B) satisfaction
    (C) satisfying
    (D) satisfyingly

12. Mr. Burbank will establish a group of ------- to handle the new clients the company has obtained.
    (A) consultant
    (B) consultants
    (C) consulting
    (D) consulted

13. Pianist Judy Watson's ------- the past three days have been widely praised by audience members.
    (A) perform
    (B) performed
    (C) performance
    (D) performances

14. In Piedmont, the ------- of some new buildings resembles that used in ancient Rome.
    (A) styling
    (B) stylist
    (C) styled
    (D) style

15. According to government -------, homes should use energy-efficient insulation materials.
    (A) recommendations
    (B) recommends
    (C) to recommend
    (D) will recommend

16. Despite his continual ------- at Weyland Aerospace for thirty years, Dan Jenkins resigned to work at another company.
    (A) employee
    (B) employing
    (C) employed
    (D) employment

17. Employees are supposed to report any ------- on business trips no matter how small.
    (A) expensive
    (B) expensively
    (C) expenses
    (D) expensed

18. Mr. Klein was asked to make a ------- regarding how to enter the South American market.
    (A) propose
    (B) proposer
    (C) proposing
    (D) proposal

19. Stores were informed that ------- of the new product line would be limited for the next two months.
    (A) distribution
    (B) distributing
    (C) distribute
    (D) distributed

20. Dr. Audrey is always eager to give her scientists ------- that they need for their experiments.
    (A) materially
    (B) materials
    (C) materialize
    (D) materialization

UNIT 02　代名詞

1　人稱代名詞

考題中經常出現人稱代名詞的主格和所有格，前者可當作主詞使用；後者則可用來修飾名詞或名詞片語。

主格	**The website** is now unavailable as **it** / he is undergoing routine maintenance. 由於網站正在進行例行性維護，目前無法使用。
受格	The department manager will **give us** / ourselves **the new schedule** for the summer season. 部門經理將會給我們新的夏季時間表。 → 動詞「give」適用句型為「give＋間接受詞＋直接受詞」，因此後方要連接兩個受詞。
所有格	Ms. Duda is persuading the executives to postpone the product launch until **her** / hers **team** is ready.　Duda女士正在說服管理高層延後產品上市時間，直到她的團隊做好準備為止。
所有格代名詞	A coworker of **mine** / me will be taking a business trip to Ulaanbaatar in a few weeks. 我的一位同事將在幾週後前往Ulaanbaatar出差。

2　不定代名詞

anyone, everyone	**Anyone** / Those **who has been** working with the company for over six months **is** eligible for a holiday bonus.　凡在公司工作超過六個月的人，都有資格領取三節獎金。 → anyone, everyone後方要連接單數動詞；those (who)後方要連接複數動詞。
one, ones	**The tire** was replaced with a new **one** / ones because it was flat. 因輪胎爆胎，所以換成新輪胎。 →「one」用來代替前方提到過的名詞「tire」，one前方一定要有限定詞。

3　指示代名詞

The commercial real estate prices in Southfield are significantly lower than **those** / that in Sherwood.
Southfield的商用不動產價格明顯低於Sherwood。
→ 空格要填入適當的字詞，用來代替前方出現過的複數名詞「The commercial real estate prices」，因此要選指示代名詞複數形態「those」。

4　反身代名詞

一般用法	For the team-building exercises, **workers** were asked to organize **themselves** / them into groups of four.　在團隊精神凝聚活動中，員工們被要求分成四人一組。 → 動詞「organize」的受詞與主詞「workers」相同，此時要使用反身代名詞「themselves」較為適當，且不能省略。

> **高分挑戰　加強語氣**
>
> The CEO of Stockton Tech usually gives new employees a building tour **himself** / him.
> Stockton科技公司的執行長通常會親自帶新進員工參觀大樓。
> → 當句子包含「主詞＋動詞＋受詞」，為結構完整的句子時，反身代名詞僅為加強語氣之用，因此可選擇省略。

108

PRACTICE

答案與解析 p.56

1. Ms. Toole is flying to Memphis tomorrow because ------- has to meet a potential client there.
   (A) her
   (B) hers
   (C) she
   (D) herself

2. ------- who is interested in a career in robotics is welcome to apply for the position.
   (A) All
   (B) Anyone
   (C) Whatever
   (D) Whomever

3. The staff meeting is mandatory, so ------- must cancel conflicting appointments and attend it tomorrow.
   (A) another
   (B) everybody
   (C) which
   (D) every

4. After reading a section of the novel, Jules Desmond ------- will autograph copies for fans.
   (A) him
   (B) he
   (C) his
   (D) himself

5. Please use the training manuals in the back of the room rather than ------- sitting on the table.
   (A) anyone
   (B) those
   (C) other
   (D) each

6. Whenever a project is complete, please contact ------- manager to receive a new assignment.
   (A) your
   (B) yours
   (C) yourself
   (D) you

7. Even though the tires are only two years old, Ms. Vernon decided to replace ------- with a new set.
   (A) them
   (B) they
   (C) their
   (D) themselves

8. The best ------- who applied for the engineering position was Rita Kraus, to whom we should offer the job.
   (A) each
   (B) one
   (C) what
   (D) another

9. The tour bus we rode in was painted red, so it was easy to locate ------- even in a full parking lot.
   (A) us
   (B) our
   (C) ours
   (D) ourselves

10. Ms. Atkins has turned ------- into a highly competent computer programmer thanks to hard work and dedication.
    (A) her
    (B) hers
    (C) herself
    (D) her own

UNIT 03　形容詞與限定詞

1　形容詞

形容詞 VS. 分詞　New employees will watch an **instructional** / instructing **video** about how to assemble the device.　新員工將觀看如何組裝設備的教學影片。
→ 空格置於形容詞的位置上，選項同時出現形容詞和分詞時，請優先選擇形容詞。

主詞補語　The recruits **seem eager** / eagerly to start their first day on the job.
新進員工似乎迫不及待要開始他們第一天的工作。

受詞補語　Attention to detail **makes Ms. Rose reliable** / reliably and easy to work with.
Rose女士善於注重細節，使她成為一個可靠且容易合作的人。
→ 句型結構為「主詞Attention to detail＋動詞makes＋受詞Ms. Rose＋受詞補語」。答題線索為對等連接詞「and」，後方連接的是形容詞「easy」。

高分挑戰　形容詞 VS. 形容詞

Without **reliable** / reliant **information**, stock traders would not be able to handle their clients' investments in a responsible manner.
若沒有可靠資訊，證券交易員將無法以負責任的方式處理客戶投資。
→ 根據文意，「reliable（可靠的）」和「reliant（依賴的）」當中，「reliable」更適合用來修飾「information」。

看起來像副詞的形容詞　Ms. Jenkins instructed her workers to respond to every e-mail in a **timely** / timer **manner**.
Jenkins女士指示她的員工及時回覆每封電子郵件。
→ 雖然「timely」的字尾為 -ly，但它並非副詞，而是形容詞。另外，還有一些看起來像副詞的形容詞，例如：costly（昂貴的）、lively（精力充沛的）、elderly（年長的）等。

比較級　The latest SUV by Eighto Motors is **more spacious** / spaciously than it looks.
Eighto汽車公司最新款的SUV比外觀看起來還寬敞。

最高級　The Mumbai branch had **the highest** / higher sales numbers out of the whole global sales team.　在整個全球銷售團隊中，孟買分公司的銷售額最高。

2　限定詞

限定詞的功能類似形容詞，用來表示後方連接的名詞具有特定性。請務必分清楚連接單數名詞和複數名詞的限定詞。

each / every
＋單數名詞　Our managers ensure that **every** / all **product** is of the highest quality.
我們經理確保每件產品都有最好的品質。

all＋複數名詞
／不可數名詞　Mr. Lambert was surprised that **all** / every **his coworkers** wrote him a letter for his retirement party.　Lambert先生對於所有同事都為他的退休派對寫了一封信感到驚訝。

any＋單複數名詞
／不可數名詞　A safety label is attached to the product to prevent **any** / each **accidents** from occurring.
產品上貼有安全標籤，以防發生任何意外。

both A and B　**Both** / Either **the design team and the marketing team** work together to make the most eye-catching book covers.　設計團隊和行銷團隊共同努力，製作出最引人注目的書籍封面。
→ either的用法為「either A or B」。

PRACTICE

1. Ms. Howell has a comprehensive understanding of even the ------- developments in technology these days.
   (A) late
   (B) lateness
   (C) lately
   (D) latest

2. After attending the workshop, ------- person has to do some hands-on training in the lab.
   (A) every
   (B) which
   (C) because
   (D) many

3. It is ------- to create an agenda before a meeting so that all important points are covered.
   (A) benefit
   (B) benefiting
   (C) beneficial
   (D) beneficially

4. Destiny Media only hires ------- applicants willing to work hard to achieve their goals.
   (A) ambition
   (B) ambitions
   (C) ambitious
   (D) ambitiously

5. It is vital that items be shipped to customers in a ------- manner.
   (A) timely
   (B) time
   (C) times
   (D) timing

6. ------- technicians are required to wear safety gear in the laboratory during the workday.
   (A) Each
   (B) All
   (C) Either
   (D) None

7. Attendees said the dance performances were the most ------- part of the festival.
   (A) impress
   (B) impression
   (C) impressive
   (D) impressively

8. After he gets promoted, Horace Powers intends to take ------- days of vacation with his family.
   (A) several
   (B) either
   (C) whatever
   (D) another

9. Ms. Cunningham has worked on multiple ------- projects during the past few years.
   (A) extensive
   (B) extend
   (C) extending
   (D) extends

10. Luxor Furniture designs ------- office chairs for individuals who remain seated most of the day.
    (A) comfort
    (B) comfortable
    (C) comforting
    (D) comfortably

UNIT 04　副詞

1　置於動詞或分詞前後方的副詞

副詞＋動詞
The food critic **favorably** / favored **reviewed** the chef's special dishes.
美食評論家對主廚的特色料理給予好評。

動詞＋副詞
BT News gets a lot of traffic to its website because it **advertises heavily** / heavy on social media.　BT 新聞在社群媒體上大量投放廣告，因此網站流量大增。

動詞＋名詞＋副詞
The factory inspector **examined** each of the manufactured items **carefully** / careful.
工廠查驗員仔細檢查每一件產品。
→ 雖然「carefully」置於名詞「items」後方，但實際上修飾的是前方的動詞「examined」。

be動詞＋副詞＋分詞
The store's refund policy **is clearly** / clear **stated** on its website.
商店的退款政策在網站上有明確說明。

be動詞＋分詞＋副詞
All elevators in the building **are inspected regularly** / regular by Mr. Jones.
Jones先生會定期檢查大樓內的所有電梯。

2　置於助動詞後方的副詞

have＋副詞＋過去分詞
The sales manager **has successfully** / success **negotiated** contracts with a variety of corporate clients.　業務經理已成功與多家企業客戶協商合約。
→ 有時也會出現「have＋過去分詞＋副詞」的形態。

助動詞＋副詞＋原形動詞
After the reading, the author **will personally** / personal **sign** copies of his new novel for fans.
說書會結束後，作者會親自為粉絲在他的新小說上簽名。

3　置於形容詞與副詞前方的副詞

副詞＋形容詞
The local bookstore has a **surprisingly** / surprising **large** selection of children's books.
當地書店的兒童讀物數量驚人。

副詞＋副詞
To the average buyer, the mini tablet is **considerably** / considerable **more** attractive than the extra-large one.　對於一般買家來說，迷你平板比超大型平板更具吸引力。
→ 「considerably」的意思與「a lot」相同。在副詞「more」前方加上considerably，表示強調的概念。

4　置於介系詞、從屬連接詞前方的副詞

Gilmore Manufacturing announced a new round of hiring **shortly after** reporting earnings that were higher than expected.　Gilmore製造公司在公布了高於預期的營收後不久，又宣布了新一輪的招募。

PRACTICE

答案與解析 p.58

1. The improvements to the website were ------- made by the director of the IT Department.
   (A) personal
   (B) personals
   (C) personality
   (D) personally

2. The audience was impressed by the ------- realistic special effects in the film.
   (A) high
   (B) higher
   (C) highest
   (D) highly

3. The sign indicates that the room is ------- off limits to unauthorized personnel.
   (A) clear
   (B) clearly
   (C) clearer
   (D) clearest

4. Mr. Olson, the office manager, ------- instructed his employees to arrive on time for special events.
   (A) repeat
   (B) repeating
   (C) repeated
   (D) repeatedly

5. Tour participants must be on time because the boat departs ------- at 7:00 A.M.
   (A) prompt
   (B) promptly
   (C) prompted
   (D) promptness

6. Since she started working at Meridian Inc., Julie Sharpe has ------- received recognition for her accomplishments.
   (A) regular
   (B) more regular
   (C) regulars
   (D) regularly

7. The waiter asked the diners ------- if they had enjoyed their meal at the restaurant.
   (A) polite
   (B) politeness
   (C) politely
   (D) most polite

8. Customer service representatives were instructed to resolve all complaints more -------.
   (A) prompt
   (B) prompts
   (C) promptness
   (D) promptly

高分挑戰

9. The warehouse supervisor had the boxes of electronics ------- removed to make space for the new shipment.
   (A) haste
   (B) hasten
   (C) hastened
   (D) hastily

高分挑戰

10. The winner of the raffle at the county fair will be determined by a ------- selected number this evening.
    (A) randomly
    (B) randomize
    (C) to randomize
    (D) random

113

UNIT 05　動詞、主動詞單複數一致性、語態、時態

1　填入動詞與形態

填入動詞　The Trimble Gallery **celebrated** / celebrating its twenty-fifth anniversary with a large reception.　Trimble美術館舉辦了大型宴會慶祝成立二十五週年。
→ 空格置於主詞後方，為該句話的動詞位置，不宜填入動名詞或不定詞to V。

填入動詞＋語態　The electronics company **has sold** / was sold **more than one million copies** of its new game console.　這家電子公司已售出一百多萬台新遊戲機。
→ 空格後方連接受詞「more than one million copies」，表示應填入主動語態。

助動詞＋原形動詞　Residents **must separate** / separates their household trash from their recyclable items.
居民應將家庭垃圾和可回收物品分開。

祈使句　Please **confirm** / confirmed that all of the items you have ordered are in the box.
請確認您所訂購的所有商品均在箱子裡。
→ 祈使句為省略主詞，以原形動詞或「Please＋原形動詞」開頭的句子。

> **高分挑戰**　特定動詞後方填入原形動詞
>
> The landlord **demanded that** tenants **give** / gave one month's notice before moving.
> 房東要求房客在搬走前一個月通知。
> → 表示建議、要求或命令的動詞包括ask, request, require, demand, suggest, propose, recommend, advise，後方連接「that子句」當作受詞。此時that子句中為「should＋原形動詞」，通常省略should。

2　主動詞單複數一致性

主詞後方連接修飾語再連接動詞　A new company policy that grants workers more rights **was enacted** / have been enacted last week.　上週頒布了新的公司政策，賦予員工更多權利。
→ 單數主詞「A new company policy」受到「形容詞子句（that ~ rights）」的修飾，後方應填入單數動詞「was enacted」。

複數形態的單數名詞　Humax Electronics **has** / have been our most reliable supplier for the past 20 years.
過去20年來，Humax電子公司一直是我們最值得信賴的供應商。
→ 專有名詞如公司名稱以s結尾時，仍視為單數名詞。

主動詞單複數一致性＋語態　An increase in profits **has allowed** / was allowed / allow **Warren Industries** to hire more employees.　收益增加使Warren工業公司得以僱用更多員工。
→ 單數主詞「An increase」受到介系詞片語「in profits」的修飾，動詞應使用單數形態，因此不宜填入複數動詞「allow」。此外，空格後方有連接受詞「Warren Industries」，因此適合填入主動語態「has allowed」。

> **高分挑戰**　主動詞單複數一致性＋時態
>
> Since Henry's Café added a drive-through window, **the number** of visitors to the coffee shop **has increased** / increases / have been increasing.
> 自從Henry's咖啡廳開設免下車取餐窗口，咖啡廳的客人數量增加了。
> → 單數主詞「the number」受到介系詞片語「of visitors ~ shop」的修飾，動詞應使用單數形態，因此不宜填入複數動詞「have been increasing」。此外，考量到前方出現副詞子句「Since ~ window」，適合搭配現在完成式使用，因此空格應填入現在完成式「has increased」。

3　主動語態與被動語態

若空格後方有連接受詞，就填入主動語態；若沒有連接受詞，就填入被動語態。

主動語態 VS. 被動語態　Mongoose LTC **established** / was established **a new branch** in Bangkok to cover the Southeast Asian market.
Mongoose有限公司在曼谷成立了新的分公司，負責東南亞市場。

> **高分挑戰**　語態＋時態
>
> **For the past few weeks**, sales of high heels **have been outperforming** / will be outperforming / are outperformed **sneakers** at Shoe Emporium.
> 在過去幾週於鞋子大百貨中，高跟鞋銷量超越了運動鞋。
> → 空格後方有連接受詞「sneakers」，表示空格應填入主動語態。加上空格前方出現副詞片語「For the past few weeks」，適合搭配現在完成式使用，因此空格應填入現在完成式的主動語態「have been outperforming」。

4　時態

該類型考題請根據出現的副詞或表示時間的副詞片語來判斷時態。

簡單式　Diesel Motors **expected** / expects to open a new factory in Colorado **last month** but faced a labor shortage. Diesel汽車公司預計上個月在科羅拉多州開設新工廠，但面臨了人力短缺問題。
→ 句中出現副詞片語「last month」，表示時間點為過去，因此要使用過去式。

進行式　The ingredients **are being shipped** / are shipped to the restaurant **later this afternoon**.
食材將於今天下午稍晚送到餐廳。
→ 現在進行式可搭配表示不久未來的時間用法，表達即將發生的事情或未來事情的安排。

完成式　VitaMint **has made** / will make some major improvements in its new supplement formula **in recent weeks**. VitaMint公司在最近幾週對新營養補充劑的配方進行了重大改進。
→ 現在完成式常與for（一段時間）、since（自從…）、already（已經）、just（剛才）、yet（尚未）、so far（至今）、over（歷經…）、in recent weeks（在最近幾週）、in just one year（時隔一年）等搭配使用。

主要子句與從屬子句的時態　After Mr. Han **gave** / has been giving his presentation, the staff **understood** the new software more clearly. 經Han先生介紹後，員工們對新軟體有更清楚的了解。
→ 主要子句的時態為過去式（understood），且根據文意，主要子句和從屬子句的情境皆為過去所發生的事，因此從屬子句也要使用過去式。

> **高分挑戰**　表示時間與條件的副詞子句時態
>
> Mr. Grantham will announce the good news to his employees **when** they **return** / will return from winter break next week. Grantham先生將在員工下週寒假回來時，向他們宣布好消息。
> → 由表示時間與條件的從屬連接詞when, before, until, once, as soon as, if, in case引導的副詞子句，需用現在式代替未來式。（有時if所引導的子句不在此限制內）。

115

PRACTICE

答案與解析 p.59

1. Danzig Office Supplies ------- cash payments for large purchases by domestic buyers.
   (A) preference
   (B) preferable
   (C) preferring
   (D) prefers

2. Many technology companies ------- new employees in spring after they graduate from college.
   (A) hirer
   (B) hiring
   (C) hires
   (D) hire

3. Daylight Media ------- news shows on the Internet and consider doing television as well.
   (A) has broadcast
   (B) is broadcasting
   (C) will broadcast
   (D) was broadcasting

4. The bid submitted by Eagle Builders ------- the requirements listed by the city government.
   (A) fulfill
   (B) fulfilling
   (C) fulfills
   (D) to fulfill

5. The work on the project will be complete as soon as David Simpson -------.
   (A) finishes
   (B) will finish
   (C) was finishing
   (D) finished

6. It is believed that Mr. Reynolds ------- several contracts with overseas corporations.
   (A) negotiating
   (B) to negotiate
   (C) is negotiated
   (D) has negotiated

7. The store's hours of operation ------- throughout the year depending on the season.
   (A) differ
   (B) differs
   (C) difference
   (D) different

8. The software from Star Technology ------- immediately after the company purchased it.
   (A) downloaded
   (B) had downloaded
   (C) was downloaded
   (D) download

9. ------- the contract if you feel that the terms in it are agreeable to you.
   (A) Signing
   (B) Signed
   (C) Signs
   (D) Sign

10. Ms. Alderson proposed that all full-time employees ------- present for the speech by the outgoing CEO.
    (A) being
    (B) had been
    (C) were
    (D) be

PRACTICE

11. Please complete the insurance paperwork you received while the orientation stage ------- set up.

(A) is being
(B) was
(C) being
(D) has been

12. The office manager ------- more desks and chairs to accommodate the newly-hired employees.

(A) will be ordered
(B) ordering
(C) will be ordering
(D) to order

13. Applicants with strong work ethics can ------- interviewers to hire them.

(A) convince
(B) to convince
(C) be convinced
(D) convincing

14. Do not submit the request for a grant to local authorities until it ------- by Ms. Parker.

(A) is reviewing
(B) reviews
(C) is reviewed
(D) will be reviewed

15. The number of computer chips ordered by foreign manufacturers ------- by thirty percent.

(A) has been reduced
(B) have been reduced
(C) is reducing
(D) were reduced

16. Dr. Morelli, the company's head scientist, ------- a large team of medical researchers.

(A) to supervise
(B) supervises
(C) supervision
(D) supervising

17. The meeting ------- because several expected attendees could not attend due to conflicting schedules.

(A) to cancel
(B) is canceling
(C) was canceled
(D) will cancel

18. Be sure to review the user's manual because ------- the precise method for installing the appliance.

(A) to explain
(B) it explains
(C) an explanation of
(D) one explaining

19. By the end of this month, Caldwell International ------- seven employees to its Singapore branch.

(A) transfers
(B) will have transferred
(C) is transferring
(D) had transferred

20. Refunds given to customers are considered valid when ------- by the store manager.

(A) processing
(B) processed
(C) process
(D) processes

UNIT 06　不定詞與動名詞

1　不定詞

在句子中，不定詞可充當名詞、形容詞或副詞。當名詞使用時，可作為主詞、受詞或補語。在多益測驗中，不定詞作為副詞使用的情況最為常見。要記住不定詞和動名詞皆不能置於動詞位置上。

名詞	The objective for this month is **to sell** / sell 5% more than we did last month. 本月目標為比我們前月的銷售量多百分之五。
形容詞	Executives at Franklin Auto agreed that it was time **to manufacture** / manufactures electric vehicles.　Franklin汽車公司的高層一致同意目前是生產電動車的時機。
副詞	The CEO does everything she can **to support** / supporting her employees. 執行長盡其所能支持她的員工。
慣用片語	The CEO does everything she can **in order to support** her employees. 為了支持她的員工，執行長盡其所能。

2　動名詞

動名詞形態是在原形動詞後加上ing。本身具有名詞特性，因此可當作主詞、補語或受詞使用。同時又具有動詞特性，可連接受詞或接受副詞的修飾。此外，還能置於介系詞後方，當作介系詞的受詞使用。在多益測驗中，出題比重最高的是當做介系詞的受詞使用。

主詞	**Creating** / Create an impressive portfolio will help you get jobs in graphic design. 製作出令人印象深刻的作品集，將有助於你在平面設計的領域中找到工作。
補語	One of the receptionist's duties is **answering** / answer every incoming call. 接待員的職責之一是接聽所有來電。
介系詞的受詞	Ms. Kirk is in charge **of overseeing** / overseen everything that happens on the assembly line. Kirk女士負責監督生產線上發生的所有事情。

> **高分挑戰　連接動名詞當作受詞的動詞**
>
> The board of trustees will **consider expanding** / to expand the business into other ventures.
> 董事會將考慮把業務擴展至其他風險事業。
>
> → 動詞「consider」後方要連接動名詞當作受詞，而非不定詞。這類動詞包含suggest（建議）、finish（結束）、enjoy（享受）、recommend（推薦）、avoid（避免）等。

PRACTICE

答案與解析 p.61

1. Ken Richards is the top candidate ------- the new team being formed in the R&D Department.
   (A) be leading
   (B) was led
   (C) will lead
   (D) to lead

2. In July, Alps Airlines will start ------- its newest routes to cities throughout Asia.
   (A) promoting
   (B) promoted
   (C) promotes
   (D) promote

3. The company's CEO plans to permit workers ------- for promotions twice a year.
   (A) applies
   (B) to apply
   (C) applying
   (D) applied

4. Mr. Solomon stated that he considers ------- the Auckland branch a mistake due to its profitability.
   (A) close
   (B) closing
   (C) to close
   (D) has closed

5. ------- guarantee faster delivery times, the company exclusively uses local courier Mercury Delivery.
   (A) In spite of
   (B) As soon as
   (C) In order to
   (D) With regard to

6. We must arrive at the airport within the next twenty minutes if we are ------- our flight to Moscow.
   (A) to make
   (B) make
   (C) made
   (D) being made

7. Since ------- a new air conditioner in the office, management has noticed a significant improvement in productivity.
   (A) installers
   (B) installation
   (C) installment
   (D) installing

8. Mr. Edwards utilized a professional architect ------- what would become the company's new research center.
   (A) designed
   (B) is designing
   (C) designs
   (D) to design

高分挑戰
9. The marketing team's goal is to advertise more online yet ------- its expenditures.
   (A) reduce
   (B) reducing
   (C) reduces
   (D) reduced

高分挑戰
10. In the past five years, Amanda Watson has gone from sweeping the floors at the store to ------ it.
    (A) owner
    (B) owning
    (C) be owning
    (D) owned

UNIT 07　分詞

1　現在分詞與過去分詞

現在分詞是在原形動詞後方加上ing，表示主動；過去分詞則是在原形動詞後方加上ed，表示被動。分詞可像形容詞一樣，修飾其後方名詞。與不定詞和動名詞一樣，分詞不可置於動詞的位置上。

修飾後方名詞　Please contact Mr. Jones immediately and e-mail him the **corrected** / correcting **agreement**.
請立即聯繫Jones先生，並將更正後的協議書透過電子郵件發送給他。
→ (○) corrected agreement 更正後的協議書 / (✗) correcting agreement 更正協議書中

Departing / Departed **passengers** must complete a security check in order to fly.
即將離境的旅客必須完成安檢才能搭乘飛機。
→ (○) departing passenger 將要離境的旅客 / (✗) departed passenger 已離境的旅客

修飾前方名詞　There are many **factors contributing** / contributed to the decrease in interest in print newspapers.
有許多因素導致人們對紙本報紙的興趣下降。
→ (○) contributing factor 導致...的因素 / (✗) contributed factor 受...影響導致的因素
　名詞後方直接連接現在分詞，是將原本關係代名詞後方的動詞改成現在分詞的形態。因此「contributing」原來是「which contribute」。

Enjoy your stay at the Bizmark Hotel and be sure to try the delicious **cookies offered** / offering in the executive lounge.
請在Bizmark飯店享受您的住宿體驗，一定要品嚐行政休息室提供的美味餅乾。
→ (○) offered cookies 被提供的餅乾 / (✗) offering cookies （親自）提供的餅乾
　名詞後方連接過去分詞，帶有被動的意涵。名詞和過去分詞間省略「關係代名詞＋be動詞」，因此該句話中「cookies」後方省略的是「which are」。

2　分詞構句

副詞子句表示時間、條件、理由或同時發生的情況等，且其主詞與主要子句的主詞相同時，可將副詞子句簡化成分詞構句。

時間　**Arriving** / Arrive at the airport, Mr. Smith called the client to postpone the meeting.
抵達機場後，Smith先生打電話給客戶，要求延後會議。
→ Arriving = When[As soon as] Mr. Smith arrived

條件　**Stored** / Storing in a cool place, these foods will last for weeks.
若將這些食物存放在陰涼處，可保存數週。
→ Stored = If these foods are stored

結果　Our startup business's stock value was up again, **marking** / mark another company record.
我們新創企業的股價再度上漲，又創下了新紀錄。
→ marking = and marked
　現在分詞引導的子句可表示連續發生的事情或結果。

> **高分挑戰**　副詞子句為過去完成式時，可簡化成「having＋過去分詞」。
>
> **Having** / Had retired, Mr. Dornan decided to travel to Europe.
> Dornan先生決定在退休後前往歐洲旅行。
> → Having retired = After Mr. Dornan had retired

PRACTICE

1. Ms. Long examined the ------- progress report that was submitted by the team leader.
   (A) revised
   (B) revising
   (C) revises
   (D) revise

2. Using professional accountants is highly recommended for ------- businesses.
   (A) expansion
   (B) expansions
   (C) expanding
   (D) expanded

3. ------- meetings should be rescheduled to mutually convenient times.
   (A) Postponed
   (B) Postpone
   (C) Postpones
   (D) Postponing

4. Any customer ------- with a product is entitled to return it within seven days of purchase.
   (A) displeases
   (B) displeased
   (C) displease
   (D) displeasing

5. Eric Murphy remained at his home during his entire vacation, ------- rest rather than travel.
   (A) prefers
   (B) had preferred
   (C) preferring
   (D) was preferred

6. Mr. Roberts has some ------- remarks he would like to share with the audience.
   (A) preparing
   (B) prepared
   (C) preparation
   (D) prepare

7. To use the electric saw properly, you need to read the instructions ------- in the manual.
   (A) include
   (B) included
   (C) inclusion
   (D) to include

8. Any employees ------- to attend the upcoming workshop on accounting must speak with Ms. Taylor.
   (A) had hoped
   (B) hoped
   (C) would hope
   (D) hoping

9. The new kiosks are expected to significantly reduce the amount of time ------- in line.
   (A) spend
   (B) spending
   (C) to spend
   (D) spent

10. ------- this Saturday, the Hamilton Department Store will offer discounts on every item in the store.
    (A) Began
    (B) Beginning
    (C) Begins
    (D) Begin

UNIT 08　介系詞

1　常考介系詞的各種字義

for	一段時間	Alex's Diamonds will be shut down **for** two months. Alex's鑽石公司將關閉兩個月。
	為了	Mr. Liu writes a weekly column **for** a local newspaper. Liu先生為當地報紙撰寫每週專欄。
from	來自	Roughly 40% of KLP & Co.'s business comes **from** overseas clients. KLP & Co.'s公司的業務中，約有40%來自海外客戶。
	from A to B	Highway 11 will soon be widened **from** two lanes **to** four. 11號高速公路很快就會從兩條車道拓寬為四條車道。
within	（期間）之內	You can expect your package **within** 3–4 business days. 你可在3至4個工作日內收到包裹。
	（距離、範圍）之內	This apartment is **within** walking distance of many popular attractions. 這間公寓可走路抵達許多熱門景點。 → within walking distance of：步行就能抵達
by	在…之前（時間）	These are the mid-year goals that we need to reach **by** the end of the quarter. 這些是我們在本季末需達到的年中目標。
	藉由…	Ms. Vowsky contributed to the project **by** taking and organizing all of the meeting notes.　Vowsky女士記錄並整理所有會議紀錄，為該專案做出了貢獻。
of	…的	Employees **of** the factory are asked to wear a safety helmet at all times. 工廠要求員工隨時配戴安全帽。
	…之中	**Of** the four new turtleneck designs, the one with white polka dots is the most popular.　在四款新的高領設計中，白色圓點設計最受歡迎。
	as of 自…起、從…開始	As **of** Monday, January 19, the company's name will be changed to Data Xpress. 從1月19日星期一開始，公司將更名為Data Xpress。
with	與…一起	Watches from Walencia come **with** a quality guarantee that lasts for five years. 來自Walencia的手錶配有五年的品質保固。 → come with：（產品）配有、附帶…
	藉由…	**With** its new logo and marketing strategy, Sistema Inc. is headed in the direction of success.　憑藉新的商標和行銷策略，Sistema公司正朝著成功的方向邁進。
	provide/replace A with B	Plymouth Supplies can **provide** your staff **with** stylish uniforms in a wide range of colors.　普利茅斯日常用品公司可為您的員工提供多種顏色的時尚制服。 → provide A with B 向A提供B／replace A with B 把A換成B

122

2 常考介系詞片語

because of	由於…	**Because of** transportation delays, some conference participants arrived late. 由於交通延誤，導致部分與會者遲到。
due to	由於…	The database is temporarily unavailable **due to** the routine system maintenance. 由於系統的例行性維護，資料庫暫時無法使用。
owing to	由於…	**Owing to** a shortage of materials, the renovations will not be finished by the original completion date. 由於材料短缺，翻修工程無法在原定完工日前完成。
prior to	在…之前、首要	The last person to leave the office must make sure the security alarm is set **prior to** locking the door. 最後一個離開辦公室的人，在鎖門前要先確認是否有設置安全警報器。
according to	根據…	**According to** recent surveys, most guests' favorite part of the resort is the rooftop lounge. 根據最近調查，度假村大多數住客最喜歡的部分是屋頂休息室。
in addition to	除了…之外	**In addition to** coming to work early, Mr. Earl sometimes works on weekends to make sure he meets deadlines. Earl先生除了提早上班外，有時還會在週末加班，以確保趕上截止日。
instead of	而非…	On weekends during the winter months, the store closes at 5:30 P.M. **instead of** 7:00 P.M. 在冬季週末，商店於下午五點半關門，而非晚上七點。
rather than	而不是…	The hotel collects payment when the guests check in **rather than** at time of booking. 飯店在客人辦理入住手續時收取費用，而非在預訂時收取。

3 以 ing 結尾的介系詞

including	包含…	It seems like Krazy Kola can be found everywhere, **including** remote parts of the world. Krazy Kola似乎在世界各地，甚至包含偏遠地區都隨處可見。
following	隨著…、 在…以後	**Following** the release of the movie, Anne Stanton became famous. 電影上映後，Anne Stanton成名了。
concerning	關於…	She plans to inform us of issues **concerning** client confidentiality. 她打算告訴我們關於客戶保密的問題。
regarding	有關…	Mr. Diaz noted that it is important to establish safety policies **regarding** the use of company vehicles. Diaz先生指出，制定有關公司車輛使用的安全政策非常重要。

PRACTICE

1. All interns must arrive by 7:30 A.M. on Monday ------ an orientation event.
   (A) for
   (B) with
   (C) as
   (D) over

2. Any returns of products sold online by Blaine Toys must be made within two weeks ------- delivery.
   (A) before
   (B) on
   (C) of
   (D) since

3. ------- serving as the firm's accountant, Melissa Standish is employed as the office manager.
   (A) As a result
   (B) Because of
   (C) With regard to
   (D) In addition to

4. ------- each performance at the county fair, a team of volunteers cleans the entire theater.
   (A) Following
   (B) Through
   (C) Around
   (D) Within

5. ------- reporting breaking news stories accurately, Melinda Carter was able to improve her reputation as a journalist.
   (A) By
   (B) On
   (C) With
   (D) About

6. Hudson Mining has seen the value of its stock double ------- its discovery of gold three months ago.
   (A) before
   (B) since
   (C) unless
   (D) therefore

7. ------- the many people on the Hardaway Textiles salesforce, Ms. Montague is the most productive.
   (A) Into
   (B) Above
   (C) For
   (D) Of

8. ------- the advice of several experts in the industry, Mr. Harrison managed to start his own business.
   (A) For
   (B) With
   (C) Along
   (D) Over

9. ------- her desire to live in Europe, Ms. Hooper volunteered for a transfer to her firm's Milan office.
   (A) Because of
   (B) During
   (C) Consequently
   (D) As well

10. Mr. Abernathy will attend graduate school on weeknights ------- his interest in furthering his education.
    (A) for
    (B) due to
    (C) since
    (D) regarding

PRACTICE

11. ------- government regulations, hard hats must be worn on the premises by everyone at all times.
(A) According to
(B) Instead of
(C) As a result
(D) However

12. Mr. Dearborn resigned his position ------- the busy holiday season.
(A) prior to
(B) except
(C) in accordance with
(D) instead of

13. The five individuals scheduled for interviews were selected ------- a pool of seventy-eight applicants.
(A) with
(B) for
(C) out
(D) from

14. Nelson Technology has a tradition of providing workers and their families ------- tickets to local cultural events.
(A) for
(B) with
(C) at
(D) on

15. ------- the popularity of its newest sneakers, Paladin Shoes decided to increase production.
(A) Everything
(B) Perhaps
(C) Owing to
(D) In all

16. Kathy Ibsen expects to be named assistant manager in her department ------- the next few months.
(A) since
(B) within
(C) approximately
(D) at

17. All individuals should clean their workspaces and turn off their computers ------- departing the office.
(A) before
(B) until
(C) over
(D) beyond

18. Marconi Textiles manufactures women's clothing from a variety of fabrics, ------- cotton and silk.
(A) including
(B) meanwhile
(C) as soon as
(D) throughout

19. A decision ------- performance bonuses will be made by the end of the month.
(A) with
(B) among
(C) concerning
(D) for

20. ------- taking on temporary staff, Mr. Flint asked his team to work overtime in March.
(A) Apparently
(B) Rather than
(C) According to
(D) Over

UNIT 09　連接詞

1　常考從屬連接詞

與對等連接詞、相關連接詞和名詞子句連接詞相比，從屬連接詞的出題比重特別高。

時間			
	when	當…的時候	The mobile application will notify you **when** the delivery driver is at your doorstep.　當送貨人員抵達你家門口時，手機應用程式會通知你。
	while	當…的時候	The bank will be closed tomorrow **while** the vault is being repaired.　明天當保險庫進行維修時，銀行將會關閉。
	whenever	每當…	**Whenever** the printer is out of ink, please report it to the maintenance department.　當印表機墨水用完時，請向維修部門報告。
	as soon as	一…就	Intercity bus services will resume **as soon as** the snow is cleared.　一旦積雪被清除，長途客運服務將立即恢復。
	since	自從…	He has worked for himself **since** he graduated from university.　自從大學畢業以來，他就一直自己獨立工作。

理由			
	as	因為…	Please wrap these vases in additional packing material **as** they are extremely fragile.　請額外用包裝材料將這些花瓶包起來，因為它們非常脆弱。
	since	因為…	I am interested in hiring your company **since** you have been in business for a long time.　我有興趣聘請貴公司，因你們已經營了很長一段時間。
	now that	既然	**Now that** I live close to my office, I walk to work.　我住的地方離辦公室很近，所以我走路上班。

讓步、對照			
	although	儘管…	**Although** the weather was rainy, a record number of people attended the parade.　儘管是下雨天，參加遊行的人數仍創新高。
	even though	即使…	**Even though** it was only 10 A.M., Hardy Bakery had already sold out of bread for the day.　即使才上午十點，Hardy烘焙坊當天的麵包已經售罄了。
	while	然而…	**While** other companies tend to follow trends, the handbags at LACY are always in classic styles.　其他公司傾向追隨潮流，然而LACY公司的手提包卻始終堅持經典風格。

條件			
	if	如果…	Orders may be delayed **if** the item is temporarily out of stock.　若商品暫時缺貨，訂單可能會延遲。
	once	一旦…	They will make an announcement **once** the date of the event is scheduled.　一旦活動日期確定，他們就會發布公告。
	unless	除非…	Visitors should not leave the lobby **unless** they are given permission.　除非得到許可，否則訪客不得離開大廳。

目的、結果			
	so that	以便…	Ms. Denton postponed her trip to France **so that** she could attend Dr. Pollard's speech.　Denton女士推遲了她的法國之行，以便能參加Pollard博士的演講。

2 對等連接詞

對等連接詞有 and（和）、but（但是）、or（或）、so（所以）、yet（然而）等。

or	或	Tickets can be purchased **at the ticket booth or through our website**. 門票可以在售票處或透過我們的網站購買。 → 對等連接詞用來連接詞性或結構相等的單字、片語、子句。
so	所以	Mr. Juan was not able to work last week, **so** Mr. Vettel filled in for him. Juan先生上週無法上班，所以由Vettel先生代替他值班。
yet	然而	Negotiating is a critical skill, **yet** many people find it a difficult one to master. 談判是一項關鍵技能，然而許多人認為它難以掌握精通。

3 相關連接詞

either A or B	A或B	Suggestions can **either** be **sent** to the company e-mail **or placed** in the feedback box. 提案書可發送到公司電子信箱或放進回饋箱中。
neither A nor B	不是A也不是B	**Neither** Mr. Herbert **nor** his employees were aware of the safety issues at the amusement park. Herbert先生和他的員工都不知道遊樂園的安全問題。

4 名詞子句連接詞

主要考的名詞子句連接詞是置於動詞後方的受詞位置上。

whether	是否…	Ms. Chomley was not sure **whether** the CFO position would be right for her. Chomley女士不確定財務長的職位是否適合她。
that		Most retailers have reported **that** the new A5 smartphone is already sold out. 多數零售商回報新的A5智慧型手機已售罄。

5 可當介系詞使用的連接詞

before、after、since 後方可省略主詞，直接連接動名詞。

before	在…之前	**Before** leaving the office, please make sure all the lights and computers have been shut off. 在離開辦公室前，請確保所有的燈和電腦都已關閉。
since	自…以來	Investgain's new CEO has made noticeable improvements **since** taking on her current role. Investgain的新任執行長自擔任目前職位以來，已取得顯著進步。

PRACTICE

1. During inclement weather, staff members should consider ------- working from home or taking public transportation to the office.
   (A) and
   (B) either
   (C) since
   (D) if

2. Jasmine Cartier worked on her presentation skills ------- is now an accomplished public speaker.
   (A) and
   (B) for
   (C) however
   (D) or

3. ------- Mr. Hamilton spent half of July on vacation, he achieved the highest sales figures on his team.
   (A) In order that
   (B) Although
   (C) Furthermore
   (D) In spite of

4. More library books are being returned on time ------- the checkout system was computerized.
   (A) around
   (B) apparently
   (C) so
   (D) since

5. ------- Emerson Inc. releases a new product, it markets the item heavily.
   (A) Because
   (B) During
   (C) Whenever
   (D) Such

6. Remember to sign up for a membership at Aubrey's Bookstore ------- you can be eligible for special offers.
   (A) so
   (B) for
   (C) or
   (D) still

7. Famed chef Andrew Hutchins states that ------- fresh ingredients are used, dishes taste much better.
   (A) when
   (B) despite
   (C) for
   (D) how

8. The board of directors must determine ------- the business climate in Canada is ideal for opening a new facility there.
   (A) around
   (B) whether
   (C) whereas
   (D) although

9. Ms. Grayson drove to the seminar in St. Louis ------- the other members of her group chose to fly there.
   (A) in spite of
   (B) such as
   (C) as well as
   (D) even though

10. ------- a customer specifies express delivery, all orders are mailed one day after being received.
    (A) Except
    (B) Because
    (C) Unless
    (D) Even

PRACTICE

11. Kevin Watts decided to remain at Nottingham Securities ------- he received a substantial pay raise.
    (A) as a result
    (B) because
    (C) not only
    (D) or

12. First-time buyers at Jupiter Groceries can receive free delivery ------- request a sample food platter at no extra cost.
    (A) or
    (B) so
    (C) both
    (D) even

13. ------- she accepted a position at Dubois Bank, Ms. Harrison studied finance at a school in Lisbon.
    (A) How
    (B) Before
    (C) Which
    (D) Rather

14. ------- Raymond Mercer runs his own restaurant, he is responsible for acquiring ingredients daily.
    (A) As if
    (B) Moreover
    (C) That
    (D) Now that

15. ------- a location for the annual shareholders' meeting is determined, an announcement will be made.
    (A) In order that
    (B) As of
    (C) Instead
    (D) Once

16. ------- interest rates are increasing, fewer people are getting mortgages on new homes.
    (A) Except
    (B) Since
    (C) However
    (D) Why

17. By the end of the day, neither Stella Reynolds ------- Jeffery Harper had submitted their proposals for the Edmund Project.
    (A) nor
    (B) and
    (C) if
    (D) so

18. Please explain the malfunction precisely with your new device ------- our technician can tell you how to repair it.
    (A) so that
    (B) since
    (C) nor
    (D) if

19. ------- Harris Manufacturing delivered the products to its client in Memphis, full payment was not made until two weeks later.
    (A) In order to
    (B) While
    (C) Thereby
    (D) Supposedly

20. Anyone is welcome to speak during the meeting but ------- they have something positive to contribute.
    (A) when
    (B) only if
    (C) even so
    (D) rather than

UNIT 10　關係詞

1　關係代名詞

關係代名詞用來連接兩個句子，身兼連接詞和代名詞兩種角色，其中出題頻率較高的為關係代名詞的主格。

主格　　Library patrons **who** / which fail to return a book by the due date will be charged a fee.
圖書館讀者未能在到期日前歸還書籍，將被收取費用。
→ 先行詞「patrons」為人物名詞，因此填入關係代名詞時，應選擇「who」或「that」較為適當。「which」用來指動物或事物，並不適合填入。

受格　　Mr. Brown carefully examined the estimate **that** / whom Millbrook Furniture **provided**.
Brown先生仔細檢視Millbrook傢俱公司提供的估價單。
→ 先行詞「the estimate」為事物名詞，且在句中為「provided」的受詞，因此適合填入「that」。「whom」用來表示人（受格），並不適合填入。請注意關係代名詞在子句中當受格時，可選擇省略。

所有格　Ms. Hayes booked the restaurant **whose** / which menu included vegetarian dishes.
Hayes女士預訂了菜單上有素食餐點的餐廳。
→ 為Ms. Hayes booked the restaurant. The restaurant's menu included vegetarian dishes. 兩句合併。

what　　Excellent customer service is **what** / that sets us apart from our competitors.
優秀的客戶服務使我們從競爭對手中脫穎而出。
→ 關係代名詞「what」本身就包含先行詞在內，因此前方不會出現先行詞。

2　關係副詞

關係副詞有when, where, why, how等，後方要連接結構完整的子句。

Mr. Wilson runs several businesses in London, **where** / which he grew up.
Wilson先生在他長大的城市倫敦，經營幾家企業。
→ 關係副詞可換成「介系詞＋關係代名詞」，因此該句話中的「where」可換成「in which」。

3　複合關係代名詞

複合關係代名詞的形態分成「關係代名詞 + ever」和「關係副詞 + ever」。「關係代名詞 + ever」後方連接不完整的子句；「關係副詞 + ever」後方則連接結構完整的子句。

whoever 無論是誰	whichever 無論是哪個	whatever 無論是什麼
whenever 無論何時	wherever 無論何地	however 無論如何

高分挑戰

Shoppers can enjoy a strong Wi-Fi signal **wherever** / however they go in the mall.
購物者可以在購物中心內的任何地方享受訊號強大的無線網路。
→ 填入「wherever」最為適當，表示「無論在購物中心何處」。「wherever」為「where（關係副詞）＋ ever」，因此後方要連接結構完整的子句。

PRACTICE

1. Mr. Cross stated that ------- recruits the highest number of new clients this month will receive a cash bonus.
   (A) whose
   (B) when
   (C) whoever
   (D) whom

2. Nantucket Construction is owned by Peter Carroll, ------- has lived in the local area since his childhood.
   (A) so
   (B) which
   (C) who
   (D) and

3. Logistics companies ------- deliver goods on time are in high demand in most parts of the country.
   (A) whom
   (B) that
   (C) what
   (D) they

4. Jessica Yeltsin established a charitable foundation ------- she attempted to use to end the local homeless crisis.
   (A) there
   (B) what
   (C) that
   (D) how

5. Jacobson Financial clients ------- make new investments in January are eligible for a free consultation.
   (A) whose
   (B) who
   (C) what
   (D) which

6. The conference will be held at the Piedmont Hotel, ------- there are modern facilities capable of handling large crowds.
   (A) except
   (B) including
   (C) where
   (D) which

7. The government ordered an investigation into the building collapse, the cause of ------- will require some time to determine.
   (A) that
   (B) who
   (C) it
   (D) which

8. Ms. Matthews decided to hire Ryan Varnum, ------- expertise in the field of corporate law is well known.
   (A) whose
   (B) himself
   (C) which
   (D) whom

9. The orientation speaker explained ------- it takes to be a success at Hollmann International.
   (A) what
   (B) that
   (C) those
   (D) their

10. Mr. Acuna teaches a training course ------- participants learn to use the firm's computer system.
    (A) who
    (B) in which
    (C) as well as
    (D) in order to

UNIT 11　高分必備名詞詞彙

associate 同事、合夥人
sales **associate** 銷售人員

occasion 情況、場合
for any **occasion** 適用任何場合
相關詞 occasionally 偶爾

durability 耐用
have a unique design and excellent **durability**
具有獨特設計和優秀的耐用性
相關詞 durable 耐用的

delegation 代表團
a member of a **delegation** 代表團成員

defect 缺點
be inspected for possible **defects**
檢查可能存在的缺陷

estimate 估價單、估計
provide free cost **estimates** 免費提供成本估價單

approval 批准
get **approval** from the CEO 獲得執行長的批准
相關詞 approve 批准、認可

benefit 優勢、利益、有益於、獲益
benefit from 從⋯獲益（V.）
generous employee **benefit** plan
優厚的員工福利制度

issue 問題、（刊物的）期號、發行
resolve technological **issues** 解決技術問題
this month's **issue** of the magazine 本月的雜誌刊號

capacity 能力、資格
make a decision in her **capacity** as president of the company 以公司總裁的身分做出決定

agenda 議程、工作事項
meeting **agenda** 會議議程

site 地點、現場
work **sites** 工作現場
oil-drilling **site** 石油開採現場

addition 附加、增加的部分
the newest **addition** to the sales team
新加入業務團隊的成員
相關詞 additional 額外的、附加的

priority 優先權、優先事項
highest **priority** 最優先事項

venue 地點、場地
a popular **venue** for athletic competitions
體育競賽的熱門場地

recipient 獲獎者、領取者
recipient of a customer service award
客戶服務獎的獲獎者

initiative 主導權、計畫
take the **initiative** 主導、掌握主導權
相關詞 initiate 開始

range 範圍
a **range** of 多樣的
offer a broad **range** of medical services
提供廣泛的醫療服務

warranty 保固（書）
one-year **warranty** that covers major repairs
提供為期一年的保固，包含重大維修

alert 警報、警覺
serve as an **alert** 起到警報的作用

location 位置、地點
have offices in more than thirty **locations**
在30多個地點設有辦事處
相關詞 locate 找出位置

profitability 獲益性
the potential **profitability** of expanding its overseas market 拓展海外市場的潛在獲利能力
相關詞 profitable 有利的、有益的

budget 預算、低價的、低廉的
budget surplus 預算盈餘
offer **budget** flights to Mexico（adj.）
提供飛往墨西哥的廉價航空

confirmation 確認、確定
receive an e-mail **confirmation** of his hotel booking 收到飯店預約確認信
相關詞 confirm 確認、確定

revision 修改、變更
make a **revision** to the agreement 修改合約書
相關詞 revise 修改、變更

dimension 大小、規模、尺寸
the **dimensions** of a swimming pool 游泳池的大小

aspect 方面、樣子
the most challenging **aspect** of managing a hotel 飯店經營上具挑戰性的方面

audit 查帳、審計
conduct an **audit** 進行會計稽核

availability 可利用性
the limited **availability** of land 可用土地有限
相關詞 available 可利用的

notice 公告、注意到
give 24 hours' **notice** 提前24小時通知
相關詞 noticeably 明顯地、顯著地

subsidy 補助金、津貼
government **subsidy** 政府補助
相關詞 subsidize 補貼、資助

application 申請（書）、應用程式
accept **applications** for entry-level positions
接受初階職位申請書
相關詞 apply 應徵、申請

reminder 提醒、通知
send patients an e-mail **reminder**
發送通知郵件給病患
相關詞 remind 提醒

exception 例外
make an **exception** 破例
with the **exception** of 除了…之外
相關詞 exceptional 例外的、特別的、卓越的

distribution 分配、分發
fast **distribution** of goods to stores
快速配送貨物至商家
相關詞 distribute 分配

renovation 翻新、維修
undergo **renovations** 進行翻修
相關詞 renovate 翻新、修復

inventory 庫存、產品目錄
inventory management software 庫存管理軟體

presence 存在
increase their **presence** on social media
增加他們社群媒體的存在感

overview 概要、概述
overview of a camera's primary features
相機主要功能的概述

panel 專門小組、板子
a **panel** of university professors
大學教授組成的小組
install solar **panels** 安裝太陽能板

emphasis 強調、重點
place an **emphasis** on 重點放在…上
相關詞 emphasize 強調

appraisal 評價
performance **appraisal** 績效考核

PRACTICE

1. Several local companies do not permit telecommuting because they prefer their employees to have a physical ------- at the office.
   - (A) appearance
   - (B) method
   - (C) work
   - (D) presence

2. A ------- of long-term customers was responsible for rating the supermarket's newest products.
   - (A) system
   - (B) version
   - (C) survey
   - (D) panel

3. The latest ------- to the company's fleet of vehicles is an SUV made by Cobra Motors.
   - (A) addition
   - (B) device
   - (C) object
   - (D) program

4. Redecorating the employee lounge is considered a low ------- at this time.
   - (A) priority
   - (B) venture
   - (C) attempt
   - (D) consequence

5. Mr. Peterson has not needed to repair his lawnmower once since buying it thanks to its -------.
   - (A) measurement
   - (B) variety
   - (C) consideration
   - (D) durability

6. Interested customers can acquire a 3-year ------- that covers all necessary repairs.
   - (A) service
   - (B) warranty
   - (C) budget
   - (D) promise

7. Edmund Blair was named the ------- of a scholarship allowing him to study in England for one year.
   - (A) recipient
   - (B) reward
   - (C) applicant
   - (D) attendee

8. Adelaide Park is a regular ------- for events such as company get-togethers and charity fundraisers.
   - (A) venue
   - (B) port
   - (C) edition
   - (D) case

9. A notable ------- of the architect's style is her reliance on the natural environment for some features.
   - (A) design
   - (B) aspect
   - (C) relief
   - (D) tradition

10. Should there be any ------- during the hiring process, Ms. Bradley needs to be consulted at once.
    - (A) possibilities
    - (B) faults
    - (C) bargains
    - (D) issues

PRACTICE

11. A financial expert questioned the ------- of Douglas Aerospace since it has been in debt for the past several years.
    (A) recurrence
    (B) profitability
    (C) issue
    (D) acceptance

12. A government ------- will be conducted next week to confirm that no laws have been broken.
    (A) method
    (B) purpose
    (C) audit
    (D) inspector

13. One ------- of working at Devlin Inc. is that the company allows its employees to work from home.
    (A) benefit
    (B) variation
    (C) impact
    (D) reminder

14. All tours of the company are suspended due to a lack of guides until further -------.
    (A) awareness
    (B) reception
    (C) provision
    (D) notice

15. All customers will receive an e-mail ------- of their orders within five minutes of placing them.
    (A) confirmation
    (B) evaluation
    (C) contribution
    (D) reception

16. Mr. Hamilton was asked to make several ------- to the grant request he submitted to the Chamberlain Group.
    (A) revisions
    (B) decisions
    (C) specifications
    (D) productions

17. ------- levels at the store have decreased on account of the shipping problems happening nationwide.
    (A) Personnel
    (B) Inventory
    (C) Management
    (D) Replacement

18. The vice president requested a rough ------- of the time required to complete the work on the new advertising campaign.
    (A) persuasion
    (B) requirement
    (C) estimate
    (D) strategy

19. Ms. Scott contacted the airline and inquired about the ------- of seats on Friday's late-night flight to Berlin.
    (A) assurance
    (B) availability
    (C) application
    (D) appearance

20. The fundraising ------- led by Denice Burns will last two months and should raise one million dollars.
    (A) league
    (B) initiative
    (C) imperative
    (D) symbol

UNIT 12　高分必備形容詞詞彙

utmost 極度的、最大限度的
be of **utmost** importance　極其重要

eligible 有資格的
be **eligible** to receive an annual bonus
有資格領取年度獎金
相關詞 eligibility　合格、適任

substantial 相當的
earn a **substantial** amount of money
賺取大量金錢

complimentary 免費的
a **complimentary** bottle of shampoo　一瓶免費洗髮精

appropriate 適當的、恰當的
programs **appropriate** for all ages
適合所有年齡層的節目

stuck 無法動彈的、卡住的
be **stuck** in traffic　卡在車陣中動彈不得

primary 主要的、首要的
the **primary** concern of the company
公司主要關心的問題

anticipated 盼望已久的、眾望所歸的
a highly **anticipated** exhibit　非常令人期待的展覽
相關詞 anticipate　預期、期望

skeptical 懷疑的
be **skeptical** of[about]　對…持懷疑態度

upcoming 即將到來的、即將來臨的
the **upcoming** holiday sale　即將到來的假期特賣

exclusive 獨家的
have an **exclusive** interview with
與…的獨家專訪

mandatory 義務性的
complete a **mandatory** training program
完成義務訓練
相關詞 mandate　命令

tentative 暫定的
tentative schedule for next year's conference
明年暫定的會議日程

consecutive 連續的
for the third **consecutive** year　連續三年

affordable 價格合理的、低廉的
affordable price　合理的價格

likely 很可能的、可望成功的
the **likely** winner of the election　有望勝選的候選人

extensive 大範圍的、龐大的
extensive knowledge of Asian history
對亞洲歷史有廣泛了解

competitive 有競爭力的
provide a **competitive** salary in the industry
提供於業界有競爭力的薪資
相關詞 competition　競爭

prestigious 有聲望的、一流的
receive a **prestigious** award　獲頒享有盛譽的獎項

rapid 快速的、迅速的
make a **rapid** change　迅速改變

preliminary 初步的
the **preliminary** results of consumer survey
消費者問卷初步調查結果

prompt 即時的
receive a **prompt** reply　立即獲得答覆

reassuring 讓人安心的、消除擔憂的
see some **reassuring** developments
看到令人安心的進展

nutritious 有營養的
nutritious vegetables　營養價值高的蔬菜
相關詞 nutrition　營養成分

overdue 逾期的、延遲的
settle an **overdue** account　結清逾期帳款

superior 優秀的、出色的
superior organizational skills　優秀的組織能力

qualifying 有資格的
pass a **qualifying** exam　通過資格考試
相關詞 qualify　具備資格、勝任

former 以前的、前任的
former vice president　前任副總

strategic 策略性的
strategic move to attract more customers
吸引更多顧客的策略性行為
相關詞 strategy　策略

incremental 遞增的
incremental improvements rather than radical changes　漸進式改善而非激進式變革

intense 強烈的、極度的
under **intense** pressure　處於極大壓力之下

frequent 頻繁的、屢次的、時常出入
frequent visitors　常客
相關詞 frequency　頻率

routine 定期的、日常的、例行公事
undergo **routine** maintenance　進行定期維護

ingenious 獨創的、機智的、巧妙的
ingenious design　獨創設計

discontinued 停產的
discontinued printer model　停產的印表機型號
相關詞 discontinue　停產

supplemental 補充的、附加的
supplemental information　補充資訊

functional 功能上的
be fully **functional**　完全正常運轉

immense 無限的、廣大的
immense lobby with a café in the center
寬廣的大廳中央有間咖啡廳

verifiable 可證實的
verifiable facts　可證明的事實

disposable 用完即丟的
disposable umbrella covers　一次性雨傘套
相關詞 dispose　丟棄、扔掉

dependent 依賴的、依靠的
be highly **dependent** on seasonal sales
高度依賴季節性銷售

overwhelming 壓倒性的、勢不可擋的
overwhelming victory　壓倒性勝利
相關詞 overwhelm　壓倒、使不知所措

PRACTICE

1. Jessica Roth, a reporter with the *Hampton Times*, had an ------- interview with Emerson Howell, the state governor.
   (A) intermittent
   (B) alternate
   (C) exclusive
   (D) imperative

2. The training program for the new marketing software is not -------, but employees are advised to take it.
   (A) mandatory
   (B) exposed
   (C) practiced
   (D) replaced

3. All customer complaints should be handled in a ------- manner by store representatives.
   (A) relative
   (B) close
   (C) prompt
   (D) various

4. Interns at Milton Technology are assigned ------- tasks to go along with the mentoring they receive.
   (A) opposing
   (B) routine
   (C) proficient
   (D) accessible

5. The CEO was satisfied with the ------- results from the customer survey conducted at the end of the year.
   (A) practical
   (B) remote
   (C) reassuring
   (D) exterior

6. One of the most highly ------- movies of the summer is the thriller directed by Martin Lincoln.
   (A) anticipated
   (B) proposed
   (C) revolutionary
   (D) revised

7. Thanks to his ------- list of contacts, Mr. Rumsfeld was able to secure several new clients for his firm.
   (A) abundant
   (B) extensive
   (C) refuted
   (D) qualified

8. Ms. Cartwright requested a ------- increase in her salary as a reward for her recent performance.
   (A) confident
   (B) costly
   (C) substantial
   (D) beneficial

9. The ------- duties of the office manager will be to supervise employees while resolving any issues between them.
   (A) eligible
   (B) comparative
   (C) primary
   (D) flexible

10. Mr. Dunlop's mechanic informed him that his truck was ------- for an oil change.
    (A) concerned
    (B) overdue
    (C) reported
    (D) clear

PRACTICE

11. Several parts of the city still have ------- housing despite being close to the financial district.
(A) possible
(B) timely
(C) coordinated
(D) affordable

12. To become an engineer, a person must pass the ------- exam that is held twice a year.
(A) qualifying
(B) repeated
(C) accomplished
(D) diverse

13. Employees at Verducci Consulting receive ------- raises depending upon their annual performance.
(A) severe
(B) advanced
(C) incremental
(D) decisive

14. Jackson Auction House requests that potential buyers make ------- offers on items they are bidding on.
(A) competitive
(B) relaxed
(C) advanced
(D) everyday

15. Those who are ------- for paid time off must receive written permission from a supervisor.
(A) revealed
(B) permitted
(C) eligible
(D) assorted

16. The programmer encountered ------- problems when trying to download the software to her computer.
(A) frequent
(B) generous
(C) alternative
(D) essential

17. Most evaluators mention the ------- performance of the new sedan manufactured by Meridian Motors.
(A) absolute
(B) integrated
(C) superior
(D) discreet

18. Several roads downtown have been closed in preparation for the ------- parade through the city.
(A) reported
(B) upcoming
(C) temporary
(D) identified

高分挑戰
19. The appliance remains ------- despite heavy usage over the years.
(A) specific
(B) functional
(C) obvious
(D) enterprising

高分挑戰
20. The new line of cosmetics by Bakersfield was ------- on account of several users suffering allergic reactions.
(A) promoted
(B) exported
(C) convinced
(D) discontinued

UNIT 13　高分必備副詞詞彙

adequately 充分地、適當地
adequately test the product　充分測試產品

remotely 遠距地、遙遠地
work **remotely**　遠距工作

frequently 經常、頻繁地
one of the most **frequently** visited places
人們最常造訪的地方之一

thoroughly 完全地、徹底地
be examined **thoroughly**　徹底檢查

shortly 馬上、不久
shortly after the meeting　會議後不久

closely 密切地、仔細地
work **closely** with marketing on the project
專案執行上，與行銷部門密切合作

seldom 很少、難得
be **seldom** late to a meeting　開會很少遲到

dramatically 極度地、戲劇性地
dramatically affect traffic in the area
嚴重影響該區交通

highly 極其、非常
a **highly** respected research organization
備受尊敬的研究組織

electronically 電子化地、採線上方式
be distributed **electronically**　線上分發

unexpectedly 意外地、未預料地
draw an **unexpectedly** large audience
意外吸引大批觀眾

directly 直接地、馬上
respond **directly** to an e-mail　馬上回覆郵件

freshly 最近、新近
the **freshly** repainted wall　最近重新粉刷的牆

mostly 主要、大多數地
customers who are **mostly** interested in science fiction novels　主要對科幻小說感興趣的顧客

definitely 明確地、確實地
definitely agree　完全同意

strictly 嚴格地
be **strictly** prohibited by law
受法律嚴格禁止

gradually 漸漸地
gradually expand vegetarian menu options
逐步增加素食菜單選項

unanimously 全體一致地
vote **unanimously**　投票一致通過

initially 最初
cost more than **initially** estimated
費用比最初預想還高

temporarily 臨時地、暫時地
be **temporarily** closed　暫時關閉

entirely 完全地
be **entirely** the fault of 完全是…的錯

currently 現在、當前
be **currently** seeking a full-time employee
當前正在尋找正式員工

beforehand 提前、事先
be notified two days **beforehand**
提前兩天接到通知

previously 事先、以前
artists who have not **previously** made a film
以前從未製作過電影的藝術家

instead 作為替代
move the meeting to 1 P.M. **instead**
會議時間改到下午一點

rapidly 快速地、迅速地
rapidly growing demand for IT specialists
對資訊科技專家的需求迅速成長

extremely 極其、非常
be **extremely** pleased 非常高興

considerably 相當、頗
vary **considerably** 截然不同

promptly 準時地、立即地
arrive **promptly** at 7:00 P.M. 晚上七點準時抵達

far 久遠地、極
reserve train tickets **far** in advance
很早之前預訂火車票

momentarily 臨時地、短暫地
She was **momentarily** surprised when her boss offered her a promotion.
當老闆提議升遷她時，她感到一陣驚訝。

randomly 隨機地
be **randomly** chosen 隨機選取

eventually 最後、終於
be **eventually** finished on schedule
終於如期結束

elsewhere 在別的地方
items that are not available **elsewhere**
其他地方買不到的東西

accordingly 相應地、照著、因此、於是
The proposals must be submitted in writing and will be responded to **accordingly**.
提案書須以書面形式繳交，並比照同等方式答覆。

alike 一樣地、相似地
children and adults **alike** 孩子和大人一樣地…

indeed 確實、真正地
be **indeed** an error in the calculation
確實為計算上的失誤

overly 過度地、極度地
be **overly** complicated 過於複雜

eagerly 渴望地、熱切地
eagerly await the results of 熱切地等待…的結果

properly 適當地、正常地
work **properly** 正常運作

significantly 相當地、顯著地
significantly increase the productivity of the staff 顯著提高員工的生產力

apparently 顯然地
Apparently, heavy rains are expected this weekend. 看來這週末會下大雨。

PRACTICE

1. Mary Hartford plans to skip the opening day of the conference and will ------- appear on the second day.
   (A) instead
   (B) variously
   (C) literally
   (D) similarly

2. Employees should submit all documents requesting the reimbursement of expenditures -------.
   (A) fortunately
   (B) gracefully
   (C) electronically
   (D) revealingly

3. Mr. Burns was ------- offered a low salary, but the company increased the amount when he rejected it.
   (A) pleasantly
   (B) entirely
   (C) initially
   (D) particularly

4. Denton Office Supplies makes sure to package and deliver all online orders -------.
   (A) seriously
   (B) promptly
   (C) hardly
   (D) really

5. The board of directors voted ------- to offer Reid Harmon the position of CEO at Watergate Industries.
   (A) enormously
   (B) possibly
   (C) unanimously
   (D) regularly

6. Please read the instructions ------- prior to attempting to install the appliance in your kitchen.
   (A) happily
   (B) almost
   (C) justly
   (D) thoroughly

7. Perkins Electronics ------- closed its factory in Mexico by order of its new president.
   (A) convincingly
   (B) accidentally
   (C) unexpectedly
   (D) preferably

8. Only those individuals ------- subscribed to the *Daily Times* are eligible for the special discount offer.
   (A) precisely
   (B) currently
   (C) merely
   (D) coincidentally

9. Ms. Galbraith ------- improved office efficiency by implementing a new filing system.
   (A) ever
   (B) significantly
   (C) shortly
   (D) exactly

10. Mr. Edwards ------- flies late at night, but he needed to arrive in Tokyo by this morning.
    (A) seldom
    (B) then
    (C) however
    (D) who

PRACTICE

11. Regular library patrons and visitors ------- are invited to see Janet Evans read from her latest novel this Friday evening.
    (A) meanwhile
    (B) alike
    (C) quite
    (D) truly

12. While he had lunch at a café with a client yesterday, Mr. Orbison ------- eats at the company cafeteria.
    (A) mostly
    (B) only
    (C) powerfully
    (D) swiftly

13. The restaurant run by chef Otto von Steuben offers dishes not available -------.
    (A) elsewhere
    (B) beyond
    (C) around
    (D) approximately

14. Since it has secured outside funding, Nano Technologies is ------- hiring more employees for its new facility.
    (A) overly
    (B) rarely
    (C) rapidly
    (D) uniquely

15. No time off will be granted in December, so make your vacation plans -------.
    (A) properly
    (B) cleanly
    (C) definitely
    (D) accordingly

16. Despite always working in Newport, Ken Dayton was concerned that he would ------- be transferred abroad.
    (A) frequently
    (B) eventually
    (C) nearly
    (D) obviously

17. The package left our warehouse two days ago and will be delivered to your office -------.
    (A) lately
    (B) fairly
    (C) shortly
    (D) formerly

18. The community parking lot was closed ------- while the surface was repaved.
    (A) finally
    (B) temporarily
    (C) cautiously
    (D) narrowly

19. After checking the budget, Ms. Jenkins determined that there is ------- enough money left for an employee gathering.
    (A) neither
    (B) else
    (C) more
    (D) indeed

20. To ensure that the application process goes smoothly, prepare all of your documents -------.
    (A) freely
    (B) beforehand
    (C) anywhere
    (D) likewise

UNIT 14　高分必備動詞詞彙

comply with 遵守⋯
comply with quality standards　遵守品質標準
相關詞 compliance　遵守、順從

equip 配備有
be **equipped** with a refrigerator
配有冰箱
相關詞 equipment　配備、設備

lack 缺乏、缺少
lack the communication skills
缺乏溝通技巧

handle 對待、處理
handle client information　處理客戶資訊

address 對付、處理、寫上姓名地址、演說
address employee concerns　處理員工的擔憂

obtain 得到、獲得
obtain a free quote　獲得免費報價

outline 概述、略述
outline the strengths and weaknesses of
略述⋯的優缺點

specify 具體指定、明確說明
specify the time of day　指定一天中的時間
相關詞 specification　規格、明細

extract 擷取、提煉
extract insights from a research report
從研究報告中擷取見解

direct 指向、直接的
direct questions to the department manager
直接向部門經理提問

waive 放棄、不適用
waive the registration fee　免註冊費

secure 獲得、確保、安全的
secure funding from foreign investors
獲得外國投資者的資金
相關詞 security　安全

grant 批准、給予
grant employees more paid leave
給予員工更多特休

admit 准許進入、承認
be **admitted** to a building　准許進入大樓內

facilitate 促進、幫助
facilitate team-building workshops
促進團隊合作的研討會

ensure 確保、保證
ensure exceptional quality　保證卓越品質

assign 分配、分派
be **assigned** a task　分配到任務
相關詞 assignment　課題、任務

encourage 鼓勵、激勵
encourage clients to report errors
鼓勵顧客回報錯誤

undergo 接受（治療）、經歷
undergo corporate restructuring
經歷企業重組

double 加倍、兩倍
double the size of the staff
當前員工人數的兩倍

bring up 提出、談到（話題）
bring up a subject at a meeting
在會議上提出議題

implement 實施
implement an extensive recycling program
實施廣泛的回收計畫

demonstrate 示範操作、說明、證明
demonstrate how to operate a camera
示範如何操作相機
[相關詞] demonstration 示範、演示

establish 建立、制定
establish guidelines regarding the handling of confidential information
制定有關處理機密資訊的原則
[相關詞] establishment 設立、確立、機構

manage 管理、經營
manage social media content 經營社群媒體內容
[相關詞] management 經營、管理部門

evolve 發展
evolve from a local supplier to a national distributor 從地區供應商發展成全國經銷商

limit 限制、限定
limit passengers to one carry-on bag
限制旅客只能攜帶一件隨身行李

post 發布、張貼
be **posted** online 線上發布

enforce 實施、執行
enforce a new regulation 實施新規定

analyze 分析
analyze project details carefully
仔細分析專案細節
[相關詞] analysis 分析

feature 以⋯為特色
feature live jazz music 主打現場爵士樂

authenticate 證明⋯為真實的
authenticate the message 證明訊息的真實性

expand 拓展、擴充
expand the international foods section
擴充海外食品專區
[相關詞] expansion 擴展

clarify 闡明
clarify the new policy on vacation days
闡明關於休假的新政策
[相關詞] clarification 澄清、說明

perform 執行、實施、表演、演奏
perform well in his job interview
在工作面試中表現優異
[相關詞] performance 業績、成果、演出

lease 出租、租借、租賃
lease a rental car 租車

coincide with 與⋯同時發生、與⋯一致
coincide with a conference 與會議時間重疊

redeem 兌換（商品或現金）
redeem a coupon 兌換優惠券

explore 探索
explore the region for investment opportunities
探索該地區的投資機會

submit 提交、繳交
submit expense reports 提交支出報告
[相關詞] submission 提交（物）

PART 5

145

PRACTICE

1. Mr. Washington ------- a strict policy of not allowing workers to arrive at meetings late.
   (A) disturbs
   (B) minimizes
   (C) enforces
   (D) reveals

2. To ------- that all individuals are treated fairly, rules must apply equally to everyone.
   (A) bargain
   (B) appoint
   (C) integrate
   (D) ensure

3. The date of the seminar will be changed so that it does not ------- with the company picnic.
   (A) collaborate
   (B) coincide
   (C) report
   (D) assign

4. Greg's Shopping Club ------- the shipping fee for all purchases of $100 or more.
   (A) clears
   (B) waives
   (C) explores
   (D) automates

5. Be sure to ------- the size and the color of each article of clothing you order.
   (A) balance
   (B) multiply
   (C) specify
   (D) reconcile

6. Discount coupons must be ------- prior to the expiration date listed on the back.
   (A) portrayed
   (B) determined
   (C) advanced
   (D) redeemed

7. Please ------- your username on the company's internet system no later than Friday afternoon.
   (A) transform
   (B) authenticate
   (C) develop
   (D) import

8. Individuals applying for the position must ------- a complete physical checkup.
   (A) approve
   (B) examine
   (C) undergo
   (D) attempt

9. Despite being highly educated, Mr. Bevers ------- the necessary leadership skills to take on an executive position.
   (A) replaces
   (B) reveals
   (C) portrays
   (D) lacks

10. Ms. Jansen ------- to contact her assistant despite having left her phone at her home.
    (A) failed
    (B) considered
    (C) managed
    (D) projected

PRACTICE

11. The facility ------- state-of-the-art workout equipment that is also easy to use.
    (A) features
    (B) removes
    (C) reports
    (D) disrupts

12. Participants in the museum tour can ------- their questions to the guide at any time.
    (A) oppose
    (B) direct
    (C) allow
    (D) prioritize

13. Brian Harper ------- the documents necessary for him to receive his accounting license.
    (A) submitted
    (B) invited
    (C) proposed
    (D) inquired

14. The user's manuals ------- the necessary steps people must take to utilize the equipment.
    (A) consider
    (B) submit
    (C) outline
    (D) attempt

15. Staff members traveling abroad can ------- company credit cards by speaking with a supervisor.
    (A) promote
    (B) obtain
    (C) apply
    (D) remain

16. Everyone who visits the factory should ------- with any instructions provided by employees there.
    (A) comply
    (B) conclude
    (C) appear
    (D) practice

17. The airline stated that it would ------- its regulations regarding carry-on baggage.
    (A) clarify
    (B) hinder
    (C) expose
    (D) participate

18. The new CEO, Deborah Burgess, promised to ------- concerns about possible layoffs at the Toronto facility.
    (A) offer
    (B) restructure
    (C) advertise
    (D) address

高分挑戰
19. The customer was ------- compensation for his loss when the shipment was damaged during delivery.
    (A) enhanced
    (B) granted
    (C) regarded
    (D) detected

高分挑戰
20. Fairmont Cab ------- a new policy requiring its drivers to have comprehensive insurance covering themselves and their passengers.
    (A) implemented
    (B) associated
    (C) instructed
    (D) transported

PRACTICE 高難度

答案與解析 p.72

1. To ensure the final draft of the magazine is printed on time, reporters should make all ------- to their texts prior to June 8.
   (A) revisions
   (B) essays
   (C) recommendations
   (D) proposals

2. Agriculture experts recommend providing the ------- environment possible for plants so that they have a good chance of thriving.
   (A) most stable
   (B) more stably
   (C) stabilizing
   (D) stability

3. Mr. Kamal will examine the incoming résumés to determine ------- reflect the necessary qualifications for the management position.
   (A) now that
   (B) even though
   (C) some such
   (D) which ones

4. Following the investigation, it was determined that the delay at the warehouse was caused by a few ------- boxes.
   (A) mislabeled
   (B) mislabeling
   (C) mislabel
   (D) mislabels

5. Nelson Recruitment insists that job applicants ------- with the recruiter to create clear employment goals.
   (A) cooperating
   (B) cooperate
   (C) cooperation
   (D) cooperated

6. Ms. Maddock's ------- for the event venue include ample parking and a state-of-the-art sound system.
   (A) preferably
   (B) preferences
   (C) preferable
   (D) preference

7. Sales of Newton Footwear increased online and in stores ------- after the launch of an ad campaign featuring professional athletes.
   (A) promptly
   (B) prompt
   (C) prompted
   (D) promptness

8. Any losses ------- the failure to correctly analyze the level of risk may be the responsibility of the investment firm.
   (A) whereabouts
   (B) apart
   (C) resulting from
   (D) in compliance with

9. ------- with a complaint regarding the effectiveness of the laundry detergent will be promptly directed to a customer service agent.
   (A) One another
   (B) Whoever
   (C) Anyone
   (D) Theirs

10. Mr. Conway was able to begin the keynote address on time ------- there were technical difficulties with the sound equipment earlier in the day.
    (A) even though
    (B) not only
    (C) owing to
    (D) while

PRACTICE

11. The controversial nature of the infrastructure project on municipal land provoked a ------- discussion at yesterday's public forum.
(A) resistant
(B) lively
(C) perishable
(D) current

12. ------- the training objectives of the session have already been met, we should use the remaining time for more casual team-building activities.
(A) Since
(B) Until
(C) Whenever
(D) Unless

13. The lifetime warranty on all washing machines from Larkin Appliances is not surprising, given that the company's products are known for -------.
(A) modification
(B) durability
(C) proximity
(D) accomplishment

14. How ------- the bus fares will increase depends on the average number of passengers and the expected fuel expenditures.
(A) substantiality
(B) substantially
(C) substance
(D) more substantial

15. All budget decisions must be approved by Tony Calderon, the ------- of the annual music festival, in advance.
(A) organizing
(B) organization
(C) organizer
(D) organize

16. Multiple rejections of the building permit forced the construction company ------- its development of the vacant lot into a luxury apartment building.
(A) abandoned
(B) abandonment
(C) to abandon
(D) abandons

17. ------- the severe weather predicted for this Saturday, the event planners for the International Food Festival have postponed the event.
(A) By means of
(B) Ever since
(C) In light of
(D) Considering that

18. Elkview Engineering has established ------- an excellent reputation that it no longer needs to allocate funds for marketing and advertising.
(A) even
(B) such
(C) yet
(D) more

19. Everyone on the product development team agrees that ------- is the most impressive prototype submitted to the national design competition.
(A) us
(B) ours
(C) we
(D) ourselves

20. ------- the international transfer request is submitted by 3 P.M., Henley Bank will finalize the transaction on the same day.
(A) Until
(B) Provided
(C) As soon as
(D) Just as

PRACTICE

21. The attractive interest rate offered by Lapointe Bank ------- customers to open new accounts and move surplus funds into them.

    (A) motivate
    (B) has motivated
    (C) is being motivated
    (D) have been motivating

22. VT Logistics plans to terminate the contract with Camden Couriers because the firm has been ------- unable to meet delivery deadlines.

    (A) intensely
    (B) steadily
    (C) consistently
    (D) tentatively

23. The department head anticipates ------- more on travel expenses next year to improve the relationships with clients through face-to-face meetings.

    (A) to spend
    (B) spend
    (C) has spent
    (D) spending

24. The majority of first-class travelers are willing to pay extra for a direct flight ------- spend additional time dealing with a layover.

    (A) in fact
    (B) as a result of
    (C) in case of
    (D) rather than

25. Murillo Incorporated's overseas expansion plan involves hiring an accounting firm ------- employees have experience with overseas tax regulations.

    (A) what
    (B) how
    (C) which
    (D) whose

26. The purchase of more equipment to enable automation has ------- the size of the workforce needed at the manufacturing facility.

    (A) gathered
    (B) regarded
    (C) monitored
    (D) decreased

27. The new policy on unpaid medical leave will go into effect immediately ------- the details are posted on the company website.

    (A) until
    (B) after
    (C) any
    (D) that

28. A review of the user information revealed that approximately forty-five percent of employees ------- the database that was announced in the e-mail.

    (A) calculated
    (B) introduced
    (C) accessed
    (D) inquired

29. Supervisors should take the time to listen to concerns from members of their team, ------- busy they may be.

    (A) rather than
    (B) indeed
    (C) however
    (D) as well

30. ------- Mr. Zhang not failed to meet reaching his sales quota for the quarter, he might have been considered for the promotion.

    (A) Having
    (B) Has
    (C) Had
    (D) Have

PART TEST

1. Mr. Cross assisted in the kitchen since ------- of his chefs arrived at the restaurant on time.
   (A) nothing
   (B) nobody
   (C) neither
   (D) anyone

2. According to financial experts, manufacturing companies should expect to make record ------- this year.
   (A) profitable
   (B) profitability
   (C) profiting
   (D) profits

3. It is expected that the automated system will make the factory workers ------- in their jobs.
   (A) product
   (B) production
   (C) productive
   (D) producer

4. The R&D team at Dayton Tech ------- a second chance to find a solution to the manufacturing problem.
   (A) gave
   (B) will give
   (C) is giving
   (D) has been given

5. The customer was fairly ------- for her loss when several items were broken during delivery.
   (A) approved
   (B) appreciated
   (C) compensated
   (D) rewarded

6. ------- members of the team felt that their ideas should be implemented at once.
   (A) Every
   (B) One
   (C) Both
   (D) Neither

7. The background noise continued ------- the speech, making it difficult for some audience members to hear anything.
   (A) throughout
   (B) around
   (C) at
   (D) since

8. Mr. Greg believes March is an appropriate time ------- the new line of products coming out in spring.
   (A) advertising
   (B) advertisement
   (C) to advertise
   (D) will advertise

9. At first glance, the design of the building seems ------- and makes good use of available space.
   (A) efficient
   (B) efficiency
   (C) efficiently
   (D) efficiencies

10. Harrison Shipbuilding saw orders increase last quarter, ------- its rival, Baden Inc., reported a record loss.
    (A) thanks to
    (B) despite
    (C) consequently
    (D) whereas

151

11. The process of ------- at Stanton Bank requires proof of residency and two forms of picture identification.
    (A) verification
    (B) withdrawal
    (C) imposition
    (D) adjustment

12. Most analysts considered Edward Hope's greatest accomplishment to be ------- his company out of bankruptcy.
    (A) get
    (B) getting
    (C) had gotten
    (D) did get

13. The Spruce Corporation agreed to work in ------- with Magpie Inc. to develop low-cost housing in Richmond.
    (A) reflection
    (B) deduction
    (C) conjunction
    (D) accumulation

14. All employees are asked to be ------- at the seminar in order to learn as much as possible.
    (A) optional
    (B) impulsive
    (C) attentive
    (D) collaborative

15. Dr. Hatfield instructed ------- who had been working nonstop since the morning to take a break.
    (A) those
    (B) one
    (C) themselves
    (D) each

16. While the seminar was considered -------, nearly everyone in the Accounting Department registered for it.
    (A) optional
    (B) concluded
    (C) progressive
    (D) responsible

17. Ms. Jacobs, one of Failsafe's top managers, ------- a class on leadership at the local university.
    (A) teach
    (B) teaches
    (C) teacher
    (D) is taught

18. The machinery must be operated ------- to prevent it from suffering a malfunction.
    (A) fairly
    (B) properly
    (C) surely
    (D) creatively

19. Ms. Oxford closely ------- random items in an effort to find flaws in the manufacturing process.
    (A) concentrates
    (B) purchases
    (C) examines
    (D) develops

20. The images captured by the magazine's new photographer are quite visually -------.
    (A) to appeal
    (B) appealed
    (C) appeals
    (D) appealing

21. Please ------- to put on your safety gear properly to avoid potential injuries.
    (A) remember
    (B) to remember
    (C) will remember
    (D) remembering

22. Mr. Hollander is the person responsible ------- confirming that proper procedures are being followed.
    (A) to
    (B) with
    (C) for
    (D) on

23. The bridge was only ------- complete when construction was halted due to the discovery of a design flaw.
    (A) partial
    (B) partially
    (C) partiality
    (D) partialness

24. Megan Reyna's major -------- to the charity was recruiting several wealthy donors.
    (A) bonus
    (B) support
    (C) contribution
    (D) variation

25. An item is considered ------- by Grossman Shipping when it is signed for by the recipient.
    (A) delivery
    (B) delivered
    (C) to deliver
    (D) was delivered

26. Jeremy Tyler's next project will be a ------- with two members of the Marketing Department.
    (A) collaborate
    (B) collaborator
    (C) collaborating
    (D) collaboration

27. All full-time employees at Focal Inc. ------- its major clients are invited to the celebration being held on December 29.
    (A) as well as
    (B) meanwhile
    (C) so that
    (D) in order to

28. We were instructed to do ------- was necessary to ensure that the festival was held successfully.
    (A) whatever
    (B) which
    (C) that
    (D) who

29. The Sales Department plans on ------- at least six members of the staff to focus on sales in North America.
    (A) commit
    (B) committed
    (C) to commit
    (D) committing

30. Mr. Davis strongly believes that ------- should be offered an executive position at Leeway's.
    (A) he
    (B) his
    (C) him
    (D) himself

PART 6

段落填空

UNIT 01 文法

UNIT 02 詞性

UNIT 03 詞彙

UNIT 04 連接副詞

UNIT 05 句子插入題

PART TEST

PART 6 段落填空

考題類型與命題方向

PART 6的考題類型介於PART 5和PART 7之間。該大題包含四篇文章，每篇文章有四道填空題。其中三道題考文法（時態、語態、代名詞等）、詞性、詞彙、連接副詞等，剩下一道題為句子插入題，要求選出符合文意的句子。

Questions 131-134 refer to the following e-mail.

答案與解析 p.77

To: All Blacktail Logistics Employees <stafflist@blacktaillogistics.com>

From: Alfred Orozco <a.orozco@blacktaillogistics.com>

Date: November 12

Subject: Performance reviews

Dear Blacktail Logistics Staff:

Throughout next week, the managers will be conducting performance evaluations of all staff members. We carry out this task ------- **131.** to ensure that you understand your role. -------, **132.** we want to make sure you are well supported in operating at your peak level. You will meet with your immediate supervisor to discuss your strengths as well as areas that need -------. **133.** Following the evaluation, you will have the opportunity to complete a comment card. This can be submitted directly to the HR department, and all comments will remain anonymous. -------. **134.** Your supervisor will inform you of the time your evaluation is scheduled.

Thank you for your cooperation,

Alfred Orozco

Office Manager, Blacktail Logistics

131. (A) occasionally
(B) occasional
(C) occasion
(D) occasions

132. (A) In contrast
(B) As a result
(C) However
(D) In addition

133. (A) proficiency
(B) improvement
(C) configuration
(D) permission

134. (A) So, please share your honest opinions.
(B) We believe you will excel in your new role.
(C) Fortunately, leadership skills can be developed over time.
(D) Policy updates are always posted online promptly.

解題策略

雖然作答PART 6需閱讀整篇文章，但其中有許多題目與PART 5類似，只需查看空格所在的句子，就能選出答案。舉例來說，若題目涉及詞性，只需確認空格所在句子的句型結構、空格前後方單字的詞性和作用，就能找出答案。但若題目涉及時態或詞彙，且有兩個或兩個以上的選項納入考量範圍時，就不得不閱讀前後方的句子，以確認前後文意。特別是涉及連接句子的連接副詞，或句子插入題時，就必須透過上下文的脈絡來解題。因此，若想答對PART 6的所有考題並取得高分，建議每篇文章都要從頭開始閱讀，並依序作答題目。

131. (A) occasionally
(B) occasional
(C) occasion
(D) occasions

詞性
詞性題由同一單字衍生出各種詞性的選項組合而成。只要確認空格在其所處的片語或子句中，適合填入什麼詞性，即能輕鬆選出答案。

132. (A) In contrast
(B) As a result
(C) However
(D) In addition

連接副詞
在連接副詞題中，空格通常置於句首。根據空格所在的句子與前一句之間的關係（如因果、轉折、舉例等），便能判斷出答案。

133. (A) proficiency
(B) improvement
(C) configuration
(D) permission

詞彙
詞彙題的選項由各種不同意思的單字組合而成。若僅從空格所在句子無法選出答案，就必須根據前後句的文意來做判斷。

134. (A) So, please share your honest opinions.
(B) We believe you will excel in your new role.
(C) Fortunately, leadership skills can be developed over time.
(D) Policy updates are always posted online promptly.

句子插入題
除了空格出現在段落開頭的情況外，通常可透過空格前方的句子來判斷適合連接的句子。因此，在作答句子插入題時，請優先確認空格前方的句子，而非空格後方的句子。

UNIT 01　文法

解析 p.77

1. e-mail（電子郵件）

> Dear Ms. Lampron,
>
> Thank you for becoming a member of the Victoria City Bookstore. ------- membership helps support small businesses and ensures that physical books remain in print. Though our storefront is modest, we offer a wide array of titles and express shipping for most books not currently on our shelves.

(A) Her　　　　(B) His　　　　(C) Your　　　　(D) Their

→ 郵件收件者為Lampron女士，郵件開頭感謝她成為Victoria城市書店的會員。而空格所在的句子說明「對方」成為會員後，為書店帶來的幫助，因此空格應填入人稱代名詞的所有格 (C) Your。

2. memo（備忘錄）

> Hogan Insurance's annual banquet will take place on Friday, December 17, at 7 P.M. All Hogan Insurance employees and their families are invited, so please RSVP to the administrative office. The top-performing employees at the company ------- at the end of the dinner. We hope to see you all there!

(A) will be recognized　　　　(B) have been recognized
(C) were recognized　　　　　(D) will recognize

→ 空格後方未連接受詞，而是直接連接介系詞片語，因此空格應填入被動語態。(A)、(B)、(C)皆為被動語態，而文章第一句話提到年度晚宴將於12月17日舉行，表示時間點為未來，因此答案要選未來式 (A) will be recognized。

3. notice（通知）

> Notice to Staff Members
>
> Please do not turn off your computers before leaving work on Friday, as the IT team is scheduled to update the software. We ------- a software update every month in order to ensure the security of our system. Should you have any questions, please direct them to Sean Hendrix, the IT manager, at extension 18.

(A) were carrying out　　(B) will be carried out　　(C) are carried out　　(D) carry out

→ 空格後方連接受詞「a software update」，因此空格應填入主動語態。(A)和(D)皆為主動語態，而後方出現副詞片語「every month」，因此答案要選現在式 (D) carry out。現在式可用來表示反覆發生及例行性的行為。

PRACTICE

答案與解析 p.78

Questions 1-4 refer to the following article.

NAPLES, Italy—Romulus Construction is a highly respected company in the region of Naples. ------- acquires and develops land and then sells completed homes in Naples and the surrounding area. These units are known for the quality of their construction ------- their affordability.
　　　1.　　　2.

Romulus Construction just announced that it ------- to acquire a large stretch of land along the coast. "We're going to construct private residences there while also maintaining the beauty of the natural environment," said Ernesto Humbert, the CEO of Romulus. "-------. We will be releasing more details in the coming weeks."
　　　　　　　　　　　　　　　　　3.　　4.

The company added that it hopes to purchase more land in the near future.

1. (A) They
   (B) It
   (C) He
   (D) There

2. (A) as well as
   (B) except for
   (C) in order to
   (D) in the meantime

3. (A) plan
   (B) is planning
   (C) will be planned
   (D) have been planned

4. (A) The buildings being constructed are nearly complete.
   (B) A decision on purchasing the land must be made soon.
   (C) One family has already moved into its new home.
   (D) We believe the homes we build will be popular with buyers.

UNIT 02 詞性

解析 p.78

1. e-mail（電子郵件）

> Your subscription to *World Travel Magazine* is due to expire on August 31. To continue ------- issues of this publication, please follow the link below and complete the online form as soon as possible. That way, you can be sure that you will not miss any of our helpful articles about the best vacation destinations around the globe.

(A) receipt　　　(B) received　　　(C) receive　　　(D) receiving

→ 空格前方為動詞「continue」、後方連接受詞「issues」，因此空格應填入動名詞。該動名詞可以當作「continue」的受詞，同時連接受詞「issues」，因此答案為(D) receiving。

2. announcement（通知）

> The city of Branchburg has approved the construction of a new apartment complex in the northern neighborhood of Rockwell. The building will contain forty-five one-bedroom units and on-site laundry facilities. The aim is to supply affordable housing for the workers at Skye Amusement Park, a popular ------- for tourists, as well as commuters who use the express bus route.

(A) attract　　　(B) attraction　　　(C) attractive　　　(D) attracts

→ 空格前方有不定冠詞「a」和形容詞「popular」，表示空格應填入名詞，因此答案為 (B) attraction。

3. article（報導）

> The R&D team at Sampson Foods has developed a new packing procedure for its line of healthy snacks. The items will now be packaged with an additional layer of plastic to maintain an airtight environment. The change is expected to provide more consistent and ------- results in the texture and taste of the food, even over a long storage period.

(A) predictable　　　(B) prediction　　　(C) predict　　　(D) predictably

→ 空格前方為形容詞「consistent」和對等連接詞「and」，空格後方連接名詞，表示空格應填入形容詞，與「consistent」一起修飾名詞「results」，因此答案為 (A) predictable。

PRACTICE

Questions 1-4 refer to the following memo.

To: Senior Staff

From: Helen Schnell

Subject: Oxford Plant Update

Date: August 10

For three months, we've advertised heavily for the positions that must be filled at our new plant in Oxford. -------. We are currently ahead of schedule and should have every position fully staffed by the end of August. We are also interested in ------- the plant with experienced workers.
1.   **2.**
Anyone interested in transferring to Oxford should contact -------. Preference in the hiring
3.
process will be given to current employees. We'll be conducting a tour of the site next week. To see it in person, reply to this e-mail, and I'll make the necessary -------.
4.

---

1. (A) Bids for the design of the facility are being accepted now.
   (B) We decided to close it down after getting negative reviews.
   (C) Our CEO will make an important announcement this afternoon.
   (D) I'm pleased to announce that half of those positions have been filled.

2. (A) replacing
   (B) designing
   (C) employing
   (D) staffing

3. (A) me
   (B) I
   (C) mine
   (D) my

4. (A) arrange
   (B) arranging
   (C) arrangements
   (D) arranged

UNIT 03　詞彙

解析 p.79

1. advertisement（廣告）

> The National History Museum offers visitors a fascinating glimpse into the lives of people from long ago. Our exhibits feature clothing items, pottery, art, and more. Admission is just $7.50 per person. The museum is easily ------- by public transportation taking bus 104 or 1288. For more information, visit our website at www.nationalhm.org.

(A) reliable　　(B) detectable　　(C) favorable　　(D) accessible

→ (A)可靠的 (B)可察覺的 (C)有利的 (D)可接近的、可進入的
　空格後方連接介系詞片語「by public transportation（搭乘大眾運輸工具）」，因此空格適合填入 (D) accessible，意指「可抵達的、可接近的」。

2. letter（信件）

> Dear Ms. Burnett,
>
> We are pleased to inform you that your application for a small business loan from Arlington Bank has been approved. The funds will be credited to your business account within 5 working days. Please retain the enclosed loan ------- for your records. Should you have any questions or concerns, feel free to contact our customer service team.

(A) institution　　(B) retrieval　　(C) agreement　　(D) excerpt

→ (A) 機構 (B) 取回 (C) 協議 (D) 摘錄
　將選項逐一套用至「enclosed loan -------」，表達「隨信附上貸款協議」最符合文意，因此答案為 (C) agreement。

3. notice（通知）

> NOTICE TO SALISBURY SUITES TENANTS
>
> We have scheduled an electrician to visit our site on January 19 in order to have the corridor lights rewired. While the work is taking place, there will be no electricity in the building. The power will be shut off at 9 A.M. and then will be ------- no later than 2 P.M. We apologize for any inconvenience this may cause.

(A) restored　　(B) shifted　　(C) enforced　　(D) surpassed

→ (A) 恢復 (B) 轉移 (C) 施行 (D) 超越
　選項中，與主詞「The power（電力、電源）」和動詞片語「be shut off（被關掉）」有關的單字為 (A) restored。

PRACTICE

Questions 1-4 refer to the following article.

HARTFORD (May 19)—Hartford-based charity Peterson House announced its annual fundraiser will be on July 1. Peterson House was ------- in 2001 and has focused on providing food, clothes, and educational supplies for children in the Hartford area.

Peterson House President Jenny Blair said, "We're going to be holding a silent auction for the first time ever. We ------- by the opportunity."

Ms. Blair added that the charity has ------- completed construction on its new office following several delays. -------. She also stated that the charity has some big plans for summer and fall and that she will discuss them at a later date.

1. (A) founded
   (B) donated
   (C) appealed
   (D) constructed

2. (A) excite
   (B) are exciting
   (C) are excited
   (D) excitement

3. (A) always
   (B) finally
   (C) instead
   (D) specially

4. (A) The work was heavily affected by poor weather this spring.
   (B) She expects to raise a million dollars at the auction.
   (C) Ms. Blair has worked at the charity since 2001.
   (D) The charity is pleased with the support it has received locally.

UNIT 04　連接副詞

解析 p.80

1. email（電子郵件）

> Hi, Ashley.
>
> Thanks for volunteering to lead the training workshop for new employees next week. I just found out that we will have employees from both our branch and the Wooddale branch. This brings the total number of participants to 25, up from 13. -------, we are moving the workshop to the main conference room, as it is larger. Please let me know if you have any questions.

(A) Even so　　(B) Therefore　　(C) For example　　(D) Otherwise

→ (A) 儘管如此 (B) 因此 (C) 舉例來說 (D) 否則
　空格前方內容為原因，後方連接結果，表示前後為因果關係，因此答案為連接副詞 (B) Therefore。

2. information（通知）

> Brisbane Hotel is having the elevators in the main lobby replaced on Thursday, August 8. Guests are asked to use the stairwell, which are located directly to the right of the front desk, to get to their rooms. -------, guests may use the elevators near the Jacobs Street entrance. Thank you for your patience.

(A) Initially　　(B) Alternatively　　(C) Unfortunately　　(D) Even if

→ (A) 最初、原本 (B) 供選擇地 (C) 不幸地 (D) 即使
　空格前方為前往客房的第一種方式，並於空格後方提供另一種方式，表示替代方案，因此答案為連接副詞 (B) Alternatively。

3. email（電子郵件）

> Dear Mr. Bradley,
>
> I would like to recommend Blake Patterson for promotion to team leader. Mr. Patterson has been working for the company for five years, and he is well respected within our department. He has excellent written communication skills. -------, he can express himself well in conversations. I believe Mr. Patterson would thrive in this role.

(A) Namely　　(B) On the other hand　　(C) Nonetheless　　(D) Likewise

→ (A) 即 (B) 另一方面 (C) 儘管如此 (D) 同樣地
　空格前一句稱讚Blake Patterson擁有優秀的書面溝通能力，而空格所在的句子補充說明他在對話時，也有很好的表達能力，因此答案要選連接副詞 (D) Likewise，表達前後內容為對等關係。

164

PRACTICE

Questions 1-4 refer to the following e-mail.

To: Carl Lambert <carl_lambert@safehold.com>

From: Harold Beemer <hbeemer@safehold.com>

Date: October 3

Subject: Scheduling

Dear Mr. Lambert,

This is in regard to next week's schedule. -------, I am unable to work next Monday. My supervisor, Brenda Malone, approved my request for time off on Monday, October 10, last week, as I ------- my parents, who live out of town then. I am departing this Friday and returning on Monday night. I assume Ms. Malone did not inform you of this matter.

-------. I would gladly exchange shifts with someone who can work in my place on Monday.

Please let me know how we can rectify this situation. I can meet you anytime to discuss our -------.

Regards,

Harold Beemer

1. (A) Unfortunately
   (B) Sincerely
   (C) Apparently
   (D) Possibly

2. (A) have visited
   (B) visit
   (C) to visit
   (D) will be visiting

3. (A) It has been a pleasure working here for you.
   (B) Thank you for understanding my situation.
   (C) I noticed I am not scheduled to work on Tuesday.
   (D) This was the first vacation of the year for me.

4. (A) options
   (B) selections
   (C) conditions
   (D) devices

UNIT 05　句子插入題

解析 p.81

1. article (報導)

> Hilltop Rentals has procured new investment funds to expand its fleet of rental cars. A spokesperson for Hilltop Rentals said that eighty small, fuel-efficient cars will be purchased. -------. The changes are in response to customer feedback indicating that a wider selection was needed. Details about rental options can be found at www.hilltop-rentals.com.

(A) They vary in price depending on the parking time.
(B) Employees are pleased with the better working hours.
(C) The company will also buy ten moving vans.
(D) He has received several complaints about the cost of renting.

→ 空格前方提到公司購買了小型節能車輛，空格後方出現複數名詞「the changes」，表示為根據顧客回饋意見所做出的變化，因此空格應填入另一項變化較符合文意，答案要選 (C)，意思為「公司還會購買十輛廂型貨車」。

2. e-mail（電子郵件）

> Dear Ms. Milton,
>
> I would like to propose moving one of the copy machines from the 5th-floor employee lounge to the 3rd-floor offices. This would help to save time, as many employees have to go up several flights of stairs just to copy documents. -------. It would solve the problem of the lounge being too crowded, which I have heard numerous complaints about.
>
> Sincerely,
>
> Keisha

(A) In addition, we could free up some space.
(B) The machines with the best reviews are usually more expensive.
(C) Many people find the instruction manual confusing.
(D) We can save paper by printing on both sides.

→ 空格後方出現代名詞「it」，請先找出它所指的東西。空格後方提到有助於解決休息室過於擁擠的問題，因此空格應填入把影印機移到三樓的優點較符合前後文意。答案要選 (A)，意思為「此外，我們還可以騰出一些空間」。

PRACTICE

答案與解析 p.81

Questions 1-4 refer to the following advertisement.

Daniels Landscaping

Daniels Landscaping ------- care of properties for more than two decades. We provide a variety of landscaping services to make your home or place of business look as nice as possible. This includes cutting grass, trimming bushes, planting trees and flowers, and watering yards. -------, we can provide other services related to caring for outdoor areas.

Our landscapers are all highly qualified with several years of experience. -------. The prices at Daniels Landscaping cannot be beat. Our work is ------- to please, or you will get your money back. Call 555-9845 for more information.

1. (A) takes
   (B) has been taking
   (C) was taken
   (D) took

2. (A) However
   (B) In addition
   (C) As a result
   (D) For instance

3. (A) Fortunately, we have a large team of workers.
   (B) Don't forget to check out our website.
   (C) Thank you for your interest in us.
   (D) They also work efficiently and cheerfully.

4. (A) guaranteed
   (B) apparent
   (C) promised
   (D) surprised

Questions 131-134 refer to the following advertisement.

International Business News Report is the best source of information on business. Find out all the latest news from around the globe and be aware of various ------- in the world of business.
131.
Our reporters are some of the top names in the industry. They write articles ------- and provide
132.
updates whenever new information becomes available. To subscribe, visit our website at www.ibnr.com/subscriptions. Joining the site gets you access to our ------- archives and allows
133.
you to take part in online chats with some of the leading individuals in various fields. Why wait? -------.
134.

131. (A) appeals
(B) trends
(C) subscriptions
(D) versions

132. (A) comparatively
(B) seriously
(C) progressively
(D) daily

133. (A) complete
(B) completion
(C) to complete
(D) completing

134. (A) We appreciate your continued dedication to our magazine.
(B) Let us tell you about the special sale that we are having.
(C) Your first issue will arrive in the mail by Monday morning.
(D) Subscribe today and start learning more about business.

Questions 135-138 refer to the following advertisement.

First Avenue Mechanics

Is your car's engine making strange noises? Would you like your car to run better? ----(135.)----. Bring your vehicle to First Avenue Mechanics. Our licensed mechanics will get your car running ----(136.)---- in no time. They can also repair both minor and major auto body issues. You don't need to make an appointment. We're open twenty-four hours a day. So just come on down to 85 First Avenue and drop off your vehicle. We'll fix it the same day in ----(137.)---- cases. Visit our website at www.firstavenuemechanics.com to see our ----(138.)---- price list.

---

135. (A) Then it's time to take a closer look into your car.
(B) Each vehicle is inspected with great care.
(C) Our new cars are offered at reasonable prices.
(D) Some parts may need to be specially ordered.

136. (A) apparently
(B) fairly
(C) conveniently
(D) smoothly

137. (A) every
(B) much
(C) most
(D) their

138. (A) comprehension
(B) comprehended
(C) comprehending
(D) comprehensive

Questions 139-142 refer to the following website.

Nantucket Seafood: Delivery Policy

Nantucket Seafood is able to ship everywhere in the country within 48 hours. -------139.-. Those individuals -------140. live within 3 hours of our factory in Nantucket can opt for same-day courier delivery. Prices vary -------141. upon the weight of the package and the distance it is traveling. All deliveries must be signed for by the recipient unless we are notified at the time the order is placed. We are not -------142. for deliveries delayed due to bad weather or other unavoidable problems. For more information, please contact a customer service representative.

139. (A) All orders are packed in dry ice and shipped by express mail.
(B) More seafood options will be available in the coming weeks.
(C) Our prices are guaranteed to be the lowest in the country.
(D) That means your order should have already arrived.

140. (A) which
(B) what
(C) who
(D) they

141. (A) considering
(B) depending
(C) waiting
(D) reporting

142. (A) responding
(B) responsive
(C) responsible
(D) responsibly

Questions 143-146 refer to the following e-mail.

To: Alexandria Houston

From: Winston Pierce

Subject: Wallpaper

Date: July 5

Dear Ms. Houston,

The wallpaper your company provided for my store has been selling very well. My customers like the designs and ------- with how the wallpaper looks in their homes. -------. Therefore, I would
             143.   144.
like a regular ------- of wallpaper each month.
               145.

I would also like to increase the number of designs. Currently, I have seven of your designs available, but I think fifteen would be better. Would you please send me some samples of your most popular designs? ------- I see them, I will be able to determine which ones I should carry.
                                146.

Regards,

Winston Pierce

Pierce Home Furnishings

143. (A) please
(B) are pleased
(C) will please
(D) are pleasing

144. (A) My store recently added a new department.
(B) Customers are trying to buy items online.
(C) Many want me to install the wallpaper for them.
(D) They also love the low prices we charge.

145. (A) ship
(B) to ship
(C) shipment
(D) shipments

146. (A) Still
(B) Before
(C) Once
(D) However

PART 7

閱讀測驗

UNIT 01 主旨或目的

UNIT 02 事實與否

UNIT 03 推論或暗示

UNIT 04 相關細節

UNIT 05 句子插入題

UNIT 06 找出同義詞

UNIT 07 雙篇閱讀

UNIT 08 多篇閱讀

PART TEST

PART 7 閱讀理解

文章類型與命題方向

PART 7共有54題，由10篇單篇閱讀文章、2組雙篇閱讀文章，以及3組多篇閱讀文章組合而成。根據近三年的命題方向分析結果顯示，在單篇閱讀中，e-mail（電子郵件）佔18%，出題比重最高，其次是article（報導）、notice（公告）、advertisement（廣告）。text-message chain（文字訊息）和online chat discussion（線上聊天）每回測驗各出1題。在雙篇閱讀和多篇閱讀中，e-mail（電子郵件）的出題比重高達40%，其次為web page（網頁）、form（表格）、article（報導）、advertisement（廣告）。

Questions 164-167 refer to the following e-mail.

答案與解析 p.83

To: Allison Holder
From: Clarissa Simpson
Date: March 16
Subject: Important Message

Dear Allison,

As of November 1, our company will no longer provide health insurance for any of our employees, both full time and part time. Instead, employees will be given small increases in their salaries that will enable them to acquire private health insurance of their own.

The cost of providing a group policy like we currently do here at Newport Technology has increased too much in recent years and is making us lose money. The board of directors has therefore decided to make this change as a cost-cutting measure. We are planning to provide consulting services for our employees to assist them in selecting the insurance provider that will be best for them and their families.

David Schuler will be in charge of the transition. He will be providing you with weekly updates until the first of November. We plan to make an announcement regarding this change in June, so we anticipate receiving many questions from employees around that time.

Regards,

Clarissa Simpson
Newport Technology

解題策略

在作答PART 7的單篇閱讀題時，最有效率的方式通常為先查看題目，接著再閱讀文章。如此可將注意力集中在相關內容上，有效縮短閱讀文章的時間。在PART 7中，答題線索通常會按照題目順序出現在文章中。因此，可根據題目出現順序，來推測答題線索位置。作答完第一題後，接著作答第二道題時，不須再從頭開始閱讀，只須從第一題答題線索後方開始閱讀即可，如此通常就能順利找到答題線索。

164. What is the purpose of the e-mail?

(A) To provide information
(B) To request assistance
(C) To schedule a meeting
(D) To ask for advice

主旨或目的
詢問主旨或目的的考題通常是文章的第一題，答題線索主要出現在文章前半段。

165. What is suggested about Newport Technology?

(A) It plans to hire new workers in the summer.
(B) It is in the healthcare industry.
(C) It has branches in other countries.
(D) It is not currently making a profit.

推論或暗示
該類型考題考的是根據文章內容，推論與事實相符選項。選項內容通常分布在文章各處，而非侷限於特定段落。因此如果遇到選項不明確的情況，可根據選項中的關鍵字，在文章中找出相對應的部分進行確認。

166. According to Ms. Simpson, what will Mr. Schuler do?

(A) Determine employees' salary increases
(B) Work together with the board of directors
(C) Provide Ms. Holder with updates
(D) Find new insurance providers for employees

相關細節
為PART 7出題比重最高的考題類型。通常會以Who（誰）、What（什麼）、Where（何處）、When（何時）、How（如何）、Why（為何）開頭的問句來詢問相關細節。

167. The word "transition" in paragraph 3, line 1, is closest in meaning to

(A) development
(B) approach
(C) change
(D) revision

找出同義詞
此類考題考的是能否找出與文中特定單字意思最為接近的單字。請注意這裡指的是單字在文章中的意思，而非字典上的解釋。

UNIT 01　主旨或目的

解題策略

通常為第一題，因此看到該類考題時，請確認文章的主旨或目的。其答題線索大多出現在文章前半段，只要確實理解內容，便能選出最適當的答案。

考題類型

What is the article **mainly about**？文章主要在講什麼？［主旨］
What is being **advertised**？正在宣傳什麼？［主旨］
What is the **purpose** of the e-mail？電子郵件的目的為何？［目的］

代表題型範例

e-mail（電子郵件）　　　　　　　　　　　　　　　　　　解析 p.84

> Dear Mr. Douglas,
>
> It has been more than six months since you have visited us for a routine checkup. You can make an appointment to have your teeth cleaned and checked for cavities by clicking here. We have five dentists on staff, and all of them are ready to assist you. Should you have a particular dentist you prefer, you can indicate that when you make your appointment.
>
> Sincerely,
>
> Tina Gooden
> White Teeth Clinic

本題詢問發送電子郵件的目的，一般會在文章開頭提及發送郵件或信件的目的。該封電子郵件是通知Douglas先生，自上次進行例行檢查至今已經超過六個月。

Q　What is the main purpose of the e-mail?
　　(A) To recommend a new location
　　(B) To provide a reminder
　　(C) To promote a new service
　　(D) To confirm a booking

目的為提醒對方接受檢查，因此答案為(B)。在多益測驗中，reminder主要指用來提醒對方的東西或內容。

176

PRACTICE

答案與解析 p.84

Questions 1-3 refer to the following press release.

FOR IMMEDIATE RELEASE

Porterhouse Manufacturing to Conduct Product Demonstration

Porterhouse Manufacturing is one of the world's leading manufacturers of advanced machinery. Today, the company announced that it will be holding a product demonstration for a machine that its engineers have just completed and that the company intends to market in winter. The event will take place at the company's headquarters in Atlanta at 3:00 P.M. on Monday, October 3. The product to be demonstrated is the newest automobile engine by the company. This engine is set to revolutionize the automobile industry as it is 35% more efficient than any other engine currently available.

Reporters and news broadcasters interested in attending the event in person must register in advance. To do so, contact company public relations employee Gregory Frye at 555-2871 during regular business hours. Individuals with podcasts and blogs and an interest in automobile technology are invited to attend as well. Jeremy Smith, the lead engineer for the project, will be available to answer questions following the demonstration. Attendees will be permitted to take pictures and film videos.

1. What is the purpose of the press release?
   (A) To inform investors of a product release
   (B) To publicize a company's updated service
   (C) To give details on how to acquire a company's product
   (D) To provide information about a product demonstration

2. How can people register for the event?
   (A) By visiting a blog that reports on technology
   (B) By calling an employee of Porterhouse Manufacturing
   (C) By signing up on the Porterhouse Manufacturing web page
   (D) By speaking with a reporter who will cover the event

3. What is indicated about the upcoming event?
   (A) It requires the payment of a fee to attend.
   (B) It will take place on a weekend.
   (C) Attendees will be allowed to ask questions.
   (D) A video will be shown to the attendees.

PART 7

177

UNIT 02　事實與否

解題策略

該類考題要求選出與文章相符或不相符的選項，需閱讀完整篇文章，逐一比對選項與文章內容。由於答題線索常常不按順序出現，因此屬於難度最高的考題類型。在作答該類考題時，需歷經「選項 (A) → 確認文章、選項 (B) → 確認文章、選項 (C) → 確認文章、選項 (D) → 確認文章」的過程，從文章中找出相對應的內容，經比對過後，才能選出正確答案。

考題類型

What is **NOT mentioned** as a feature of the program?　文中沒有提到的節目特色為何？

What is **true** about the job?　關於工作的敘述，何者正確？

What is **indicated** about the contest?　關於比賽，文中指出什麼？

代表題型範例

advertisement（廣告）　　　　　　　　　　　　　　　　　解析 p.84

Greenbrier Writing Workshop, Meeting 1

1:00–3:00 P.M.
Greenbrier Public Library
April 11

Would you like to write like a professional? Do you have great ideas for stories but don't know how to put them into words? Then the upcoming workshop hosted by Allison Herbst is for you. Ms. Herbst has published more than ten novels and also teaches at Greenbrier Community College.

To register and to see the complete schedule for the entire series, go to www.greenbrierlibrary.org. All workshops are free, but advance registration is a must. Ms. Herbst will answer questions after the workshop concludes.

本文為一則寫作課程廣告，文中提供了日期、時間、人物、大學等相關資訊。選項(A)與文中「All workshops are free」的敘述相矛盾；文中有提到明確的地點「Greenbrier Public Library」，因此選項(B)也不正確；文中並未提到寫作課程是由「Greenbrier Community College」主辦，因此選項(D)也不正確。

Q　What is indicated about the workshop?
　(A) People must pay to attend it.
　(B) It will take place online.
　(C) It will be led by an author.
　(D) A college is hosting it.

由Allison Herbst主持寫作課程，她是位已出版多本小說的作家，因此選項(C)的敘述正確，課程會由作家主導。

178

PRACTICE

Questions 1-3 refer to the following information.

Silverwood Botanical Garden Pass

Silverwood Botanical Garden is the largest in the entire state. Covering more than 200 acres, the garden features not only trees, flowers, and plants native to the Southeast but also a wide variety of non-native species, including those from the tropics. Visitors to the garden can enjoy hiking through the wooded areas, picnicking by our five ponds, and seeing some of the wildlife that inhabits the area.

A Silverwood Botanical Garden pass costs only $50 per year and covers an entire family of four. It permits daily access to the garden as well as free parking. Your contribution will allow us to maintain the plants in the garden and acquire new ones.

A pass may be purchased at the ticket office or online at www.silverwoodbg.org. Please note that special discounts on food or other products sold at the stores near the ticket office are not available.

1. Which activity is mentioned in the information?

    (A) Hiking
    (B) Swimming
    (C) Hunting
    (D) Camping

2. What is indicated about the Silverwood Botanical Garden?

    (A) It only has plants from the local area.
    (B) It relies solely on donations from its members.
    (C) It allows guests to go fishing in the ponds.
    (D) It is larger than other nearby botanical gardens.

3. What is a benefit of a Silverwood Botanical Garden pass?

    (A) Lower prices on food
    (B) Guided tours of the garden
    (C) Discounts on souvenirs
    (D) Complimentary parking

UNIT 03　推論或暗示

💡 解題策略

該類型考題要根據文章內容，揣摩其中隱含意義，再選出最相符的選項。選項通常會採換句話說的方式，也就是把文中出現的字詞，改寫成其他說法。當改寫後的選項難度較高時，有效解題方式為刪去法，逐一排除錯誤選項，直到找出正確答案。如果題目中有提到關鍵字，就可從文章中找出相關內容。如果沒有提到，就需從頭開始閱讀文章，逐一對照每個選項的內容。當文章篇幅很長且內容複雜時，最好的作答方式為當成「事實與否」考題，採取「選項 (A) → 確認文章、選項 (B) → 確認文章、選項 (C) → 確認文章、選項 (D) → 確認文章」的解題過程，必定能有效節省時間。

🔍 考題類型

Who **mostly likely** is Mr. Martin?　Martin先生最有可能是誰？

What is **suggested** about Ms. Barrett?　關於Barrett女士，文中暗示什麼？

Where would the notice **most likely** appear?　公告最有可能出現在哪？

📎 代表題型範例

text-message chain（文字訊息）　　　　　　　　　　　　解析 p.85

> **Emily Hudson (2:24 P.M.)**
> David, the budget reports for September were due yesterday. I'm still waiting for yours, though.
>
> **David Weber (2:25 P.M.)**
> I'm sorry. I just returned from a trip to Helsinki. I'm working on it now.
>
> **Emily Hudson (2:26 P.M.)**
> I didn't know you were traveling abroad. I hope your trip was successful. Do you think your department went over budget?
>
> **David Weber (2:27 P.M.)**
> I'll let you know by the end of the day.
>
> **Emily Hudson (2:28 P.M.)**
> Thanks. I need to finish my final report by Friday, but I can't do that until I get your numbers.

題目關鍵字為Ms. Hudson，請從文章中找尋相關內容。Ms. Hudson實際上指的是Emily Hudson，因此答題線索可能會出現在Emily Hudson所說的話中，即以「I（我）」開頭的句子。而對話的對象為David Weber，因此在他的訊息中，以「you（你）」開頭的句子，也可能出現答題線索。

Q　What can be inferred about Ms. Hudson?
　　(A) She will take a business trip to Helsinki.
　　(B) She knew Mr. Weber was away from the office.
　　(C) She has not completed her own report yet.
　　(D) She will meet her supervisor on Friday.

Emily Hudson在訊息最後提到她需在星期五前完成最終報告，表示她目前尚未完成報告。另外，開頭處提到的「budget reports」，指的是各部門交給Emily Hudson的成本報告。

PRACTICE

答案與解析 p.85

Questions 1-3 refer to the following online chat discussion.

Bill Hagler (2:03 P.M.)	Hello, everyone. How is the work on the property coming along? Are we going to finish on time? I'd really like to be able to open on March 1.
Susan Denton (2:06 P.M.)	Everything is looking good, Bill. The kitchen is almost entirely installed. The tables and chairs are going to arrive tomorrow. We'll need someone to help set them up.
Dallas Blair (2:08 P.M.)	Chris and I can do that, Susan. Just let me know what time I should be there.
Susan Denton (2:09 P.M.)	Thanks, Dallas. I really appreciate your being willing to work on your day off.
Dallas Blair (2:10 P.M.)	Oh, I spoke with the owner of the shop right next to ours. He said that he's planning to retire in the next couple of months.
Bill Hagler (2:11 P.M.)	Is his shop going to be available for rent?
Dallas Blair (2:12 P.M.)	That's what he said. We should probably check into it. It might be possible to connect the two places. That would give us more space, so we could expand the dining room.
Susan Denton (2:13 P.M.)	I'll get in touch with a real estate agent.
Bill Hagler (2:14 P.M.)	Sounds great, Susan.

1. Where do the writers most likely work?
   (A) At a restaurant
   (B) At a real estate agency
   (C) At a supermarket
   (D) At a bakery

2. What is Mr. Hagler concerned about?
   (A) Paying for the installation of some equipment
   (B) Opening an establishment by a certain date
   (C) Finding workers willing to set up some tables
   (D) Getting along with the shopkeeper next door

3. At 2:13 P.M., why does Ms. Denton write, "I'll get in touch with a real estate agent"?
   (A) To say she will ask about lowering the monthly rent
   (B) To indicate she can sign a rental agreement
   (C) To state she needs to find a new apartment
   (D) To offer to check on an available property

UNIT 04　相關細節

💡 解題策略

為PART 7出題比重最高的考題類型。通常會以Who（誰）、What（什麼）、Where（何處）、When（何時）、How（如何）、Why（為何）等疑問詞開頭的問句詢問相關細節。作答該類題型時，需根據題目關鍵字，在文章中找出相關內容。關鍵字通常是名詞，如人名或公司名，有時也可能是動詞或動詞片語。在找到與關鍵字相關的內容時，建議先確認其所在句子以及前後文的內容，再選出答案。

🔍 考題類型

Who is Mr. McClellan?　McClellan先生是誰？
What does Cregar sell?　Cregar販售什麼東西？
Why did Ms. Cairns send the memo?　Cairns女士為何會發送備忘錄？
How should Mr. Thurman respond to the request?　Thurman先生該如何回應要求？

📎 代表題型範例

article（報導）　　　　　　　　　　　　　　　　　　　解析 p.86

> *Stamford Daily*
>
> June 28—The city of Stamford has declared that the house located at 86 Bellevue Drive is a historical structure. The home, currently owned by Mark Whitman, was constructed in 1772. It has been the ancestral home of the Whitman family since that time. Mayor Thomas Whittaker stated that the home is now protected and cannot be torn down. Mr. Whitman no longer lives in the house but intends to refurbish it and will provide tours for those interested in learning about life in colonial times. According to Mr. Whitman, many furnishings are from the time when the house was built.

> 題目關鍵字為Mr. Whitman和house on Bellevue Drive。確認完關鍵字後，請迅速瀏覽文章內容，從中找出答題線索。

Q　What does Mr. Whitman plan to do with the house on Bellevue Drive?

　(A) Renovate it so that he can live in it
　(B) Sell it to the city of Stamford
　(C) Let people visit it
　(D) Transform it into a furniture museum

> Whitman先生不會繼續住在位於Bellevue大道的房子，他打算在重新裝修後，開放人們參觀並提供導覽，因此答案選(C)。

PRACTICE

答案與解析 p.86

Questions 1-3 refer to the following e-mail.

To:	All Dearborn Finance Employees
From:	Jefferson Grant, CEO
Date:	July 27
Subject:	David Stillman

To all Dearborn Finance employees,

I regret to inform you that David Stillman has informed me he is stepping down from his position here at Dearborn Finance. Mr. Stillman has worked as our chief researcher for more than twelve years. He has decided to take a position near his hometown so that he can help care for his elderly parents. Please be sure to let David know how much you valued his time here and wish him good luck.

Due to David's departure, we need to find a replacement as soon as possible. Anyone interested in the research position should send an e-mail to Susan Westmoreland at susan@dearbornfinance.com. Be sure to explain why you are qualified for the position and attach a copy of your résumé as well.

David has agreed to help train his replacement, so we are hoping to fill the position within the next three weeks so that he can work with the new employee for a few weeks after that.

Sincerely,

Jefferson Grant
CEO
Dearborn Finance

1. What is one purpose of the e-mail?
   (A) To announce a job opportunity
   (B) To request volunteers
   (C) To schedule a company outing
   (D) To describe a change in the company's structure

2. What is Mr. Stillman doing?
   (A) Getting transferred to the company's head office
   (B) Returning to school to get a degree
   (C) Retiring to spend time with his family
   (D) Resigning to take another position

3. What is NOT indicated about Mr. Stillman?
   (A) He will leave Dearborn Finance in three weeks.
   (B) He is a lead researcher at the company.
   (C) He has worked at Dearborn Finance for more than a decade.
   (D) He is willing to train another employee.

183

UNIT 05　句子插入題

解題策略

此類考題要為根據題目所提供的句子，在文章中找出最適當的位置，通常會出現在題組最後一道題。作答時，首先要確實理解引號中的句子，接著在文章中找出適合填入的位置。如果句子中含有代名詞，如it、this等，建議先找出相應名詞所在句子，再將引號中的句子置於其後方。若句中包含連接副詞，如additionally（此外）、alternatively（或者）等，則建議根據前一句話是否符合文意來確定答案。

考題類型

In which of the positions marked [1], [2], [3], and [4] does the following sentence best belong? "It took a while for the concept to catch on."

[1]、[2]、[3]和[4]當中，何處最適合填入下方句子？

「這個概念在一段時間後才受到歡迎。」

代表題型範例

article（報導）

解析 p.87

PENSACOLA (April 19)—Atlantic Shipping made a shocking announcement last night. —[1]—. The company stated that CEO Kevin Davenport would be stepping down immediately. Mr. Davenport had just started working at Atlantic in March, so his sudden decision to resign has left everyone surprised. —[2]—. Melissa Samuels, a company spokesperson, said that Bradley Wellman, the company's vice president of operations, would act as the interim CEO until a permanent replacement could be found. —[3]—. She did not provide a timeline for when the company expects to have a new leader. —[4]—.

題目提供的句子為「對於他離開的原因，並未發布任何公告。」，適合將其置於提及某人決定辭職的句子之後。

Q　In which of the positions marked [1], [2], [3], and [4] does the following sentence best belong?

"No announcement regarding the reason for his departure was given."

(A) [1]
(B) [2]
(C) [3]
(D) [4]

請先查看題目提供的句子，找出解題關鍵字。本題關鍵字為「his departure（他的離開）」，請迅速查看文章中是否提及相關內容。由於resign意思和departure相同，因此可將其套用至resign所在的句子之後，答案選[2]。

PRACTICE

答案與解析 p.87

Questions 1-3 refer to the following article.

NORFOLK (September 4)—A new restaurant has just opened in Norfolk, and it is rapidly becoming one of the city's most popular eateries. The name of the establishment is Kirk's Diner. Owned by Stephanie Kirk, the restaurant specializes in Italian and Spanish food. —[1]—.

Almost all of the food served at the restaurant comes from local farmers, something that Ms. Kirk is very proud of. —[2]—. "The Norfolk area produces lots of great food, and I'm pleased that my restaurant can serve it to our customers," she said.

Ms. Kirk is not only the owner but also the head chef. She studied culinary arts at the Milan Cooking School in Italy. Later, she worked as a chef in London, Paris, and Athens. —[3]—. She came back home to Norfolk last year, where she worked at Italian Delights. Now, she has her own restaurant. —[4]—. Judging from the long waits for tables, it is going to be a successful place.

1. What is the purpose of the article?
   (A) To review a meal at a restaurant
   (B) To describe a business's grand opening
   (C) To promote a new product
   (D) To introduce a dining establishment

2. What is stated about Ms. Kirk?
   (A) She is the owner of a restaurant.
   (B) She speaks Italian and Spanish.
   (C) She has a farm in Norfolk.
   (D) She studied cooking in London.

3. In which of the positions marked [1], [2], [3], and [4] does the following sentence best belong?
   "She spent more than twenty years living abroad."
   (A) [1]
   (B) [2]
   (C) [3]
   (D) [4]

UNIT 06　找出同義詞

💡 解題策略

請先在文章中找出題目引號內的單字。請注意，電子郵件的收件者、寄件者、日期、主旨，以及報導或廣告的標題並不算在段落（paragraph）中。如果單字是片語動詞或特定詞組（collocation）的一部分，只需確認前後方字詞即可找出答案，否則就要先理解單字所在子句或句子的意思。若仍無法解答，則需逐一將選項帶入以確認答案。

🔍 考題類型

此類考題特點是題目最後方沒有問號，若是多篇閱讀題，前方會標示所屬文章的類型。

[單篇閱讀] The word "measure" in paragraph 1, line 4, is closest in meaning to
　　　　第一段第4行中的「measure」一詞，意思最接近何者？

[多篇閱讀] In the memo, the word "courtesy" in paragraph 2, line 3, is closest in meaning to
　　　　在備忘錄中，第二段第3行中的「courtesy」一詞，意思最接近何者？

📎 代表題型範例

web page（網頁）　　　　　　　　　　　　　　　　　　　　解析 p.88

> Thank you for registering to become a member of the online shopping club at Lux Warehouse. All of our members receive automatic 10% discounts on all purchases as well as free express shipping. For a complete list of benefits, click here. Be sure to check your e-mail every Sunday night, as you will receive a members-only special offer then. Members are also frequently asked to **grade** new products and may receive requests to complete customer satisfaction surveys. We want to ensure our most loyal customers are happy with our service.

> grade後方連接new products當作受詞，可確認grade為動詞。再根據句中另一個動詞片語「complete customer satisfaction surveys（完成客戶滿意度調查）」，可推測出「grade new products」的意思為「對新產品進行評分」。

Q　The word "grade" in line 7 is closest in meaning to
　　(A) purchase
　　(B) sample
　　(C) rate
　　(D) consider

> 與grade意思最為相近的是rate（評價），因此答案要選(C)。

186

PRACTICE

Questions 1-3 refer to the following advertisement.

CHAMBERLIN MARKETING

Many small businesses have outstanding products and services they would like to sell. However, their owners have neither the time nor the ability to market these goods and services. Fortunately, Chamberlin Marketing can handle all of their needs.

Chamberlin Marketing has been in business for thirty-five years. We have provided assistance to more than 500 small businesses during that time. We have assisted companies in marketing themselves locally, nationwide, and internationally. Our employees have experience in numerous markets, and each of them is familiar with at least one foreign language.

If you would like a one-hour consultation, please call us at 555-0271 during regular business hours. Tell us about your company, and we'll come up with a preliminary marketing plan at no cost to you. There's no obligation to use our services. But if you do, you won't regret it.

1. The word "handle" in paragraph 1, line 3, is closest in meaning to
   (A) take care of
   (B) think about
   (C) promote
   (D) reveal

2. What is indicated about Chamberlin Marketing?
   (A) It focuses on marketing products online.
   (B) It can promote goods in foreign countries.
   (C) It was established in the past decade.
   (D) It has more than 500 employees.

3. What is Chamberlin Marketing offering to small business owners?
   (A) A discount on creating a web page
   (B) Reduced rates
   (C) A free consultation
   (D) A cash refund

UNIT 07　雙篇閱讀

💡 解題策略

第176題至第185題為雙篇閱讀題，共有10道題。每篇文章包含5道考題，其中有4題為詢問目的或主旨、事實與否、相關細節、找出同義詞，另外1題為雙篇文章整合題，需從兩篇文章中找出答題線索，才能選出答案。當中不會出現句子插入題。若題目詢問目的或主旨，答題線索通常會在文章前半段。若題目要求選出同義詞，只要正確理解所在句子的意思，通常能順利選出答案。因此，若作答時間不足，請務必把握好這兩類題型，以順利取得分數。至於雙篇文章整合題，最佳作答方式為專注於數字。若一篇文章提到價格、數量、時間、日期等數字，另一篇文章通常也會出現相關答題線索。

📎 代表題型範例

Questions 1-5 refer to the following article and label. 　　　　　　　　　　　　解析 p.88

Calico Crackers to Change Labels

LOS ANGELES (September 5)—Calico Crackers, the popular whole-wheat snack food, has announced plans to change its product labels. The packaging will now provide pairing suggestions, such as which variety of cheese goes best with each Calico Crackers flavor. The company's aim is to get customers to try the crackers with other foods instead of just on their own.

The move is intended to help Calico Crackers regain market share after Crispy Dreams overtook the company as the top snack cracker on the market. The heavy competition has prompted Calico Crackers officials to look for new ways to promote the product.

"Calico Crackers are a great snack when you're on the go," said company spokesperson Jocelyn Watkins. "But when you're at home, you can create more elaborate recipes and food combinations with our crackers. All the labels we make after September 25 will have these added ideas, and we would love to see our customers' own creations on our social media platforms."

CALICO CRACKERS
Herb and Garlic Flavor

100g
Packaged in Toronto, Canada

Pairing Suggestion: Why not try these crackers with cream cheese or topped with sun-dried tomatoes?

Visit www.calicocrackers.com to find step-by-step video recipes of more dishes you can make with Calico Crackers!

1. According to the article, what does Calico Crackers hope to do for customers?

   (A) Reduce the amount of packaging in their purchases
   (B) Make it easier for those with allergies to check the ingredients
   (C) Inspire them to try their product with new foods
   (D) Quickly determine which cracker flavor they may like

   第一題的答題線索通常會在文章開頭部分，尤其是第一段前半部。題目中提到：「According to the article」，明確指出了文章，因此只需要查看該篇文章即可找到答案。文中的答題線索為：「The company's aim is to get customers to try the crackers with other foods」。

2. What does the article suggest about Crispy Dreams?

   (A) It has recently started producing snacks.
   (B) It sells more goods than Calico Crackers.
   (C) It is currently based in Los Angeles.
   (D) It is the cheapest brand on the market.

   題目關鍵字為「Crispy Dreams」，請在文章中找出相關內容，其答題線索為：「Crispy Dreams overtook the company as the top snack cracker on the market.」。

3. In the article, the word "prompted" in paragraph 2, line 2, is closest in meaning to

   (A) assisted
   (B) caused
   (C) rushed
   (D) reminded

   動詞「promoted」出現在句子「The heavy competition has prompted Calico Crackers officials to look for new ways to promote the product.」，表示激烈的競爭促使Calico餅乾的高層人員尋找宣傳該產品的新方法。

4. What is suggested about the package's label?

   (A) It was made in a new food factory.
   (B) Its weight was listed incorrectly.
   (C) It is for a newly released product.
   (D) It was printed after September 25.

   本題為整合題。題目關鍵字為「label」，請在文章中找出相關內容，並特別留意是否出現數字。第一篇文章中提到從9月25日開始，所有標籤都會附上食物搭配的資訊。接著查看第二篇的標籤，當中有提及搭配建議。

5. According to the label, what can customers do on a website?

   (A) Suggest new cracker flavors
   (B) Write product recipe reviews
   (C) Watch instructional videos
   (D) Download a coupon

   最後一題的答題線索通常會在文章最後一段。第二篇的標籤中，「Visit ~ with Calico Crackers!」提到可在網站上找到料理的逐步食譜影片。

PRACTICE

Questions 1-5 refer to the following e-mail and report.

E-Mail

To: information@jasperrealty.com
From: samjackson@hoffmanassociates.com
Date: August 18
Subject: Office Space

To Whom It May Concern,

My firm has plans to open a small branch office in Lincoln. One of my colleagues suggested that I contact your agency to assist in the process of finding an acceptable office.

The branch office will have ten people working there. The space needs to have a minimum of six individual offices as well as an open workspace that can accommodate the other employees. The building needs to be within a couple of blocks of a bus stop since that is how many of the employees commute to work. It would be ideal if there's a parking lot for clients to park in, but it's not a must. Being close to local restaurants and coffee shops would be ideal as well.

Please let me know what properties are available that fit my criteria. I would also like to know roughly how much the utilities will cost on a monthly basis. We would like to open the office within two months, so we need to find a place soon. We can sign a two-year lease as well.

Sam Jackson
Hoffman Associates

Possible Office Spaces for Hoffman Associates
Prepared by Alice Moreno

88 Rhubarb Avenue
Four individual offices and a large open space for six people. Free parking in the basement. Right in front of a bus stop.

192 Catfish Lane
Seven individual offices and one open space for five people. Electricity provided by solar power. One block away from a bus stop and the train station.

27 Hamilton Boulevard
Two open spaces for twelve people. No individual offices. Daycare center located in the same building. Four blocks away from a bus stop. Public parking lot nearby.

64 Maple Street
Brand-new building. Twelve individual offices. Restaurants located in the basement. Great view of the oceanfront. Near a bus stop.

PRACTICE

1. In the e-mail, the word "accommodate" in paragraph 2, line 2, is closest in meaning to

   (A) locate
   (B) approve
   (C) fit
   (D) satisfy

2. What does Mr. Jackson request?

   (A) The prices of utilities
   (B) A sample contract
   (C) A map of the local region
   (D) Telephone numbers of office owners

3. What information about the office spaces is NOT provided?

   (A) The nearby facilities
   (B) The number of individual offices
   (C) The location of public transportation
   (D) The monthly rent

4. According to the report, what is true about the office space located on Hamilton Boulevard?

   (A) It has twelve individual offices.
   (B) There is enough room for twelve people.
   (C) It is close to the bus station.
   (D) There is no parking lot close to it.

5. Which office space would Mr. Jackson most likely be interested in?

   (A) 88 Rhubarb Avenue
   (B) 192 Catfish Lane
   (C) 27 Hamilton Boulevard
   (D) 64 Maple Street

UNIT 08　多篇閱讀

解題策略

第186題至第200題為多篇閱讀題，每組文章包含5道考題。在雙篇閱讀中，每5題僅有1題為整合題；但在多篇閱讀中，每5題有2題為整合題。當中不會出現句子插入題和找出同義詞考題。多篇閱讀與雙篇閱讀的解題策略相同，看到詢問目的或主旨題目時，請務必好好把握，拿下分數。

代表題型範例

Questions 1-5 refer to the following website, form, and e-mail.　　　　　　　　　　解析 p.90

International Association of Biomedical Engineers (IABE)
Fifteenth Annual Conference

Location: Bayside Hotel, Athens, Greece
Date: September 22–25
Theme: New Trends in Biomedical Engineering

Please note the following important dates:
* Proposal submissions – March 1
* Proposal acceptance – May 1
* Complete paper submissions – June 30

All proposals should be between 400 and 500 words and should be submitted online at our website at www.iabe.org/proposals. Please follow the instructions on the website regarding how to write the proposal.

Registration for the conference begins on June 1. The fee includes a conference T-shirt, refreshments, the luncheon, attendance at all sessions, and a copy of all papers. Please register at www.iabe.org/registration.

Attendee — $500 / early registration before June 20
Attendee — $600 / registration after June 20
Presenter — $400
Student — $300

---

https://www.iabe.org/registration

International Association of Biomedical Engineers
Fifteenth Annual Conference Registration

Name: Susanna Madsen
Company: Klein Pharmaceuticals
Area of Interest: Pharmaceutical Development
Telephone Number: 805-555-8573
E-mail: smadsen@klein.com
Registration Fee: $500

To: Susanna Madsen
From: Sunshine Hotel
Date: August 14
Subject: RE: Questions

Dear Ms. Madsen,

We are looking forward to having you as a guest here next month. To respond to your questions, the hotel is a five-minute walk from the sea. You will find all kinds of places to shop and eat near the hotel. We are also located right across the street from the conference you are attending. You can therefore walk there with ease. If you have any other questions, please let me know.

Sincerely,

Ioannis Papadopoulos
Customer Service Representative
Sunshine Hotel

1. According to the web page, what is true about the conference?

   (A) A lunch event will be held during the conference.
   (B) It is open only to IABE members.
   (C) Some people can attend it for free.
   (D) It will last for one week.

   詢問事實與否的考題，其答題線索未必會按照順序出現。本題的答題線索在文章第一段中間：「The fee includes ~ all papers.」。

2. When will individuals most likely be notified whether their proposals have been accepted?

   (A) On March 1
   (B) On May 1
   (C) On June 1
   (D) On June 30

   請特別注意文中提及日期之處。

3. What is suggested about Ms. Madsen?

   (A) She is not a member of the IABE.
   (B) She is attending the conference for a second time.
   (C) She signed up for the conference before June 20.
   (D) She is going to present a paper at the conference.

   本題為整合題，題目關鍵字為Madsen。第二篇文章有出現Susanna Madsen，當中提到她的報名費為500美元。接著查看第一篇文章，最下面提及各類人士報名費用的部分，便能找到答題線索。

4. Why did Mr. Papadopoulos send the e-mail?

   (A) To confirm a room reservation
   (B) To offer a special discount
   (C) To respond to some inquiries
   (D) To change the date of a booking

   題目關鍵字為Papadopoulos。第三篇文章的寄件者為Ioannis Papadopoulos，從信件主旨欄位及內容可得知，他發送郵件是為了回答Susanna Madsen的問題。

5. What is indicated about the Sunshine Hotel?

   (A) It is located close to the Bayside Hotel.
   (B) It recently underwent renovations.
   (C) It offers a discount to conference attendees.
   (D) It does not have any vacancies in September.

   本題為整合題，題目關鍵字為Sunshine Hotel。第三篇信件中提及該飯店位於舉辦研討會的飯店對面，再查看第一篇文章可得知為Bayside Hotel。

193

PRACTICE

答案與解析 p.91

Questions 1-5 refer to the following web page and e-mails.

https://www.bostontours.com/tours

Boston Tours has over thirty-three years of experience providing tours of the city and the surrounding area. Every tour is led by a guide who is a native of the area and has a strong familiarity with all of the most notable places to see in Boston. We offer four tours for people to choose from.

Package 1 A half-day tour of downtown Boston and an aquarium visit - $50/person

Package 2 A half-day tour of Boston with a focus on shopping downtown - $40/person

Package 3 A one-day tour of Boston and Cambridge with visits to Harvard, MIT, the aquarium, and Beacon Hill - $80/person

Package 4 A one-day tour of Boston and the surrounding area that includes visits to historical sites related to the American Revolution - $100/person

For more information or to arrange a booking, send an e-mail to information@bostontours.com.

To: information@bostontours.com
From: Marcus Cartwright <marcus_c@prometheus.com>
Date: June 11
Subject: Tour

Hello,

I'm planning a family trip to New England this summer, and your company was recommended by a friend who has used your services before. She said your guides are knowledgeable and the tour she went on was entertaining and educational.

We're going to be in the Boston area from June 28 to July 1. I'd prefer to take a tour on the first day we're there. But if there are no available spots that day, the next day is fine with us. There are five of us in my family. My wife and three children will be accompanying me. The children love history, so we hope you have a tour that can accommodate us.

Regards,

Marcus Cartwright

PRACTICE

TO:	Marcus Cartwright <marcus_c@prometheus.com>
FROM:	Cynthia Potter <cynthia@bostontours.com>
DATE:	June 15
SUBJECT:	Re: Tour

Dear Mr. Cartwright,

Thank you for contacting Boston Tours. We have a one-day tour that is perfect for your children's interests. Unfortunately, the tour is already fully booked on the first day of your stay in Boston. But there are still five openings for the tour on the second day. To confirm your reservation, you need to pay a nonrefundable deposit of half the amount of the fee for each ticket. How old are your children? They may be eligible for our children's rate, which is half the regular price. Please let me know whether you want to book the tour, and then we can make the payment arrangements.

Regards,

Cynthia Potter
Boston Tours

1. What does the web page indicate about Boston Tours?

   (A) It hires guides that can speak foreign languages.
   (B) It recently started giving tours of Boston.
   (C) It accepts both cash and credit card payments.
   (D) It has been in business for more than three decades.

2. What is indicated about Mr. Cartwright?

   (A) He grew up in the Boston area.
   (B) He will be traveling with his family.
   (C) He is visiting Boston for the first time.
   (D) He will spend one week in Boston.

3. Which package will Mr. Cartwright most likely select?

   (A) Package 1
   (B) Package 2
   (C) Package 3
   (D) Package 4

4. When most likely will Mr. Cartwright go on a tour?

   (A) On June 15
   (B) On June 28
   (C) On June 29
   (D) On July 1

5. What does Ms. Potter request from Mr. Cartwright?

   (A) His credit card information
   (B) The names of his family members
   (C) The place where he should be picked up
   (D) The ages of his children

PART TEST

Questions 147-148 refer to the following notice.

Asbury Road Parking Lot Update

The recent poor weather conditions this spring have caused the renovation work on the Asbury Road parking lot to be significantly delayed. The work was expected to be completed by May 1. However, construction crews were unable to access the site during the snowy weather. Furthermore, some structural issues were identified by engineers, further delaying the work. As a result, the project is now scheduled for completion by August 15. Anyone who has questions is welcome to contact Russell Mayer of Vanderbilt Construction at 802-555-9361.

147. What is the purpose of the notice?

(A) To report on recent weather conditions
(B) To explain a change in some plans
(C) To apologize for missing a deadline
(D) To provide details on work to be done

148. What is indicated about the Asbury Road parking lot project?

(A) It is not going to be finished on time.
(B) It will expand the size of the parking lot.
(C) It will be completed in May.
(D) It is expected to go over its budget.

Questions 149-151 refer to the following form.

Purchase Request Form

Employee Name: Kenneth Dumont
Department: IT

Request Date: November 11
E-mail: kdumont@dmr.com

Item	Vendor	Quantity
Syntax 4000 Digital Camera	MTR Technology	1
Xtreme 1000G Laptop Computer	CompuServe	1
4TB External Hard Drive	CompuServe	2
Steady Sound Headphones	Techno Sound	1

- When submitting this form, please attach other relevant information necessary for purchase of the items. This includes the addresses of the web pages where the items can be acquired and captured images of the items.
- No requests will be approved without the signature of your immediate supervisor.
- The items purchased are for work use only and not for personal use.

Employee Signature: Kenneth Dumont

Department Head Signature: Leslie Wheeler

---

149. Which item does Mr. Dumont request more than one of?

(A) The digital camera
(B) The laptop computer
(C) The external hard drive
(D) The headphones

150. What did Mr. Dumont most likely submit along with the form?

(A) A cash payment
(B) Receipts
(C) Images of the items
(D) A credit card number

151. Who most likely is Ms. Wheeler?

(A) An employee at MRT Technology
(B) A client of Mr. Dumont's
(C) A member of the Purchasing Department
(D) The IT Department supervisor

Questions 152-155 refer to the following article.

Brentwood News
February 26

Grant Autos, one of the country's biggest vehicle manufacturers, will be opening a manufacturing facility in Brentwood. The facility will be where Roth Textiles was once located. The existing buildings are in the process of being demolished, and three new manufacturing centers will be erected in their place. The first center will be operational within eighteen months, while the other two will take up to two years before they are complete.

Jefferson Trent, a senior vice president at Grant Autos, stated, "We hope to produce up to 300 vehicles a day when all three facilities are operational. We're making a big investment in Brentwood, and we expect it to pay off for us."

Grant Autos will hire more than 2,500 full-time employees to work at the complex. Most of them will work on the manufacturing line. However, over the next two years, the company will also be seeking designers, engineers, executives, and others to employ.

152. What is the purpose of the article?

(A) To report on a business merger
(B) To describe a problem in Brentwood
(C) To announce the opening of a factory
(D) To promote some Grant Autos vehicles

153. Who is Mr. Trent?

(A) A factory manager
(B) A Grant Autos executive
(C) An automobile maker spokesperson
(D) A Brentwood government official

154. The phrase "pay off" in paragraph 2, line 6, is closest in meaning to

(A) reimburse
(B) develop
(C) recall
(D) succeed

155. According to the article, what will Grant Autos do?

(A) Hire a variety of workers
(B) Renovate an existing facility
(C) Request a loan from the city
(D) Design a new line of vehicles

Questions 156-159 refer to the following e-mail.

To: Tim Chapman <timchapman@chapmandesigns.com>
From: Dustin Peters <d_peters@beaumontconsulting.com>
Date: August 19
Subject: August 19 Design Decision

Dear Mr. Chapman,

I want to thank you and your team for the five options you presented to us for the redesign of the interior of our office. In addition, I appreciate your being patient and waiting for our response. I'm very sorry for the delay. Several individuals involved in the decision-making process were on vacation and only returned to the office this week. Still, we have made our decision and hope you can begin working on the project before the end of the month. — [1] —.

We have decided to go with the third option, entitled "Futuristic Design." — [2] —. We love the unique appearance of this design and think that it will go well with our company's image. It also has plenty of open space, which makes the office look bigger than it is in reality. — [3] —.

Before the work begins, we need to discuss a few aspects of the design. I wonder if you and your team are available to come here and meet us in person this week. — [4] —. Please let me know if you have time for that.

Sincerely,

Dustin Peters

156. Who most likely is Mr. Chapman?

(A) A financial consultant
(B) An interior designer
(C) A property agent
(D) A residential architect

157. Why does Mr. Peters apologize to Mr. Chapman?

(A) He made a mistake in a previous e-mail.
(B) He forgot to attend a scheduled meeting.
(C) He failed to submit a payment on time.
(D) He did not respond for a long time.

158. What is indicated about "Futuristic Design"?

(A) It was favored by everyone at the company.
(B) It will take a short time to implement.
(C) It matches the image that the company has.
(D) It can be done within the company's budget.

159. In which of the positions marked [1], [2], [3], and [4] does the following sentence best belong?

"That will give us the opportunity to go over the design in detail."

(A) [1]
(B) [2]
(C) [3]
(D) [4]

Questions 160-164 refer to the following advertisement and e-mail.

Sanderson Home Improvement

Sanderson Home Improvement has been helping homeowners in the Sturbridge area for more than twelve years. We provide a wide variety of services on both a regular and one-time basis.

Some of the services we provide are:
- Air conditioning installation and maintenance
- Roof installation and repair
- Chimney cleaning
- Swimming pool construction
- Home expansion and repair

Contact Information
General Information: Cody Wilde, cwilde@sandersonhomes.com
Air Conditioning: Julius Clover, jclover@sandersonhomes.com
Roof and Chimney: Eric Blaine, eblaine@sandersonhomes.com
Swimming Pools: Carla Crow, ccrow@sandersonhomes.com
Home Renovation: Douglas Montana, dmontana@sandersonhomes.com

---

E-Mail

To: Carla Crow <ccrow@sandersonhomes.com>
From: Alyson Roswell <a_roswell@moderntimes.com>
Date: April 11
Subject: Tomorrow

Good afternoon, Carla.

I'm afraid I need to delay tomorrow's visit by Jack Haley's work crew. I have to take a trip out of town. I'm leaving tonight and won't return until late tomorrow, so there won't be anyone home to let the workers in tomorrow. I'm terribly sorry about that.

I know there are only two more days to go until the project is complete. That's what Mr. Haley told me this morning. I'll be home the rest of the week, so I think the crew can finish up everything by the weekend.

Once the work is complete, I'll make the final payment.

Regards,

Alyson Roswell

160. What is suggested about Sanderson Home Improvement?

(A) It is located in Sturbridge.
(B) It offers discounts to customers.
(C) It offers a chimney design service.
(D) It installs heaters in homes.

161. According to the advertisement, who should be contacted about cooling systems?

(A) Julius Clover
(B) Douglas Montana
(C) Cody Wilde
(D) Eric Blaine

162. What is the main purpose of Ms. Roswell's e-mail?

(A) To postpone some work
(B) To schedule a meeting
(C) To arrange a payment
(D) To discuss a job opportunity

163. What is Ms. Roswell most likely having done at her house?

(A) Air conditioning installation
(B) Chimney cleaning
(C) Home expansion
(D) Swimming pool construction

164. Who most likely is Mr. Haley?

(A) A construction supervisor
(B) A roof installer
(C) The CEO of Sanderson Home Improvement
(D) A customer of Sanderson Home Improvement

Questions 165-169 refer to the following e-mail, invoice, and memo.

E-Mail

TO:	Preston Peterson <ppeterson@tristatemedia.com>
FROM:	Curtis Harrier <curtis_harrier@vanguardautos.com>
DATE:	October 11
SUBJECT:	Notes
ATTACHMENT:	@comments

Dear Mr. Peterson,

My team and I watched the initial version of the video your team at Tristate Media made for Vanguard Auto's newest vehicle. We were impressed with your work. The video clearly shows how well the Stallion handles, especially in off-road situations. There are a few issues in the video I would like for you to address.

* At 10 seconds: Please include the company name and logo in large print at the bottom of the screen.
* At 25 seconds: The shots of the vehicle's interior are not clear. We want viewers to see how comfortable the interior is. Could you please reshoot that part?
* At 1 minute: There is too much dust in the off-road scene. It makes the car difficult to see.

I've outlined these issues further in the attached document. I'm looking forward to seeing the final version of the video by October 19. We're sending it to all our dealers around the country as well as some top clients. Please get in touch with me if you have any questions regarding my suggested changes.

Regards,

Curtis Harrier
Media Department
Vanguard Autos

Vanguard Autos

Invoice 5433

Billing Date: November 15

Delivery Date: November 19

Bill To: Silverado Ranch
       45 Buffalo Lane
       Billings, Montana

Quantity	Item Number	Description	Unit Price	Total
5	57231	Stallion SUV	$53,000	$265,000

                                     Tax $10,600
                                     Total $275,600

MEMO

To: All Employees
From: Christina Wilson, Vice President of Sales
Date: November 20
Re: Congratulations

I'd like to thank everyone for the work you did in creating the recent informational video for the Stallion. Our national dealers love it, and so do the clients to whom we sent it. I'd especially like to thank Mr. Harrier for the work he did in getting the video done.

The Stallion doesn't officially go on sale until December 1, but we have already sold some units. They were delivered yesterday to a long-term customer. Ben Freeman, who made the purchase, told us the video was instrumental in getting him to buy the vehicles without even test-driving them. We're going to need some commercials for the Stallion done soon, so I'm expecting great things from you in December.

---

165. What is attached to the e-mail?

(A) An invoice
(B) A description of a new vehicle
(C) A review of a video production
(D) A copy of a receipt

166. Why does Mr. Harrier want to reshoot the scene at 25 seconds?

(A) The vehicle is moving too fast.
(B) The image in the video is unclear.
(C) There is too much dust in the scene.
(D) The company logo does not appear.

167. What does the invoice indicate about the Stallion?

(A) The purchaser ordered five of them.
(B) A discount was provided.
(C) There was a fee for delivery.
(D) They were delivered on November 15.

168. Who does Ms. Wilson specifically praise?

(A) A member of the Media Department
(B) A long-term client
(C) A video producer
(D) A national salesperson

169. Where does Mr. Freeman most likely work?

(A) At Vanguard Autos
(B) At Silverado Ranch
(C) At Tristate Media
(D) At a test-driving center

實戰模擬試題

實戰模擬試題 聽力與閱讀篇

LISTENING TEST

In the Listening test, you will be asked to demonstrate how well you understand spoken English. The entire Listening test will last approximately 45 minutes. There are four parts, and directions are given for each part. You must mark your answers on the separate answer sheet. Do not write your answers in your test book.

PART 1

Directions: For each question in this part, you will hear four statements about a picture in your test book. When you hear the statements, you must select the one statement that best describes what you see in the picture. Then find the number of the question on your answer sheet and mark your answer. The statements will not be printed in your test book and will be spoken only one time.

Statement (C), "He's making a phone call," is the best description of the picture, so you should select answer (C) and mark it on your answer sheet.

1.

2.

3.

4.

5.

6.

PART 2

Directions: You will hear a question or statement and three responses spoken in English. They will not be printed in your test book and will be spoken only one time. Select the best response to the question or statement and mark the letter (A), (B), or (C) on your answer sheet.

7. Mark your answer on your answer sheet.
8. Mark your answer on your answer sheet.
9. Mark your answer on your answer sheet.
10. Mark your answer on your answer sheet.
11. Mark your answer on your answer sheet.
12. Mark your answer on your answer sheet.
13. Mark your answer on your answer sheet.
14. Mark your answer on your answer sheet.
15. Mark your answer on your answer sheet.
16. Mark your answer on your answer sheet.
17. Mark your answer on your answer sheet.
18. Mark your answer on your answer sheet.
19. Mark your answer on your answer sheet.
20. Mark your answer on your answer sheet.
21. Mark your answer on your answer sheet.
22. Mark your answer on your answer sheet.
23. Mark your answer on your answer sheet.
24. Mark your answer on your answer sheet.
25. Mark your answer on your answer sheet.
26. Mark your answer on your answer sheet.
27. Mark your answer on your answer sheet.
28. Mark your answer on your answer sheet.
29. Mark your answer on your answer sheet.
30. Mark your answer on your answer sheet.
31. Mark your answer on your answer sheet.

PART 3

Directions: You will hear some conversations between two or more people. You will be asked to answer three questions about what the speakers say in each conversation. Select the best response to each question and mark the letter (A), (B), (C), or (D) on your answer sheet. The conversations will not be printed in your test book and will be spoken only one time.

32. Where most likely are the speakers?
    (A) At a shipping company
    (B) At a national park
    (C) At a hardware store
    (D) At a cleaning service

33. According to the man, what has caused a problem?
    (A) A staff shortage
    (B) A scheduling conflict
    (C) Some poor reviews
    (D) Some broken equipment

34. What does the woman say she will do?
    (A) Print a document
    (B) Hire a specialist
    (C) Check a manual
    (D) Process a payment

35. Who most likely is the man?
    (A) A building owner
    (B) An art instructor
    (C) An interior designer
    (D) A journalist

36. What is the woman concerned about?
    (A) Increased costs
    (B) Safety issues
    (C) Unavailable materials
    (D) A missed deadline

37. What does the woman suggest doing?
    (A) Taking a training session
    (B) Looking at some images
    (C) Contacting a manufacturer
    (D) Placing a rush order

38. Who are the men meeting with?
    (A) A real estate agent
    (B) A mechanic
    (C) A safety inspector
    (D) An accountant

39. What are the men concerned about?
    (A) A location is difficult to find.
    (B) A site is not large enough.
    (C) A form is missing information.
    (D) A parking fee is too high.

40. What will the speakers most likely do next?
    (A) Enter a building
    (B) View a document
    (C) Go to another site
    (D) Take some measurements

41. Why is the woman calling?
    (A) To request a discount
    (B) To reschedule a delivery
    (C) To make a payment
    (D) To inquire about returns

42. Why did the woman order some items?
    (A) She plans to transport some items.
    (B) She must repair some machinery.
    (C) She will give gifts to employees.
    (D) She is redecorating her office.

43. What will the man do next?
    (A) Drive to the woman's business
    (B) Update a company website
    (C) Speak to the woman's manager
    (D) Check an employee's availability

44. Where does the man work?
    (A) At a computer repair shop
    (B) At a medical clinic
    (C) At a bank
    (D) At an employment agency

45. Why does the woman need to make a change?
    (A) She is having car problems.
    (B) She will take a business trip.
    (C) She must teach a class.
    (D) She is not feeling well.

46. What will the woman most likely do next?
    (A) Make a formal complaint
    (B) Provide new contact information
    (C) Confirm an expiration date
    (D) Contact another branch

47. Where do the speakers most likely work?
    (A) At a farm
    (B) At a warehouse
    (C) At a café
    (D) At an appliance store

48. Why does the woman say, "the training period is already quite long"?
    (A) To reject a suggestion
    (B) To reassure the man
    (C) To offer her assistance
    (D) To suggest changing a schedule

49. What does the man mention about Steven?
    (A) He has a lot of experience.
    (B) He is dissatisfied with the work conditions.
    (C) He can recommend a supplier.
    (D) He may have trouble with a workload.

50. Where are the speakers?
    (A) At a movie theater
    (B) At a library
    (C) At a restaurant
    (D) At a gym

51. What does Joseph give the woman information about?
    (A) Meeting staff members
    (B) Participating in group classes
    (C) Accessing an account
    (D) Touring a facility

52. What does the woman say she did last month?
    (A) She moved to a different city.
    (B) She started a new job.
    (C) She received a certification.
    (D) She began studying online.

53. What industry do the speakers most likely work in?
    (A) Advertising
    (B) Technology
    (C) Energy
    (D) Pharmaceuticals

54. What change are the speakers discussing?
    (A) Relocating to another site
    (B) Purchasing some machinery
    (C) Extending the hours of operation
    (D) Raising salaries for employees

55. What does the woman offer to do?
    (A) Set up some sale items
    (B) Contact a specialist
    (C) Review some financial data
    (D) Gather feedback from the staff

56. What problem is the man calling about?
(A) He has forgotten a password.
(B) He provided some incorrect information.
(C) He lost his most recent bill.
(D) He has been overcharged.

57. Where does the woman work?
(A) At a shipping service
(B) At a moving company
(C) At an Internet provider
(D) At an accounting firm

58. What did the man do last month?
(A) He moved to a new address.
(B) He upgraded a service package.
(C) He launched his own business.
(D) He visited the woman's company.

59. What are the speakers discussing?
(A) A job opening
(B) A product release
(C) A company relocation
(D) An annual event

60. What department does the woman most likely work in?
(A) Finance
(B) Marketing
(C) Information technology
(D) Operations management

61. Why does the woman say, "The project manager has already moved up our deadline"?
(A) To demonstrate urgency
(B) To show appreciation
(C) To propose a compromise
(D) To express confusion

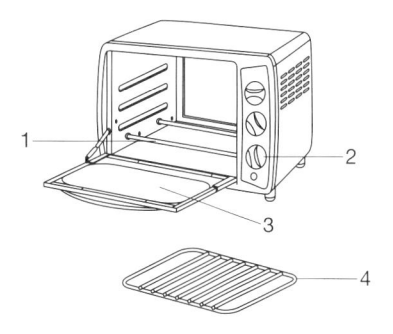

62. Where does the man work?
(A) At a research institute
(B) At a restaurant
(C) At a department store
(D) At a law firm

63. Look at the graphic. Which part has been damaged?
(A) Part 1
(B) Part 2
(C) Part 3
(D) Part 4

64. What will the woman probably do next?
(A) Look for a product manual
(B) Order replacement parts
(C) Send a list of locations
(D) Check an item's availability

New Arrivals!	
Circles: code G33	**Stripe:** code H18
Colors: blue, green	Colors: brown, blue
Waves: code N29	**Stars:** code P77
Colors: blue, gray	Colors: red, gray

Performance Schedule	
7:00 P.M.	Tango Treats
7:30 P.M.	Marlana Music
8:00 P.M.	BC Dance Troupe
8:30 P.M.	The Chapmans

65. What will Tahoka Manufacturing change?

(A) A shipping schedule
(B) A warranty period
(C) An office location
(D) A storage fee

66. What does the woman like about Tahoka Manufacturing?

(A) The speed of deliveries
(B) The wide selection of patterns
(C) The friendliness of the staff
(D) The quality of its materials

67. Look at the graphic. Which design do the speakers agree to order?

(A) G33
(B) H18
(C) N29
(D) P77

68. Why does the man want to have a party?

(A) A team has completed a project.
(B) A colleague received a promotion.
(C) A company was nominated for an award.
(D) A sales goal was exceeded.

69. Look at the graphic. Which group is Libby a member of?

(A) Tango Treats
(B) Marlana Music
(C) BC Dance Troupe
(D) The Chapmans

70. What problem does the man mention?

(A) A venue is in a remote area.
(B) A transportation service is unavailable.
(C) The price of admission is high.
(D) Some team members will be absent.

PART 4

Directions: You will hear some talks given by a single speaker. You will be asked to answer three questions about what the speaker says in each talk. Select the best response to each question and mark the letter (A), (B), (C), or (D) on your answer sheet. The talks will not be printed in your test book and will be spoken only one time.

71. What type of business is being advertised?
(A) A catering service
(B) An event space
(C) A rental home
(D) A movie theater

72. What does the speaker say the business is most known for?
(A) Its talented staff
(B) Its convenient location
(C) Its lengthy history
(D) Its original architecture

73. What can listeners do on a website?
(A) Look at pictures
(B) Read reviews
(C) Find a discount code
(D) Make a booking

74. What is the podcast episode about?
(A) Online advertising
(B) Computer programming
(C) Starting a business
(D) Expanding overseas

75. What does the speaker say Ms. Dambe is good at?
(A) Solving technical glitches
(B) Getting funding
(C) Understanding customers
(D) Negotiating with suppliers

76. What will the speaker discuss next?
(A) A subscription service
(B) A research project
(C) A listener question
(D) A news report

77. What will happen next Monday?
(A) A presentation will be delivered.
(B) A product will be purchased.
(C) A new location will be opened.
(D) An office space will be redesigned.

78. What inspired the speaker?
(A) An advertisement
(B) A famous book
(C) An employee suggestion
(D) A media report

79. How can listeners learn about the benefits of the new lights?
(A) By reading an email
(B) By visiting a website
(C) By looking at a handout
(D) By watching a video

80. What type of business is the listener calling?
(A) A cable provider
(B) A consulting company
(C) A utility company
(D) An automobile manufacturer

81. What does the speaker imply when she says, "We thank you for your patience"?
(A) The responders are untrained.
(B) The company is closing soon.
(C) Many people are complaining.
(D) The repairs are not yet complete.

82. How can the listener stay updated?
(A) By getting automated e-mails
(B) By calling again later
(C) By receiving text messages
(D) By checking a website

83. Why have some citizens complained?

(A) Street parking is unavailable.
(B) The roads are damaged.
(C) Street cleaning is too infrequent.
(D) Parking garages are too expensive.

84. What is John Daly concerned about?

(A) Higher taxes
(B) Environmental damage
(C) Increased traffic
(D) Construction noise

85. What will certain residents receive?

(A) Parking passes
(B) Hotel room fees
(C) Event tickets
(D) Transportation services

86. What is the topic of the seminar?

(A) Manufacturing
(B) Shipping
(C) Publishing
(D) Journalism

87. Why does the speaker thank some of the listeners?

(A) They raised questions.
(B) They shared their experience.
(C) They attended previous talks.
(D) They gave feedback on the slides.

88. Why does the speaker mention the back of the room?

(A) Refreshments are available there.
(B) A worker is sitting there.
(C) Informational materials are there.
(D) A book is on sale there.

89. Why is Matteo away from his business?

(A) He is meeting a supplier.
(B) He is delivering a lecture.
(C) He is at a job interview.
(D) He is viewing real estate.

90. Why does the speaker say, "Fettuccini alfredo has always been a hit with our regulars"?

(A) To make a suggestion
(B) To provide a compliment
(C) To demonstrate a problem
(D) To congratulate an achievement

91. What good news does the speaker share about the restaurant?

(A) It won an annual award.
(B) It had an influx of customers.
(C) It received attention online.
(D) It appeared in a television show.

92. What type of business does the speaker most likely work at?

(A) A hardware store
(B) A construction company
(C) A furniture store
(D) A delivery service

93. What does the speaker imply when he says, "I have experience in sales"?

(A) He will mentor some employees.
(B) He will take over for some shifts.
(C) He will interview candidates soon.
(D) He will offer extra pay for overtime work.

94. What does the speaker expect the listeners to do?

(A) Reorganize the store layout
(B) Clean an area
(C) Organize a luncheon
(D) Plan a hiring event

	Innersville Bus Station
Terminal A	Fulton Bus Lines
Terminal B	Kiwi Bird Bus Travel
Terminal C	Speedy Friends Buses
Terminal D	Clockwork Bus Company

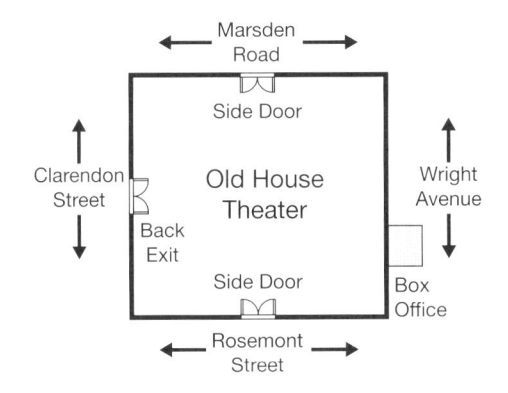

95. Who most likely is the speaker?

(A) A bus operator
(B) A tour guide
(C) A rideshare driver
(D) A train conductor

96. Look at the graphic. Where does the speaker want to meet?

(A) On Clarendon Street
(B) On Wright Avenue
(C) On Rosemont Street
(D) On Marsden Road

97. How can the listener confirm the change?

(A) By calling the company
(B) By sending a message
(C) By using an app
(D) By standing outside

98. Who is the audience for the talk?

(A) Travel agents
(B) Employees
(C) Town residents
(D) Investors

99. According to the speaker, why was the facility needed?

(A) The government wants to reduce car traffic.
(B) The old bus station was in bad condition.
(C) The town lacks public transportation options.
(D) The local airport recently closed.

100. Look at the graphic. Which terminal will have the first departure?

(A) Terminal A
(B) Terminal B
(C) Terminal C
(D) Terminal D

READING TEST

In the Reading test, you will read a variety of texts and answer several different types of reading comprehension questions. The entire Reading test will last 75 minutes. There are three parts, and directions are given for each part. You are encouraged to answer as many questions as possible within the time allowed.

You must mark your answers on the separate answer sheet. Do not write your answers in your test book.

PART 5

Directions: A word or phrase is missing in each of the sentences below. Four answer choices are given below each sentence. Select the best answer to complete the sentence. Then mark the letter (A), (B), (C), or (D) on your answer sheet.

101. The consulting firm intends to hold a training ------- for its newest employees next week.

(A) session
(B) method
(C) approach
(D) way

102. The order coming from Europe is ------- going to arrive no later than tomorrow evening.

(A) fairly
(B) severely
(C) accurately
(D) supposedly

103. Ms. Patterson ------- her desire to attend the marketing seminar in Dallas to her supervisor.

(A) asked
(B) submitted
(C) expressed
(D) alerted

104. Sylvester Deli's selection of meats is ------- than all other stores in the city.

(A) greatly
(B) greater
(C) greatest
(D) great

105. We regret to announce Mr. Carpenter's ------- from his position in the R&D Department.

(A) resign
(B) to resign
(C) resignation
(D) will resign

106. Nearly ------- individual at the logistics conference is directly involved in the industry.

(A) almost
(B) all
(C) those
(D) every

107. All transactions with clients are ------- both on paper and electronically.

(A) record
(B) recorded
(C) recording
(D) records

108. Mr. Anderson scheduled a staff meeting for the ------- of discussing this month's budget.

(A) purpose
(B) view
(C) opinion
(D) appointment

109. As soon as the seminar attendees arrive, ------- will be divided into groups for a role-playing activity.
(A) they
(B) them
(C) their
(D) themselves

110. A government inspection must be conducted ------- new regulations have just been enacted.
(A) however
(B) in spite of
(C) because
(D) as soon as

111. The new law resulted in increased ------- in the financial industry by foreigners.
(A) supply
(B) method
(C) possession
(D) investment

112. It is well known that Mr. Jackson, one of the new managers, ------- to work evening shifts at the restaurant.
(A) prefer
(B) prefers
(C) is preferred
(D) is being preferred

113. Ms. Chamberlain will be absent ------- roughly one week while she travels to Madrid on business.
(A) within
(B) on
(C) during
(D) for

114. The engineer must determine the precise ------- of the crack in the pipe.
(A) location
(B) locate
(C) locating
(D) located

115. Ms. Lopez described the new product ------- when asked about it by the board of directors.
(A) tremendously
(B) certainly
(C) thoughtfully
(D) ultimately

116. Those part-timers ------- work contracts expire next month should speak with Ms. Matisse by this Thursday.
(A) which
(B) whose
(C) when
(D) that

117. Executives who transfer to foreign branches receive higher salaries ------- are responsible for their own housing.
(A) but
(B) since
(C) as well
(D) in order to

118. Each bolt must be attached ------- to ensure that the shelf stays together.
(A) tights
(B) tightness
(C) tightly
(D) tighten

119. The cargo cannot be unloaded from the ship ------- permission from local authorities.
(A) without
(B) between
(C) instead of
(D) except

120. Since no funding is currently available, the bridge is only ------- constructed.
(A) partial
(B) partially
(C) partials
(D) partialness

121. ------- the latest information from the sales team, the new cosmetics line is selling better than anticipated.

(A) Because
(B) Consequently
(C) In spite of
(D) According to

122. Domestic ------- in the computer industry has been increasing over the past four months.

(A) employable
(B) employment
(C) employee
(D) employer

123. After considering the formal request, management ------- agreed to provide its employees with extra paid vacation days.

(A) eventual
(B) eventuality
(C) eventually
(D) event

124. Industry experts believe exports ------- in the coming months due to issues with the supply chain.

(A) decline
(B) declined
(C) will decline
(D) have been declining

125. Local farmers reported ------- high crop yields despite the relatively cool summer weather.

(A) surprisingly
(B) imperatively
(C) annually
(D) gradually

126. Despite market research indicating that customers were ------- about the item, Gladden Technology ceased production.

(A) impressed
(B) fantastic
(C) determined
(D) enthusiastic

127. Skylar Electronics plans to manufacture more computers locally yet ------- them to countries in Europe.

(A) distribute
(B) distributing
(C) distributes
(D) distributed

128. Concert attendees were ------- with the performances of both bands.

(A) maintained
(B) expected
(C) admired
(D) satisfied

129. To organize the maintenance request forms, Mr. Gibson created a ------- folder for storing the documents.

(A) designate
(B) designated
(C) designating
(D) designates

130. When Ms. Sulla received her monthly electric bill, she ------- her power usage had declined from the previous month.

(A) noticed
(B) glanced
(C) appeared
(D) repeated

PART 6

Directions: Read the texts that follow. A word, phrase, or sentence is missing in parts of each text. Four answer choices for each question are given below the text. Select the best answer to complete the text. Then mark the letter (A), (B), (C), or (D) on your answer sheet.

Questions 131-134 refer to the following notice.

To All Customers,

We regret ------- you that the Kensington branch of Marigold Bakery will be closed as of March 31. We will no longer be able to provide pastries, cakes, and ------- items to our customers there. The building in which the bakery is located is being renovated, so we have no choice in this matter.

-------. They are in Mayfield, Westside, and Haywood. You can also order online and have your items delivered for free. Thank you again for your ------- support during the past seventeen years.

131. (A) inform
(B) will inform
(C) have informed
(D) to inform

132. (A) all
(B) other
(C) another
(D) every

133. (A) Please be aware that we have three other locations nearby.
(B) We have decided to expand the store to let more customers dine in.
(C) The cost of doing business in Kensington has increased greatly.
(D) It is no longer possible to remain in the food-supply business.

134. (A) continue
(B) continues
(C) continual
(D) continually

Questions 135-138 refer to the following memo.

To: All Employees

From: Eric Horner

Date: February 11

Subject: Gym Membership

I am pleased to announce that management has agreed to sponsor gym memberships for full-time employees. This perk ------- by a number of you in the January employee satisfaction survey. Starting on March 1, employees can receive a voucher for a free membership at Westfield Gym. Please request one only if you ------- to work out regularly. The voucher is good for a half-year membership. When the ------- ends, you can ask for an additional one. It does not include working out with a personal trainer. -------.

135. (A) is requested
(B) requested
(C) was requested
(D) has been requested

136. (A) anticipate
(B) appear
(C) intend
(D) approve

137. (A) period
(B) coupon
(C) training
(D) tour

138. (A) We hope you all use the facilities here.
(B) Thank you for your support.
(C) A voucher has been sent to each of you.
(D) You must pay for that yourself.

Questions 139-142 refer to the following notice.

It is time once again to submit nominations for end-of-the-year awards. This year, two awards ------- (139).

The first is the employee of the year. The second is the newcomer of the year. All nominations must be received by Maryanne Carter by November 30. Please include a brief statement explaining ------- (140) the person you nominate should receive the award.

The winners will be announced at our annual get-together on December 29. ------- (141). Each winner will receive a cash ------- (142) and several other prizes.

139. (A) were presented
 (B) are presenting
 (C) present
 (D) will be presented

140. (A) why
 (B) how
 (C) where
 (D) when

141. (A) Mr. Anderson, our CEO, hosted the ceremony.
 (B) We had nearly perfect attendance at last year's party.
 (C) This year's event will be at the Hillsdale Restaurant.
 (D) Invitations will be sent to all of the winners.

142. (A) salary
 (B) trophy
 (C) medal
 (D) reward

Questions 143-146 refer to the following information.

Thank you for purchasing an appliance from Madison Electronics. We take ------- in the quality
143.
of our products. Should you experience any problems with your appliance, please contact us
at 1-888-555-8473. Our toll-free hotline is open twenty-four hours a day. Our customer service
representatives ------- to assist you anytime.
144.

Your appliance comes with a full two-year warranty. However, if an unauthorized person services
the item, the warranty will ------- be in effect.
145.

For more information, visit our website at www.madisonelectronics.com. -------.
146.

143. (A) proud
(B) proudness
(C) prided
(D) pride

144. (A) have stood by
(B) stood by
(C) are standing by
(D) will stand by

145. (A) never
(B) such
(C) no longer
(D) still

146. (A) Refunds must be requested within 10 days of purchase.
(B) You can also e-mail us at info@madisonelectronics.com.
(C) Please be sure to keep your receipt.
(D) You must send the item in its original packaging.

PART 7

Directions: In this part, you will read a selection of texts, such as magazine and newspaper articles, e-mails, and instant messages. Each text or set of texts is followed by several questions. Select the best answer for each question and mark the letter (A), (B), (C), or (D) on your answer sheet.

Questions 147-148 refer to the following notice.

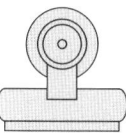

Attention: All City Lifeguards

Your work schedules will be sent to your phones by text message starting on April 30. Schedules will arrive every Sunday night no later than 6:00 P.M. Should you have any scheduling conflicts or issues, please respond to the message within an hour. In case of inclement weather, text messages indicating that pools or beaches are closed may be sent at any time.

Please contact Wendy Sullivan in the City Parks and Recreation office to make sure that your phone number currently on file is accurate.

147. What is one thing that lifeguards will be notified about by text message?
(A) Overtime opportunities
(B) Staff meetings
(C) Schedules
(D) Government inspections

148. Why should lifeguards contact the office?
(A) To request time off work
(B) To confirm certain information
(C) To inquire about weather conditions
(D) To request assistance

Questions 149-150 refer to the following article.

Bradenton Times

October 11—Local businessman Harold Grimes has just announced that he intends to establish another business in Bradenton. Mr. Grimes owns four restaurants in town as well as two supermarkets. His new venture, however, will not be in the food industry. Instead, he is opening a medical clinic. Grimes Medical Care will be located at 67 Easton Drive across from the Bradenton Library. While Mr. Grimes himself has no medical background, he stated that the people of the city are in need of quality, affordable medical care. The clinic will employ five full-time doctors and have state-of-the-art medical equipment.

Mr. Grimes said he expects the clinic to open in November. Interested individuals can call 539-9573 for more information about the specialties of the doctors and making appointments.

149. What is indicated about Mr. Grimes?

(A) He studied medicine at university.
(B) He will replace some doctors at a clinic.
(C) He has several business establishments.
(D) He is involved in local politics.

150. Why is Grimes Medical Care being opened?

(A) To give local residents good health care
(B) To replace a hospital that is closing
(C) To provide specialized surgical options
(D) To fulfill a request from Bradenton residents

Questions 151-154 refer to the following article.

TORONTO (April 23)—In an effort to break into the European market, Canadian electronics manufacturer Galleon, Inc. has signed an agreement with Baldrick to examine the markets in several countries.

Baldrick is a consulting firm headquartered in London, England, and has offices in Madrid, Rome, Paris, and several other major European cities. —[1]—. "We feel like we understand what Europeans want," said CEO Ian Smythe. "We've assisted numerous other North American firms in their efforts to succeed in Europe, and we're positive we can assist Galleon as well."

Baldrick has been in business for more than three decades and is the largest family-owned consulting company in England. —[2]—.

"It's not easy to switch from one market to another," said Mr. Smythe. "For instance, American consumers may expect certain functions from their electronic devices whereas European customers have no interest in those at all. —[3]—. We'll identify how Galleon can adapt its products in order to be successful."

Galleon anticipates receiving a report from Baldrick by December of this year. —[4]—. Once it analyzes the data, it will begin efforts to produce products tailor-made for export next year.

---

151. How is Baldrick helping Galleon, Inc.?

(A) By analyzing production trends
(B) By recruiting new employees
(C) By determining consumer preferences
(D) By improving its computer database

152. What does the article mention about Baldrick?

(A) Its main office is located in Toronto.
(B) It manufactures electric appliances.
(C) It is owned by another company.
(D) It opened over thirty years ago.

153. According to Mr. Smythe, what is different about European and American consumers?

(A) The brand names they buy
(B) The functions they want in devices
(C) The instruction details they need
(D) The prices they want to pay

154. In which of the positions marked [1], [2], [3], and [4] does the following sentence best belong?

"It also has branches in Asia and North America."

(A) [1]
(B) [2]
(C) [3]
(D) [4]

Questions 155-156 refer to the following text-message chain.

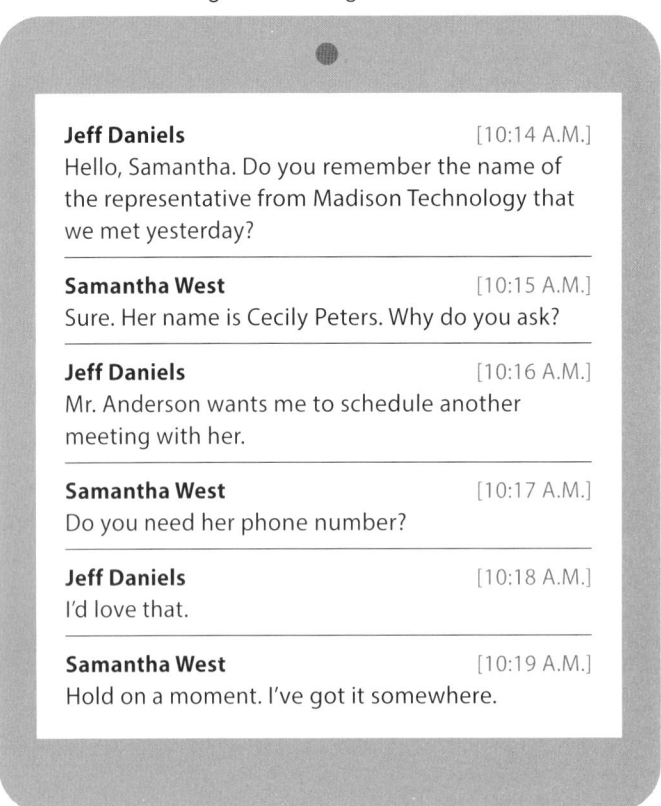

Jeff Daniels [10:14 A.M.]
Hello, Samantha. Do you remember the name of the representative from Madison Technology that we met yesterday?

Samantha West [10:15 A.M.]
Sure. Her name is Cecily Peters. Why do you ask?

Jeff Daniels [10:16 A.M.]
Mr. Anderson wants me to schedule another meeting with her.

Samantha West [10:17 A.M.]
Do you need her phone number?

Jeff Daniels [10:18 A.M.]
I'd love that.

Samantha West [10:19 A.M.]
Hold on a moment. I've got it somewhere.

155. What is suggested about the writers?

(A) They work for Madison Technology.
(B) They have to submit a report to Mr. Anderson.
(C) They attended a meeting together the previous day.
(D) They will give Ms. Peters a product demonstration.

156. At 10:18 A.M., what does Mr. Daniels most likely mean when he writes, "I'd love that"?

(A) He wants a person's contact information.
(B) He is willing to meet Ms. West sometime today.
(C) He is happy Ms. West will schedule a meeting.
(D) He is eager to purchase a new phone.

Questions 157-159 refer to the following advertisement.

Graham's Custom Shoes

Graham's Custom Shoes are the ideal gift for someone special in your life. They are made with soft leather in a variety of colors. The shoes are sized perfectly for each customer's feet. —[1]—. They are guaranteed to last for at least three years. —[2]—. Since the shoes are custom made, customers must either visit the store in person or send precise measurements of their feet to us online. —[3]—. To learn more about the styles available, visit us at 58 Rochester Road or go to www.grahamscustomshoes.com. —[4]—. Try us once, and you'll never purchase shoes from anyone else again.

157. What is indicated about the items in the advertisement?

(A) They are made from the same type of material.
(B) They all have the same price.
(C) They require around two weeks to make.
(D) They can be mailed to international addresses.

158. What does the advertisement recommend that some customers do?

(A) Call for more information
(B) Submit pictures of their preferred style
(C) Ask about the product guarantee
(D) Provide accurate information

159. In which of the positions marked [1], [2], [3], and [4] does the following sentence best belong?

"Be sure to check each foot since individual feet are slightly different in size."

(A) [1]
(B) [2]
(C) [3]
(D) [4]

Questions 160-163 refer to the following letter.

March 11

Patrick Peterson
546 Mercer Avenue
Sacramento, CA 94258

Dear Mr. Peterson,

As a long-time shopper at Daniel's Green Grocer, you must be aware that we sell a variety of domestic and international foods. You should also know that we have a deli and a bakery, where we create many foods.

We would like to receive your input regarding the foods we make. We are therefore extending an opportunity to you to become a food taster.

Simply show up here on your designated weekend. You'll be given samples of between five and ten different foods to try. The foods you'll be sampling will include baked goods, pastries, cheeses, meats, and cooked foods such as lasagna and ziti. Then, you provide your frank opinion of each item by completing a short survey. The entire process should take ten minutes.

To sign up for this opportunity, drop by Daniel's anytime within the next two weeks and speak with Marjorie Benson, the store manager. In return for your assistance, you'll receive a $10 store coupon as well as free samples you can take home.

We hope to receive a positive response soon.

Regards,

Eric Quinn
CEO, Daniel's Green Grocer

160. What is the purpose of the letter?

(A) To announce a special sale
(B) To advertise some new products
(C) To discuss an employment opportunity
(D) To request participation in an activity

161. What is indicated about Daniel's Green Grocer?

(A) It has multiple branches in the city.
(B) It is the city's largest grocery store.
(C) It sells food from other countries.
(D) It will construct a new bakery soon.

162. The word "sampling" in paragraph 3, line 2, is closest in meaning to

(A) tasting
(B) providing
(C) attending
(D) reporting

163. What can Mr. Peterson receive from Daniel's Green Grocer?

(A) An express delivery service
(B) Monthly coupons
(C) Free food
(D) Membership in a shopper's club

Questions 164-165 refer to the following web page.

---

www.axlerentalcar.com

Axle Rental Car Membership

Welcome, Allen Darcy, to Axle Rental Car's members-only club. Your application for membership has been accepted, and you are now eligible for all kinds of special deals.

Your account number is 75234ADP23. You need to use this number every time you make a booking with us and when you pick up or drop off a vehicle. We also recommend downloading our mobile app for your smartphone. That way, you'll always be able to log in to your account no matter where you are.

Every week, we will have special offers only for members of this club. The deals for the week change every Sunday at midnight. You can choose to have them sent to you by e-mail by clicking here. The more you use your membership, the more points you'll accrue. That will enable you to qualify for even more discounts.

---

164. What must Mr. Darcy do when renting a vehicle?

(A) Present his account number
(B) Show a valid driver's license
(C) Pay with a credit card
(D) Prove that he has insurance

165. What is indicated about Axle Rental Car's members-only club?

(A) It lets members rent vehicles for free.
(B) It is open only to long-term customers.
(C) It requires payment of an annual fee.
(D) It offers multiple deals each week.

Questions 166-168 refer to the following article.

Haverford Construction to Build New Apartment Complex

SUDBURY (November 12)—The mayor's office in Sudbury announced last night that it had sold a large plot of land on the outskirts of town to Haverford Construction. The land covers fourteen acres and is located alongside Highway 32 on the eastern side of town near Darlington Mountain. A spokesperson for Haverford said that the company intends to develop the land into an apartment complex containing no fewer than seven buildings. The company expects to release its designs for the new complex sometime early next year. According to a source in the mayor's office, there was only one other bidder for the land. That was a private individual who wanted to use the land for farming. The city, however, is desperate for new housing. With several companies announcing plans to construct facilities near town, the local population is expected to increase greatly soon. Thus, securing more housing is of the utmost importance to the mayor's office.

166. Where is the land that was acquired located?

(A) On Darlington Mountain
(B) Opposite the mayor's office
(C) Near a farm
(D) On the eastern side of Sudbury

167. According to the article, why is there a need for housing in Sudbury?

(A) Many homes in the town are in poor condition.
(B) Some apartment complexes burned down recently.
(C) Housing prices in the local area are rising too fast.
(D) Many people will move there in the near future.

168. The word "securing" in line 12 is closest in meaning to

(A) preserving
(B) obtaining
(C) inspecting
(D) guarding

Questions 169-171 refer to the following information.

E-Z Wash Laundry

E-Z Wash Laundry is proud to announce that it is no longer necessary for customers to carry coins to use our washers and dryers. Instead, customers can purchase cards and top up. Then, these cards can be used to operate the machines.

To use our new system, simply do the following:

1. Go to one of the machines at the back of the store. Select the amount of money you want to top up and then insert the necessary cash.
2. You will then receive a card with credit on it.
3. Put your laundry in a washer or dryer and select the setting you would like.
4. Insert your card in the slot and press the "Use" button. The machine will begin running, and the fee will be deducted from your card.

You can use the machines to receive a refund for any funds on your card that you do not use.

169. What is the purpose of the information?
(A) To apologize for a mistake
(B) To explain the results of a survey
(C) To announce a new service
(D) To promote a branch opening

170. What should a person do after choosing the cycle for their clothing?
(A) Put money in a slot
(B) Insert a card
(C) Speak with an employee
(D) Add laundry detergent

171. What is indicated about the cards?
(A) They can be used only one time.
(B) Users can get their money back from them.
(C) They have an expiration date.
(D) Credit cards can be used to put money on them.

Questions 172-175 refer to the following online chat discussion.

Dieter Kimball [1:12 P.M.] Hi, everyone. I just got back to the office and noticed someone left some folders on my desk. Who was that?

Sally Beecher [1:15 P.M.] George and I did that, Mr. Kimball. We need your approval for some expenditures. As you know, the company picnic is fast approaching, and we were chosen to organize it.

George White [1:16 P.M.] Do you have time to look at everything today? We could be in your office in five minutes.

Dieter Kimball [1:17 P.M.] I'm meeting Sylvester Mann at 1:30.

George White [1:18 P.M.] Do you know how long that's going to take?

Dieter Kimball [1:19 P.M.] It's hard to say. We have a lot to go over. Is there anything I should know about in the folder you gave me?

Sally Beecher [1:20 P.M.] The only issue is that we're going to exceed our budget a bit. More people than usual have committed to attending with their families. So we need to purchase more food and other supplies than normal.

George White [1:21 P.M.] That's our primary concern, but there are a couple of other minor issues we'd like to discuss, too.

Dieter Kimball [1:22 P.M.] Drop by my office at four thirty. We can go over everything then.

172. Who most likely is Mr. Kimball?

(A) A job applicant
(B) A supervisor
(C) An event planner
(D) A client

173. What does Mr. White want to do?

(A) Change the date of an event
(B) Receive extra funding
(C) Meet Mr. Kimball in person
(D) Move a venue to another place

174. At 1:17 P.M., why does Mr. Kimball write, "I'm meeting Sylvester Mann at 1:30"?

(A) To reject a suggestion
(B) To approve a request
(C) To describe his schedule tomorrow
(D) To offer to cancel his plans

175. What is suggested about the company picnic?

(A) It will happen in August.
(B) It is held near the company.
(C) It has taken place before.
(D) Only employees may attend.

Questions 176-180 refer to the following letter and e-mail.

Sunfield Golf Resort
1603 Westway Drive
Mesa, AZ 85209

June 23

Lawrence Mercado
294 Hickory Road
Florence, AZ 85143

Dear Mr. Mercado,

Thank you for registering for Sunfield Golf Resort's annual Sun and Fun Tournament on July 17. Your confirmation number is 0638. Please find enclosed your parking pass and name badge. You must wear the name badge at all times while on the resort's grounds to show that you are participating in the tournament.

You should check in at the reception desk in the clubhouse between 7:00 A.M. and 8:30 A.M., and a photo ID will be required. The tournament consists of four categories with the following start times at the first hole: 9:00 A.M. [Semi-Pro], 10:00 A.M. [Advanced], 11:00 A.M. [Intermediate], and noon [Beginner].

There will be tea, coffee, soda, and bottled water available at the reception desk for free. However, you must show your name badge to be served. Food will be available for purchase in our restaurant.

We look forward to seeing you at Sunfield Golf Resort!

Sincerely,

The Sunfield Golf Resort Event Staff

E-Mail

To: Lawrence Mercado <l.mercado@shermansales.com>
From: Nancy Aldridge <nancy@sunfieldgolf.com>
Date: July 6
Subject: Sun and Fun Tournament

Dear Mr. Mercado,

We are excited to welcome our golfers soon for the Sun and Fun Tournament! Your assigned start time is 10:00 A.M. If you are driving to the tournament, please note that you should park in the lot off Avis Street. The one connected to Mooney Street is temporarily closed to make space for the crews working on the expansion of our indoor driving range. To download a map of our site, please click here.

Warmest regards,

Nancy Aldridge

176. What is the purpose of the letter?

   (A) To apologize for an error
   (B) To confirm registration
   (C) To recommend a service
   (D) To request funds

177. What will Mr. Mercado be asked to do on July 17 when he arrives?

   (A) Show a form of identification
   (B) Sign an official document
   (C) Choose some group members
   (D) Inspect his equipment

178. What is suggested about the reception desk?

   (A) Its beverages are for participants only.
   (B) It will collect donations for charity.
   (C) Its employees can provide parking passes.
   (D) It opens daily at 7:00 A.M.

179. What is most likely true about Sunfield Golf Resort?

   (A) It has recently changed ownership.
   (B) It is holding a competition for the first time.
   (C) It provides discounts on events to its members.
   (D) It has a building currently under construction.

180. What most likely is Mr. Mercado's skill level in golf?

   (A) Beginner
   (B) Intermediate
   (C) Advanced
   (D) Semi-pro

Questions 181-185 refer to the following web pages.

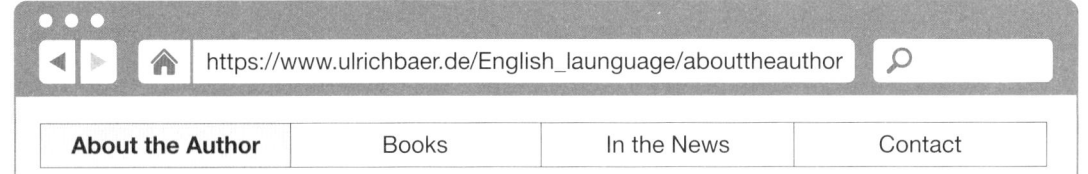

https://www.ulrichbaer.de/English_launguage/abouttheauthor

| **About the Author** | Books | In the News | Contact |

Ulrich Baer was born in Leipzig, Germany, to Sebastian and Ines Baer. His father was in the military, so throughout his childhood he lived in many different parts of the world, moving every couple of years. While at university, one of his friends was planning a trip to Argentina. Mr. Baer had lived there, so he made notes for his friend. They were so useful that he figured he could turn them into a travel guide.

Since that time, Mr. Baer has written eight travel guides for various countries/regions. He also published a collection of historical photos entitled *Through the Lens*, which was highly praised by critics.

Mr. Baer will release his newest travel guide, *Footprints in Asia*, on May 10. It will contain some photos from *Through the Lens* so readers can see how areas have changed. The book will contain maps along with tips about the best times to visit tourist attractions and where to shop for unique souvenirs. It will also feature fifty restaurant reviews for those wanting to try the local cuisine.

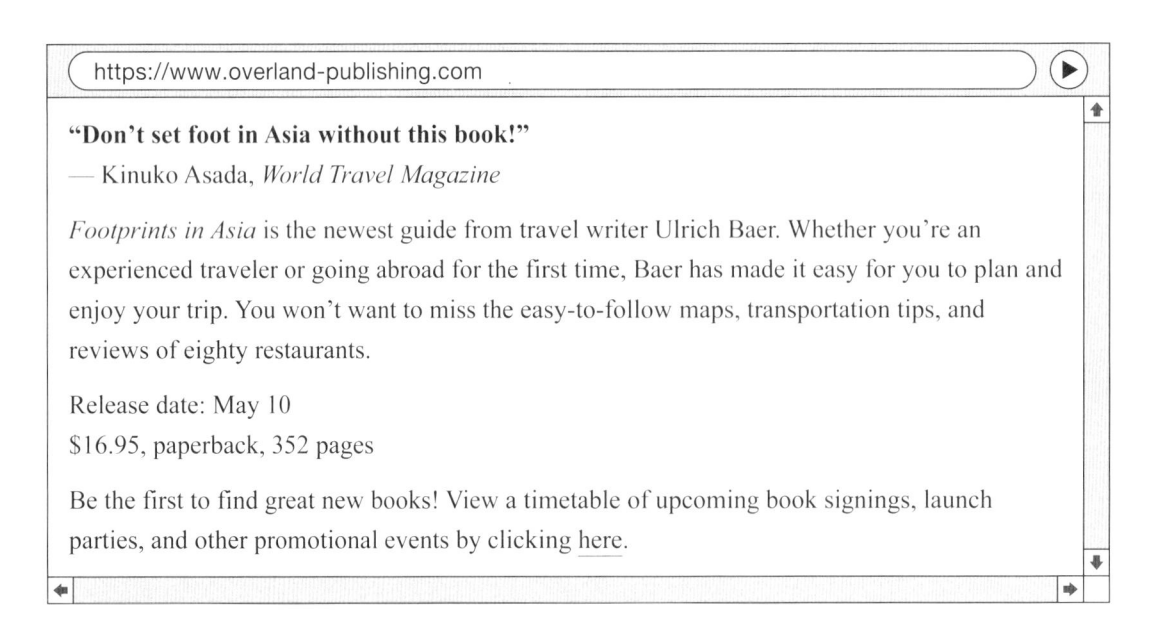

---

https://www.overland-publishing.com

"Don't set foot in Asia without this book!"
— Kinuko Asada, *World Travel Magazine*

Footprints in Asia is the newest guide from travel writer Ulrich Baer. Whether you're an experienced traveler or going abroad for the first time, Baer has made it easy for you to plan and enjoy your trip. You won't want to miss the easy-to-follow maps, transportation tips, and reviews of eighty restaurants.

Release date: May 10
$16.95, paperback, 352 pages

Be the first to find great new books! View a timetable of upcoming book signings, launch parties, and other promotional events by clicking here.

181. What is true about Mr. Baer?

(A) He moved around a lot when he was young.
(B) He attended a university in Argentina.
(C) He followed the same job as his father.
(D) He wrote fiction in his early career.

182. What is suggested about Mr. Baer's new travel guide?

(A) It received mixed reviews from critics.
(B) It includes historical photos.
(C) It comes with a free souvenir.
(D) It was published in German and English.

183. On the first web page, the word "figured" in paragraph 1, line 5, is closest in meaning to

(A) appeared
(B) performed
(C) contributed
(D) decided

184. What is true about Overland Publishing?

(A) It is accepting work from new writers.
(B) It has an event schedule online.
(C) It is headquartered in Leipzig.
(D) It publishes *World Travel Magazine*.

185. How did Mr. Baer's latest travel guide change?

(A) It received a new title.
(B) Its publishing date was postponed.
(C) Some maps were featured in it.
(D) More restaurant reviews were added.

Questions 186-190 refer to the following report, e-mail, and invoice.

Brandywine Finance

Report on Staff Survey Results

Issues in the Workplace

Employees had the following major workplace concerns as described in September's survey:

1. They have little privacy in open-space office areas. (62% of respondents)
2. The employee lounge is insufficient in size and lacks enough seating capacity. (57% of respondents)
3. Computers are old and break down frequently, thereby causing employees to be less productive at times. (49% of respondents)
4. Employee IDs sometimes fail to work, leaving employees locked out of buildings or individual rooms. (27% of respondents)
5. There are not enough recycling bins, so employees must often dispose of recyclable items in trash cans. (15% of respondents)

Employees also complained about high noise levels due to employees talking or listening to music (7%), insufficient break periods (5%), and a drab office interior (3%).

From: jchandler@brandywinefinance.com
To: jasminehoward@brandywinefinance.com
Subject: Report on Staff Survey Results
Date: October 11

Dear Ms. Howard,

Thank you for providing the data in the report on the recent staff survey. I spoke with Luis Guarino in the IT Department, and he assured me he would do his best to maintain the computers better in the future. He emphasized that many machines should be replaced, however. Do we have enough funding for that? Perhaps by replacing a few each month, we can minimize the stress on the budget. What are your thoughts on this matter?

Regarding the fourth concern listed, I recall we had similar problems last year. I was under the impression that this problem had been solved, but I was apparently wrong.

We need to have a meeting about this soon. When are you available?

Sincerely,

Jennifer Chandler

Aaron's Supplies

Customer: Brandywine Finance
Date: October 17

Item Description	Quantity	Unit Price	Total
Comfortable Chair, Black	8	$95.00	$760.00
		Tax	$45.60
		Total	$805.60

Thank you for ordering from us. Your order will be delivered within two business days. If you have any questions, please call us at 1-888-555-9375.

---

186. What does the report suggest about Brandywine Finance?

(A) It occupies at least two different buildings.
(B) Protecting the environment is a major concern there.
(C) Staff members can park in its employee parking lot.
(D) Many of its employees do not have their own offices.

187. What percentage of respondents were unhappy about loud noises?

(A) 62%
(B) 27%
(C) 15%
(D) 7%

188. What does Ms. Chandler ask Ms. Howard about?

(A) How much money remains in this year's budget
(B) Who she should send the report to
(C) When she has time to discuss some issues
(D) Why problems are not being solved

189. According to Ms. Chandler, what problem happened last year?

(A) ID cards did not work on occasion.
(B) Employee computers broke down.
(C) There was not enough privacy for workers.
(D) Employees worked overtime too much.

190. What concern mentioned in the report most likely resulted in Brandywine Finance's purchase from Aaron's Supplies?

(A) Concern 1
(B) Concern 2
(C) Concern 3
(D) Concern 5

Questions 191-195 refer to the following brochure and e-mails.

The Rosemont Amusement Park provides fun and entertainment for children and adults. Located in the city of Oxford, the park has more than twenty rides, arcades and entertainment areas, a zoo, eating facilities, and souvenir shops.

We have special programs for all visitors to attend.

June 19—Horses and ponies from Jasper Farm will be at the zoo for visitors to pet and ride on. Members pay $3. Nonmembers pay $5.

June 26—Come see the elephant show. There will be three shows throughout the day. See what the elephants can do. After the show, come down to the stage and feed the elephants. Members pay $10. Nonmembers pay $20.

Reserve tickets for each event online at our website. You can also sign up to become a member of the Rosemont Amusement Park. Membership provides many benefits, including discounts on entrance tickets, food, and souvenirs as well as access to special events. Visit www.rosemontap.com/membership to learn more.

E-Mail

To: rcraig@gladden.com
From: membership@rosemontap.com
Subject: Welcome
Date: June 14

Dear Mr. Craig,

Thank you for becoming a member of the Rosemont Amusement Park. You selected a family membership, so you, your wife, son, and daughter will gain the advantages of membership. Each of you will receive a membership card in the mail within the next three days. You must use it when applying for a discount at the park, or you'll have to pay full price.

The first time you visit the amusement park, stop by the information center to pick up a special gift for you and your family.

Regards,

Tina Southern
Rosemont Amusement Park

TO:	Tina Southern <tina_s@rosemontap.com>
FROM:	Robert Craig <rcraig@gladden.com>
SUBJECT:	Request
DATE:	July 5

Dear Ms. Southern,

When my family and I recently visited your park as members, imagine our surprise when we were informed that my wife, whose card was at home, had to pay the nonmember price to see the elephant show. I paid the extra cost, but I would appreciate a refund. I can pick up the payment the next time I visit the park.

By the way, thank you for the picnic basket we were given. It was a thoughtful gift.

Regards,

Robert Craig

---

191. What is indicated about the Rosemont Amusement Park?

(A) It charges extra for special programs.
(B) It gives discounts to first-time visitors.
(C) It has plans to build a zoo soon.
(D) It has rides that are mostly for children.

192. What is NOT a benefit of becoming a member at the Rosemont Amusement Park?

(A) A lower price on admission
(B) Access to special events
(C) Discounts on food items
(D) An invitation to a year-end celebration

193. What is true according to the first e-mail?

(A) The price of membership recently increased.
(B) The information center has been closed for repairs.
(C) Membership cards can be picked up at the park.
(D) Everyone in the Craig family is a new member.

194. Why will Mr. Craig's request most likely be rejected?

(A) The application date has already passed.
(B) The park refuses to give any refunds.
(C) A membership card was not presented.
(D) Adults are not eligible for lower prices.

195. What can be inferred about the Craig family?

(A) They reserved tickets for the elephant show online.
(B) They rode on several rides at the amusement park.
(C) They visited the information center on June 26.
(D) They had dinner at the amusement park.

Questions 196-200 refer to the following website and e-mails.

http://www.blackforestpark.gov

Black Forest State Park is the biggest local park, yet it gets the fewest visitors in the state. To help potential tourists explore the park, we have created a virtual guide. It allows visitors to see the best spots in the park and find out what they can do there. The guide also provides links to local campgrounds, hotels, and restaurants.

To use the virtual guide, first, register on our website here. Then, you will have total access to the guide. You will be able to make bookings not only at places inside the park but also at those surrounding it.

Check out the guide when you have time, and let us know what you think. We'll be adding the ability to comment soon, so visitors can see what others think.

Contact us at information@blackforestpark.gov with your questions or comments.

E-Mail

To: information@blackforestpark.gov
From: lkeller@miltonhikingclub.org
Subject: Hiking Trail
Date: March 28

To Whom It May Concern,

I am impressed with your virtual guide. I have been to the park on numerous occasions, and I was unaware of several places, particularly dining establishments. I will check them out in the future.

I am curious about one thing. I could not locate the hiking trail around Swan Lake. Has the trail been closed due to the inclement winter weather? I'm planning to visit the park on April 4, and that trail is at the top of my list. Please let me know because our group includes twenty-seven people and may need to make some changes.

Sincerely,

Lisa Keller
President, Milton Hiking Club

To:	lkeller@miltonhikingclub.org
From:	information@blackforestpark.gov
Subject:	Re: Hiking Trail
Date:	March 29

Dear Ms. Keller,

Thank you for bringing that oversight to our attention. The necessary information will be added to the guide at once. If you find anything else wrong, please contact me at fchapman@blackforestpark.gov. I'll handle any other issues immediately.

Be advised that there is a new admission fee for groups. The following rates now apply:

Group Size	Fee
10 — 15	$20
16 — 25	$30
26 — 40	$50
41 or more	$70

I hope you have a wonderful time at the park.

Regards,

Fred Chapman
Park Ranger

196. According to the website, what is true about Black Forest State Park?

(A) All visitors must complete a form.
(B) Not many people go there.
(C) Park rangers provide tours there.
(D) It is the largest park in the country.

197. What are users of the virtual guide requested to do?

(A) Upload pictures
(B) Send a link to others
(C) Provide feedback
(D) Buy a membership

198. What is suggested about Ms. Keller?

(A) She has volunteered at the park before.
(B) She signed up on the park's website.
(C) She recently started a hiking club.
(D) She visits the park on a weekly basis.

199. What is one purpose of the second e-mail?

(A) To confirm a booking
(B) To acknowledge a mistake
(C) To request contact information
(D) To propose a new attraction

200. How much will Ms. Keller's group most likely pay when they visit the park?

(A) $20
(B) $30
(C) $50
(D) $70

ANSWER SHEET

測驗日期	20 . .
姓名	
答對題數	/200

TOEIC 實戰模擬試題

LISTENING (Part I ~ IV)

READING (Part V ~ VII)

ANSWER SHEET

TOEIC 實戰模擬試題

測驗日期 20 . .
姓名
答對題數 /200

LISTENING (Part I ~ IV)

READING (Part V ~ VII)

ANSWER SHEET

TOEIC 實戰模擬試題

測驗日期	20 . .
姓名	
答對題數	/200

LISTENING (Part I ~ IV)

#		#		#		#		#	
1	ⓐⓑⓒⓓ	21	ⓐⓑⓒ	41	ⓐⓑⓒⓓ	61	ⓐⓑⓒⓓ	81	ⓐⓑⓒⓓ
2	ⓐⓑⓒⓓ	22	ⓐⓑⓒ	42	ⓐⓑⓒⓓ	62	ⓐⓑⓒⓓ	82	ⓐⓑⓒⓓ
3	ⓐⓑⓒⓓ	23	ⓐⓑⓒ	43	ⓐⓑⓒⓓ	63	ⓐⓑⓒⓓ	83	ⓐⓑⓒⓓ
4	ⓐⓑⓒⓓ	24	ⓐⓑⓒ	44	ⓐⓑⓒⓓ	64	ⓐⓑⓒⓓ	84	ⓐⓑⓒⓓ
5	ⓐⓑⓒⓓ	25	ⓐⓑⓒ	45	ⓐⓑⓒⓓ	65	ⓐⓑⓒⓓ	85	ⓐⓑⓒⓓ
6	ⓐⓑⓒⓓ	26	ⓐⓑⓒ	46	ⓐⓑⓒⓓ	66	ⓐⓑⓒⓓ	86	ⓐⓑⓒⓓ
7	ⓐⓑⓒⓓ	27	ⓐⓑⓒ	47	ⓐⓑⓒⓓ	67	ⓐⓑⓒⓓ	87	ⓐⓑⓒⓓ
8	ⓐⓑⓒ	28	ⓐⓑⓒ	48	ⓐⓑⓒⓓ	68	ⓐⓑⓒⓓ	88	ⓐⓑⓒⓓ
9	ⓐⓑⓒ	29	ⓐⓑⓒ	49	ⓐⓑⓒⓓ	69	ⓐⓑⓒⓓ	89	ⓐⓑⓒⓓ
10	ⓐⓑⓒ	30	ⓐⓑⓒ	50	ⓐⓑⓒⓓ	70	ⓐⓑⓒⓓ	90	ⓐⓑⓒⓓ
11	ⓐⓑⓒ	31	ⓐⓑⓒ	51	ⓐⓑⓒⓓ	71	ⓐⓑⓒⓓ	91	ⓐⓑⓒⓓ
12	ⓐⓑⓒ	32	ⓐⓑⓒ	52	ⓐⓑⓒⓓ	72	ⓐⓑⓒⓓ	92	ⓐⓑⓒⓓ
13	ⓐⓑⓒ	33	ⓐⓑⓒ	53	ⓐⓑⓒⓓ	73	ⓐⓑⓒⓓ	93	ⓐⓑⓒⓓ
14	ⓐⓑⓒ	34	ⓐⓑⓒ	54	ⓐⓑⓒⓓ	74	ⓐⓑⓒⓓ	94	ⓐⓑⓒⓓ
15	ⓐⓑⓒ	35	ⓐⓑⓒ	55	ⓐⓑⓒⓓ	75	ⓐⓑⓒⓓ	95	ⓐⓑⓒⓓ
16	ⓐⓑⓒ	36	ⓐⓑⓒ	56	ⓐⓑⓒⓓ	76	ⓐⓑⓒⓓ	96	ⓐⓑⓒⓓ
17	ⓐⓑⓒ	37	ⓐⓑⓒ	57	ⓐⓑⓒⓓ	77	ⓐⓑⓒⓓ	97	ⓐⓑⓒⓓ
18	ⓐⓑⓒ	38	ⓐⓑⓒ	58	ⓐⓑⓒⓓ	78	ⓐⓑⓒⓓ	98	ⓐⓑⓒⓓ
19	ⓐⓑⓒ	39	ⓐⓑⓒ	59	ⓐⓑⓒⓓ	79	ⓐⓑⓒⓓ	99	ⓐⓑⓒⓓ
20	ⓐⓑⓒ	40	ⓐⓑⓒ	60	ⓐⓑⓒⓓ	80	ⓐⓑⓒⓓ	100	ⓐⓑⓒⓓ

READING (Part V ~ VII)

#		#		#		#		#	
101	ⓐⓑⓒⓓ	121	ⓐⓑⓒⓓ	141	ⓐⓑⓒⓓ	161	ⓐⓑⓒⓓ	181	ⓐⓑⓒⓓ
102	ⓐⓑⓒⓓ	122	ⓐⓑⓒⓓ	142	ⓐⓑⓒⓓ	162	ⓐⓑⓒⓓ	182	ⓐⓑⓒⓓ
103	ⓐⓑⓒⓓ	123	ⓐⓑⓒⓓ	143	ⓐⓑⓒⓓ	163	ⓐⓑⓒⓓ	183	ⓐⓑⓒⓓ
104	ⓐⓑⓒⓓ	124	ⓐⓑⓒⓓ	144	ⓐⓑⓒⓓ	164	ⓐⓑⓒⓓ	184	ⓐⓑⓒⓓ
105	ⓐⓑⓒⓓ	125	ⓐⓑⓒⓓ	145	ⓐⓑⓒⓓ	165	ⓐⓑⓒⓓ	185	ⓐⓑⓒⓓ
106	ⓐⓑⓒⓓ	126	ⓐⓑⓒⓓ	146	ⓐⓑⓒⓓ	166	ⓐⓑⓒⓓ	186	ⓐⓑⓒⓓ
107	ⓐⓑⓒⓓ	127	ⓐⓑⓒⓓ	147	ⓐⓑⓒⓓ	167	ⓐⓑⓒⓓ	187	ⓐⓑⓒⓓ
108	ⓐⓑⓒⓓ	128	ⓐⓑⓒⓓ	148	ⓐⓑⓒⓓ	168	ⓐⓑⓒⓓ	188	ⓐⓑⓒⓓ
109	ⓐⓑⓒⓓ	129	ⓐⓑⓒⓓ	149	ⓐⓑⓒⓓ	169	ⓐⓑⓒⓓ	189	ⓐⓑⓒⓓ
110	ⓐⓑⓒⓓ	130	ⓐⓑⓒⓓ	150	ⓐⓑⓒⓓ	170	ⓐⓑⓒⓓ	190	ⓐⓑⓒⓓ
111	ⓐⓑⓒⓓ	131	ⓐⓑⓒⓓ	151	ⓐⓑⓒⓓ	171	ⓐⓑⓒⓓ	191	ⓐⓑⓒⓓ
112	ⓐⓑⓒⓓ	132	ⓐⓑⓒⓓ	152	ⓐⓑⓒⓓ	172	ⓐⓑⓒⓓ	192	ⓐⓑⓒⓓ
113	ⓐⓑⓒⓓ	133	ⓐⓑⓒⓓ	153	ⓐⓑⓒⓓ	173	ⓐⓑⓒⓓ	193	ⓐⓑⓒⓓ
114	ⓐⓑⓒⓓ	134	ⓐⓑⓒⓓ	154	ⓐⓑⓒⓓ	174	ⓐⓑⓒⓓ	194	ⓐⓑⓒⓓ
115	ⓐⓑⓒⓓ	135	ⓐⓑⓒⓓ	155	ⓐⓑⓒⓓ	175	ⓐⓑⓒⓓ	195	ⓐⓑⓒⓓ
116	ⓐⓑⓒⓓ	136	ⓐⓑⓒⓓ	156	ⓐⓑⓒⓓ	176	ⓐⓑⓒⓓ	196	ⓐⓑⓒⓓ
117	ⓐⓑⓒⓓ	137	ⓐⓑⓒⓓ	157	ⓐⓑⓒⓓ	177	ⓐⓑⓒⓓ	197	ⓐⓑⓒⓓ
118	ⓐⓑⓒⓓ	138	ⓐⓑⓒⓓ	158	ⓐⓑⓒⓓ	178	ⓐⓑⓒⓓ	198	ⓐⓑⓒⓓ
119	ⓐⓑⓒⓓ	139	ⓐⓑⓒⓓ	159	ⓐⓑⓒⓓ	179	ⓐⓑⓒⓓ	199	ⓐⓑⓒⓓ
120	ⓐⓑⓒⓓ	140	ⓐⓑⓒⓓ	160	ⓐⓑⓒⓓ	180	ⓐⓑⓒⓓ	200	ⓐⓑⓒⓓ

ANSWER SHEET

TOEIC 實戰模擬試題

測驗日期	20 . .
姓名	
答對題數	/200

LISTENING (Part I ~ IV)

1 ⓐⓑⓒⓓ	21 ⓐⓑⓒ	41 ⓐⓑⓒⓓ	61 ⓐⓑⓒⓓ	81 ⓐⓑⓒⓓ
2 ⓐⓑⓒⓓ	22 ⓐⓑⓒ	42 ⓐⓑⓒⓓ	62 ⓐⓑⓒⓓ	82 ⓐⓑⓒⓓ
3 ⓐⓑⓒⓓ	23 ⓐⓑⓒ	43 ⓐⓑⓒⓓ	63 ⓐⓑⓒⓓ	83 ⓐⓑⓒⓓ
4 ⓐⓑⓒⓓ	24 ⓐⓑⓒ	44 ⓐⓑⓒⓓ	64 ⓐⓑⓒⓓ	84 ⓐⓑⓒⓓ
5 ⓐⓑⓒⓓ	25 ⓐⓑⓒ	45 ⓐⓑⓒⓓ	65 ⓐⓑⓒⓓ	85 ⓐⓑⓒⓓ
6 ⓐⓑⓒⓓ	26 ⓐⓑⓒ	46 ⓐⓑⓒⓓ	66 ⓐⓑⓒⓓ	86 ⓐⓑⓒⓓ
7 ⓐⓑⓒ	27 ⓐⓑⓒ	47 ⓐⓑⓒⓓ	67 ⓐⓑⓒⓓ	87 ⓐⓑⓒⓓ
8 ⓐⓑⓒ	28 ⓐⓑⓒ	48 ⓐⓑⓒⓓ	68 ⓐⓑⓒⓓ	88 ⓐⓑⓒⓓ
9 ⓐⓑⓒ	29 ⓐⓑⓒ	49 ⓐⓑⓒⓓ	69 ⓐⓑⓒⓓ	89 ⓐⓑⓒⓓ
10 ⓐⓑⓒ	30 ⓐⓑⓒⓓ	50 ⓐⓑⓒⓓ	70 ⓐⓑⓒⓓ	90 ⓐⓑⓒⓓ
11 ⓐⓑⓒ	31 ⓐⓑⓒⓓ	51 ⓐⓑⓒⓓ	71 ⓐⓑⓒⓓ	91 ⓐⓑⓒⓓ
12 ⓐⓑⓒ	32 ⓐⓑⓒⓓ	52 ⓐⓑⓒⓓ	72 ⓐⓑⓒⓓ	92 ⓐⓑⓒⓓ
13 ⓐⓑⓒ	33 ⓐⓑⓒⓓ	53 ⓐⓑⓒⓓ	73 ⓐⓑⓒⓓ	93 ⓐⓑⓒⓓ
14 ⓐⓑⓒ	34 ⓐⓑⓒⓓ	54 ⓐⓑⓒⓓ	74 ⓐⓑⓒⓓ	94 ⓐⓑⓒⓓ
15 ⓐⓑⓒ	35 ⓐⓑⓒⓓ	55 ⓐⓑⓒⓓ	75 ⓐⓑⓒⓓ	95 ⓐⓑⓒⓓ
16 ⓐⓑⓒ	36 ⓐⓑⓒⓓ	56 ⓐⓑⓒⓓ	76 ⓐⓑⓒⓓ	96 ⓐⓑⓒⓓ
17 ⓐⓑⓒ	37 ⓐⓑⓒⓓ	57 ⓐⓑⓒⓓ	77 ⓐⓑⓒⓓ	97 ⓐⓑⓒⓓ
18 ⓐⓑⓒ	38 ⓐⓑⓒⓓ	58 ⓐⓑⓒⓓ	78 ⓐⓑⓒⓓ	98 ⓐⓑⓒⓓ
19 ⓐⓑⓒ	39 ⓐⓑⓒⓓ	59 ⓐⓑⓒⓓ	79 ⓐⓑⓒⓓ	99 ⓐⓑⓒⓓ
20 ⓐⓑⓒ	40 ⓐⓑⓒⓓ	60 ⓐⓑⓒⓓ	80 ⓐⓑⓒⓓ	100 ⓐⓑⓒⓓ

READING (Part V ~ VII)

101 ⓐⓑⓒⓓ	121 ⓐⓑⓒⓓ	141 ⓐⓑⓒⓓ	161 ⓐⓑⓒⓓ	181 ⓐⓑⓒⓓ
102 ⓐⓑⓒⓓ	122 ⓐⓑⓒⓓ	142 ⓐⓑⓒⓓ	162 ⓐⓑⓒⓓ	182 ⓐⓑⓒⓓ
103 ⓐⓑⓒⓓ	123 ⓐⓑⓒⓓ	143 ⓐⓑⓒⓓ	163 ⓐⓑⓒⓓ	183 ⓐⓑⓒⓓ
104 ⓐⓑⓒⓓ	124 ⓐⓑⓒⓓ	144 ⓐⓑⓒⓓ	164 ⓐⓑⓒⓓ	184 ⓐⓑⓒⓓ
105 ⓐⓑⓒⓓ	125 ⓐⓑⓒⓓ	145 ⓐⓑⓒⓓ	165 ⓐⓑⓒⓓ	185 ⓐⓑⓒⓓ
106 ⓐⓑⓒⓓ	126 ⓐⓑⓒⓓ	146 ⓐⓑⓒⓓ	166 ⓐⓑⓒⓓ	186 ⓐⓑⓒⓓ
107 ⓐⓑⓒⓓ	127 ⓐⓑⓒⓓ	147 ⓐⓑⓒⓓ	167 ⓐⓑⓒⓓ	187 ⓐⓑⓒⓓ
108 ⓐⓑⓒⓓ	128 ⓐⓑⓒⓓ	148 ⓐⓑⓒⓓ	168 ⓐⓑⓒⓓ	188 ⓐⓑⓒⓓ
109 ⓐⓑⓒⓓ	129 ⓐⓑⓒⓓ	149 ⓐⓑⓒⓓ	169 ⓐⓑⓒⓓ	189 ⓐⓑⓒⓓ
110 ⓐⓑⓒⓓ	130 ⓐⓑⓒⓓ	150 ⓐⓑⓒⓓ	170 ⓐⓑⓒⓓ	190 ⓐⓑⓒⓓ
111 ⓐⓑⓒⓓ	131 ⓐⓑⓒⓓ	151 ⓐⓑⓒⓓ	171 ⓐⓑⓒⓓ	191 ⓐⓑⓒⓓ
112 ⓐⓑⓒⓓ	132 ⓐⓑⓒⓓ	152 ⓐⓑⓒⓓ	172 ⓐⓑⓒⓓ	192 ⓐⓑⓒⓓ
113 ⓐⓑⓒⓓ	133 ⓐⓑⓒⓓ	153 ⓐⓑⓒⓓ	173 ⓐⓑⓒⓓ	193 ⓐⓑⓒⓓ
114 ⓐⓑⓒⓓ	134 ⓐⓑⓒⓓ	154 ⓐⓑⓒⓓ	174 ⓐⓑⓒⓓ	194 ⓐⓑⓒⓓ
115 ⓐⓑⓒⓓ	135 ⓐⓑⓒⓓ	155 ⓐⓑⓒⓓ	175 ⓐⓑⓒⓓ	195 ⓐⓑⓒⓓ
116 ⓐⓑⓒⓓ	136 ⓐⓑⓒⓓ	156 ⓐⓑⓒⓓ	176 ⓐⓑⓒⓓ	196 ⓐⓑⓒⓓ
117 ⓐⓑⓒⓓ	137 ⓐⓑⓒⓓ	157 ⓐⓑⓒⓓ	177 ⓐⓑⓒⓓ	197 ⓐⓑⓒⓓ
118 ⓐⓑⓒⓓ	138 ⓐⓑⓒⓓ	158 ⓐⓑⓒⓓ	178 ⓐⓑⓒⓓ	198 ⓐⓑⓒⓓ
119 ⓐⓑⓒⓓ	139 ⓐⓑⓒⓓ	159 ⓐⓑⓒⓓ	179 ⓐⓑⓒⓓ	199 ⓐⓑⓒⓓ
120 ⓐⓑⓒⓓ	140 ⓐⓑⓒⓓ	160 ⓐⓑⓒⓓ	180 ⓐⓑⓒⓓ	200 ⓐⓑⓒⓓ

ENERGY

生命的每個瞬間，
都該是美好的結束，
亦是嶄新的開始。

—— 法頂禪師

EZ TALK

New TOEIC 一本攻克新制多益聽力＋閱讀850+：
完全比照最新考題趨勢精準命題

| 作　　者：Eduwill語學研究所
| 譯　　者：關亭薇
| 主　　編：潘亭軒
| 責任編輯：鄭雅方
| 封面設計：兒日設計
| 內頁排版：簡單瑛設
| 行銷企劃：張爾芸

發　行　人：洪祺祥
副總經理：洪偉傑
副總編輯：曹仲堯
法律顧問：建大法律事務所
財務顧問：高威會計師事務所

出　　版：日月文化出版股份有限公司
製　　作：EZ叢書館
地　　址：臺北市信義路三段151號8樓
電　　話：(02)2708-5509
傳　　真：(02)2708-6157
網　　址：www.heliopolis.com.tw
郵撥帳號：19716071日月文化出版股份有限公司

總　經　銷：聯合發行股份有限公司
電　　話：(02)2917-8022
傳　　真：(02)2915-7212
印　　刷：中原造像股份有限公司
初　　版：2024年11月
定　　價：520元
Ｉ Ｓ Ｂ Ｎ：978-626-7516-47-8

> New TOEIC 一本攻克新制多益聽力＋閱讀850+：完全比照最新考題趨勢精準命題 /Eduwill語學研究所著；關亭薇譯. -- 初版. -- 臺北市：日月文化出版股份有限公司, 2024.11
> 384 面；　19x25.7 公分. -- (EZ talk)
> ISBN 978-626-7516-47-8（平裝）
> 1.CST: 多益測驗

Copyright © 2023 by Eduwill Language Institute
All rights reserved.
Traditional Chinese Copyright © 2024 by HELIOPOLIS CULTURE GROUP
This Traditional Chinese edition was published by arrangement with Eduwill through Agency Liang

◎版權所有 翻印必究
◎本書如有缺頁、破損、裝訂錯誤，請寄回本公司更換

NEW TOEIC
一本攻克新制多益
聽力 ＋ 閱讀
850⁺
解析本

完全比照
最新考題趨勢精準命題

不容錯過的多益應考攻略，透過短期密集訓練，培養高效解題思維，
一網打盡聽力閱讀 Part 1~Part 7 所有題型！

Eduwill語學研究所——著　關亭薇——譯

LC PART 1

照片描述　　題本 p.16

1. 單人獨照
(A) 她正在修理印表機。
(B) 她正在穿夾克。
(C) 她正在檢查資料。
(D) 她正在影印文件。

單字 fix 修理　put on 穿上　examine 檢查　photocopy 影印

2. 雙人照片
(A) 他們正在摘下安全帽。
(B) 他們正在摺紙。
(C) 其中一名男子正在圖紙上做標記。
(D) 其中一名男子正在測量窗玻璃的大小。

單字 remove 摘下、移除　mark 標記　measure 測量　windowpane 窗玻璃

3. 多人照片
(A) 顧客正在挑選一些食品雜貨。
(B) 顧客在排隊等候。
(C) 收銀員正在取出現金。
(D) 收銀員正在打開收銀機。

單字 pick out 挑選、選擇　take out 取出

4. 事物與風景照
(A) 牆上掛著一些畫作。
(B) 有些藝術品倚靠著沙發。
(C) 牆上安裝著燈具。
(D) 桌上放著盆栽。

單字 hang 懸掛　prop against 倚靠…　light fixture 燈具

UNIT 01　人物照片

CHECK-UP　題本 p.19

1. (C)　**2.** (A)

1. 🎧 英國女子

(A) A toolbox has been left on the ground.
(B) He is putting on knee pads.
(C) He is removing some floor tiles.
(D) Some debris is being cleared from the floor.

(A) 工具箱放在地上。
(B) 他正在穿上護膝。（動作）
(C) 他正在拆除一些地磚。
(D) 正從地板上清除殘骸。

單字 put on 穿戴（動作）…　knee pad 護膝　remove 拆除　debris 殘骸　clear 清除

2. 🎧 美國男子

(A) A customer is handing a worker some cash.
(B) A woman is looking through her purse.
(C) A customer is trying on a patterned blouse.
(D) A man is arranging merchandise on shelves.

(A) 顧客正在給服務人員現金。
(B) 女子正在翻找她的手提包。
(C) 顧客正在試穿有圖案的襯衫。
(D) 男子正在整理貨架上的商品。

單字 hand A B 把 B 給 A　look through 翻找　try on 試穿　arrange 整頓

UNIT 02　事物照與風景照

CHECK-UP　題本 p.21

1. (C)　**2.** (D)

1. 🎧 英國女子

(A) Some fishing poles have been left on a deck.
(B) Some boats are sailing in the ocean.
(C) Some chairs have been placed on a dock.
(D) A house overlooks a fishing pier.

(A) 有些釣竿被留在甲板上。
(B) 有些船隻在海上航行。
(C) 有些椅子被放置在碼頭上。
(D) 一棟可俯瞰釣魚碼頭的房子。

單字 fishing pole 釣竿　dock 碼頭、船塢
overlook 眺望、俯瞰

2. 🎧 美國男子

(A) A top drawer has been closed.
(B) A faucet is running water.
(C) There are some cooking utensils on the ground.
(D) There is some fruit on a countertop.

(A) 上方抽屜已關閉。
(B) 水從水龍頭流出。
(C) 地上有些廚房用具。
(D) 流理台上有些水果。

單字 faucet 水龍頭　cooking utensil 廚房用具
countertop 流理台

PRACTICE 高難度　題本 p.23

1. (C)　**2.** (D)　**3.** (B)　**4.** (D)　**5.** (C)　**6.** (A)

1. 🎧 美國男子

(A) He's loading crates into a vehicle.
(B) He's stocking shelves in a storage room.
(C) Some boxes are stacked in a vehicle.
(D) A car is exiting a parking garage.

(A) 他正在把箱子裝進車裡。
(B) 他正在儲藏室的貨架上架商品。
(C) 有些箱子被堆放在車上。
(D) 有輛汽車正駛出停車場。

單字 load 裝載　stock 進貨　stack 堆放　exit 離開
parking garage 停車場

2. 🎧 英國女子

(A) A watering can has been placed next to a hanger.
(B) The woman is carrying a vase filled with flowers.
(C) There is a clock on top of a shelf.
(D) The woman is watering a plant on a desk.

(A) 澆水壺被放在衣架旁。
(B) 女子拿著裝滿花的花瓶。
(C) 架子上有個時鐘。
(D) 女子正在為桌上的植物澆水。

單字 watering can 澆水壺　on top of 在⋯上
water 為⋯澆水

3. 🎧 澳洲男子

(A) A man is unpacking a suitcase.
(B) A woman is resting her hand on a railing.
(C) They're standing in a doorway.
(D) They're parking bicycles next to a building.

(A) 男子正在打開手提箱。
(B) 女子把手靠在欄杆上。
(C) 他們站在出入口。
(D) 他們把腳踏車停在大樓旁。

單字 unpack 打開、從（包包中）取出　rest 支撐
doorway 出入口

4. 🎧 美國男子

3

(A) Some people are viewing some artwork.
(B) A woman is drawing a graph on a whiteboard.
(C) The people are seated across from one another.
(D) The audience is facing a screen.

(A) 有些人正在觀看藝術作品。
(B) 有名女子正在白板上畫圖。
(C) 人們面對面坐著。
(D) 觀眾面對著螢幕。

單字 view（仔細地）觀看

5. 🎧 英國女子

(A) Some tables are being wiped down.
(B) Some potted plants are being rearranged.
(C) An outdoor area has been set up for dining.
(D) Some chairs on a patio are occupied.

(A) 有些桌子正在被擦拭。
(B) 有些盆栽正在被重新排列。
(C) 戶外設有用餐區。
(D) 露台上的一些椅子正被佔用。

單字 wipe down 擦拭乾淨　rearrange 重新排列、重新整理　be occupied 使用中的

6. 🎧 澳洲男子

(A) Some shelves are lined up in a hallway.
(B) Some equipment has been set up on a stage.
(C) Some packages are being unloaded from a cart.
(D) Some items are being removed from storage units.

(A) 一些貨架沿著走道排列。
(B) 舞台上已架設一些設備。
(C) 正從購物車上卸下一些包裹。
(D) 正從倉儲中拿出物品。

單字 line up 排成一列　set up 架設　unload 從（車子或架上）卸下貨物　storage unit 倉儲

PART TEST 1　題本 p.24

1. (A)　**2.** (C)　**3.** (D)　**4.** (B)　**5.** (D)　**6.** (B)

1. 🎧 美國男子

(A) He's mowing the lawn.
(B) He's kneeling on the grass.
(C) He's pruning a bush.
(D) He's pushing a cart.

(A) 他正在修整草坪。
(B) 他正在跪在草地上。
(C) 他正在修剪灌木叢。
(D) 他正推著手推車。

單字 mow 修剪、割（草坪、草）　kneel 跪下　prune 修剪、修整

2. 🎧 英國女子

(A) There's a sign posted on a fence.
(B) One of the men is putting on his helmet.
(C) Some snow is being shoveled off a walkway.
(D) The men are sweeping the floor.

(A) 柵欄上張貼著標誌。
(B) 其中一名男子正在戴安全帽。
(C) 人行道上的雪正被剷除。
(D) 幾名男子正在掃地。

單字 post 張貼（公告）　shovel 鏟除　sweep 清掃

3. 🎧 澳洲男子

(A) The women are facing each other.
(B) One of the women is handing out flyers.
(C) A server is tying an apron.
(D) A server is taking an order.

(A) 幾名女子相互面對面。
(B) 其中一名女子正在發傳單。
(C) 服務員正在繫圍裙。（動作）
(D) 服務員正在幫客人點餐。

單字 hand out 發放　tie 繫上　take an order 點餐

4. 🎧 美國女子

(A) They're seated in a line.
(B) A man is pointing at a board.
(C) They're examining some documents.
(D) A woman is gesturing towards a chalkboard.

(A) 他們坐成一排。
(B) 一名男子正指著白板。
(C) 他們正在檢查文件。
(D) 一名女子正指向黑板。

單字 point at 指向⋯　examine 檢查

5. 🎧 美國男子

(A) She's opening a drawer.
(B) She's fixing an office equipment.
(C) She's emptying a trash bin.
(D) She's refilling a copy machine with paper.

(A) 她正在開抽屜。
(B) 她正在修理辦公設備。
(C) 她正在清空垃圾桶。
(D) 她正在為影印機加紙。

單字 fix 修理　empty 清空　refill A with B 為 A 裝滿 B

6. 🎧 英國女子

(A) Some stairs are being cleaned.
(B) Some chairs are arranged in a circle.
(C) A pathway is being repaired.
(D) A fence is being installed alongside a building.

(A) 正在清掃樓梯。
(B) 有些椅子被排成一圈。
(C) 正在修繕步道。
(D) 正在大樓旁安裝柵欄。

單字 in a circle 圍成一圈　pathway 步道、人行道

PART TEST 2　　題本 p.27

1. (B)　2. (C)　3. (A)　4. (C)　5. (D)　6. (B)

1. 🎧 美國男子

(A) He's reaching into a shopping basket.
(B) He's holding a refrigerator door open.
(C) He's putting some groceries in a cart.
(D) He's carrying a jacket over his arm.

(A) 他正把手伸進購物籃裡。
(B) 他正開著冰箱門。
(C) 他正把食品放進購物車裡。
(D) 他在手臂上掛著夾克。

單字 reach into 把手伸進⋯　is holding a door open 開著門

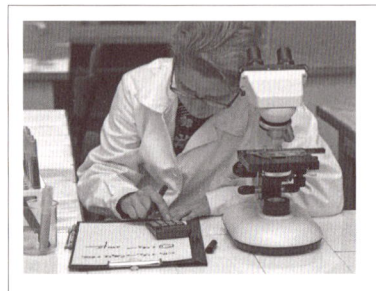

2. 🎧英國女子

(A) The woman is picking up a test tube.
(B) The woman is adjusting a microscope.
(C) The woman is using a calculator.
(D) The woman is writing on a notepad.

(A) 女子正拿起一根試管。
(B) 女子正在調整顯微鏡。
(C) 女子正在使用計算機。
(D) 女子正在記事本上寫字。

單字 pick up 拿起⋯　adjust 調整、校準

3. 🎧澳洲男子

(A) The man is vacuuming the floor.
(B) They are putting away some cleaning tools.
(C) One of the women is sweeping a walkway.
(D) One of the women is crouching under a desk.

(A) 男子正在用吸塵器吸地。
(B) 他們正在收拾清潔用品。
(C) 其中一名女子正在清掃通道。
(D) 其中一名女子正蹲在桌子底下。

單字 vacuum 用吸塵器清掃　put away 收拾、歸位
sweep 清掃　crouch 蹲下

4. 🎧美國女子

(A) Some display areas are being restocked.
(B) A woman is loading some furniture onto a cart.
(C) Some boxes are stacked in a warehouse.
(D) A man is handing some papers to a woman.

(A) 正在為部分展示區補貨。
(B) 女子正在把傢俱裝到手推車上。
(C) 有些箱子被堆放在倉庫裡。
(D) 男子正在把文件交給女子。

單字 restock 補貨、重新進貨　load A onto B 把 A 裝到 B 上
warehouse 倉庫　hand A to B 把 A 遞給 B

5. 🎧美國男子

(A) Some of the men are putting on ties.
(B) They're looking at posts on a bulletin board.
(C) A man is organizing documents in a folder.
(D) One of the men is pointing at a monitor.

(A) 幾名男子正在繫領帶。
(B) 他們正在看公告欄上的貼文。
(C) 一名男子正在整理文件夾裡的文件。
(D) 其中一名男子正指著螢幕。

單字 put on 穿戴、戴上　organize 整理　point at 指向⋯

6

6. 🎧 美國女子

(A) A rug is being removed from the floor.
(B) Some potted plants are hanging from a ceiling.
(C) Some artwork has been propped up on a shelf.
(D) A blanket is hanging on a table.

(A) 正在把地毯從地板上移開。
(B) 有些盆栽懸掛在天花板上。
(C) 有些藝術品被架在架上。
(D) 桌上掛著毯子。

單字 remove A from B 把 A 從 B 移除　potted plant 盆栽　artwork 藝術品　prop up 架、支撐

LC　PART 2

UNIT 01　Who/What/Which 問句

CHECK-UP
題本 p.35

1. (A)　**2.** (A)　**3.** (B)　**4.** (A)　**5.** (C)　**6.** (A)

1. 🎧 美國男子／英國女子

Who's going to select a candidate for the position?
(A) The marketing team.
(B) That option would be best.
(C) I have her résumé here.

由誰來挑選該職位的人選？
(A) 行銷團隊。
(B) 那個選項最好。
(C) 我這裡有她的履歷。

2. 🎧 美國男子／英國女子

What was the total charge for the car rental?
(A) I'd have to look at the receipt.
(B) It looks like a compact vehicle.
(C) Yes, for any amount you'd like.

租車的總費用是多少？
(A) 我需要查看收據。
(B) 它看起來像一輛小型車。
(C) 是的，金額不限。

3. 🎧 美國男子／英國女子

Which floor is Chetwood Financial Services located on?
(A) The financial report will be done this week.
(B) They've already closed for the day.
(C) The department budget for February.

Chetwood 金融服務公司在哪一層樓？
(A) 財務報告預計於本週完成。
(B) 他們今天已經關門了。
(C) 二月的部門預算。

4. 🎧 美國女子／澳洲男子

Who needs a copy of the lease contract?
(A) Marty does.
(B) Yes, I already signed up.
(C) At least $5,000.

誰需要租賃合約副本？
(A) Marty 需要。

7

(B) 是的，我已經報名了。
(C) 至少 5000 美元。

單字 sign up 報名、簽約、（在資料上）簽名

5. 🎧 美國女子／澳洲男子

> What kind of restaurants do you usually go to?
> (A) Mark made the reservation instead.
> (B) Mainly on weekends or holidays.
> **(C) I'm a big fan of Thai cuisine.**

你通常會去什麼類型的餐廳？
(A) 改由 Mark 訂位了。
(B) 主要在週末或假日。
(C) 我非常喜歡泰式料理。

單字 make a reservation 預約

6. 🎧 美國女子／澳洲男子

> Which building did Margaret move her office to?
> **(A) The tall one on the corner.**
> (B) Thanks, I appreciate that.
> (C) Show the parking pass at the gate.

Margaret 把辦公室搬到哪棟樓了？
(A) 街角的高樓。
(B) 謝謝，我很感激。
(C) 請在入口處出示停車證。

UNIT 02　When/Where 問句

CHECK-UP　　　　　　　　　題本 p.37

1. (B)　**2.** (B)　**3.** (C)　**4.** (B)　**5.** (C)　**6.** (A)

1. 🎧 美國男子／英國女子

> Where did these pineapples come from?
> (A) It's in aisle nine.
> **(B) From a supplier in Florida.**
> (C) Here's a cart you can use.

這些鳳梨來自何處？
(A) 在九號走道。
(B) 來自佛羅里達州的供應商。
(C) 你可使用這台推車。

2. 🎧 美國男子／英國女子

> When are they going to decide who to hire?
> (A) Lift it up a little higher.
> **(B) Quite a few résumés have come in.**
> (C) The department managers.

他們何時決定要僱用誰？
(A) 把它抬高一點。
(B) 收到了相當多的履歷。
(C) 部門經理

解說 (B) 收到了相當多的履歷，表示還需要一段時間才能決定要僱用誰，屬於間接回答的方式。

3. 🎧 美國男子／英國女子

> Where did you first learn about the job opening?
> (A) No, I didn't apply.
> (B) I'm going to open a business account.
> **(C) I subscribe to a weekly career magazine.**

你從哪裡首次得知該職缺？
(A) 不，我沒有應徵。
(B) 我要開設一個企業帳戶。
(C) 我有訂閱職業週刊。

解說 表示在職業週刊上得知該職缺的消息，屬於間接回答。

單字 subscribe to 訂閱⋯

4. 🎧 美國女子／澳洲男子

> When do you need the blueprints for the lobby renovation?
> (A) No, the printer is broken right now.
> **(B) By early afternoon, please.**
> (C) That's not as expensive as we thought.

你何時需要大廳的裝修設計圖？
(A) 不用，印表機現在壞了。
(B) 請在下午早些時候給我。
(C) 沒有我們想像的那麼貴。

單字 blueprint 藍圖　broken 故障

5. 🎧 美國女子／澳洲男子

> Where is the engineering team?
> (A) At the end of this quarter.
> (B) More than 20 people.
> **(C) They're at a training session.**

工程團隊在哪裡？
(A) 在本季度末。
(B) 超過二十人。
(C) 他們在上培訓課程。

6. 🎧 美國女子／澳洲男子

> When will construction on this road finish?
> **(A) In the spring.**
> (B) The back entrance of this building.
> (C) I'll take the elevator.

這條路何時能完工？
(A) 春天。
(B) 該棟大樓的後門。
(C) 我要搭電梯。

UNIT 03　How/Why問句

CHECK-UP　　　　　　　　　　　題本 p.39

1. (C)　**2.** (A)　**3.** (C)　**4.** (A)　**5.** (B)　**6.** (A)

1. 🎧 美國男子／英國女子

How many tickets do we need for tomorrow's concert?
(A) We're meeting at two o'clock sharp.
(B) The theater's on William Street.
(C) I'll buy mine at the door.

明天的音樂會需要幾張票？
(A) 我們兩點整見。
(B) 劇院位在William街。
(C) 我會在現場買我的。

單字 sharp （時刻）整點

2. 🎧 美國男子／英國女子

How are the website updates coming along?
(A) I've been tied up with the other accounts.
(B) That date works for me.
(C) I was stuck in a traffic jam.

網站更新的進度如何？
(A) 我忙於處理其他客戶。
(B) 我那天可以。
(C) 我遇到塞車了。

單字 tied up with 忙於…　account 帳戶、客戶

3. 🎧 美國男子／英國女子

How did your presentation for Raymond Financial Group go this morning?
(A) Our main client.
(B) That was a nice present.
(C) It went very well.

今天早上你對Raymond金融集團的演講進行得如何？
(A) 我們的主要客戶。
(B) 那是一份很好的禮物。
(C) 進展得非常順利。

4. 🎧 美國女子／澳洲男子

Why did our company decide to offer a free newsletter?
(A) To expand our customer base.
(B) That sounds like a great idea.
(C) The other side of town.

為什麼我們公司決定免費提供電子報？
(A) 為擴大我們的客戶群。
(B) 聽起來是個好主意。
(C) 城鎮的另一邊。

單字 customer base 客戶群

5. 🎧 美國女子／澳洲男子

Why isn't Ms. Watts available to meet the client?
(A) She's a regular customer.
(B) Because she's on a business trip this week.
(C) Tomorrow would be good.

為何Watts女士沒辦法跟客戶見面？
(A) 她是常客。
(B) 因為她這週去出差了。
(C) 明天可以。

單字 regular customer 常客

6. 🎧 美國女子／澳洲男子

Why did our sales targets increase this month?
(A) Check with the manager.
(B) No, I'm taking time off at the end of the month.
(C) I'm working on their performance reviews.

為何我們本月的銷售目標額提高了？
(A) 請跟經理確認一下。
(B) 不，我月底要請假。
(C) 我正在對他們進行績效考核。

單字 sales target 銷售目標（額）
performance review 績效考核

UNIT 04　Yes/No問句

CHECK-UP　　　　　　　　　　　題本 p.41

1. (A)　**2.** (A)　**3.** (C)　**4.** (C)　**5.** (A)　**6.** (B)

1. 🎧 美國男子／英國女子

Does the shop open on Saturdays?
(A) Yes. At 11:00.
(B) Close to the train station.
(C) The fundraiser's on Friday.

商店星期六有開嗎？
(A) 有，11 點。
(B) 靠近火車站。
(C) 募款活動於星期五舉行。

2. 🎧 美國男子／英國女子

> Will Dr. Miller be late today?
> **(A) No, you shouldn't have to wait long.**
> (B) I haven't seen them lately.
> (C) Sure, I'm free now.

Miller醫生今天會晚到嗎？
(A) 不，你應該不會等太久。
(B) 我最近沒見到他們。
(C) 當然，我現在有空。

3. 🎧 美國男子／英國女子

> Aren't there locker rooms at this library?
> (A) You have to return the books by May 3.
> (B) The door is unlocked.
> **(C) Yes, they're on the second floor.**

這間圖書館沒有置物間嗎？
(A) 你需要在5月3日前還書。
(B) 門沒有鎖。
(C) 有，他們在二樓。

4. 🎧 美國女子／澳洲男子

> Hasn't anyone called you back for the second interview yet?
> (A) Here's the phone number.
> (B) Yes, we had several positions open.
> **(C) I'm still waiting.**

你還沒接到第二次面試的電話通知嗎？
(A) 這是電話號碼。
(B) 是的，我們有幾個職缺。
(C) 我還在等。

5. 🎧 美國女子／澳洲男子

> This shipment will arrive by this Friday, won't it?
> **(A) Definitely.**
> (B) I'll sign for the delivery.
> (C) It won't fit in my car.

這批貨物將於本週五前到貨，不是嗎？
(A) 當然。
(B) 交貨單由我來簽收。
(C) 它放不進我的車。

6. 🎧 美國女子／澳洲男子

> Should I bring anything to the trade fair?
> (A) Probably in the maintenance room.
> **(B) Do we have enough handouts?**
> (C) That sounds like a fair price.

我需要帶些什麼去貿易展覽會嗎？
(A) 應該在維修室裡。
(B) 我們有足夠的傳單嗎？
(C) 聽起來價格很合理。

單字 maintenance room 維修室

UNIT 05 表示建議或要求的問句、選擇疑問句

CHECK-UP 題本 p.43

1. (C) **2.** (C) **3.** (B) **4.** (A) **5.** (A) **6.** (B)

1. 🎧 美國男子／英國女子

> Could you call Ms. Thomson and let her know we're in the hotel lobby?
> (A) Sorry, it's under repair.
> (B) I ordered a room service.
> **(C) Yes, of course.**

你可以打電話給Thomson女士，告訴她我們在飯店大廳嗎？
(A) 抱歉，正在維修中。
(B) 我叫了客房服務。
(C) 當然可以。

2. 🎧 美國男子／英國女子

> Could I take a look at some sample floral arrangements?
> (A) It's a third floor apartment.
> (B) No. I believe Edward is doing that.
> **(C) Certainly, I have them right here.**

我可以看一下插花樣品嗎？
(A) 這是三層樓的公寓。
(B) 不，我確信Edward正在做。
(C) 當然，我這裡就有。

單字 floral 用花做的、花裝飾的

3. 🎧 美國男子／英國女子

> Should I make the dinner reservation for Thursday or Friday?
> (A) The bistro across the street.
> **(B) Friday is better.**
> (C) I enjoyed the pasta salad.

10

我應該預訂星期四還是星期五的晚餐？
(A) 街道對面的餐酒館。
(B) 星期五比較好。
(C) 我享用了義大利麵沙拉。

4. 🎧 美國女子／澳洲男子

> Would you prefer a train in the morning or the afternoon?
> **(A) I'd better leave early.**
> (B) Because of the traffic jam.
> (C) Every morning at ten o'clock.

中譯
你喜歡早上還是下午的火車？
(A) 我希望能早點出發。
(B) 因為交通堵塞。
(C) 每天早上十點。

5. 🎧 美國女子／澳洲男子

> Why don't we provide more samples of the tile patterns for our clients?
> **(A) There are plenty in the binders.**
> (B) Because it's out of stock.
> (C) I like the striped blanket.

我們何不為客戶提供更多磁磚圖案樣品呢？
(A) 活頁夾中有很多。
(B) 因為缺貨了。
(C) 我喜歡條紋毯子。

6. 🎧 美國女子／澳洲男子

> Would you like to make a reservation for this Friday?
> (A) The flight was cancelled.
> **(B) Does 8 P.M. work?**
> (C) Next week's train schedule.

你想預訂這週五嗎？
(A) 航班被取消了。
(B) 晚上8點可以嗎？
(C) 下週的火車時刻表。

UNIT 06 直述句

CHECK-UP　　　　　　　　題本 p.44

1. (A)　2. (C)　3. (C)　4. (B)　5. (B)　6. (A)

1. 🎧 美國男子／英國女子

> Your expense report seems a bit short.
> **(A) I didn't spend much this quarter.**
> (B) I'm leaving shortly.
> (C) Maybe one and a half meters?

你的開銷報告似乎有點少。
(A) 這一季我沒花費很多。
(B) 我很快要走了。
(C) 大約一米半？

2. 🎧 美國男子／英國女子

> I'd like to attend the tech conference next month.
> (A) There was a problem with the projector.
> (B) The speech starts at noon.
> **(C) Registration closed yesterday.**

我想參加下個月的科技會議。
(A) 投影機出了問題。
(B) 演講於中午開始。
(C) 昨天報名截止了。

3. 🎧 美國男子／英國女子

> I had a chance to look over the proposal this morning.
> (A) We're under budget.
> (B) I'm doing well, thanks.
> **(C) What did you think of it?**

今天上午我有機會仔細查看提案。
(A) 我們預算不足。
(B) 我過得很好，謝謝。
(C) 你覺得怎麼樣？

4. 🎧 美國女子／澳洲男子

> The market on Maple Street is closed for a week.
> (A) Please order more tablecloths.
> **(B) Is there another one nearby?**
> (C) That's market price.

Maple街上的市集將休市一週。
(A) 請再訂購一些桌布。
(B) 附近還有別家嗎？
(C) 這是市場價格。

5. 🎧 美國女子／澳洲男子

> This agreement needs a signature before it's sent out.
> (A) I received it.
> **(B) OK, I'll do that now.**
> (C) A roofing contractor.

11

這份協議需在發送前簽名。
(A) 我收到了。
(B) 好,我現在就簽名。
(C) 屋頂承包商。

單字 send out 發送、寄送

6. 🎧 美國女子／澳洲男子

That film has received excellent reviews.
(A) Why don't we go see it?
(B) The department director.
(C) I'd like a room with a view of the sea.

那部電影獲得了好評。
(A) 我們去看看怎麼樣?
(B) 部門主管。
(C) 我想要海景房。

PRACTICE 高難度
題本 p.45

1. (C)	2. (C)	3. (A)	4. (B)	5. (A)	6. (B)
7. (C)	8. (C)	9. (A)	10. (A)	11. (B)	12. (A)
13. (A)	14. (C)	15. (A)	16. (C)	17. (B)	18. (A)
19. (C)	20. (B)	21. (A)	22. (A)	23. (C)	24. (C)
25. (B)	26. (A)	27. (C)	28. (C)	29. (B)	30. (C)

1. 🎧 美國男子／英國女子

When can I move these supplies into the storage room?
(A) The warehouse on Lancaster Avenue.
(B) It's a new supplier.
(C) We'll need to clear some space.

我何時可以把這些用品搬進儲藏室?
(A) Lancaster大道上的倉庫。
(B) 這是新的供應商。
(C) 我們需要騰出一些空間。

單字 supplies 用品、備品、補給品　supplier 供應商

2. 🎧 英國女子／美國男子

Where did you go after luncheon yesterday?
(A) Of course I'd be willing to do that.
(B) I'm afraid I just ate.
(C) I had a dentist's appointment.

你昨天午餐會後去了哪裡?
(A) 我當然願意那樣做。
(B) 抱歉我剛吃過了。
(C) 我有預約牙醫。

3. 🎧 澳洲男子／美國女子

Who's giving the first part of the sales pitch?
(A) I'm handling the presentation on my own.
(B) It's for a prospective client.
(C) That would be really helpful.

誰負責商品推銷演說的第一部分?
(A) 由我一個人發表演說。
(B) 這是為了潛在客戶。
(C) 那會很有幫助。

單字 on my own 單獨地　prospective client 潛在客戶

4. 🎧 美國女子／澳洲男子

How did Ms. Carter enjoy her stay at our hotel?
(A) No, five days and four nights.
(B) She didn't check out yet.
(C) Until the end of the month.

Carter女士滿意我們飯店的住宿嗎?
(A) 不,是五天四夜。
(B) 她還沒退房。
(C) 到這個月底。

5. 🎧 美國男子／英國女子

What's the status of our grant application?
(A) It should be approved early next week.
(B) An interest-free loan.
(C) To my work e-mail address.

我們補助金的申請情況如何?
(A) 應該會在下週初獲得批准。
(B) 無息貸款。
(C) 寄到我公司的電子郵件地址。

單字 grant (政府或團體提供的)補助金

6. 🎧 英國女子／美國男子

Why are the lights out in the hallway?
(A) He just went out for lunch.
(B) Because they're doing some maintenance work.
(C) We should've turned left.

為何走廊的燈熄滅了?
(A) 他剛出去吃午餐。
(B) 因為他們正在進行維護工作。
(C) 我們應該要左轉。

7. 🎧 澳洲男子／美國女子

Which photograph should we use for the article?
(A) It's a pretty town with a picturesque lake.
(B) For several women's magazines.
(C) The third one on the right.

12

我們應在文章中使用哪張照片？
(A) 有著景致優美湖泊的美麗城鎮。
(B) 用在幾本女性雜誌。
(C) 右邊第三個。

8. 🎧 美國女子／澳洲男子

> Who's attending Rohan's retirement party?
> (A) This calls for celebration.
> (B) Three o'clock sharp.
> **(C) It should be noted on the guest list.**

誰會參加Rohan的退休派對？
(A) 這值得慶祝。
(B) 三點整。
(C) 賓客名單上應會提到。

單字 sharp 整點（= on the dot）

9. 🎧 美國男子／英國女子

> Who was in the break room last?
> **(A) I noticed that it was messy, too.**
> (B) I think the brake is broken.
> (C) It won't last long.

最後一個在休息室的人是誰？
(A) 我也有注意到那裡很亂。
(B) 我認為煞車壞了。
(C) 它不會持續太久。

10. 🎧 英國女子／美國男子

> What's the best way to get to Roxbury Convention Center?
> **(A) I'd take the bus.**
> (B) That one is way better.
> (C) Ten people from the sales department.

前往Roxbury會議中心的最佳方式為何？
(A) 我會搭公車。
(B) 那個比較好。
(C) 來自銷售部門的十個人。

11. 🎧 澳洲男子／美國女子

> How did the sales presentation go yesterday?
> (A) At the City Convention Center.
> **(B) Greenwood Motor Company is now one of our clients.**
> (C) I thought it was on sale.

昨天的銷售演說情況如何？
(A) 在城市會議中心。
(B) Greenwood 汽車公司現在是我們的客戶之一。
(C) 我以為有打折。

解說 指的是銷售介紹很成功，才能順利與 Greenwood 汽車公司簽約。

12. 🎧 美國女子／澳洲男子

> When are you moving to your new office?
> **(A) As early as February.**
> (B) This equipment is not mobile.
> (C) On the second floor.

你何時會搬到新辦公室？
(A) 最快會在二月。
(B) 這不是移動式設備。
(C) 在二樓。

13. 🎧 美國男子／英國女子

> When is the library construction starting?
> **(A) We're a bit behind schedule.**
> (B) A well-known author.
> (C) To construct a bridge.

圖書館何時開始施工？
(A) 我們的進度有點落後。
(B) 知名作家。
(C) 為了建造橋樑。

14. 🎧 英國女子／美國男子

> Where's the main entrance to the library?
> (A) The entrance fee is $10.
> (B) On top of the bookcase.
> **(C) There's a pretty long line over there.**

圖書館的正門在哪裡？
(A) 入場費為10美元。
(B) 在書櫃最上方。
(C) 那裡排著很長的隊伍。

單字 on top of 在⋯上方

15. 🎧 澳洲男子／美國女子

> Why was the shipment late?
> (A) I was charged a late fee.
> (B) Could you sign for me?
> **(C) Traffic was really bad this morning.**

為什麼出貨延遲了？
(A) 我被收取了滯納金。
(B) 你可以幫我簽名嗎？
(C) 今天早上的交通狀況非常差。

單字 late fee 滯納金

13

16. 🎧 美國女子／澳洲男子

> Does the company pay for employee travel?
> (A) The fee is $200.
> (B) It's a week-long business trip.
> **(C) Only for work-related expenses.**

公司會支付員工差旅費用嗎？
(A) 費用為 200 美元。
(B) 出差一星期。
(C) 僅支付公務相關費用。

17. 🎧 美國男子／英國女子

> Sales of our cold-brew iced coffee rose by fifteen percent last month.
> (A) It's very chilly outside.
> **(B) I didn't know it was so popular.**
> (C) Close the coffee shop an hour earlier.

冷萃冰咖啡上個月的銷售業績成長了 15%。
(A) 外面非常冷。
(B) 我不知道它這麼受歡迎。
(C) 提前一小時打烊咖啡廳。

18. 🎧 英國女子／美國男子

> Has the job ad for the accountant position been posted?
> **(A) Not yet, but by noon.**
> (B) Sharon's a great candidate.
> (C) I like the account management software.

已經發布會計師職缺的徵才廣告了嗎？
(A) 還沒有，但會在中午之前發布。
(B) Sharon 是個很好的人選。
(C) 我喜歡帳戶管理軟體。

單字 accountant 會計師、會計人員

19. 🎧 澳洲男子／美國女子

> Are we ready to begin production on the summer clothing line?
> (A) Many people are in line.
> (B) It comes in various sizes.
> **(C) Sure, the designs are almost finalized.**

我們準備好開始生產夏季服裝了嗎？
(A) 很多人在排隊。
(B) 它有各種尺寸。
(C) 當然，幾乎快完成設計了。

20. 🎧 美國女子／澳洲男子

> Don't you want to buy the rocking chair?
> (A) Yes, the living room furniture's new.
> **(B) We already have one.**
> (C) We charge cancellation fees.

你不想買搖椅嗎？
(A) 是的，客廳傢俱是新的。
(B) 我們已經有一個了。
(C) 我們會收取消手續費。

單字 cancellation fee 取消手續費

21. 🎧 美國男子／英國女子

> You haven't always worn glasses, have you?
> (A) Two glasses of juice, please.
> **(B) No, only since last month.**
> (C) The brake pads are very worn.

你不是一直都戴眼鏡，對吧？
(A) 請給我兩杯果汁。
(B) 不，是從上個月開始。
(C) 煞車片嚴重磨損。

單字 worn 磨損、舊的

22. 🎧 英國女子／美國男子

> Can you show me how to fill out this registration form?
> **(A) I'm about to join a video conference call.**
> (B) At the management seminar.
> (C) That position has been filled.

你能告訴我如何填寫註冊表嗎？
(A) 我正要去參加電話視訊會議。
(B) 在管理研討會上。
(C) 該職位已經補人。

23. 🎧 澳洲男子／美國女子

> Isn't Priscilla coming to this meeting?
> (A) Sure, we've met before.
> (B) In the conference room down the hall.
> **(C) Yes, she'll be here soon.**

Priscilla 不來參加這次會議嗎？
(A) 當然，我們之前見過面。
(B) 在走廊盡頭的會議室裡。
(C) 會，她快來了。

24. 🎧 美國女子／澳洲男子

> Do you have this winter coat in a smaller size?
> (A) It's so cold inside.
> (B) A large number of orders.
> **(C) Oh, I'm not a sales associate.**

這件冬季大衣有更小一點的尺寸嗎？
(A) 裡面太冷了。
(B) 大量訂單。
(C) 喔，我不是銷售人員。

單字 sales associate 銷售人員

25. 🎧 美國男子／英國女子

> Would you mind forwarding me a summary of the results of your research?
> (A) We'll visit Belgium this summer.
> **(B) I don't think I have your e-mail address.**
> (C) Sure, I'll remind her later.

你能否轉寄研究成果摘要給我？
(A) 我們將於今年夏天造訪比利時。
(B) 我好像沒有你的電子郵件地址。
(C) 當然，我稍後會提醒她。

26. 🎧 英國女子／美國男子

> I'd like to schedule an appointment for next week.
> **(A) How about Thursday at ten?**
> (A) Director of international sales.
> (C) No, it's a week-long business trip.

我想預約下個星期會面。
(A) 星期四十點如何？
(A) 國際銷售總監。
(C) 不，是出差一星期。

27. 🎧 澳洲男子／美國女子

> Could you change the location of the board meeting?
> (A) I have difficulty locating this book.
> (B) The board meets once a month.
> **(C) Lewis books the conference rooms.**

你能更改董事會會議的地點嗎？
(A) 我很難找到這本書。
(B) 每月召開一次董事會。
(C) 是Lewis在預約會議室。

28. 🎧 美國女子／澳洲男子

> Do you want to take a morning or afternoon flight to Toronto?
> (A) The shuttle is on its way.
> (B) A round-trip ticket.
> **(C) Which one's less expensive?**

你想搭乘上午還是下午飛往多倫多的航班？
(A) 接駁車在路上了。
(B) 來回票。
(C) 哪個比較便宜？

29. 🎧 美國男子／英國女子

> I didn't see you at the company picnic yesterday.
> (A) I'll prepare some sandwiches.
> **(B) Oh, there was an urgent meeting.**
> (C) Every spring.

昨天公司野餐會沒看到你。
(A) 我會準備一些三明治。
(B) 喔，有個緊急會議。
(C) 每年春天。

30. 🎧 英國女子／美國男子

> We're behind schedule, aren't we?
> (A) Yes, it's behind the building.
> (B) Thanks for your extra work.
> **(C) No, everything's right on time.**

我們進度落後了，不是嗎？
(A) 是的，就在大樓後方。
(B) 謝謝你加班。
(C) 不，一切都按時進行。

單字 behind schedule 進度落後

PART TEST 題本 p.46

1. (C)	**2.** (B)	**3.** (A)	**4.** (C)	**5.** (B)	**6.** (A)
7. (A)	**8.** (B)	**9.** (A)	**10.** (C)	**11.** (A)	**12.** (A)
13. (C)	**14.** (C)	**15.** (A)	**16.** (B)	**17.** (C)	**18.** (A)
19. (B)	**20.** (C)	**21.** (A)	**22.** (C)	**23.** (B)	**24.** (C)
25. (B)					

1. 🎧 美國男子／英國女子

> Where do you park when you go to Jackson Stadium?
> (A) I like spending time at the park.
> (B) The restroom is just around the corner.
> **(C) It's easier to just take the subway.**

你去Jackson體育場時把車停在哪裡？
(A) 我喜歡在公園裡消磨時光。
(B) 洗手間就在轉角處。
(C) 搭地鐵比較方便。

2. 🎧 英國女子／美國男子

> Who's going to interview candidates for the position?
> (A) For two weeks.
> **(B) Is the position not filled yet?**
> (C) My office is just next door.

誰來面試該職缺的求職者？
(A) 兩星期。
(B) 該職位還沒有補人嗎？
(C) 我的辦公室就在隔壁。

3. 🎧 澳洲男子／美國女子

> Can you help me clean the break room?
> **(A) Sure, I have time right after lunch.**
> (B) The other one's broken.
> (C) I put it in the storage room.

你能幫我打掃休息室嗎？
(A) 當然，我午餐後有空。
(B) 另一個壞掉了。
(C) 我把它放在儲藏室裡。

4. 🎧 美國女子／澳洲男子

> Does the entrée have meat in it?
> (A) No, I'll meet them tomorrow.
> (B) The back entrance is over there.
> **(C) The chef can use a substitute.**

主菜裡有肉嗎？
(A) 不，我明天會跟他們見面。
(B) 後門在那裡。
(C) 主廚可用其他食材代替。

解說 表示雖然主菜含有肉，但可要求主廚換成其他食材，屬於間接回答的方式。

5. 🎧 美國男子／英國女子

> Would you prefer I send the report electronically or by mail?
> (A) To the marketing team.
> **(B) I'll print it out myself.**
> (C) Only if you have to.

你希望我用電子郵件還是紙本信件寄送報告？
(A) 給行銷團隊。
(B) 我會自行印出來。
(C) 僅在必要時才這樣做。

解說 表示選擇電子郵件（electronically），收到後自行印出。

6. 🎧 英國女子／美國男子

> I need the phone number for the sales team.
> **(A) I left it on your desk.**
> (B) My degree is in mechanical engineering.
> (C) A large number of orders.

我需要銷售團隊的電話號碼。
(A) 我把它放在你桌上了。
(B) 我的學位是機械工程。
(C) 大量訂單。

7. 🎧 澳洲男子／美國女子

> Don't you want to look at the draft before the meeting?
> **(A) My computer is down at the moment.**
> (B) They already left.
> (C) I reserved the meeting room.

你不想在開會前看一下草案嗎？
(A) 我的電腦現在不能用。
(B) 他們已經離開了。
(C) 我預約了會議室。

8. 🎧 美國女子／澳洲男子

> Are you printing out the lease contract?
> (A) The computer login information.
> **(B) No, the printer is broken right now.**
> (C) That's my least favorite place.

你正在列印租賃合約嗎？
(A) 電腦登入資訊。
(B) 沒有，印表機現在壞了。
(C) 那是我最不喜歡的地方。

9. 🎧 美國男子／英國女子

> What do you plan to discuss with Mr. Allen?
> **(A) We're going over the training schedule.**
> (B) Yes, I just finished the floor plan.
> (C) Tomorrow would work for him.

你打算與Allen先生討論什麼？
(A) 我們會檢視培訓計畫。
(B) 是的，我剛完成平面圖。
(C) 他明天有時間。

10. 🎧 英國女子／美國男子

> Why wasn't Brian's proposal approved?
> (A) Would you like to pose next to the sign?
> (B) Yes, I double checked it.
> **(C) Because we don't have enough funding.**

為什麼Brian的提議沒有被批准？
(A) 你想在招牌旁擺個姿勢嗎？
(B) 是的，我有再次確認過。
(C) 因為我們沒有足夠的資金。

11. 🎧 澳洲男子／美國女子

> Did you book a campsite?
> **(A) Yes, I have the confirmation number right here.**
> (B) No, the one near the station.
> (C) The book is out of stock now.

你預約露營地了嗎？
(A) 是的，我這裡有確認號碼。
(B) 不，是車站附近那家。
(C) 這本書現在沒有庫存。

12. 🎧 美國女子／澳洲男子

> Do I register for the conference online or in person?
> **(A) You can register online.**
> (B) No, I'll be at a seminar.
> (C) Yes, a small fee.

會議是線上報名還是親自報名？
(A) 你可以線上報名。
(B) 不，我會在研討會。
(C) 是的，有少許費用。

13. 🎧 美國男子／英國女子

> When is Thomas going to the airport?
> (A) Use Gate 22.
> (B) By bus, I think.
> **(C) Right after the team meeting.**

Thomas什麼時候去機場？
(A) 請使用22號登機門。
(B) 搭公車吧，我覺得。
(C) 團隊會議結束後。

14. 🎧 英國女子／美國男子

> Where did you buy that handmade soap?
> (A) There may be a discount.
> (B) Just last week.
> **(C) At the farmer's market.**

你在哪裡買手工肥皂的？
(A) 可能會打折。
(B) 就在上週。
(C) 在農夫市集。

15. 🎧 澳洲男子／美國女子

> This model is selling well, isn't it?
> **(A) We spend a fortune on advertising.**
> (B) It's a marketing position.
> (C) Sure, I'll stop by the store.

這款型號賣得很好，不是嗎？
(A) 我們在廣告上花了一大筆錢。
(B) 這是個行銷職位。
(C) 當然，我會順道去一趟商店。

單字 fortune 巨款、財富　stop by 順路造訪⋯

16. 🎧 美國女子／澳洲男子

> I can help set up the stage if you'd like.
> (A) Yes, it was a great performance.
> **(B) Thanks, but you don't have to do that.**
> (C) A new assistant manager.

如果你願意，我可以幫忙搭建舞台。
(A) 是的，這是場很棒的表演。
(B) 謝謝，但你不必那樣做。
(C) 新任副經理。

17. 🎧 美國男子／英國女子

> Why was the delivery late?
> (A) Gillian signed the delivery receipt.
> (B) At least 5 hours.
> **(C) Did you see all the traffic?**

為什麼配送延遲了？
(A) Gillian在交貨單上簽名了。
(B) 至少五個小時。
(C) 你有看到都在塞車嗎？

18. 🎧 英國女子／美國男子

> You're leaving for Taiwan soon, aren't you?
> **(A) The conference was canceled.**
> (B) Just leave it to me.
> (C) No, Friday doesn't work.

你馬上就要去臺灣了，不是嗎？
(A) 會議被取消了。
(B) 交給我吧。
(C) 不，星期五沒時間。

解說 表示在臺灣的會議被取消。

19. 🎧 澳洲男子／美國女子

> Ms. Hill will be a great division executive.
> (A) The personnel department.
> **(B) She does hold the company's sales record.**
> (C) No, I can't remember the exact date.

Hill女士將成為一名優秀的部門主管。
(A) 人事部。
(B) 她確實維持了公司的銷售記錄。
(C) 不，我不記得確切日期了。

20. 🎧 美國女子／澳洲男子

> When did that hotel open?
> (A) I'm sorry, but we're fully booked.
> (B) The price includes accommodation.
> **(C) There was an article in the paper last week.**

那間飯店何時開業的？
(A) 不好意思，我們的預定滿了。
(B) 包含住宿的價格。
(C) 上週的報紙上有報導。

解說 (C) 表示上週的報紙上有報導開業的消息，屬於間接回答的方式。

21. 🎧 美國男子／英國女子

> This contract was reviewed by our legal team, wasn't it?
> **(A) Betty left her comments on some issues.**
> (B) Yes, it has an excellent view.
> (C) I'll contact my doctor.

這份合約是由我們法務組審核的，不是嗎？
(A) Betty對某些問題留下了意見。
(B) 是的，景色很好。
(C) 我會聯絡醫生。

解說 表示法務組的 Betty 看完合約後，留下了相關意見，屬於間接回答的方式。

22. 🎧 英國女子／美國男子

> Which dates would you like to book the conference room for?
> (A) The department budget for March.
> (B) Yes, we close at 6 o'clock.
> **(C) From the sixth to the eighth, please.**

你想預約哪天的會議室？
(A) 三月的部門預算。
(B) 是的，我們六點關門。
(C) 麻煩請預約六到八號。

23. 🎧 澳洲男子／美國女子

> How many new employees are you training today?
> (A) The gym on the third floor.
> **(B) Jason developed an online instruction module instead.**
> (C) She approved it.

你今天要培訓多少名新員工？
(A) 三樓的健身房。
(B) Jason開發了線上教學單元。
(C) 她批准了。

解說 表示改採線上方式培訓，屬於間接回答的方式。

24. 🎧 美國女子／澳洲男子

> Why hasn't Paul updated the database?
> (A) Just about two weeks, I think.
> (B) Yes, there's a sale on electronics tomorrow.
> **(C) Didn't you hear that the computer servers are down?**

Paul為何沒有更新資料庫？
(A) 我想大約兩星期。
(B) 是的，明天有電子產品的促銷活動。
(C) 你沒聽說電腦伺服器當機了嗎？

25. 🎧 美國男子／英國女子

> I can give you a discount if you increase your order to 50 chairs.
> (A) At the new furniture store.
> **(B) I'm not authorized to make that decision.**
> (C) This place looks great.

如果你把椅子訂購量增加到50張，我可以給你打折。
(A) 在新開的傢俱店。
(B) 我沒有權限做出該決定。
(C) 這個地方看起來很棒。

LC PART 3

簡短對話

題本p.51

1. (B)　**2.** (C)　**3.** (A)

範例

女　感謝您造訪Kaysville水族館。請問有什麼需要幫忙的嗎？
男　我想買兩張成人票。
女　普通票為22美元。不過，您可以只用75美元買到季票。一年內不限造訪次數。
男　嗯… 我們住在附近，所以應該會常來參觀。我會買。
女　太好了！你只需填寫這張申請表即可。

1. 對話發生在何處？
(A) 在電影院
(B) 在水族館
(C) 在美術館
(D) 在體育場

2. 男子最有可能購買什麼？
(A) 團體票
(B) 半日票
(C) 季票
(D) 學生票

3. 女子要求男子做什麼？
(A) 填寫表格
(B) 致電另一間分館
(C) 出示身分證
(D) 撥打電話

UNIT 01　說話者的職業或對話地點

CHECK-UP

題本 p.53

1. (C)　**2.** (D)

1. 🎧 美國男子／英國女子
Question 1 refers to the following conversation.

M　Betty, I just heard at the staff meeting our company won the bid to build the bridge over Rivanna River.
W　It's great news. That's the biggest construction project we've had in a while.
M　Exactly. Do you happen to know when construction will begin?
W　We have to wait until the contract is officially signed. It will be a while before we actually get started.

男　Betty, 我剛在員工會議上聽說Rivanna河川大橋的建案由我們公司得標。
女　真是個好消息。這是我們近年來最大的建設項目。
男　沒錯。你知道何時開始施工嗎？
女　我們要等到正式簽訂合約後。離我們實際開始還有一段時間。

單字　win a bid 得標　happen to do 有可能⋯

1. 說話者從事什麼行業？
(A) 出版業
(B) 運輸業
(C) 建築業
(D) 金融業

2. 🎧 澳洲男子／美國女子
Question 2 refers to the following conversation.

M　Hello. Lake Park Apartments management office. How can I help you?
W　Hi. I'm Helen Thomson. I live in Unit 325B. I'm a new tenant here.
M　Are you enjoying your new apartment?
W　Yes, I love it. However, I lost my key card for the main entrance. Do you happen to have an extra one?
M　No, we don't, but we can get that reissued. It'll take a few days.
W　Thank you. How much is it for reissuing that?
M　This is your first reissue, so there's no extra charge for that.

男　您好，這裡是湖畔公園公寓管理辦公室。有什麼需要幫忙的嗎？
女　你好，我是Helen Thomson。我住在325B，是新入住的住戶。
男　你對新公寓還滿意嗎？
女　是的，我很喜歡。但我弄丟了主入口的鑰匙卡。你還有備用的卡片嗎？
男　不，沒有，但可以補辦。這會需要幾天時間。
女　謝謝你。補辦的話要多少錢？
男　這是你第一次補辦，所以不用額外付費。

單字　management office 管理辦公室　tenant 住戶　reissue 重新發放

2. 男子最有可能是誰？
(A) 室內設計師
(B) 房屋仲介
(C) 安全檢查員
(D) 公寓管理員

19

UNIT 02 對話目的或主旨

CHECK-UP 題本 p.55

1. (B)   2. (A)

1. 🎧 英國女子／美國男子
Question 1 refers to the following conversation.

> W Hello, Mr. Lewis? This is Karen Miller calling from Siemens Technologies. I reviewed your application for the mechanical engineer position and would like to interview you.
> M Oh, I'm so pleased to hear that.
> W Good. I'm wondering if Thursday at 10 A.M. works for you.
> M Actually, I have a dentist appointment that morning. Do you mind if I call you back after I reschedule it?

女　你好，是Lewis先生嗎？我是Siemens科技公司的Karen Miller。我審閱過你對機械工程師一職的申請表，**想與你面談**。
男　哦，我很高興聽到這個消息。
女　很好。我想知道你星期四上午10點是否方便。
男　事實上，我那天早上有預約牙醫，我可以重新安排後再回電給你嗎？

單字　review 審閱　　application 申請表

1. 這通電話的目的為何？
(A) 下訂單
(B) 安排面談
(C) 確認合約
(D) 取消預約

2. 🎧 澳洲男子／美國女子
Question 2 refers to the following conversation.

> M The lights in my office just went out.
> W The power seems to be out in the whole building. I just called the maintenance office and they said it would take at least one hour until the power is restored.
> M Oh, I have a meeting with a client in 10 minutes.
> W Why don't you have a meeting at the coffee shop across the street?
> M That's a good idea.

男　剛剛我辦公室的燈熄滅了。
女　**整棟大樓好像都停電了**。我剛打電話給維修室，他們說至少要一小時才能恢復供電。
男　啊，我十分鐘後要跟客戶開會。
女　你要不要在對街的咖啡廳開會？
男　那是個好主意。

單字　go out 熄滅　　restore 恢復、使復原（過往的狀況、情感等）

2. 他們正在討論什麼問題？
(A) 停電
(B) 道路封閉
(C) 惡劣的天氣
(D) 故障的車輛

UNIT 03 建議或要求

CHECK-UP 題本 p.57

1. (A)   2. (C)

1. 🎧 美國男子／英國女子
Question 1 refers to the following conversation.

> M Hello. This is Marcus from Special Edge Marketing. I just sent you an e-mail with the design for your new advertising campaign. Did you get a chance to look at it?
> W Hi, Marcus. I was just about to call you. I wanted to tell you that we have a new slogan.
> M That's not a problem. Can you send it to me before the end of the day? Then I can finalize everything by tomorrow.
> W Definitely! After you're finished, please update the contract to reflect the changes.

男　你好，我是特殊優勢行銷公司的Marcus。我剛把新廣告活動的設計用電子郵件寄給你了。你看過了嗎？
女　你好，Marcus。我正要打電話給你。我想告訴你，我們有新的廣告標語。
男　那不成問題。你能在今天之內將它寄給我嗎？這樣我可以在明天前完成。
女　當然可以！麻煩你在完成後，**根據變更事項更新合約**。

單字　be about to 正要⋯
reflect the changes 反映出變更事項

1. 女子要求男子做什麼？
(A) 修改合約
(B) 完成付款
(C) 延長期限
(D) 獲得主管批准

2. 🎧 澳洲男子／美國女子

Question 2 refers to the following conversation.

> M　Cindy, have you analyzed the results from the customer satisfaction questionnaire?
>
> W　I did, and it seems like customers are satisfied with our service, but they wish we offered more discounts. Compared to other stores, we hardly ever have sales.
>
> M　Wow. I actually watched a video about this recently. It said that frequent sales can get more people in the door to your business.
>
> W　In that case, why don't we start a rewards program? That way, people will be tempted to come in more often to receive discounts.

男　Cindy，你分析過客戶滿意度問卷調查結果了嗎？
女　我分析過了，客戶似乎很滿意我們的服務，但希望我們提供更多優惠。與其他店家相比，我們很少打折促銷。
男　哇。其實我最近才看了關於這個的影片。據說頻繁的折扣會吸引更多顧客上門。
女　既然如此，**我們何不啟用回饋制度呢？** 如此一來客人就會為了想獲得折扣更常光顧。

單字　questionnaire 問卷調查　compared to 與…相比
tempt 引誘、吸引

2. 女子建議做什麼事？
(A) 進行市場調查
(B) 雇用更多員工
(C) 提供回饋制度
(D) 尋找顧問

UNIT 04 疑難問題或擔憂

CHECK-UP　　　　　　　　　　　題本 p.59

1. (B)　　**2.** (C)

1. 🎧 英國女子／美國男子

Question 1 refers to the following conversation.

> W　Kevin, have you ordered the mugs for our guests yet? Our gallery's grand opening is just around the corner.
>
> M　I called the Lolly Ceramics yesterday but unfortunately, the style we picked out is sold out. They said they aren't sure when they'll have more available.
>
> W　Well, we need the gifts here by the 2nd of July. We can't afford to wait.
>
> M　OK, I'll search the Internet to see if any other suppliers have a similar style right away.

女　Kevin，你有為我們的客人訂購馬克杯了嗎？我們的畫廊就快開幕了。
男　我昨天有打電話給Lolly陶器廠，但**遺憾的是，我們挑選的杯款已經售罄**。他說不確定什麼時候會有存貨。
女　嗯，我們需要在7月2日前收到禮品。我們沒辦法等了。
男　好的，我會立即上網搜尋其他供應商有沒有賣類似的款式。

單字　just around the corner 即將到來　pick out 挑選
sold out 售罄　supplier 供應商

1. 男子提到什麼問題？
(A) 錯過了截止日。
(B) 產品缺貨。
(C) 訂單未送達。
(D) 有些工作人員無法上班。

2. 🎧 澳洲男子／美國女子

Question 2 refers to the following conversation.

> M　I appreciate the invitation to your place of business. Like I wrote in my e-mail, I'm searching for a landscaping company to help modernize some of the properties I'm selling.
>
> W　No problem. My company is well-known for providing the most up-to-date landscaping possible.
>
> M　That sounds wonderful. I'm a little concerned about the price, though. Do you have different options depending on the budget?
>
> W　Of course. I'm sure we can find something within your price range. I'll show you a slideshow of some of our work and you can decide what you want done.

男　感謝你邀請我到你的公司。正如我在電子郵件中所寫，我目前在尋找一家景觀美化公司，來幫助我為正在銷售的房產進行現代化改造。
女　沒問題。我公司正以提供最新的景觀美化而聞名。
男　聽起來很棒。**不過，我還是有點擔心價格**。是否會根據預算提供多種選擇？
女　當然。我相信一定可以找到你價格範圍內的方案。我會向你展示一些作品的投影片，以便你決定想要哪種。

單字　place of business 工作場合　search for 尋找…
up-to-date 最新的　depending on 根據…

2. 男子說他擔心什麼？
(A) 位置
(B) 可行日期
(C) 價格
(D) 尺寸

UNIT 05 特定時間

CHECK-UP 題本 p.61

1. (C) **2.** (D)

1. 🎧 美國男子／英國女子
Question 1 refers to the following conversation.

> M Hello, and thank you for calling Carol's, the customized gift-making shop. What can I do for you?
> W I'm calling to order 150 pens with my company's logo. It's our fifth year of being in business, so we're having a small anniversary party. Would it be possible to have them in three weeks?
> M Sure. That won't be a problem. And since you plan to order over 100 items, I can give you a 10% discount.
> W That's wonderful! How can I pay for my purchase? Do I have to visit the shop or can I provide my credit card details online?

男 你好，感謝你致電Carol's客製化禮品店。有什麼需要幫忙的嗎？
女 我想訂購150支印有我們公司標誌的原子筆。**在迎來創業五週年之際，我們要舉辦一個小型週年紀念派對。請問能在三週之內拿到嗎？**
男 當然沒問題。而且，由於你打算訂購超過100項商品，我可以提供你九折優惠。
女 太棒了！我該如何支付購買費用呢？我需要親自前往商店，還是可線上提供信用卡資料？

單字 customized 客製化的

1. 根據女子所述，三週後會發生什麼事？
(A) 盤點庫存
(B) 年度清倉拍賣
(C) 週年紀念派對
(D) 盛大開幕

2. 🎧 美國女子／澳洲男子
Question 2 refers to the following conversation.

> W You've reached the Allendale Community Center. What can I do for you?
> M Hello, I'm looking to start a bird-watching club.
> W Sure. To start your own club, you can come to the center and fill out some paperwork.
> M Perfect. I'll come by later today. Can I reserve a space at the center?
> W Sure, but since you're starting a new club, you might not have a lot of initial members.
> M I understand. Also, does the community center have AV equipment? I want to project some pictures of birds on a screen.
> W Yes. You can borrow our AV equipment free of charge.

女 這裡是Allendale社區中心。有什麼需要幫忙的嗎？
男 你好，我想創辦一個賞鳥社團。
女 沒問題。如果你想創辦社團，**只要到中心填寫文件即可。**
男 太好了。**我今天晚點會過去一趟。**我可以在社區中心預約空間嗎？
女 當然可以，但因為是新成立的社團，初期可能不會有太多成員。
男 我明白。另外，社區中心有視聽設備嗎？我想在螢幕上投影鳥類的照片。
女 有的。你可以免費借用我們的視聽設備。

單字 fill out 填寫（資料等）　　come by 順道過去
free of charge 免費

2. 男子說他今天晚點會做什麼事？
(A) 發表演說
(B) 線上填寫調查表
(C) 預約車輛
(D) 造訪社區中心

UNIT 06 下一步的行動

CHECK-UP 題本 p.63

1. (D) **2.** (B)

1. 🎧 美國男子／英國女子
Question 1 refers to the following conversation.

> M Hey, Eleanor. I want you to attend the annual book publishing conference in New York. It will be a great chance for you to connect with other publishers.
> W That's wonderful! I appreciate the opportunity. Do you mind if we push back the deadline for our latest children's book project? If I'm away for the conference, I won't be able to work on it.
> M That's a good point. Let's move the deadline back one week so you have enough time to work on the project. I'll send out an e-mail notice to the rest of the staff.

男 嘿，Eleanor。我希望你能參加在紐約舉行的年度圖書出版會議。這對你來說是個能與其他出版社交流的好機會。
女 太好了！我很感激有這個機會。那你介意延後我們最新的兒童讀物專案截止日嗎？如果我去參加會議，就無法繼續

22

作業。

男 有道理。我們把截止日延後一週，這樣你就有足夠的時間完成該專案。**我會發電子郵件通知其他員工。**

單字 push back the deadline 延後截止日（=move the deadline back）　send out 發送

1. 男子接下來最有可能做什麼？
(A) 打電話
(B) 為會議做準備
(C) 去吃午餐
(D) 發送通知

2. 🎧 美國女子／澳洲男子
Question 2 refers to the following conversation.

> W Good morning, Jeremy. The final blueprints for our sorting robot and driverless forklift are ready. We'll be able to show them to our clients from Redhawk Logistics at today's meeting.
>
> M Actually, none of the conference rooms are available. I forgot to book one for today's meeting.
>
> W I see. I'll speak with the other department heads to see if we can take one of their slots. The clients have a tight schedule and we need to have the meeting today.
>
> M Thanks a bunch. I think the marketing and human resource departments reserved the conference room.
>
> W OK.

女 早安，Jeremy。我們分類機器人和無人駕駛堆高機的最終設計圖已準備就緒。我們可以在今天的會議上展示給紅鷹物流公司的客戶看。
男 事實上，沒有任何可用的會議室。我忘了預約今天開會要用的會議室了。
女 我知道了。**那我會跟其他部門主管商量，看看他們能否給我們已預約的空間。**客戶的行程緊湊，所以我們今天一定要開會。
男 非常感謝。我想行銷部門和人力資源部門有預約會議室。
女 好的。

單字 sort 分類　driverless 無人駕駛的　forklift 堆高機
slot 位置（時間、空間）　have a tight schedule 行程緊湊
reserve 預約

2. 女子接下來最有可能做什麼事？
(A) 檢查部分設備
(B) 與同事談話
(C) 接送客戶
(D) 重新安排演示時間

PRACTICE　UNIT 01-06　題本 p.64

1. (C)	2. (A)	3. (B)	4. (B)	5. (A)	6. (C)
7. (A)	8. (C)	9. (D)	10. (A)	11. (B)	12. (B)
13. (D)	14. (D)	15. (B)	16. (C)	17. (C)	18. (B)
19. (B)	20. (C)	21. (D)	22. (C)	23. (A)	24. (A)

1-3. 🎧 英國女子／美國男子
Questions 1-3 refer to the following conversation.

> W Good morning. ¹Do you know when you and your crew will be finished with the renovations to our library?
>
> M I can't say for sure. The project is running behind schedule. ²We're waiting for wooden frames to arrive before we can install new windows in the reading room.
>
> W That's too bad. Our temporary facility across the street is quite small, so our library staff is eager to return to the building as soon as possible.
>
> M I understand. ³I'll call the supplier to see if they can make a rush delivery of the frames by the end of the week.

女 早安。¹請問你和你的團隊何時能完成我們圖書館的翻修工程呢？
男 我不確定。該專案的進度落後了。²**我們正在等木製窗框抵達**，才能在閱覽室安裝新窗戶。
女 這真是個壞消息。我們位於對街的臨時設施場所太小，所以圖書館工作人員想要盡快回到大樓。
男 我理解。³**我會打電話給供應商**，看看窗框能否在本週結束前交貨。

單字 run behind schedule 進度落後
be eager to do... 渴望做某件事
make a rush delivery 緊急出貨

1. 男子最有可能是誰？
(A) 行銷顧問
(B) 新聞記者
(C) 建設經理
(D) 網頁開發人員

2. 男子提到什麼問題？
(A) 缺少部分材料。
(B) 專案費用過高。
(C) 天候不佳。
(D) 工作人員辭職。

3. 男子接下來會做什麼事？
(A) 發送電子郵件
(B) 打電話

23

(C) 撰寫報告
(D) 造訪政府機關

4-6. 🎧 英國女子／美國男子

Questions 4-6 refer to the following conversation.

> W　Hi. [4]I'm here with my documentary crew. I'm putting together a series on innovative designs in contemporary medical facilities. I'm here to get footage of your hospital.
>
> M　Oh, right. [5]An agent from your film studio e-mailed me this morning to say you were coming.
>
> W　Can you please direct me to the newly renovated intensive care unit?
>
> M　Sure. [6]I can also introduce you to our Assistant Director. He was in charge of designing the East Wing.

女　你好，[4]我們是紀錄片製作組。目前正在製作一系列關於當代醫療設施的創新設計。我來拍攝你們醫院的影片。

男　哦，對。[5]今天早上你們電影工作室的經紀人有發郵件說你們要過來。

女　你能帶我去新裝修的加護病房嗎？

男　當然可以。[6]我還可以為你介紹我們的副主任。他負責東館的設計。

單字 put together 整理、匯集起來　footage 影片的鏡頭（畫面、影像）　direct 指路

4. 女子最有可能是誰？
(A) 內科醫生
(B) 電影導演
(C) 建築師
(D) 室內設計師

5. 男子說今天早上發生了什麼事？
(A) 他收到了電子郵件。
(B) 他發現了問題。
(C) 他跟承包商碰面。
(D) 他上班遲到了。

6. 男子提議做什麼事？
(A) 進行面談
(B) 繳交報告
(C) 安排談話
(D) 分享數據

7-9. 🎧 澳洲男子／美國女子

Question 7-9 refer to the following conversation.

> M　Thanks for meeting with me today, Lydia. I'd like to discuss your products' performance in the Backpackers' Online Marketplace.
>
> W　Sure, Mike. The marketplace has been a great way for me to distribute [7]my apparel to backpackers worldwide.
>
> M　Your Shoe Hop boots are among our best-selling items. [8]Customers praise their durability. [7, 8] Customers describe using your boots on rough terrain and in extreme weather, with the boots showing minimal signs of wear and tear.
>
> W　I'm glad. [9]I've been getting rubber from a different company recently. I'm pleased with the results and plan to continue working with them.

男　Lydia，謝謝你今天來見我。我想討論一下貴公司產品在背包客線上市集的銷售表現。

女　當然好，Mike。線上市集一直是我把[7]服裝銷售給世界各地背包客的好方法。

男　貴公司的Shoe Hop靴子是我們公司最暢銷的商品之一。[7,8]客戶稱讚其耐用性非常好，據稱在崎嶇地形和極端氣候下穿著你們家的靴子，磨損程度微乎其微。

女　我很榮幸。[9]我最近向另一家公司購買橡膠。結果令我滿意，所以我打算繼續與他們合作。

單字 marketplace 市場、市集　apparel 服裝、服飾
durability 耐用性　terrain 地形、地域　wear and tear 磨損

7. 女子的公司在賣什麼東西？
(A) 登山裝備
(B) 行動應用程式
(C) 保健食品
(D) 兒童服裝

8. 男人強調哪一點？
(A) 網站有所更動。
(B) 顧客不滿意。
(C) 產品值得信賴。
(D) 價格上漲。

9. 女子對什麼感到滿意？
(A) 廣告活動
(B) 送貨服務
(C) 熟練的員工
(D) 新的供應商

10-12. 🎧 美國女子／澳洲男子

Questions 10-12 refer to the following conversation.

> W [10]Welcome to the Brighton Senior Center. Are you here to visit a family member?
>
> M Actually, [11]I'm here because I heard there's an opening for a lifeguard position.
>
> W That's right. Do you have previous experience working as a lifeguard for senior citizens?
>
> M I worked at Sunny Side Beach over in Roslindale for more than three years. The population there was mostly elderly.
>
> W I see. Well, the application process is pretty simple. [12]But first, I can show you around the pool and the rest of the building to give you a clearer idea of what the position requires.
>
> M Thanks, that sounds great.

女 [10]歡迎光臨Brighton樂齡中心。你是來探望家人的嗎？
男 事實上，[11]我來這裡是因為聽說有救生員的職缺。
女 好的。你以前擔任過老年人的救生員嗎？
男 我曾在Roslindale的陽光海灘工作超過三年的時間。那裡大多數為老年人。
女 我明白了。嗯，申請流程非常簡單。[12]不過，我先帶你參觀游泳池和大樓其他地方，讓你能更清楚了解職位的需求。
男 謝謝，聽起來很不錯。

單字 opening 職缺　elderly 年長　give you a clearer idea of 讓…更清楚地了解

10. 女子在哪裡工作？
(A) 退休社區
(B) 大學
(C) 招募機構
(D) 醫院

11. 男子的來訪目的為何？
(A) 他來見親戚。
(B) 他正在詢問工作。
(C) 他正在送貨。
(D) 他正在付款。

12. 男子接下來可能會做什麼？
(A) 觀看短片
(B) 參觀設施
(C) 填寫申請表
(D) 撰寫電子郵件

13-15. 🎧 美國男子／英國女子

Questions 13-15 refer to the following conversation.

> M Good morning. [13]I'm wondering if you could repair my custom-designed business suit. There's a tear along the right shoulder line, and some frayed ends inside the pocket.
>
> W I see… Yes, I can fix this, but it will take some time to make sure I get the stitching right. How soon do you need it?
>
> M [14]I'll be traveling to a business conference in Sao Paulo next weekend. I'd like to take the item with me if possible.
>
> W It shouldn't be a problem. [15]Just fill out this order form with any special instructions and leave the suit in the basket along the back wall.

男 早安。[13]我想知道你能否幫我修補我的訂製西裝。右肩線上有一處撕裂痕，口袋內側有破損。
女 我明白了…是，我可以修補好它，但縫要花一些時間。你最快何時需要？
男 [14]我下週末要去聖保羅參加商務會議。如果可以的話，我想把這套西裝帶過去。
女 沒問題。[15]請填寫訂單，並在上方註明特殊事項，然後把西裝放在後牆的籃子即可。

單字 tear 撕裂處、撕裂　fray 磨損、被磨損

13. 女子是誰？
(A) 服飾店店員
(B) 雜貨店店主
(C) 旅行社仲介
(D) 裁縫師

14. 男子說下週會發生什麼事？
(A) 他將會休假。
(B) 他將主辦會議。
(C) 他將簽署合約。
(D) 他將參加活動。

15. 男子接下來可能會做什麼事？
(A) 付款
(B) 填寫表格
(C) 領取收據
(D) 撰寫評論

16-18. 🎧 英國女子／美國男子

Questions 16-18 refer to the following conversation.

W Greetings, Mr. Valdez, and thank you for coming out to Willow Country Club to meet with me today. I hope our businesses can develop a long-lasting partnership.

M Me, too. I hear there have been some recent changes at your club.

W Yes. [16]Our membership population has doubled over the last six months. Now, we simply don't have enough kitchen staff members to meet our clientele's needs.

M Well, my company's award-winning chefs are among the best in the county. [17]We could come up with new high-end menu items to impress your members and their guests.

W That would be great. [18]I could announce the partnership by launching a televised ad campaign, to our mutual benefit.

女 你好，Valdez先生，謝謝你今天來柳樹鄉村俱樂部與我碰面。希望我們的事業能夠發展為長期合作夥伴關係。

男 我也是。聽說你們俱樂部最近發生了一些變化。

女 是的。[16]在過去的六個月裡，我們的會員數增加了一倍。現在我們的廚房員工短缺，無法滿足客戶的需求。

男 嗯，我公司的獲獎廚師稱得上是全縣最優秀的廚師。[17]我們可以推出新的高級餐點，讓俱樂部會員和同行賓客留下深刻印象。

女 這是個好主意。[18]我想藉由電視廣告來宣布這項合作夥伴關係，這樣做對雙方都有好處。

單字 long-lasting 長久的　membership population 會員數　award-winning 獲獎的　come up with 提出、想出　televised ad campaign 電視廣告

16. 根據女子所述，最近她的俱樂部發生了什麼事？
(A) 找到投資者。
(B) 員工要求加薪。
(C) 客戶群增長。
(D) 地點有所更動。

17. 男子的公司可以做什麼？
(A) 提供服務人員
(B) 安排餐廳
(C) 準備高級餐點
(D) 送餐服務

18. 女子說她可以做什麼來宣布合作關係？
(A) 策劃特別活動
(B) 製作廣告
(C) 發起社群媒體活動
(D) 在報紙刊登廣告

19-21. 🎧 澳洲男子／美國女子

Questions 19-21 refer to the following conversation.

M Hi, and [19]welcome to Speedsters Athletic Club. How can I help you?

W [19]I've belonged to this gym for a while, but I've never signed up for individual training sessions before. Can you tell me about them?

M Sure. Here.[20]You just need to fill out this document listing your exercise goals and available time slots. Then we'll match you up with a personal trainer who's a perfect fit for your needs.

W Exciting! Is it possible to meet any of the trainers beforehand? I have some specific questions about training programs.

M Yes. [21]Steve, one of our most popular trainers, is right over here. I'll introduce you.

W Thanks. Lead the way!

男 [19]歡迎光臨Speedsters健身俱樂部。請問有什麼需要幫忙的嗎？

女 [19]我加入健身房已經有一段時間了，但之前從未報名參加過個人訓練。你能跟我說明一下嗎？

男 當然可以。[20]請你先在這份文件上填寫你的訓練目標和有空的時段。接著我們會為你提供最符合需求的私人教練。

女 太令人興奮了！請問能不能提前與任何一位教練見面？我有一些關於訓練項目的特定問題想要請教。

男 好。[21]我們最受歡迎的教練之一Steve人就在這裡。我來為你介紹一下。

女 謝謝。請帶路！

單字 sign up for 報名、加入　fill out 填寫（表格）　match A up with B 幫 A 與 B 配對　a perfect fit for 對⋯適合的人選　lead the way 帶路、領先

19. 談話最有可能發生在哪裡？
(A) 辦公大樓
(B) 健身中心
(C) 滑雪場
(D) 體育用品店

20. 男子交給女子什麼東西？
(A) 電話號碼
(B) 收據
(C) 表格
(D) 網站連結

21. 女子接下來最有可能做什麼事？
(A) 打電話
(B) 前往等候區
(C) 繳交求職申請書
(D) 與工作人員交談

22-24. 🎧 澳洲男子／美國女子

Questions 22-24 refer to the following conversation.

> M Hey, Karina. Sorry I'm late. It's been a stressful morning.
>
> W What happened?
>
> M I stopped for gas on the way to work. [22]When I got back in my car, it wouldn't start. A stranger helped me get the engine going, but now it's making loud clunking noises.
>
> W Hmm… [23]do you know Stevenson's Auto Body on 71st street? The owner is really knowledgeable. I bet he can fix your car.
>
> M Thanks, I'll ask him. But first, [24]I'll try to find the invoice from the last time I got the car repaired so I can show it to him. This is a recurring issue.

男 嘿，Karina。不好意思我來晚了。早上就讓人壓力很大。
女 發生什麼事了？
男 我在上班途中順道去加油。[22]當我回到車上時，發動不了車子。一位陌生人幫我發動引擎，但現在它會發出響亮的咔噠聲。
女 那…[23]你知道在71街上的Stevenson's修車廠嗎？老闆非常博學。我敢肯定他能修好你的車。
男 謝謝，我會去問他。但我要先[24]找出上次修車的發票，然後拿給他看。這是個反覆出現的問題。

單字 on the way to work 上班途中
get the engine going 發動引擎
knowledgeable 博學多聞的
get the car repaired （在車廠）修車
recurring 反覆出現的（recur 反覆出現、再發生）
（recurrent 復發的、定期重複的）

22. 男子提到什麼問題？
(A) 他受傷了。
(B) 他的輪胎爆胎了。
(C) 他的引擎失靈了。
(D) 他的油箱漏油了。

23. 女人提出什麼建議？
(A) 前往特定的維修店
(B) 檢查保固資訊
(C) 購買新保險
(D) 要求退款

24. 男子說他會找出什麼東西？
(A) 發票
(B) 說明書
(C) 名片
(D) 警方報告

UNIT 07 掌握意圖

Example 01   題本 p.66

1. (A)   **2.** (C)   **3.** (D)

> 男 Heather，我們還沒為下週末舉行的Sheffield夏季音樂節做任何計劃。這會是個很好的宣傳機會。
> 女 肯定會有很多人去。
> 男 沒錯。我想免費發放我們的罐裝系列汽水。我們還可以在限量版飲料罐上印音樂節的標誌。
> 女 這可能需要長達兩週的時間。
> 男 沒錯。也許我們可想出其他能脫穎而出的辦法。

單字 take place 發生、舉行   publicity 宣傳   give out 發放
get A printed with B 在A上刻印B   stand out 脫穎而出

1. 下週末將舉辦什麼活動？
(A) 音樂節
(B) 慈善募款活動
(C) 週年紀念派對
(D) 公司野餐會

2. 說話者的公司生產什麼東西？
(A) 運動裝備
(B) 服裝
(C) 飲料
(D) 戶外傢俱

3. 女子為何會說：「這可能需要長達兩週的時間」？
(A) 為失誤道歉
(B) 建議延長期限
(C) 對服務表達不滿
(D) 表達對計畫的擔憂

PRACTICE 高難度   題本 p.67

1. (C)   **2.** (D)   **3.** (B)   **4.** (D)   **5.** (D)   **6.** (A)
7. (D)   **8.** (A)   **9.** (D)   **10.** (C)   **11.** (A)   **12.** (B)

1-3. 🎧 英國女子／美國男子

Questions 1-3 refer to the following conversation.

> W Hello, Daniel. [1]This is Sabrina from Arch Publishing. We were highly impressed with your résumé and interview, so we wish to offer you a position at our Los Angeles branch.
>
> M Thank you so much! It's great to hear that. [2]But I think I need some time to think about moving all the way to Los Angeles before I make a decision.
>
> W Actually, we're looking to hire as soon as possible.

M　Ah, I see.

W　Working for our company has a lot of perks. As I'm sure you know, [3]the company provides both a housing and transportation stipend for all workers. A huge chunk of your expenses would already be covered by the company.

女　您好，Daniel。[1]我是拱門出版社的Sabrina。您的履歷和面試讓我們留下了深刻印象，所以希望提供您洛杉磯分公司的職位。

男　太感謝了！很高興聽到這個消息。[2]不過在做出決定前，我需要一些時間來考慮搬到洛杉磯的事情。

女　其實我們希望能盡快錄用。

男　啊，我明白。

女　在我們公司工作有很多福利。如您所知，[3]公司為全體員工提供住宿和交通津貼。有很大一部分的花費會由公司負擔。

單字　look to 期望某事發生　perk（薪資外的）福利
stipend 津貼

1. 女子在什麼類型的公司上班？
(A) 行銷公司
(B) 旅行社
(C) 出版社
(D) 法律事務所

2. 女子說：「我們希望能盡快錄用」，意味著什麼？
(A) 她很快要退休了。
(B) 將會更動時間表。
(C) 需要額外資金。
(D) 男子應迅速做出決定。

3. 根據女子所述，公司有提供什麼？
(A) 免費餐食
(B) 差旅補貼
(C) 公司信用卡
(D) 員工折扣

4-6. 🎧美國男子／英國女子

Questions 4-6 refer to the following conversation.

M　Hey, Elois. [4]How are the designs for the new swimsuit line coming along? I was hoping to begin production soon.

W　Not great, actually. We finalized the patterns, but we can't decide on what colors to use. We don't know if we should go with bright colors or more neutral tones. [5]I'm a little annoyed because we can't reach a decision.

M　So what are you going to do? Summer is coming in a few months.

W　I was hoping you could give us some advice since you stay up to date with trends.

男　嘿，Elois。[4]新泳裝系列的設計進度如何？我一直希望能盡快開始生產。

女　其實不太順利。我們確定好了圖案，但還沒決定用什麼顏色。不知道該使用明亮色還是更中性的色調。[5]因為我們拿不定主意，使我有點困擾。

男　那你接下來打算怎麼辦？幾個月後夏天就要來臨了。[6]

女　我希望你能給我們一些建議，因為你掌握了最新流行趨勢。

單字　How are ~ coming along? …的進展如何？
go with 伴隨　reach a decision 做決定
stay up to date with trends 掌握最新流行趨勢

4. 說話者最有可能從事什麼行業？
(A) 傢俱
(B) 健身
(C) 化妝品
(D) 服裝

5. 女子為什麼感到困擾？
(A) 有些材料的品質不佳。
(B) 有些設備損壞。
(C) 無法使用某些設計。
(D) 尚未做出某些決定。

6. 男子為何會說：「幾個月後夏天就要來臨了」？
(A) 強調緊迫性
(B) 提醒女子截止日
(C) 調整行程安排錯誤
(D) 表達對假期的渴望

7-9. 🎧美國女子／澳洲男子

Questions 7-9 refer to the following conversation.

W　Ben, our game testers are reporting slow load times and [7]faulty mechanics for the new Mars Hunters computer game.

M　That's bad news. Our developers will need to fix the problems soon if we want to stay on track for a November release date.

W　The project has already been a long haul. We might want to offer extra incentives to anyone who is willing to work overtime this month.

M　Good idea. [9]I'll go speak with the human resource manager. Hopefully she can come up with a special offer for our workers.

女　Ben，我們的遊戲測試人員說新的火星獵人電腦遊戲，有載入時間緩慢和[7]機制缺陷的問題。

男　這是個壞消息。如果我們想趕上十一月的上市日期，開發人員需盡快解決這些問題。

女　這個項目已經耗時很久了。我們可能要為這個月願意加班的人提供額外獎勵。

男　好主意。[9]我會跟人力資源經理商量。希望她能為我們員工

開出不錯的條件。

單字 mechanics 機制、技術、機械學　stay on track 進展順利
haul 距離（旅程、路）　come up with 提出、想出…

7. 女子提到什麼問題？
(A) 銷量下降。
(B) 送貨延遲。
(C) 資料遺失。
(D) 產品有缺陷。

8. 女子說：「這個項目已經耗時很久了」，意味著什麼？
(A) 員工一直在努力工作。
(B) 公司雇用了新員工。
(C) 應該終止項目。
(D) 遊戲適合高階玩家。

9. 男子接下來會做什麼事？
(A) 進行線上調查
(B) 撰寫正式投訴
(C) 發送電子郵件
(D) 開會

10-12. 🎧 美國女子／澳洲男子
Questions 10-12 refer to the following conversation.

> W Hey, Allen. I know we were supposed to look over [10] the blueprints for the new library, but I'm way too busy today.
> M Why are you so busy?
> W Well, I'm in charge of designing the new bridge for Kline River, but a materials shortage messed up my original plan. Plus, I have the monthly meeting with the company executives. Do you mind looking at the blueprints tomorrow?
> M [11] It will only be a few minutes. I've narrowed everything down to two designs, so we just have to decide which one will suit the new library the best.
> W Ahh, OK. I think I can find time around 5:30. [12] But I have to leave right after work because I need to pick up dinner for my family.

單字 be supposed to 應該要做…　mess up 打亂
narrow something down 縮小、減少（可選擇範圍）
suit 適合

10. 說話者從哪個領域的工作？
(A) 製造業
(B) 金融
(C) 建築
(D) 農業

11. 男子為何會說：「我已把所有內容減少到兩種設計」？
(A) 向女子保證不會花很長時間開會。
(B) 徵求女子同意。
(C) 表現出對設計圖的驚訝。
(D) 表達對計劃的失望。

12. 女子說她會在下班後做什麼？
(A) 參加週年紀念晚宴
(B) 帶餐點回家
(C) 去看醫生
(D) 為休假計劃

UNIT 08　三人對話

Example 01　題本 p.68

1. (D)　**2.** (C)　**3.** (B)

> 男　Washington女士，幸好你的手臂已經痊癒了。我們將在您下次就診時開始進行物理治療。
> 女1　喔，但我以為物理治療也是預約今天。
> 男　對此我感到非常抱歉。一定是在安排預約時出了差錯。我們只為您預約了X光檢查。
> 女1　啊，原來是這樣。
> 男　Rislov女士，你能幫Washington女士預約物理治療嗎？
> 女2　當然。但我應該更新您的聯絡資訊。我們一般會發送預約提醒，但我們的紀錄上似乎沒有您的手機號碼。能請您填寫這張聯絡表格嗎？
> 女1　沒問題。

1. 說話者最有可能在哪裡？
(A) 社區中心
(B) 健身俱樂部
(C) 律師事務所
(D) 醫院

2. 男子為何要道歉？
(A) 某些設備無法運轉。
(B) 有位同事遲到了。
(C) 安排預約上發生錯誤。
(D) 帳單有誤。

29

3. Washington女士接下來會做什麼？
(A) 預約
(B) 填寫表格
(C) 順道去藥局
(D) 聯絡保險公司

2. 男子的工作為何？
(A) 銷售代表
(B) 大樓管理經理
(C) 軟體工程師
(D) 餐廳主廚

3. Jolene下午打算做什麼？
(A) 造訪房地產
(B) 進行演示
(C) 回到辦公室
(D) 觀看演講

PRACTICE 高難度   題本 p.69

| 1. (C) | 2. (A) | 3. (D) | 4. (C) | 5. (B) | 6. (B) |
| 7. (C) | 8. (A) | 9. (D) | 10. (D) | 11. (A) | 12. (B) |

1-3. 🎧 英國女子／美國女子／美國男子

Questions 1-3 refer to the following conversation with three speakers.

W1　[1]Jolene, I've really been enjoying the annual interior design conference.

W2　Me too! I hope our company will attract more customers after this. Hey, let's take a look at this booth about sustainable furniture.

M　Hello! My name is Jerry Harvest, and [2]I'm head of the sales team at Brothers Furniture. I'm happy to answer any questions you have.

W2　What makes your company different from others?

M　We custom-make each piece of furniture specifically to meet the needs of our clients. [3]I'll be giving a talk in the main hall later today about the ordering process.

W1　I have an investor meeting at two, but [3]Jolene, you should go.

W2　That sounds great.

女1　[1]Jolene，我真的很享受年度室內設計大會。
女2　我也是！希望我們公司將來能吸引更多客戶。嘿，我們來看一下展示永續傢俱的攤位。
男　你好！我叫Jerry Harvest，[2]我是兄弟傢俱公司銷售團隊的**負責人**。我很樂意回答您的任何問題。
女2　貴公司與其他公司有何不同之處？
男　我們專門訂製每一件傢俱，來滿足客戶的需求。[3]**今天稍晚我會在主廳演說訂購流程。**
女1　我兩點有個投資者會議，[3]但Jolene，你應該去參加。
女2　好主意。

單字 sustainable 永續的　　ordering process 訂購流程

1. 女子在哪裡工作？
(A) 化工廠
(B) 建設公司
(C) 室內設計公司
(D) 會議中心

4-6. 🎧 美國男子／英國女子／美國女子

Questions 4-6 refer to the following conversation with three speakers.

M　Hi, Florence and Nicki. [4]I recently heard that our design for the additional storehouse at the local factory has been approved. Florence, any updates for the next step?

W1　Yes, we conducted a preliminary survey with the surrounding residents, and [5]it turns out they're very concerned about the noise during building construction.

M　Nicki, how about we set up a meeting at the town hall to discuss these issues with residents?

W2　I already wanted to schedule a meeting for April ninth, [6]but the town hall was booked for then. Luckily, the recreation center offered to provide a venue for free.

男　你好，Florence和Nicki。[4]**我最近聽說在當地工廠增設倉庫的設計已獲批准。**Florence，關於後續有什麼新進展嗎？
女1　是的，我們對附近居民進行了初步調查，[5]**結果發現他們非常擔心建築施工過程中所產生的噪音。**
男　Nicki，我們要不要在鎮政廳安排一場會議，與居民討論這個問題？
女2　我本來想把會議排在4月9日，[6]**但那天鎮政廳已被預約了。**幸好娛樂中心願意免費提供場地。

單字 preliminary 初步的　　surrounding 附近的、周圍的
it turns out that... 結果發現、顯示為⋯
set up a meeting 安排會議　　town hall 鎮政廳、市民大會
schedule a meeting 安排會議

4. 工廠附近將建造什麼？
(A) 停車場
(B) 加油站
(C) 倉儲設施
(D) 垃圾掩埋場

5. 居民最擔憂的事情為何？
(A) 安全
(B) 噪音
(C) 資金
(D) 交通

6. 為何選擇新的會議地點？
(A) 提供更多空間。
(B) 原場地已被預訂。
(C) 交通更方便。
(D) 居民偏好新地點。

7-9. 🎧 美國男子／英國女子／澳洲男子
Questions 7-9 refer to the following conversation with three speakers.

> M1　⁷Hello, P.J.'s Electronics Factory. This is Raymond Daniels. How may I help you?
>
> W　Hello, Mr. Daniels. I'm Linda Patterson. ⁸I e-mailed you to ask if it was possible for my students to tour your facilities.
>
> M1　Oh, Ms. Patterson! Right. I've been waiting for your call. Actually, my secretary Kevin is in charge of that. I'll transfer you to him. He'll be able to set everything up for you.
>
> W　Thank you!
>
> M2　Hello, Ms. Patterson. This is Mr. Daniels' secretary, Kevin. Would your class be able to visit the factory on September 15? That's about a month from now.
>
> W　Yes, that would be perfect. But I'm a bit worried about the safety of my students. ⁹Are there any guidelines I should know about?
>
> M2　Absolutely. I'll send those to you in an e-mail.

男1 ⁷您好這裡是P.J.'S電子廠。我是Raymond Daniels。請問有什麼需要幫忙的嗎？
女 您好，Daniels先生。我是Linda Patterson。⁸我有發郵件給您，詢問我的學生能否參觀貴公司的設施。
男1 喔，Patterson女士！是，我一直在等您的電話。目前是由我的秘書Kevin負責此事。我幫您轉接電話，他會為您安排好一切。
女 謝謝您！
男2 您好，Patterson女士。我是Daniels先生的祕書Kevin。您的班級方便在9月15日參觀工廠嗎？大約是一個月後。
女 沒問題，太好了。不過我有點擔心學生的安全。⁹有什麼我應該知道的安全守則嗎？
男2 當然有。我會用電子郵件發送給您。

單字 tour 參觀、巡視、觀光　transfer 轉接電話給其他人　set up 準備、安排

7. 男子最有可能從事何種行業？
(A) 服務業
(B) 媒體業
(C) 電子業
(D) 建築業

8. 來電目的為何？
(A) 詢問實地參觀事宜
(B) 下訂單
(C) 安排面試
(D) 退回部分商品

9. 會發送給女子什麼東西？
(A) 保固書
(B) 前往地點的路線圖
(C) 合約影本
(D) 安全指南

10-12. 🎧 美國女子／美國男子／澳洲男子
Questions 10-12 refer to the following conversation with three speakers.

> W　Hello. ¹⁰I got an e-mail advertisement for this Crystal Clear 2000 television, ¹¹but I don't see any of the televisions on the shelves.
>
> M1　Let me check the computer to see if we have more in the back... Looks like we're all sold out. I'll get my manager to help you. Mr. Dowell? Could you come here please? The customer here is looking for the Crystal Clear 2000.
>
> M2　Hi. So sorry about that. That television has been on sale for a few days, so many people came to the store to buy it. ¹¹That's why we're completely out of stock.
>
> W　Is there any way I could still buy it?
>
> M2　Sure. If you pay now, we can ship the television to your preferred address. ¹²I can even offer you free express shipping for your trouble.

女　你好，¹⁰我有收到這款Crystal Clear 2000電視的廣告郵件，¹¹但我沒有在貨架上看到任何電視。
男1 我用電腦確認一下還有沒有庫存…看來已經賣完了。我請經理過來協助您。Dowell先生？可以請你過來一下嗎？顧客正在尋找Crystal Clear 2000電視。
男2 你好，真的很不好意思。那款電視這幾天在打折，有很多人來店裡購買，¹¹所以才會沒有存貨。
女　我還有辦法買到嗎？
男2 當然。如果您現在付款，我們會把電視送到您指定的地址。¹²由於造成您的麻煩，我會提供您免費快遞服務作為補償。

單字 be sold out 完售　on sale 打折的　out of stock 沒有庫存

10. 說話者正在討論何種產品？
(A) 傢俱
(B) 辦公用品
(C) 廚具
(D) 家電

11. 女子提到什麼問題？
(A) 商品缺貨。
(B) 尚未公布販售價格。
(C) 物品損壞。
(D) 帳單金額有誤。

12. 經理會提供女子什麼？
(A) 保固書
(B) 快遞服務
(C) 商店會員資格
(D) 全額退款

UNIT 09 圖表題

Example 01
題本 p.70

1. (C) **2.** (B) **3.** (D)

女　嘿，Marcus。下週新員工要來參加入職培訓，我們必須決定迎新午餐的菜單。你覺得這些餐點中哪一道最好？
男　嗯。上次辦新員工培訓時，我們選擇牛排和馬鈴薯，當時大受歡迎。
女　我記得那次。今年我們的預算有點少，所以我想我們必須點些不一樣的。
男　那義大利麵怎麼樣？
女　我覺得是個好主意。雞肉咖哩聽起來也不錯，但那些餐廳離這裡有點遠。
男　沒錯。還有在你打電話跟餐廳訂位前，我們還要準備好確切的入職培訓時間表，所以最好現在馬上開始。

餐點選項	價格
雞肉咖哩	每人7美元
義大利麵	每人10美元
炸雞	每人11美元
牛排和馬鈴薯	每人16美元

1. 說話者正在準備什麼？
(A) 退休晚宴
(B) 鄉村市集
(C) 入職培訓
(D) 客戶來訪

2. 請查看圖表。說話者最有可能買每人幾元的餐點？
(A) 7美元
(B) 10美元
(C) 11美元
(D) 16美元

3. 說話者接下來會做什麼？
(A) 與他們的主管談話
(B) 請客人進行問卷調查
(C) 訂位
(D) 安排時間表

PRACTICE 高難度
題本 p.71

1. (C) **2.** (D) **3.** (C) **4.** (A) **5.** (D) **6.** (D)
7. (A) **8.** (C) **9.** (D) **10.** (B) **11.** (B) **12.** (C)
13. (A) **14.** (D) **15.** (A) **16.** (A) **17.** (D) **18.** (A)

1-3. 英國女子／美國男子
Questions 1-3 refer to the following conversation and catalogue page.

W Thank you for calling Pristine Plates. How can I help you?
M I came across your company's catalogue and was considering ordering some dishes for the grand re-opening of my restaurant. [1]I'm interested in the circular ones with the polka dots around the edge.
W No problem. But just so you know, [2]our shipping prices are going to increase soon.
M Oh, really?
W Starting next week, the price of shipping will increase based on the weight of your order. Since you're ordering for a restaurant, the shipping price could be much higher.
M That's a good point. How much for 100 of those plates? [3]My re-opening isn't until September, but I think I should order them now.

女　感謝您致電純樸瓷盤公司。請問有什麼需要幫忙的嗎？
男　我偶然看到貴公司的商品目錄，為了餐廳的重新開幕，正在考慮訂購一些餐盤。**我對邊緣有圓點的圓盤很感興趣**。
女　沒問題。不過讓您知道一下，**我們的運費馬上要調漲了**。
男　啊，真的嗎？
女　從下週開始，運費將會根據您的訂單重量而增加。由於您是訂購用於餐廳的商品，運費可能會更高。
男　說得有道理。100個圓盤的價格多少？**我要到九月才重新開幕**，但我想現在就應該訂購了。

單字　come cross 偶然發現　based on 根據…

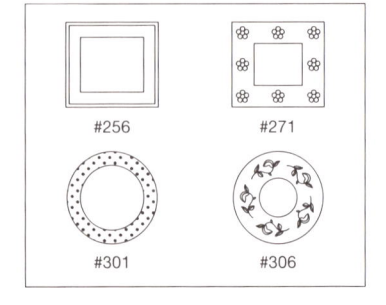

#256　#271
#301　#306

1. 請查看圖表。男子對哪種盤子感興趣？
(A) 圖案#256
(B) 圖案#271
(C) 圖案#301
(D) 圖案#306

2. 女子提到什麼問題？
(A) 部分商品缺貨。
(B) 商品目錄並非最新版本。
(C) 部分商品為限量版。
(D) 將會調漲運費。

3. 根據男子所述，九月會發生什麼事？
(A) 新員工將加入他的公司。
(B) 將推出新產品。
(C) 餐廳將重新開幕。
(D) 將在市中心開設購物中心。

4-6. 🎧 英國女子／美國男子

Questions 4-6 refer to the following conversation and event space layout.

> **W** Hi! Welcome to Jan's Tavern.
>
> **M** Hello. I made a reservation for Julian, party of two, for 7 p.m. ⁴But I'm late because of the icy road conditions on the highway.
>
> **W** No problem. There are plenty of tables available. We've got local jazz musicians performing tonight. Do you want to be near the stage?
>
> **M** Actually, that might be too loud for us. ⁵My business partner and I are here to talk about launching our start-up, so we need to be able to hear each other.
>
> **W** I'll put you away from the bar, too, then. ⁶Is near the bathroom okay?
>
> **M** ⁶Sure!

女 你好！歡迎光臨Jan's小酒館。
男 你好。我有訂位，名字是Julian，預約晚上7點兩位。⁴但因為高速公路上結冰的關係，所以我來晚了。
女 沒關係。還有很多桌可供選擇。今晚我們有當地的爵士樂手表演，你想坐在靠近舞台的座位嗎？
男 事實上，那對我們來說可能會太吵。⁵我是來和生意夥伴討論新創公司的創業事宜，所以需要聽得見彼此的聲音。
女 那我也為你們安排離酒吧遠一點的座位。⁶靠近洗手間附近的可以嗎？
男 ⁶當然！

單字 make a reservation for 預約　plenty of 大量的
put ~ away from 安排在遠離…

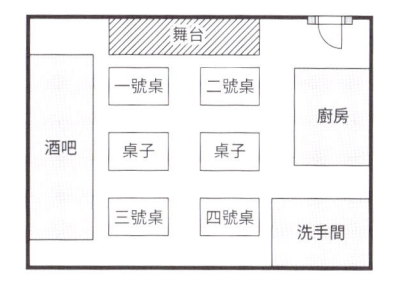

（event space layout: 舞台, 一號桌, 二號桌, 廚房, 酒吧, 桌子, 桌子, 三號桌, 四號桌, 洗手間）

4. 根據男子所述，什麼原因導致遲到？
(A) 道路濕滑。
(B) 未提供停車位。
(C) 尖峰時段路況不佳。
(D) 地點有變動。

5. 男子為何要與他的生意夥伴見面？
(A) 討論潛在併購
(B) 談論應徵人選
(C) 分析產品銷售狀況
(D) 為成立公司做準備

6. 請查看圖表。男子會坐在哪裡？
(A) 一號桌
(B) 二號桌
(C) 三號桌
(D) 四號桌

7-9. 🎧 美國女子／澳洲男子

Questions 7-9 refer to the following conversation and team directory.

> **W** Alan, thanks for taking over during practice today. ⁷You did a great job of leading the drills while I had to step out for a family emergency.
>
> **M** I was only imitating your leadership style. Still, I don't think the team is playing with enough energy right now.
>
> **W** You're right. It's been a long season, and ⁸our players are exhausted.
>
> **M** What should we do?
>
> **W** I think the team will need a morale boost during our upcoming road trip to the West Coast. Since you're in charge of scheduling, ⁹could you find us some fancy hotel options for Friday's game in Phoenix?
>
> **M** I'll get right on it.

女 Alan，感謝你接手今天的訓練。⁷在我家中有緊急狀況暫時離開時，你在指導訓練上表現優異。
男 我只是在模仿你的指導風格而已。不過我認為球隊現在沒有足夠的精力比賽。

33

女　你說得沒錯。這是一個漫長的賽季，[8]**我們的球員已經精疲力盡了。**
男　我們該怎麼做？
女　我認為需要在這趟去西海岸的公路之旅中，提振球隊士氣。既然你是負責安排行程的，[9]**能為我們週五在鳳凰城的比賽找到一些不錯的飯店選擇嗎？**
男　我馬上去找。

單字 take over 代替、接手　drill 訓練、操練
step out 暫時離開、外出　morale boost 提振士氣
get right on 馬上開始做

名冊
- Inez Garcia: 籃球教練
- Amala Kalil: 球員
- Suki Tanoko: 設備經理
- Jennifer Snell: 行銷企劃專員

---

7. 請查看圖表。女子是誰？
(A) Inez Garcia
(B) Amala Kalil
(C) Suki Tanoko
(D) Jennifer Snell

8. 說話者在討論什麼問題？
(A) 比賽延期。
(B) 球迷很生氣。
(C) 球員感到疲憊。
(D) 球隊被出售。

9. 男子接下來最有可能做什麼事？
(A) 刊登廣告
(B) 購買新制服
(C) 機票升等
(D) 尋找住宿

10-12. 🎧 美國女子／澳洲男子
Questions 10-12 refer to the following conversation and brochure.

> W　Good morning. Are there any units available for rent in your building?
>
> M　Let me check. When are you looking to move in?
>
> W　As soon as possible. [10]My husband and I are going to have a baby at the end of the year, and our current place is too small for the three of us.
>
> M　Congratulations! It looks like we have two open units: a two-bedroom apartment on the third floor, and a three-bedroom unit on the fifth floor.

> [11]Personally, I recommend the bigger unit, since it has a huge window looking out on the ocean. Here's a brochure listing the prices.
>
> W　[12]I don't think we can afford the bigger one. Can I take a look at the unit now?

女　早安。你們大樓裡還有出租公寓嗎？
男　我確認一下。您打算何時搬進來？
女　越快越好。[10]**我和丈夫的孩子年底就要出生了**，現在住的地方對我們三人來說太小了。
男　恭喜您！看起來我們目前有兩間房：三樓的兩臥室公寓和五樓的三臥室公寓。[11]**就我個人而言，我推薦較大的那間，因為它有一扇大型窗戶，可以眺望大海。**這本手冊上有列出價格。
女　[12]**我想我們無法負擔較大的那間。現在方便看一下公寓嗎？**

單字 available for rent 可供出租　look to 打算

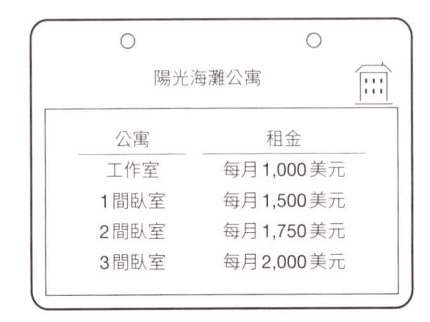

陽光海灘公寓

公寓	租金
工作室	每月 1,000 美元
1 間臥室	每月 1,500 美元
2 間臥室	每月 1,750 美元
3 間臥室	每月 2,000 美元

---

10. 女子為何想趕快搬家？
(A) 她找到新工作。
(B) 她懷孕了。
(C) 她住的大樓不太安全。
(D) 她的房租太高。

11. 男人喜歡較大公寓的哪一點？
(A) 室內設計
(B) 景觀
(C) 現代家電
(D) 寬敞的浴室

12. 請查看圖表。女子想租的公寓價格為何？
(A) 每月 1,000 美元
(B) 每月 1,500 美元
(C) 每月 1,750 美元
(D) 每月 2,000 美元

13-15. 🎧 英國女子／美國男子

Questions 13-15 refer to the following conversation and schedule.

> W [13]Thank you for attending today's lecture series on eco-friendly developments in industrial cleaning. Can I have your name?
>
> M Hi, I'm Gerald. Do you have a schedule listing today's presenters?
>
> W Sure, here you go.
>
> M Thanks… [14]Uh-oh. I have to make a call to a client overseas during Leopold Fritz's talk. That's bad timing.
>
> W I'm sorry to hear it. Also, please note that Kate Marrone's talk may be moved to the afternoon. [15]She's currently experiencing travel delays due to the extreme weather that's been hitting the region this week.

女 [13]感謝您今天來參加工業清潔環保發展的系列講座。請問您的大名是？
男 你好，我是Gerald。請問有包含今天演講者名單的時間表嗎？
女 當然有，給你。
男 謝謝… [14]天啊。在Leopold Fritz演講期間，我要打電話給海外客戶。時間真不湊巧。
女 我很遺憾聽到這個消息。另外請注意一下，Kate Marrone的演講可能會移至下午。[15]由於本週該地區天候惡劣，她目前的旅程有所延誤。

單字 eco-friendly 環保的 list 名單、列出 hit 襲擊

時間表	
Emilio Lopez	上午9點
Kate Marrone	上午11點
Yeonsu Lee	下午2點
Leopold Fritz	下午4點

13. 正在舉辦什麼類型的活動？
(A) 商務研討會
(B) 電影節
(C) 頒獎典禮
(D) 慈善募款活動

14. 請查看圖表。男子何時要打電話給客戶？
(A) 上午9點
(B) 上午11點
(C) 下午2點
(D) 下午4點

15. 女子提到什麼問題？
(A) 演講者可能會晚到。
(B) 會議室已關閉。

16-18. 🎧 美國男子／英國女子

Questions 16-18 refer to the following conversation and information board.

> M Welcome to Saffron Air. How can I help you?
>
> W [16]I'm scheduled to fly to New York on Flight 156 later, but I'm in a rush. Are there any earlier departures?
>
> M Hmm… There's a flight leaving in 30 minutes that goes to New Jersey, which is a short taxi ride away from New York. You'll need to hurry, though. [17]I'll contact transportation security and tell them to put you at the front of the line.
>
> W Wow, that's a huge help.
>
> M [18]I'll just need your current flight information so I can access your records.

男 歡迎來到藏紅花航空。請問有什麼需要幫忙的嗎？
女 [16]我本來打算搭乘稍晚飛往紐約的156航班，但我要趕時間。有沒有更早出發的班機？
男 嗯… 30分鐘後有一班飛往紐澤西的航班，從那裡再搭乘計程車過去紐約的車程不遠。不過，你要抓緊時間。[17]我會聯絡運輸安全官，請他們把你安排在隊伍最前方。
女 哇，真是幫了我一個大忙。
男 [18]我需要你目前的航班資訊，以便查閱你的紀錄。

單字 be in a rush 趕時間 a huge help 幫大忙

航班	出發地	目的地
156	底特律	紐約市
205	亞特蘭大	邁阿密
310	檀香山	洛杉磯
644	舊金山	西雅圖

16. 請查看圖表。女子從哪裡出發？
(A) 底特律
(B) 亞特蘭大
(C) 檀香山
(D) 舊金山

17. 男子如何幫助女子？
(A) 提供退款
(B) 托運額外行李
(C) 安排她搭乘頭等艙
(D) 知會機場安檢人員

18. 女子接下來最有可能給男子什麼？
(A) 她的機票
(B) 她的信用卡

(C) 她的優惠券
(D) 她的電子郵件地址

PART TEST
題本 p.74

1. (A)	2. (B)	3. (A)	4. (D)	5. (D)	6. (C)
7. (A)	8. (B)	9. (B)	10. (B)	11. (B)	12. (A)
13. (C)	14. (C)	15. (A)	16. (B)	17. (C)	18. (B)
19. (A)	20. (B)	21. (A)	22. (C)	23. (B)	24. (B)
25. (B)	26. (D)	27. (B)	28. (D)	29. (A)	30. (A)
31. (A)	32. (C)	33. (C)	34. (B)	35. (B)	36. (C)
37. (B)	38. (D)	39. (C)			

1-3. 🎧 美國男子／英國女子
Questions 1-3 refer to the following conversation.

> M Hey, Lizzie. Did you hear about the new company policy?
> W ¹I heard that each of us can now choose when our workday starts.
> M Right! Personally, I'm leaning toward starting at 10 a.m. to avoid rush hour traffic.
> W I bet many people will want that slot. ²You should put in your request soon. Our team has a limit on the number of people for each slot.
> M Good call. Oh, there goes Pedro from Accounting. ³I'm going to ask if he wants to continue carpooling with me.

男　嘿，Lizzie。你聽說公司的新政策了嗎？
女　¹**我聽說現在我們各自可選擇開始工作的時間**。
男　沒錯！我個人傾向從上午10點開始，以避免尖峰時段的交通堵塞。
女　我敢保證有很多人會想要那個時段。²**你應該盡快提出你的要求**。我們團隊對每個時段都有人數限制。
男　你說得對。喔，正好會計部的Pedro來了。³**我要問他是否願意繼續跟我共乘**。

單字 lean toward 傾向…　　put in a request 提出要求

1. 公司正在做出哪些改變？
(A) 提供彈性上班時間。
(B) 開設新分公司。
(C) 提供打折餐食。
(D) 可報銷差旅費。

2. 女子建議做什麼事？
(A) 向管理階層報告擔憂事宜
(B) 迅速繳交偏好時段
(C) 研究一些產品
(D) 參加工作面試

3. 男子接下來最有可能做什麼事？
(A) 與同事交談
(B) 打電話給客戶
(C) 要求退款
(D) 舉辦培訓課程

4-6. 🎧 英國女子／美國男子
Questions 4-6 refer to the following conversation.

> W Humberto, have you noticed that ⁴our figs are taking a long time to ripen this year?
> M Yeah, I think it's because of all the storms we've had this summer. ⁵Maybe we should install some southern-facing white walls around the fig trees to make sure they're getting maximum sunlight.
> W Good idea. ⁶I'll get the contractor who built our greenhouse to do it for us. He always charges fair prices.

女　Humberto，你有沒有注意到今年⁴**我們的無花果**需要很長時間才能成熟？
男　對，我想這是因為我們今年夏天有暴風雨所導致。也許我們應在無花果樹周圍⁵**裝設朝南的白牆**，盡可能讓無花果樹有陽光照射。
女　好主意。⁶**我會拜託建造溫室的承包商來做**。他總是收取合理的價格。

單字 fig 無花果　　ripen 成熟、熟成

4. 說話者最有可能從事什麼行業？
(A) 超商
(B) 造景公司
(C) 五金行
(D) 農場

5. 男子建議做什麼事？
(A) 購買更多土地
(B) 推出新產品
(C) 添加更多植物
(D) 裝設新的建物

6. 女子說她會做什麼事？
(A) 確認庫存
(B) 購買材料
(C) 聘請專業人員
(D) 更新合約

7-9. 🎧 美國女子／澳洲男子

Questions 7-9 refer to the following conversation.

> W Good afternoon. [7]I just saw your post about the office space on Brooklane Avenue. Are there any other businesses in the building?
>
> M You'd be on the same floor as two other small businesses. [8]There's a shared kitchen. If you want access to it, that would increase the rental price by $100 per month.
>
> W Okay. When can you show me the place?
>
> M How about tomorrow evening? [9]Just make sure to bring your driver's license so we can do a background check in case you want to get the application process started right away.

女　午安。[7]我剛看到你刊登位於Brooklane大道的辦公空間。大樓裡還有其他企業嗎？

男　你會和另外兩家小型企業在同一層樓。[8]有一個共用廚房。若你想使用廚房，每月租金會加收100美元。

女　好的，什麼時候能帶我參觀那個地方？

男　明天晚上怎麼樣？因為你可能會想馬上申請，所以[9]請務必攜帶駕照，以便我們進行背景調查。

單字 rental price 租金
get ~ started right away 馬上開始做⋯

7. 女子為何打電話來？
(A) 討論房產列表
(B) 預訂飯店客房
(C) 確認申請狀態
(D) 繳款

單字 listing 清單、列表

8. 根據男子所述，影響價格的因素為何？
(A) 停車位數量
(B) 使用共享空間
(C) 客戶數量
(D) 有無廣告

9. 男子建議明晚要帶什麼東西？
(A) 推薦信
(B) 身分證件
(C) 訂金
(D) 收入證明

10-12. 🎧 澳洲男子／美國女子

Questions 10-12 refer to the following conversation.

> M Hi, I'm trying to purchase a train pass, [10]but the automated kiosk isn't working. Can you please help me?
>
> W I'll call in a maintenance worker. It should be back up and running soon.
>
> M Ugh… [11]This is frustrating. I have an important meeting in 30 minutes, and there's no way I'll make it on time.
>
> W Since you're in a hurry, [12]I would recommend downloading the Subway Rider mobile app. You can put in your credit card information and access the platform that way.
>
> M I'll do that.

男　你好，我打算購買火車票，[10]但自動售票機無法正常使用。能請你幫我一下嗎？

女　我打電話叫維修人員。應該很快就會恢復運作。

男　啊⋯[11]真令人沮喪。30分鐘後有個重要會議，但我沒辦法準時參加了。

女　你趕時間的話，[12]我建議你下載地鐵通手機應用程式。只要輸入你的信用卡資訊，進入線上平台就行了。

男　我會的。

單字 train pass 火車票　call in 打電話叫⋯
be back up and running 重新啟動
There's no way~ 沒辦法⋯
make it on time 準時抵達

10. 為何男子需要幫助？
(A) 辦公室搬走了。
(B) 機器故障了。
(C) 火車路線變動。
(D) 東西不見了。

11. 男子說他對什麼感到沮喪？
(A) 花太多錢
(B) 會議遲到
(C) 接收錯誤資訊
(D) 排隊隊伍很長

12. 男子接下來最有可能做什麼事？
(A) 使用應用程式
(B) 搭計程車
(C) 打電話給經理
(D) 搭公車

13-15. 🎧 美國男子／英國女子／澳洲男子

Questions 13-15 refer to the following conversation with three speakers.

> **M1** Table 2 just made a request about allergens. Is it possible to [13]make the penne dish without risking any exposure to shellfish?
>
> **W** It's possible, but the timing is bad. The dinner party in the back room just placed their orders, and [14]there are a lot of off-menu requests.
>
> **M2** I can take care of it, Gerald. I just finished making the tiramisu for Table 6.
>
> **M1** Thanks. You know, [15]maybe we should think about adding some specifically allergen-free dishes to the menu. These requests seem to be getting more common nowadays.

男1 二號桌剛剛針對過敏原提出了要求。能否在完全不使用貝類的情況下[13]**製作通心粉**？

女 可以，但時機點不太好。後方包廂晚宴的客人剛點完餐，[14]**而且點了很多菜單上沒有的品項**。

男2 我能處理好，Gerald。我剛完成六號桌的提拉米蘇。

男1 謝謝。所以說，[15]**我們可能該考慮在菜單中加入一些不含過敏原的餐點**。這些要求最近似乎變得越來越普遍了。

單字 allergen 過敏原　risk 冒著…風險
place an order 點餐　off-menu 菜單上沒有的
take care of 負責處理…
allergen-free 不含過敏原的、不會誘發過敏的

13. 說話者最有可能在哪裡工作？
(A) 音樂廳
(B) 食品雜貨店
(C) 餐廳
(D) 送貨公司

14. 女子正在做什麼？
(A) 清洗設備
(B) 與供應商交談
(C) 準備特殊訂單
(D) 培訓新進員工

15. Gerald建議做什麼事？
(A) 增加供應的餐點
(B) 補充庫存
(C) 發起行銷活動
(D) 開設第二間分店

16-18． 🎧 美國女子／澳洲男子

Questions 16-18 refer to the following conversation.

> **W** Is everyone almost ready to film [16]tonight's episode of *Kids' Trivia Show*? We're supposed to start in 20 minutes.
>
> **M** Yes. The stage crew is just finishing up, and all of our cameras are ready.
>
> **W** Where are the contestants? [17]They still haven't been given instructions about the rules. That could be a big problem.
>
> **M** Don't worry. I asked [18]our temp, José Carrasco, to prep them backstage.
>
> **W** Ah, that's good news. I've been impressed with José's work for us, so I trust him. You know, we should think about giving him a permanent position on the team.

女 [16]**今晚《兒童冷知識節目》**的拍攝準備好了嗎？我們預計20分鐘後開始。

男 是的。舞台工作人員正在進行最後潤飾，所有的攝影機都準備就緒。

女 參賽者在哪裡？[17]**他們還沒收到關於規則的指示。這可能會是個大問題。**

男 別擔心。我有請[18]**臨時工作人員José Carrasco**在後台幫他們做好準備。

女 啊，太好了。José幫我們做的事都使我印象刻，因此我十分信賴他。我們應該考慮讓他成為團隊的正式成員。

單字 be supposed to do 預計做…　contestant 參賽者
instructions 指示、指南

16. 說話者在準備什麼？
(A) 標準化測驗
(B) 益智節目
(C) 體育賽事
(D) 公開講座

17. 女子提到什麼問題？
(A) 部分廣告有誤。
(B) 腳本有缺陷。
(C) 參賽者未做好準備
(D) 攝影機壞了。

18. José Carrasco是誰？
(A) 工程師
(B) 臨時員工
(C) 經理
(D) 編劇

19-21. 🎧 英國女子／美國男子
Questions 19-21 refer to the following conversation.

> W　Ahmed, I just finished reading through [19]your recommendation to add a company gym on the first floor of our building. You make a strong case. Thanks for your work on this.
>
> M　No problem. I think it could really improve staff morale.
>
> W　Speaking of boosting people's spirits: A lot of folks are sad about [20]Jim Harlow's upcoming retirement. I'd like to have a party to celebrate his achievements at the company.
>
> M　That's a great idea. We could get Frank's Restaurant and Grill to cater the event.
>
> W　Actually, I would be happy to prepare some homemade dishes. Then, we could use our budget to hire a performer.

女　Ahmed，[19]我剛讀完你提出在大樓一樓增設公司健身房的建議。你提出強而有力的論點。感謝你為此所做的努力。
男　沒什麼。我認為這能確實提振員工士氣。
女　說到提振員工士氣：很多員工[20]對Jim Harlow即將退休感到難過。我想舉辦派對來慶祝他在公司的成就。
男　好主意。我們可以交給Frank's燒烤餐廳來準備這場活動的餐點。
女　事實上，我很樂意準備一些家常菜。如此一來，我們就可以用預算來聘請表演者。

單字　read through　仔細閱讀
make a strong case　提出充分有理的主張
cater　（為活動）供應餐點

19. 女子感謝男子做了什麼？
(A) 繳交提案
(B) 完成銷售
(C) 推薦供應商
(D) 主導會議

20. 為何要安排聚會？
(A) 公司銷售紀錄創新高。
(B) 有員工即將退休。
(C) 經理將過生日。
(D) 部分員工需要休息。

21. 女子說：「我很樂意準備一些家常菜」，意味著什麼？
(A) 餐飲服務非必要開支。
(B) 餐廳的評價不太好。
(C) 公司將拒絕支付餐飲費用。
(D) 每個人都應自備餐點。

22-24. 🎧 英國女子／美國男子
Questions 22-24 refer to the following conversation.

> W　The rumor at headquarters is that fewer people are signing up for [22]gym memberships. How bad is the situation?
>
> M　This was a rough quarter. Membership dropped by 11％. [23]I would suggest offering reduced annual fees as a way to attract new sign-ups.
>
> W　I see. What's your projection for next quarter? I'm particularly curious about the Burbank Street facility that opened last month.
>
> M　That location gets a lot of foot traffic, so [24]enrollment should remain the same there for the foreseeable future.

女　總公司有傳言說報名[22]健身房會員的人數越來越少。情況有多嚴重呢？
男　此季度很艱辛。會員數減少了11％。[23]我想建議調降年費，以此方式吸引新會員加入。
女　我明白了。你預期下一季會如何？我對位於Burbank街上個月開幕的健身場所特別好奇。
男　那個地區的人流量很大，所以預計近期[24]會員人數應該能維持。

單字　headquarters　總公司　sign up for　報名、加入…
annual fee　年費　sign-up　報名、加入　projection　預測、預期
foot traffic　人流量　the foreseeable future　可預見的未來

22. 說話者在哪裡工作？
(A) 銀行
(B) 運動用品店
(C) 健身房
(D) 信用卡公司

23. 男子建議做什麼？
(A) 更改營業時間
(B) 調降價格
(C) 製作新廣告
(D) 販售未使用的設備

24. 男人預測什麼事？
(A) 公司將調降薪資。
(B) 新場所將維持會員數。
(C) 分店租金將會上漲。
(D) 顧客將留下正面評價。

39

25-27. 🎧 英國女子／美國男子／美國女子

Questions 25-27 refer to the following conversation with three speakers.

> **W1** The R&D team just reported that they're having trouble [25]accessing the cloud platform while working in the conference room. Could somebody help them out?
>
> **M** I can do it. I wonder why that's happening, though.
>
> **W1** [26]We recently updated the operating system on the computer in that room. But apparently the teams haven't been trained on how to use the new operating system.
>
> **W2** [27]I have some experience creating user guides. I could write one up and post it on the conference room wall for anyone who needs assistance in the future.
>
> **W1** That would be great. Thanks, Mei Ling.

女1 研發團隊剛才報告說，他們在會議室工作期間，無法 [25]**連上雲端平台**。有沒有人可以幫他們？

男 我可以幫忙。但我很好奇為什麼會發生那種狀況。

女1 [26]**我們最近更新了那間會議室的電腦作業系統**。但顯然團隊還沒接受如何操作新作業系統的訓練。

女2 [27]**我有撰寫使用者指南的經驗。我可以寫一篇**張貼在會議室牆上，供往後需要協助的人使用。

女1 太好了。謝謝，美玲。

單字 have trouble -ing 在⋯有問題
help ~ out 幫忙　write ~ up 撰寫

25. 說話者最有可能從事哪個領域的工作？
(A) 行銷
(B) 資訊科技
(C) 研究調查
(D) 人力資源

26. 最近發生了什麼事？
(A) 錄用了新員工。
(B) 部門被搬遷。
(C) 裝修公司大樓。
(D) 更新了電腦。

27. 美玲建議做什麼事？
(A) 刊登徵人啟事
(B) 撰寫說明指示
(C) 打電話給客戶
(D) 主辦會議

28-30. 🎧 澳洲男子／美國女子

Questions 28-30 refer to the following conversation.

> **M** Hey, Midori. Can I ask your thoughts on something?
>
> **W** Sure. What's up?
>
> **M** [28]I've been offered a minor role in a romantic comedy, but the pay is much lower than I would expect for this kind of part. It's barely enough to cover travel expenses. On the other hand, taking it could help me gain some traction in the industry.
>
> **W** When I was just starting out, I took some really bad roles. You know, my cousin is a lawyer, and he often helps me out by looking at my contracts before I sign them. [30]I could share his e-mail address with you. I'm sure he'd be happy to offer advice.

男 嘿，Midori。我可以問你對某事的想法嗎？

女 當然可以，是什麼事？

男 [28]**我收到某部浪漫喜劇小配角的邀約**，但片酬遠低於我對這類角色的預期，頂多只能勉強支付旅費。另一方面，答應邀約的話，能幫我在業界獲得一定程度的關注。

女 我剛開始工作時，演過一些非常糟糕的角色。你也知道，我表弟是律師，他經常在我簽合約前，幫我審閱合約。[30]**我可以把他的電子郵件地址給你**。相信他會很樂意提供建議。

單字 barely 幾乎不、勉強、僅僅　start out 開始

28. 男子是什麼人？
(A) 音樂家
(B) 攝影師
(C) 影評者
(D) 演員

29. 男子說：「答應邀約的話，能幫我在業界獲得一定程度的關注。」意味著什麼？
(A) 他沒有太多經驗。
(B) 他仍在攻讀學位。
(C) 他的經紀人給了他不好的建議。
(D) 他想轉行。

30. 女子說她會做什麼事？
(A) 提供聯絡資訊
(B) 參加活動
(C) 寫推薦信
(D) 閱讀合約

31-33. 🎧 美國男子／英國女子

Questions 31-33 refer to the following conversation and product list.

> **M** Hi there. Enjoying the game?
>
> **W** Yes, it's a good one! So, ³¹I work at Caldwell Assisted Living Facility in town, and we're currently on a special outing to the local ballpark with some of our senior citizens. We have enough in our budget to ³¹get them souvenirs, but I'm not sure what to get.
>
> **M** ³²These caps are always popular. The size is adjustable.
>
> **W** Great! I'll take ten of them.
>
> **M** Okay. ³³I'll throw in a free tote bag for you. I'm a big supporter of what you all do over at Caldwell.

男　你好。享受觀賞比賽嗎？
女　是的，很有意思！³¹**我在鎮上的Caldwell輔助生活公司工作，今天我們特地帶著一群年長者到當地的棒球場郊遊**。我們有足夠的預算³¹**買紀念品給他們**，但我不知道該買什麼。
男　³²**這些帽子一直都很受歡迎。尺寸可調整。**
女　太好了！那我要買十頂。
男　好的，³³**我免費贈送你一個手提袋**。我非常支持你們在Caldwell所做的事。

單字 outing 郊遊　　ballpark 棒球場　　souvenir 紀念品　　throw in 額外贈送

鑰匙圈 $5
水瓶 $15
棒球帽 $20
襯衫 $40

31. 女子會把禮物送給誰？
(A) 設施居民
(B) 高階管理人員
(C) 家庭成員
(D) 生意夥伴

32. 請查看圖表。男子推薦的商品多少錢？
(A) 5美元
(B) 15美元
(C) 20美元
(D) 40美元

33. 男子說他會做什麼？
(A) 聯絡經理
(B) 檢查庫存
(C) 提供額外物品
(D) 提供付款計畫

34-36. 🎧 美國男子／英國女子

Questions 34-36 refer to the following conversation and pricing list.

> **M** I'm getting excited for the farmer's market in Scantonville this weekend. ³⁴I think our apples are going to be a big hit.
>
> **W** Me too. We still have to decide on how to package them. Last week, in Mapleton, we tried to sell in large portions, and revenue was lower than I expected.
>
> **M** I noticed that too. ³⁵Let's go with the small baskets this time. They're visually appealing and a manageable size.
>
> **W** Okay. I'll take care of gathering up all our product. ³⁶Do you mind driving the van on Saturday? I want to go down early in my own car and get a sense of the event space layout.

男　這個週末要去Scantonville的農夫市集真令人興奮。³⁴**我覺得我們的蘋果會大受歡迎。**
女　我也是。不過我們需要決定如何包裝它們。上週在Mapleton，我們嘗試以大份量販售，結果收益低於我的預期。
男　我也注意到這一點。³⁵**此次我們就用小籃子裝**。這樣在視覺上既有吸引力份量也方便管理。
女　好的。我會負責把所有的商品收集起來。³⁶**星期六你方便開貨車嗎？**我想早點開自己的車下去，了解活動現場的佈置。

單字 a big hit 熱賣　　in large portions 大量的　　manageable 方便管理的、容易處理的　　gather up 聚集起來　　get sense of 了解

售價	
塑膠袋	$3
小籃子	$4
大籃子	$6
桶子	$8

34. 說話者販售什麼東西？
(A) 咖啡豆
(B) 水果
(C) 堅果
(D) 乳製品

41

35. 請查看圖表。說話者將售價定為多少？
(A) 3 美元
(B) 4 美元
(C) 6 美元
(D) 8 美元

36. 女子需要什麼幫助？
(A) 卡車裝貨
(B) 佈置展位
(C) 運送產品
(D) 宣傳活動

水下潛水者	
關卡名稱	關卡編號
珊瑚冒險	1
與鯨魚共游	2
深海	3
埋藏的寶藏	4

37. 說話者主要在討論什麼？
(A) 研究項目
(B) 產品上市
(C) 廣告活動
(D) 供應商變更

37-39. 🎧 美國女子／澳洲男子
Questions 37-39 refer to the following conversation and chart.

> **W** So, Reynaldo, we're going to ³⁷release the new installment of the Underwater Diver video game series in just a few weeks.
>
> **M** That's great. I can't wait to hear what gamers think of it. How are the beta tests going?
>
> **W** According to our testers, the graphics on the level with the coral look amazing. ³⁸But there are still some issues with the level where players search for treasure in a sunken pirate ship. Apparently, there are glitches in the gameplay.
>
> **M** We can get one of the freelancers to work on that, but the project is getting expensive. Can we afford it?
>
> **W** ³⁹I can talk to management and see if they're willing to expand the budget.

38. 請查看圖表。哪個關卡出了問題？
(A) 珊瑚探險
(B) 與鯨魚共游
(C) 深海
(D) 埋藏的寶藏

39. 女人提議做什麼事？
(A) 聯絡銷售團隊
(B) 延後活動
(C) 要求更多資金
(D) 撰寫徵人啟事

女 Reynaldo，我們在幾週後³⁷**將推出新水下潛水者電玩系列的新版本**。
男 太好了。我等不及要聽聽玩家的意見。試測進展得如何？
女 根據測試人員的說法，在珊瑚出現的關卡，視覺設計看起來令人驚豔。³⁸**但玩家在沉沒海盜船上尋找寶藏的關卡仍存在一些問題**。顯然遊戲本身還是有些缺陷。
男 我們可以找一名自由工作者來做此事，但該項目的成本越來越高，我們負擔得起嗎？
女 ³⁹**我可以跟管理階層商量，看看他們是否有意願增加預算**。

單字 I can't wait to do 我等不及要… sunken 沈沒的 glitch 缺陷、小毛病 gameplay 遊戲玩法

LC PART 4

簡短獨白

題本p.81

Example 01

很高興大家能和我一起參觀我們的珍稀藏書。在Jonestown圖書館，我們相信保存過往文獻的價值。這就是我們收藏這些需要特別注意和處理之獨特書籍的原因。請務必避免觸碰這裡的任何東西，因為所有材料都非常容易受影響。首先，我們來看一下地下室的中世紀檔案保存館。請跟我來。

UNIT 01 會議摘錄

CHECK-UP

題本p.83

1. (A)　2. (A)　3. (D)　4. (C)　5. (A)　6. (C)

1-3. 🎧 澳洲男子

Questions 1-3 refer to the following excerpt from a meeting.

M Hi, everyone. I've got something exciting to share with you. Our company will be moving in a new direction, and it's going to affect [1]all current and future investors, like you all. You may have heard that we've had great success with our new line of luxury vehicles. [2]Now, the company has decided to develop its own line of electric cars. This is an attempt to be more environmentally friendly and appeal to younger consumers. You may be concerned that our existing customers may not be happy with the change, but you'll probably change your mind if you look at this. [3]Here are the results of our recent survey showing more than 90% of our customers are interested in electric cars.

大家好。我有件令人振奮的事情要和大家分享。我們公司將朝新方向發展，且會影響[1]所有當前及未來的投資者。你們可能有聽說，我們的新款豪華車系列取得了極大成功。[2]現在公司決定自主研發電動車系列。此舉旨在變得更加環保，並嘗試吸引年輕消費者。各位可能擔心現有客戶會不滿意這項變化，但若你們看一下這個，也許會改變想法。[3]此為最近的調查結果，顯示有超過90%的客戶對電動車感興趣。

單字 have great success with 在…上取得極大的成功

1. 聽者最有可能是誰？
(A) 投資者
(B) 行銷專家
(C) 管理階層
(D) 產品設計師

2. 根據說話者所述，公司會做出哪些改變？
(A) 生產的汽車類型
(B) 總部所在地
(C) 產品型錄出版商
(D) 收集客戶意見的方式

3. 說話者為何會說：「你們看一下這個，也許會改變想法」？
(A) 更正錯誤
(B) 提出疑問
(C) 拒絕提議
(D) 提供保證

4-6. 🎧 英國女子

Questions 4-6 refer to the following excerpt from a meeting

W I'm happy everyone made it to today's meeting. I'm thrilled with the way [4]our new software came out. Everyone did their part to make its launch a success. I also read through your responses to [5]the employee questionnaire I handed out last week. Thank you for taking the time to complete them. A lot of you suggested increasing our social media presence. I think that's a great idea, but we do have a limited hiring budget. [6]If anyone is interested in working overtime to help with the company's social media, please let me know at the end of the meeting.

很高興各位都來參加今天的會議。[4]對於我們新軟體的推出，我感到十分興奮。為了讓它成功上市，每個人都盡了本分。我還詳讀了大家對上週發放的[5]員工調查問卷的回應。感謝各位抽空完成。很多人建議提升我們的社群媒體影響力。我認為這是好主意，但我們的招募預算有限。[6]如果有人有意願加班，協助公司的社群媒體事宜，請於會議結束後告訴我。

單字 be thrilled with 對…感到興奮　read through 詳讀

4. 說話者從事什麼行業？
(A) 廣告
(B) 建設
(C) 軟體
(D) 運輸

5 說話者感謝聽者的原因為何？
(A) 填寫問卷
(B) 達成銷售目標
(C) 確定合約
(D) 創造新設備

6. 說話者為何會說：「我們的招募預算有限」？
(A) 鼓勵聽者創造更多銷售
(B) 提醒聽者注意損失
(C) 告知聽者她不會僱用更多員工。
(D) 建議聽者購買新軟體

PART 4

43

UNIT 02　電話留言

CHECK-UP　　　　　　　　　　題本 p.85

1. (D)　**2.** (B)　**3.** (A)　**4.** (B)　**5.** (B)　**6.** (D)

1-3. 🎧 美國男子
Questions 1-3 refer to the following telephone message.

> M How's it going, Bruce? I just got off a phone call with a candidate for the marketing specialist position. She wants to interview this week, but I know you're quite busy. ¹Do you think you could free up your schedule for just an hour to join in on the interview? ²She's the first candidate who's trilingual. She speaks English, Spanish, and French! I want to have the chance to interview her before she chooses another company. ³I just sent you an e-mail with her available dates and times. Let me know if any of them works for you.

Bruce，你好嗎？我剛剛跟一名應徵行銷專員職位的人通過電話。雖然她想約這週面試，但我知道你很忙。¹你能否騰出一小時來參加面試？²她是第一個會說三國語言的應徵者。她會說英語、西班牙語和法語！在她選擇其他公司前，我希望有機會與她面談。³我剛發了一封郵件給你，上面寫了她方便面試的日期和時間。請告訴我當中你何時有空。

1. 說話者為何會打電話來？
(A) 更正錯誤
(B) 規劃即將到來的旅程
(C) 徵求意見
(D) 請求更改日程

2. 關於應徵者，說話者提到什麼？
(A) 她有很好的推薦信。
(B) 她會說多種語言。
(C) 她決定去別的地方工作。
(D) 她不住在該地區。

3. 說話者在電子郵件中發送了什麼？
(A) 時程表
(B) 費用估算
(C) 合約
(D) 履歷表

4-6. 🎧 澳洲男子
Questions 4-6 refer to the following recorded message.

> M You've reached the voicemail of Henry Raynor. ⁴I am currently taking my annual summer vacation and will return to the office on Monday, August 3rd. If you are interested in participating in the photography contest announced in ⁵our January issue, please visit our website. ⁶There you can complete a form to enter the contest as well as find out the details about the judging criteria. For other matters, please leave a message after the tone. Thank you.

您已轉接至 Henry Raynor 的語音信箱。⁴我目前正在放年度暑假，將於8月3日星期一重回辦公室。如果您有興趣參加我們發表在⁵一月刊號中的攝影比賽，請造訪我們的網站。⁶您可以在網站上填寫參加比賽的報名表，並了解審查標準的詳細資訊。若有其他事宜，請於嗶聲後留言，謝謝。

單字 judging criteria 審查標準

4. 說話者現在為何無法接聽電話？
(A) 他正在參加產業活動。
(B) 他正在休假。
(C) 他的團隊正在受訓。
(D) 他的辦公設備故障。

5. 說話者最有可能從事何種行業？
(A) 電腦軟體經銷商
(B) 雜誌出版社
(C) 電子產品製造商
(D) 錄音工作室

6. 根據說話者所述，網站上可以找到什麼？
(A) 職務說明
(B) 活動日曆
(C) 圖庫
(D) 報名表

UNIT 03　廣播通知與公告

CHECK-UP　　　　　　　　　　題本 p.87

1. (B)　**2.** (A)　**3.** (A)　**4.** (D)　**5.** (C)　**6.** (B)

1-3. 🎧 英國女子

> W Attention patrons. The library will close an hour early this evening. We'll be using this time to ¹update the layout of the bookshelves, making it easier for you to find what you're looking for. To learn more about how the stacks will look after the work is complete, ²you can ask a staff member before leaving. And for those of you planning to participate in ³tomorrow morning's book club meeting, don't worry. The gathering will still take place as scheduled. Thank you.

44

各位讀者請注意。今晚圖書館將提前一小時關門。我們將利用這段時間 [1]**更新書架陳列**，讓您能更輕鬆地找到所需內容。如欲了解更多關於作業完成後書架的變化，請在離開前 [2]**詢問工作人員**。另外，計畫參加 [3]**明天早上讀書會**的人，請別擔心。讀書會將如期舉行。謝謝。

單字 patron 主顧、常客　the stack （圖書館）書架、書庫　gathering 聚會　as scheduled 按原定時間

1. 說話者說今晚會發生什麼事？
(A) 將上架新書。
(B) 重新排列書架。
(C) 更新線上目錄。
(D) 移動查詢櫃檯的位置。

2. 根據說話者所述，聽者如何獲得更多資訊？
(A) 與圖書管理員交談
(B) 查看網站
(C) 領取傳單
(D) 致電櫃檯

3. 明天會發生什麼事？
(A) 團體討論會
(B) 簽書會
(C) 學術講座
(D) 電影放映會

4-6. 🎧 英國女子
Questions 4-6 refer to the following announcement.

> W I have a couple of announcements before we get started with [4]this month's farmer's market. Joe from Joe's Pickles is under the weather, so [5]he won't be able to make it this weekend. If customers ask for his booth, please let them know that he will be back next month. Also, most of the booths have been set up already, but I want you all to walk down the aisles to make sure everything is running smoothly. Remember that, as volunteers, you're often the first person customers see or talk to at the farmer's market, so [6]greet people warmly and with a smile.

[4]**在本月農夫市集**開張前，有幾項通知。Joe's 醃漬酸黃瓜攤販的 Joe 身體不太舒服，所以 [5]**這個週末他無法參加**。若有顧客詢問他的攤位，請告知他們他下個月會回來。另外，大部分攤位都已搭建完畢，但我希望大家能沿著走道走走，確保一切順利進行。請記住，作為志工，你通常是顧客在農夫市集第一個看到或交談的對象，所以 [6]**請熱情微笑與人們打招呼**。

單字 under the weather 身體不舒服　set up 設置　run smoothly 順利進行

4. 最有可能在哪裡發布該通知？
(A) 美容院
(B) 食品雜貨店
(C) 會議中心
(D) 農夫市集

5. 關於 Joe's 醃漬酸黃瓜攤販，通知提到了什麼？
(A) 他將舉辦優惠活動。
(B) 他僅收現金。
(C) 他不會參加。
(D) 他破產了。

6. 說話者建議聽者做什麼事？
(A) 提前到達
(B) 親切地與人打招呼
(C) 加班
(D) 尋求幫助

UNIT 04 電視、廣播節目與網路廣播

CHECK-UP　題本 p.89

1. (C)　**2.** (B)　**3.** (D)　**4.** (C)　**5.** (C)　**6.** (D)

1-3. 🎧 英國女子
Questions 1-3 refer to the following broadcast.

> W In other news, tomorrow marks the final day of our town's Theater Festival, which has been taking place in the town park. The festival is sponsored by [1]Discover Works, a company that funds outdoor theater performances and highlights the work of lesser-known playwrights. Anyone who plans to attend tomorrow's shows may want to arrive early, because [2]an early-bird discount is available for those who show up before 11 a.m. The Theater Festival is only one of many festivities hosted in the park this summer. [3]You can visit the town park website to see the full series of activities that are offered.

下一則新聞，明天是我們鎮上戲劇節的最後一天，該慶典一直在鎮公園舉行。該慶典 [1]**由發現作品公司贊助，他們資助戶外戲劇表演，並關注鮮為人知劇作家的作品**。計畫明天觀賞演出的人，建議儘早抵達，[2]**因為上午11點前到場者可享有早鳥優惠**。戲劇節只是今年夏天在鎮公園舉行的眾多慶典之一。[3]**您可以造訪鎮公園的網站，查看所提供的一系列活動**。

單字 highlight 關注、強調　lesser-known 不太知名的　playwright 劇作家　may want to do 應該要做…（等同於 should）　show up 出現、到場

1. 發現作品公司贊助什麼？
(A) 公園整修

45

(B) 音樂團體
(C) 舞台表演
(D) 短篇電影

2. 根據說話者所述，聽者為何要早到？
(A) 找到好位置
(B) 省錢
(C) 與表演者見面
(D) 避免交通壅塞

3. 鎮公園網站上可找到什麼內容？
(A) 討論區
(B) 一系列影片
(C) 會員資料
(D) 活動列表

4-6. 🎧 美國男子
Questions 4-6 refer to the following podcast.

> M Welcome to Space Cadets, a podcast for those who love studying ⁴planets, stars, and everything in between. I've got an exciting guest coming on today. Her name is Kiran Buttar, and ⁵she has just designed a new rocket propulsion system that will get humans closer to exploring Mars than ever before. Aspiring engineers will be particularly interested in this interview. The first fifteen minutes are available for free, ⁶but the rest of the interview is reserved for those with annual memberships. So if you're not a member, subscribe today!

歡迎收聽太空學員，這是專為熱愛研究⁴行星、恆星和其間一切事物人們所準備的網路廣播。今天我們請到一位令人興奮的嘉賓。她的名字叫Kiran Buttar，⁵她剛設計出新的火箭推進系統，讓人類比以往更加邁進火星探險。有志成為工程師的人會對這次訪談特別感興趣。前十五分鐘可免費收聽，⁶但後面的訪談僅保留給持有年度會員資格者。因此，若您尚未成為會員，請立即訂閱！

單字 cadet 見習生、培訓生　propulsion 推進、推進力
aspiring 有志成為⋯的
reserve 為（擁有某種權限者）⋯保留、預約

4. 網路廣播主要在談論什麼內容？
(A) 化學
(B) 電玩
(C) 旅遊
(D) 天文學

5. Kiran Buttar最近做了什麼事？
(A) 她主持了公共募款活動。
(B) 她開始做生意。
(C) 她創造了創新技術。
(D) 她獲得了獎學金。

6. 根據說話者所述，聽者為何要訂閱年度會員？
(A) 了解非公開活動
(B) 下載錄音稿
(C) 與其他會員見面
(D) 收聽完整節目

UNIT 05　廣告

CHECK-UP　題本 p.91

1. (A)　**2.** (B)　**3.** (C)　**4.** (C)　**5.** (B)　**6.** (B)

1-3. 🎧 美國男子
Questions 1-3 refer to the following advertisement.

> M If you've spotted moths, termites, or any other ¹unwanted insects inside your home, you might have a pest problem. Bug-Finder Pest Control is here to help. ²We offer an initial consultation at no cost to you. During that appointment, we'll complete ²a thorough sweep of your home and come up with a treatment plan. Also, for a limited time, ³you can receive a 10% discount if you enter the word "MOSQUITO" when you book your first appointment online.

如果您在家中發現了飛蛾、白蟻或其他任何¹不樂見的昆蟲，表示您可能遇到蟲害問題。驅蟲專家隨時能協助您。²我們提供免費的初步諮詢。在諮詢期間，²我們將仔細檢查您的家，並制定滅蟲計畫。另外，在限定期間內，於網站上進行首次預約時，³輸入「蚊子」一詞，便能享有九折優惠。

單字 spot 發現　moth 飛蛾　unwanted 不樂見的、不需要的
at no cost 免費　sweep 環視、掃過
come up with 準備好（計畫）

1. 廣告內容為何？
(A) 除蟲業者
(B) 清潔工
(C) 寵物照顧服務
(D) 室內設計師

2. 免費提供什麼？
(A) 清潔產品
(B) 房屋檢查
(C) 作業一小時
(D) 會員卡

3. 聽者如何享有優惠？
(A) 推薦朋友
(B) 發布社群媒體貼文
(C) 使用促銷代碼
(D) 多次預約

4-6. 🎧 英國女子

Questions 4-6 refer to the following advertisement.

> **W** If you're looking for a one-of-a-kind experience, come visit us at Walter's Coffee Factory. [4]Every tour begins with a special lecture about our beans by our resident coffee expert, Joe Walters. After that, our staff will guide you to the factory floor and show you around. [5]At the very end, everyone will receive a discount coupon to purchase our amazing coffee beans at the gift shop. Due to safety regulations, [6]children under 10 years old are not allowed to participate in the tour, so please keep that in mind when making your plans.

如果您正在尋找獨一無二的體驗，請前來參觀Walter's咖啡工廠。[4]**每次導覽都會由**我們的常駐咖啡專家Joe Walters帶來的咖啡豆**特別講座開始**。隨後，我們的工作人員將帶您前往工廠現場參觀。[5]**最後，每人都會拿到一張優惠券**，可在禮品店購買我們絕妙的咖啡豆。根據安全規定，[6]**10歲以下的兒童不得參加此行程**，所以請在安排計畫時謹記此點。

單字 one-of-a-kind 獨一無二的
show someone around 帶某人參觀
safety regulation 安全規定
children under 10 years old 十歲以下的兒童
keep something in mind 謹記

4. 每次的導覽如何開始？
(A) 供應茶點。
(B) 播放影片。
(C) 進行講座。
(D) 發放安全裝備。

5. 行程結束後，參加者會收到何種禮物？
(A) 海報
(B) 優惠券
(C) 一袋咖啡
(D) 明信片

6. 說話者提醒聽者什麼事？
(A) 健康風險
(B) 年齡限制
(C) 關閉的可能性
(D) 停車位有限

UNIT 06 演說、介紹、參訪／觀光導覽

CHECK-UP 題本 p.93

| 1. (A) | 2. (C) | 3. (C) | 4. (B) | 5. (C) | 6. (C) |

1-3. 🎧 英國女子

Questions 1-3 refer to the following tour information.

> **W** Thank you for coming down to Daisy Marie's [1]All-Natural Dairy Farm. I'm excited to introduce you to this four-acre plot of land which is home to the best organic dairy products on Earth. Here, in the field, you can see our herd of cows grazing peacefully in the afternoon sun. This is a lucky day for you visitors, because [2]you'll get the chance to hand-feed these amazing creatures their favorite snack — oats! [3]Now, I'm handing out a pamphlet on the best ways to handle dairy cows, to ensure you develop a happy relationship with these loveable animals.

感謝您來到Daisy Marie的[1]**全自然牧場**。我很高興向您介紹這片佔地四英畝的土地，它是**地球上最好的有機乳製品的發源地**。在田野裡，您可以看到我們的牛群在午後陽光下靜靜地吃草。這對遊客來說是個幸運的日子，[2]**因為您將有機會親手給這些美妙的生物餵食牠們最喜愛的零食— 燕麥！**[3]**現在，我將會發放一本小冊子**，上面寫著對待乳牛的最佳方法，讓您能與這些可愛的動物建立幸福關係。

單字 plot （特定用途的）小塊土地、腹地
be home to …的發源地、所在地
dairy product 乳製品　oat 燕麥

1. 農場生產什麼？
(A) 有機牛奶
(B) 棉花
(C) 牛肉乾
(D) 新鮮水果

2. 聽者將有機會做什麼？
(A) 與動物一起散步
(B) 試吃產品
(C) 為動物提供食物
(D) 與業主見面

3. 聽者會收到什麼？
(A) 影片連結
(B) 零食沾醬
(C) 傳單
(D) 刷子

4-6. 🎧 澳洲男子

Questions 4-6 refer to the following speech.

> **M** Hi, everyone! Thanks for coming to the grand opening of Elephant World, [4]a theme park featuring rides and games for people of all ages. I know you're excited to get inside. Before opening the gates, I want to let you know about a special

promotion. We're trying to encourage a social atmosphere, ⁵so we're offering tickets at half-price for anyone who comes in a group of six or more. It's perfect for a birthday party or your next social gathering. We also have a major event coming up: ⁶this Friday, there will be a performance by famous singing group The Fluffy Bears. Don't miss it!

各位朋友，大家好！感謝蒞臨大家世界的開幕式，這是為所有年齡層人們提供遊樂設施和遊戲的 ⁴**主題公園**。我知道大家都迫不及待想進去。在開門之前，我想告訴大家一項特別的促銷活動。我們鼓勵營造出社交氛圍，⁵**因此將會提供六人以上的團體半價門票**。非常適合生日派對或您的下一次社交聚會。還有另一項即將到來的重大活動：⁶**本週五，知名歌唱團體毛茸熊將舉行表演**。千萬別錯過！

單字 feature 以⋯為特色　at half-price 半價

4. 說話者在討論什麼地方？
(A) 美術館
(B) 遊樂園
(C) 可愛動物園
(D) 運動場

5. 說話者提到什麼特別優惠？
(A) 免費餐點
(B) 給朋友的優惠券
(C) 團體優惠
(D) 年度會員計畫

6. 星期五會發生什麼事？
(A) 藝術工作坊
(B) 導覽服務
(C) 現場音樂會
(D) 電影放映

PRACTICE 高難度　題本 p.94

1. (D)	2. (B)	3. (A)	4. (C)	5. (A)	6. (A)
7. (B)	8. (D)	9. (A)	10. (D)	11. (A)	12. (A)
13. (D)	14. (D)	15. (D)			

1-3. 🎧 美國男子
Questions 1-3 refer to the following telephone message.

M Hi, I'm calling about ¹the pickup truck you dropped off at Sotheby's this afternoon. We looked it over, and it turns out your radiator is leaking coolant. We can do some patchwork now, but you're going to need to get the radiator replaced, which will be a major job. If you want to do it with us, let me know and ²I'll suggest some possible times for next week. In the meantime, ³Benny will be working late this evening, so you can pick the vehicle up anytime before 8 p.m.

您好，我打電話詢問¹**今天下午寄放在Sotheby's的小貨車**。我們檢查了一下，發現散熱器有冷卻劑滲出。我們現在可以做一些臨時修繕工作，但最終仍需要更換散熱器，而**這是一項重大的工作**。如果您想委託我們請告知，²**我會告訴您下週的可行時間**。同時，³**Benny今晚會工作到很晚**，所以晚上8點前您隨時都可來取車。

單字 drop something off somewhere 把某物放在某處後離開
look over 檢查　leak 滲出
patchwork 拼湊物（此處指臨時補救滲出冷卻劑的工作）
patch 修補、補丁　major 重大的、主要的、重要的

1. 說話者最有可能在哪裡工作？
(A) 洗車場
(B) 搬家公司
(C) 租車服務處
(D) 汽車修理廠

2. 說話者提到：「這是一項重大的工作」，意味著什麼？
(A) 必須先付訂金。
(B) 該項工作費時。
(C) 他需要雇用更多人。
(D) 他馬上要去度假。

3 關於今晚，說話者提到了什麼？
(A) 有名員工會在場。
(B) 有零件會送達。
(C) 將結束營業。
(D) 將更新付款系統。

4-6. 🎧 澳洲男子
Questions 4-6 refer to the following talk.

M Hello, customer support center. As you're probably aware, a recent news report about environmental damage caused by the plastic utensils manufacturing industry has many people upset. ⁴You can expect to receive a lot of calls from angry consumers today. Please assure them that ⁵our company's products do not contain any of the toxic chemicals on this document I'm handing out now. We've radically changed our production process over the last five years. To help you, ⁶I'm also providing a list of talking points to emphasize during challenging calls. ⁶Please look it over and feel free to ask questions.

客服中心的各位，你們好。大家應該都知道，最近關於塑膠器具製造業造成環境破壞的新聞報導讓許多人感到不悅。⁴**今天大家可能會接到很多憤怒消費者打來的電話**。請向他們保證，

48

⁵我們公司的產品不含我現在發放文件上列出的任何有毒化學物質。在過去五年間,我們從根本上改變了我們的生產流程。為了幫助各位,我還整理一些在難以應對的通話中,⁶請需強調的要點清單。請仔細閱讀,並歡迎隨時提出問題。

單字 utensil 器具　assure 向…保證　contain 包含
hand out 發放　radically 激進地　talking points 談話重點

4. 本段演說的目的為何?
(A) 告訴聽者關於訴訟的事
(B) 宣布新的退貨政策
(C) 請聽者做好被投訴的準備
(D) 提議擴充團隊

5. 說話者說:「我們從根本上改變了我們的生產流程。」,意味著什麼?
(A) 公司曾使用過危險的化學物質。
(B) 產品正以更高的利潤出售。
(C) 生產力急遽提高。
(D) 新聞報導內容有誤。

6. 聽者被要求做什麼事?
(A) 閱讀發放的資料
(B) 稍作休息
(C) 撰寫報告
(D) 回覆一些電子郵件

7-9. 🎧 美國男子
Questions 7-9 refer to the following talk and design plan.

> M I'm Raja Abdul from WMTH. I'm here reporting on ⁷the construction of a series of walking paths, which are being funded by the city. Together, the paths extend 5 miles, stretching from Alpha Hospital to Lake Capra. ⁸The project was launched after a recent study showed that Coolidge City is less pedestrian-friendly than others in the region. ⁹Work has already been completed between Alpha Hospital and the Market District. Meanwhile, the areas surrounding Lake Capra are expected to be finished by the end of the month.

我是WMTH的Raja Abdul。我在此報導由該市資助⁷所建設的一系列人行步道的情況。這些路徑從Alpha醫院一路延伸到Capra湖,總長5英里。⁸該專案的啟動始於最近一項研究,其指出Coolidge市與該地區其他城市相比,對行人不夠友善。⁹Alpha醫院和市場區之間的施工已經完成了。與此同時,Capra湖周邊地區預計將於本月底完工。

單字 walking path 人行步道　fund 資助、贊助
stretch 延伸、綿延

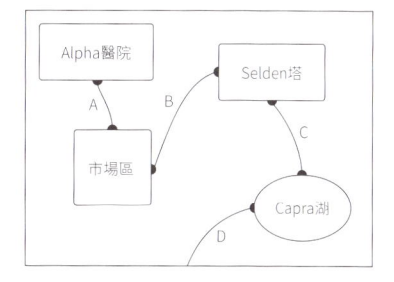

```
┌─────────────────────────────────┐
│  ┌────────┐                      │
│  │Alpha醫院│      ┌──────┐       │
│  └────┬───┘      │Selden塔│       │
│       │ A    B   └───┬──┘        │
│       │              │ C         │
│   ┌───┴───┐          │           │
│   │市場區 │          │           │
│   └───┬───┘      ┌───┴───┐       │
│       │          │Capra湖│       │
│       └────D─────┘       │       │
│                  └───────┘       │
└─────────────────────────────────┘
```

7. 說話者主要討論什麼專案?
(A) 市政廳
(B) 步道
(C) 河濱公園
(D) 運動場

8. 為何會啟動該專案?
(A) 有公司願意支付費用。
(B) 由納稅民眾決定。
(C) 市長提出有其必要性。
(D) 由研究報告所促成。

9. 請查看圖表。根據說話者所述,該專案哪一路段已完工?
(A) A路段
(B) B路段
(C) C路段
(D) D路段

10-12. 🎧 英國女子
Questions 10-12 refer to the following telephone message and table.

> W Hi. Thanks for inquiring about staying at La Vida Tropica Hotel. Unfortunately, our facilities don't contain any three-bedroom units. However, we do have some units ¹⁰with two large bedrooms that also offer stunning views of the ocean. ¹¹Our hotel caters mainly to young families, so I think it would be a perfect spot for your vacation. If you'd like to book a room through me, I'll be available until the end of the day. ¹²I'm out of the office tomorrow, but you can also call the front desk at 555-0196.

您好。感謝您詢問入住La Vida Tropica飯店。很抱歉,我們飯店沒有任何三間臥室的客房。不過,我們確實有些客房¹⁰設置兩間大臥室,還可以欣賞到壯麗的海景。¹¹我們飯店的客層主要針對年輕家庭,所以我認為這會是您理想的度假地點。若您想透過我預訂房間,都可在今天結束前與我聯絡。¹²我明天不在辦公室,但您可以撥打555-0196至櫃檯。

單字 inquire about 詢問
stunning 壯麗的、極為漂亮的、驚人的　unit 客房、單元

客房特色	房型 A	房型 B	房型 C	房型 D
兩間臥房	✓			✓
海景			✓	✓
按摩椅	✓		✓	

10. 請查看圖表。說話者提到哪種客房？
(A) A房型
(B) B房型
(C) C房型
(D) D房型

11. 說話者強調飯店的哪一點？
(A) 家庭友善的氛圍
(B) 價格低廉
(C) 高品質餐食
(D) 整潔度

12. 明天會發生什麼事？
(A) 說話者將休假一天。
(B) 飯店不會營業。
(C) 說話者將拜訪客戶。
(D) 飯店將被訂滿。

13-15. 🎧 英國女子
Questions 13-15 refer to the following excerpt from a meeting and map.

> **W** Hello, everyone. I called this meeting to talk about expanding our customer base in various regions of the country. Word of mouth has gotten [13] our medicinal products a long way in our home state, but on the other side of the country, sales are lagging. Take a look at this map. [14] You'll see that sales were lowest in the Northeast last quarter, where we generated only 2% of the company's total revenue. [15] Now, our marketing team plans to launch a new digital promotional campaign at the end of the year. That should help to improve brand awareness with younger generations in the regions where sales are struggling.

大家好。我召開本次會議是為討論如何在全國各地擴展我們的客戶群。[13] 我們的藥品在本州已取得良好的口碑，但在其他州的銷售不太樂觀。請看一下這張地圖。[14] 你會發現上一季度我們在東北地區的銷量最低，僅創造出公司總收入的2%。[15] 現在我們的行銷團隊打算在年底推出新的數位宣傳活動。這將有助於在銷售不佳的地區，提升我們品牌在年輕一代中的知名度。

單字 call a meeting 召開會議　word of mouth 口耳相傳　medicinal product 藥品　lag 落後、低迷

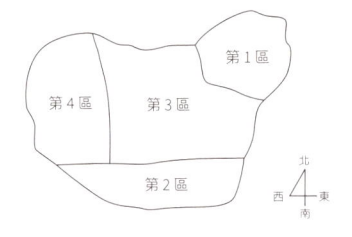

13. 說話者的公司販售什麼東西？
(A) 文具
(B) 美容產品
(C) 汽車零件
(D) 藥品

14. 請查看圖表。上一季哪個地區的銷售量最少？
(A) 第1區
(B) 第2區
(C) 第3區
(D) 第4區

15. 根據說話者所述，年底將推出什麼產品？
(A) 研究項目
(B) 數位家電
(C) 新的產品系列
(D) 線上廣告

PART TEST　題本 p.96

1. (C)	2. (D)	3. (A)	4. (B)	5. (C)	6. (D)
7. (D)	8. (B)	9. (D)	10. (A)	11. (D)	12. (A)
13. (B)	14. (D)	15. (C)	16. (D)	17. (B)	18. (A)
19. (B)	20. (D)	21. (C)	22. (B)	23. (C)	24. (A)
25. (C)	26. (D)	27. (B)	28. (B)	29. (C)	30. (C)

1-3. 🎧 美國男子
Questions 1-3 refer to the following talk.

> **M** On the screens in front of you, you'll see the reservation software [1] you'll be using to book rooms when customers call the front desk. The first time you log in, you'll be asked to create [2] a password. Please write it down for today, as you'll be logging in and out frequently. But eventually, you'll need to memorize it. [3] We've just upgraded the system, so it's a lot more user-friendly than it used to be.

各位面前的螢幕上顯示，[1] 當顧客撥打電話至櫃檯時用於訂房的軟體。首次登入時，系統會要你建立[2] 密碼。各位會經常登入和登出，因此[2] 今天請先寫下來。但最終還是需要記住它。[3] 我們剛升級完系統，所以介面對使用者來說，比過往更為友善。

1. 聽者受僱為何種職務？
(A) 導遊
(B) 客房清潔人員
(C) 櫃檯接待員
(D) 超市店員

2. 聽者被要求寫下什麼？
(A) 偏好工作日
(B) 制服尺寸
(C) 聯絡電話
(D) 密碼

3. 針對系統，說話者提到什麼？
(A) 最近升級了。
(B) 僅供經理使用。
(C) 重新啟動需花一段時間。
(D) 不太常用。

4-6. 🎧 澳洲男子
Questions 4-6 refer to the following telephone message.

> M Hi, ⁴this is Robert Jensen from the marketing department. When I arrived at my office this morning … um … number 203, ⁵my overhead lights wouldn't turn on. They were fine yesterday, so I'm not sure what the problem is. I'll be working in the conference room temporarily, so that's where you can find me if you have any questions. ⁶But please note that I'll only be on site until 2 P.M., as I'm leaving then to catch the express train to Dover. Thank you.

你好，⁴**我是行銷部的Robert Jensen**。今天早上我到辦公室時……嗯……是203號辦公室，⁵**我頭頂上方的燈不會亮**。昨天還好好的，所以我不確定問題出在哪裡。我會暫時在會議室工作，所以如果你有任何問題，可以去那裡找我。⁶**不過我只會在會議室待到下午2點，之後我要出發去搭乘前往Dover的特快列車**。謝謝你。

單字 overhead 在頭頂上方的　on site 在現場

4. 說話者在哪個部門工作？
(A) 採購
(B) 行銷
(C) 資料管理
(D) 產品開發

5. 說話者提到什麼問題？
(A) 他必須加班。
(B) 會議室門被鎖住。
(C) 有些燈不會亮。
(D) 有些文件暫時遺失。

6. 說話者在下午2點最有可能去哪裡？
(A) 百貨公司
(B) 演講廳
(C) 銀行
(D) 火車站

7-9. 🎧 英國女子
Questions 7-9 refer to the following excerpt from a meeting.

> W Our advertising campaign on social media has been a major success. We have several large orders from shop owners for ⁷our handmade jewelry. We don't have enough merchandise in stock, ⁸so everyone will be working overtime to get these items made. I know you were planning on starting our new line of necklaces this week, but those won't go on the website until April. ⁹In hindsight, we shouldn't have offered express shipping, especially since we have no maximum order size. We'll adjust this policy to prevent issues in the future.

我們在社群媒體上的廣告活動取得了巨大的成功。我們從店長那裡收到了幾筆⁷**手工珠寶**的大型訂單。因為商品庫存不足，⁸**所以每個人都要加班來製作這批商品**。我知道你們打算在本週開始製作新的項鍊系列，但這批項鍊要到四月才會發布上線。⁹**現在回想起來，我們不應提供快遞配送服務**，特別是因為我們沒有設定訂單尺寸上限。我們會調整此項政策，以免往後出現問題。

單字 have something in stock 有…的庫存
work overtime 加班　plan on doing 打算做…
in hindsight 回想起來、回過頭來看
express shipping 快遞配送

7. 說話者的公司販售什麼？
(A) 油漆
(B) 陶器
(C) 傢俱
(D) 珠寶

8. 說話者說：「這批項鍊要到四月才會發布上線」，意味著什麼？
(A) 她遇到技術上的困難。
(B) 她認為另一項任務更為重要。
(C) 她發現時間表出錯。
(D) 她想為延誤道歉。

9. 說話者認為公司犯了什麼錯誤？
(A) 把價格定太低。
(B) 在廣告上花太多錢。
(C) 換成不可靠的供應商。
(D) 提供了快速送貨的選擇。

51

10-12. 🎧 美國男子

Questions 10-12 refer to the following announcement.

> M Hello, passengers. Unfortunately, we're coming into bad weather, with a storm just on the horizon. There will be choppy waves and some heavy winds [10]on the top deck for the next twenty minutes or so. [11]I encourage everyone to take a break from their mobile devices to avoid getting seasick. Those of you who are standing may also want to look for a seat. [12]One of our attendants, Malia, will now provide updated estimates on our arrival times at each stop.

各位乘客您好。非常遺憾，我們正面臨惡劣的天氣，暴風雨即將來臨。在接下來的二十分鐘左右，會出現更加猛烈的海浪，[10]頂層甲板上將出現強風。[11]建議大家暫時停止使用行動裝置，以免暈船。也請站著的乘客找座位入座。[12]現在我們的服務人員Malia將提供各站變更後的抵達時間。

單字 choppy 波濤洶湧的　get seasick 暈船

10. 該通知最有可能在哪裡發布？
(A) 在渡輪上
(B) 在火車上
(C) 在飛機上
(D) 在公車上

11. 說話者向聽者建議做什麼？
(A) 避免進食
(B) 繫好安全帶
(C) 移動到其他層
(D) 停止使用手機

12. 接下來最可能發生什麼事？
(A) 將提供更多資訊。
(B) 變更路線。
(C) 載更多乘客。
(D) 將行李聚集起來。

13-15. 🎧 美國女子

Questions 13-15 refer to the following advertisement.

> W Are you ready to explore the history and culture of Europe? Leave the planning to our experts and enjoy an all-inclusive [13]bus tour from Graystone. We'll show you the top attractions in amazing cities such as Rome, Milan, and Paris. And if you have a large group, [14]you can customize the itinerary to include only the sites you're interested in. Take advantage of our special offer [15]in March. Book any trip to receive a complimentary T-shirt with the Graystone logo.

你準備好探索歐洲的歷史和文化了嗎？把計畫行程交給專業人士，享受由Graystone提供的全包式[13]巴士之旅。我們將帶你參觀羅馬、米蘭和巴黎等迷人城市的熱門景點。如果你是人數較多的團體，[14]可以自訂行程，僅選擇你感興趣的景點。請使用我們[15]三月份的特別優惠。只要預訂任何行程，即可獲得印有Graystone標誌的免費T恤。

單字 all-inclusive 全包式　attraction 觀光景點
take advantage of 利用（機會、好處、優惠等）
special offer 特別優惠　complimentary 免費的

13. 廣告內容為何？
(A) 音樂廳
(B) 旅行社
(C) 飯店
(D) 航空公司

14. 說話者提到企業的哪些優勢？
(A) 取消時可全額退款。
(B) 可接受臨時的要求。
(C) 採用環保材料。
(D) 提供客製化選擇。

15. 三月份會提供什麼？
(A) 餐券
(B) 團體優惠
(C) 免費衣服
(D) 保險

16-18. 🎧 英國女子

Questions 16-18 refer to the following talk.

> W Now that everyone is here, [16]I'm ready to begin this hike through the beautiful Clarion National Park. [17]Unfortunately, due to some fallen trees from the storm a few days ago, the Haven Trail is closed. This was supposed to be part of our hike today, so I'm sorry about that. Before we leave, don't forget that there is a water fountain here in case anyone needs to [18]fill up their water bottle.

現在大家都到齊了，[16]我們準備開始在美麗的Clarion國家公園徒步健行。[17]可惜的是，幾天前的暴風雨導致一些樹木倒下，Haven步道因而關閉。這本來是我們今天徒步路線的一部分，為此我感到抱歉。在離開之前，別忘記這裡有噴泉，需要的話[18]可以裝滿水瓶。

單字 be supposed to do 本來要做…　in case 萬一
fill up 填滿

16. 說話者最有可能是誰？
(A) 健身教練
(B) 山林管理員
(C) 公車司機
(D) 研究科學家

17. 說話者為何道歉？
(A) 費用增加
(B) 意外的關閉
(C) 延後出發
(D) 列印錯誤

18. 一些聽者接下來最有可能做什麼事？
(A) 填滿容器
(B) 觀看現場示範
(C) 挑選零食
(D) 配戴名牌

19-21. 🎧 澳洲男子
Questions 19-21 refer to the following excerpt from a meeting.

> M Good morning, everyone. I'd like to take this opportunity to introduce [19]our latest addition to the team, Mr. Terrance Hickman. Since graduating from the prestigious Edsel University, he has built an impressive career background in a short time. He will be helping you with [20]reviewing contracts to ensure they are in compliance with the law. Although he'll receive training from me, [21]he may also have a lot of questions for the rest of you about our process. I know that you all have busy schedules and it's difficult to be interrupted, but when you started here you all had the same opportunity.

大家早安。我想藉此機會向大家介紹[19]**新加入我們團隊的成員Terrance Hickman先生**。他從知名的Edsel大學畢業後，在短時間內累積了令人印象深刻的職業生涯。他會幫助各位[20]**審閱合約，確認是否符合法律規範**。他會接受我的培訓，[21]**但對於我們的流程，他可能會有很多疑問想請教大家**。我知道你們的工作都很忙，很難抽出時間，但各位最初來到這裡時，你們都享有同等的機會。

單字 addition 新加入的成員
in compliance with 符合、遵守… interrupt 妨礙、中斷

19. Terrance Hickman是誰？
(A) 潛在投資者
(B) 新進員工
(C) 大學教授
(D) 董事會成員

20. 聽者最有可能在哪個部門工作？
(A) 平面設計
(B) 技術支援
(C) 廣告
(D) 法務

21. 說話者為何會說：「你們都享有同等的機會」？
(A) 對截止日提出警示
(B) 表揚優秀員工
(C) 鼓勵聽者提供協助
(D) 解釋誤解

22-24. 🎧 美國女子
Questions 22-24 refer to the following telephone message.

> W Hi, this is Evelyn Owens from Edgewood Financial. I've been showing [22]the blueprints you made for our new headquarters building, and everyone loves them. As I mentioned a few weeks ago, we may add an extension out the back instead of having additional parking. It depends on approval from the board to increase the budget. [23]I know you've been waiting to find out whether more work is needed on this project. Well, the board meeting is tomorrow. If you need to get a hold of me today, please note that you should call my mobile phone. I won't be in the office because [24]I'm going to a conference this afternoon.

你好，我是Edgewood理財公司的Evelyn Owens。我已經向大家展示過[22]**你為我們新的總公司大樓製作的設計圖**，大家都很喜歡。正如我幾週前所提到，我們可能會在大樓後方擴建，而非增加停車場。任何預算的增加均須經過董事會批准。[23]**我知道你一直在等待，確認這項專案是否需要增加更多工程。嗯，明天將會召開董事會**。如果你今天有事需要與我聯絡，麻煩請撥打我的手機。[24]**我今天下午要去參加一個會議**，所以不在辦公室中。

單字 headquarter 總公司　extension 擴張
get a hold of 聯絡、通電話

22. 說話者最有可能打電話給誰？
(A) 翻譯人員
(B) 建築師
(C) 會計師
(D) 財務顧問

23. 說話者提到：「明天將會召開董事會」，意味著什麼？
(A) 她沒辦法訂到她想要的房間。
(B) 她需要重新安排與聽者的會議。
(C) 她很快就會得到一些資訊。
(D) 她想讓聽者進行演講。

24. 說話者今天下午打算做什麼事？
(A) 參加會議
(B) 培訓同事
(C) 簽訂合約
(D) 探望家庭成員

25-27. 🎧 美國男子

Questions 25-27 refer to the following speech and report.

> **M** Good afternoon. I'm Salvador Carlson, the head of research and development at Crenshaw Industries, and I'd like to thank you for your attendance [25]here at this press conference. [26]In February, we acquired our competitor, Renzelli Enterprises. Members of that team as well as ours have been working to create an efficient battery-powered bike. Well, the design we created will hit the market later this year, and our testing has had amazing results so far. In fact, I was the rider for one of the tests and traveled [27]one hundred twenty-one miles, breaking an industry record.

午安。我是Crenshaw工業公司的研發負責人Salvador Carlson，感謝各位參加[25]本次的記者會。[26]我們於二月時收購了競爭對手Renzelli企業。該團隊成員以及我們的團隊一直致力於開發一款高效能的電動自行車。我們創造的設計作品將於今年下半年上市，且至目前為止，我們的測試取得了不錯的結果。事實上，其中一場測試由我親自騎乘了[27]一百二十一英里，打破了產業記錄。

單字 acquire 收購　battery-powered 電池驅動的
hit the market 上市　break a record 打破紀錄

測試結果	
測試	距離
1	95 英里
2	121 英里
3	103 英里
4	99 英里

25. 聽者在哪裡？
(A) 新進員工培訓
(B) 就業面試
(C) 記者會
(D) 頒獎晚宴

26. 根據說話者所述，二月發生了什麼事？
(A) 發明專利獲批准。
(B) 發表了安全報告。
(C) 更換部門負責人。
(D) 完成企業收購。

27. 請查看圖表。說話者參與了哪一場測試？
(A) 測試1
(B) 測試2
(C) 測試3
(D) 測試4

28-30. 🎧 美國女子

Questions 28-30 refer to the following excerpt from a meeting and map.

> **W** Let's get this meeting started. This morning, [28]I had a conference call with all of the managers of our department store's branches. Fortunately, operations are running smoothly at most places. [29]However, our branch in Flanigan is temporarily closed because of damage from last night's storm. Actually, a lot of buildings and roads in that district were damaged. Therefore, some of the shipments intended for that branch will be redirected here. [30]We need to make space in the main section of our storage facility for those deliveries. Annabelle, could your team handle that?

我們開始進行本次會議。今天早上，[28]我和我們百貨公司所有分館的經理開了電話會議。幸好大部分分館的營運都很順利。[29]然而，由於昨晚的暴風雨，造成位於Flanigan的分館有所損壞，因此暫時關閉。事實上，該地區有許多建築物和道路皆遭到破壞。因此，本應運往該分館的貨物將改送至這裡。[30]我們需在倉庫設施的主要區域，騰出空間來存放這批貨物。Annabelle，能麻煩你的團隊處理嗎？

單字 get something started 開始…
conference call （三人以上的）電話會議　operation 營運
run smoothly 進展順利　redirect （改方向、地址）重新寄送

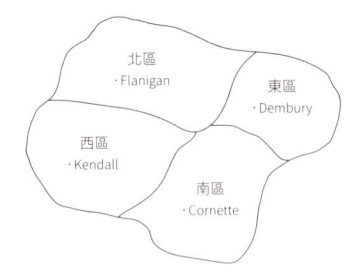

```
        北區
       ·Flanigan     東區
                    ·Dembury
   西區
  ·Kendall
              南區
            ·Cornette
```

28. 說話者早上與誰交談過？
(A) 公用事業員工
(B) 百貨公司經理
(C) 緊急救援人士
(D) 工廠管理人員

29. 請查看圖表。哪個地區受到暴風雨的襲擊？
(A) 東部地區
(B) 西部地區
(C) 北部地區
(D) 南部地區

30. 說話者要求Annabelle的團隊做什麼事？
(A) 審閱文件
(B) 打電話給客戶
(C) 清空區域
(D) 修理車輛

RC PART 5

UNIT 01 名詞

PRACTICE
題本 p.106

1. (C)　2. (B)　3. (B)　4. (B)　5. (C)　6. (D)
7. (C)　8. (B)　9. (C)　10. (D)　11. (B)　12. (B)
13. (D)　14. (D)　15. (A)　16. (D)　17. (C)　18. (D)
19. (A)　20. (B)

1. (C)
中譯 根據公司的電子報，副總將於本週四召開關於公司發展的討論會。
解說 空格前方有不定冠詞 a，因此答案要選 (C) discussion。
單字 newsletter 電子報、商務通訊　firm 公司
progress 進行、進展

2. (B)
中譯 如果在生產組裝線上發生任何安全違規行為，請與主管溝通。
解說 空格前方為名詞，後方連接動詞，表示空格適合填入名詞，與前方名詞 safety 組合成複合名詞，因此答案為 (B) violations。
單字 supervisor 主管、管理人　safety 安全　violation 違規
occur 發生　assembly line（工廠的）生產組裝線

3. (B)
中譯 律師仔細審查談好的協議，確認是否存在任何問題。
解說 句子的主詞為 The lawyers、動詞為 review，空格為 review 的受詞，且受到 negotiated 的修飾，應填入名詞，因此答案為 (B) agreements。
單字 review 審查　negotiated 洽談的
agreement 協議、合約

4. (B)
中譯 Irene Krakow打算明天早上與健身房的教練見面。
解說 空格受到前方不定冠詞 a 的修飾，且為動詞 meet 的受詞，因此答案為名詞 (B) trainer。不定冠詞 a 無法修飾 (D) training，該選項填入後亦不符合題意，因此並不適當。
單字 intend 打算、意圖　gym 健身房、體育館

5. (C)
中譯 銀行櫃員猶豫是否要接受管理層提出的合約提議。
解說 there is 後方應連接單數名詞，因此答案為 (C) hesitation。
單字 hesitation 猶豫、躊躇　teller 銀行櫃員　contract 合約
put forth 提出

6. (D)
中譯 Cromwell先生在成功完成Maxell項目後，獲得了任務選擇權。
解說 空格前方為介系詞，表示空格應填入名詞或動名詞，當作介系詞的受詞，因此答案可能是 assigning 或 assignments。動名詞後方要連接受詞，但空格後方並未連接受詞，因此答案要選 (D) assignments。
單字 choice 選擇權　complete 完成

7. (C)
中譯 Dover運動用品店與當地的幾支棒球隊為長期合作關係。
解說 空格受到不定冠詞 a 和形容詞 long-term 的修飾，應填入名詞。選項中，affiliate（附屬機構）和 affiliation（合作、聯盟）皆為名詞，但根據題意，空格適合填入 (C) affiliation。
單字 sporting goods 運動用品　long-term 長期的
affiliation 合作、聯合

8. (B)
中譯 由於預計會下大雪，建議旅客避開山區道路。
解說 空格為句子的主詞，同時為接受建議的對象。Travel 和 Travelers 皆為名詞，答案應選人物名詞 (B) Travelers。
單字 advised 建議、勸告　avoid 避開
on account of 由於…　expected 預期的
heavy snowfall 大雪

9. (C)
中譯 根據執行長的決定，所有員工都額外獲得一天特休。
解說 空格前後方皆為介系詞，空格適合填入名詞，當作介系詞的受詞，因此答案為 (C) accordance。
單字 in accordance with 根據　extra 額外的
paid leave 有薪假、特休

10. (D)
中譯 假期間，所有飯店的線上訂房均不予退款。
解說 空格應與名詞 hotel 組合成複合名詞，當作句子的主詞，並受到限定詞 all 的修飾。all 後方可連接複數名詞或不可數名詞，因此答案要選複數名詞 (D) bookings。
單字 making a booking 預訂　completely 完全地、徹底地
nonrefundable 不可退還的

11. (B)
中譯 Hightower先生對於市長選擇他的橋樑設計表示滿意。
解說 空格為動詞 expressed 的受詞，因此答案要選名詞 (B) satisfaction。
單字 express 表現、表示　select 挑選　mayor 市長

12. (B)
中譯 Burbank先生將成立一個顧問團隊，負責處理公司獲得的新客戶。
解說 空格前方為介系詞 of，空格應填入名詞，當作介系詞的受

55

詞。選項中，consultant 和 consultants 皆為名詞，而 group 指的是多人組成的團體，因此答案要選複數名詞 (B) consultants。

單字 establish 成立　handle 處理　obtain 獲得、得到

13. (D)
中譯 鋼琴家Judy Watson於過去三天的演奏受到觀眾的廣泛好評。
解說 空格前方為所有格 Judy Watson's，表示空格應填入名詞。performance 和 performances 皆為名詞，但句中的動詞 have 為複數動詞，因此答案要選複數名詞 (D) performances。
單字 performance 表演　widely 廣泛地　praise 稱讚
audience 觀眾

14. (D)
中譯 在皮埃蒙特，有些新建築的風格類似於古羅馬時期。
解說 空格受到定冠詞 the 的修飾，應填入名詞。stylist 和 style 皆為名詞，但根據題意，加上後方受到介系詞片語 of some new buildings 的修飾，空格適合填入 (D) style。
單字 resemble 類似　ancient 古代的

15. (A)
中譯 根據政府建議，家庭應使用節能隔熱材料。
解說 According to 為介系詞，從 According to 至空格為片語，並非子句，因此動詞形態 (B)、(D) 和不定詞 (C) 皆不適合填入空格。空格與 government 組合成複合名詞，因此答案為 (A) recommendations。
單字 according to 根據⋯　recommendation 建議、推薦
energy-efficient 節能的　insulation material 隔熱材料

16. (D)
中譯 儘管Dan Jenkins在Weyland航空公司連續工作了三十年，他還是辭職去另一家公司工作。
解說 空格前方為形容詞，後方連接介系詞片語，表示空格應填入名詞，受到形容詞和介系詞片語的修飾。employee 和 employment 皆為名詞，而根據文意，答案要選 (D) employment。
單字 continual 連續的、不間斷的　resign 辭職、卸任

17. (C)
中譯 無論出差的開支多少，員工都應該要呈報。
解說 空格前方為限定詞 any，因此答案要選名詞 (C) expenses。
單字 be supposed to 應該要⋯　report 報告、呈報
business trip 出差

18. (D)
中譯 Klein先生被要求提出關於如何打入南美市場的建議。
解說 空格為動詞 make 的受詞，且受到不定冠詞 a 的修飾，表示空格應填入名詞。proposer 和 proposal 皆為名詞，根據文意，答案要選 (D) proposal。
單字 make a proposal 提議　regarding 關於⋯　enter 進入、進去

19. (A)
中譯 商店被告知在未來兩個月，將限制新產品線的流通。
解說 空格置於名詞子句中的主詞位置，且後方受到介系詞片語的修飾，因此答案要選 (A) distribution。distributing 為動名詞，後方要直接連接受詞，因此不適合填入。
單字 inform 通知、告知　distribution 流通、分配
product line 產品線　limit 限制

20. (B)
中譯 Audrey博士總是想為她的科學家提供實驗所需的材料。
解說 該句話的句型結構為「動詞（give）＋間接受詞（her scientists）＋直接受詞」，空格後方連接形容詞子句，因此空格應填入適當的名詞，當作關係代名詞 that 的先行詞。materials 和 materialization 皆為名詞，而根據文意，答案選 (B) materials 較為適當。
單字 be eager to 渴望去做⋯　experiment 實驗

UNIT 02 代名詞

PRACTICE
題本 p.109

1. (C)　**2.** (B)　**3.** (B)　**4.** (D)　**5.** (B)　**6.** (A)
7. (A)　**8.** (B)　**9.** (C)　**10.** (C)

1. (C)
中譯 Toole女士明天要飛往曼非斯，因為她必須與一位潛在客戶見面。
解說 空格置於副詞子句中的主詞位置，因此答案為人稱代名詞主格 (C) she。
單字 potential 潛在的　client 客戶

2. (B)
中譯 歡迎任何有興趣從事機器人技術產業的人應徵此職位。
解說 空格後方為關係代名詞 who，其後方連接單數動詞 is，表示該句應為 anyone who 開頭的句子，因此答案要選 (B) Anyone。
單字 career 職業、職涯　robotics 機器人技術
apply for 應徵⋯

3. (B)
中譯 員工會議是強制性的，因此每個人都必須取消撞期會議，並參加明天的員工會議。
解說 空格後方連接動詞 must cancel，表示空格應填入主詞，因此答案為 (B) everybody。
單字 staff 員工　mandatory 強制的
conflicting 衝突的、撞期的

4. (D)
中譯 Jules Desmond在讀完小說的部分段落後，將為粉絲親自在書上簽名。

56

解說 句中包含主詞（Jules Desmond）、動詞（will autograph）和受詞（copies），表示該句話為結構完整的句子。因此空格可填入反身代名詞，表示強調語氣，答案要選 (D) himself。

單字 section 段落　novel 小說　autograph 簽名　copies 副本、一本

5. (B)
中譯 請使用房間後方的訓練手冊，而非放在桌上的那些。

解說 空格應填入適當的代名詞，代替前方出現過的複數名詞 the training manuals，因此答案為 (B) those。空格與 sitting 之間省略了「關係代名詞＋ be 動詞（that[which] are）」。

單字 training 訓練　manual 手冊、說明書

6. (A)
中譯 每次項目完成後，請與你的經理聯絡以獲取新任務。

解說 空格用來修飾 manager，因此答案要選人稱代名詞所有格 (A) your。

單字 complete 完成　assignment 任務、課題

7. (A)
中譯 儘管這些輪胎只用了兩年，Vernon女士還是決定更換一套新的輪胎。

解說 空格置於 replace 後方的受詞位置上，用來指 tires，因此答案要選人稱代名詞受格 (A) them。

單字 replace 更換、替換

8. (B)
中譯 應徵工程師職位的人中，最佳人選為 Rita Kraus，我們應向她提出工作邀約。

解說 形容詞子句 who ~ position 用來修飾主詞 The best -------。空格應填入適當的名詞，當作形容詞子句的先行詞，且受到形容詞 best 的修飾，因此答案為不定代名詞 (B) one。形容詞無法修飾其他選項，文法上亦不正確。

單字 apply for 應徵⋯　engineering 工程師、工程　offer 提供、給予

9. (C)
中譯 我們搭的觀光巴士被漆成紅色，所以即使在停滿的停車場，也很容易辨識出它的位置。

解說 空格置於 to locate 後方的受詞位置上，表示空格可填入 us, ours, ourselves。而根據文意，ours 代表「our tour bus」，因此答案要選所有格代名詞 (C) ours。

單字 locate 確定⋯的地點

10. (C)
中譯 由於Atkins女士認真工作和付出，使她自己成為一名非常有能力的電腦程式設計師。

解說 動詞 turned 的受詞與主詞相同，同為 Ms. Atkins，因此答案為反身代名詞 (C) herself。

單字 turn A into 把 A 變成 B　highly 非常　competent 有能力的　thanks to 由於⋯　dedication 奉獻

UNIT 03 形容詞與限定詞

PRACTICE　題本 p.111

1. (D)　**2.** (A)　**3.** (C)　**4.** (C)　**5.** (A)　**6.** (B)
7. (C)　**8.** (A)　**9.** (A)　**10.** (B)

1. (D)
中譯 Howell女士對當今最新的科技發展都有全面的了解。

解說 空格修飾後方名詞 developments，表示應填入形容詞。空格前方有定冠詞 the，因此答案要選 (D) latest，組合成形容詞最高級。

單字 comprehensive 全面的

2. (A)
中譯 參加完研討會後，每個人都要在實驗室中進行一些實作訓練。

解說 空格與 person 組合成主詞，因此答案要選限定詞 (A) every，用來修飾單數名詞。which 當作限定詞使用時，要置於問句中；many 要修飾複數名詞，並不適當。

單字 hands-on 親自動手的、實作的　lab 實驗室

3. (C)
中譯 最好在開會前建立好議程，這樣即可確保已涵蓋所有重要事項。

解說 空格置於主詞補語的位置上，適合填入形容詞，因此答案為 (C) beneficial。選項中同時出現形容詞和分詞時，要以形容詞為優先考量，因此 benefiting 並非答案。

單字 agenda 議程　cover 涵蓋、包含

4. (C)
中譯 命運媒體公司只雇用有雄心壯志、願意努力工作實現自身目標的應徵者。

解說 空格置於動詞 hires 後方，表示可填入形容詞，修飾後方受詞 applicants；或是填入名詞，與 applicants 組合成複合名詞。名詞 ambition 不適合搭配 applicants 一起使用，因此答案要選 (C) ambitious。

單字 ambitious 有雄心的　applicant 應徵者　willing 願意的　achieve 達成　goal 目標

5. (A)
中譯 重要的是及時把物品出貨給客戶。

解說 空格前方有不定冠詞 a，後方連接名詞 manner，表示空格可填入形容詞，修飾後方名詞；或是填入名詞，與 manner 組合成複合名詞。time 和 times 都不適合與 manner 組合成複合名詞，因此答案為形容詞 (A) timely。建議直接記下片語 in a timely manner。

單字 vital 重要的、必要的　items 物品　ship 出貨、配送　in a timely manner 及時

6. (B)

中譯 所有在工作中的技術人員都必須在實驗室內穿戴安全裝備。

解說 空格用來修飾主詞 technicians，因此答案為限定詞 (B) All，可修飾複數名詞。其餘選項皆不適當：each 用來修飾單數名詞；none 的用法為「none of 複數名詞」；either 可修飾某些特定名詞，像是 side，但本題空格後方為數量不明確的複數名詞，不適合修飾。

單字 technician 技術人員、技師
be required to do 被要求做⋯　safety gear 安全裝備
laboratory 實驗室　workday 工作日、平日

7. (C)

中譯 參加者表示，慶典中最令人印象深刻的部分是舞蹈表演。

解說 空格前方為限定詞 most，後方連接名詞 part，表示空格應填入形容詞，受到 most 的修飾，同時修飾後方的名詞，因此答案為 (C) impressive。

單字 performance 表演

8. (A)

中譯 Horace Powers 打算在升遷後與家人一起度假幾天。

解說 空格用來修飾複數名詞 days，因此答案為 (A) several。

單字 get promoted 升遷　intend 打算、意圖
take a vacation 度假

9. (A)

中譯 Cunningham 女士在過去幾年裡參與了多個大型專案。

解說 空格可填入形容詞，修飾後方名詞 projects；或是填入名詞，與 projects 組成複合名詞，因此答案選擇 (A) extensive 較為適當。選項中有形容詞，因此不可選分詞 extending。

單字 multiple 複合的、多樣的　extensive 廣大的、廣泛的

10. (B)

中譯 Luxor 傢俱公司設計舒適的辦公椅給幾乎整天都坐著的人。

解說 空格用來修飾後方名詞 office chairs，因此答案為形容詞 (B) comfortable。選項中有形容詞，因此不可選分詞 (C) comforting。

單字 individual 個人、個體　remain seated 維持坐著

UNIT 04 副詞

PRACTICE　題本 p.113

| 1. (D) | 2. (D) | 3. (B) | 4. (D) | 5. (B) | 6. (D) |
| 7. (C) | 8. (D) | 9. (D) | 10. (A) |

1. (D)

中譯 網站的改善是由資訊科技部門的負責人親自進行。

解說 空格置於 be 動詞和分詞之間，應填入副詞，因此答案為 (D) personally。

單字 make improvements 改善、改進
personally 親自、直接　director 負責人、主管

2. (D)

中譯 電影中極為逼真的特效讓觀眾留下了深刻的印象。

解說 空格應填入副詞，用來修飾後方的形容詞 realistic，因此答案為 (D) highly。

單字 audience 觀眾、聽眾
be impressed by 對⋯留下深刻的印象　highly 極度地
realistic 逼真的、現實的　special effect 特效　film 電影

3. (B)

中譯 該招牌清楚指出此房間禁止未經授權的人員出入。

解說 空格置於 be 動詞後方，且後方連接形容詞片語 off limits，因此答案要選副詞 (B) clearly。

單字 sign 標誌牌、招牌　indicate 指出、顯示
clearly 清楚地、明確地　off limits 禁止出入的
unauthorized 未經授權的、沒有權限的　personnel 人員

4. (D)

中譯 辦公室經理 Olson 先生多次指示員工準時參加特別活動。

解說 該句話的主詞為 Mr. Olson，動詞為 instructed，名詞片語 the office manager 用來修飾主詞。而空格置於動詞前方，因此答案要選副詞 (D) repeatedly。

單字 repeatedly 多次地、反覆地　instruct 指示
on time 準時

5. (B)

中譯 因為船在早上 7 點會準時出發，所以參加行程的遊客必須準時抵達。

解說 空格置於動詞 departs 後方做修飾，因此答案要選副詞 (B) promptly。

單字 on time 準時　depart 出發　promptly 準時地、立即地

6. (D)

中譯 自 Julie Sharpe 開始在 Meridian 公司工作以來，她的成就經常受到認可。

解說 空格置於助動詞 has 和過去分詞 received 之間，因此答案要選副詞 (D) regularly。

單字 regularly 經常地、定期地　recognition 認可、肯定
accomplishment 成就、業績

7. (C)

中譯 服務生有禮貌地詢問客人是否享受在餐廳用餐的時光。

解說 雖然空格置於名詞 diners 後方，但真正修飾的對象為動詞 asked，因此答案要選副詞 (C) politely。

單字 diner 用餐的人　politely 有禮貌地

8. (D)
中譯 客服代表接獲指示要更迅速解決所有投訴。
解說 該句話的句型結構為「動詞（solve）＋名詞（complaints）＋副詞」，因此答案要選 (D) promptly。
單字 customer service representative 客服代表　instruct 指示　solve 解決　complaint 投訴、不滿

9. (D)
中譯 倉庫管理員急忙把電子設備箱搬走，為新貨物騰出空間。
解說 該句話中的主詞為 The warehouse supervisor、動詞為 had、受詞為 the boxes of electronics，過去分詞 removed 為受詞補語。而空格置於動詞與過去分詞之間，因此答案要選副詞 (D) hastily。
單字 warehouse 倉庫　supervisor 管理員、監督者　electronics 電子設備　remove 移開、搬走　make space for 為⋯騰出空間　shipment 貨物

10. (A)
中譯 縣博覽會的抽獎中獎者，將由今晚隨機抽出的號碼決定。
解說 該句話的句型結構為「不定冠詞（a）＋分詞（selected）＋名詞（number）」，當中的分詞扮演形容詞的角色，而空格置於分詞前方，因此答案要選副詞 (A) randomly。
單字 raffle 抽獎　fair 博覽會　randomly 隨機地

UNIT 05 動詞、主動詞單複數一致性、語態、時態

PRACTICE　題本 p.116

1. (D)	2. (D)	3. (C)	4. (C)	5. (A)	6. (D)
7. (A)	8. (D)	9. (D)	10. (D)	11. (A)	12. (C)
13. (A)	14. (C)	15. (A)	16. (B)	17. (C)	18. (B)
19. (B)	20. (B)				

1. (D)
中譯 針對國內買家的大量採購訂單，Danzig 辦公用品公司偏好現金付款。
解說 空格置於動詞的位置上，雖然主詞 Danzig Office Supplies 的形態為複數形，但該名詞屬於公司名稱，應視為單數，因此答案要選單數動詞 (D) prefers。
單字 prefer 偏好、喜歡　cash 現金　payment 付款、結帳　domestic 國內的

2. (D)
中譯 許多科技公司都在春季招募剛從大學畢業的新員工。
解說 主詞 Many technology companies 為複數名詞，空格置於後方動詞的位置上，因此答案要選複數動詞 (D) hire。
單字 technology 科技　hire 招募　graduate from 畢業於⋯

3. (C)
中譯 日光媒體公司將在網路上播放新聞節目，並考慮製作電視節目。
解說 雖然主詞 Daylight Media 為單數名詞，但後方出現對等連接詞 and，且後方連接的是原形動詞 consider，並非單數動詞 considers，表示空格應填入助動詞加上原形動詞，因此答案要選 (C) will broadcast。
單字 broadcast 播放　consider 考慮　as well 也、同時

4. (C)
中譯 老鷹建設公司繳交的投標書符合市政府列出的要求。
解說 該句話的主詞為 The bid，後方的過去分詞 submitted by Eagle Builders 用來修飾主詞，因此空格應填入動詞。(B) 為分詞、(D) 為不定詞，可先刪去這兩個選項。主詞為單數名詞，因此答案為單數動詞 (C) fulfills。
單字 bid 投標（書）　submit 繳交　fulfill 符合　requirement 要求、必要條件　list 列出清單

5. (A)
中譯 待 David Simpson 完成時，該專案的工作就算完成了。
解說 as 至句末為表示時間的副詞子句，該類型子句中可用現在式代替未來式，因此答案要選 (A) finishes。
單字 complete 完成、結束

6. (D)
中譯 相信 Reynolds 先生已與海外企業談成了幾份合約。
解說 空格置於名詞子句中的動詞位置上，選項中 (A) 為分詞、(B) 為不定詞，因此可先刪去。空格後方有受詞 several contracts，因此答案要選主動語態 (D) has negotiated。
單字 negotiate 談成、協商　contract 合約　corporation 企業、公司

7. (A)
中譯 商家全年的營業時間因季節而異。
解說 該句話的主詞 hours 為複數名詞，因此答案為複數動詞 (A) differ。請特別注意，切勿看到空格前方為單數名詞 operation，就直接選擇 differs 作為答案。
單字 operation 營運　differ 不同　throughout the year 全年　depending on 取決於⋯

8. (C)
中譯 在公司購買星耀科技公司的軟體後，便立即下載了。
解說 該句話的主詞為 The software，空格置於其後方的動詞位置上，且空格後方沒有連接受詞，因此答案要選被動語態 (C) was downloaded。
單字 immediately after ⋯之後立即　purchase 購買

9. (D)
中譯 如果你可以接受合約中的條款，請在合約上簽名。
解說 空格至 the contract 為主要子句，if ~ to you 為副詞子句。

59

子句需要包含主詞和動詞，但是主要子句中並未出現，表示主要子句應為祈使句，省略掉主詞，僅保留原形動詞，因此答案要選 (D) Sign。

單字 contract 合約　term（合約中的）條款
agreeable 可接受的、同意的

10. (D)
中譯 Alderson女士建議所有全職員工都參加即將卸任執行長的演講。

解說 空格置於名詞子句中的動詞位置上，該句話主要動詞為 proposed，表示提議、要求或命令，後方子句的動詞要使用「should＋原形動詞」，表示空格應填入 should be，而當中的 should 可省略，因此答案要選 (D) be。

單字 propose 建議　full-time 全職的、專任的
employee 員工　present 在場的
outgoing 即將卸任的、外出的

11. (A)
中譯 請在培訓活動舞台準備期間填寫您收到的保險文件。

解說 連接詞 while 的意思為「在…期間」，表示兩件事情同時發生，而選項 (B) 和 (D) 分別為過去式和現在完成式，並不適當。本題的主要子句為祈使句，表達現在發生的事情，因此答案要選現在進行式的被動語態 (A) is being。

單字 complete 完成、填寫　insurance 保險
paperwork 文件　stage 舞台　set up 準備、設置

12. (C)
中譯 為容納新進員工，辦公室經理將訂購更多的桌椅。

解說 空格置於該句話的動詞位置上，而選項 (B) 和 (D) 皆不是動詞形態，可優先刪去。空格後方有受詞 more desks and chairs，所以可刪去被動語態 (A)。綜合上述，答案要選主動語態 (C) will be ordering。

單字 accommodate 容納

13. (A)
中譯 具有強烈職業道德的應徵者，能說服面試官錄取他們。

解說 空格置於動詞位置上，且前方為助動詞 can，因此答案要選原形動詞 (A) convince。空格後方連接受詞 interviewers，因此不可填入被動語態 (C)。

單字 applicant 應徵者　work ethics 職業道德
convince 說服、使確信

14. (C)
中譯 在Parker女士審核之前，不要向地方當局繳交補助金申請文件。

解說 空格後方沒有連接受詞，因此可先刪去主動語態 (A) 和 (B)。連接詞 until 引導表示時間的副詞子句，當中的動詞可用現在式代替未來式，因此答案為 (C) is reviewed。

單字 submit 繳交　grant 補助金　authority 當局、政府
review 審核

15. (A)
中譯 外國製造商訂購的電腦晶片數量減少了百分之三十。

解說 該句話的主詞為 The number，後面 of computer ~ manufacturers 用來修飾主詞。因為主詞為單數名詞，所以答案有可能是選項 (A) 或 (C)。而空格後方並未連接受詞，因此答案要選被動語態 (A) has been reduced。根據文意，表達的是「從外國製造商下單的時間點到現在減少了百分之三十」，時態適合使用現在完成式。請注意勿把複數名詞 computer chips 當作主詞。

單字 manufacturer 製造商、製造業者　reduce 減少

16. (B)
中譯 公司的資深科學家Morelli博士，負責監督一支由醫學研究員組成的大型團隊。

解說 該句話的主詞為 Dr. Morelli，the company's head scientist 用來修飾主詞，而空格置於後方動詞位置上，且連接受詞，因此答案要選 (B) supervises。

單字 supervise 監督　researcher 研究員

17. (C)
中譯 由於幾名預期參加的與會者在時間安排上有衝突，導致會議被取消了。

解說 空格置於主要子句的動詞位置上，後方並未連接受詞，因此答案要選被動語態 (C) was canceled。

單字 expected 預期的　attendee 與會者　due to 由於…
conflicting schedule 時間安排有衝突

18. (B)
中譯 請務必查看使用說明書，因為當中有解釋安裝設備的確切方法。

解說 由連接詞 because 引導的副詞子句中，缺少主詞和動詞，表示空格應填入主詞加上動詞。主要子句的 the user's manual 為單數名詞，可用單數代名詞 it 表示。而後方要搭配單數動詞，因此答案要選 (B) it explains。

單字 be sure to 務必做…　user's manual 使用說明書
precise 明確的　method 方法　install 安裝
appliance 設備

19. (B)
中譯 Caldwell國際公司將在本月底之前，把七名員工調到新加坡分公司。

解說 副詞片語 By the end of this month，表示未來的時間點，因此答案要選未來完成式 (B) will have transferred。

單字 transfer 調動、搬遷　branch 分公司、分店

20. (B)
中譯 由商店經理處理後，付給顧客的退款被視為有效。

解說 空格置於由連接詞 when 引導的副詞子句中，而副詞子句中缺少主詞和動詞。四個選項皆為動詞的變化形，加上空格後方並未連接受詞，只有介系詞片語，表示空格可能是省略「主

詞＋ be 動詞」的被動語態，因此答案要選 (B) processed。該句話省略了代名詞 they（指前方出現過的 refunds）以及 be 動詞 are。

單字 give a refund 退款　consider 視為、考慮
valid 有效的　process 處理

UNIT 06 不定詞與動名詞

PRACTICE　　　　　　　　　題本 p.119

| 1. (D) | 2. (A) | 3. (B) | 4. (B) | 5. (C) | 6. (A) |
| 7. (D) | 8. (D) | 9. (A) | 10. (B) |

1. (D)
中譯 Ken Richards 是帶領研發部門組成之新團隊的最佳人選。
解說 該句話的主詞為 Ken Richards，動詞為 is，補語為 the top candidate，空格至句末用來修飾 candidate，因此答案要選不定詞 (D) to lead，為形容詞用法，修飾名詞。
單字 candidate 人選　lead 帶領、領導　form 組成、形成
R&D 研究開發（= research and development）

2. (A)
中譯 Alps 航空公司將於七月開始宣傳其飛往亞洲各城市的最新航線。
解說 空格前方為動詞 start，後方連接 its newest routes，表示空格要成為動詞 start 的受詞，同時能搭配受詞 its newest routes，因此答案要選動名詞 (A) promoting。
單字 promote 宣傳　route 航線、路線

3. (B)
中譯 該公司的執行長打算允許員工每年申請升遷兩次。
解說 動詞 permit 的用法為「permit ＋受詞＋不定詞 to V」，因此答案要選不定詞 (B) to apply，而非動名詞 applying。
單字 permit 允許　apply for 申請…　promotion 升遷
twice 兩次

4. (B)
中譯 Solomon 先生表示，他認為由於奧克蘭分公司擁有獲利能力，關閉它是個錯誤。
解說 空格置於動詞 considers 後方的受詞位置上，同時連接 the Auckland branch 當作受詞，空格應填入動名詞較為適當，因此答案為 (B) closing。consider 可連接動名詞當作受詞。
單字 state 陳述　consider 認為、考慮
branch 分公司、分店　due to 由於…　profitability 獲利能力

5. (C)
中譯 為了保證更快的交貨時間，該公司獨家使用當地的水星快遞公司。
解說 空格後方沒有主詞，而是直接連接動詞 guarantee。In spite of 為介系詞、As soon as 為連接詞，可優先刪去。In order to 後方可連接動詞；With regard to 後方則要連接名詞，因此答案要選 (C) In order to。
單字 guarantee 保證　exclusively 專門地、獨佔地
courier 快遞公司、快遞員

6. (A)
中譯 如果我們要搭乘飛往莫斯科的班機，就必須在接下來的二十分鐘內抵達機場。
解說「be 動詞＋不定詞 to V」可用來表示預定、義務、可能或意圖，因此答案要選不定詞 (A) to make。其他選項皆不符合文法規定。
單字 make a flight 搭機飛往…

7. (D)
中譯 管理階層注意到辦公室自從安裝新冷氣後，生產力有顯著的提升。
解說 空格後方連接 a new air conditioner 當作受詞，因此答案要選動名詞 (D) installing。since 除了可以當連接詞外，還可以當介系詞使用。
單字 since 自…以後　install 安裝　management 管理階層
notice 注意到　significant 顯著的、重大的
improvement 增進、改善　productivity 生產力

8. (D)
中譯 Edwards 先生運用專業建築師來設計公司的新研究中心。
解說 該句話的主詞為 Mr. Edwards，動詞為 utilized、受詞為 a professional architect，而選項 (A)、(B) 和 (C) 皆為動詞，所以可優先刪去。空格連接關係代名詞 what 當作副詞，因此答案要選 (D) to design，適用不定詞的副詞用法。
單字 utilize 善用、運用　architect 建築師

9. (A)
中譯 行銷團隊的目標是在網路上投放更多的廣告，同時減少支出。
解說 yet 為對等連接詞，連接 to advertise 和空格，表示空格應填入不定詞。因此答案要選不定詞 to 可連接的原形動詞 (A) reduce。
單字 goal 目標　advertise online 在網路上投放廣告
yet 然而、卻　reduce 減少　expenditure 支出

10. (B)
中譯 在過去的五年裡，Amanda Watson 已經從店內的打掃人員轉變成店主。
解說 該句話適用句型「go from A to B」，當中 A 和 B 的詞性需一致。A 對應的是 sweeping，因此答案要選動名詞 (B) owning。
單字 sweep 打掃、掃地　own 擁有、持有

UNIT 07 分詞

PRACTICE　題本 p.121

1. (A)　**2.** (C)　**3.** (A)　**4.** (B)　**5.** (C)　**6.** (B)
7. (B)　**8.** (D)　**9.** (D)　**10.** (B)

1. (A)
中譯 Long女士審閱了組長繳交的修訂版進度報告。

解說 空格應填入適當的分詞，用來修飾 progress report。report 為東西，不會自行修改，而是被修改的對象，因此答案要選過去分詞 (A) revised。

單字 revise 修改　progress 過程、進行　submit 繳交

2. (C)
中譯 強烈建議擴展中的公司使用專業會計師。

解說 名詞 expansion 無法和 businesses 組成複合名詞，所以可先刪去選項 (A) 和 (B)。形容詞或分詞皆可修飾空格後方的 business（業務），因此 expanding 和 expanded 可納入考量。而根據文意，建議擴展中的公司使用專業會計師，而非建議已擴展的公司，因此答案要選 (C) expanding。

單字 accountant 會計師　highly 非常　recommend 推薦

3. (A)
中譯 延期的會議應重新安排在雙方都方便的時間。

解說 該句話的動詞為 should be rescheduled，所以可先刪去動詞 (B) 和 (C)。若填入 Postponing，為動名詞連接 meeting 當作受詞，表示「正在延期的會議」，不符合文意。根據文意，表示「已延期的會議」較為適當，因此答案要選過去分詞 (A) Postponed。

單字 postpone 延期　reschedule 重新安排　mutually 互相、彼此間　convenient 方便的

4. (B)
中譯 任何對產品不滿意的客戶都有權在購買後七天內退貨。

解說 該句話的主詞為 Any customer、動詞為 is entitled、空格至 product 用來修飾主詞，所以可先刪去動詞 (A) 和 (C)。根據文意，表達顧客對產品感到不滿，應使用過去分詞，因此答案要選 (B) displeased。

單字 displeased 不滿意的、不愉快的　be entitled to 有權⋯　purchase 購買

5. (C)
中譯 Eric Murphy整個假期都待在家裏，他寧願休息也不要去旅行。

解說 空格前方沒有主詞，所以可先刪去動詞 (A)、(B) 和 (D)。空格置於分詞構句的結構中，省略連接詞和主詞，表示空格應填入分詞，因此答案要選 (C) preferring。省略前的句子為「because[since] he preferred」。

單字 remain 留下、繼續存在、保持　entire 整個的、所有的　prefer 偏好、喜歡　rest 休息

6. (B)
中譯 Roberts先生有一些準備好的發言想與聽眾分享。

解說 空格前方已有動詞 has，所以可先刪去動詞 (D)。名詞 preparation 無法與 remarks 組成複合名詞，所以也可刪去 (C)。根據文意，表達「準備好的評論」較為適當，因此答案要選過去分詞 (B) prepared。

單字 remark 評論、發言　share with 與⋯分享　audience 觀眾、聽眾

7. (B)
中譯 為了正確使用電鋸，你需要閱讀操作手冊中的說明。

解說 空格至 manual 用來修飾前方的 the instructions，因此答案要選分詞 (B) included，可置於名詞後方做修飾。另外，也可視為空格前方省略「關係代名詞＋be動詞（which[that] are）」。空格後方並未連接受詞，因此不能選不定詞 (D)。

單字 electric saw 電鋸　properly 正確地　instruction 說明、指示　include 包含　manual 使用說明書、操作手冊

8. (D)
中譯 任何希望參加即將舉行之會計研討會的員工，都必須與Taylor女士交談。

解說 該句話的主詞為 Any employees、動詞為 must speak、空格至 accounting 用來修飾主詞，所以要填入適當的分詞，置於名詞後方做修飾。選項中的分詞有 hoped 和 hoping，主詞 employees 為人物應使用主動，因此答案要選現在分詞 (D) hoping。

單字 upcoming 即將來臨、即將到來的　accounting 會計

9. (D)
中譯 新的自助服務機台有望顯著減少排隊時間。

解說 spend 為及物動詞，表示「花費時間或金錢」之意。該句話中，「the amount of time」為 spend 的受詞，受到 spend 的修飾，屬於被動關係，因此答案要選過去分詞 (D) spent。

單字 kiosk 售票亭、機台　expected 預計、期待　significantly 顯著地　reduce 減少

10. (B)
中譯 從本週六開始，Hamilton百貨公司將特價出售店內的每件商品。

解說 「Starting / Beginning ＋時間」為慣用片語，置於句首表示「從⋯（何時）開始」，強調事情開始的時間點。

單字 discount 折扣　item 商品、物品

UNIT 08 介系詞

PRACTICE　題本 p.124

1. (A)	2. (C)	3. (D)	4. (A)	5. (A)	6. (B)
7. (D)	8. (B)	9. (A)	10. (B)	11. (A)	12. (A)
13. (D)	14. (B)	15. (C)	16. (B)	17. (A)	18. (A)
19. (C)	20. (B)				

1. (A)
中譯 所有實習生必須在週一上午七點半前抵達，以參加迎新活動。
(A) 為了 (B) 與…一起 (C) 作為 (D) 在…之上
單字 orientation 迎新　event 活動

2. (C)
中譯 Blaine玩具商店在網路上銷售的所有產品，皆需在收到貨品後的兩週內提出退貨。
(A) 在…之前 (B) 有關、在…之上 (C) …的 (D) 自從
單字 make a return 退貨、退還

3. (D)
中譯 Melissa Standish除了擔任公司的會計師外，還擔任辦公室經理。
(A) 因此 (B) 因為 (C) 關於 (D) 除了…之外
單字 serve 服務　firm 公司　accountant 會計師、會計人員

4. (A)
中譯 在縣博覽會上，每場演出結束後，由志工組成的團隊都會清掃整個劇場。
(A) 接著的 (B) 透過 (C) 在…四周 (D) 在…裡面
單字 performance 演出　county（行政區域）縣　fair 博覽會　volunteer 志工　entire 整體的　theater 劇場

5. (A)
中譯 經由準確報導新聞快報，Melinda Carter得以提高她作為新聞記者的聲譽。
(A) 經由 (B) 在…之上 (C) 與…一起 (D) 關於
單字 breaking news 新聞快報　accurately 準確地　reputation 聲譽

6. (B)
中譯 Hudson礦產公司自三個月前發現黃金以來，股價翻漲了一倍。
(A) 在…之前 (B) 自從 (C) 除非 (D) 因此
單字 value 價值　stock 股票　double 加倍

7. (D)
中譯 在Hardaway紡織公司銷售團隊的眾多人員中，Montague女士的工作效率最高。
(A) 在…裡面 (B) 在…之上 (C) 為了 (D) 在…之中

單字 salesforce 銷售人員、銷售部門　productive 有成效的

8. (B)
中譯 在業界幾位專家的建議下，Harrison先生成功創辦了自己的公司。
(A) 為了 (B) 帶著 (C) 沿著 (D) 在…之上、超過
單字 expert 專家　industry 產業、業界

9. (A)
中譯 由於Hooper女士渴望在歐洲生活，她自願調到公司的米蘭辦事處。
(A) 由於 (B) 在…期間 (C) 因此 (D) 也
單字 volunteer 自願　transfer 調動

10. (B)
中譯 由於Abernathy先生有興趣繼續深造，他將在平日晚上去讀研究所。
(A) 為了 (B) 由於 (C) 自從 (D) 關於
單字 graduate school 研究所　weeknight 平日晚上　further 促進

11. (A)
中譯 根據政府規定，每個人在此場地內都要隨時配戴安全帽。
(A) 根據 (B) 而不是 (C) 因此 (D) 然而
單字 regulation 規定　hard hat 安全帽　on the premises 在建築物內、在用地內　at all times 隨時

12. (A)
中譯 Dearborn先生在繁忙的假期來臨前辭去了職務。
(A) 在…之前 (B) 除外 (C) 依照 (D) 而不是
單字 resign 辭去、放棄

13. (D)
中譯 安排面試的五個人是從七十八名申請者中選出來的。
(A) 與…一起 (B) 為了 (C) 在…之外 (D) 來自、從…起
單字 individual 個人、個體　scheduled 安排的　select 挑選　pool 一群（可用人才）

14. (B)
中譯 Nelson科技公司有向員工和他們家人提供當地文化活動門票的傳統。
解說 該句話適用句型「provide A with B（向 A 提供 B）」，因此答案要選 (B) with。
單字 tradition 傳統　provide 提供、給予　local 當地的

15. (C)
中譯 由於Paladin製鞋公司的最新款運動鞋十分受歡迎，便決定增加生產量。
(A) 一切 (B) 也許 (C) 由於 (D) 總共
單字 popularity 歡迎、流行　sneakers 運動鞋

16. (B)
中譯 Kathy Ibsen預計在未來幾個月內被任命為部門副理。
(A) 自從 (B) 在…之內 (C) 大約 (D) 在
單字 expect 期待、預計　name 任命

17. (A)
中譯 所有人在離開辦公室前，都要打掃辦公區域並關閉電腦。
(A) 在…之前 (B) 直到 (C) 超過 (D) 超越
單字 workspace 辦公空間　turn off 關閉　depart 離開

18. (A)
中譯 Marconi紡織公司用棉和絲等各種布料生產女裝。
(A) 包含 (B) 同時 (C) 一…就 (D) 遍布、貫穿
單字 manufacture 生產　a variety of 各式各樣的
fabric 布料、織品　cotton 棉

19. (C)
中譯 月底之前將會做出關於績效獎金的決定。
(A) 與…一起 (B) 在…之間 (C) 關於 (D) 為了
單字 make a decision 做決定
performance bonus 績效獎金

20. (B)
中譯 Flint先生沒僱用臨時工，而是要求他團隊在三月加班。
(A) 顯然地 (B) 而不是 (C) 根據 (D) 超過
單字 take on 僱用　temporary 臨時的　staff 員工
work overtime 加班

UNIT 09 連接詞

PRACTICE 題本 p.128

1. (B)	2. (A)	3. (B)	4. (D)	5. (C)	6. (A)
7. (A)	8. (B)	9. (D)	10. (C)	11. (B)	12. (A)
13. (B)	14. (D)	15. (D)	16. (B)	17. (A)	18. (A)
19. (B)	20. (B)

1. (B)
中譯 天候不佳之際，員工應考慮在家辦公或搭乘大眾運輸工具前往辦公室。
(A) 而且 (B) 兩者擇一 (C) 因為、自從 (D) 如果

解說 空格前方出現動詞 consider，其後方要連接動名詞當作受詞。空格後方的 working 和 taking 以連接詞 or 連接，可得知是「either A or B」的用法，因此答案要選相關連接詞 (B) either。

單字 inclement weather 天候不佳、惡劣氣候
work from home 在家辦公
public transportation 大眾運輸工具

2. (A)
中譯 Jasmine Cartier努力提升自己的演講技巧，現在已成為一名有成就的公眾演講者。
(A) 和 (B) 為了 (C) 然而 (D) 或

解說 該句話的主詞為 Jasmine Cartier，後方缺少連接詞，連接兩個動詞 worked 和 is，因此空格應填入適當的對等連接詞。選項中的對等連接詞有 and 和 or，根據文意，答案要選 (A) and。

單字 work on 努力…　presentation 演講
accomplished 有成就的

3. (B)
中譯 雖然Hamilton先生七月有一半的時間都在休假，他仍創下了團隊中的最高銷量。
(A) 為了 (B) 雖然 (C) 此外 (D) 儘管

解說 空格後方連接主詞（Mr. Hamilton）和動詞（spent），而選項 (C) 和 (D) 並非連接詞，可優先刪去。前段話提到有一半的時間都在休假，表示他工作的時間不多，後方卻提到他創下最高銷量，前後內容相反，因此答案要選 (B) Although，表達前後對比。

單字 on vacation 休假　sales 銷量、銷售額

4. (D)
中譯 自從有電腦借閱系統後，更多的圖書能按時歸還。
(A) 周圍 (B) 顯然地 (C) 所以 (D) 自從、因為

解說 空格連接前後兩個子句，應填入連接詞。選項中，so 和 since 為連接詞，而根據文意，表示「自從…」較為適當，因此答案要選 (D) since。

單字 on time 準時　checkout （圖書）借閱
computerize 電腦化

5. (C)
中譯 Emerson公司每次推出新產品時，都會大力宣傳該產品。
(A) 因為 (B) 在…期間 (C) 每當 (D) 如此的

解說 空格後方連接主詞（Emerson Inc.）和動詞（releases），表示空格應填入連接詞。選項中，Because 和 Whenever 為連接詞，而根據文意，表達「每當推出新產品時，都會大力宣傳」較為適當，因此答案要選 (C) Whenever。

單字 release 推出　market 宣傳、行銷
heavily 大力地、沉重地

6. (A)
中譯 記得在Aubrey's書店註冊會員，這樣你就有資格享有特別優惠。
(A) 所以 (B) 為了 (C) 或者 (D) 仍然

解說 空格後方連接主詞（you）和動詞（can be），表示空格應填入連接詞，所以可先刪去選項 (B) 和 (D)。查看空格前後方子句的關係，屬於因果關係，因此答案要選 (A) so。

單字 sign up for 註冊　membership 會員
be eligible for 具有…的資格
special offer 特別優惠、特惠品

64

7. (A)
中譯 知名廚師Andrew Hutchins表示，使用新鮮食材時，餐點嚐起來更加美味。
(A) 當…的時候 (B) 儘管 (C) 為了 (D) 如何
解說 空格置於名詞子句當中，用來引導副詞子句，因此答案要選副詞子句連接詞 (A) when。
單字 famed 知名的　chef 廚師　state 敘述　ingredient 食材　taste 嚐起來

8. (B)
中譯 董事會必須確定加拿大的商業環境是否適合開設新的營業場所。
(A) 周圍 (B) 是否 (C) 然而 (D) 雖然
解說 空格應填入適當的連接詞，用來引導名詞子句，當作動詞 determine 的受詞，因此答案要選名詞子句連接詞 (B) whether。
單字 board of directors 董事會　climate 氣候、環境氛圍　ideal 理想的　facility 場所、設施

9. (D)
中譯 儘管Grayson女士所屬團隊的其他成員選擇搭飛機前往聖路易斯，她還是開車前往那裡參加研討會。
(A) 儘管 (B) 例如 (C) 並且 (D) 儘管
解說 空格應填入連接詞，連接前後方的子句，因此答案要選 (D) even though。其他選項皆為介系詞。
單字 drive 開車　fly 搭飛機

10. (C)
中譯 除非客戶指定要快速出貨，否則所有訂單均在收到後一天郵寄。
(A) 除了 (B) 因為 (C) 除非 (D) 甚至
解說 空格置於連接詞的位置上，根據文意，空格所在的副詞子句表示條件，因此答案要選 (C) Unless。
單字 specify 指定、明確說明　express delivery 快遞、快速運送　order 訂單　mail 郵寄、郵件

11. (B)
中譯 Kevin Watts決定留在Nottingham證券公司，因為他獲得了大幅加薪。
(A) 因此 (B) 因為 (C) 不僅 (D) 或是
解說 空格前後方皆有主詞和動詞，且前後方子句屬於因果關係，因此答案要選連接詞 (B) because。
單字 substantial 大幅的　pay raise 加薪

12. (A)
中譯 木星超市的首購者可享有免運費服務，或免費索取食物拼盤樣品。
解說 助動詞 can 後方出現兩個動詞 receive 和 request，表示空格應填入對等連接詞，所以答案可能是 or 或 so。而根據文意，前後兩個子句為二者擇一，因此答案要選 (A) or。
單字 platter 餐盤　extra cost 額外費用

13. (B)
中譯 在接受Dubois銀行的工作前，Harrison女士在里斯本的學校學習金融。
(A) 如何 (B) 在…之前 (C) 哪一個 (D) 相當、寧願
解說 空格後方連接結構完整的子句，表示空格應填入連接詞，因此答案為 (B) Before。其他選項當作副詞、代名詞或限定詞使用，並不適當。
單字 accept 接受、同意　position 職務、職位　finance 金融、財務

14. (D)
中譯 既然Raymond Mercer自行經營餐廳，他每天都要負責採購食材。
(A) 好像 (B) 此外 (C) 那個 (D) 由於
解說 空格後方連接子句，表示空格應填入連接詞。且兩個子句屬於因果關係，因此答案要選 (D) Now that。
單字 run 經營、營運　acquire 取得、獲得　ingredient 材料

15. (D)
中譯 一旦確認年度股東大會的地點，將予以公告。
(A) 為了 (B) 自…起 (C) 作為替代 (D) 一旦
解說 空格應填入連接詞，因此答案可能是 In order that 或 Once。根據文意，兩個子句表達時間先後，因此答案要選 (D) Once。
單字 location 地點　annual 年度的　shareholder 股東　determine 決定　make an announcement 發布公告

16. (B)
中譯 由於利率上升，越來越少人以新房抵押來借貸款。
(A) 除了 (B) 由於 (C) 然而 (D) 為何
解說 空格應填入連接詞，而根據文意，兩個子句屬於因果關係，因此答案要選 (B) Since。
單字 interest rate 利率　mortgage 抵押貸款

17. (A)
中譯 到下班時，Stella Reynolds和Jeffery Harper都沒有繳交Edmund項目的提案。
解說 該句話使用句型「neither A nor B」，因此答案要選 (A) nor。
單字 submit 繳交　proposal 提案

18. (A)
中譯 請準確說明新設備出現的故障，以便我方技術人員告知維修方式。
(A) 以便 (B) 自從 (C) 也不是 (D) 如果
解說 空格應填入連接詞，而前後方子句屬於因果關係，因此答案要選 (A) so that。
單字 malfunction 故障、失靈　precisely 準確地　device 機器、設備　technician 技術人員、技師

65

19. (B)
中譯 雖然Harris製造公司已把產品交到位於曼菲斯的客戶手上，但直到兩週後他們才完成全額付款。
(A) 為了 (B) 雖然 (C) 因此 (D) 可能
解說 空格後方連接結構完整的子句，表示空格應填入連接詞，因此答案要選 (B) While。(A) 為片語動詞、(C) 和 (D) 為副詞。
單字 client 客戶　make a payment 付款
full payment 全額付款

20. (B)
中譯 歡迎任何人在會議發言，但前提是他們要有正面貢獻。
(A) 當⋯的時候 (B) 只要、只有 (C) 即使 (D) 而不是
解說 空格應填入連接詞，根據文意，空格所屬的子句表示條件，因此答案要選 (B) only if。
單字 positive 正面的、積極的　contribute 貢獻

UNIT 10　關係詞

PRACTICE　題本 p.131

| 1. (C) | 2. (C) | 3. (B) | 4. (C) | 5. (B) | 6. (C) |
| 7. (D) | 8. (A) | 9. (A) | 10. (B) |

1. (C)
中譯 Cross先生表示，本月招收到最多新客戶的人，將獲得現金獎勵。
解說 空格置於名詞子句中的主詞位置上，表示應填入適當的單字，當作主格。根據文意，答案要選複合關係代名詞 (C) whoever，可扮演主詞的角色，表示「無論是誰」。
單字 state 述說、陳述　recruit 招收　cash 現金

2. (C)
中譯 Nantucket建築公司的所有權人為Peter Carroll，他從小就住在當地。
解說 空格置於主詞的位置上，且先行詞 Peter Carroll 為人物，因此答案要選 (C) who，為表示人物的關係代名詞主格。
單字 own 所有、擁有　childhood 童年

3. (B)
中譯 全國大部分地區對按時送貨之物流公司的需求很高。
解說 空格前方為主詞 Logistics companies、後方連接動詞 deliver，表示空格應填入適當的關係代名詞，代替先行詞 Logistics companies，因此答案要選 (B) that。
單字 logistics 物流　goods 商品、物品
on time 按時、準時　be in high demand 需求高的

4. (C)
中譯 Jessica Yeltsin創立了慈善基金會，並試圖用它來結束當地無家可歸者的危機。
解說 空格後方有主詞（she）和動詞片語（attempted to use），但缺少 use 的受詞，表示空格應填入適當的關係代名詞，代替先行詞 a charitable foundation，因此答案為 (C) that。(B) what 兼具先行詞和關係代名詞的作用，所以前方不能有 a charitable foundation。
單字 establish 創立　charitable 慈善的　foundation 基金會
attempt 試圖　homeless 無家可歸的、露宿的　crisis 危機

5. (B)
中譯 一月份新投資Jacobson金融公司的客戶有資格獲得免費諮詢。
解說 空格置於主詞 clients 和動詞 make 之間，應填入適當的關係代名詞主格，代替先行詞 clients，因此答案要選 (B) who。
單字 make an investment 投資　eligible for 有資格⋯
consultation 諮詢

6. (C)
中譯 會議將於Piedmont飯店舉行，那裡有現代化的設施能容納大批群眾。
解說 空格前後方各連接一個子句，表示空格應填入連接詞，或具備連接詞功能的字詞。except 為連接詞，但並不符合文意。空格用來代替先行詞 Piedmont Hotel，因此答案要選表示地點的關係副詞 (C) where。
單字 conference 會議　facility 設施　capable of 能夠⋯

7. (D)
中譯 政府已下令對建築倒塌事件進行調查，還需要一段時間才能查明原因。
解說 空格用來代替先行詞 building collapse，應填入關係代名詞主格，因此答案為 (D) which。如果本題的逗點後方出現「名詞／代名詞＋介系詞＋關係代名詞」時，通常是針對前方子句的內容補充說明，若改成有連接詞的句子則為「and the cause of it ~」。
單字 investigation 調查　collapse 倒塌　cause 原因
require 需要

8. (A)
中譯 Matthews女士決定僱用Ryan Varnum，他在公司法領域的專業性廣為人知。
解說 空格前後方的 Ryan Varnum 和 expertise，指的是「Ryan Varnum 的專業知識」，因此答案要選關係代名詞所有格 (A) whose。
單字 expertise 專業性　field 領域　corporate 公司的

9. (A)
中譯 迎新活動的講者說明了該如何在Hollmann國際公司取得成功。
解說 空格為動詞 explained 的受詞，同時也是名詞子句內 takes 的受詞，表示空格應填入適當的關係代名詞。空格前方沒有先行詞，因此要選擇包含先行詞在內的複合關係代名詞 (A) what。

10. (B)

中譯 Acuna先生教授培訓課程，讓參加者學會如何使用公司的電腦系統。

解說 空格後方連接子句，所以可先刪去選項 (C) 和 (D)。空格後方有主詞 participants，所以也可刪去 (A) who。該句話原本是兩個句子「Mr. Acuna teaches a training course. Participants learn to use the firm's computer system in it.」，如要連接成一個句子，需把句末的「介系詞＋代名詞（in it）」改成 in which，因此答案為 (B)。in which 也可改成關係副詞 where，建議一併記下。

單字 participant 參加者　firm 公司

UNIT 11 高分必備名詞詞彙

PRACTICE 題本 p.134

1. (D)	2. (D)	3. (A)	4. (A)	5. (D)	6. (B)
7. (A)	8. (A)	9. (B)	10. (D)	11. (B)	12. (C)
13. (A)	14. (D)	15. (A)	16. (A)	17. (B)	18. (C)
19. (B)	20. (B)				

1. (D)

中譯 有些當地公司不允許遠距工作，因為他們希望員工親自到辦公室工作。

(A) 外觀、出現 (B) 方法 (C) 工作 (D) 存在、在場

解說 遠距工作指的是在家工作，而公司反對遠距工作，表示希望員工在辦公室現場，因此答案要選 (D) presence，表示「存在、在場」。

單字 permit 允許　telecommuting 遠距工作　physical 身體上的

2. (D)

中譯 由老顧客組成的專門小組負責評估超市的最新產品。

(A) 系統 (B) 版本 (C) 調查 (D) 面板、專門小組

單字 long-term 長期的　rate 評估

3. (A)

中譯 該公司擁有的車輛中，最新增加的是Cobra引擎公司製造的運動型多功能車款。

(A) 增加物 (B) 設備 (C) 對象、物體 (D) 方案、程序

解說 空格適合表示「新增的車輛」，因此答案要選 (A) addition。除了表示東西之外，addition 也可用來表示公司新加入的員工。

單字 fleet 車隊　vehicle 車輛

4. (A)

中譯 重新裝修員工休息室目前被認為是次要的事情。

(A) 優先順位 (B) 冒險事業、風險 (C) 試圖 (D) 結果

單字 redecorate 重新裝修　lounge 休息室、會客廳　consider 考慮、認為

5. (D)

中譯 由於除草機的耐用度高，Peterson先生從購買以來從未需要修理。

(A) 測量 (B) 多樣化 (C) 考慮 (D) 耐用度

單字 lawnmower 除草機　once 一次　thanks to 由於…

6. (B)

中譯 有興趣的顧客可獲得三年保固，涵蓋所有必要的維修。

(A) 服務 (B) 保固 (C) 預算 (D) 承諾

單字 interested 有興趣的　acquire 獲得、得到　cover 涵蓋、包含

7. (A)

中譯 Edmund Blair被選為獎學金得主，可在英國留學一年。

(A) 受領者、接受者 (B) 獎項 (C) 申請者 (D) 參加者

單字 name 指名、提名　scholarship 獎學金　allow 允許

8. (A)

中譯 Adelaide公園是個定期舉行公司聚會或慈善募款等活動的場所。

(A) 場所 (B) 港口 (C) 版本、刊號 (D) 案件

單字 regular 定期的、週期的　get-together 聚會　charity 慈善　fundraiser 募款活動

9. (B)

中譯 那位建築師的風格中，有個顯著的特點是她對自然環境的依賴。

(A) 設計 (B) 方面、面向 (C) 緩和 (D) 傳統

單字 notable 值得注意的、顯著的　architect 建築師　reliance 依賴　feature 特色、特點

10. (D)

中譯 如果在招募過程中出現任何問題時，應立即諮詢Bradley女士。

(A) 可能性 (B) 缺陷、缺點 (C) 議價 (D) 問題、議題

單字 process 過程　consult 諮詢、商量　at once 立即

11. (B)

中譯 有名金融專家質疑Douglas航空公司的獲利能力，因為該公司過去幾年一直負債累累。

(A) 復發 (B) 獲利能力 (C) 發行、問題 (D) 接受

單字 financial 金融的　expert 專家　be in debt 欠債

12. (C)

中譯 下週將進行政府審計，以確認沒有違法行為。

(A) 方法 (B) 目的 (C) 審計 (D) 調查員

單字 conduct 實施　confirm 確認、確定　break a law 違法

13. (A)
中譯 在Devlin公司工作的其中一個好處，就是公司允許員工在家辦公。
(A) 好處、優勢 (B) 變化 (C) 影響、衝擊 (D) 提醒
單字 work from home 在家辦公

14. (D)
中譯 由於導遊人數不足，公司暫停所有行程，直至另行通知。
(A) 認知、察覺 (B) 接待 (C) 供應 (D) 公告、通知
單字 suspend 中斷、暫停　due to 由於⋯　lack 不足
until further notice 直至另行通知

15. (A)
中譯 所有顧客會在下單後五分鐘內收到訂單確認郵件。
(A) 確認、確定 (B) 評價 (C) 貢獻 (D) 接待
單字 place an order 下單

16. (A)
中譯 Hamilton先生被要求修改他向Chamberlain集團提交的補助金申請。
(A) 修改 (B) 決定 (C) 規格 (D) 生產
單字 make revisions to 修改⋯　several 幾個的
grant 補助金　submit 繳交

17. (B)
中譯 由於全國內發生的運送問題，商店的庫存量有所下降。
(A) 人事、員工 (B) 庫存 (C) 管理 (D) 更換
單字 level 水準　decrease 減少　on account of 由於⋯
shipping 運送　nationwide 在全國

18. (C)
中譯 副總要求粗略估算完成新廣告活動所需的時間。
(A) 說服 (B) 必要條件、需要 (C) 估價、估算 (D) 策略
單字 vice president 副總、副社長　rough 大略的
advertising campaign 廣告活動

19. (B)
中譯 Scott女士聯絡了航空公司，詢問週五深夜飛往柏林的班機是否有座位。
(A) 保證、把握 (B) 可利用性 (C) 應用程式、申請 (D) 出現
單字 contact 聯絡　airline 航空公司　inquire 詢問

20. (B)
中譯 由Denice Burns領導的募款活動將持續兩個月，預計募得100萬美元。
(A) 聯盟、同盟 (B) 主動的行為、倡議 (C) 必要的事 (D) 象徵
單字 fundraising 募款　last 持續　raise 募集（資金）

UNIT 12 高分必備形容詞詞彙

PRACTICE　　　　　　　　　　　　題本 p.138

1. (C)　**2.** (A)　**3.** (C)　**4.** (B)　**5.** (C)　**6.** (A)
7. (B)　**8.** (C)　**9.** (C)　**10.** (B)　**11.** (D)　**12.** (A)
13. (C)　**14.** (A)　**15.** (C)　**16.** (A)　**17.** (C)　**18.** (B)
19. (B)　**20.** (D)

1. (C)
中譯 《Hampton時報》的記者Jessica Roth可以獨家專訪州長Emerson Howell。
(A) 間歇的 (B) 輪流的 (C) 獨有的、唯一的 (D) 必要的、緊急的
單字 state 州　governor 長官、管轄者

2. (A)
中譯 雖然新行銷軟體的培訓計畫並非強制性活動，但建議員工參加。
(A) 強制的 (B) 暴露的 (C) 練習的 (D) 替換的
單字 be advised to do 建議去做⋯

3. (C)
中譯 所有顧客的投訴應由商店負責人及時處理。
(A) 相對的 (B) 接近的 (C) 及時的 (D) 各式各樣的
單字 complaint 投訴、抱怨　handle 處理
manner 方式、態度　representative 負責人

4. (B)
中譯 Milton科技公司的實習生被分配到例行任務中，同時接受相應的指導。
(A) 反對的 (B) 例行的 (C) 熟練的 (D) 可接近的
單字 assign 分配、指派　task 任務　go along 繼續（活動）

5. (C)
中譯 年底實施的客戶調查得出令人安心的結果，執行長對此感到滿意。
(A) 實用的 (B) 遠距的 (C) 安心的 (D) 外部的
單字 survey 調查　conduct 實施

6. (A)
中譯 夏天最受期待的電影之一是由Martin Lincoln所執導的驚悚片。
(A) 期待的、預期的 (B) 提議的 (C) 革命性的 (D) 修改的
單字 highly anticipated 高度期待的　direct 執導

7. (B)
中譯 多虧Rumsfeld先生擁有龐大的聯絡人名單，讓他的公司可以獲得幾名新客戶。
(A) 豐富的 (B) 龐大的、廣泛的 (C) 反駁的 (D) 有資格的
單字 thanks to 由於⋯　secure 獲得、到手

68

8. (C)
中譯 Cartwright女士要求大幅加薪,以獎勵她最近的成果。
(A) 有信心的 (B) 昂貴的 (C) 大量的 (D) 有益的
單字 reward 獎勵　performance 成果、業績

9. (C)
中譯 辦公室經理的主要職責為監督員工,同時解決他們之間的任何問題。
(A) 符合資格的 (B) 相對的 (C) 主要的 (D) 彈性的
單字 supervise 監督　resolve 解決　issue 問題

10. (B)
中譯 Dunlop先生的機械維修人員告訴他,他的卡車已經逾期換油了。
(A) 擔憂的 (B) 逾期的 (C) 報導的 (D) 清晰的
單字 mechanic 機械維修員　inform 告知、通報

11. (D)
中譯 儘管該市有些地區靠近金融區,仍有價格合理的住宅。
(A) 可能的 (B) 適時的 (C) 同等的、協調的 (D) 價格經濟實惠的、負擔得起的
單字 several 幾個、一些　housing 住宅　despite 儘管　financial 金融的、財務的　district 地區、區域

12. (A)
中譯 要成為工程師,必須通過每年舉行兩次的資格考試。
(A) 取得資格的 (B) 反覆的 (C)有成就的、熟練的 (D) 多樣化的
單字 engineer 工程師　twice 兩次

13. (C)
中譯 Verducci諮詢公司會根據員工年度工作表現等量加薪。
(A) 嚴重的 (B) 進步的、先進的 (C) 遞增的 (D) 決定性的
單字 raise 增加（薪資）　depending upon 取決於…
annual 年度的　performance 業績、成果

14. (A)
中譯 Jackson拍賣行要求潛在買家為他們競標的物品提出有競爭力的報價。
(A) 有競爭力的 (B) 放鬆的 (C) 先進的 (D) 每天的
單字 auction 拍賣　potential 潛在的
make an offer 報價、提案　bid on 競標

15. (C)
中譯 有資格享受有薪假的人,必須得到主管的書面批准。
(A) 揭露的 (B) 許可的 (C) 有資格的 (D)各式各樣的、分類的
單字 paid 有薪的　time off 休假、休息　permission 批准
supervisor 主管、上司

16. (A)
中譯 程式設計師試圖將軟體下載到她的電腦上時,經常遇到一些問題。

(A) 頻繁的 (B) 慷慨的 (C) 替代的 (D) 必需的
單字 encounter 遇到、遭遇

17. (C)
中譯 大多數評估員都提到了Meridian引擎公司製造的新型轎車性能優秀。
(A) 絕對的 (B) 結合的 (C) 優秀的 (D) 謹慎的
單字 evaluator 評估員　mention 提到、提出
performance 性能　manufacture 製造

18. (B)
中譯 市中心有幾條道路已經關閉,準備迎接即將穿越城市的遊行。
(A) 報告的 (B) 即將到來的、快到的 (C) 暫時的 (D) 確認的
單字 downtown 市中心　in preparation for 為…準備

19. (B)
中譯 該設備儘管多年來使用頻繁,仍維持正常運作。
(A) 特定的 (B) 正常運作的、功能上的 (C) 明顯的、顯著的 (D) 富有進取心的
單字 appliance 設備　remain 維持
heavy usage 使用頻繁

20. (D)
中譯 由於多名使用者出現過敏反應,Bakersfield的新系列化妝品已停產。
(A) 宣傳 (B) 出口 (C) 確信 (D) 終止
單字 line〔產品的〕類別、系列　cosmetics 化妝品
on account of 由於…　suffer 遭受
allergic reactions 過敏反應

UNIT 13　高分必備副詞詞彙

PRACTICE　題本 p.142

1. (A)	2. (C)	3. (A)	4. (B)	5. (C)	6. (D)
7. (C)	8. (B)	9. (B)	10. (A)	11. (B)	12. (A)
13. (A)	14. (C)	15. (D)	16. (B)	17. (C)	18. (B)
19. (D)	20. (B)				

1. (A)
中譯 Mary Hartford打算略過會議召開日,改在第二天出席。
(A) 作為代替 (B) 各式各樣地 (C) 字面上地 (D) 相似地
單字 skip 跳過、略過　conference 會議、學會

2. (C)
中譯 員工應以電子方式繳交所有要求報銷支出的文件。
(A) 幸運的是 (B) 優雅地 (C) 透過電子方式地 (D) 暴露地
單字 submit 繳交　reimbursement 報銷
expenditure 支出、費用

3. (C)
中譯 最初開給Burns先生的薪資很低，但當他拒絕後，公司又調高了薪資。
(A) 愉快地 (B) 完全地 (C) 最初 (D) 尤其
單字 offer 提議　reject 拒絕

4. (B)
中譯 Denton辦公用品公司確保所有的線上訂單都能迅速包裝並出貨。
(A) 認真地 (B) 迅速地 (C) 幾乎不 (D) 非常
單字 make sure 確保、一定會　package 包裝、包裹

5. (C)
中譯 董事會投票一致通過讓Reid Harmon擔任水門工業公司的執行長。
(A) 龐大地 (B) 也許 (C) 全體一致地 (D) 定期地
單字 board of directors 董事會　vote 投票

6. (D)
中譯 嘗試在廚房安裝設備前，請仔細閱讀使用說明書。
(A) 幸福地 (B) 幾乎 (C) 公平地 (D) 仔細地、徹底地
單字 instructions 使用說明書、指南　prior to 在…之前　attempt 試圖　install 安裝　appliance 設備

7. (C)
中譯 Perkins電子公司在新任總裁的命令下，突然關閉了墨西哥的工廠。
(A) 有說服力地 (B) 偶然地 (C) 突如其來地、意外地 (D) 反而、寧可
單字 factory 工廠　order 命令、指示

8. (B)
中譯 只有現在訂閱《每日時報》的人，才有資格享有特別優惠。
(A) 確切地 (B) 現在、目前 (C) 僅僅 (D) 巧合地
單字 individual 個人　subscribe to 訂閱　be eligible for 有資格

9. (B)
中譯 Galbraith女士藉由實行新歸檔系統，顯著提高辦公效率。
(A) 在任何時候、從來 (B) 顯著地 (C) 很快地 (D) 確切地
單字 improve 提升、改善　efficiency 效率　implement 實施　file 整理文件

10. (A)
中譯 Edwards先生很少在深夜搭乘飛機，但他需在今天早上抵達東京。
(A) 很少 (B) 那時 (C) 然而 (D) 誰

11. (B)
中譯 本週五晚上，圖書館的常客和訪客都受邀去看Janet Evans朗讀她的最新小說。
(A) 與此同時 (B) 同樣地、相似地 (C) 相當 (D) 真正地
單字 regular 定期地、經常地　patron 常客

12. (A)
中譯 Orbison先生昨天和客戶在咖啡廳共進午餐，但他大多是在公司的員工餐廳內用餐。
(A) 大部分地 (B) 只有 (C) 有力地 (D) 迅速地
單字 while 然而　cafeteria 員工餐廳

13. (A)
中譯 由主廚Otto von Steuben經營的餐廳供應其他地方吃不到的餐點。
(A) 其他地方 (B) 超越 (C) 周圍 (D) 約莫
單字 dish 餐點、料理　available 可使用的、可得到的

14. (C)
中譯 Nano科技公司得到了外部資金，因此正在迅速為新營業場所招募更多員工。
(A) 過度地 (B) 很少地 (C) 迅速地 (D) 獨特地
單字 since 由於、自從…　secure 得到　funding 資金　facility 設施

15. (D)
中譯 十二月份的休假皆不會被核准，所以請制定相應的假期計畫。
(A) 適當地 (B) 乾淨地 (C) 明確地 (D) 相應地
單字 time off 休假　grant 准予

16. (B)
中譯 儘管Ken Dayton一直都在Newport工作，但他還是擔心自己最終會被調到國外。
(A) 頻繁地 (B) 最終 (C) 幾乎 (D) 明顯地
單字 concerned 擔心的、擔憂的　transfer 調動　abroad 國外

17. (C)
中譯 包裹兩天前離開我們倉庫，很快就會送到你們辦公室。
(A) 最近 (B) 公平地 (C) 很快地 (D) 先前地
單字 package 包裹　warehouse 倉庫

18. (B)
中譯 社區停車場在重新鋪設地面期間暫時關閉。
(A) 最後 (B) 暫時地 (C) 謹慎地 (D) 狹窄地
單字 community 社區　while 在…期間　surface 表面　repave 重新鋪設

19. (D)
中譯 Jenkins女士檢查預算過後，確定確實有足夠的錢用於員工聚會。
(A) 兩者皆非 (B) 另外、其他 (C) 更多地 (D) 確實地
單字 budget 預算　determine 確定、查明　gathering 聚會

20. (B)
中譯 為了確保申請過程順利進行，請提前準備好所有文件。
(A) 自由地 (B) 事先、提前 (C) 任何地方 (D) 同樣地

單字 ensure 確保、保障　application 申請
process 過程、流程　smoothly 順利地

UNIT 14 高分必備動詞詞彙

PRACTICE　　　　　　　　　　　題本 p.146

1. (C)	2. (D)	3. (B)	4. (B)	5. (C)	6. (D)
7. (B)	8. (C)	9. (D)	10. (C)	11. (A)	12. (B)
13. (A)	14. (C)	15. (B)	16. (A)	17. (A)	18. (D)
19. (B)	20. (A)				

1. (C)
中譯 Washington先生嚴格執行了不允許員工在開會時遲到的政策。
(A) 妨礙、打擾 (B) 最小化 (C) 實施 (D) 透露、展現

單字 strict 嚴格的　policy 政策、方針　allow 允許

2. (D)
中譯 為了確保所有人都受到公平的待遇，規則應該平等地適用於每個人。
(A) 議價 (B) 任命 (C) 整合 (D) 確保、保證

單字 individual 人、個人　treat 對待、待遇　fairly 公平地
apply 適用　equally 同樣地、平等地

3. (B)
中譯 將更改研討會日期，避免與公司的野餐活動時間重疊。
(A) 合作 (B) 同時發生 (C) 報告 (D) 分配

單字 date 日期　company picnic 公司野餐活動

4. (B)
中譯 Greg's購物俱樂部對所有購物滿100美元以上的訂單免收運費。
(A) 清除 (B) 放棄、不適用 (C) 探險 (D) 自動化

單字 shipping 運送　fee 費用　purchase 購買

5. (C)
中譯 請務必註明你訂購的每件衣服的尺寸和顏色。
(A) 平衡 (B) 相乘 (C) 指定、指明 (D) 調解

單字 article 物品、商品

6. (D)
中譯 折價券必須在背面列出的有效期限之前兌換。
(A) 描寫 (B) 下定決心 (C) 前進 (D) 兌換（商品）

單字 prior to 在…之前　expiration 到期、屆期
list 列出、記載

7. (B)
中譯 請最遲於星期五下午在公司內部網路系統上驗證你的使用者名稱。
(A) 轉變 (B) 驗證 (C) 開發 (D) 進口

單字 username 使用者名稱　no later than 不遲於…

8. (C)
中譯 應徵該職位的人必須接受全身健康檢查。
(A) 批准 (B) 檢查 (C) 歷經、接受 (D) 嘗試

單字 apply for 應徵…　complete 完整的、徹底的
physical checkup 健康檢查

9. (D)
中譯 儘管Bevers先生受過高等教育，但他缺乏擔任高階主管職所需的領導能力。
(A) 代替 (B) 展現、顯露 (C) 描寫 (D) 缺乏

單字 highly 高度地、非常　take on 擔任…
executive 管理階層的

10. (C)
中譯 儘管Jansen女士把手機忘在家裡，她還是設法聯絡上她的助理。
(A) 失敗 (B) 考慮 (C) 設法 (D) 計畫、預計

單字 contact 聯絡　assistant 助理、秘書

11. (A)
中譯 該設施的特色為配有最先進的健身設備，而且易於使用。
(A) 以…為特色 (B) 移除 (C) 報告 (D) 中斷

單字 facility 設施　state-of-the-art 最先進的
workout 運動　equipment 設施、設備

12. (B)
中譯 參加博物館導覽的遊客可以隨時向導遊提問。
(A) 反對 (B) 指向 (C) 允許 (D) 按優先順序

單字 at any time 隨時

13. (A)
中譯 Brian Harper繳交了取得會計執照所需的文件。
(A) 繳交 (B) 邀請 (C) 提議 (D) 詢問

單字 accounting 會計　license 執照

14. (C)
中譯 使用說明書概述了人們使用該設備時必須採取的步驟。
(A) 考慮 (B) 繳交 (C) 概述、略述 (D) 嘗試

單字 user's manual 使用說明書　utilize 使用、應用
equipment 設備

15. (B)
中譯 出差到國外的員工可與主管談話，以取得公司信用卡。
(A) 升遷 (B) 得到、取得 (C) 適用、應用 (D) 保持

單字 credit card 信用卡　supervisor 主管、上司

16. (A)
中譯 所有參觀工廠的人，都應遵守工廠員工提出的任何指示。
(A) 遵守 (B) 下結論 (C) 出現 (D) 練習

單字 instruction 指示　provide 提供、提出

17. (A)
中譯 航空公司表示將闡明關於隨身行李的規定。
(A) 闡明 (B) 妨礙 (C) 暴露 (D) 參加

單字 state 述說、表示　regulation 規定　regarding 關於…
carry-on 隨身的　baggage 行李

18. (D)
中譯 新任執行長Deborah Burgess承諾處理多倫多廠可能裁員的擔憂。
(A) 提供 (B) 重建、調整 (C) 廣告 (D) 處理、對付

單字 concern 擔憂、憂慮　layoff 裁員

19. (B)
中譯 貨物在運送過程中損壞時，同意補償顧客的損失。
(A) 提升 (B) 同意、給予 (C) 認為 (D) 察覺

單字 compensation 補償、賠償　loss 損失
shipment 運送、貨品

20. (A)
中譯 Fairmont計程車公司實施了新政策，要求司機購買綜合保險，為自己和乘客提供保障。
(A) 實施 (B) 相關聯 (C) 指示 (D) 運送

單字 policy 政策　require 要求、需要
comprehensive insurance 綜合保險　cover 給…保險
passenger 乘客

PRACTICE 高難度　題本 p.148

1. (A)	2. (A)	3. (D)	4. (A)	5. (B)	6. (B)
7. (A)	8. (C)	9. (C)	10. (A)	11. (B)	12. (A)
13. (B)	14. (B)	15. (C)	16. (C)	17. (C)	18. (B)
19. (B)	20. (B)	21. (B)	22. (C)	23. (D)	24. (D)
25. (D)	26. (D)	27. (B)	28. (C)	29. (C)	30. (C)

1. (A)
中譯 為確保雜誌最終定稿按時印刷，記者應在6月8日前完成對文檔的全面編修。
(A) 修改 (B) 論文 (C) 建議 (D) 提案

單字 ensure 確保、保障　draft 原稿、初稿　print 印刷
on time 按時、準時　reporter 記者　make a revision 編修
text 文檔、文章　prior to 在…之前

2. (A)
中譯 農業專家建議為植物盡可能提供最穩定的環境，讓植物有機會茁壯成長。

解說 空格用來修飾名詞 environment，表示空格可填入形容詞，或是填入名詞，與後方名詞組合成複合名詞。而空格受到定冠詞 the 的修飾，因此答案要選形容詞 (A) most stable，組合成形容詞最高級。選項有形容詞時，以形容詞為優先，所以不可選分詞 stabilizing。名詞 stability 無法與 environment 組合成複合名詞，所以也不是答案。

單字 agriculture 農業　expert 專家　recommend 建議
provide 提供、給予　stable 穩定的　plant 植物
thrive 茁壯成長、繁榮

3. (D)
中譯 Kamal先生將檢視收到的履歷表，確定哪些人符合管理職位所需的資格條件。

解說 空格前後方分別有動詞 determine 和 reflect，表示空格應填入適當的字詞，當作 determine 的受詞，同時當作 reflect 的主詞。now that 和 even though 為連接詞，所以可優先刪去；剩下的選項為 some such 和 which ones，當中符合前述條件的是 (D) which ones，故為正解。

單字 incoming 進來的、到來的　résumé 履歷表
determine 確定、決定　reflect 反映出
qualifications 資格條件

4. (A)
中譯 調查結果顯示，倉庫的延誤為有幾個箱子貼錯標籤所致。

解說 空格和限定詞 a few 一起修飾後方的 boxes。mislabeled 和 mislabeling 皆為分詞，可修飾名詞，但是 boxes 為物品，無法自行做出動作，因此答案要選過去分詞 (A) mislabeled。

單字 investigation 調查　delay 延誤　warehouse 倉庫
cause 導致　mislabel 貼錯標籤

5. (B)
中譯 Nelson招聘公司堅持求職者要與招募人員合作，共同制定明確的就業目標。

解說 本題的選項使用相同單字，但以不同詞性呈現。空格前方的 job applicants 為名詞子句的主詞，後方缺少動詞，表示空格應填入動詞，所以可先刪去 cooperating 和 cooperation。insist 屬於表示建議、主張、要求、命令的動詞，其用法為後方連接 that 子句。而子句中要使用「should ＋原形動詞」，當中的 should 可省略，因此答案要選原形動詞 (B) cooperate。

單字 applicant 應徵者　cooperate 合作
recruiter 招募人員　employment 就業、僱用

6. (B)
中譯 Maddock女士對活動場地的偏好為擁有充足的停車位和最先進的音響系統。

解說 空格應填入適當的名詞，受到所有格 Ms. Maddock's 的修飾，所以答案可能是複數名詞 preferences 或單數名詞 preference。而該句話的動詞 include 為複數動詞，因此答案要選 (B) preferences。

單字 preference 偏好　venue 場地　ample 充足的
state-of-the-art 最先進的

7. (A)
中譯 Newton鞋子公司在推出以職業運動選手為特色的廣告後,線上和實體店面的銷售額迅速增加。

解說 本題的選項使用相同單字,但以不同詞性呈現。該句話即使缺少空格,仍為結構完整的句子,表示空格應填入副詞,因此答案要選 (A) promptly。promptly after 的意思為「之後立即…」。

單字 promptly 迅速地、立即地　launch 推出、開始　feature 以…為特色　athlete 運動選手

8. (C)
中譯 任何由於未能正確分析風險等級所致的損失,可能會由投資公司承擔責任。
(A) 在哪裡 (B) 分隔兩地 (C) 產生、起因於 (D) 遵守

解說 該句話的主詞為 Any losses、動詞片語為 may be,空格至 risk 皆用來修飾主詞。只有介系詞能連接名詞的修飾語,所以要先刪去非介系詞的選項 whereabouts 和 apart。剩餘選項為 resulting from 和 in compliance with,而根據文意,答案選 (C) resulting from。

單字 loss 損失、損害　failure 失敗　analyze 分析　risk 風險　investment 投資　firm 公司

9. (C)
中譯 任何對於洗衣精效果不滿的人,都會被立即轉接至客服人員。

解說 空格應填入主詞,受到後方介系詞片語 with ~ detergent 的修飾。代名詞可當作主詞,因此答案要選 (C) Anyone。Whoever 後方要直接連接動詞,因此並非答案。

單字 complaint 不滿、投訴　laundry 送洗的衣服　detergent 洗潔劑　promptly 立即　direct 連接、指向

10. (A)
中譯 即使當天稍早時音響設備出現技術性問題,Conway先生還是能夠準時開始主題演講。
(A) 即使 (B) 不僅 (C) 由於 (D) 在…期間

解說 空格用來連接前後方的子句,表示應填入連接詞。even though 和 while 皆為連接詞,而根據文意,答案要選 (A) even though。

單字 keynote address 主題演講　on time 準時、按時　technical 技術上的　equipment 設備

11. (B)
中譯 在昨天的公共論壇上,位於市用地上基礎設施工程的爭議性,引發了熱烈的討論。
(A) 抵抗的 (B) 熱烈的 (C) 易腐爛的 (D) 現在的

單字 controversial 有爭議的　nature 性質、特性　infrastructure 基礎設施　municipal 市政的、地方自治的　provoke 引發、激起　forum 討論會、論壇

12. (A)
中譯 由於本次的訓練目標已達成,我們可用剩下的時間做更多輕鬆的團隊建設活動。
(A) 由於 (B) 直到 (C) 無論何時 (D) 除非

解說 空格前後方子句的內容屬於因果關係,因此答案要選表示原因的連接詞 (A) Since。

單字 training 訓練　meet an objective 達成目標　session (訓練) 時間　casual 休閒的、非正式的　team-building 團隊建設　activity 活動

13. (B)
中譯 Larkin家電公司的所有洗衣機均享有終身保固並不令人意外,因為該公司的產品以耐用性而聞名。
(A) 修改 (B) 耐用 (C) 接近 (D) 成果

單字 lifetime 終身的　warranty (品質) 保固

14. (B)
中譯 公車票價的漲幅視平均乘客人數和預計燃料支出而定。

解說 該句話的主詞為 How ~ increase、動詞為 depends on。當中使用「how ＋形容詞／副詞」的用法,而本題應填入副詞,修飾當中的動詞 increase,因此答案要選 (B) substantially。

單字 substantially 實質上、相當多地、大量地　passenger 乘客　fuel 燃料　expenditure 支出

15. (C)
中譯 任何預算決定都必須事先得到年度音樂節主辦者Tony Calderon的批准。

解說 空格前方為定冠詞 the,後方連接介系詞片語,表示空格應填入名詞。選項中的名詞有 organization 和 organizer,而空格指的是前方人物 Tony Calderon,因此答案要選人物名詞 (C) organizer。

單字 budget 預算　approve 批准　organizer 主辦者、組織者　annual 年度　in advance 事先

16. (C)
中譯 建築許可申請遭到多次拒絕,迫使建築公司放棄將空地開發成豪華公寓大廈的計畫。

解說 該句話的主詞為 Multiple ~ permit、動詞為 forced。動詞 force 的用法為「force A ＋不定詞 to」,表示「迫使A不得不做…」,因此答案要選不定詞 (C) to abandon。

單字 multiple 多次的　rejection 拒絕　permit 許可　abandon 放棄　vacant lot 空地　luxury 豪華的

17. (C)
中譯 考量到本週六可能出現惡劣天氣,國際美食節的活動策劃者已把活動延期。
(A) 透過…方法 (B) 自…以後 (C) 考量到、有鑑於 (D) 考慮到

解說 雖然選項 (D) 也符合文意,但連接詞 that 後方應連接子句,因此並非答案。

單字 severe 劇烈的、嚴峻的　predict 預測　planner 策劃者　postpone 延期

18. (B)
中譯 Elkview工程公司已經建立非常出色的聲譽，因此不再需要分配資金來用於行銷和廣告上。
解說 「such a/an 形容詞＋名詞」和「so 形容詞 a/an 名詞」表示「非常⋯」。
單字 allocate 分配、分派

19. (B)
中譯 產品研發團隊所有人都同意，我們繳交的產品是全國設計大賽上最令人印象深刻的原型樣機。
解說 空格置於名詞子句中的主詞位置上，作為名詞子句前方動詞 agrees 的受詞。空格後方連接動詞 is，因此答案要選所有格代名詞 (B) ours，表示「我們的東西」。we 和 ourselves 為複數，不能連接 is。
單字 impressive 印象深刻的　prototype 原型樣機
submit 繳交　competition 比賽、競賽

20. (B)
中譯 如果在下午3點前繳交國際轉帳申請，Henley銀行將在當天完成交易。
(A) 直到 (B) 如果 (C) 一⋯就 (D) 正如
解說 空格後方連接包含主詞和動詞的子句，表示空格應填入連接詞。選項中的連接詞有 Provided 和 As soon as，而根據文意，前方子句表示「條件」較為適當，因此答案要選 (B) Provided。請注意 provided 當作連接詞使用時，意思為「如果⋯」。
單字 transfer 移動、轉帳　submit 繳交　finalize 完成
transaction 交易

21. (B)
中譯 Lapointe銀行提出具有吸引力的利率，促使客戶開立新帳戶，並將剩餘資金存入其中。
解說 主詞 The attractive interest rate 為單數名詞，受到 offered by Lapointe Bank 的修飾，所以可先刪去複數動詞 (A) 和 (D)。而空格後方連接受詞 customers，因此答案要選主動語態 (B) has motivated。
單字 attractive 有吸引力的　interest rate 利率
motivate 促使　account 帳戶　surplus 剩餘的、過剩的

22. (C)
中譯 VT物流公司打算解除與Camden快遞公司的合約，因為該公司一直無法按時交貨。
(A) 強烈地 (B) 穩定地 (C) 一貫地 (D) 試驗性地、暫時地
單字 logistics 物流　terminate 終止、解除　contract 合約
courier 快遞公司　meet the deadline 按時

23. (D)
中譯 該部門負責人預計明年在差旅費用上支出更多，以透過面對面會議改善與客戶的關係。
解說 動詞 anticipate 後方並非連接不定詞，而是要連接動名詞當作受詞，因此答案要選 (D) spending。
單字 department head 部門負責人　anticipate 預期
client 客戶　face-to-face 面對面的

24. (D)
中譯 大多數頭等艙旅客願意為直飛航班支付額外費用，而不是花額外時間來處理轉機事宜。
(A) 事實上 (B) 因此 (C) 如果發生 (D) 而不是
單字 the majority of 大多數的　extra 額外的、另外的
direct flight 直飛航班　additional 額外的　deal with 處理
layover 轉機

25. (D)
中譯 Murillo公司的海外擴張計畫包含委任一家會計師事務所，其員工具有處理海外稅務法規的經驗。
解說 空格後方連接的 employees 屬於前方出現的先行詞 accounting firm，因此答案要選所有格代名詞 (D) whose。what 當作關係代名詞使用時，不能連接先行詞；兩空格後方缺少主詞或受詞時，才能選擇關係代名詞 which。
單字 overseas 海外的　expansion 擴張
involve 包含、伴隨　accounting firm 會計事務所
regulation 規定

26. (D)
中譯 購買更多能夠自動化的設備，減少了生產設施所需的人力規模。
(A) 聚集 (B) 視為 (C) 監測 (D) 減少
單字 purchase 購買　equipment 設備　enable 能夠
automation 自動化　workforce 人力
manufacturing 生產、製造　facility 設施

27. (B)
中譯 關於無薪病假的新政策，將於公司網站上刊登詳情後立即生效。
解說 空格後方連接子句，表示空格應填入連接詞。而根據文意，答案要選 (B) after。immediately after 意思為「⋯後立即」，建議記下此用法。
單字 policy 政策、方針　unpaid 無報酬的
medical leave 病假　go into effect 生效、實施
immediately 立即　details 詳情　post 刊登

28. (C)
中譯 針對使用者資訊的檢查結果顯示，約有百分之四十五的員工登入了電子郵件中公告的資料庫。
(A) 計算 (B) 介紹 (C) 進入、存取 (D) 詢問
單字 review 檢查　reveal 顯示、展現
approximately 大約、約莫

29. (C)
中譯 無論主管有多忙，都應該抽出時間傾聽團隊成員的擔憂。
解說 空格後方連接形容詞 busy，接著又連接「主詞＋動詞（they may be）」，可以推測為「however＋形容詞＋主詞＋動詞」的用法，因此答案要選 (C) however。
單字 supervisor 主管、管理者　concern 擔憂、關心事宜

30. (C)

中譯 如果Zhang先生有達成這一季的銷售額，他可能會被列入升遷候選。

解說 逗號後方的子句使用「might have + 過去分詞」，為對過去事實做出的推測，表示與過去事實相反的假設語氣，因此答案要選 (C) Had。該句話原本的寫法為：「If Mr. Zhang had not failed to meet ~」。

單字 miss 錯過　　sales 銷售　　quota 額度、配額
quarter 季度　consider 考慮　promotion 升遷

PART TEST
題本 p.151

1. (C)	2. (D)	3. (C)	4. (D)	5. (C)	6. (C)
7. (A)	8. (C)	9. (A)	10. (D)	11. (A)	12. (B)
13. (C)	14. (C)	15. (A)	16. (A)	17. (B)	18. (B)
19. (C)	20. (D)	21. (A)	22. (C)	23. (B)	24. (C)
25. (B)	26. (D)	27. (A)	28. (A)	29. (D)	30. (A)

1. (C)

中譯 Cross先生在廚房裡幫忙，因為兩名廚師都沒有準時抵達餐廳。

解說 空格置於副詞子句的主詞位置上，雖然 nobody 和 neither 皆符合文意，但是只有後者可受到介系詞片語 of his chefs 的修飾，因此答案要選 (C) neither。

單字 assist 幫忙、協助　since 因為　on time 準時

2. (D)

中譯 金融專家表示，預期製造產業公司今年能夠實現創紀錄的利潤。

解說 空格為動詞 make 的受詞，同時受到 record 的修飾，應填入名詞。選項中，profitability 和 profits 皆為名詞，而根據文意，後者適合作為 make 的受詞，因此答案要選 (D) profits。在該句話中，record 當作形容詞使用，而非名詞，請特別留意。

單字 financial 金融的、財務的　　expert 專家
manufacturing 製造（業）　　record 創紀錄的

3. (C)

中譯 自動化系統有望使工廠人員提高工作效率。

解說 該句話的句型結構為「動詞（make）＋受詞（the factory workers）＋受詞補語」，表示空格應填入名詞或形容詞，當作受詞補語使用。而根據文意，表達「使工廠員工變成某種狀態」最為適當，因此答案要選形容詞 (C) productive。

單字 expect 期待、預期　　productive 有生產力的

4. (D)

中譯 Dayton科技公司的研發團隊獲得第二次找出生產問題解決方案的機會。

解說 空格置於動詞位置上，give 使用主動語態時，可使用「give ＋間接受詞＋直接受詞」或「give ＋直接受詞＋ to 對象」兩種句型。該句話中的直接受詞為 a second chance，後方並未連接對象，而是連接不定詞，所以主動語態的選項 (A)、(B)、(C) 皆不適當。如果把句子改寫成被動語態，原本的間接受詞 The R&D team at Dayton Tech 會變成主詞，因此答案要選 (D) has been given。

單字 R&D 研究開發（= research and development）
solution 解決方案　manufacturing 製造、生產

5. (C)

中譯 在送貨過程中有多件物品受損，顧客的損失得到了相應的補償。

(A) 獲准　(B) 感激　(C) 補償　(D) 報酬

解說 compensate 和 reward 的差異在於：compensate 用於表示補償損失；reward 則是作為某件事的獎勵、回報。

單字 fairly 相當地、頗為　　loss 損失　item 物品
delivery 運送、配送

6. (C)

中譯 團隊中的兩位成員都認為他們的想法應立刻被付諸執行。

解說 選項中，只有限定詞 (C) Both 可修飾複數名詞。(A) 和 (B) 只能修飾單數名詞；(D) 的用法為 neither A nor B，或是後方直接連接單數名詞。

單字 implement 執行　　at once 立刻

7. (A)

中譯 整個演講過程中，背景噪音持續不斷，使得一些聽眾聽不清楚任何聲音。

(A) 從頭到尾、貫徹　(B) 周圍　(C) 在　(D) 自從

單字 background 背景　noise 噪音、雜音　speech 演講
audience member 聽眾

8. (C)

中譯 Greg先生認為三月份是宣傳即將於春季上市新品系列的適當時機。

解說 空格用來修飾前方的 an appropriate time，並連接 the new line 當作受詞，因此答案要選不定詞 (C) to advertise，屬於形容詞的用法。名詞子句的動詞為 is，因此並不適合選擇未來式 (D)。

單字 appropriate 適當的　　line 產品系列

9. (A)

中譯 乍看之下，建築物的設計看起來既有效率，又充分利用了可用空間。

解說 空格應填入名詞或形容詞，當作該句話的補語，因此答案要選形容詞 (A) efficient。名詞 efficiency 和 efficiencies 指的是效率，無法與 design（設計）劃上等號，因此不能作為答案。

單字 at first glance 乍看之下
make good use of 充分利用⋯　available 可用的
space 空間

10. (D)

中譯 Harrison造船公司上一季的訂單有所增加，而其競爭對手Baden公司則報告了創紀錄的損失。

(A) 由於、幸虧 (B) 儘管 (C) 因此 (D) 然而

解說 空格前後連接的子句內容形成對比，應填入表示轉折的連接詞，因此答案為 (D) whereas。(A) 和 (B) 為介系詞、(C) 為副詞，詞性皆不適當。

單字 quarter 季度　record 創紀錄的　loss 損失

11. (A)

中譯 在Stanton銀行，其驗證過程需要居住證明和附有照片的兩種身分證明。

(A) 驗證、核實 (B) 撤回 (C) 徵收、施加 (D) 調整

單字 process 過程　proof 證明　residency 居住
form 形式、種類　identification 身分證

12. (B)

中譯 大多數分析師認為Edward Hope最大的成就是把他的公司從破產中拯救出來。

解說 該句話的句型結構為「consider ＋ 受詞 ＋ 受詞補語（to be）」，空格當作 be 的補語，同時連接受詞 his company，因此答案要選動名詞 (B) getting。

單字 analyst 分析師、分析者　accomplishment 成就、業績
bankruptcy 破產、倒閉

13. (C)

中譯 Spruce公司同意與Magpie公司合作，在Richmond地區開發低價住宅。

(A) 反射、反映 (B) 扣除、推論 (C) 結合、共同 (D) 累積

解說 選項為四個不同意思的名詞，應選擇適當的名詞，填入「in ~ with」之間，因此答案要選 (C) conjunction，in conjunction with 意思為「與⋯合作、與⋯一起」。

單字 low-cost 低價的　housing 住宅、房屋

14. (C)

中譯 所有員工都應專注在研討會上，盡可能去學習。

(A) 可選擇的 (B) 衝動的 (C) 專心的 (D) 合作的

15. (A)

中譯 Hatfield博士指示那些從早開始就不停工作的人休息一下。

解說 空格為動詞 instructed 的受詞，同時也是關係代名詞主格 who 的先行詞，因此答案要選 (A) those，以「those who」表達「那些⋯的人」。

單字 instruct 指示　nonstop 不停地　take a break 休息

16. (A)

中譯 雖然研討會可自行選擇是否參加，但會計部幾乎所有人都有報名參加。

(A) 可選擇的 (B) 已有結論的 (C) 進步的 (D) 有責任的

單字 while 然而　register for 報名參加…

17. (B)

中譯 Jacobs女士是Failsafe的高階經理之一，她在當地大學教授一門關於領導能力的課程。

解說 空格後方連接受詞 a class，表示空格應填入主動語態，且主詞 Ms. Jacobs 為單數名詞，因此答案要選單數動詞 (B) teaches。

單字 manager 經理

18. (B)

中譯 機器必須正確操作，以免發生故障。

(A) 公平地、相當地 (B) 適當地 (C) 確實地 (D) 有創造力地

單字 machinery 機械、機器設備　operate 操作、運作
suffer 遭受、歷經　malfunction 故障、功能失常

19. (C)

中譯 Oxford女士仔細檢查隨機抽選的物品，以找出製造過程中的缺陷。

(A) 專注 (B) 採購 (C) 檢查 (D) 開發

單字 closely 仔細地、緊密地　random 隨機的
in an effort to 為⋯而努力　flaw 缺陷、缺點
manufacturing 製造、生產

20. (D)

中譯 該雜誌新攝影師拍攝的照片在視覺上頗具吸引力。

解說 空格置於該句話主詞補語的位置上，受到副詞 visually 的修飾，因此答案要選形容詞 (D) appealing。

單字 capture 捕捉　quite 相當地、頗為　visually 視覺上地
appealing 有吸引力的

21. (A)

中譯 請記得正確穿戴安全裝備，以避免潛在的傷害。

解說 please 開頭的句子為祈使句，因此答案要選原形動詞 (A) remember。

單字 put on 穿戴　gear 裝備　properly 正確地、適當地
potential 潛在的　injury 傷害

22. (C)

中譯 Hollander先生負責確認是否有遵循適當的流程。

解說 看到空格前方出現形容詞 responsible，便可聯想到搭配使用的介系詞為 for，因此答案要選 (C) for。

單字 confirm 確認、證實　proper 適當的、適合的
procedure 流程、過程

23. (B)

中譯 由於發現設計缺陷而停止施工時，這座橋僅有部分完工。

解說 空格用來修飾形容詞 complete，因此答案要選副詞 (B) partially。

單字 halt 停止　flaw 缺陷

24. (C)

中譯 Megan Reyna對慈善機構的主要貢獻為招募到幾名富有的捐贈者。

(A) 獎金 (B) 支持 (C) 貢獻 (D) 變化

單字 major 主要的　charity 慈善機構　recruit 招募
donor 捐贈者

25. (B)
中譯 當收件人簽收物品後，即視為已由Grossman貨運公司送達完成。
解說 空格後方連接介系詞 by 加上執行動作者，表示應使用被動語態，因此答案要選 (B) delivered，其前方省略 to be。該句話有動詞 is，因此不能選 (D)。
單字 item 物品　consider 視為、看作
recipient 收件人、接收者

26. (D)
中譯 Jeremy Tyler的下個專案將與行銷部的兩名成員合作。
解說 空格前方為不定冠詞 a，表示空格應填入單數名詞。collaborator 為人物名詞、collaboration 為事物名詞，而根據文意，表達「合作專案」較為適當，因此答案要選 (D) collaboration。
單字 collaboration 合作

27. (A)
中譯 Focal公司所有正式員工以及其主要客戶均受邀參加於12月29日舉行的慶祝活動。
(A) 以及、並且 (B) 同時 (C) 以便 (D) 為了
解說 空格後方連接片語 its major clients，表示空格應填入介系詞，因此答案要選介系詞 (A) as well as。
單字 full-time 全職的、專任的　celebration 慶祝活動

28. (A)
中譯 我們接獲指示，要盡一切可能確保慶典成功舉行。
解說 空格置於動詞 do 後方的受詞位置上，後方連接缺少主詞的不完整子句，因此答案要選複合關係代名詞 (A) whatever。其他選項皆需要先行詞，所以並不適當。
單字 instruct 指示　ensure 確保、保障

29. (D)
中譯 銷售部門計畫至少安排六名員工專注於北美的銷售。
解說 空格前方為介系詞 on、後方有受詞 six members，因此答案要選動名詞 (D) committing，當作介系詞的受詞。
單字 commit ~ to do 致力於⋯　at least 至少

30. (A)
中譯 Davis先生堅信，Leeway's公司應提供他高階主管的職位。
解說 空格置於名詞子句的主詞位置上，因此答案要選人稱代名詞主格 (A) he。
單字 executive 經營管理的、高層的

RC　PART 6

段落填空　題本p.156

收件者：Blacktail物流公司全體員工
　　　　<stafflist@blacktaillogistics.com>
寄件者：Alfred Orozco <a.orozco@blacktaillogistics.com>
日期：11月12日
主旨：績效評估

親愛的Blacktail物流公司員工：

下週期間，經理將對全體員工進行績效評估。我們**偶爾**會執行這項任務，以確保你了解自己的職責。**此外**，我們也想確保你能夠得到充分的支援，以最佳狀態作業。各位將與你的直屬主管會面，討論自己的優勢以及需要**改進**的地方。評估結束後，你將有機會填寫意見卡。此卡會直接交給人力資源部，意見將採匿名方式進行。**因此請各位分享你最真實的想法**。你的主管將通知你評估的時間安排。

感謝各位的合作。

Alfred Orozco

行政經理 Blacktail物流公司

131. (A)
解說 空格前方有主詞（We）、動詞（carry out）、受詞（this task），表示該句話為結構完整的子句，空格應填入副詞，因此答案要選副詞 (A) occasionally，用來修飾前方的動詞 carry out。

132. (D)
(A) 相反地 (B) 因此 (C) 然而 (D) 此外、又

133. (B)
(A) 熟練 (B) 改進 (C) 配置、結構 (D) 許可

134. (A)
(A) 因此請各位分享你最真實的想法。
(B) 我們相信你會在新職位上表現出色。
(C) 幸運的是，領導能力可隨著時間的推進而提升。
(D) 政策更新總會及時於線上發布。

UNIT 01 文法　題本p.158

1. (C)

Lampron女士您好，

感謝您成為Victoria城市書店的會員。**您的**會員資格有助於支持小型企業，並確保實體書籍能繼續出版。儘管我們的店面規模不大，但我們提供的書籍種類繁多，且目前未陳列在架上的書籍，大多數都有提供快遞服務。

單字 membership 會員身分、會員資格　ensure 確保、保障
in print 印刷出版　storefront 店面　modest 不太大（或多）的
a wide array of 種類多的　title 書籍、出版品　shelf 架子

2. (A)

> Hogan保險公司的年度宴會將於12月17日星期五晚上7點舉行。邀請所有Hogan保險公司的員工及其家屬參加，敬請回覆行政辦公室確認出席。晚宴結束時，**將會表揚**公司表現最優秀的員工。我們期待見到各位！

單字 annual 年度的　banquet 晚宴、宴會
take place 舉行、發生　RSVP 敬請回覆
administrative office 行政辦公室　perform 表現
recognize 表揚、認可

3. (D)

> 致員工的通知
> 請不要在週五下班前關閉你的電腦，因為資訊科技團隊已排定要更新軟體。我們每個月都會**進行**一次軟體更新，以確保系統安全。若你有任何問題，請直接聯絡資訊科技部經理Sean Hendrix，分機號碼為18。

單字 turn off 關閉　leave work 下班
be scheduled to 排定要…　update 更新　ensure 確保、保障
security 安全　direct 指向　extension 分機號碼

PRACTICE　題本 p.159

1. (B)　**2.** (A)　**3.** (B)　**4.** (D)

1-4. 報導

> 義大利那不勒斯—Romulus建設公司在那不勒斯地區備受尊敬。**它**取得土地並進行開發，然後在那不勒斯和周邊地區出售完工的成屋。這些房屋以其建築品質**以及**經濟實惠的價格而聞名。
> Romulus建設公司在不久前宣布**計畫**在沿海地區收購一大片土地。Romulus執行長Ernesto Humbert表示：「我們將在那裡建造私人住宅，同時保持自然環境的美麗。」「**相信我們所建造的房屋會受到買家歡迎**。我們將在未來幾週內公布更多詳細資訊」。
> 該公司還補充道，希望在不久的將來購買更多土地。

單字 highly 相當　acquire 取得、得到
complete 完工的、完整的　unit 住宅單位
affordability 經濟實惠　a stretch of 一大片　along 沿著
residence 住宅　release 公布、發表　add 補充、追加
in the near future 在不久的將來

1. (B)
解說 空格用來代替前方出現過的主詞 Romulus Construction，其為單數名詞，因此答案要選的人稱代名詞主格為 (B) It。

2. (A)
(A) 以及　(B) 除外　(C) 為了　(D) 在此期間
解說 選項中包含介系詞和副詞兩種詞性，空格後方連接的是名詞片語，表示答案可能為介系詞 as well as 或 except for。而根據文意來判斷，except for 並不適合填入，因此答案要選 (A) as well as。

3. (B)
解說 空格前方的 it 為名詞子句的主詞，而空格置於動詞的位置上。主詞為單數名詞，所以可先刪去複數動詞 plan, have been planned。空格後方連接不定詞當作受詞，屬於不定詞的名詞用法，因此答案要選主動語態 (B) is planning。

4. (D)
(A) 正在建設的房屋即將完工。
(B) 必須盡快做出購買土地的決定。
(C) 已經有一戶人家搬進新家。
(D) 相信我們所建造的房屋會受到買家歡迎。
單字 make a decision 做決定

UNIT 02 詞性　題本 p.160

1. (D)

> 您所訂閱的《世界旅遊雜誌》將於8月31日到期。若要繼續**收到**本刊物，請盡快點選下方連結，並填寫線上表格。如此一來，您就不會錯過任何關於全球最佳度假勝地的實用文章。

單字 subscription 訂閱　be due to 預計在…　expire 到期
issue 刊物、刊號　publication 出版品、刊物
complete 填寫、完成　form 表格　miss 錯過　article 文章
destination 目的地、終點

2. (B)

> Branchburg市已批准在Rockwell的北部社區建造一棟新公寓大樓社區。該大樓將包含45間一臥室房及大樓內部洗衣設施。其目的不僅是為深受遊客歡迎的**景點**Skye遊樂園的工作人員，還有搭乘高速巴士路線的通勤者，提供價格實惠的住房。

單字 approve 批准　apartment complex 公寓大樓社區
neighborhood 區域、鄰近　contain 包含、含有　unit 住房、單位　on-site 建築物內、現場的　laundry 洗衣　facility 設施
aim 目標　supply 提供　affordable 價格實惠的
attraction 觀光景點、名勝　commuter 通勤者　route 路線

78

3. (A)

> Sampson食品公司的研發團隊已為其健康零食系列開發了一種新的包裝流程。現在這些物品將會增加一層塑膠包裝，以保持其密封環境。這項變化預計在食品的質地和口感上提供更一致和**可預測的**結果，即使長期儲藏也是如此。

單字 R&D 研究開發　packing 包裝　procedure 流程
line 產品系列　healthy 有益健康的　snack 零食
package 包裝　additional 增加的　layer 層　plastic 塑膠
maintain 維持　airtight 密封的、密閉的
consistent 一致的、一貫的　predictable 可預測的
texture 質地　storage 保存、儲存　period 期間

PRACTICE　　　題本 p.161

1. (D)　**2.** (D)　**3.** (A)　**4.** (C)

1-4. 備忘錄

> 收件者：高階員工
>
> 寄件者：Helen Schnell
>
> 主旨：Oxford工廠最新消息
>
> 日期：8月10日
>
> 過去三個月以來，我們一直在極力宣傳Oxford新工廠需要填補的職缺。**很高興宣布，已有一半的職缺已經補人**。目前我們領先於原計畫，應會在八月底前補滿每個職缺。我們也想用經驗豐富的員工來**填補**工廠的職位。有意轉調Oxford的人都可以聯絡**我**。在招募過程中，將優先考慮現職員工。下週我們將進行現場視察。若想親自查看現場的人，請回覆此電子郵件，我會進行必要的**安排**。

單字 plant 工廠　update 最新消息　heavily 猛烈地
fill a position 填補職缺　staff 員工、補充人力
transfer 調動、轉調　preference 優先、偏好
conduct 進行　tour 參觀、參訪　site 現場
in person 親自　arrangement 安排、準備

1. (D)
(A) 目前接受該設施的建築設計投標。
(B) 在收到負面評論後，我們決定關閉它。
(C) 我們的執行長將於今天下午發表重要聲明。
(D) 我很高興宣布，已有一半的職缺已經補人。

單字 bid 投標　facility 設施　close down 關閉
negative 負面的　review 評論
make an announcement 發表

2. (D)
(A) 取代 (B) 設計 (C) 僱用 (D) 補充人力

3. (A)

解說 空格位在動詞 contact 後方，應填入適當的受詞，因此答案要選人稱代名詞受格 (A) me。

4. (C)

解說 空格受到定冠詞 the 和形容詞 necessary 的修飾，因此答案要選名詞 (C) arrangements。

UNIT 03 詞彙　　　題本 p.162

1. (D)

> 國家歷史博物館讓遊客有機會一睹早期人們的生活。我們的展品以服裝、陶器、藝術等為特色。每人的門票票價僅需7.50美元。透過大眾運輸工具搭乘104或1288號公車，即可輕鬆**抵達**博物館。如欲了解更多資訊，請造訪我們的網站www.nationalhm.org。

單字 fascinating 迷人的　glimpse 看一眼、一瞥
exhibit 展品　feature 以⋯為特色　pottery 陶器
admission 門票　public transportation 大眾運輸工具

2. (C)

> Burnett女士您好，
>
> 我們很高興通知您，您向Arlington銀行申請的小型企業貸款已獲批准。資金將於5個工作日內匯入您的企業帳戶。請自行留存隨信附上的貸款**協議**。如果您有任何問題或疑慮，歡迎隨時與我們的客戶服務團隊聯絡。

單字 pleased 高興的、開心的　inform 告知、通知
application 申請　small business 小型企業
loan 貸款　fund 錢、資金　credit 把⋯計入貸方
account 帳戶　retain 保留、維持　enclose 隨信附上
record 紀錄　concern 擔憂、疑慮　feel free to 隨時⋯
contact 聯絡

3. (A)

> 致SALISBURY套房住戶的通知
>
> 我們已經安排一名電工於1月19日造訪我們的公寓，以重新安裝走廊燈。在施工期間，大樓將會斷電。電源將於上午9點關閉，最晚於下午2點前**恢復**。對造成不便，我們深表歉意。

單字 tenant 住戶、租客　schedule 安排　electrician 電工
site 地點、現場　corridor 走廊　rewire 重裝電線
while 在⋯期間　take place 發生、舉辦　electricity 電力
shut off 關閉　no later than 不遲於⋯
apologize for 對⋯致歉　inconvenience 不便

PRACTICE
題本 p.163

1. (A) **2.** (C) **3.** (B) **4.** (A)

1-4. 報導

HARTFORD（5月19日）— 總部位於Hartford的慈善機構Peterson House宣布將於7月1日舉行年度募款活動。Peterson House**成立**於2001年，致力於為Hartford地區的兒童提供食物、衣物和教育用品。

Peterson House的總裁Jenny Blair表示：「這是我們首次舉行無聲競標拍賣。我們對這個機會**感到興奮**」。

Blair女士補充道，慈善機構在歷經幾次工程延誤後，新的辦公室**終於**完工。**今年春天的天候狀況不佳，嚴重影響到工程進度**。她還表示，慈善機構在夏季和秋季有一些重大計畫，她將於日後討論。

單字 based 總部位在　charity 慈善機構　annual 年度的
fundraiser 募款活動　supplies 用品、補給品
silent auction 無聲競標拍賣　present 呈現　state 敘述
at a later date 日後

1. (A)
(A) 成立 (B) 捐贈 (C) 上訴 (D) 建設

2. (C)
解說 空格後方沒有連接受詞且主詞為人物代名詞，因此要選擇包含 be 動詞在內的被動語態，答案為 (C) are excited。

3. (B)
(A) 總是 (B) 終於 (C) 代替 (D) 特別地

4. (A)
(A) 今年春天的天候狀況不佳，嚴重影響到工程進度。
(B) 她預計在拍賣會上募得一百萬美元。
(C) Blair女士自2001年以來一直在該慈善機構工作。
(D) 該慈善機構對於在當地獲得支持感到滿意。

單字 affect 影響　raise 募款　locally 在當地

UNIT 04 連接副詞
題本 p.164

1. (B)

你好，Ashley

感謝你自願主持下週的新進員工培訓研會。我剛得知我們分公司和Wooddale分公司的員工都會參加。這使總參加人數從13人增加至25人。**因此**，我們會把研討會移動到空間更大的主會議室。若你有任何疑問，請告訴我。

單字 volunteer 自願　lead 主持、帶領　training 培訓
branch 分公司、分店　bring 導致（結果）　total 總計的

main 主要的　conference room 會議室

2. (B)

Brisbane飯店將於8月8日星期四更換中央大廳的電梯。請房客使用櫃檯右側的樓梯前往客房。**或者**，房客也可使用Jacobs街入口附近的電梯。感謝您的耐心。

單字 replace 更換　stairwell 樓梯間　locate 位於
directly 直接地、正好　entrance 入口　patience 耐心

3. (D)

Bradley先生您好，

我想推薦Blake Patterson晉升為組長。Patterson先生已在公司工作了五年，於我們部門內備受尊敬。他擁有優秀的書面溝通能力，**同時也**擅長在對話中表達個人意見。我相信Patterson先生一定能成功勝任此職位。

單字 recommend 推薦　promotion 升遷
communication 溝通　express 表達　thrive 成功、繁盛

PRACTICE
題本 p.165

1. (A) **2.** (D) **3.** (C) **4.** (A)

1-4. 電子郵件

收件者：Carl Lambert <carl_lambert@safehold.com>

寄件者：Harold Beemer <hbeemer@safehold.com>

日期：10月3日

主旨：班表安排

Lambert先生你好，

關於下週的班表安排。**不幸的是**，我下週一不能上班。我的主管Brenda Malone已在上週批准了我於10月10號所提出的週一休假申請，因為我那天**要去探望**住在外地的父母。我預計在本週五出發，並於週一晚上回來。我想Malone女士可能沒有通知你這件事。

我發現我週二沒有安排工作。如果週一有人可以替我值班，我很樂意和對方換班。請告訴我可以如何調整此情況。我隨時可以與你碰面，討論我們**可選擇的方案**。

祝好，

Harold Beemer

單字 in regard to 關於　supervisor 主管、上司
approve 批准　time off 休假　out of town 在外地
depart 出發、離開　assume 猜測、認為
inform A of B 告知 A 人 B 事　matter 問題、事情　shift 排班
rectify 調整、矯正

1. (A)
(A) 不幸的是、遺憾的是 (B) 真誠地 (C) 顯然 (D) 大概

2. (D)
解說 電子郵件傳送日期為10月3日，休假的日期為10月10日，表示空格應填入未來式動詞，因此答案為 (D) will be visiting。

3. (C)
(A) 很高興能在此為你工作。
(B) 謝謝你體諒我的情況。
(C) 我發現我週二沒有安排工作。
(D) 這是我今年的第一個假期。

單字 notice 發現

4. (A)
(A) 選擇方案 (B) 被挑選出的人或物 (C) 情況 (D) 設備

UNIT 05 句子插入題   題本p.166

1. (C)

山頂租車行已獲得新的投資資金，以擴大其租車車隊。山頂租車行的發言人表示，將會購買八十輛小型節能汽車。**公司還將購買十輛廂型貨車**。這些變化是為了回應客戶於回饋中提出需要更廣泛選擇的需求。有關租賃選項的詳細資訊，請上www.hilltop-rentals.com。

(A) 價格隨停車時間而變動。
(B) 員工對更好的工作時間感到滿意。
(C) 公司還將購買十輛廂型貨車。
(D) 他收到了好幾次關於租金的投訴。

單字 procure 獲得、入手 fund 資金 expand 擴大 fleet 車隊 spokesperson 發言人 fuel-efficient 節能的 in response to 回應… feedback 回饋、意見 indicate 指出 vary 變化 moving van 廂型貨車 block 阻擋、封鎖

2. (A)

Milton女士你好，

我建議把5樓員工休息室裡的其中一台影印機搬到3樓的辦公室。這將有助於節省時間，因為有許多員工為了影印文件不得不爬好幾層樓梯。**此外，我們還可以騰出一些空間**。這將解決我曾多次聽聞他人抱怨過，休息室過於擁擠的問題。

祝好，

Keisha

(A) 此外，我們還可以騰出一些空間。
(B) 評價最好的機器通常比較貴。
(C) 許多人覺得使用說明書令人困惑。
(D) 我們可以透過雙面列印來節省紙張。

單字 propose 建議 lounge 休息室 save 節省 flight 樓梯、樓層 crowded 擁擠的 numerous 多次的 complaint 抱怨 in addition 此外、另外 free up 騰出、空出 instruction manual 使用說明書

PRACTICE   題本 p.167

1. (B)   **2.** (B)   **3.** (D)   **4.** (A)

1-4. 廣告

Daniels景觀公司

Daniels景觀公司**從事**物業管理已超過二十年。我們提供各種景觀美化服務，盡可能讓您的住宅或工作場所看起來賞心悅目。服務項目包含除草、修剪灌木、種植樹木和花卉、以及澆灌庭院等。**此外**，我們還提供其他與戶外區域養護相關的服務。

我們的景觀設計師皆擁有多年的經驗，具備一定的資質。**他們的工作效率高，且樂在其中**。Daniels景觀公司的價格無人能敵。我們的作業**保證**讓您滿意，不滿意可以退費。如欲了解更多資訊，請致電555-9845。

單字 landscaping 景觀美化 property 房產、財產 decade 十年 a variety of 多樣的 trim 修剪 bush 灌木 water 澆水 yard 庭院 outdoor 戶外的、室外的 qualified 有資格的 beat 擊敗

1. (B)
解說 空格後方出現介系詞 for，連接一段時間，表示空格應填入現在完成進行式，因此答案為 (B) has been taking。

2. (B)
(A) 然而 (B) 此外 (C) 因此 (D) 舉例來說

3. (D)
(A) 幸運的是，我們有一支人數眾多的大團隊。
(B) 別忘了查看我們的網站。
(C) 感謝您對我們的關注。
(D) 他們的工作效率高，且樂在其中。

單字 check out 查看、確認 efficiently 有效率地 cheerfully 享受地

4. (A)
(A) 保證 (B) 明顯的 (C) 承諾 (D) 驚訝

PRACTICE   題本 p.168

131. (B) **132.** (D) **133.** (A) **134.** (D) **135.** (A) **136.** (D)
137. (C) **138.** (D) **139.** (A) **140.** (C) **141.** (B) **142.** (C)
143. (B) **144.** (D) **145.** (C) **146.** (C)

131-134. 廣告

《國際商業新聞報導》是取得商業資訊的最佳來源。了解世界各地的最新消息，並關注商業世界的各種**趨勢**。我們的記者都是業界的頂尖人物。他們**每天**撰寫文章，並在收到新資訊時更新消息。如欲訂閱，請上我們的網站www.ibnr.com/subscriptions。加入網站後，您可以存取**完整**的資料庫，並與各領域的優秀人士一起參與線上討論。還在等什麼？**今日訂閱，開始了解更多關於商業的資訊**。

單字 source 來源、源頭　be aware of 了解
industry 業界、產業　article 文章　update 最新消息
subscribe 訂閱　access 進入、利用
archive 資料庫、記錄保管處　field 領域

131. (B)
(A) 魅力、吸引力　(B) 趨勢、動向　(C) 訂閱　(D) 版本

132. (D)
(A) 相對地、比較地　(B) 嚴重地　(C) 漸進地　(D) 每日

133. (A)
解說 空格後方連接名詞 archives，因此答案要選形容詞 (A) complete，修飾後方名詞。

134. (D)
(A) 感謝您一直支持我們的雜誌。
(B) 向您介紹我們正在進行的特別優惠活動。
(C) 您將於週一早上透過郵件收到第一期電子報。
(D) 今日訂閱，開始了解更多關於商業的資訊。

單字 appreciate 感謝、感激　continued 持續的
dedication 好感、奉獻　issue（報章雜誌）刊號、期數

135-138. 廣告

第一大道維修廠

您的汽車引擎有發出奇怪的聲音嗎？想讓您的汽車跑得更順暢嗎？**是時候仔細檢查一下您的車輛了**。請把您的車開到第一大道維修廠。我們持有證照的機械維修人員會快速讓您的汽車恢復**平穩**行駛。車身的大小問題他們都可以幫您處理。您無需預約。我們24小時全天候營業。所以，直接來第一大道85號，把您的車交給我們即可。在**大多數**情況下，我們當天就能修好。請上我們的網站www.firstavenuemechanics.com查看我們的**綜合**價目表。

單字 mechanic 機械維修員　licensed 有證照的、得到許可的
minor 輕微的、較小的　major 主要的
make an appointment 預約
twenty-four hours a day 全天候　fix 維修
comprehensive 綜合的

135. (A)
(A) 是時候仔細檢查一下您的車輛了。
(B) 每輛車都經過仔細檢查。
(C) 我們的新車售價合理。
(D) 有些零件可能需要特別訂購。

單字 inspect 檢查　reasonable 合理的

136. (D)
(A) 顯然地　(B) 頗為　(C) 方便地　(D) 平穩地、順暢地

137. (C)
解說 空格用來修飾名詞 cases，因此答案要選形容詞 (C)。every 用來修飾單數名詞、much 用來修飾不可數名詞，皆不適當。空格前方未出現 their 所指的單字，所以也不能選。

138. (D)
解說 空格用來修飾名詞 price list，因此答案要選形容詞 (D) comprehensive。選項中同時出現形容詞和分詞時，要以形容詞為優先考量，因此分詞 comprehended 和 comprehending 並非答案。

139-142. 網頁

Nantucket海鮮公司：配送規範

Nantucket海鮮公司能在48小時內將貨物運送到全國各地。**所有訂單均以乾冰包裝，並採用快遞運送**。居住在距離Nantucket工廠三小時內的人可選擇當日快遞送貨。價格**根據**包裹重量和運送距離有所不同。除非在下單時另有告知，否則所有貨物都必須由收件人簽收。因天候不佳或其他不可抗力因素導致延遲交貨，我們概不**負責**。如欲了解更多資訊，請聯絡客服人員。

單字 seafood 海鮮　policy 規範、政策　ship 配送
opt 選擇、挑選　courier 快遞公司　vary 變化
recipient 收件人　notify 告知、通知　place an order 下單
unavoidable 不可避免的　contact 聯絡

139. (A)
(A) 所有訂單均以乾冰包裝，並採用快遞運送。
(B) 未來幾週將有更多的海鮮種類以供選擇。
(C) 我們的價格保證是全國最低價。
(D) 這表示您的訂單應該已經送達。

單字 order 訂單、訂購品　pack 包裝
express mail 快遞運送　guarantee 保證

140. (C)
解說 空格前方的先行詞 individuals 為人物，空格後方連接動詞，因此答案要選表示人物的關係代名詞主格 (C)。

141. (B)
(A) 考慮　(B) 根據、取決　(C) 等待　(D) 報告
解說 空格後方連接介系詞 upon，要選出適合搭配使用的選項，因此答案為 (B) depending。

142. (C)

解說 空格前方為 be 動詞 are，後方連接介系詞 for，表示空格應填入適當的形容詞，當作補語，因此答案為 (C) responsible。responsive 的意思為「反應的」，並不符合文意。

143-146. 電子郵件

> 收件者：Alexandria Houston
> 寄件者：Winston Pierce
> 主旨：壁紙
> 日期：7月5日
>
> Houston女士您好，
>
> 貴公司提供給本店的壁紙賣得很好。我的顧客喜歡這些設計，並對壁紙呈現在家中的樣子**感到滿意**。**他們也很喜愛我們的定價偏低**。因此，我希望每個月都能定期收到**一批壁紙**。
>
> 我還想增加設計樣式的數量。目前有七款設計可供選擇，但我認為十五款會更好。您能否寄給我一些你們最受歡迎的設計樣品？**一旦**看過樣品，我就能決定哪些款式適合販售。
>
> 祝好，
>
> Winston Pierce
>
> Pierce居家裝潢

單字 wallpaper 壁紙　as such 因此、結果
set up 準備、安裝　shipment 貨物　currently 目前、現在
available 可使用的　carry 出售（商品）

143. (B)
解說 空格後方並未連接受詞，而是連接介系詞片語，表示空格應使用被動語態，因此答案要選 (B) are pleased。

144. (D)
(A) 我的店裡最近增加了新的櫃位。
(B) 顧客嘗試在網路上購買商品。
(C) 很多人希望我幫他們鋪設壁紙。
(D) 他們也很喜愛我們的定價偏低。

單字 department（商店的）櫃位、賣場　charge 收取

145. (C)
解說 空格前方有動詞 like 和形容詞 regular，空格當作動詞的受詞，同時受到形容詞修飾，表示應填入名詞。空格前方有不定冠詞 a，因此答案要選單數名詞 (C) shipment。

146. (C)
(A) 仍然　(B) 在⋯之前　(C) 一旦　(D) 然而

RC　PART 7

閱讀理解

題本p.174

164-167 電子郵件

> 收件者：Allison Holder
> 寄件者：Clarissa Simpson
> 日期：3月16日
> 主旨：重要訊息
>
> 親愛的Allison：
>
> 自11月1日起，本公司將不再為任何員工提供健康保險，包含全職和兼職員工。相反地，我們將進行薪資微幅調整，以便員工購買自己的私人健康保險。
>
> 像我們目前在Newport科技公司所提供的團體保單，近年來的運作成本增加過多，**導致我們虧損**。董事會因此決定做出此項變更，以降低成本。我們打算為員工提供諮詢服務，協助他們選擇最適合自己和家人的保險公司。
>
> **David Schuler將負責此次的保險轉換工作。他將於11月1日之前，每週向你提供最新消息。**我們將於六月份發布有關此次變更的公告，屆時預計將收到許多員工的提問。
>
> 祝好，
> Clarissa Simpson 敬上
> Newport科技公司

單字 as of 自⋯起　no longer 不再
health insurance 健康保險
enable 以便　acquire 得到、獲得
policy 保單　currently 目前、現在
board of directors 董事會　therefore 因此
measure 方法、措施　assist 協助　select 選擇
provider 提供者、供應者　transition 轉換、過渡
update 最新消息　make an announcement 發布
regarding 關於　anticipate 預計、預測

164. 電子郵件的目的為何？ (A)
(A) 提供資訊
(B) 請求協助
(C) 安排會議
(D) 徵求意見

165. 關於Newport科技公司，文中提到什麼？ (D)
(A) 計畫於夏季僱用新員工。
(B) 屬於醫療產業。
(C) 在其他國家設有分公司。
(D) 目前尚未獲利。

166. 根據Simpson女士所述，Schuler先生將會做什麼事？ (C)
(A) 決定員工的加薪幅度
(B) 與董事會合作

83

(C) 提供Holder女士最新消息
(D) 為員工尋找新的保險公司

167. 第三段第1行中的「transition」一詞的意思最接近何者？(C)
(A) 發展
(B) 方法
(C) 改變
(D) 修訂

UNIT 01　主旨或目的
題本 p.176

代表題型範例

> 親愛的Douglas先生：
>
> **距離您上次來訪接受例行檢查以來，已經超過六個月了。您可以點選此處預約洗牙**，並檢查是否有蛀牙。我們診所有五名牙醫，他們都準備好隨時可為您提供協助。如果您有特別指定的牙醫，可於預約時註明。
>
> Tina Gooden
> 潔白牙醫診所

單字　routine 例行的　checkup 檢查
make an appointment 預約　cavity 蛀牙　dentist 牙醫
staff 員工　prefer 偏好　indicate 表明

Q. 電子郵件的主要目的為何？
(A) 推薦新地點
(B) 提供提醒
(C) 宣傳新服務
(D) 確認預約

單字　recommend 推薦　location 地點
provide 提供、給予　reminder 提醒
promote 宣傳　confirm 確認　booking 預約

PRACTICE
題本 p.177

1. (D)　　**2.** (B)　　**3.** (C)

1-3 新聞稿

> 即時發布
>
> **Porterhouse製造公司預計進行產品示範**
>
> Porterhouse製造公司是世界領先的高科技機械製造商之一。該公司今天**宣布將為其工程師剛完成的機器舉行產品演示**，並打算在冬季上市。活動將於10月3日星期一下午3點在公司位於亞特蘭大的總部舉行。本次示範的產品為公司最新的汽車引擎。與目前市面上其它任何引擎相比，它的效率高出35%，將為汽車產業帶來一場革命。
>
> 有意親自參加活動的記者和新聞媒體必須事先登記。**請在上班時段撥打555-2871與公司公關人員Gregory Frye聯繫**。
>
> 同時也歡迎有網路廣播節目和部落格，並對汽車技術感興趣的人參加。**該項目的首席工程師Jeremy Smith將於演示結束後回答問題**。與會者可以拍照和錄影。

單字　release 公開、發布　conduct 進行、實施
demonstration 示範　leading 先進的　advanced 進步的
machinery 機械　intend 打算、計畫　headquarter 總部
be set to 預計將…　revolutionize 發起革命
efficient 有效率的　broadcaster 電視台、廣播節目
register 登記　in advance 事先、提前
public relation 公關　business hours 營業時間
as well 且、也

1. 該篇新聞稿的目的為何？
(A) 通知投資者有產品推出
(B) 宣傳公司的最新服務
(C) 詳細說明如何購買公司的產品
(D) 提供有關產品演示的資訊

單字　detail 細節、詳情　acquire 取得、入手

2. 人們如何報名參加活動？
(A) 造訪報導科技的部落格
(B) 打電話給Porterhouse製造公司的員工
(C) 在Porterhouse製造公司的網頁上註冊
(D) 與將報導該活動的記者交談

換句話說　contact → calling

單字　report 報告、告知　technology 技術

3. 關於即將到來的活動，文中指出什麼？
(A) 需要付費才能參加。
(B) 將在週末舉行。
(C) 與會者可以提問。
(D) 將播放影片給與會者。

單字　upcoming 即將到來的、即將來臨的　payment 支付
fee 費用　take place 舉行、發生

UNIT 02　事實與否
題本 p.178

代表題型範例

> Greenbrier寫作工作坊，第1次會議
> 下午1:00-3:00
> Greenbrier公共圖書館
> 4月11日
>
> 你是否想要像專業作家一樣寫作？你是否有許多很棒的故事點子，卻不知道如何用文字表達？那麼，**由Allison Herbst主持的工作坊非常適合你**。Herbst女士已出版超過十本小說，目前任教於Greenbrier社區大學。
>
> 如欲報名及查看全系列工作坊的完整時間表，請上www.greenbrierlibrary.org。所有工作坊皆免費，但需提前報名。Herbst女士將在工作坊結束後回答問題。

單字 put into words 用文字表達　host 主持
publish 出版　register 報名　complete 完整的
advance 提前　conclude 結束、完成

Q. 關於工作坊，文中指出什麼？
(A) 人們需付費參加。
(B) 在線上進行。
(C) 將由作家主導。
(D) 由大學主辦。

單字 take place 進行、舉行　lead 主導

PRACTICE　題本 p.179

1. (A)　**2.** (D)　**3.** (D)

1-3 資訊

> Silverwood植物園通行證
>
> **Silverwood植物園是全州規模最大的植物園。** 佔地超過200英畝，園內不僅有原產於東南部的樹木、花卉和植物，還有各式各樣包含熱帶植物在內的外來品種。[1] **來到園區的遊客可以享受穿越森林的徒步健行，** 在五個池塘邊野餐，並觀賞棲息在該地區的野生動物。
>
> Silverwood植物園通行證每年僅50美元，適用一家四口。**遊客每天都可以進入園區並享有免費停車。** 您的貢獻將幫助我們維護園內的植物，並引進新植物。
>
> 通行證可於售票處，或上www.silverwoodbg.org線上購買。請注意，售票處附近商店販售的食品或其他產品不能享有特別優惠。

單字 botanical garden 植物園　pass 通行證
state （行政區）州　cover 涵蓋、包含　feature 以⋯為特色
native 原生的、原有的　a wide variety of 各式各樣的
species 物種　tropics 熱帶　wooded 樹木繁茂的
picnic 野餐　pond 池塘　wildlife 野生動物　inhabit 棲息
contribution 貢獻、捐款　maintain 維持
acquire 取得　note 注意　available 可取得的

1. 資訊中提到哪項活動？
(A) 徒步健行
(B) 游泳
(C) 狩獵
(D) 露營

2. 關於Silverwood植物園，文中指出什麼？
(A) 只有當地的植物。
(B) 完全依賴會員的捐款。
(C) 遊客可在池塘裡釣魚。
(D) 比附近其他植物園還大。

單字 rely on 依賴　solely 僅僅　donation 捐款
go fishing 釣魚　nearby 附近的

3. Silverwood植物園通行證有什麼好處？
(A) 較低的食品價格
(B) 園區導覽
(C) 紀念品折扣
(D) 免費停車

換句話說 free → complimentary

單字 benefit 好處、利益　guided 有導覽的
souvenir 紀念品　complimentary 贈送的

UNIT 03　推論或暗示　題本 p.180

代表題型範例

> Emily Hudson（下午2:24）
> David，九月份的預算報告昨天就要交了。我目前還在等你的報告。
>
> David Weber（下午2:25）
> 對不起，我剛從赫爾辛基出差回來。我現在正在處理。
>
> Emily Hudson（下午2:26）
> 我不知道你去國外出差。希望出差一切順利。你覺得你的部門有沒有超出預算？
>
> David Weber（下午2:27）
> 我會在今天結束前告訴你。
>
> Emily Hudson（下午2:28）
> 謝謝。**我需要在星期五之前完成我的最終報告，但我要先收到你的數據，才能做到。**

單字 budget 預算　submit 繳交

Q. 關於Hudson女士，可以推斷出什麼？
(A) 她要去赫爾辛基出差。
(B) 她知道Weber先生不在辦公室。
(C) 她還沒完成自己的報告。
(D) 她將於週五與她的主管會面。

單字 complete 完成

PRACTICE　題本 p.181

1. (A)　**2.** (B)　**3.** (D)

1-3 線上聊天

> Bill Hagler（下午2:03）
> 大家好，關於建築的工作進展如何？我們能準時完成嗎？**我真的很希望能在3月1日開幕。**
>
> Susan Denton（下午2:06）
> 一切看起來都很好，Bill。**廚房幾乎都安裝好了。** 桌椅會在明天送達。我們需要有人幫忙安裝。
>
> Dallas Blair（下午2:08）
> Chris和我能幫忙，Susan。只要告訴我應該幾點到那裡。
>
> Susan Denton（下午2:09）
> 謝謝你，Dallas。非常感謝你願意在休假日工作。

85

Dallas Blair（下午 2:10）
喔，我和我們隔壁店家的老闆談過了。他說他打算在未來幾個月內退休。
Bill Hagler（下午 2:11）
他的店會出租嗎？
Dallas Blair（下午 2:12）
他是這麼說的。**我們應該要確認一下**。也許可以把兩個地方連接起來。**這樣我們就會有更多空間，可以擴張餐廳。**
Susan Denton（下午 2:13）
我會跟房屋仲介聯絡一下。
Bill Hagler（下午 2:14）
好的，Susan。

單字 property 建築、房地產　on time 準時　install 安裝　appreciate 感謝　day off 休假日、休息日　next to 在旁邊　retire 退休　available 可使用的　rent 出租　connect 連接　expand 擴張　real estate agent 房屋仲介

1. 傳送訊息者最有可能在哪裡工作？
(A) 餐廳
(B) 房屋仲介公司
(C) 超市
(D) 麵包店

2. Hagler先生擔心什麼？
(A) 支付部分設備的安裝費用
(B) 在特定日期前開放場所
(C) 尋找願意安裝桌子的人員
(D) 與隔壁店主相處融洽

單字 pay for 支付　installation 安裝　equipment 設備　establishment 公司、機關　certain 特定的　get along with 與…相處融洽　shopkeeper 店主

3. Denton女士為何會在下午2點13分時寫道：「我會跟房屋仲介聯絡一下」？
(A) 表示她會要求降低月租
(B) 表明她可以簽署租賃合約
(C) 聲明她需要尋找新公寓。
(D) 提議確認可用的房產

單字 lower 降低　indicate 表明、指出　agreement 合約（書）　state 聲明

UNIT 04　相關細節

題本 p.182

代表題型範例

Stamford日報

6月28日 — Stamford市 宣 布，位 於Bellevue大 道86號 的房屋是一座歷史建築。該房屋建於1772年，目前為Mark Whitman所有。從那時起，它一直是Whitman家族的祖居。市長Thomas Whittaker表示，該棟房屋現在受到保護，無法拆除。雖然**Whitman先生已不住在這棟房子裡，但他打算重新翻修，並為有興趣了解殖民時期生活的人提供導覽。**據Whitman先生所述，許多傢俱是在建設房屋時已經就有的。

單字 declare 宣布、宣言　structure 建築、結構　currently 現在、目前　own 擁有　ancestral 祖先的、祖傳的　tear down 拆除　intend 打算　refurbish 重新翻修　colonial 殖民地的　furnishing 傢俱、室內陳設

Q. Whitman先生打算如何處理Bellevue大道上的房子？
(A) 翻新它以便入住
(B) 賣給Stamford市
(C) 供人們參觀
(D) 改造成傢俱博物館。

單字 renovate 翻新、修理　transform 改造、轉換

PRACTICE

題本 p.183

1. (A)　**2.** (D)　**3.** (A)

1-3 電子郵件

收件者：Dearborn金融公司全體員工
寄件者：執行長Jefferson Grant
日期：7月27日
主旨：David Stillman

致Dearborn金融公司全體員工：

我很遺憾地通知各位，David Stillman已告知我他將辭去Dearborn金融公司的職務。**Stillman先生擔任本公司的首席研究員已超過十二年。他決定在老家附近找工作，以便照顧年邁的父母。**請務必讓David知道各位有多麼珍惜他在這裡的時光，並祝他好運。
由於David即將辭職，我們需要盡快找到繼任者。任何對研究職位感興趣的人，請發送電子郵件給Susan Westmoreland，郵件地址為susan@dearbornfinance.com。請務必說明你能夠勝任該職位的理由，並附上你的履歷表。
David已同意協助培訓他的繼任者，因此我們希望在接下來的三週內填補該職位，讓他能與新員工一起工作交接幾個星期。

祝好，
Jefferson Grant
執行長
Dearborn金融公司

單字 regret 感到遺憾　inform 通知　step down 辭去、離職
chief 首要的　care for 照顧　elderly 年邁的
value 珍視、重視　departure 離開、卸任
be qualified for 勝任　attach 附加　copy 副本
résumé 履歷表　as well 也、且　replacement 繼任者

1. 電子郵件的其中一個目的為何？
(A) 告知工作機會
(B) 要求志工
(C) 安排公司的短期旅遊
(D) 解釋公司結構的變化

單字 volunteer 志工　schedule 安排　outing 短期旅遊

2. Stillman先生在做什麼？
(A) 調到公司總部
(B) 為取得學位重返校園
(C) 退休與家人共度時光
(D) 辭職以轉換其他工作職務

單字 degree 學位　resign 辭職

3. 關於Stillman先生，文中並未指出什麼？
(A) 他將在三週後離開Dearborn金融公司。
(B) 他是公司的首席研究員。
(C) 他在Dearborn金融公司工作超過十年。
(D) 他願意培訓其他員工。

單字 decade 十年

UNIT 05 句子插入題　　題本p.184

代表題型範例

PENSACOLA（4月19日）— 大西洋航運昨晚宣布了一項令人震驚的消息。公司表示，執行長Kevin Davenport將立即辭職。Davenport先生在今年3月才開始在大西洋航運工作，因此他突然辭職的決定讓所有人都感到驚訝。對於他離開的原因，並未發布任何公告。公司發言人Melissa Samuels表示，在找到正式替代的繼任者前，將由公司營運副總Bradley Wellman擔任臨時執行長一職。她並未提供公司預期計時會有新領導者的確切時間。

單字 make an announcement 宣布
step down 辭職、卸任　immediately 立刻
spokesperson 發言人　vice president 副總
operation 營運　interim 臨時的　permanent 正職的
replacement 繼任者　timeline 時間表

Q. [1]、[2]、[3]和[4]當中，何處最適合填入下方句子？
「對於他離開的原因，並未發布任何公告」。
(A) [1]
(B) [2]
(C) [3]
(D) [4]

PRACTICE　　題本 p.185

1. (D)　**2.** (A)　**3.** (C)

1-3 報導

NORFOLK（9月4日）— **Norfolk新開了一家餐廳，正迅速成為該城市最受歡迎的餐廳之一。**這家餐廳的名字叫Kirk's餐館。餐廳老闆為Stephanie Kirk，主打義大利和西班牙美食。

餐廳供應的所有食材幾乎都來自當地農民，Kirk女士對此感到非常自豪。她說：「Norfolk地區生產很多很棒的食材，我很高興我的餐廳能夠把它提供給顧客」。

Kirk女士不僅是老闆，也是主廚。她在義大利米蘭烹飪學校學習廚藝。 後來她在倫敦、巴黎和雅典等城市擔任廚師。她在國外生活超過二十年。去年她回到老家Norfolk，在義大利饗宴工作。現在她擁有自己的餐廳。從需要長時間候位的情況來看，這將是一家成功的餐廳。

單字 rapidly 迅速地　eatery 餐廳　establishment 機構
specialize in 主打…　serve 供應　chef 廚師、主廚
culinary arts 廚藝

1. 該篇報導的目的為何？
(A) 針對餐廳的餐點評論
(B) 描述企業盛大開幕的情形
(C) 宣傳新產品
(D) 介紹餐飲場所
換句話說 restaurant → dining establishment

單字 review 評論　meal 餐點　describe 描述
grand opening 盛大開幕（式）　promote 宣傳
dining 餐飲

2. 關於Kirk女士，文中提到什麼？
(A) 她是餐廳的老闆。
(B) 她會說義大利語和西班牙語。
(C) 她在Norfolk有農場。
(D) 她在倫敦學習烹飪。

3. 在[1]、[2]、[3]和[4]當中，何處最適合填入下方句子？
「她在國外生活超過二十年。」
(A) [1]
(B) [2]
(C) [3]
(D) [4]

UNIT 06 找出同義詞

題本p.186

代表題型範例

感謝您註冊成為Lux倉庫線上購物俱樂部的會員。我們的所有會員在購物時均自動享有九折優惠，還有免費的快遞配送服務。欲了解完整的會員福利，請點擊此處。請務必在每週日晚上查看您的電子郵件，屆時您將收到會員專屬的特別優惠。會員可能會經常被要求對新產品進行**評分**，或是收到填寫客戶滿意度調查的請求，我們想確保我們最忠實的客戶對服務感到滿意。

單字 register 註冊　automatic 自動的
purchase 購物、購買　as well as 不僅、還有
express shipping 快遞配送　complete 完整的
benefit 福利、好處　special offer 特別優惠
frequently 經常、頻繁地　grade 評分、評價
complete 完成填寫　survey 調查　ensure 確保、保證
loyal customer 忠實顧客

Q 第7行中「grade」一詞的意思最接近何者？
(A) 購買
(B) 試用
(C) 評分
(D) 考慮

PRACTICE

題本 p.187

1. (A)　**2.** (B)　**3.** (C)

1-3 廣告

CHAMBERLIN行銷公司

許多小型企業都擁有優秀的產品和服務，希望將其銷售出去。然而，這些企業的老闆既沒有時間，也沒有能力去推銷這些商品和服務。幸運的是，Chamberlin行銷公司能夠**處理**他們的所有需求。

Chamberlin行銷公司已經營了三十五年。在此期間，我們已為超過500家的小型企業提供協助。**我們協助公司在當地、全國和國際上進行自我行銷。**我們的員工在許多市場上擁有經驗，每個人都至少熟悉一門外語。

如果您想進行一小時的諮詢，請在平日上班時間內撥打555-0271與我們聯絡。**告訴我們貴公司的情況，我們會為您提供免費的初步行銷計畫。**您並沒有義務要使用我們的服務。但如果您選擇我們，一定不會後悔。

單字 outstanding 優秀的　market 行銷　handle 處理
be in business 經營　provide 提供、給予
assistance 協助、幫忙　numerous 大量的
consultation 諮詢　business hours 上班時間、營業時間
come up with 準備、想出　preliminary 初步的
obligation 義務　regret 後悔

---

1. 第一段第3行中「handle」一詞的意思最接近何者？
(A) 處理、照顧
(B) 思索
(C) 宣傳、推廣
(D) 展現、曝露

2. 關於Chamberlin行銷公司，文中指出什麼？
(A) 專注於網路行銷產品。
(B) 可以在國外推廣商品。
(C) 成立近十年。
(D) 擁有500多名員工。
換句話說 internationally → in foreign countries

單字 focus on 專注　establish 成立　decade 十年

3. Chamberlin行銷公司能為小型企業業主提供什麼？
(A) 網頁製作優惠
(B) 費用降低
(C) 免費諮詢
(D) 現金退款
換句話說 at no cost → free

單字 reduced 打折的、減少的　rate 費用　cash 現金
refund 退款

UNIT 07 雙篇閱讀

題本p.188

代表題型範例

1-5 報導、標籤

Calico餅乾將更換標籤

洛杉磯（9月5日）—廣受歡迎的全麥零食品牌Calico餅乾宣布更換其產品標籤的計畫。新的包裝上將提供搭配建議，例如每種口味的Calico餅乾最適合搭配哪一種起司。**公司的目標是讓顧客嘗試將餅乾與其他食物搭配，而不僅僅是單獨食用。**

此舉旨在幫助Calico餅乾被Crispy Dreams超越，成為市場上最暢銷的零食餅乾後，重新奪回市佔率。激烈的競爭促使Calico餅乾的高層人員尋找新方法來宣傳該產品。

公司發言人Jocelyn Watkins表示：「當您忙不停沒時間休息時，Calico餅乾是一款絕佳的零食。但是當您在家時，可以用我們的餅乾創造出更為精緻的食譜和食物組合。從9月25日開始，我們生產的所有標籤都將會附上這些新點子，我們也很樂意在社群媒體平台上看到顧客的創意。」

單字 label 標籤　whole wheat 全麥
packaging 包裝（材料）　pair 搭配　variety 種類
go with 適合　flavor 味道、風味　intend 打算
regain 找回、恢復　market share 市佔率　overtake 超越
prompt 促使　promote 宣傳　on the go 忙不停
spokesperson 發言人　elaborate 精緻的
combination 組合　social media 社群媒體

```
          Calico餅乾
         香草大蒜風味

100克
於加拿大多倫多包裝
搭配建議：何不嘗試將這些餅乾加上奶油起司或日曬番茄乾呢？
請上www.calicocrackers.com，以找到更多使用Calico餅乾製作料理的逐步教學食譜影片！
```

單字 garlic 大蒜　package 包裝　top 放上
step-by-step 逐步的

1. 根據報導所述，Calico餅乾希望為顧客做些什麼？
(A) 減少購買商品中的包裝數量
(B) 讓過敏者能更容易確認成分
(C) 鼓勵他們嘗試用新食物搭配他們的產品
(D) 迅速決定他們可能喜歡的餅乾口味

單字 reduce 減少　amount 數量　purchase 購買
ingredient 成分、材料　inspire 鼓勵、激勵

2. 關於Crispy Dreams，文中提到什麼？
(A) 最近開始生產零食。
(B) 銷售量高於Calico餅乾。
(C) 目前總部設於洛杉磯。
(D) 為市場上最便宜的品牌。

單字 goods 產品、商品　currently 現在、目前
be based in 總部設在、根基於…

3. 在報導中，第二段第2行中「prompted」一詞意思最接近何者？
(A) 協助
(B) 引起、使
(C) 匆忙
(D) 提醒

4. 關於包裝上的標籤，文中提到什麼？
(A) 在新的食品工廠製造。
(B) 重量標示有誤。
(C) 為新上市產品製作的。
(D) 9月25日以後印製的。

單字 weight 重量　list 標示、記載
incorrectly 有誤地、不正確地　release 上市

5. 根據標籤，顧客可以在網站上做什麼？
(A) 提議新的餅乾口味
(B) 撰寫產品食譜評論
(C) 觀看教學影片
(D) 下載優惠券

單字 instructional 教學用的

PRACTICE 題本 p.190

1. (C)　**2.** (A)　**3.** (D)　**4.** (B)　**5.** (B)

1-5 電子郵件、報告書

```
收件者：information@jasperrealty.com
寄件者：samjackson@hoffmanassociates.com
日期：8月18日
主旨：辦公空間

敬啟者：
本公司計畫在Lincoln開設一間小型分公司。有位同事建議我聯絡貴公司，以協助尋找合適的辦公室。
預計有十名員工在分公司工作。**辦公空間需要至少六個獨立辦公室，以及一個可容納其他員工的開放式辦公空間。大樓需位於距離公車站幾個街區範圍內**，因為許多員工都是搭公車通勤上下班。理想狀況是配有停車場可供客戶停車，但並非必要。靠近當地餐廳和咖啡廳也是理想的條件。
請告訴我有哪些房產符合我的標準。**我還想知道每個月的水電費大約為多少**。我們希望在兩個月內開設辦公室，因此需盡快找到合適的地方。我們也可以簽訂兩年的租約。
Sam Jackson
Hoffman合夥人公司
```

單字 To Whom It May Concern（無法確定收件者是誰）敬啟者
firm 公司　branch office 分公司　colleague 同事
agency 仲介、代理商　acceptable 適當的、可接受的
minimum 至少、最少　individual 獨立的、個別的
workspace 辦公空間　accommodate 容納
commute 通勤　ideal 理想的　property 房地產
fit 符合、適合　criteria 標準　roughly 大約
utility 水電費、公共事業費　on a monthly basis 每月
lease 租約

```
          Hoffman合夥人公司可用的辦公空間
              準備者：Alice Moreno

Rhubarb大道88號
四個獨立辦公室和一個可供六人使用的大型開放空間。地下室有免費停車場。**位於公車站正前方**。
Catfish巷192號
七個獨立辦公室和一個可供五人使用的開放空間。太陽能供電。距離公車站和火車站僅一個街區。
Hamilton大道27號
兩個可供十二人使用的開放空間。沒有獨立辦公室。同棟大樓內有托嬰中心。距離公車站有四個街區。附近有公共停車場。
Maple街64號
全新大樓。十二個獨立辦公室。**地下室有餐廳**。面向海邊的美景。鄰近公車站。
```

單字 basement 地下室　electricity 電力
solar power 太陽能發電　daycare center 托嬰中心
nearby 鄰近　brand-new 全新的　oceanfront 面海

1. 在電子郵件中，第二段第2行中「accommodate」一詞的意思最接近何者？
(A) 找出位置
(B) 批准
(C) 符合、適合
(D) 滿足

2. Jackson先生要求什麼？
(A) 水電費價格
(B) 合約範本
(C) 當地的地圖
(D) 辦公室所有者的電話號碼

3. 關於辦公空間，文中未提供的資訊為何？
(A) 週邊設施
(B) 獨立辦公室的數量
(C) 大眾交通運輸的地點
(D) 月租

單字 public transportation 大眾交通運輸　rent 租金

4. 根據報告書，位在Hamilton大道上辦公空間的敘述何者正確？
(A) 有十二個獨立辦公室。
(B) 空間足以容納十二人。
(C) 離公車站很近。
(D) 附近沒有停車場。

5. Jackson先生最有可能對哪個辦公空間感興趣？
(A) Rhubarb大道88號
(B) Catfish巷192號
(C) Hamilton大道27號
(D) Maple街64號

解說 本題為整合題。根據第一篇文章要求的條件，對照第二篇文章的內容，從中找出條件相符的辦公空間。(A) 和 (C) 的獨立辦公室數量不足，所以並不符合條件；(D) 沒有開放式辦公空間，所以也不是答案。(B) 有獨立辦公室和開放式辦公空間，且鄰近大眾交通運輸，故為正解。雖然 (B) 沒有停車場，但第一篇文章中有提到停車場非必要條件，因此該辦公空間仍符合Jackson先生的要求。

UNIT 08 多篇閱讀

題本p.192

代表題型範例

1-5 網頁、表格、電子郵件

國際生物醫學工程師協會（IABE）
第十五屆年會

地點：希臘雅典Bayside飯店
日期：9月22日至25日
主題：生物醫學工程的新趨勢
請注意以下重要日期：
* 提案繳交 — 3月1日
* 提案受理 — 5月1日
* 完整論文繳交 — 6月30日
所有提案應在400字至500字之間，且應線上繳交到我們的網站www.iabe.org/proposals。請按照網站上的說明來撰寫提案。
會議報名自6月1日開始。**費用包括會議T恤、茶點、午宴、所有會議的出席費，以及所有論文的影本一份**。請至www.iabe.org/registration報名。
與會者 — 500美金／6月20日前註冊
與會者 — 600美金／6月20日後註冊
演講者 — 400美金
學生 — 300美金

單字 association 協會　biomedical 生物醫學的
annual 年度的　conference 學會、會議　note 注意
proposal 提案　submission 繳交　acceptance 受理、接受
regarding 關於　registration 報名
refreshment 茶點、點心　session 會期

---

https://www.iabe.org/registration

國際生物醫學工程師協會
第十五屆年會報名

姓名：Susanna Madsen
公司：Klein製藥公司
感興趣的領域：藥物開發
電話號碼：805-555-8573
電子郵件：smadsen@klein.com
報名費：500美元

單字 pharmaceutical 製藥的、藥學的

收件者：Susanna Madsen
寄件者：陽光飯店

日期：8月14日

主旨：回覆：詢問

親愛的Madsen女士：
我們期待您下個月的光臨。**在此回覆您的問題**，飯店距離海邊僅需五分鐘步行時間。附近有各式各樣的購物和餐飲場所。**此外，飯店就在您參加會議場地的正對面。因此您可以輕鬆步行前往**。若您還有其他問題，請隨時告訴我。
祝好，
Ioannis Papadopoulos 敬上
客戶服務代表
陽光飯店

單字 therefore 因此、因而　with ease 輕鬆地

1. 根據網頁內容，關於會議的敘述何者正確？
(A) 期間將舉行午餐活動。
(B) 僅開放IABE會員參加。
(C) 有些人可免費參加。
(D) 時間將會持續一週。
換句話說 luncheon → lunch event
單字 for free 免費

2. 何時最有可能收到提案受理的通知？
(A) 3月1日
(B) 5月1日
(C) 6月1日
(D) 6月30日

3. 關於Madsen女士，文中提到什麼？
(A) 她不是IABE的會員。
(B) 她是第二次參加會議。
(C) 她在6月20日前報名參加會議。
(D) 她將在會議上發表論文。
單字 sign up for 報名參加　present 發表

4. Papadopoulos先生為何會發送電子郵件？
(A) 確認客房預訂
(B) 提供特別折扣
(C) 回覆一些詢問
(D) 更改預約日期
單字 confirm 確認　reservation 預訂　respond to 回覆
booking 預約

5. 關於陽光飯店，文中指出什麼？
(A) 鄰近Bayside飯店。
(B) 近期重新翻修過。
(C) 提供會議參加者優惠。
(D) 九月份沒有空房。

單字 close to 鄰近…　recently 近期　undergo 歷經
renovation 翻修、修理　vacancy 空房

PRACTICE
題本 p.194

1. (D)　**2.** (B)　**3.** (D)　**4.** (C)　**5.** (D)

1-5 網頁、電子郵件

波士頓旅遊公司擁有超過三十三年的經驗，提供城市及周邊地區導覽服務。每趟旅遊均由為當地人的導遊帶領，他對所有波士頓最為著名的景點都非常熟悉。我們有四種行程供您選擇。

套裝行程1　波士頓市中心半日遊及參觀水族館——每人50美元

套裝行程2　波士頓市中心購物半日遊——每人40美元

套裝行程3　波士頓及劍橋一日遊，參觀哈佛大學、麻省理工學院、水族館和燈塔山——每人80美元

套裝行程4　波士頓及周邊地區一日遊，包括參觀與美國獨立革命有關的歷史遺跡——每人100美元

如欲了解更多資訊或安排預訂，請發送電子郵件至information@bostontours.com。

單字 surrounding 周邊的、鄰近的　native 當地的、本土的
familiarity 熟悉　notable 著名的、值得關注的
package 套裝行程　aquarium 水族館　downtown 市中心
the American Revolution 美國獨立革命

收件者：information@bostontours.com
寄件者：Marcus Cartwright <marcus_c@prometheus.com>
日期：6月11日
主旨：行程

你好，
今年夏天我計畫帶全家人去新英格蘭地區旅行，以前使用過你們服務的朋友向我推薦貴公司。她說你們的導遊知識淵博，她參加的行程兼具娛樂性與教育意義。
我們預計於6月28日至7月1日在波士頓地區。我希望在我們到達的第一天參加旅遊。但如果當天沒有空位，我們也可以安排在隔天。我們家有五個人。我的妻子和三個孩子會陪同我一起參加。孩子們非常喜歡歷史，所以希望你們能安排適合我們的旅遊行程。
祝好，
Marcus Cartwright

單字 recommend 推薦　knowledgeable 知識淵博的
entertaining 娛樂的、有趣的　accompany 陪同
accommodate 容納、符合

收件者：Marcus Cartwright <marcus_c@prometheus.com>
寄件者：Cynthia Potter <cynthia@bostontours.com>
日期：6月15日
主旨：回覆：行程

Cartwright先生您好：
感謝您連絡波士頓旅遊公司。我們有個一日遊行程非常符合您孩子們的興趣。**遺憾的是，在您抵達波士頓首日，該行程已全部被訂滿了。但第二天的行程尚有五個空位**。為確認您的預約，您需要支付每張門票一半的費用，作為不可退款的訂金。[5]**請問您的孩子年紀多大呢？**他們可能符合兒童票價，為一般價格的一半。請告知我是否想預約該行程，接下來我們才能安排付款事宜。
祝好，
Cynthia Potter
波士頓旅遊公司

單字 contact 聯絡　fully booked 全部被訂滿
opening 空位　confirm 確認、確定　reservation 預約
nonrefundable 不可退款的　deposit 訂金
be eligible for 符合…的資格　rate 費用
regular price 一般定價　arrangement 安排

1. 關於波士頓旅遊公司，網頁上指出什麼？
(A) 僱用會說外語的導遊。
(B) 最近開始提供遊覽波士頓的行程。
(C) 接受現金和信用卡付款。
(D) 已經營超過三十年。

單字 hire 僱用　cash 現金　payment 付款、結帳
be in business 經營　decade 十年

2. 關於Cartwright先生，文中指出什麼？
(A) 他在波士頓地區長大。
(B) 他將與家人一起旅行。
(C) 他第一次造訪波士頓。
(D) 他會在波士頓待一個星期。

3. Cartwright先生最有可能選擇哪個套裝行程？
(A) 套裝行程1
(B) 套裝行程2
(C) 套裝行程3
(D) 套裝行程4

解說 本題為整合題，請從文章中找出Cartwright, package 等關鍵字。在第二篇文章中，Cartwright先生表示自己的孩子非常喜歡歷史，希望可以安排符合條件的行程。回到第一篇文章，與歷史有關的套裝行程為 Package 4，因此答案要選 (D)。

4. Cartwright先生最有可能參加哪天的行程？
(A) 6月15日
(B) 6月28日
(C) 6月29日
(D) 7月1日

解說 本題為整合題，請特別注意數字，並從文章中找出Cartwright, go on a tour 等關鍵字。在第二篇文章中，Cartwright先生表示他想參加6月28日的行程，但如果當天沒有名額，參加隔天6月29日的行程也可以。而在第三篇文章中，提到Cartwright先生抵達波士頓當日的行程沒有空位，第二天的話行程才有名額，表示Cartwright先生最有可能參加6月29日的行程。

5. Potter女士向Cartwright先生提出什麼要求？
(A) 他的信用卡資訊
(B) 家庭成員的名字
(C) 派車接送的地點。
(D) 他孩子們的年紀

單字 pick up 派車接送、接駁

PART TEST
題本 p.196

147. (B)　**148.** (A)　**149.** (C)　**150.** (C)　**151.** (D)　**152.** (C)
153. (B)　**154.** (D)　**155.** (A)　**156.** (B)　**157.** (D)　**158.** (C)
159. (D)　**160.** (A)　**161.** (A)　**162.** (A)　**163.** (D)　**164.** (A)
165. (C)　**166.** (B)　**167.** (B)　**168.** (A)　**169.** (B)

147-148 公告

Asbury路停車場最新消息

今年春季的天氣狀況不佳，導致位於Asbury路的停車場翻新工程嚴重延宕。該工程原本預計於5月1日完工。然而，在下雪期間施工人員無法進入工地。此外，工程師還發現一些結構性問題，更加延遲了工程進度。**因此，該項目當前計畫將於8月15日完工**。如有任何疑問，歡迎聯絡Vanderbilt建設公司的Russell Mayer，電話為802-555-9361。

單字 update 最新消息　recent 近期的　cause 導致
renovation 翻新、翻修　significantly 嚴重地
delay 延遲　crew 工作人員　access 進入　site 工地、現場
furthermore 此外、而且　structural 結構性的
issue 問題、爭議　identify 確認　further 進一步
as a result 因此、結果

147. 該公告的目的為何？
(A) 報告近期的天氣情況
(B) 說明某些計畫的變化
(C) 為錯過截止日期而道歉
(D) 提供待辦事項的詳情

單字 apologize for 針對…道歉
miss a deadline 錯過截止日　details 詳情

148. 關於Asbury路的停車場項目，文中指出什麼？
(A) 無法準時完成。
(B) 預計擴大停車場的規模。
(C) 將於五月份完成。
(D) 預期會超出預算。

單字 on time 準時　expand 擴大、擴張　budget 預算

149-151 表格

採購申請表

員工姓名：Kenneth Dumont　申請日期：11月11日
部門：資訊科技部　電子郵件：kdumont@dmr.com

品項	供應商	數量
Syntax 4000 數位相機	MTR科技公司	1
Xtreme 1000G 筆記型電腦	CompuServe	1
4TB外接式硬碟	CompuServe	2
Steady Sound耳機	Techno音響公司	1

- 繳交此表格時，請附上其他關於購買商品的必備資訊。包含可購買商品的網址和商品截圖。
- 未經直屬主管簽名，任何請求均不予批准。
- 所購物品僅限於工作用途，不得作為個人用途。

員工簽名：Kenneth Dumont
部門主管簽名：Leslie Wheeler

單字 item 品項　vendor 供應商　quantity 數量
laptop 筆記型電腦　submit 繳交　attach 附上
relevant 相關的　enable 使得以…　captured image 截圖
approve 批准　signature 簽名
immediate supervisor 直屬主管

149. Dumont先生要求購買多於一件的品項是？
(A) 數位相機
(B) 筆記型電腦
(C) 外接式硬碟
(D) 耳機

150. Dumont先生最有可能隨表格一起繳交什麼？
(A) 現金付款
(B) 收據
(C) 物品圖片
(D) 信用卡號碼

單字 along with 與…一起　receipt 收據

151. Wheeler女士最有可能是誰？
(A) MRT科技公司的員工
(B) Dumont先生的客戶
(C) 採購部成員
(D) 資訊科技部主管

換句話說 department head → department supervisor

152-155 報導

Brentwood新聞
2月26日

美國最大的汽車製造商之一Grant Autos將在Brentwood開設一座製造工廠。該工廠將設在Roth紡織公司曾經的所在地。現有建築正在進行拆除，預計在其位置上建造三個新製造中心。第一個中心將在十八個月內開始營運，而另外兩個中心則需長達兩年的時間才能完成。

Grant Autos資深副總Jefferson Trent表示：「我們希望在三個工廠全部啟用後，每天能夠生產多達300輛汽車。我們在Brentwood進行大規模的投資，並期待這能為我們獲利。」

Grant Autos將僱用超過2500名全職員工在該綜合園區工作。當中大部分的人將在生產線工作。然而，在接下來的兩年內，該公司還將招募設計師、工程師、高階主管和其他職位的人員。

單字 manufacturer 製造商　facility 設施　existing 現有的
be in the process of 正在進行…　demolish 拆除
erect 建立、蓋　operational 啟用的、運作的
vice president 副總　state 陳述、聲明　investment 投資
pay off 回報、清償　complex 綜合園區、建築群
executive 高階主管、經理

152. 該篇報導的目的為何？
(A) 報導企業合併
(B) 說明Brentwood的問題
(C) 宣布工廠開業
(D) 宣傳Grant Autos的部分車輛

解說 告知製造設施的啟用，因此答案要選 (C)。
換句話說 manufacturing facility → factory

單字 report 告知、報告　merger 合併
describe 說明、描述　promote 宣傳

153. Trent先生是誰？
(A) 工廠經理
(B) Grant Autos的高階主管
(C) 汽車製造商發言人
(D) Brentwood的政府官員

換句話說 vice president → executive

單字 spokesperson 發言人

154. 第二段第6行中「pay off」一詞的意思最接近何者？
(A) 償還
(B) 發展
(C) 回收
(D) 成功

155. 根據報導所述，Grant Autos將做什麼？
(A) 僱用各種職位的員工
(B) 改造現有設施

(C) 向市府申請貸款
(D) 設計新車系

換句話說 employees → workers

單字 a variety of 各式各樣的　renovate 改造
existing 現有的　loan 貸款　line（產品的）系列

156-159 電子郵件

收件者：Tim Chapman
　　　　　<timchapman@chapmandesigns.com>
寄件者：Dustin Peters
　　　　　<d_peters@beaumontconsulting.com>
日期：8月19日
主旨：設計決定

Chapman先生您好：

我想感謝您和您的團隊為我們辦公室提供五個新室內設計的選項。此外，感謝您耐心等待我們的回覆。我對延誤感到非常抱歉。有幾位參與決策過程的人員正在休假，本週才回到辦公室。不過，我們已經做出了決定，希望您能在月底前開始進行該項目。

我們決定採用第三個選項，名為「前衛設計」。我們非常喜歡這項設計獨特的外觀，認為它非常符合我們公司的形象。這項設計擁有許多開放空間，讓辦公室看起來比實際上還寬敞。

在開始動工之前，我們有幾個設計方面的事宜需要討論。不知您和您的團隊本週是否有時間親自過來與我們見面。這樣會讓我們有機會仔細審視設計。請告訴我您是否有空。

祝好，

Dustin Peters

單字 option 選項、選擇權　present 提供、呈現
in addition 此外　appreciate 感謝、感激
involve 牽涉、相關、包含　entitle 給⋯名稱
unique 獨特的　appearance 外觀、外表　go with 與⋯合適
in reality 實際上　aspect 方面、面向
available 有空的、可利用的　in person 親自

156. Chapman先生最有可能是誰？
(A) 財務顧問
(B) 室內設計師
(C) 房屋仲介
(D) 住宅建築師

單字 property 房產、財產　residential 住宅的、居住的

157. Peters先生為何要向Chapman先生道歉？
(A) 他在先前發的電子郵件中出了錯。
(B) 他忘記參加預定的會議。
(C) 他未能按時付款。
(D) 他很久沒有回覆。

單字 previous 先前的、以前的　submit 繳交

158. 關於前衛設計，文中指出什麼？
(A) 受到公司所有人的青睞。
(B) 執行時間短。
(C) 與公司形象相符。
(D) 可在公司預算內完成。

單字 favor 贊成、獲得青睞　implement 執行
match 相符、一致　budget 預算

159. 在[1]、[2]、[3]和[4]當中，何處最適合填入下方句子？
「這樣會讓我們有機會仔細審視設計。」
(A) [1]
(B) [2]
(C) [3]
(D) [4]

單字 go over 審視　in detail 仔細地、詳細地

160-164 廣告、電子郵件

Sanderson居家環境改善公司
Sanderson居家環境改善公司為Sturbridge地區的屋主提供協助已經超過十二年。我們提供各種定期以及一次性的服務。
我們提供的部分服務包含：
- 冷氣安裝和維護
- 屋頂安裝和維修
- 煙囪清潔
- 游泳池建設
- 房屋擴建和維修
聯絡資訊
一般資訊：Cody Wilde，cwilde@sandersonhomes.com
冷氣：Julius Clover，jclover@sandersonhomes.com
屋頂和煙囪：Eric Blaine，eblaine@sandersonhomes.com
游泳池：Carla Crow，ccrow@sandersonhomes.com
房屋裝修：Douglas Montana，
　　　　　　dmontana@sandersonhomes.com

單字 improvement 改善、提升
a wide variety of 各式各樣的　on a regular basis 定期地
installation 安裝　maintenance 維護　chimney 煙囪
expansion 擴建　general 一般的　renovation 裝修、改造

收件者：Carla Crow <ccrow@sandersonhomes.com>
寄件者：Alyson Roswell
<a_roswell@moderntimes.com>
日期：4月11日
主旨：明天

Carla午安，

很抱歉，我需要延期明天Jack Haley施工團隊的來訪，因為我要去外地出差。我今晚出發，要到明天晚些時候才會回來，所以明天沒有人在家，無法讓施工人員進來。對此我感到非常抱歉。

我知道只剩下兩天的時間就能完成工程。今天早上Haley先生告知我的。 這星期的其他時間我都會在家，所以我想施工人員應該能在週末前完成所有工作。

待施工完畢後，我會支付最後的款項。

祝好，

Alyson Roswell

單字 work crew 施工團隊　take a trip 出差、旅遊　out of town 到外地

160. 關於Sanderson居家環境改善公司，文中提到什麼？
(A) 位於Sturbridge。
(B) 提供顧客折扣。
(C) 提供煙囪設計服務。
(D) 可在家中安裝暖氣。

單字 install 安裝

161. 根據廣告所述，有關冷氣系統的問題應該聯絡誰？
(A) Julius Clover
(B) Douglas Montana
(C) Cody Wilde
(D) Eric Blaine

換句話說 air conditioning → cooling systems

162. Roswell女士的電子郵件主要目的為何？
(A) 延後部分工程
(B) 安排會議
(C) 安排付款
(D) 討論工作機會

換句話說 delay → postpone

單字 arrange 安排、處理

163. Roswell女士最有可能在她家做什麼？
(A) 冷氣安裝
(B) 煙囪清潔
(C) 房屋擴建
(D) 游泳池建設

解說 本題為整合題。Roswell 女士為第二篇文章的寄件者，發送電子郵件給 Carla Crow。回到第一篇文章，Carla Crow 為游泳池施工的聯絡對象，因此答案要選 (D)。

164. Haley先生最有可能是誰？
(A) 監工人員
(B) 屋頂安裝工人
(C) Sanderson居家環境改善公司的執行長
(D) Sanderson居家環境改善公司的顧客

單字 supervisor 監督人員、管理者

165-169 電子郵件、發票、備忘錄

收件者：Preston Peterson
<ppeterson@tristatemedia.com>
寄件者：Curtis Harrier
<curtis_harrier@vanguardautos.com>
日期：10月11日
主旨：筆記
附加檔案：@評論

Peterson先生您好，

我和我的團隊觀看了Tristate媒體公司團隊為Vanguard汽車公司的最新車輛製作的初版影片，我們都對其印象深刻。影片清楚展示出Stallion在越野的情況下出色的處理能力。不過影片中有幾個問題，想麻煩你們處理。

* 10秒處：請在畫面底部用大字體顯示公司名稱和標誌。
* 25秒處：**車輛內部的畫面不夠清晰。我們希望觀眾能看到內部的舒適性。** 能請您重新拍攝此部分嗎？
* 1分鐘處：越野場景的灰塵過多，導致難以看清楚車輛。

我在附檔中進一步詳細說明了這些問題。 期待能在10月19日之前看到最終版的影片。我們會把影片發送給全國的經銷商以及一些重要客戶。如果您對我的修改建議有任何疑問，請與我聯絡。

祝好，

Curtis Harrier
媒體部門
Vanguard汽車公司

單字 attachment 附加檔案　initial 最初的、初期的　handle 處理、承擔　off-road 越野的　issue 問題、議題　address 處理、處置　print 字體　shot 鏡頭、畫面

Vanguard汽車公司
發票 5433
請款日期：11月15日
發貨日期：11月19日
請款地址：Silverado Ranch
　　　　　45 Buffalo Lane
　　　　　Billings, Montana

數量	產品編號	產品規格	單價	合計
5	57231	Stallion 休旅車	$53,000	$265,000

税金　$10,600
總計　$275,600

單字 invoice 請款單、發票　bill 開帳單　quantity 數量　description 說明、產品規格　unit price 單價

> 備忘錄
>
> 收件者：全體員工
> 寄件者：銷售副總 Christina Wilson
> 日期：11月20日
> 回覆：祝賀
>
> 感謝所有致力於製作近期 Stallion 宣傳影片的人。我們發送給全國經銷商和客戶，他們都非常喜歡這段影片。**我想特別感謝為完成這段影片而努力的 Harrier 先生。**
>
> 雖然 Stallion 要到12月1日才正式開賣，但我們已經賣出了幾輛。昨天已經把這些車輛交給一位老客戶。購買車輛的客戶 Ben Freeman 告訴我們，這段影片起到了關鍵性的作用，讓他在沒有試駕的情況下就決定購入車輛。我們很快就需要為 Stallion 製作廣告了，所以期待各位在十二月份的出色表現。

單字 recent 近期的　informational 宣傳資訊的　officially 正式地　go on sale 販賣　unit (單位) 台　instrumental 關鍵的　test-drive 試駕　commercial 廣告

165. 電子郵件的附件檔案為何？
(A) 發票
(B) 新車說明
(C) 影片製作評論
(D) 收據副本

單字 review 評論、回覆　copy 副本、一份　receipt 收據

166. 為何 Harrier 先生想重新拍攝25秒處的場景？
(A) 車輛行駛速度過快。
(B) 影片中的影像不夠清晰。
(C) 場景中的灰塵過多。
(D) 未出現公司標誌

換句話說 shots → image

單字 unclear 不清晰的　scene 場景　appear 出現

167. 關於 Stallion，發票上指出什麼？
(A) 買方訂購5台。
(B) 有提供折扣。
(C) 需支付運費。
(D) 於11月15日送達。

單字 purchaser 買方　fee 費用

168. Wilson 女士特別稱讚誰？
(A) 媒體部員工
(B) 老客戶
(C) 影片製作人
(D) 全國銷售人員

解說 本題為整合題。在最後一篇文章中，提到她特別想感謝 Harrier 先生。回到第一篇文章，Curtis Harrier 是媒體部門的員工，因此答案要選 (A)。

169. Freeman 先生最有可能在哪裡工作？
(A) 在 Vanguard 汽車公司
(B) 在 Silverado Ranch
(C) 在 Tristate 媒體公司
(D) 在試駕中心

解說 本題為整合題。在最後一篇文章中，提到已經賣出幾台 Stallion 給一位叫做 Ben Freeman 的老客戶。而在第二篇文章中，出現的地址為 Silverado Ranch，因此答案要選 (B)。

題本 p.207

LISTENING TEST

1. (D)	2. (A)	3. (C)	4. (B)	5. (A)
6. (B)	7. (A)	8. (A)	9. (A)	10. (B)
11. (C)	12. (C)	13. (B)	14. (B)	15. (B)
16. (B)	17. (A)	18. (C)	19 (B)	20. (C)
21. (B)	22. (A)	23. (B)	24. (A)	25. (C)
26. (C)	27. (B)	28. (C)	29. (A)	30. (B)
31. (A)	32. (C)	33. (D)	34. (C)	35. (C)
36. (C)	37. (B)	38. (A)	39. (B)	40. (B)
41. (B)	42. (A)	43. (D)	44. (B)	45. (B)
46. (C)	47. (C)	48. (A)	49. (A)	50. (D)
51. (B)	52. (C)	53. (B)	54. (D)	55. (C)
56. (D)	57. (C)	58. (A)	59. (A)	60. (C)
61. (A)	62. (D)	63. (C)	64. (C)	65. (A)
66. (D)	67. (C)	68. (B)	69. (B)	70. (C)
71. (B)	72. (D)	73. (D)	74. (A)	75. (C)
76. (A)	77. (A)	78. (D)	79. (C)	80. (C)
81. (D)	82. (C)	83. (B)	84. (D)	85. (B)
86. (C)	87. (A)	88. (B)	89. (B)	90. (A)
91. (C)	92. (C)	93. (B)	94. (B)	95. (C)
96. (A)	97. (B)	98. (C)	99. (C)	100. (D)

READING TEST

101. (A)	102. (D)	103. (C)	104. (B)	105. (C)
106. (D)	107. (B)	108. (A)	109. (A)	110. (C)
111. (D)	112. (B)	113. (D)	114. (A)	115. (C)
116. (B)	117. (A)	118. (C)	119. (A)	120. (B)
121. (D)	122. (B)	123. (C)	124. (C)	125. (A)
126. (D)	127. (A)	128. (D)	129. (B)	130. (A)
131. (D)	132. (B)	133. (A)	134. (C)	135. (C)
136. (D)	137. (A)	138. (D)	139. (D)	140. (A)
141. (C)	142. (D)	143. (D)	144. (C)	145. (C)
146. (B)	147. (C)	148. (B)	149. (C)	150. (A)
151. (C)	152. (D)	153. (B)	154. (A)	155. (C)
156. (A)	157. (A)	158. (D)	159. (C)	160. (D)
161. (C)	162. (B)	163. (C)	164. (A)	165. (D)
166. (D)	167. (D)	168. (B)	169. (C)	170. (B)
171. (B)	172. (B)	173. (C)	174. (A)	175. (C)
176. (B)	177. (A)	178. (A)	179. (C)	180. (C)
181. (A)	182. (B)	183. (D)	184. (B)	185. (D)
186. (D)	187. (D)	188. (C)	189. (A)	190. (B)
191. (A)	192. (C)	193. (D)	194. (C)	195. (C)
196. (B)	197. (C)	198. (B)	199. (B)	200. (C)

1. 🎧 美國女子

(A) She's writing some notes on a pad of paper.
(B) She's rolling up her sleeves.
(C) Some cartons have been stacked on the floor.
(D) Ceramic pots have been arranged on shelves.

(A) 她正在便條本上寫筆記。
(B) 她正在捲起袖子。
(C) 有些紙箱被堆放在地板上。
(D) 架上正擺放著一些瓷器。

2. 🎧 美國男子

(A) They're lifting a sofa.
(B) They're moving some chairs.
(C) They're assembling some furniture.
(D) They're walking through a doorway.

(A) 他們正在抬起沙發。
(B) 他們正在搬椅子。
(C) 他們正在組裝傢俱。
(D) 他們正在穿過出入口。

3. 🎧 英國女子

(A) She's examining a price tag.
(B) She's removing her sunglasses.
(C) She's reaching for a vegetable on a shelf.
(D) She's pushing a cart filled with items.

(A) 她正在檢視標價牌。
(B) 她正在摘下太陽眼鏡。
(C) 她正在伸手去拿架上的蔬菜。
(D) 她正在推著裝滿物品的推車。

4. 🎧 澳洲男子

(A) The woman is drinking from a cup.
(B) The man is pointing at a menu.
(C) Some food is being served at a table.
(D) Flowers have been stitched on a tablecloth.

(A) 女子正用杯子喝水。
(B) 男子正指著菜單。
(C) 餐桌上正供應著一些食物。
(D) 餐桌布上縫著花朵。

5. 🎧 美國女子

(A) One of the men is giving a presentation.
(B) One of the men is putting on a jacket.
(C) One of the women is adjusting a computer monitor.
(D) One of the women is putting away her laptop.

97

(A) 其中一名男子正在演講。
(B) 其中一名男子正在穿夾克。（動作）
(C) 其中一名女子正在調整電腦螢幕。
(D) 其中一名女子正在收起她的筆電。

6. 🎧 美國男子

> (A) Kitchen towels have been placed on a countertop.
> **(B) Some lamps are hanging from the ceiling.**
> (C) A cupboard door has been left open.
> (D) Some cooking utensils are being arranged on a table.

(A) 廚房紙巾被放在流理台上。
(B) 天花板上掛著幾盞燈。
(C) 櫥櫃的門保持敞開。
(D) 桌上擺放著一些廚房用具。

7. 🎧 美國男子／英國女子

> Have the company vehicles in the parking lot been cleaned?
> **(A) No, not yet.**
> (B) I just parked it on the street.
> (C) I put it in the recycling bin.

停車場內的公司車輛都洗好了嗎？
(A) 不，還沒有。
(B) 我剛把它停在街上。
(C) 我把它放進回收箱裡了。

8. 🎧 英國女子／美國男子

> How much will the budget increase next year?
> **(A) About 10 percent.**
> (B) Sorry, I must have dropped it.
> (C) At the end of this quarter.

明年的預算會增加多少？
(A) 大約10%。
(B) 抱歉，我好像弄掉了。
(C) 在此季度末。

9. 🎧 澳洲男子／美國女子

> You're going to have a meeting with Mr. Woodman before you leave, aren't you?
> **(A) Yes, right after lunch.**
> (B) I'd better take the bus.
> (C) Three months' parental leave.

你離開前要和Woodman先生開會，不是嗎？
(A) 對，就在午餐後。
(B) 我最好搭公車。
(C) 三個月的育嬰假。

10. 🎧 美國女子／澳洲男子

> Aren't you going to schedule an eye doctor appointment?
> (A) These glasses are not expensive.
> **(B) I already scheduled one.**
> (C) The new manager was appointed today.

你不打算預約眼科嗎？
(A) 這些眼鏡並不貴。
(B) 我已經約好了。
(C) 今天任命了新的經理。

11. 🎧 美國男子／英國女子

> I'm going to try to fix this copy machine.
> (A) Double-sided copies.
> (B) Light fixtures for the lobby.
> **(C) Are you sure it can be repaired?**

我打算修理這台影印機。
(A) 雙面影印。
(B) 安裝在大廳的燈具。
(C) 你確定可以修理嗎？

12. 🎧 英國女子／美國男子

> What should we do with these brochures?
> (A) Sure, I have time this afternoon.
> (B) It's close to the seashore.
> **(C) Let me leave them at the front desk.**

我們該如何處理這些小冊子？
(A) 當然，我今天下午有時間。
(B) 離海邊很近。
(C) 讓我把它們放在櫃檯。

13. 🎧 澳洲男子／美國女子

> Has the policy meeting been rescheduled?
> (A) The staffing policy.
> **(B) Yes, it's happening next Monday instead.**
> (C) The entire management team.

是否已重新安排政策會議的時間？
(A) 人員配置政策。
(B) 是，改到下週一舉行。
(C) 整個管理團隊。

單字 staffing 人員配置（staff 員工）

14. 🎧 美國女子／澳洲男子

> Why don't we stop by the warehouse on our way to the workshop?
> (A) The store on Oak Street.
> **(B) Sure, we have time for that.**
> (C) The topic has just changed.

我們在去研討會的路上順便去一趟倉庫如何？
(A) Oak街上的商店。
(B) 當然，我們有時間那樣做。
(C) 剛剛換了主題。

單字 on our way to 在去…的路上

15. 🎧 美國男子／英國女子

> Have you tried our famous salmon dish?
> (A) I'm afraid I can't make it on time.
> **(B) Yes, it was delicious.**
> (C) We need a table for six.

你吃過我們有名的鮭魚料理嗎？
(A) 我恐怕無法準時抵達。
(B) 有，很美味。
(C) 我們需要一張六人桌。

單字 make it 準時、及時抵達

16. 🎧 英國女子／美國男子

> Who's the opening act at tonight's concert?
> (A) It's too crowded here.
> **(B) Sandra booked tickets.**
> (C) There're several job openings on our design team.

今晚音樂會的開場表演者是誰？
(A) 這裡太擁擠了。
(B) Sandra訂票的。
(C) 我們的設計團隊有幾個職缺。

單字 act 表演

解說 表示音樂會的票是由 Sandra 預訂，所以她知道開場表演者是誰。

17. 🎧 澳洲男子／美國女子

> When do the software demonstrations start?
> **(A) The schedule was e-mailed to everyone.**
> (B) A lot of attractive features.
> (C) In the conference room, I think.

軟體演示什麼時候開始？
(A) 時間表已發送電子郵件給所有人了。
(B) 有許多吸引人的功能。
(C) 我想是在會議室裡。

解說 已發送郵件給所有人，表示要求對方自行確認時間。

18. 🎧 美國女子／澳洲男子

> The health inspector will be visiting the restaurant soon.
> (A) Take this to table three.
> (B) I'm fine, thanks for asking.
> **(C) We're all set.**

衛生檢查員很快會造訪餐廳。
(A) 把這個拿到三號桌。
(B) 我很好，感謝詢問。
(C) 我們都準備好了。

19. 🎧 美國男子／英國女子

> Did you find a good welding specialist?
> (A) I have some wedding invitation templates.
> **(B) Yes, he starts next week.**
> (C) The list of special guests.

你找到好的焊接專家了嗎？
(A) 我有一些結婚請帖範本。
(B) 是的，他下週開始工作。
(C) 特別嘉賓名單。

單字 welding specialist 焊接專家（welder 焊工）

20. 🎧 英國女子／美國男子

> How was the tile pattern for the restroom chosen?
> (A) The service was good.
> (B) I like this checkered shirt.
> **(C) I wasn't involved.**

廁所的磁磚圖案是怎麼選出來的？
(A) 服務很好。
(B) 我喜歡這件格子襯衫。
(C) 我沒有參與。

21. 🎧 澳洲男子／美國女子

> When are we ordering office supplies for new employees?
> (A) In front of the storage closet.
> **(B) Next week on Tuesday.**
> (C) They're training now.

我們何時訂購辦公用品給新員工？
(A) 在置物櫃前。
(B) 下週二。
(C) 他們現在正在受訓。

單字 office supplies 辦公用品　train 受訓、訓練

22. 🎧 美國女子／澳洲男子

> The garden lights are going to be solar-powered, right?
> **(A) We are still in the planning stages.**
> (B) Yes, this plant grows best in the shade.
> (C) $250 per year.

花園的燈光將採用太陽能供電，對吧？
(A) 目前仍處於規劃階段。
(B) 是的，這種植物在陰涼處生長得最好。
(C) 每年250美元。

單字 solar-powered 太陽能的

23. 🎧 美國男子／英國女子

> Where can I buy a charger for this camera?
> (A) This has excellent resolution.
> **(B) I can order one for you.**
> (C) Around 2:30.

哪裡可以買到這款相機的充電器？
(A) 具備優秀的解析度。
(B) 我可以幫你訂一個。
(C) 兩點半左右。

24. 🎧 英國女子／美國男子

> Do I need to reserve a conference room?
> **(A) Yes, Jeff will show you how.**
> (B) I booked the trip already.
> (C) There's room for improvement.

我需要預約會議室嗎？
(A) 是的，Jeff會告訴你怎麼做。
(B) 我已經訂好旅遊行程了。
(C) 還有改善空間。

25. 🎧 澳洲男子／美國女子

> When's the new department director supposed to start?
> (A) Yes, for a summer vacation.
> **(B) Mr. Anderson is not retiring until May.**
> (C) No, he should be in the office.

新任部門主管何時開始工作？
(A) 是的，為了暑假。
(B) Anderson先生要到五月才退休。
(C) 不，他應該在辦公室裡。

解說 現任部門主管 Anderson 先生要到五月才退休，表示新任部門主管最快會於五月才開始工作，屬於間接回答的方式。

26. 🎧 美國女子／澳洲男子

> Should I finish designing these fliers now, or can it wait until tomorrow?
> (A) I'm flying to San Francisco.
> (B) In the waiting room.
> **(C) Tomorrow's fine.**

我應該現在就完成這些傳單的設計，還是可以等到明天？
(A) 我要飛往舊金山。
(B) 在等候室。
(C) 明天做也行。

27. 🎧 美國男子／英國女子

> This laptop is becoming quite slow.
> (A) Attendance was low.
> **(B) When did you last check for viruses?**
> (C) No, you shouldn't have to wait long.

這台筆電的運作速度變得好慢。
(A) 出席率很低。
(B) 你最後一次檢查電腦病毒是什麼時候？
(C) 不，你不用等太久。

28. 🎧 英國女子／美國男子

> How much will the repairs cost?
> (A) In about three days.
> (B) I'd like you to do this in pairs.
> **(C) Everything is covered under the warranty plan.**

維修費是多少？
(A) 大約三天後。
(B) 我希望你們兩人一組做此事。
(C) 所有維修費用都包含在保固方案內。

29. 🎧 澳洲男子／美國女子

> Why don't you check the prices at a different hardware store?
> **(A) Do you know of a good one?**
> (B) She's a software engineer.
> (C) You can check in after 10 o'clock.

何不去別間五金行看一下價格呢？
(A) 你知道不錯的店嗎？
(B) 她是名軟體工程師。
(C) 你可在十點後辦理入住手續。

30. 🎧 美國女子／澳洲男子

> Can you give me a tour of the property on Abbey Street this afternoon?
> (A) It has a large backyard.
> **(B) Sorry, I won't have time until Friday.**
> (C) Over 20 people.

今天下午你可以帶我參觀一下Abbey街上的房子嗎？
(A) 它有個很大的後院。
(B) 抱歉，我在星期五前都沒時間。
(C) 超過二十個人。

31. 🎧 美國男子／英國女子

> Who's scheduled to do the product demonstration tomorrow?
> **(A) We're waiting for confirmation.**
> (B) At the Wilson Hotel.
> (C) Let me show you a few more.

明天由誰來進行產品示範？
(A) 我們正在等待確認。
(B) 在Wilson飯店。
(C) 我再給你看一些。

32-34. 🎧 英國女子／美國男子

Questions 32-34 refer to the following conversation.

> W Hassan, ³²I've finished restocking the power tools. Ted said that you wanted to talk to me about an issue we're having in the paint section.
> M That's right. ³³The paint-mixing machine has broken down. So, we can't mix any custom paints for customers at the moment.
> W Hmm … I wonder if it's something easy to fix. ³⁴I'll take a look at the user manual to see if I can figure out the problem.

女 Hassan，³²我已經把電動工具重新補貨了。Ted說你想找我談談在油漆區域遇到的問題。
男 沒錯。³³油漆混合機壞了。所以現在我們無法為客戶製作任何訂製混合油漆。
女 嗯… 不知道它是否很容易就能修好。³⁴我會先查看使用說明手冊，看看能否解決問題。

單字 restock（庫存）重新補貨   power tool 電動工具
section 區域、部分   break down 損壞
at the moment 現在、目前   fix 修理   take a look at 查看

32. 說話者最有可能在哪裡？
(A) 運輸公司
(B) 國家公園
(C) 五金行
(D) 清潔公司

33. 根據男子所述，是什麼造成了問題？
(A) 人員短缺
(B) 日程衝突
(C) 負面評價
(D) 設備損壞

34. 女子說她會做什麼事？
(A) 列印文件
(B) 聘請專家
(C) 查看使用說明手冊
(D) 處理付款

35-37. 🎧 英國女子／美國男子

Questions 35-37 refer to the following conversation.

> W ³⁵I've reviewed your design for Ms. Osborne's living room, and I think you've done a great job. I love the unique style!
> M Thank you. She had a clear vision for that room, so I tried to follow it.
> W There's just one adjustment needed, though. ³⁶We can't use the wood panels you selected because they've been discontinued by the manufacturer.
> M I hadn't realized that. They're a major feature of my design.
> W Well, you might be able to achieve the same look with wallpaper. ³⁷Check out the photos of the room that Yuki did for Mr. Harris. Then you can see what I mean.

女 ³⁵我已經審閱過你為Osborne女士客廳的設計，我覺得你做得很棒。我很喜歡你獨特的風格！
男 謝謝你。她清楚知道她想要的客廳樣貌，所以我試著按照她的想法來設計。
女 不過，只有一點需要調整。³⁶你所選的木製板無法使用，因為製造商已停產了。
男 我沒有發現到。那是我設計的主要特色。
女 嗯，也許你可使用壁紙，創造出同樣的外觀。³⁷你查看一下Yuki為Harris先生設計的房間照片，就明白我的意思了。

單字 review 審閱   unique 獨特的、有個性的
adjustment 調整、修正   panel 板子、嵌板
discontinue 停產   major 主要的   feature 特色
wallpaper 壁紙

35. 男子最有可能是誰？
(A) 大樓業主
(B) 藝術指導員
(C) 室內設計師
(D) 記者

101

36. 女子擔心什麼事？
(A) 費用增加
(B) 安全問題
(C) 無法取得的材料
(D) 錯過截止日

37. 女子建議做什麼事？
(A) 參加培訓課程
(B) 查看一些圖片
(C) 聯絡製造商
(D) 緊急下單

38-40. 🎧 澳洲男子／美國男子／美國女子
Questions 38-40 refer to the following conversation with three speakers.

> **M1** I'm glad we were both able to visit this site in person.
> **M2** Me, too. I hope it'll be suitable for our car dealership.
> **M1** Well, ³⁸the real estate agent said that it is in an excellent location. Oh, here she is now. Hi, Cindy.
> **W** Good morning. So, what's your first impression?
> **M2** It's a great neighborhood. ³⁹But we need a lot of space to display our vehicles. I'm worried about the small size.
> **M1** Right. We'll need extra room for customer parking as well.
> **W** You know, there's a grassy area on the east side that could be paved. ⁴⁰Let me show you the property line on the map.

男1 我很高興我們能親自造訪此地。
男2 我也是。我希望它是合適的汽車經銷據點。
男1 嗯，³⁸房地產經紀人說這裡地點極佳。喔，她人來了。你好，Cindy。
女 早安。所以，你們的第一印象如何呢？
男2 這是個很棒的社區。³⁹但我們需要非常大的空間來展示我們的汽車。我擔心它太小。
男1 沒錯。我們還需要額外空間讓客戶停車。
女 你知道，東邊有一塊綠地可以鋪設地面。⁴⁰我給你看地圖上的地界線。

單字 site 地點、腹地　in person 親自　dealership 經銷商
real estate agent 房地產經紀人　location 地點、位置

38. 男子們與誰見面？
(A) 房地產經紀人
(B) 機械維修師
(C) 安全檢查員
(D) 會計師

39. 男子們在擔心什麼事？
(A) 地點很難找。
(B) 佔地不夠大。
(C) 表格上遺漏資訊。
(D) 停車費過高。

40. 說話者接下來最有可能做什麼事？
(A) 進入大樓
(B) 檢視文件
(C) 前往其他地點
(D) 測量尺寸

41-43. 🎧 美國女子／澳洲男子
Questions 41-43 refer to the following conversation.

> **W** Good morning. This is Pamela at Lubbock Sales. ⁴¹You were supposed to deliver some boxes today, but I'm wondering if you can do it tomorrow instead. They're carrying out emergency repairs on our road, so it's difficult to access our entrance.
> **M** Don't you need the items urgently?
> **W** We can wait another day. ⁴²They're containers for moving our office items, and we aren't quite ready to start packing anyway.
> **M** I see. ⁴³Then, let me call our driver, Milton, to see if he can do it.

女 早安。我是Lubbock銷售公司的Pamela。⁴¹本來請你今天送幾個箱子，但我想知道能否改成明天再送。因為我們這邊的路段正在進行緊急搶修，所以很難從入口進來。
男 您不是急需這些東西嗎？
女 我們可以再等一天。⁴²這些箱子是用來搬運我們辦公室的物品，而我們也還沒準備開始打包。
男 我明白了。⁴³那我打電話給司機Milton，看看他能否配合。

單字 carry out 進行　pack 打包

41. 女子為何打電話來？
(A) 要求打折
(B) 重新安排配送時間
(C) 付款
(D) 詢問退貨事宜

42. 女子訂購東西的理由為何？
(A) 她打算搬運一些物品。
(B) 她必須修理機器。
(C) 她要發禮物給員工。
(D) 她在裝修她的辦公室。

43. 男子接下來會做什麼事？
(A) 開車去女子的公司
(B) 更新公司網站
(C) 與女子的經理談話
(D) 確認員工是否有時間

44-46. 🎧 美國男子／英國女子

Questions 44-46 refer to the following conversation.

> M　Good morning, [44]Chapman Health Center.
>
> W　Hi, I have a doctor's appointment on Thursday at ten, but I need to reschedule it.
>
> M　I can help you with that. Could you please tell me your name?
>
> W　It's Bonnie Phillips. [45]I'm supposed to have my annual checkup, but now I need to fly to Sacramento for a work conference.
>
> M　Are you available next Wednesday at nine o'clock?
>
> W　Yes. Thanks.
>
> M　Okay. Let's see … [46]your insurance policy expires in November, right?
>
> W　[46]I'll have to check. Just a moment.

男　早安，[44]這裡是Chapman健康中心。
女　你好，我星期四十點有預約看診，但我需要重新約診。
男　我可以協助您。方便告訴我您的姓名嗎？
女　我是Bonnie Phillips。[45]我本該進行年度體檢，但現在我需要飛往Sacramento參加工作會議。
男　下星期三九點您有空嗎？
女　有的，謝謝。
男　好的，[46]我來看看…您的保單將於十一月到期，對嗎？
女　[46]我要確認一下。請稍等。

單字 doctor's appointment 預約看診
reschedule 重新安排時間　be supposed to do 應該要…
annual 年度的、每年的　checkup 健康檢查
insurance policy 保險單　expire 到期、屆期

44. 男人在哪裡工作？
(A) 電腦維修店
(B) 醫療診所
(C) 銀行
(D) 職業介紹所

45. 女子為何想要變更預約時間？
(A) 她的汽車出問題。
(B) 她要去出差。
(C) 她必須授課。
(D) 她身體不舒服。

46. 女子接下來最有可能做什麼事？
(A) 提出正式投訴
(B) 提供新的聯絡資訊
(C) 確認到期日
(D) 聯絡其他分店

47-49. 🎧 美國男子／英國女子

Questions 47-49 refer to the following conversation.

> M　Christina, most of the feedback on the customer comment cards is positive. [47]However, there were quite a few complaints about our menu being so limited.
>
> W　I didn't realize that was an issue.
>
> M　[47]Well, I thought maybe we could add a better variety of main dishes.
>
> W　Hmm … All of our cooks would have to learn how to make those, and the training period is already quite long.
>
> M　Then how about just adding more desserts? [49]Steven makes all of them, so the change wouldn't affect others. I'm sure he could handle it, as he's worked in the industry for a long time.

男　Christina，顧客意見卡上大部分的回饋都是正面的。[47]但也有不少人抱怨我們的菜單選擇太少。
女　我沒有意識到這會是個問題。
男　[47]嗯…我想我們應該加入更多種類的主菜。
女　嗯…但是所有廚師都要學習如何製作，而訓練時間已經夠長了。
男　那加入更多甜點如何？[49]所有甜點都由Steven負責製作，所以這項更動不會影響到其他人。他在這個行業已經工作了很長一段時間，所以我相信他可以應對。

單字 comment 意見、評論　quite a few 相當多的
limited 有限的　a variety of 多樣的　main dish 主菜
affect 影響　handle 應付、處理

47. 說話者最有可能在哪裡工作？
(A) 農場
(B) 倉庫
(C) 咖啡廳
(D) 電器行

48. 女子為何會說：「訓練時間已經夠長了」？
(A) 拒絕提議
(B) 讓男人安心
(C) 提供她的協助
(D) 建議更改時間表

49. 關於Steven，男子提到什麼？
(A) 他的經驗豐富。
(B) 他對工作條件不滿意。
(C) 他可以推薦供應商。
(D) 他可能在工作量上遇到困難。

50-52. 🎧 美國男子／美國女子／澳洲男子

Questions 50-52 refer to the following conversation

with three speakers.

> **M1** Good afternoon. [50]Do you have a pass to our gym?
>
> **W** Not yet. I'd like to know more about your classes.
>
> **M1** Of course. My colleague can tell you more. [51]Joseph, could you please explain our system for group exercise classes?
>
> **M2** Sure. [51]You can sign up online and attend up to five per week. These are included in your membership fees.
>
> **W** That's great. Also, I heard that you give discounts to Wesley Sales employees. [52]I just began working there last month. Am I eligible?

男1 午安。[50]你有我們健身房的出入證嗎？
女 還沒有。我想了解更多關於你們的課程。
男1 沒問題。我同事可以告訴你更多相關內容。[51]Joseph，你能說明一下我們團體運動課程的制度嗎？
男2 當然。[51]你可以在線上報名，每週最多參加5次。這些通通包含在你的會費裡。
女 太好了。另外，我聽說有給Wesley行銷公司的員工提供折扣。[52]我從上個月開始在那裡工作。我有符合資格嗎？

單字 pass 出入證、通行證　gym 健身房、體育館
colleague 同事　sign up 報名　membership fee 會費
eligible 有資格的

50. 說話者在哪裡？
(A) 電影院
(B) 圖書館
(C) 餐廳
(D) 健身房

51. Joseph提供女子什麼樣的資訊？
(A) 與工作人員會面
(B) 參加團體課程
(C) 存取帳戶
(D) 參觀設施

52. 女子說她上個月做了什麼事？
(A) 她搬到另一個城市。
(B) 她開始做新工作。
(C) 她取得了證書。
(D) 她開始在線上學習。

53-55. 🎧 澳洲男子／美國女子
Questions 53-55 refer to the following conversation.

> **M** [53]Demand for our software programs is still growing, Danielle. We need to expand our team of programmers, but we're having a lot of problems filling the positions.
>
> **W** [54]You know, if we want to remain competitive, we need to increase the annual salary we offer to the staff. That would help to retain good workers as well as attract the top talent for new workers.
>
> **M** That sounds like a good idea, but would our current situation support that change?
>
> **W** I believe so, since our sales have been strong. [55]I'll look over our budget categories to see what's possible.

男 Danielle，[53]市場對我們軟體的需求不斷增長。我們需要擴大程式設計師團隊，但在填補職位方面碰到很多問題。
女 [54]我跟你說，若我們想保持競爭力，需提高員工的年薪。這將有助於留住優秀員工，並吸引頂尖人才成為新員工。
男 聽起來是個好主意，但我們目前的狀況能支持此改變嗎？
女 因為我們的銷量一直很不錯，所以我相信可以。[55]我先檢查一下我們的預算類別，查看可能性。

單字 demand 需求　expand 擴大　competitive 有競爭力的
annual salary 年薪　retain 維持、保持
talent 有天賦的人、才能　look over 檢查、瀏覽
budget 預算

53. 說話者最有可能從事何種行業？
(A) 廣告
(B) 科技
(C) 能源
(D) 藥品

54. 說話者正在討論哪些變化？
(A) 搬遷至其他地點
(B) 購買機械設備
(C) 延長營業時間
(D) 提高員工薪資

55. 女子提議做什麼事？
(A) 準備優惠品項
(B) 聯絡專家
(C) 查看財務數據
(D) 收集員工意見

56-58. 🎧 美國男子／英國女子

Questions 56-58 refer to the following conversation.

> **M** Hi, I'm calling because I just got my bill for September and there's an issue. ⁵⁶I've been charged twice my normal amount.
>
> **W** I'm sorry about that, sir. ⁵⁷Our Internet company strives to ensure accuracy. Could you please tell me your account number?
>
> **M** Yes, it's 47801. ⁵⁸I moved to a new home on the fifteenth of last month, and it looks like I've been charged the full fee at both places.
>
> **W** I see. Please wait while I look into this further.

男　你好，我剛收到九月份的繳款通知單，且發現有點問題，所以打電話過來。⁵⁶我被收取了正常金額的兩倍。

女　先生，我很抱歉。⁵⁷我們的網路公司會努力確保準確性。能告訴我您的帳號嗎？

男　好的，是47801。⁵⁸我上個月15日搬到新家，看來是向我收取了兩個地方的全額費用。

女　我明白了。請稍等，我會進一步調查此事。

單字 bill 帳單、請款單　charge 收費、索取　ensure 確保、保證　accuracy 準確度　account 帳戶、帳號

56. 男子打電話詢問什麼問題？
(A) 他忘了密碼。
(B) 他提供了一些錯誤資訊。
(C) 他弄丟了近期的帳單。
(D) 他被多收取了費用。

57. 女子在哪裡工作？
(A) 運輸公司
(B) 搬家公司
(C) 網路服務供應商
(D) 會計師事務所

58. 男子上個月做了什麼事？
(A) 他搬到了新住址。
(B) 他升級了服務組合方案。
(C) 他創辦了自己的企業。
(D) 他造訪了女子的公司。

59-61. 🎧 英國女子／美國男子

Questions 59-61 refer to the following conversation.

> **W** Good morning, Andrew. ⁵⁹ ⁶⁰I want to talk to you about the software developer position that my team is currently interviewing candidates for.
>
> **M** Sure. What's up?
>
> **W** So far, none of the applicants we've seen have had sufficient experience in web development. I think we need to expand the applicant pool. Can HR increase the salary listed in the job posting?
>
> **M** I'll need to discuss it with my team members. How soon do you need a response?
>
> **W** Well, the project manager has already moved up our deadline.
>
> **M** Understood. I'll e-mail you as soon as a decision is reached.

女　早安，Andrew。⁵⁹ ⁶⁰我想和你談談我的團隊目前正在面試的軟體開發人員職位。

男　當然可以，怎麼了？

女　截至目前為止，我們所見過的應徵者都沒有足夠的網頁開發經驗。我認為我們需要擴增應徵者的人選。人資部可以調高該職缺列出的薪資嗎？

男　我需要和我的團隊成員討論一下。我需要何時回覆你？

女　嗯，專案經理已經提前了最後期限。

男　我明白了。有結論後，我就立刻發郵件通知你。

單字 currently 現在、目前　so far 截至目前為止　applicant 應徵者　sufficient 充足的　expand 擴大、增加　pool 人才庫、水池　job posting 徵人啟示　move up 提前　reach a decision 做出決定

59. 說話者正在討論什麼？
(A) 職缺
(B) 產品上市
(C) 公司搬遷
(D) 年度活動

60. 女子最有可能在哪個部門工作？
(A) 財務
(B) 行銷
(C) 資訊科技
(D) 營運管理

61. 女子為何會說：「專案經理已經提前了最後期限」？
(A) 表示急迫性
(B) 表達感謝
(C) 提出折衷方案
(D) 表達困惑

105

62-64. 🎧 美國女子／澳洲男子

Questions 62-64 refer to the following conversation and diagram.

> W Phoenix Appliances. How can I help you?
>
> M Hi, [62]last week I ordered a toaster oven for the break room at my law firm ... uh ... model D-670. We already have an issue. It was order 49522.
>
> W All right. What seems to be the problem?
>
> M When I was using it this morning, [63]the door panel suddenly cracked.
>
> W I'm sorry for the inconvenience. Unfortunately, that model is currently out of stock, but it can be repaired at one of our centers. The e-mail address we have on file is tedfletcher@wagner.com. Is that the best way to reach you?
>
> M Yes, it is.
>
> W Okay. [64]I'll e-mail you the addresses of the repair centers nearest to you.

女　Phoenix電器行您好，請問有什麼需要幫忙的嗎？
男　你好，[62]我上週訂購了一台電烤箱，放在我的律師事務所休息室使用。呃… 型號是D-670。已經出現問題了，訂單號碼是49522。
女　好的，請問問題出在哪呢？
男　我今天早上使用時，[63]烤箱門板突然裂開了。
女　很抱歉造成您的不便。遺憾的是，該型號目前缺貨，但可以在我們的中心進行維修。我們已存檔的電子郵件地址是tedfletcher@wagner.com。這是聯絡您的最佳方式嗎？
男　是的。
女　好的。[64]我會用電子郵件發送離您最近的維修中心地址。

單字 appliances 家電　break room 休息室
panel 面板、板子　crack 裂開　inconvenience 不便
out of stock 缺貨　reach 聯絡

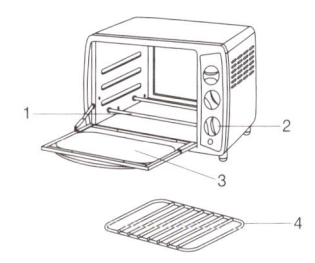

62. 男人在哪裡工作？
(A) 研究機構
(B) 餐廳
(C) 百貨公司
(D) 律師事務所

63. 請查看圖表。哪一部分受損了？
(A) 第一部分
(B) 第二部分
(C) 第三部分
(D) 第四部分

64. 女子接下來可能會做什麼？
(A) 尋找產品使用手冊
(B) 訂購替換零件
(C) 發送地點清單
(D) 檢查某商品是否有貨

65-67. 🎧 美國女子／澳洲男子

Questions 65-67 refer to the following conversation and catalog.

> W [65]I've just spoken to a representative from Tahoka Manufacturing. They plan to begin sending our shipments on the first Monday of every month instead of every Friday.
>
> M When does that start?
>
> W Next month. We'd have to place larger orders and figure out where to store the items.
>
> M I think it's still worth buying their wool rugs for our shop. Their products are excellent.
>
> W I agree. [66]I like that they only use high-quality wool. And didn't they just release some new designs?
>
> M Yes. I've got the new catalog here. [67]I like this wavy design. How about getting that?
>
> W [67]Sure. It's nice that it's available in both blue and gray.

女　[65]我剛和Tahoka製造公司的負責人談過了。他們打算在每個月的第一個星期一開始發貨，而非每個星期五。
男　從什麼時候開始？
女　下個月。除了訂購更多商品之外，我們還需設想哪裡可以存放物品。
男　我還是覺得購買他們公司的羊毛地毯很值得。他們的產品很出色。
女　我也這麼認為。[66]我喜歡他們只使用高品質的羊毛。他們不久前不是推出了一些新設計嗎？
男　對。我這裡有新目錄。[67]我喜歡這種波浪紋的設計。要不要買這個？
女　[67]當然好。有藍色和灰色兩種顏色可供選擇，這一點很好。

單字 representative 負責人　shipment 運送的貨物
place an order 下訂單　figure out 想出　store 存放、保管
item 物品　rug 地毯、毯子　release 推出　wavy 波浪的

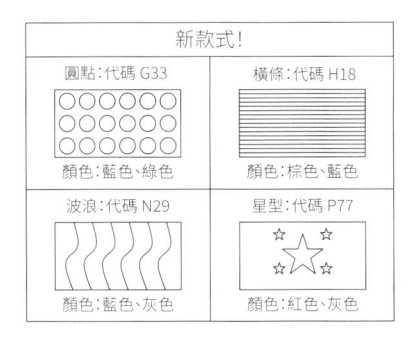

新款式！	
圓點：代碼 G33 顏色：藍色、綠色	橫條：代碼 H18 顏色：棕色、藍色
波浪：代碼 N29 顏色：藍色、灰色	星型：代碼 P77 顏色：紅色、灰色

65. Tahoka製造公司將更改什麼？
(A) 出貨時間
(B) 保固期
(C) 辦公地點
(D) 倉儲費

66. 女子喜歡Tahoka製造公司的哪一點？
(A) 交貨速度
(B) 圖案的選擇眾多
(C) 員工友善
(D) 材料品質

67. 請查看圖表。說話者同意訂購哪種設計？
(A) G33
(B) H18
(C) N29
(D) P77

68-70. 🎧 美國男子／英國女子
Questions 68-70 refer to the following conversation and schedule.

> M [68]Did you hear about Victor's promotion?
>
> W Yes, I'm glad he was offered the team leader role. He'll do a great job.
>
> M I agree. [68]I'd like to have a small party this Friday to celebrate.
>
> W You know, Libby from HR just told me that she's participating in a dance show this Friday.
>
> M Oh, really? Where's that?
>
> W It's at the Murphy Center. Let's see … here's the schedule on the website. [69]Her group goes on at 7:30.
>
> M Hmm … [70]but it costs twenty-five dollars per person to get in. That's quite a lot.
>
> W We might be able to use some company funds, since it'll be a team-building event.

男　[68]你有聽說Victor升遷的消息嗎？
女　有，我很高興他被任命為團隊的領導者。他會做得很好。
男　我同意。[68]我想在本週五開個小型派對慶祝。
女　我跟你說，人資部的Libby剛告訴我她週五要參加一場舞蹈表演。
男　喔，真的嗎？在哪裡？
女　在Murphy中心。我看一下… 網站上有時間表。[69]她所屬的團體在7點30分登場。
男　嗯… [70]不過每個人要花25美元才能進去。費用有點高。
女　這次活動是為凝聚團隊關係，也許我們可以動用一些公司的資金。

單字 promotion 升遷　HR 人資部　(= human resources)
cost 花費　fund 資金　team building 團隊凝聚

節目表	
7:00 P.M.	探戈饗宴
7:30 P.M.	Mariana音樂
8:00 P.M.	BC舞蹈團
8:30 P.M.	商人團

68. 男子為何想開派對？
(A) 團隊完成了專案。
(B) 有位同事升遷。
(C) 公司獲得獎項提名。
(D) 超越銷售目標。

69. 請查看圖表。Libby是哪個團體的成員？
(A) 探戈饗宴
(B) Mariana音樂
(C) BC舞蹈團
(D) 商人團

70. 男子提到什麼問題？
(A) 場地位在偏遠地區。
(B) 無法提供交通服務。
(C) 入場費用高昂。
(D) 部分團隊成員將會缺席。

71-73. 🎧 美國男子
Questions 71-73 refer to the following advertisement.

> M Whether you're planning a wedding reception, a corporate function, or anything in between, it can be hard to find the perfect venue. At King's Convention Center, we're here to help. [71]Equipped with the latest technology and luxury furniture, our site is sure to satisfy all of your attendees. [72]King's Convention Center is famous for having a unique building design, featuring high ceilings and stained glass windows that make you feel like you're in a royal court. [73]For reservations, simply go to our website. We hope to see you soon!

男　無論您正在籌畫婚宴、企業活動，或是介於兩者之間的任

107

何活動，找到完美的場地可能是件難事。在國王會議中心，我們隨時為您提供協助。⁷¹**我們的場地配有最新技術和豪華傢俱，一定能讓所有與會者滿意。**⁷²**國王會議中心以獨特的建築設計聞名，**設有挑高天花板和彩色玻璃窗，讓您彷彿置身於皇家宮廷。⁷³**如需預約，請造訪我們的網站。**希望不久後就能見到您！

單字 wedding reception 婚宴　corporate 公司的
function 活動、集會　in between 之間　venue 場地
equip 具備　attendee 與會者　feature 以⋯為特色
ceiling 天花板　royal court 皇家宮廷　simply 僅僅、只

71. 正在宣傳什麼類型的業務？
(A) 外燴餐飲服務
(B) 活動空間
(C) 出租房屋
(D) 電影院

72. 說話者表示該企業最出名的是什麼？
(A) 才華洋溢的員工
(B) 地理位置便利
(C) 歷史悠久
(D) 獨創的建築風格

73. 聽者可以在網站上做什麼事？
(A) 查看圖片
(B) 閱讀評論
(C) 尋找折扣碼
(D) 預約

74-76. 🎧 澳洲男子
Questions 74-76 refer to the following podcast.

> M　Welcome back to the Entrepreneurial Ventures podcast. ⁷⁴Today, my topic is digital self-promotion. When is the right time to start a new viral marketing campaign, and how can you do so effectively in the modern world? To answer these questions and more, I'll be introducing a special guest: Amara Dambe. The founder of the famous tech start-up, Financing Together, ⁷⁵Ms. Dambe is known for her ability to get into the mentalities of consumers when they're using virtual spaces. I think you'll enjoy this episode. But before getting started, ⁷⁶I'm going to briefly talk about a new service that I'm offering for a small monthly fee.

男　歡迎回到創業投資網路廣播。⁷⁴**我今天的主題是數位自我行銷。**什麼時候是適合開始新廣泛行銷活動的時機？以及在現代世界中如何有效地做到這一點？為了回答這些問題，我將介紹一位特別來賓：Amara Dambe。Dambe女士為知名科技新創公司，一起理財的創辦人，⁷⁵**她以能深入了解消費者在使用虛擬空間時的思考方式而聞名。**我想大家會喜歡這集節目。但在開始前，⁷⁶**我想簡單介紹一項由我提供，**只需支付小額月費即可享有的新服務。

單字 promotion 宣傳　founder 創辦人　start-up 新創公司
get into 進入　mentality 心態、思考方式
virtual space 虛擬空間　episode 集數
briefly 簡短地、簡略地

74. 本集的網路廣播主題為何？
(A) 網路廣告行銷
(B) 電腦程式設計
(C) 創業
(D) 拓展海外市場

75. 說話者提到Dambe女士擅長什麼？
(A) 解決技術問題
(B) 獲取資金
(C) 了解消費者
(D) 與供應商談判

76. 說話者接下來會討論什麼？
(A) 訂閱服務
(B) 研究項目
(C) 聽眾提問
(D) 新聞報導

77-79. 🎧 美國女子
Questions 77-79 refer to the following excerpt from a meeting.

> W　⁷⁷Next Monday, we'll have the first in a series of seminars about reducing stress in the workplace. Our first guest lecturer will help you learn to use meditative breathing exercises to calm your body and mind. ⁷⁸I was inspired to launch this series when I read a recent news story about the effects of physical and mental health on employee productivity. As part of the initiative, we've also started installing mood-enhancing lighting throughout the building. ⁷⁹I'm distributing a pamphlet that talks about the scientific reason for the change.

女　⁷⁷**下週一，我們將舉行一系列有關減少職場壓力研討會中的首場。**我們的第一位客座講師將幫助各位，學會使用冥想呼吸練習來平靜身心。⁷⁸**我發起此系列的靈感，來自於我最近讀到一篇關於身心健康對員工生產力影響的新聞報導。**作為該計畫的一部分，我們還開始在整棟大樓內安裝改善情緒的照明設施。⁷⁹**我會發放一本小冊子，當中有講述關於這項變化的科學原因。**

單字 workplace 職場　lecturer 講師、講者
meditative 冥想的　breathing 呼吸　inspire 賦予靈感
launch 發起　productivity 生產力　initiative 計畫
enhance 改善　distribute 發放、分發

77. 下週一會發生什麼事？
(A) 將會有場演講。
(B) 將會購買產品。
(C) 將開設新分店。
(D) 將重新設計辦公空間。

78. 賦予說話者靈感的是什麼？
(A) 廣告
(B) 知名書籍
(C) 員工建議
(D) 媒體報導

79. 聽者如何了解新照明設施的好處？
(A) 透過閱讀電子郵件
(B) 透過造訪網站
(C) 透過查看講義
(D) 透過觀看影片

80-82. 🎧英國女子
Questions 80-82 refer to the following recorded message.

> W Good afternoon. [80]You've reached the Blandensville County Power Company. Please note that a telephone pole was recently knocked down near McArthur Avenue as a result of a traffic accident. A team of responders is on site. We thank you for your patience. [82]If you'd like to receive updates about the electric grid in your area, press 1 to sign up for our automatic texting service.

女　午安。[80]您已接通至Blandensville郡電力公司。請注意，最近McArthur大道附近有根電線桿因交通事故而倒塌。現場有一組緊急搶修人員。感謝您的耐心等候。[82]如果您想收到有關您所在地區電力網的最新消息，請按 1 註冊我們的簡訊自動發送服務。

單字 reach 聯絡　note 留意　telephone pole 電線桿
knock down 倒塌　as a result of 由於
responder 現場應急人員　update 最新消息
electric grid 電力網　sign up for 註冊…　text 傳送簡訊

80. 聽者打電話給什麼類型的公司？
(A) 電纜供應商
(B) 顧問公司
(C) 水電公司
(D) 汽車製造商

81. 說話者說：「感謝您的耐心等候」，表示了什麼？
(A) 緊急搶修人員未經訓練。
(B) 公司即將結束營業。
(C) 有很多人在抱怨。
(D) 尚未完成維修工作。

82. 聽者如何收到最新消息？
(A) 接收自動發送的電子郵件
(B) 稍後回電
(C) 接收簡訊
(D) 查看網站

83-85. 🎧美國女子
Questions 83-85 refer to the following excerpt from a meeting.

> W The City Council will now discuss the issue of street maintenance. [83]A group of citizens submitted a petition to repair and repave a number of the town's streets. In particular, Main Street has been reported as a dangerous area due to the presence of potholes in various locations. While the motion has been approved, [84]Chairperson John Daly has raised a concern that the requested work will be obtrusively loud for Main Street residents. [85]To compensate these residents, the city will reimburse up to a one week stay at the nearby Comfort Plus Inn for those who live within a 50-meter radius of the work site.

女　市議會現在要討論街道維護問題。[83]有一些市民繳交了請願書，要求修復和重新鋪設多處鎮上的街道。尤其是主街道被報告為危險區域，因為地上有多處坑洞。雖然該提議已獲得批准，但[84]議長John Daly擔心，該工程將會產生噪音，影響主街道的居民。[85]為補償這些居民，該市將為住在工程區半徑50公尺範圍內的居民，提供無償入住附近的 Comfort Plus旅社一週。

單字 submit 繳交　petition 請願書、陳情書、申請書
in particular 尤其是　pothole 道路上的坑洞　motion 提議
obtrusively 顯著地、引人注目地　radius 半徑

83. 為何有市民提出投訴？
(A) 未提供路邊停車位。
(B) 道路有損壞。
(C) 不常進行街道清潔。
(D) 停車場太貴。

84. John Daly擔心什麼事？
(A) 高額稅收
(B) 環境破壞
(C) 車流量增加
(D) 施工噪音

85. 某些居民會得到什麼？
(A) 停車證
(B) 飯店住宿費
(C) 活動門票
(D) 交通接送服務

109

86-88. 🎧 美國男子

Questions 86-88 refer to the following speech.

> M　Hi! [86]Welcome to today's seminar about the future of publishers in our increasingly paperless society. I'm Jean Couturier, and I've been working in the publishing industry for over thirty years. [87]Before I get started, I want to thank those of you who submitted anonymous inquiries through my website. Those questions helped me design my slides for today's presentation. [88]I also want to express my gratitude for my assistant, Melanie Grichuk, who worked hard to make this event happen. There's Melanie in the back corner—let's give her a round of applause.

男　大家好！[86]歡迎來參加今天的研討會，探討在日益無紙化的社會中，出版社的未來。我是Jean Couturier，我在出版業工作超過三十年。[87]在開始之前，我想感謝那些透過我的網站繳交匿名提問的人。這些問題幫助我設計了今天的簡報投影片。[88]我還想感謝我的助理Melanie Grichuk，她為促成本次活動付出很多努力。Melanie坐在後面的角落—讓我們給她熱烈的掌聲。

單字 publisher 出版社　increasingly 日益地、增加地　submit 繳交、提交　anonymous 匿名的　inquiry 提問、詢問　presentation 簡報　gratitude 感謝　assistant 助理　give a round of applause 鼓掌

86. 研討會的主題為何？
(A) 製造
(B) 運送
(C) 出版
(D) 新聞

87. 為何說話者要感謝某些聽眾？
(A) 他們提出了問題。
(B) 他們分享了自身經驗。
(C) 他們參加過以前的講座。
(D) 他們對投影片提出意見回饋。

88. 為何說話者要提及會場的後方？
(A) 那裡有供應茶點。
(B) 有員工坐在那裡。
(C) 附有資訊的資料放在那裡。
(D) 那裡正在銷售書籍。

89-91. 🎧 英國女子

Questions 89-91 refer to the following telephone message.

> W　Hi, [89]Matteo. I hope your university talk goes well tonight. Everything's fine here at Vezia Bistro while you're away, but I want to follow up on the instructions you left behind. I know you wanted to offer chicken marsala as our weekly special, but some of the supplies for that dish are running low. Fettuccini alfredo has always been a hit with our regulars. Also, I've got good news. [91]An influential blogger visited the restaurant last night and wrote up some major praise for us on his site this morning.

女　嗨，[89]Matteo。祝你今晚在大學的演講能順利進行。你不在的期間，Vezia餐酒館的一切都很好，但我想對你留下的指示進行後續報告。我知道你想將瑪薩拉香料雞作為我們的每週特色料理，但這道菜中使用的部分材料已經所剩無幾了。義式奶油白醬寬麵一直深受我們常客的喜愛。我還有個好消息。[91]昨晚有位具影響力的部落客來訪餐廳，今天早上他在自己的網站上寫下對我們餐廳的讚譽。

單字 follow up on 採取後續行動、跟進　instruction 指示　leave behind 留下　supplies 備料、庫存　run low 不足、快用完　regular 常客

89. 為何Matteo不在他的公司？
(A) 他正在與供應商見面。
(B) 他正在演講。
(C) 他正在參加工作面試。
(D) 他正在看房地產。

90. 為何說話者會說：「義式奶油白醬寬麵一直深受我們常客的喜愛」？
(A) 提出建議
(B) 給予讚美
(C) 展示問題所在
(D) 慶祝成果

91. 說話者分享什麼有關餐廳的好消息？
(A) 榮獲年度獎項。
(B) 大批顧客湧入。
(C) 在網路上受到關注。
(D) 出現在電視節目中。

92-94. 🎧 澳洲男子

Questions 92-94 refer to the following excerpt from a meeting.

> M Hello everyone. ⁹²We've got a busy week ahead, with the new Delillo models of beds and shelving units arriving soon, and all of our dining sets on sale. There should be plenty of customers streaming in. Now, with Enrico having moved on to another company, we're short-staffed until we find his replacement. But don't worry: I have experience in sales, even though most of you haven't seen it. I also need to mention that the back room is starting to get disorganized. ⁹⁴I want everyone to spend a few minutes straightening it after lunch today.

男 大家好。⁹²我們將迎來忙碌的一週，因為新款的Delillo床鋪和床架組即將到貨，還有我們所有的餐桌椅組都在打折促銷。肯定會有大量顧客湧入。現在由於Enrico跳槽到別間公司，在找到他的繼任者前，我們會人手不足。但別擔心：儘管你們大多數人沒見識過，但⁹³我也有銷售經驗。我還想提出，後面的房間開始變得有點雜亂。⁹⁴我希望大家在今天午餐後，抽出幾分鐘時間整理一下。

單字 shelving unit 層架　dining set 餐桌椅組
stream in 湧入　short-staffed 人手不足的
replacement 繼任者、替代者
disorganized 雜亂的、無秩序的　straighten 整頓、清理

92. 說話者最有可能從事何種類型的工作？
(A) 五金行
(B) 建築公司
(C) 傢俱店
(D) 送貨服務

93. 說話者說：「我也有銷售經驗」，意味著什麼？
(A) 他會指導員工。
(B) 他會接手一些輪班工作。
(C) 他很快就會面試應徵者。
(D) 他會增加班費。

94. 說話者希望聽者做什麼事？
(A) 重新調整店面佈局
(B) 清潔某個區域
(C) 舉辦午餐會
(D) 策劃招募活動

95-97. 🎧 美國男子

Questions 95-97 refer to the following telephone message and map.

> M Hi, my name is Phil, ⁹⁵and I'm supposed to pick you up in front of Old House Theater by the box office in a few minutes. The problem is, there's a major accident on Wright Avenue. ⁹⁶I'm wondering if you're willing to go out the back exit of the theater and meet me there instead so we can avoid a major delay. ⁹⁷All you need to do is text "YES" to this number to agree to the change.

男 你好，我叫Phil，⁹⁵原本預計幾分鐘後我會在Old House劇院的售票處旁接你上車。但問題是，Wright大道上發生了一起重大車禍。⁹⁶我想知道你是否願意從劇院後門出來與我碰面，如此可避免時間上耽擱過久。⁹⁷若你同意此項更動，只要發送文字簡訊「是」至該號碼即可。

單字 be supposed to do 預計做⋯　pick up（開車）接送
box office 售票處

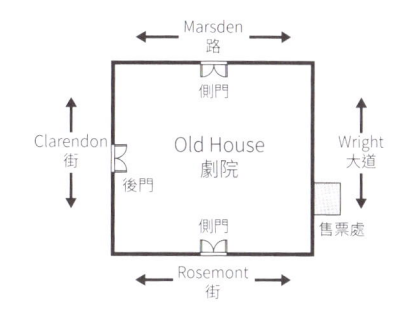

```
            Marsden
              路
         ┌─────────┐
Clarendon│  側門   │ Wright
   街    │ Old House│  大道
         │  劇院   │
         │  後門   │ 售票處
         └─────────┘
            側門
           Rosemont
              街
```

95. 說話者最有可能是誰？
(A) 公車司機
(B) 導遊
(C) 共乘車輛司機
(D) 列車長

96. 請查看圖表。說話者希望在哪裡碰面？
(A) 在Clarendon街
(B) 在Wright大道
(C) 在Rosemont街
(D) 在Marsden路

97. 聽者如何確定變更事項？
(A) 打電話至公司
(B) 發送簡訊
(C) 使用應用程式
(D) 站在外面

98-100. 🎧 美國女子

Questions 98-100 refer to the following talk and schedule.

> W ⁹⁸Greetings, people of Innersville, and thanks for coming out to the opening of our brand-new bus station in the heart of downtown. This facility will drastically improve travel conditions throughout the region. ⁹⁹Right now, there are limited resources in terms of public transportation in the area. To compensate, these private bus lines offer comfortable rides at very affordable prices. We are excited to welcome Kiwi Bird Bus Travel and Clockwork Bus Company to the area for the first time. ¹⁰⁰The first departure, from Clockwork Bus Company, leaves in 30 minutes, so check the schedule and happy travels!

女 ⁹⁸Innersville的居民們你們好，感謝各位前來參加我們位於市中心的全新巴士站開幕式。該設施將大大改善整個地區的交通狀況。⁹⁹目前該地區在大眾交通運輸方面的資源有限。為彌補此點，這些私人巴士路線會以非常實惠的價格，提供舒適的乘車體驗。我們很高興歡迎首次來到該地區的Kiwi Bird巴士之旅和Clockwork巴士公司。¹⁰⁰第一班車將由Clockwork巴士公司負責，預計於30分鐘後發車，請確認時刻表，祝各位旅途愉快！

單字 greetings 問候　brand-new 最新的
in the heart of 在…中心　downtown 市中心、市區
drastically 大幅地　limited 有限的　in terms of 在…的方面
public transportation 大眾交通運輸
affordable 經濟實惠的

Innersville 巴士站	
總站A	Fulton巴士線
總站B	Kiwi Bird巴士之旅
總站C	Speedy Friends巴士
總站D	Clockworkss巴士公司

98. 該段獨白針對的聽者是誰？
(A) 旅行社員工
(B) 員工
(C) 居民
(D) 投資者

99. 根據說話者所述，為何需要該設施？
(A) 政府希望減少汽車車流量。
(B) 舊巴士站的狀況不佳。
(C) 該城鎮缺乏大眾交通運輸設施。
(D) 當地機場最近關閉了。

100. 請查看圖表。首班車會從哪個巴士站出發？
(A) 總站A
(B) 總站B
(C) 總站C
(D) 總站D

101. (A)
中譯 該顧問公司打算在下週為新進員工舉辦培訓課程。
(A) 集會、會議　(B) 方法　(C) 接近、方法　(D) 路、方式
解說 training session （培訓課程）、informational session （說明會） 皆為常見用法，因此答案要選 (A) session。
單字 intend 打算、意圖　hold 舉辦、召開

102. (D)
中譯 來自歐洲的訂單應該會在明天晚上前抵達。
(A) 相當地　(B) 嚴格地　(C) 準確地　(D) 大概
單字 no later than 不遲於…

103. (C)
中譯 Patterson女士向她的主管表達她想要參加在達拉斯的行銷研討會。
(A) 詢問　(B) 繳交　(C) 表達　(D) 提醒
單字 attend 參加　supervisor 主管、上司

104. (B)
中譯 Sylvester熟食店嚴選的肉類比該城市其他商店都要好。
解說 空格置於補語位置上，且後方連接 than，因此答案要選形容詞的比較級 (B) greater。
單字 selection 精選品項

105. (C)
中譯 我們很遺憾地宣布Carpenter先生辭去研發部的職務。
解說 空格前方為限定詞，因此答案要選名詞 (C) resignation，受到所有格的修飾。
單字 regret 感到遺憾、懊悔　resign 辭職
R&D Department 研發部

106. (D)
中譯 物流會議上幾乎每位參加者都與該行業有直接關聯。
解說 空格後方連接單數名詞，因此答案要選可修飾單數名詞的 (D) every。almost 為副詞，不能修飾名詞。all 和 those 用來修飾複數名詞，也不適當。
單字 nearly 幾乎　attendee 參加者　logistics 物流
conference 會議、學會　directly 直接地
be involved in 與…有關　industry 行業、產業

107. (B)
中譯 與客戶的所有交易均以紙本和電子方式紀錄。
解說 空格前方為 be 動詞，後方未連接受詞，而是連接介系詞片語，因此答案要選過去分詞 (B) recorded，與 be 動詞組合成

被動語態。

單字 transaction 交易　client 客戶　record 記錄
electronically 以電子方式、用電腦

108. (A)
中譯 Anderson先生安排了一場員工會議，目的是為討論本月的預算。
(A) 目的 (B) 觀點、視野 (C) 意見 (D) 約定

解說 本題使用片語 for the purpose of（目的為…），因此答案要選 (A) purpose。

單字 schedule 安排　staff 員工
for the purpose 目的為、為了…　budget 預算

109. (A)
中譯 研討會的與會者一到達，就會分組進行角色扮演活動。

解說 空格置於該句話的主詞位置上，因此答案要選人稱代名詞主格 (A) they。

單字 divide 分開、劃分　activity 活動

110. (C)
中譯 因為新法規剛頒布，政府必須進行檢驗。
(A) 然而 (B) 儘管 (C) 因為 (D) 一…就

解說 選項包含連接詞、介系詞和副詞。空格後方連接結構完整的子句，表示空格應填入連接詞，所以可先刪去連接副詞 (A) 和介系詞 (B)。根據文意，主要子句和副詞子句屬於因果關係，因此答案要選 (C) because。

單字 government 政府　inspection 檢驗、調查
conduct 進行（特定活動）　regulation 規定　enact 頒布

111. (D)
中譯 新法規使外國人對金融產業的投資增加。
(A) 供應 (B) 方法 (C) 擁有、所有物 (D) 投資

單字 result in 導致　financial 金融的

112. (B)
中譯 眾所周知，最近有位新上任的經理Jackson先生偏好上餐廳的晚班。

解說 空格置於 that 子句中的動詞位置上，that 子句的主詞 Mr. Jackson 為單數名詞，因此答案要選單數動詞 (B) prefers。因空格後方連接不定詞當作受詞，所以被動語態的 (C) 和 (D) 皆不適當。

單字 prefer 喜歡、偏好　shift 輪班工作

113. (D)
中譯 Chamberlain女士前往馬德里出差，大約一週不在。
(A) 在…範圍內 (B) 在 (C) 期間 (D) 期間

解說 空格後方連接一段時間 one week，因此答案要選介系詞 (D) for。介系詞 for 可置於數字前方，而 during 則要置於特定期間前，例如：during the winter（冬季期間）。

單字 absent 缺勤的　roughly 大約、幾乎

on business 出差

114. (A)
中譯 工程師必須確定管道中裂縫的確切位置。

解說 空格前方為定冠詞和形容詞 precise，表示空格應填入名詞，因此答案要選 (A) location。

單字 determine 確定、弄清楚　precise 確切的
location 位置、地點　locate 確定地點　crack 裂縫

115. (C)
中譯 當董事會問及新產品時，Lopez女士仔細地進行描述。
(A) 極其、非常 (B) 確實地 (C) 仔細地、考慮周到地 (D) 最終地

單字 describe 描述　board of directors 董事會

116. (B)
中譯 工作合約在下個月到期的兼職人員，應於本週四前與Matisse女士交談。

解說 該句話的主詞為 Those part-timers、動詞為 should speak，空格至 month 為形容詞子句，用來修飾主詞。先行詞 part-timers 指人物，所以可先刪去指事物的 (A) which 和副詞 (C) when。考量先行詞 part-timers 和 work contracts 的關係，答案要選關係代名詞所有格 (B) whose。

單字 part-timer 兼職人員、工讀生　contract 合約（書）
expire 到期

117. (A)
中譯 調到國外分公司的高階主管薪資較高，但要負責自己的住處費用。
(A) 但是 (B) 自從、因為 (C) 也、同樣地 (D) 為了

解說 該句話的主詞為 Executives、動詞為 receive 和 are，who transfer to foreign branches 為形容詞子句，用來修飾主詞。空格應填入對等連接詞，連接空格前後的動詞，因此答案要選 (A)。

單字 executive 高階主管、管理人員　transfer 調動、移動
branch 分公司、分店　housing 住宅

118. (C)
中譯 每個螺栓都必須牢牢拴緊，以確保貨架牢固。

解說 空格置於動詞後方，且後方連接不定詞，表示空格應填入副詞，修飾前方動詞，因此答案為 (C) tightly。

單字 attach 貼上、固定　tightly 緊緊地、牢固地
ensure 確保、保障　shelf 貨架

119. (A)
中譯 未經地方當局許可，不得從船上卸下貨物。
(A) 沒有 (B) 在…之間 (C) 而不是 (D) 除外

單字 cargo 貨物　unload 卸下　permission 許可
authorities 當局

113

120. (B)
中譯 由於目前無法取得資金，該座橋僅修建了部分。
解說 空格置於 be 動詞 is 和過去分詞 constructed 組合而成的被動語態之間，因此答案要選副詞 (B) partially。
單字 since 由於　funding 資金　currently 目前、現在
available 可取得、可利用的

121. (D)
中譯 根據銷售團隊的最新消息，新化妝品系列的銷售情況優於預期。
(A) 因為　(B) 因此　(C) 儘管　(D) 根據
解說 空格後方連接名詞片語，表示空格適合填入介系詞。(C) 和 (D) 皆為介系詞，而根據文意，答案要選 (D) According to。
單字 sales 銷售的　cosmetics 化妝品　line（商品的）系列
anticipate 預期、期待

122. (B)
中譯 過去四個月，電腦產業的國內就業人數一直在增加。
解說 空格前方為形容詞、後方連接介系詞片語，表示空格應填入名詞，受到前方形容詞的修飾，所以可先刪去 (A)。其餘選項 (B)、(C)、(D) 皆為名詞，而根據文意，最適合填入空格的是 (B) employment。
單字 domestic 國內的　employment 就業、僱用

123. (C)
中譯 管理層考慮正式請求後，最終同意為員工提供額外的有薪假。
解說 空格置於主詞 management 和動詞 agreed 之間，表示空格應填入副詞，修飾後方的動詞，因此答案要選 (C) eventually。
單字 consider 考慮　formal 正式的、官方的
management 管理層　provide 提供、給予
extra 額外的、外加的　paid vacation 有薪假

124. (C)
中譯 業界專家認為由於供應鏈發生問題，未來幾個月的出口將會減少。
解說 空格置於名詞子句的動詞位置上，子句中的主詞為 exports。空格後方為副詞片語 in the coming months，表示時態為未來式，因此答案要選 (C) will decline。
單字 expert 專家　export 出口　decline 減少
in the coming months 未來幾個月　due to 由於
issue 問題　supply chain 供應鏈

125. (A)
中譯 當地農民報告，儘管夏季天氣相對涼爽，作物收穫量卻出人意料地高。
(A) 出乎意料地　(B) 極重要地　(C) 每年　(D) 逐漸
單字 report 報告　crop 作物　yield 收穫量
relatively 相對地、比較地

126. (D)
中譯 儘管市場調查顯示消費者對該產品懷有熱忱，但 Gladden 科技公司還是停止了生產。
(A) 印象深刻的　(B) 幻想的　(C) 果斷的　(D) 熱情的
解說 (A) impressed 搭配的介系詞為 with 或 by。
單字 indicate 指出、顯示　cease 停止

127. (A)
中譯 Skylar 電子公司計畫在當地製造更多電腦，但會把它們分銷至歐洲國家。
解說 該句話以對等連接詞 yet，連接 to manufacture 和空格，因此答案要選省略 to 的不定詞 (A) distribute。
單字 manufacture 製造、生產　locally 在當地
yet 但是　distribute 分銷、流通

128. (D)
中譯 演場會觀眾很滿意這兩支樂團的表演。
(A) 維持　(B) 預期　(C) 欽佩的　(D) 滿意的
單字 attendee 觀眾、參加者　performance 表演

129. (B)
中譯 為了整理維護申請表，Gibson 先生建立了一個指定的資料夾來儲存文件。
解說 空格前方為不定冠詞、後方連接名詞，表示空格應填入適當的形容詞，修飾後方名詞。designated 和 designating 為分詞，皆可扮演形容詞的角色，而根據文意，表達「（被人）指定的資料夾」較為適當，因此答案要選 (B) designated。
單字 organize 整理　maintenance 維護　form 表格
designated 指定的　store 儲存、保管

130. (A)
中譯 當 Sulla 女士收到每個月的電費帳單時，她注意到她的用電量有比上個月減少。
(A) 注意到　(B) 瞥見　(C) 出現　(D) 重複
單字 electric bill 電費帳單　usage 用量、使用
decline 減少　previous 先前的

131-134 公告

致所有顧客，

我們很遺憾通知您，Marigold 烘焙坊的 Kensington 分店將於 3 月 31 日關閉。我們將無法再向該分店的顧客提供糕點、蛋糕和其他產品。烘焙坊所在的大樓正在裝修，所以我們別無選擇。

請注意，附近還有其他三間分店。分別位於 Mayfield、Westside 和 Haywood。您也可以線上訂購，我們會免費送貨。再次感謝您十七年以來持續的支持。

單字 regret 感到遺憾、感到後悔　inform 通知、告知
branch 分店、分公司　as if 宛如　provide 提供、給予
renovate 裝修、翻新　matter 問題　continual 持續的

131. (D)
解說 空格前方為動詞 regret，後方可連接不定詞或動名詞當作受詞，因此答案要選 (D) to inform，屬於不定詞的副詞用法。該句話的動詞為 regret，所以作答時，可先刪去其他動詞選項。

132. (B)
解說 空格後方連接複數名詞 items，而 another 和 every 僅可修飾單數名詞，所以可先刪去這兩個選項。根據文意，除了 pastries 和 cakes 之外，還有「其他」產品，因此答案要選 (B) other。

133. (A)
(A) 請注意，附近還有其他三間分店。
(B) 我們決定擴大商店規模，讓更多顧客進來用餐。
(C) 在Kensington做生意的成本大幅增加。
(D) 不可能再繼續從事食品供應產業。

解說 空格後方依序列出三個地名 Mayfield、Westside、Haywood，表示應填入與此相關的句子，因此答案要選 (A)。

單字 be aware that 注意⋯　location 地點、位置
nearby 附近的　expand 擴大　dine 用餐
do business 做生意、經營事業

134. (C)
解說 空格前方為限定詞 your，後方連接名詞 support，表示空格可填入形容詞，修飾後方的名詞；或填入名詞，與 support 組合成複合名詞。根據文意，答案要選形容詞 (C) continual。

135-138 備忘錄

> 收件者：所有員工
> 寄件者：Eric Horner
> 日期：2月11日
> 主旨：健身房會員
>
> 我很高興宣布，管理層已同意為全職員工贊助健身房的會員資格。在一月份的員工滿意度調查中，許多人**有要求**這項福利。從3月1日起，員工可以獲得一張Westfield健身房的免費會員優惠券。請**確定**你會定期運動再索取。該會員優惠券的效期為半年。**期限**屆滿後，你可以申請額外的優惠券。該優惠券不包含私人教練訓練服務。**該部分需由你自行付費。**

單字 gym 健身房、體育館　membership 會員（資格）
sponsor 贊助　full-time 全職的　perk（薪資外的）福利
survey 調查　voucher 優惠券、折抵券　work out 運動
regularly 定期地、規律地　additional 額外的

135. (C)
解說 空格置於句子的動詞位置上，後方並未連接受詞，而是連接介系詞片語，表示空格應填入被動語態。發送備忘錄的時間為2月11日，而員工滿意度調查的時間為一月份，表示時態要用過去式，因此答案要選 (C) was requested。

136. (C)
(A) 預期　(B) 出現　(C) 意圖、打算　(D) 批准

137. (A)
(A) 期間　(B) 優惠券　(C) 培訓　(D) 導覽、參觀

138. (D)
(A) 希望大家都能使用這裡的設施。
(B) 感謝各位的支持。
(C) 優惠券已發給你們所有人。
(D) 該部分需由你自行付費。

單字 facilities 設施

139-142 通知

> 又到了繳交年度獎項提名名單的時候。今年**將會頒發**兩個獎項。
>
> 第一個是年度最佳員工獎，第二個是年度最佳新進員工獎。所有提名名單須在11月30日前交給Maryanne Carter。請附上一份簡短說明，解釋**為什麼**你提名的人選應該獲獎。
>
> 預計將於12月29日的年度聚會上公布獲獎者。**今年的活動將在Hillsdale餐廳舉行。**每位獲獎者將獲得現金**獎勵**和其他多項獎品。

單字 submit 繳交　nomination 提名、推薦　award 獎項
present 給予、頒發　newcomer 新來的人、新手
brief 簡短的　statement 說明、陳述　annual 年度的
get-together 聚會　cash 現金

139. (D)
解說 空格後方未連接受詞，表示空格應填入被動語態。而頒獎活動為之後才會發生的事情，時態要用未來式，因此答案為未來被動式 (D) will be presented。

140. (A)
解說 根據文意，應表達說明提名者應該獲獎的理由，因此答案要選 (A) why。

141. (C)
(A) 由我們的執行長Anderson先生主辦活動。
(B) 去年的派對幾乎全員出席。
(C) 今年的活動將在Hillsdale餐廳舉行。
(D) 將發送邀請函給所有獲獎者。

單字 host 主辦　attendance 出席　invitation 邀請函

142. (D)
(A) 薪水　(B) 獎盃　(C) 獎牌　(D) 獎勵（金）

143-146 公告

感謝您購買Madison電器行的電器。我們以產品的品質為榮。如果您的電器出現任何問題,請撥打 1-888-555-8473 與我們聯絡。我們的免費熱線24小時全天候開放。我們的客服人員隨時**準備好**為您提供協助。

您的電器享有兩年完整保固。然而,若有未經授權的人員對該產品進行維修,保固將**不再**具有效力。

如欲了解更多資訊,請至我們的網站www.madisonelectronics.com。**您也可以發送電子郵件至info@madisonelectronics.com**。

單字 purchase 購買　appliance 電器、設備
toll-free 免費的　hotline 熱線電話
customer service 客戶服務　assist 協助
come with 附有　warranty 保固　unauthorized 未經授權的
service 維修、檢修　no longer 不再　in effect 有效的

143. (D)
解說 空格前方為動詞 take,後方連接介系詞,表示空格應填入名詞,當作動詞的受詞,因此答案要選 (D) pride。

144. (C)
解說 主詞 customer service representatives 為一天24小時隨時都能服務,因此答案要選用在進行式 (C) are standing by。

145. (C)
解說 根據文意,表達「若有未經授權的人員對產品進行維修,保固將<u>不再具有效力</u>」較為適當,因此答案要選 (C) no longer。

146. (B)
(A) 退款需在購買後10天內提出。
(B) 您也可以發送電子郵件至info@madisonelectronics.com。
(C) 請務必保留您的收據。
(D) 您必須使用原包裝寄送產品。

147-148 公告

注意事項:所有城市救生員

從4月30日起,您的工作時間表將透過簡訊發送至您的手機。時間表最晚將於每週日晚上6點前發送。如果您有任何排班衝突或問題,請在一小時內回覆訊息。若遇到惡劣天氣,隨時可能會發送游泳池或海灘關閉的簡訊通知。

請聯絡城市公園和娛樂項目辦公室的Wendy Sullivan,確認您目前存檔的電話號碼正確無誤。

單字 lifeguard 救生員　text message 簡訊
no later than 不晚於…
scheduling conflict 時間衝突、行程重疊
issue 問題　respond to 回覆
in case of 若發生…　inclement weather 惡劣天氣
indicate 指出、告知　make sure 確認

currently 現在、目前　on file 存檔紀錄　accurate 正確的

147. 救生員會收到簡訊通知的事情為何?
(A) 加班機會
(B) 員工會議
(C) 時間表
(D) 政府視察

單字 overtime 加班、超時工作　inspection 檢查、視察

148. 救生員為什麼要聯絡辦公室?
(A) 要求休假
(B) 確認某些資訊
(C) 查詢天氣狀況
(D) 請求協助

換句話說 make sure → confirm / phone number → information

單字 time off work 休假　confirm 確認
inquire about 詢問…　assistance 協助

149-150 報導

Bradenton時報

10月11日— 本地事業家Harold Grimes剛剛宣布,他打算在Bradenton再創辦一家公司。**Grimes先生在鎮上擁有四家餐廳和兩家超市**。然而,他的新事業將不再涉足食品業。取而代之的是,他要開設一家醫療診所。Grimes醫療中心將位於Easton Drive 67號,Bradenton圖書館對面。儘管Grimes先生本人沒有醫學背景,**但他表示市民需要品質優良且可負擔的醫療服務**。診所將聘請五名全職醫生,並配有最先進的醫療設備。

Grimes先生表示,診所預計將於十一月開業。有興趣的人可撥打539-9573,了解更多關於醫生專業的資訊,並進行約診。

單字 intend 打算、計畫　establish 創辦　business 公司
own 擁有　venture 企業、事業　while 儘管
background 背景、經歷　state 表明　quality 品質優良的
affordable 可負擔的　medical care 醫療服務
specialty 專業、專攻　make a appointment 約診

149. 關於Grimes先生,文中指出什麼?
(A) 他曾在大學中學習醫學。
(B) 他想更換診所裡的一些醫生。
(C) 他擁有多家商業機構。
(D) 他有參與地方政治。

解說 文中提到他有餐廳和超市,因此答案要選 (C)。文中僅提到會聘請醫生,並未提及要更換掉醫生,因此不能選 (B)。

換句話說 restaurants, supermarkets → business establishments

單字 medicine 醫學、內科學　be involved in 參與…
politics 政治(學)

116

150. 為何要開設Grimes醫療中心？
(A) 為當地居民提供良好的醫療服務
(B) 取代即將關閉的醫院
(C) 提供專業的手術選擇
(D) 滿足Bradenton居民的要求

換句話說 quality, affordable medical care → good health care

單字 replace 取代、換掉　specialized 專業的
surgical 手術的、外科的　option 選擇、選項
fulfill 滿足、實現

151-154 報導

> 多倫多（4月23日）— 為了努力打入歐洲市場，加拿大電子產品製造商Galleon公司已與Baldrick簽署了協議，以調查諸多國家的市場。
>
> Baldrick是一家顧問公司，總部位於英國倫敦，並在馬德里、羅馬、巴黎和其他幾個歐洲主要城市設有辦事處。<u>同時在亞洲和北美地區也設有分公司。</u>
>
> 執行長Ian Smythe表示：「我認為我們了解歐洲人的需求。我們已協助過許多其他北美公司在歐洲取得成功，我們也有信心能幫助Galleon。」
>
> Baldrick已經營超過三十年，是英國最大的家族企業顧問公司。
>
> 「從一個市場轉換到另一個市場並不容易，例如，美國消費者可能期望他們的電子設備具有某些功能，而歐洲消費者對這些功能根本毫無興趣。我們將找出Galleon如何調整其產品以取得成功的方法。」Smythe先生說道
>
> Galleon預計將於今年十二月收到Baldrick的報告。分析完資料後，公司將於明年開始生產專為出口而設計的產品。

單字 in an effort 努力…　break into 打入、進入
agreement 協議（書）　be headquartered in 總部位於…
major 主要的　numerous 許多的　positive 有信心的
as well 也　be in business 經營　decade 十年
switch 轉換、變更　function 功能
electronic device 電子設備　identify 找出、確認
adapt 調整　anticipate 期待、預期　analyze 分析
tailor-made 特製的

151. Baldrick如何幫助Galleon公司？
(A) 透過分析生產趨勢
(B) 透過招募新員工
(C) 透過掌握消費者偏好
(D) 透過改善電腦資料庫

單字 trend 趨勢、傾向　recruit 招募、僱用
determine 判定、確定　preference 偏好

152. 關於Baldrick，報導中提到什麼？
(A) 主要辦事處位於多倫多。
(B) 製造家電產品。
(C) 所屬另一家公司。

(D) 三十多年前開業。

換句話說 three decades → thirty years

單字 manufactures 製造　electric appliance 家電產品

153. 根據Smythe先生所述，歐洲與美國消費者之間有何差異？
(A) 他們購買的品牌名稱
(B) 他們想要的設備功能
(C) 他們需要的使用說明細節
(D) 他們願意支付的價格

單字 brand name 品牌名稱　instructions 使用說明

154. 在[1]、[2]、[3]和[4]當中，何處最適合填入下方句子？
「同時在亞洲和北美地區也設有分公司。」
(A) [1]
(B) [2]
(C) [3]
(D) [4]

解說 題目提供的句子中出現代名詞it，指的是Baldrick。先提到在歐洲各城市設有辦事處，再補充其他國家的狀況，因此句子適合填入 [1]。

155-156 文字簡訊

> Jeff Daniels（上午 10:14）
> 哈囉，Samantha。<u>你還記得我們昨天見過的Madison科技公司代表的名字嗎？</u>
> Samantha West（上午 10:15）
> 當然。她叫Cecily Peters。你為什麼要問？
> Jeff Daniels（上午 10:16）
> Anderson先生希望我再安排一次與她的會議。
> Samantha West（上午 10:17）
> <u>你需要她的電話號碼嗎？</u>
> Jeff Daniels（上午 10:18）
> <u>我很需要。</u>
> Samantha West（上午 10:19）
> 稍等，我找一下。

單字 representative 代表　schedule a meeting 安排會議
hold on（電話上）稍等

155. 關於撰寫者，文中提到什麼？
(A) 他們在Madison科技公司工作。
(B) 他們需繳交報告給Anderson先生。
(C) 他們前一天一起參加了會議。
(D) 他們將為Peters女士進行產品演示。

解說 訊息中提到「that we met yesterday」，可推論出昨天Jeff Daniels和Samantha West兩人一起見了Cecily Peters，因此答案要選 (C)。

換句話說 yesterday → the previous day

單字 submit 繳交　attend a meeting 參加會議
previous 先前的　give a demonstration 演示、示範

117

156. 上午10點18分，Daniels先生寫道：「我很需要」，最有可能意味著什麼？
(A) 他想要某人的聯絡資訊。
(B) 他願意在今天之內與West女士見面。
(C) 他很高興West女士會安排會議。
(D) 他急著要買新手機。

換句話說 phone number → contact information

單字 contact 聯絡　be eager to 急著要做⋯

157-159 廣告

> **Graham's客製鞋子**
> Graham's客製鞋子是送給您生命中特別之人的理想禮物。**鞋子由柔軟的皮革製成，有各種顏色可供選擇**。鞋子尺寸根據每位顧客的腳型特別訂製，保證至少可以穿三年。**由於鞋子是訂製品，顧客必須親自到店測量或在網站上提供精確的腳部尺寸。請務必確認每隻腳的尺寸，因為每人雙腳的大小略有差異。**如欲了解更多可供選擇的款式，請造訪我們位於Rochester路58號的店面或上我們的網站www.grahamscustomshoes.com。試穿過一次後，您將不再於其他地方購買鞋子。

單字 custom 客製化、訂製的　ideal 理想的　leather 皮革
a variety of 各式各樣的　guarantee 保證　last 維持
in person 親自　precise 精確的　measurement 尺寸
once 一次

157. 關於產品，廣告中指出什麼？
(A) 由同一種材料所製成。
(B) 都有相同價格。
(C) 大約需要兩週的時間來製作。
(D) 可以郵寄到海外地址。

單字 type 種類　material 材料　mail 郵寄

158. 廣告建議一些顧客做什麼？
(A) 致電獲取更多資訊
(B) 繳交喜歡款式的照片
(C) 詢問產品保固
(D) 提供準確的資訊

換句話說 precise → accurate

單字 guarantee 保固、保證　accurate 準確的

159. 在[1]、[2]、[3]和[4]當中，何處最適合填入下方句子？
「請務必確認每隻腳的尺寸，因為每人雙腳的大小略有差異。」
(A) [1]
(B) [2]
(C) [3]
(D) [4]

160-163 信件

> 3月11日
> Patrick Peterson
> Mercer大道546號
> Sacramento, CA 94258
>
> Peterson先生您好，
>
> 作為Daniel's綠色食品雜貨店的老顧客，**您一定知道我們銷售各種國內外食品**。您應該也知道我們有一間熟食店和一間麵包店，並在那裡製作了許多食物。
>
> 我們希望收到您對我們所製作食品的意見。因此，我們想提供一個機會，邀您成為美食試吃員。
>
> 只需在指定週末來到我們店裡，將有五到十種不同食品的樣品供您試吃。
>
> **試吃**的食品包含烘焙食品、糕點、起司、肉類以及千層麵和筆管麵等熟食。然後會請您完成一份簡短的問卷調查，對每樣食品如實提出您的意見。整個過程需要十分鐘。
>
> 如欲報名參加此試吃機會，請在接下來兩週內的任何時間前往Daniel's，並告知店經理Marjorie Benson。**作為協助的回報，您將會收到一張十美元的商店優惠券，以及可帶回家的免費樣品。**
>
> 我們期待很快就能收到您的正面答覆。
>
> 祝好，
> Eric Quinn
> Daniel's綠色食品雜貨店執行長

單字 grocer 食品雜貨商　be aware that 知道⋯
a variety of 各式各樣的　domestic 國內的
deli 熟食店　bakery 麵包店、烘焙坊　input 意見
regarding 關於　extend 提供、擴展　taster 試吃員
show up 出現　designated 指定的　sample 樣品、試吃
baked goods 烘焙食品　frank 誠實的　complete 完成
survey 問卷調查　drop by 順道經過　in return for 作為回報

160. 這封信件的目的為何？
(A) 告知特價販售
(B) 宣傳某些新產品
(C) 討論就業機會
(D) 要求參加某項活動

161. 關於Daniel's綠色食品雜貨店，文中指出什麼？
(A) 在城市中有多家分店。
(B) 為該城市最大的食品雜貨店。
(C) 有販售其他國家的食品。
(D) 很快就會建造新的麵包店。

換句話說 international foods → food from other countries

單字 multiple 多數的、複數的　branch 分店、分公司

162. 第三段第2行中「sampling」一詞的意思最接近何者？
(A) 試吃
(B) 提供
(C) 參加
(D) 報告

163. Peterson先生能從Daniel's綠色食品雜貨店獲得什麼？
(A) 快遞服務
(B) 每月優惠券
(C) 免費食品
(D) 顧客俱樂部的會員資格

單字 express 快遞的　coupon 優惠券、禮券
membership 會員（資格）

164-165 網頁

> Axle租車公司會員資格
>
> Allen Darcy，歡迎您加入Axle租車公司的會員專屬俱樂部。您的會員申請已通過，現在您可以享有各種特別優惠。
>
> 您的帳號為75234ADP23。每次預約車輛以及取車或還車時，您都需要使用此號碼。我們還建議您在智慧型手機上下載我們的行動應用程式。如此一來，無論您身在何處，隨時都能登錄您的帳戶。
>
> 我們每週都會為俱樂部的會員提供特別優惠。每週的優惠會於星期日午夜更換。您可以點擊此處選擇透過電子郵件發送給您。您使用會員資格的次數越多，就能累積越多點數，從而獲得更多折扣。

單字 rental car 租車　membership 會員（資格）
application 申請　be eligible for 享有…
special deal 特別優惠　account 帳戶
make a booking 預約　drop off 返還　log in to 登錄…
accrue 獲得、累積　enable 能夠　qualify 取得資格

164. Darcy先生租車時應該要做什麼？
(A) 出示他的帳號
(B) 出示有效駕照
(C) 使用信用卡付款
(D) 證明他有保險

單字 present 出示　valid 有效的　driver's license 駕照
prove 證明　insurance 保險

165. 關於Axle租車公司的會員專屬俱樂部，文中指出什麼？
(A) 允許會員免費租用車輛。
(B) 僅開放老客戶加入。
(C) 需要繳交年費。
(D) 每週提供多項優惠。
換句話說 special offers → deals

單字 for free 免費　annual 年度的、每年的　deal 優惠商品

166-168 報導

> Haverford 建設公司將建造新的公寓大樓社區
>
> SUDBURY（11月12日）Sudbury市長辦公室昨晚宣布，已將城鎮郊區的一大塊土地出售給Haverford建設公司。**這塊土地佔地十四英畝**，位於城鎮東側的32號高速公路旁，鄰近Darlington山。Haverford公司的發言人表示，公司打算將這塊土地開發為一個至少有七棟建築的公寓大樓社區。公司預計將於明年年初公開新社區的設計。據市長辦公室某位消息人士透露，這塊土地僅有另一名競標者，是一位想用土地來農耕的人。然而，這座城市迫切需要新的住房。隨著多家公司宣布計畫在城鎮附近建設設施，**預計當地人口很快就會大幅增加**。因此對市長辦公室來說，**確保有更多住房至關重要**。

單字 apartment complex 公寓大樓社區　mayor 市長
plot 土地　on the outskirts 在郊區　alongside 在…旁邊
spokesperson 發言人　contain 包含　no fewer than 至少
release 公開、發表　source 消息來源　bidder 競標者
desperate 迫切的、渴望的　facility 設施　population 人口
secure 確保　be of the utmost importance 至關重要的

166. 取得的土地位於哪裡？
(A) Darlington山
(B) 市長辦公室對面
(C) 農場附近
(D) 在Sudbury的東側

單字 acquire 取得、入手　farm 農場

167. 根據報導所述，為什麼Sudbury需要住房？
(A) 鎮上有許多房子的屋況不佳。
(B) 最近有一些公寓大樓被燒毀。
(C) 當地房價上漲飆快。
(D) 在不久的將來會有許多人搬到此處。

單字 burn down 燒毀、焚燒　recently 最近

168. 第12行中的「securing」一詞意思最接近何者？
(A) 保存
(B) 獲得
(C) 檢查
(D) 保衛

169-171 公告

> E-Z 洗衣店
>
> E-Z洗衣店很自豪地宣布，顧客不再需要攜帶銅板即可使用我們的洗衣機和烘衣機。取而代之的是，顧客可以購買卡片並儲值。然後，這些卡片可以用來操作機器。
>
> 欲使用我們的新系統，請按照以下步驟操作：
> 1. 前往商店後方的任一台機器，選擇您想要儲值卡片的金額，並放入相應的現金。
> 2. 您會收到一張附有餘額的卡片。
> 3. **把衣物放入洗衣機或烘衣機中，選擇您想要的設定。**

119

4. 把卡片插入插槽中，並按下「使用」的按鈕。機器便會開始運轉，費用將會從您的卡片中扣除。
您可以使用這些機器來接收退款或退還卡片中未使用的餘額。

單字 laundry 洗衣店、衣物　no longer 不再
carry 攜帶、帶著　washer 洗衣機　dryer 烘衣機
instead 取而代之的是　operate 操作　select 選擇
cash 現金　credit（等同現金的）點數　insert 插入、放入
slot 插槽、洞口　deduct 扣除、減除　refund 退款

169. 該公告的目的為何？
(A) 為錯誤道歉
(B) 說明調查結果
(C) 宣布新服務
(D) 宣傳分公司開業

單字 apologize for 為⋯道歉　survey 調查　promote 宣傳

170. 在選擇完洗衣功能後需做什麼？
(A) 把錢放進插槽
(B) 插入卡片
(C) 與員工交談
(D) 加入洗衣粉

解說 步驟寫道「把卡片插入插槽中，並按下按鈕」，因此答案要選 (B)。把錢放進插槽，為的是取得卡片，所以不能選 (A)。
換句話說 select the setting → choosing the cycle

單字 cycle（洗衣機、烘衣機的）一輪　add 加入
detergent 洗衣粉、洗潔劑

171. 關於卡片，文中指出什麼？
(A) 只能使用一次。
(B) 使用者可以拿回裡面的錢。
(C) 具備有效期限。
(D) 可用信用卡來儲值。

換句話說 receive a refund → get their money back

單字 expiration 到期、截止

172-175 線上聊天

Dieter Kimball（下午 1:12）
大家好。我剛回到辦公室，注意到有人把一些資料夾留在我桌上。那是誰放的？
Sally Beecher（下午 1:15）
Kimball先生，是我和George放的。**我們需要您批准幾項支出**。如您所知，公司的野餐會快到了，而我們被選中負責準備。
George White（下午 1:16）
您今天有空看一下嗎？**我們可以在五分鐘內去辦公室找您。**
Dieter Kimball（下午 1:17）
我跟Sylvester Mann約好一點半見面。
George White（下午 1:18）

您知道需要花多久時間嗎？
Dieter Kimball（下午 1:19）
很難說。我們有很多事項要討論。資料夾裡面有什麼我需要知道的內容嗎？
Sally Beecher（下午 1:20）
唯一的問題是我們會略微超出預算。**表示要帶家人一起參加的人比以往還多。**所以我們不得不購買比以往更多的食物和其他用品。
George White（下午 1:21）
那是我們最擔心的問題，但還有其他一些小問題我們也想一起討論。
Dieter Kimball（下午 1:22）
四點半來我辦公室。到時候我們再討論所有問題。

單字 notice 注意到　folder 資料夾、文件夾　approval 批准
expenditure 支出　organize 準備、籌劃　go over 討論
issue 問題　exceed 超過　budget 預算
commit 表態、承諾　supplies 用品　primary 主要的
concern 擔憂、關心的事　minor 較小的

172. Kimball先生最有可能是誰？
(A) 求職者
(B) 主管
(C) 活動策劃者
(D) 客戶

解說 Sally Beecher 和 George White 要請 Dieter Kimball 批准幾項支出，由此可推論出 Kimball 先生可能是 (B) 主管。

173. White先生想做什麼？
(A) 更改活動日期
(B) 取得額外資金
(C) 與Kimball先生親自見面
(D) 把場地移到其他地方

單字 extra 額外的　funding 資金　in person 親自、直接
venue（活動）場地

174. Kimball先生為何在下午1點17分寫道：「我跟Sylvester Mann約好一點半見面」？
(A) 拒絕提議
(B) 批准請求
(C) 說明他明天的行程安排
(D) 提議取消他的計畫

解說 George White 表示他們可以去辦公室找 Kimball 先生，而後 Kimball 先生回答自己有約，等於拒絕對方的提議，因此答案要選 (A)。

單字 reject 拒絕　suggestion 提議　describe 說明、描述
offer 提議　cancel 取消

175. 關於公司野餐會，文中提到什麼？
(A) 將於八月舉行。
(B) 在公司附近舉行。

120

(C) 以前有舉辦過。
(D) 只有員工才能參加。

解說 文中出現的答題線索為「than usual（比往常）」，因此答案要選 (C)。

單字 take place 舉行、發生　employee 員工

176-180. 信件、電子郵件

Sunfield高爾夫度假村
Westway Drive 1603 號
Mesa, AZ 85209

6 月 23 日
Lawrence Mercado
Hickory路 294 號
Florence, AZ 85143

Mercado先生您好，

感謝您報名參加 7 月 17 日在 Sunfield 高爾夫度假村舉辦的年度 Sun and Fun 錦標賽。您的確認號碼為 0638。請確認隨信附上的停車證和名牌。在度假村場地內，您必須全程佩戴名牌，以顯示您正在參加比賽。

您應於上午 7 點至 8 點 30 分之間，至會所的接待櫃檯報到，並需要出示有照片的身分證件。比賽分為四個組別，各組別的第一洞開球時間如下：上午 9 點〔半職業組〕、上午 10 點〔高級組〕、上午 11 點〔中級組〕、中午〔初級組〕。

接待櫃檯將免費提供茶、咖啡、汽水和瓶裝水。不過，您必須出示名牌才能取用。還可以在餐廳購買食物。

我們期待在 Sunfield 高爾夫度假村見到您！

祝好，
Sunfield高爾夫度假村 全體活動員工

單字 register 報名參加　annual 年度的　confirmation 確認　enclose 隨信附上　pass 通行證　at all times 全程、總是　while 在⋯期間　grounds 場地、區域　check in 報到　reception desk 接待櫃檯　photo ID 有照片的身分證件　consist of 由⋯組成　category 組別、類型　intermediate 中級的　bottled water 瓶裝水　serve 供應（食物）

收件者：Lawrence Mercado
　　　　<l.mercado@shermansales.com>
寄件者：Nancy Aldridge <nancy@sunfieldgolf.com>
日期：7 月 6 日
主旨：Sun and Fun 錦標賽

Mercado先生您好，

我們非常高興歡迎即將參加 Sun and Fun 錦標賽的高爾夫球手！您的指定開球時間為上午 10 點。如果您開車前來參加比賽，請注意您應把車停在 Avis 街旁邊的停車場。與 Mooney 街相連的停車場暫時關閉，以便為擴建室內練球場的施工人員騰出空間。如欲下載我們場地的地圖，請點擊此處。

祝好，
Nancy Aldridge

單字 assigned 指定的、分配的　note 注意、留意　lot 停車場　temporarily 暫時地、臨時地　make space for 為⋯騰出空間　crew 施工人員　expansion 擴建　indoor 室內　driving range 高爾夫練習場　site 場地

176. 該信件的目的為何？
(A) 為錯誤道歉
(B) 確認報名
(C) 推薦服務
(D) 請求資金

單字 apologize for 為⋯道歉　registration 報名　fund 資金、基金

177. Mercado先生被要求在 7 月 17 日抵達時做什麼？
(A) 出示一項身分證明
(B) 簽署正式文件
(C) 選擇一些會員
(D) 檢查他的設備

換句話說 a photo ID → a form of identification

單字 form 種類、形式　identification 身分證（=ID）　inspect 檢查　equipment 設備

178. 關於接待櫃檯，文中提到什麼？
(A) 飲料僅供參加者取用。
(B) 將為慈善團體募款。
(C) 員工會提供停車證。
(D) 每天早上 7 點開放。

單字 beverage 飲料　donation 捐款　charity 慈善團體

179. 關於 Sunfield 高爾夫度假村的敘述何者正確？
(A) 最近變更了所有權。
(B) 第一次舉辦比賽。
(C) 提供會員活動折扣。
(D) 目前有正在施工的建築。

單字 recently 最近　ownership 所有權　competition 比賽　currently 現在、目前　under construction 施工中

180. Mercado先生的高爾夫程度最有可能為何？
(A) 初級
(B) 中級
(C) 高級
(D) 半職業

解說 本題為整合題。第二篇文章的收件者為 Mercado 先生，當中提到指定開球時間為上午 10 點。回到第一篇文章，上午 10 點對應的級數為高級，因此答案要選 (C)。

121

181-185 網頁

| 關於作者 | 書籍 | 新聞報導 | 聯絡方式 |

Ulrich Baer出生於德國萊比錫，父母親為Sebastian Baer和Ines Baer。他的父親是軍人，**所以他在童年時期經常搬家，每隔兩年就會搬到世界各地不同的地方居住**。在大學期間，他有位朋友計畫去阿根廷旅行。由於Baer先生曾住在阿根廷，他便為朋友做了旅遊筆記。這些筆記非常有用，使他**認為**可以把它們變成一本旅遊指南。

從那時起，Baer先生為多個國家或地區撰寫了八本旅遊指南。**他還出版了一本名為《透過鏡頭》的歷史照片集**，該書受到評論家的高度讚賞。

Baer先生將於5月10日出版他最新的旅遊指南《亞洲足跡》。此書將收錄一些《透過鏡頭》中的照片，讓讀者看到各地區的變化。書中將附上地圖以及旅遊景點的最佳參觀時間，還有購買獨特紀念品的最佳地點建議。

它還會包含50篇餐廳評論，供想要品嘗當地美食的人參考。

單字 author 作者、作家　note 筆記、便條
figure 認為、判斷　turn A into B 把A變成B
guide 指南手冊、導覽書　collection 收集　entitled 書名為⋯
highly 相當地　critic 評論家　release 出版、推出
footprint 足跡　contain 包含　along with 附上⋯
tip 建議、技巧　tourist attraction 旅遊景點
unique 獨特的　souvenir 紀念品　feature 特別包含
review 評論、心得　cuisine 料理

---

https://www.overland-publishing.com
「沒有這本書，就別踏上亞洲！」
── Kinuko Asada《世界旅遊雜誌》

《亞洲足跡》是旅遊作家Ulrich Baer的最新指南。無論您是經驗豐富的旅行者還是第一次出國，Baer都能讓您輕鬆規畫並享受您的旅程。您一定不能錯過可以輕鬆照著走的地圖、交通建議和**80家餐廳的評論**。

出版日期：5月10日
16.95美元，平裝本，352頁
成為第一個發現精彩新書的人！**點擊此處查看即將舉辦的新書簽名會、出版派對和其他宣傳活動的時間表**。

單字 set foot 踏上　experienced 經驗豐富的、熟練的
miss 錯過　easy-to-follow 易於仿效的
transportation 交通　timetable 時間表
upcoming 即將到來的　launch 出版、發表
promotional 宣傳的

181. 關於Baer先生的敘述何者正確？
(A) 他小時候經常搬家。
(B) 他曾就讀阿根廷的大學。
(C) 他和他父親從事同樣的工作。
(D) 他在早期職業生涯中寫過小說。

單字 attend 上（大學）、參與　fiction 小說
career 職業生涯

182. 關於Baer先生的新旅遊指南，文中提到什麼？
(A) 評論家對它的評價褒貶不一。
(B) 其中包含歷史照片。
(C) 附贈免費紀念品。
(D) 以德語和英語出版。

單字 mixed 混雜的　come with 附上⋯

183. 在第一則網頁中，第一段第5行中「figured」一詞的意思最接近何者？
(A) 出現
(B) 執行
(C) 貢獻
(D) 決定

184. 關於Overland出版社的敘述何者正確？
(A) 正在接受新作家的作品。
(B) 網路上有活動時間表。
(C) 總部位於萊比錫。
(D) 出版了世界旅遊雜誌。

單字 headquarter 總部設於

185. Baer先生最新的旅遊指南有何變化？
(A) 獲得了新標題。
(B) 出版日期延期了。
(C) 當中有附上地圖。
(D) 新增了更多餐廳評論。

解說 本題為整合題。在第一篇文章中提到在《亞洲足跡》中，收錄了旅遊景點、購物地點建議、地圖以及50篇餐廳評論。而在第二篇文章中，可以發現增加為80篇餐廳評論，因此答案要選(D)。

單字 title 標題　postpone 延期　add 新增、加入

186-190 報告書、電子郵件、發票

Brandywine金融公司
員工問卷調查報告
工作場所問題
根據九月份的問卷調查，員工提出在工作場所存在以下主要問題：
1. 開放式辦公區缺乏隱私。（佔回答者62%）
2. 員工休息室的空間不足，且座位數量不夠。（佔回答者57%）
3. 電腦老舊且經常故障，導致員工有時工作效率降低。（佔回答者49%）
4. **員工識別證有時會失效，導致員工被鎖在建築物或個人辦公室外。**（佔回答者27%）
5. 回收箱數量不足，員工經常不得不將可回收物品扔進垃圾桶（佔回答者15%）
員工還抱怨**由於某些員工交談或聽音樂，導致噪音過大（7%）**、休息時間不足（5%）和辦公室內部裝潢單調乏味（3%）。

單字 survey 問卷調查　workplace 工作場所、職場
concern 問題、擔憂　describe 說明、描述
respondent 回答者　insufficient 不足的
lack 缺乏　seating capacity 座位數量　break down 故障
frequently 經常、頻繁地　thereby 因此
productive 有生產力的　at times 有時　ID 身分識別證
fail 失效　lock out of 鎖在…之外　dispose of 處理掉…
recyclable item 可回收物品　break 休息
period 一段時間　drab 單調乏味的

> 寄件者：jchandler@brandywinefinance.com
> 收件者：jasminehoward@brandywinefinance.com
> 主旨：員工問卷調查結果報告書
> 日期：10月11日
>
> Howard女士您好，
>
> 感謝您提供最近員工調查報告中的資料。我已與資訊科技部門的Luis Guarino談過，他向我保證今後會盡力維護好電腦。但他強調許多機器需要更換。我們有足夠的資金進行更換嗎？也許每月更換幾台，可以減少預算上的壓力。您對此有何看法？
>
> 關於報告中的第四個問題，我記得去年我們也遇過類似的問題。我以為這個問題已經解決了，但顯然沒有。
>
> 我們需要盡快開會討論這個問題。您何時有空呢？
>
> 祝好，
>
> Jennifer Chandler

單字 assure 保證、肯定　maintain 維護　emphasize 強調
replace 更換、替換　funding 資金　minimize 縮減到最小
budget 預算　matter 問題、事情　regarding 關於
list 列出　recall 回想
be under the impression that 有…的想法
apparently 顯然地　available 有空的

> Aaron's用品公司
> 顧客：Brandywine金融公司
> 日期：10月17日
>
> | 產品描述 | 數量 | 單價 | 合計 |
> |---|---|---|---|
> | 休閒椅，黑色 | 8 | 95.00美元 | 760.00美元 |
> | | | 稅金 | 45.60美元 |
> | | | 總計 | 805.60美元 |
>
> 感謝您的訂購。您的訂單將於兩個工作日內送達。如有任何疑問，請撥打1-888-555-9375與我們聯絡。

單字 supplies 用品、備品　item 品項
description 描述、說明　quantity 數量
unit price 單價　business day 工作日、平日

186. 關於Brandywine金融公司，報告書中提到什麼？
(A) 佔據至少兩棟不同的建築物。
(B) 主要關心的問題為環境保護。
(C) 員工可以把車停在員工停車場。
(D) 許多員工沒有自己的辦公室。

解說 第一篇文章中提到「open-space office areas」，指的是開放式辦公區，因此答案要選 (D)。

單字 occupy 佔據、佔用　at least 至少、最少

187. 有多少比例的回答者對噪音感到不滿？
(A) 62%
(B) 27%
(C) 15%
(D) 7%

換句話說 high noise levels → loud noises

188. Chandler女士向Howard女士詢問什麼？
(A) 今年的預算還剩下多少
(B) 她應該把報告寄給誰
(C) 她何時有空討論問題
(D) 問題沒有解決的原因

單字 budget 預算

189. 根據Chandler女士所述，去年發生了什麼問題？
(A) 識別證有時無法使用。
(B) 員工電腦壞掉。
(C) 員工沒有足夠的隱私。
(D) 員工太常加班。

解說 本題為整合題，請先確認 Chandler 是誰。在第二篇文章的電子郵件中，寄件者為 Jennifer Chandler。她表示去年也遇過類似第四點的問題。回到第一篇文章，第四點問題指的是員工識別證有時會失效，因此答案要選 (A)。

換句話說 sometimes → on occasion

單字 on occasion 有時、偶爾　work overtime 加班

190. 報告中提到哪個問題最有可能導致Brandywine金融公司向Aaron's用品公司採購？
(A) 問題1
(B) 問題2
(C) 問題3
(D) 問題5

解說 本題為整合題。在第三篇文章中，可以得知 Brandywine 金融公司買了八張休閒椅。回到第一篇文章中，尋找與椅子有關的問題，對應的是員工休息室的座位數量（seating capacity）不夠，因此答案要選 (B)。

單字 result in 導致

191-195 手冊、電子郵件

> Rosemont遊樂園為小孩和大人提供樂趣和娛樂。遊樂園位於Oxford市，擁有二十多項遊樂設施、遊樂場和娛樂區、動物園、餐飲設施和紀念品商店。
> **我們有為所有遊客安排特別的活動。**
> 6月19日— 來自Jasper農場的馬和小馬將來到動物園，供遊客撫摸和騎乘。會員價3美元。非會員價5美元。

123

6月26日— 前來觀看大象表演。全天共有三場表演。來看看大象能做什麼。表演結束後，您可以到舞台下餵食大象。會員價10美元。 非會員價20美元。

您可以在我們的網站上預訂每場活動的門票。也可以註冊成為Rosemont遊樂園的會員。會員可享有多項福利，包含門票、食物和紀念品折扣，以及參加特別活動的機會。詳情請上www.rosemontap.com/membership。

單字 amusement park 遊樂園　provide 提供、給予　entertainment 娛樂　ride 遊樂設施　arcade 遊樂場　facility 場所　souvenir 紀念品　pet 撫摸　nonmember 非會員　feed 餵食　reserve 預訂　sign up 註冊　benefit 福利、好處　access 入場、接近

收件者：rcraig@gladden.com
寄件者：membership@rosemontap.com
主旨：歡迎
日期：6月14日

Craig先生您好，

感謝您成為Rosemont遊樂園的會員。您選擇的是家庭會員資格，因此您、您的妻子、兒子和女兒將享有會員的各種優惠。每人將在接下來的三天內收到一張郵寄的會員卡。申請園內折扣時，請務必出示此卡，否則將需支付全額。

在您首次造訪遊樂園時，請順道前往服務中心一趟，領取為您和家人準備的特別禮品。

Tina Southern
Rosemont遊樂園

單字 select 選擇、挑選　apply for 申請　stop by 順道前往　pick up 領取、拿起

收件者：Tina Southern <tina_s@rosemontap.com>
寄件者：Robert Craig <rcraig@gladden.com>
主旨：要求
日期：7月5日

Southern女士您好，

我和我的家人最近以會員身分造訪遊樂園時，我太太的會員卡忘在家裡，於是我們被告知必須支付非會員價格才能觀看大象表演，請想像一下我們有多驚訝。我支付了額外的費用，但希望能獲得退款。我可以在下次前往遊樂園時領取退款。

順帶一提，感謝您送給我們的野餐籃。這是一份貼心的禮物。

Robert Craig

單字 inform 告知、通知　appreciate 感謝、感激　refund 退款　thoughtful 貼心的

---

191. 關於Rosemont遊樂園，文中指出什麼？
(A) 特別節目需要額外收費。
(B) 為首次來訪者提供折扣。
(C) 計畫不久後要建造動物園。
(D) 多為適合兒童的遊樂設施。

解說 第一篇文章中有提到與馬和大象有關的特別活動，皆需額外付費，因此答案要選 (A)。第一篇文章開頭，提到遊樂設施適合大人和小孩，因此 (D) 並不正確。

單字 charge 收費　extra 額外的、附加的　first-time 首次　mostly 大多地

192. 何者並非成為Rosemont遊樂園會員的好處？
(A) 入場價格較便宜
(B) 可以參加特別活動
(C) 食品的優惠
(D) 邀請參加年末慶祝活動

單字 admission 入場　access to 進入、使用　celebration 慶祝活動

193. 根據第一封電子郵件的內容，何者敘述正確？
(A) 會員價格近期有上漲。
(B) 已關閉服務中心進行維修。
(C) 可以在園區領取會員卡。
(D) Craig家族的每個人都是新會員。

194. 為何Craig先生的要求很有可能遭到拒絕？
(A) 已超過申請期限。
(B) 遊樂園拒絕任何退款。
(C) 未出示會員卡。
(D) 成人無資格享有較低的價格。

解說 本題為整合題。在第二篇文章中，提到申請園內折扣時，務必要出示會員卡，否則將支付全額。而在第三篇文章中，Robert Craig 提到他太太把會員卡忘在家裡，因而付了非會員價格，要求退回差額。但因未出示會員卡，其退款要求極有可能遭拒，因此答案要選 (C)。

單字 application 申請　give a refund 提供退款　present 出示　be eligible for 有…的資格

195. 關於Craig一家人，可以推論出什麼？
(A) 他們在網路上預訂了大象表演的門票。
(B) 他們在遊樂園裡玩了好幾項遊樂設施。
(C) 他們在6月26日造訪了服務中心。
(D) 他們有在遊樂園吃晚餐。

解說 本題為整合題。在第三篇文章中，Robert Craig 提到他們全家前往遊樂園，觀看大象表演，還有領取禮物野餐籃。回到第一篇文章，可確認大象表演的活動日期為6月26日。而在第二篇文章，當中提到新會員可於首次造訪遊樂園時，至服務中心領取特別禮。綜合上述，Craig一家人於6月26日首次造訪遊樂園，並於當天前往服務中心領取禮物，因此答案要選 (C)。

單字 reserve 預訂

196-200 網頁、電子郵件

黑森林州立公園是當地最大的公園,但卻是該州遊客數量最少的。為了幫助潛在遊客探索公園,我們建立了虛擬指南。這將讓遊客看到公園裡的最佳景點,並了解他們可以在那裡做什麼。該指南還提供當地的露營地、飯店和餐廳的連結。

如要使用虛擬指南,請先在我們的網站上註冊。然後,您將能完整存取該指南。您不僅可以預約公園裡的各項設施,還可以預約周邊的場所。

請在您有空時查看該指南,並告訴我們您的想法。我們很快就會新增評論功能,讓遊客能看到其他人的意見。

如有任何疑問或意見,請透過information@blackforestpark.gov與我們聯絡。

單字 state 州　yet 但是　potential 潛在的、可能性的　explore 探索、探險　virtual 虛擬的　guide 指南、導覽　spot 地方、場所　campground 露營地　register 註冊　have access to 可存取、可進入…　comment 意見、評論

收件者:information@blackforestpark.gov
寄件者:lkeller@miltonhikingclub.org
主旨:健行步道
日期:3月28日

敬啟者,

我對你們的虛擬指南印象深刻。我去過公園好幾次,但對於某些地方,尤其是餐飲場所還不太了解。往後我會去看看這些地方。

我有一個疑問。我找不到環繞天鵝湖的健行步道。這條步道是否因為冬季的惡劣天氣而關閉了?我計畫於4月4日造訪公園,這條步道是我行程中的首選。**請告訴我步道的情況,因為我們的團體有二十七人,可能需要做出一些變更。**

祝好,
Lisa Keller
Milton健行俱樂部會長

單字 hiking trail 健行步道　to whom it may concern 敬啟者　impressed 感到印象深刻的　numerous 許多的　occasion 情況、時候　be unaware of 不了解　dining establishment 餐飲場所　locate 找出位置　inclement 惡劣的、嚴酷的

收件者:lkeller@miltonhikingclub.org
寄件者:information@blackforestpark.gov
主旨:回覆:健行步道
日期:3月29日

Kelly女士您好,

感謝您提醒我們這項疏漏。必要的資訊將立刻新增至指南中。如果您發現其他錯誤,請透過fchapman@blackforestpark.gov與我聯絡。我會立即處理其他任何問題。

請注意,團體需要支付新的入園費用,目前適用費率如下:

團體規模	收費
10-15人	20美元
16-25人	30美元
26-40人	**50美元**
41人以上	70美元

希望您在公園度過愉快的時光。

祝好,
Fred Chapman
公園管理員

單字 bring to one's attention 讓人知道…　oversight 疏忽、疏漏　add 新增、加入　at once 立刻　be advised that 記住…　admission fee 入園費　rate 費用　apply 適用　ranger 公園管理員

---

196. 根據網站內容,關於黑森林州立公園的敘述何者正確?
(A) 所有訪客都必須填寫表格。
(B) 去那裡的人並不多。
(C) 公園管理員有提供導覽服務。
(D) 為全國最大的公園。

197. 虛擬指南的使用者被要求做什麼?
(A) 上傳圖片
(B) 發送連結給其他人
(C) 提供意見回饋
(D) 購買會員資格

換句話說 let us know what you think → provide feedback

單字 upload 上傳

198. 關於Keller女士,文中提到什麼?
(A) 她以前曾在公園當過志工。
(B) 她有在公園的網站上註冊。
(C) 她最近創立了健行俱樂部。
(D) 她每週都會造訪公園。

解說 本題為整合題。Keller女士為第一封電子郵件的寄件者,她提到對虛擬指南印象深刻。回到第一篇文章,當中提到要先在網站上註冊,才能使用虛擬指南,表示Lisa Keller有在網站上註冊,並使用虛擬指南,因此答案要選(B)。

換句話說 register → signed up

單字 volunteer 志願　recently 最近　on a weekly basis 每週

199. 第二封電子郵件的其中一個目的為何?
(A) 確認預訂
(B) 承認錯誤
(C) 索取聯絡資訊
(D) 提議新景點

單字 confirm 確認　booking 預訂　acknowledge 承認　attraction 景點

200. Keller女士的團體造訪公園時,最有可能付多少錢?
(A) 20 美元
(B) 30 美元
(C) 50 美元
(D) 70 美元

解說 本題為整合題。在第二篇文章中,Lisa Keller 表示她計畫造訪公園健行,團體有 27 人。而在第三篇文章中,27 人對應的入園費為 50 美元,因此答案要選 (C)。

EZ TALK

New TOEIC 一本攻克新制多益聽力＋閱讀850+：
完全比照最新考題趨勢精準命題

作　　　者：Eduwill語學研究所	New TOEIC 一本攻克新制多益聽力＋閱讀
譯　　　者：關亭薇	850+：完全比照最新考題趨勢精準命題 /Eduwill
主　　　編：潘亭軒	語學研究所著；關亭薇譯 . -- 初版 . -- 臺北市：
責任編輯：鄭雅方	日月文化出版股份有限公司, 2024.11
封面設計：兒日設計	384 面；　19x25.7 公分 . -- (EZ talk)
內頁排版：簡單瑛設	ISBN 978-626-7516-47-8（平裝）
行銷企劃：張爾芸	1.CST: 多益測驗

發 行 人：洪祺祥
副總經理：洪偉傑
副總編輯：曹仲堯
法律顧問：建大法律事務所
財務顧問：高威會計師事務所

出　　版：日月文化出版股份有限公司
製　　作：EZ 叢書館
地　　址：臺北市信義路三段151號8樓
電　　話：(02)2708-5509
傳　　真：(02)2708-6157
網　　址：www.heliopolis.com.tw
郵撥帳號：19716071日月文化出版股份有限公司

總 經 銷：聯合發行股份有限公司
電　　話：(02)2917-8022
傳　　真：(02)2915-7212
印　　刷：中原造像股份有限公司
初　　版：2024年11月
定　　價：520元
Ｉ Ｓ Ｂ Ｎ：978-626-7516-47-8

Copyright © 2023 by Eduwill Language Institute
All rights reserved.
Traditional Chinese Copyright © 2024 by HELIOPOLIS CULTURE GROUP
This Traditional Chinese edition was published by arrangement with Eduwill through Agency Liang

◎版權所有 翻印必究
◎本書如有缺頁、破損、裝訂錯誤，請寄回本公司更換